STEPHEN JONES lives in London, England. A Hugo Award nominee, he is the winner of four World Fantasy Awards, three International Horror Guild Awards, five Bram Stoker Awards, twenty-one British Fantasy Awards and a Lifetime Achievement Award from the Horror Writers Association. One of Britain's most acclaimed horror and dark fantasy writers and editors, he has more than 140 books to his credit, including *The Art of Horror: An Illustrated History*; the film books of Neil Gaiman's *Coraline* and *Stardust*, *The Illustrated Monster Movie Guide* and *The Hellraiser Chronicles*; the non-fiction studies *Horror: 100 Best Books* and *Horror: Another 100 Best Books* (both with Kim Newman); the single-author collections *Necronomicon* and *Eldritch Tales* by H.P. Lovecraft, *The Complete Chronicles of Conan* and *Conan's Brethren* by Robert E. Howard, and *Curious Warnings: The Great Ghost Stories of M.R. James*; plus such anthologies as *Horrorology: The Lexicon of Fear*, *Fearie Tales: Stories of the Grimm and Gruesome*, *A Book of Horrors*, *The Mammoth Book of Vampires*, the *Zombie Apocalypse!* series and twenty-seven volumes of *Best New Horror*. You can visit his web site at *www.stephenjoneseditor.com* or follow him on Facebook at *Stephen Jones-Editor*.

BEST NEW
HORROR

#27

BEST NEW HORROR

#27

EDITED AND WITH
AN INTRODUCTION BY
STEPHEN JONES

DIP

BEST NEW HORROR
Volume №27

This paperback edition published in February 2017 by PS Publishing Ltd.
by arrangement with Stephen Jones.

2 4 6 8 10 9 7 5 3 1

ISBN 978-1-786360-66-3

Design and Layout by Michael Smith
Cover design by Smith & Jones

Printed and bound in England by T. J. International

PS PUBLISHING
Grosvenor House, 1 New Road
Hornsea HU18 1PG, England

editor@pspublishing.co.uk
www.pspublishing.co.uk

CONTENTS

ACKNOWLEDGEMENTS

THE EDITOR WOULD like to thank Kim Newman, David Barraclough, Andrew I. Porter, Mandy Slater, Amanda Foubister, Jo Fletcher, Sara Broecker, Gordon Van Gelder, Robert Morgan, Rosemary Pardoe, R.B. Russell, David A. Riley, Shawn Garrett (*Pseudopod*), Andy Cox, Michael Kelly, David Longhorn and, especially, Peter and Nicky Crowther, Michael Smith, Marie O'Regan and Michael Marshall Smith for all their help and support. Special thanks are also due to *Locus*, *Ansible*, *Classic Images*, *Entertainment Weekly* and all the other sources that were used for reference in the Introduction and the Necrology.

This one has to be for
VIOLET REBECCA JONES
(1926-2016)
Thank you for all your love, encouragement
and support over the years.

"You see? No shock. No engulfment. No tearing asunder.
What you feared would come like an explosion is like a whisper.
What you thought was the end is the beginning."
—*The Twilight Zone:* 'Nothing in the Dark'
by George Clayton Johnson

INTRODUCTION

HORROR IN 2015

I N 2015, HARPERCOLLINS finally came to a new, multi-year
agreement with Amazon.com regarding both print and digital
books. Starting in April, the publisher returned to full agency pricing
for all its retailers, who would no longer be allowed to discount the
publisher's set price.

Six months later, Amazon announced that it planned to sue more
than 1,000 people it claimed were paid to write fake product reviews.
In April, the online company had sued four websites for selling
favourable reviews.

Well-respected horror editor Don D'Auria was let go by Samhain
Publishing in early November. Some reports suggested that this was
because D'Auria had spent too much time actually editing the books
he published and neglected such things as social-media promotion.

In May, the late John Wyndham was commemorated by a
passageway in north London being officially named "Triffid Alley"
after it was apparently identified as a location in his 1951 novel *The
Day of the Triffids*.

Meanwhile, Godzilla (aka Gojira) was made an official resident of
Tokyo's Shinjuku Ward for "promoting the entertainment of and
watching over the Kabuki-cho neighbourhood and drawing visitors
around the globe in the form of the (eighty ton) Godzilla head built
atop the Shinjuku Toho Building".

The week before Hallowe'en, a branch of UK supermarket Tesco was forced to remove from display a rubber mask of a rat-eating zombie after one mother complained that it scared her two-year-old son and four-year-old daughter. "I would not let my children watch zombie films on TV," she said, "so why should they be exposed to them when I am taking them round a local store?"

In America, almost $7 billion was spent on Halloween in 2015 (down from an $8 billion high in 2012), with more than 157 million people celebrating the holiday. Perhaps the most scary thing was that twenty million of those planned on dressing-up as a pet.

Meanwhile, a Dutch study based around the movie *Insidious* found that horror films could be bad for your health. Exposure to scary movies boosts a protein in the body called Factor VIII that congeals the blood and can raise the risk of a clot by around a fifth. It is, literally, "blood-curdling"!

Stephen King's initial publication of the year was the psychological thriller *Finders Keepers*, the second in a proposed trilogy linked to the author's 2014 novel *Mr. Mercedes*. After an obsessed fan murdered a reclusive writer during a break-in, years later he crossed paths with a ten-year-old boy who had discovered the author's hidden notebooks and refused to let them go.

King followed that with his sixth short story collection, *The Bazaar of Bad Dreams*, which contained twenty short stories (nine original), each with brief introductions by the author.

Stephen King was also amongst the year's ten recipients of the US National Medal of Arts from President Obama on September 10.

Joyce Carol Oates' short novel *Jack of Spades*, loosely inspired by Edgar Allan Poe and, presumably, the work of one Stephen King, was another psychological thriller concerning a successful author, who had a second career under a secret pseudonym. After being sued by a crazy woman claiming he stole her ideas by breaking into her house, the writer uncovered hidden secrets of his own.

Clive Barker's long-awaited *The Scarlet Gospels* united his two most famous characters, the demonic Cenobite Pinhead and psychic investigator Harry D'Amour, in a descent into Hell itself.

Earthling published a deluxe limited edition, signed by the author, illustrated by Les Edwards, and featuring a Foreword by actor Doug Bradley.

Saint Odd was the seventh and final volume in the "Odd Thomas" series by Dean Koontz. The paperback edition included the first printing of a bonus prequel story.

Visitors could go in, but they could never leave, as various people disappeared every eight years inside the eponymous edifice in David Mitchell's novella *Slade House*, a sequel-of-sorts to the author's novel *The Bone Clocks*.

British bookseller Waterstones produced an exclusive 2,500-copy hardcover edition of *A Song of Shadows*, the thirteenth book in John Connolly's "Charlie Parker" series, signed by the author and containing a bonus CD.

Christopher's Diary: Echoes of Dollanganger was the sixth in the "Dollanganger" series and *Secret Brother* was the third in "The Diaries" series by V.C. Andrews^Æ or, more likely, Andrew Niederman. *Bittersweet Dreams* was a stand-alone novel under the same, long-dead author's, byline.

The sign of any good writer is coming up with something new and inter-esting to say, which is probably why both Stephanie Meyer and E.L. James decided to simply recycle their previous work from different gender perspectives in *Life and Death: Twilight Reimagined* and *Fifty Shades of Grey*, respectively.

Favourably compared to Stephen King, Michael Crichton and Patricia Highsmith, *Under Ground* by "S.L. Grey" (Sarah Lotz and Louis Greenberg) was a high-concept horror novel set in a subterranean survival condominium in rural Maine, where those escaping a global super-flu virus discovered that something even worse might be waiting for them underground.

A cruise shop was lost into an alternate, apocalyptic world in Lotz's solo novel *Day Four*, which was set in the same world as *The Three*, and The Mariana Trench hid the potential cure to a deadly plague in *The Deep* by Nick Cutter (Craig Davidson).

Academic book thief and savant Anna Verco found herself on a quest to find a medieval volume written in the language of witches in *The Serpent Papers* by Jessica Cornwall.

Kim Newman's *The Secret of Drearcliff Grange School* was set in the titular 1920s boarding school for Unusual Girls, where a secret super-powered society of pupils called the "Moth Club" uncovered a Hooded Conspiracy that ran through the strange Somerset establishment.

A young boy was taken from his family and subjected to examinations for a genetic sickness in *The Death House* by Sarah Pinborough, which came with a glowing recommendation from Stephen King.

Alison Littlewood's *The Hidden People* was set in the mid-19th century and involved a man looking into the mysterious murder of his cousin, while the same author's *Zombie Apocalypse! Acapulcalypse Now* was the third spin-off novel set in the shared world created by Stephen Jones.

A race of subterranean creatures guided by sound laid waste to Europe in Tim Lebbon's novel *The Silence*, and the world suddenly became full of doppelgangers in Christopher Golden's *Dead Ringers*.

An agent for Satan investigated a nasty murder in Hell in Simon Kurt Unsworth's *The Devil's Detective*, *The Devil's Only Friend* was the first volume in a new "John Cleaver" trilogy by Dan Wells, and a man shared his soul with an evil Aztec priest in Adam Mansbach's *The Devil's Bag Man*.

A woman recalled what really happened when her older sister had her demonic possession filmed by a popular reality TV show in Paul Tremblay's *A Head Full of Ghosts*.

The Society of Blood was the second book in Mark Morris' "Obsidian Heart" series, and *For a Few Souls More* was the third and final book in the "Heaven's Gate" trilogy by Guy Adams.

The print edition of Shaun Hutson's new novel *Monolith* contained an original short story as well.

A private detective inherited a bookstore in Providence, Rhode Island, run by the last female descendant of H.P. Lovecraft in *Carter & Lovecraft* by Jonathan L. Howard.

Chapelwood was the second volume in Cherie Priest's Lovecraftian

"Borden Dispatches" series, while Austin Grossman's *Crooked* pitted US President Richard M. Nixon against Lovecraftian monsters.

Melinda Snodgrass' *The Edge of Dawn* was the third in the occult thriller series about paladin Richard Oort battling the inter-dimensional Old Ones.

A person could take over other people's bodies in *Touch* by "Claire North" (Catherine Webb), while *The Touched* by Joanna Briscoe was a Hammer novella about a family who moved to a haunted cottage in the country.

Of Sorrow and Such was a new novella by Angela Slatter, set in the author's "Sourdough" universe.

A boy's drawings of monsters became real in Keith Donohue's *The Boy Who Drew Monsters*, while John Birmingham's *Dave vs. the Monsters: Emergence* was the first book in the "Dave Hooper" trilogy, followed by *Resistance* and *Ascendance*.

The Rules by Nancy Holder and Debbie Vigué was about a deadly high school scavenger hunt.

In *Dead Spots* by Rhiannon Frater, a woman mourning her stillborn child discovered a "dead spot" where dreams or nightmares could be brought to life, and a boy was haunted by his psychopathic twin sister in Andrew Pyper's *The Damned*.

Stallo by journalist Stefan Sjput involved children kidnapped by trolls in an ancient forest in northern Sweden.

Heather Graham's *The Dead Play On* was part of the "Cafferty & Quinn" series, while *The Forgotten* and *The Hidden* were entries in the same author's "Krewe of Hunters" series.

The Last American Vampire, author Seth Grahame-Smith's sequel to *Abraham Lincoln, Vampire Hunter*, wandered into Kim Newman's "Anno Dracula" territory as the author took an alternate look at American history using such real-life characters as Jack the Ripper, Arthur Conan Doyle, Rasputin and Nikola Tesla.

An antiques dealer searched for a vampire's treasure in *The Fifth House of the Heart* by Ben Tripp, while *Vampires of Manhattan* by Melissa de la Cruz was the first volume in the "New Blue Bloods Coven" series, a spin-off from the YA "Blue Bloods" series.

Dracula of the Apes, Book One: The Urn, Book Two: The Ape and *Book Three: The Curse* was a trilogy of pastiches by G. Wells Taylor, and *The Originals: The Rise, The Loss* and *The Resurrection* comprised the packaged prequel trilogy to *The Vampire Diaries*, credited to that series' creator Julie Plec.

The Dark Arts of Blood was the fourth volume in Freda Warrington's "Blood" series.

Cherry Bomb was the third book in the series about werepire demon hunter Siobhan Quinn by "Kathleen Tierney" (Caitlín R. Kiernan), and a detective found himself cursed in *Werewolf Cop* by Andrew Klavan.

A screenwriter working on a script about the walking dead got carried away in Alexsandar Haydon's comic novel *The Making of Zombie Wars*, while *World War Moo* was the second volume of Michael Logan's "Apocalypse Cow" series, about bovine zombies.

The New Hunger was a prequel to Isaac Marion's 2011 post-apocalypse zombie romance *Warm Bodies*, which was reissued in a movie tie-in edition.

David Towsey's *Your Brother's Blood* was the first book in "The Walkin'", a post-apocalyptic Western zombie series. Joe McKinney's *The Dead Won't Die* was the second novel in the "Deadlands" series, and *Drifters* and *Crossbones* were the third and fourth books, respectively, in John L. Campbell's "Omega Days" zombie series.

Strands of Sorrow was the fourth and final volume in John Ringo's "Black Tide Rising" zombie apocalypse series. *White Trash Zombie Gone Wild* was the fifth volume in Diana Rowland's series featuring zombie Angel Crawford, while *The Remaining: Allegiance* and *The Remaining: Extinction* were the fifth and sixth and final volumes, respectively, in the zombie series by D.J. Molles.

The daughter of Henry Jekyll and her uncultured alter-ego Lizzie Hyde hunted a serial killer in an alternate 19th-century London in Viola Carr's steampunk debut novel, *The Diabolical Miss Hyde*. It was followed by *The Devious Dr. Jekyll*.

Shutter was a first novel by Courtney Alameda, about teenage ghost hunters, while Henry Turner made his debut with the YA horror novel *Ask the Dark*.

A girl being stalked could see the ghost of her older sister in Shannon Grogan's *From Where I Watch You*, and a girl could travel through other people's dreams in Robert L. Anderson's first novel *Dreamland*.

A man revisited his childhood home and discovered strange secrets in Robert Levy's debut *The Glittering World*, and a pregnant teenager and her family moved into an apparently haunted prairie house in Amy Lukavics' *Daughters Unto Devils*.

Indra Das' *The Devourers* was a first novel about werewolves, published by Penguin India.

Stephen King supplied a new Introduction to *The Rim of Morning: Two Tales of Horror*, an omnibus of the novels *To Walk the Night* (1937) and *Edge of Running Water* (1939) by William Sloane.

Edited with an Introduction by Mike Ashley, *The Face of the Earth and Other Imaginings* from Stark House collected eighteen stories and twelve essays by Algernon Blackwood. The book also included a useful Chronology of Blackwood's published works.

From the same PoD publisher, *The King in Yellow/The Mystery of Choice* was an omnibus of two 19th-century collections, introduced by Stefan Dziemianowicz. It was the first volume in "The Complete Weird Fiction of Robert W. Chambers".

With another Introduction by Dziemianowicz, *Classic Horror Stories* from Barnes & Noble was a gilt-edged, leather-bound anthology of forty-one stories by M.R. James, H.P. Lovecraft, E. Nesbit and others.

In the Shadow of Edgar Allan Poe, edited by Leslie S. Klinger, contained twenty stories from 1816-1914 by Joseph Sheridan Le Fanu, Robert W. Chambers, Arthur Conan Doyle and Charlotte Perkins Gilman, amongst others. *The Annotated Poe* collected stories and poems by the author, edited and extensively annotated by Kevin J. Hayes. William Giraldi contributed a Foreword.

Angela Carter's classic collection *The Bloody Chamber* was reissued in a deluxe paperback edition by Penguin to celebrate the 75th anniversary of the author's birth. Kelly Link supplied a new Introduction.

Issued as part of the Penguin Classics imprint, *Perchance to Dream* collected twenty-three stories by Charles Beaumont along with a 1981 Foreword by Ray Bradbury and a new Afterword by William Shatner.

Published as part of the same series, Laird Barron supplied a Foreword to Ray Russell's 1962 novel *The Case Against Satan*, while *Songs of a Dead Dreamer and Grimscribe* was an omnibus edition of two early collections by Thomas Ligotti, with a new Foreword by Jeff VanderMeer.

Edited by Scott Connors and Ron Hilger, *The End of the Story* was the first of five volumes in "The Collected Fantasies of Clark Ashton Smith" from Night Shade Books. Presenting the late poet and author's work in chronological order, the volume featured an Introduction by Ramsey Campbell and various notes and appendices by the editors.

From Flame Tree Publishing, *Chilling Horror Short Stories* and *Chilling Ghost Short Stories* were two beautiful-looking hardcover anthologies of new and classic tales in the publisher's "Gothic Fantasy" deluxe gift-book series (there was a third volume devoted to science fiction). With Forewords by Gothic expert Dr. Dale Townshend, the books included stories by, amongst others, E.F. Benson, Ambrose Bierce, Robert W. Chambers, Wilkie Collins, F. Marion Crawford, James Dorr, Arthur Conan Doyle, Sheridan Le Fanu, Nathaniel Hawthorne, William Hope Hodgson, W.W. Jacobs, Henry James, M.R. James, D.H. Lawrence, H.P. Lovecraft, A. Merritt, Edith Nesbit, Edgar Allan Poe, Bram Stoker, Lucy Taylor, Edith Wharton, Oscar Wilde and Andrew J. Wilson. Biographical sources were given, although individual copyright notices were noticeable by their absence.

Holly Black's *The Darkest Part of the Forest* was a dark fairy tale set in a town where humans and fair folk co-existed, while *Doll Bones* from the same author was about a sinister children's game.

Monsters were loose in San Bernardino, California, in the young adult novel *Trollhunters* by Guillermo del Toro and Daniel Kraus.

Derek Landy's *Demon Road*, the first volume in a new series, was also available in a signed, limited "Platinum" edition.

A girl's new home turned out to be an asylum with a mind of its own in Katie Alender's *The Dead Girls of Hysteria Hall*, and a girl found herself stuck in the body of a dying woman in an insane asylum in Ilsa J. Blick's *The Dickens Mirror*, the second book in the "Dark Passages" series.

A teenager inherited his father's collection of ghosts in Leo Hunt's *13 Days of Midnight*, while a group of children making a ghost film discovered that the location was really haunted in *Ghostlight* by Sonia Gensler.

A girl searching for a rare flower in the Okefenokee swamp discovered something nasty lurking in the water in Robert Lettrick's *The Murk*. A teenager began to recall what happened to her and her missing sister years earlier in *The Creeping* by Alexandra Sirowy, and a group of high school girls found themselves trapped in a subterranean rave with a killer in *Survive the Night* by Danielle Vega.

Michael Grant's *The Tattooed Heart* was the second book in the "Messenger of Fear" series, and Hillary Monahan's *Mary Unleashed* was the second volume in the "Bloody Mary" trilogy.

Library of Souls was the third volume in Ransom Riggs' "Miss Peregrine's Peculiar Children" series, while *Catacomb* was the third volume in Madeleine Roux's "Asylum" series, featuring "found" photographs. This was also available in a Barnes & Noble exclusive edition containing a bound-in map and evidence board.

In Daniel Kraus' *The Death and Life of Zebulon Finch Volume One: At the Edge of Vampire*, a 19th-century Chicago gangster returned from the dead in a slowly-decomposing body.

A young girl fell down a hole into a fantasy world of zombies in *Once Upon a Zombie Book One: The Color of Fear* by Billy Phillips and Jenny Nissenson, while *A Mad Zombie Party* was the fourth and final book in "The White Rabbit Chronicles" mash-up series.

Zom-B Bride and *Zom-B Fugitive* were the tenth and eleventh volumes, respectively, in the YA series by Darren Shan (Darren O'Shaughnessy), illustrated by Warren Pleece. The author also had an adult horror novel out, *Sunburn*, under the name "Darren Dash".

Susan Dennard's 1800's-set steampunk zombie novel *Strange and Ever After* was a sequel to *Something Strange and Deadly*, and

Kathleen Peacock's *Willowgrave* was the third in the werewolf mystery series.

Edited by April Genevieve Tucholke, *Slasher Girls and Monster Boys* was a young adult anthology containing fourteen original stories.

Neil Gaiman's latest collection, *Trigger Warning: Short Fiction and Disturb-ances*, contained a selection of fiction, poems, sketches and commentary, including a *Doctor Who* story.

Night Music was the second volume of the "Nocturnes" series and collected thirteen stories by John Connolly with illustrations by Jim Tierney.

Get in Trouble featured nine stories (one original) by Kelly Link, and *Three Moments of an Explosion* was China Miéville's first collection of short stories.

Edited by Joseph Nassise and Del Howison, *Midian Unmade: Tales of Clive Barker's Nightbreed* was exactly what the title said, featuring stories based on the author's 1990 movie and earlier novella by Amber Benson, Nancy Holder, Seanan McGuire, Weston Ochse, David J. Schow and others, along with an Introduction by Barker.

Boasting a cover and interior illustrations by Barker, *Horrorology: The Lexicon of Fear* edited by Stephen Jones collected within a wraparound narrative twelve original stories and novellas based on the language of horror by Barker, Ramsey Campbell, Joanne Harris, Kim Newman, Lisa Tuttle, Pat Cadigan, Michael Marshall Smith, Muriel Gray, Reggie Oliver, Robert Shearman, Angela Slatter and Mark Samuels.

The Doll Collection, edited and introduced by Ellen Datlow, contained seventeen stories by an impressive line-up of contributors that included Tim Lebbon, Stephen Gallagher, Joyce Carol Oates, Gemma Files, Pat Cadigan, John Langan and others, along with photos by the editor, Ellen Klages and Richard Bowes.

Edited by Jason Blum, *The Blumhouse Book of Nightmares: The Haunted City* contained seventeen urban horror stories by Sarah Langan, Simon Kurt Unsworth and others.

The Mammoth Book of Jack the Ripper Stories was a new anthology from Maxim Jakubowski, who had previously edited another compilation on the subject. It included thirty-seven stories by Steve Rasnic Tem, Rhys Hughes and others.

Ghostly, edited, introduced and illustrated by Audrey Niffenegger, collected sixteen ghost stories by, amongst others, M.R. James, Edgar Allan Poe, Edith Wharton, P.G. Wodehouse, Neil Gaiman and Kelly Link.

Edited by Marjorie Sandor, *The Uncanny Reader: Stories from the Shadows* contained thirty-one stories by Edgar Allan Poe, Joan Aiken, Kelly Link, China Mièville and others.

Dead But Not Forgotten, edited by Charlaine Harris and Toni P. Kelner, was subtitled *Stories from the World of Sookie Stackhouse* and included contributions from Rachel Caine, Jonathan Maberry and Sean McGuire.

Edited by Christopher Golden, *Seize the Night: New Tales of Vampiric Terror* contained twenty stories by Charlaine Harris, John Ajvide Lindqvist and others.

Paula Guran edited *Blood Sisters: Vampire Stories by Women,* which contained twenty-five tales by Caitlín R. Kiernan, Laurell K. Hamilton and Tanya Huff, amongst others. From the same editor, *New Cthulhu 2* reprinted nineteen Lovecraftian stories from 2010-14.

The Madness of Cthulhu Volume Two, edited and introduced by S. T. Joshi, featured fourteen original stories "inspired by H.P. Lovecraft" by Greg Bear, Alan Dean Foster, Kevin J. Anderson, Nancy Kilpatrick, William F. Nolan, Steve Rasnic Tem and others. Kim Newman provided an Introduction.

For fans of Arthur Conan Doyle's consulting detective, *The Big Book of Sherlock Holmes Stories* edited by Otto Penzler was the largest collection of Sherlock Holmes stories ever assembled. It included more than eighty stories by, amongst others, Stephen King, Neil Gaiman, August Derleth, Michael Moorcock, Anthony Boucher, Tanith Lee, Poul Anderson, Peter Tremayne, Manly Wade Wellman, Davis Grubb, Peter Cannon and Doyle himself (with two parodies and an essay).

Best New Horror #26 was the first volume in the series to be originally published—in signed and slipcased and regular hardcover editions—by PS Publishing. Edited by Stephen Jones, it included nineteen stories and novellas, along with the usual historical Introduction, Necrology and Useful Addresses.

Ellen Datlow's *The Best Horror of the Year: Volume Seven* featured twenty-two contributions, plus the editor's Summation of the year and the inevitable Honourable Mentions, while Paula Guran's *The Year's Best Dark Fantasy & Horror* collected twenty-eight stories.

The second and reportedly final volume in series editor Johnny Mains' *Best British Horror* featured twenty-two tales, including a tribute to the late Graham Joyce, and the *Year's Best Weird Fiction Volume Two* edited by Kathe Koja and Michael Kelly contained twenty stories.

The Jones and Datlow anthologies overlapped by just one story (by Dale Bailey), the Jones and Mains books both featured the same story by Simon Kurt Unsworth under different titles, and the Datlow and Koja/Kelly both used the same story by Nathan Ballingrud.

Dale Bailey had the distinction of appearing in four "Year's Best" horror volumes, and he was followed by Nathan Ballingrud, Caitlín R. Kiernan, Helen Marshall and Angela Slatter, who were represented in three. Laird Barron, Gemma Files, Stephen Graham Jones, John Langan, Alison Littlewood, Robert Shearman, Simon Strantzas, Steve Rasnic Tem, Lavie Tidhar and Simon Kurt Unsworth all had stories reprinted in two volumes.

Apparently everybody's feeling the squeeze . . . even J.K. Rowling, whose online Pottermore site made a loss of around £6 million in 2015, down from a profit of £14.9 million the previous year. Much of the loss was blamed on the end of an agreement with Sony to package licensed "Harry Potter" video games and e-books with its Sony Reader.

John Joseph Adams' free monthly online *Nightmare Magazine* featured new fiction by, amongst others, Kealan Patrick Burke, Alison Littlewood, Chuck Palahniuk and Silvia Moreno-Garcia; reprints from Brian Everson, Halli Villegas, Robert Shearman, Lynda E.

Rucker, Nancy Kilpatrick, Stephen Graham Jones, Chet Williamson, Lisa Tuttle, Christopher Golden, Steve Rasnic Tem, Richard Christian Matheson, Reggie Oliver, Caitlín R. Kiernan, Poppy Z. Brite, Tim Lebbon, Gemma Files and F. Paul Wilson; columns on horror by Helen Marshall, Lynda E. Rucker, Paul Tremblay, Nancy Holder and Lucy A. Snyder, and interviews with Helen Marshall, Chuck Palahniuk, Richard Chizmar, William F. Nolan, Lucy A. Snyder, Clive Barker and Jason Blum. The October issue was a special "Queers Destroy Horror!" issue edited by Wendy N. Wagner.

Jeani Rector's monthly online magazine *The Horror Zine* presented fiction and poetry from, amongst many others, Sarah Pinborough, Terry Grimwood, Yvonne Navarro, Piers Anthony and Graham Masterton.

The free bi-monthly online magazine *The Dark*, edited by Jack Fisher and Sean Wallace, featured dark fantasy and strange fiction from Lisa L. Hannett, Angela Slatter and others.

Two years after being revived as a print "sampler", John Gilbert's *Fear* magazine finally re-appeared in a digital format. It included interviews with Barbie Wilde, Adam Nevill, Christopher Rice, Jack Ketchum, John Jarrold, and associate editor Dean M. Drinkel, along with news and reviews.

The same day that the first season of *Fear the Walking Dead* ended in early October, AMC launched the sixteen-part online companion series *Fear the Walking Dead: Flight 462*. Featuring a group of aeroplane passengers dealing with an on-board outbreak of the zombie virus, one of its characters was slated to join the sophomore season of the TV series.

Channel 4 streamed *A Moment of Horror*, an anthology of six short-short films online over Hallowe'en.

The latest volume of editor Paul Finch's excellent series of print-on-demand anthologies for Gray Friar Press was *Terror Tales of the Ocean*, which included thirteen stories (four reprints) by, amongst others, Peter James, Terry Grimwood, Robert Shearman, Stephen Laws, Adam Nevill, Simon Strantzas, Lynda E. Rucker and Conrad Williams.

Publisher Charles Black selected fourteen often gruesome tales for *The Eleventh Black Book of Horror* by, amongst others, Thana Niveau, John Llewellyn Probert, Kate Farrell, David A. Riley, Tony Earnshaw, Marion Pitman and Sam Dawson.

Perhaps best known for playing the female Cenobite in *Hellbound: Hellraiser II*, Barbie Wilde's debut collection of stories, *Voices of the Damned*, was impressively published by Birmingham's Short, Scary Tales Publications. Featuring eleven tales (two original), the book boasted a cover painting by Clive Barker, a Foreword by *Fangoria* editor-in-chief Chris Alexander, an Afterword from film-makers the Soska Sisters, and full-colour illustrations by various artists, including Barker, Ben Baldwin, Daniele Serra and others.

Also from SST Publications, *Blood Red* was a werewolf retelling of 'Little Red Riding Hood' and collected Paul Kane's original 2008 novella *Red*, the titular sequel, and two Introductions by Alison Littlewood and Tim Lebbon. The signed, limited hardcover also included extracts from an award-winning screenplay adaptation by Sundae Jahant-Osborn, excerpts from a graphic novel script with character sketches by the author, and a portion of another novella by Kane. Dave McKean supplied the cover art.

Published in hardcover and boasting a terrific cover painting by Clive Barker and an Introduction by Nicholas Vince, *Monsters* from The Alchemy Press collected eighteen stories (one original) and an Afterword by Paul Kane. It came with a bonus DVD of the short film *The Weeping Woman*, directed by Mark Steensland from a story and script by Kane.

Music in the Bone and Other Stories collected twenty stories (one original) by Marion Pitman, who also included author notes on each one.

Evocations featured seventeen tales (one original) and story notes by James Brogden, while Mike Chinn's *Give Me These Moments Back* contained eighteen stories (two original) and an Afterword by the author.

Also from Alchemy, *Leinster Gardens and Other Subtleties* included fourteen stories (one original) and an Afterword by Jan Edwards, with an Introduction by David A. Sutton.

Dead Water and Other Weird Tales from the same imprint collected eighteen career-spanning stories (two original) by Sutton, along with an Introduction by David A. Riley, story notes by the author, and a frontispiece illustration by Jim Pitts.

From David Sutton's own Shadow Publishing, *Creeping Crawlers* was a hefty anthology edited and introduced by Allen Ashley, featuring nineteen stories (one reprint) about insects, arachnids, arthropods and other slithering things by Storm Constantine, Adrian Cole, Dennis Etchison, John Grant, Andrew Darlington and others.

Edited by Pete Kahle, *Not Your Average Monster! A Bestiary of Horrors* was an attractive PoD trade paperback featuring twenty-two stories about unusual creatures by Christine Morgan, Adrian Cole, Billie Sue Mosiman and others, including the editor himself.

Published by Tickety Boo Press and boasting dust-jacket artwork by Jim Burns, Spectral Press founder Simon Marshall-Jones' episodic novel *Biblia Longcrofta* was set in the titular town on the northern coastline of Britain.

From Surinam Turtle Press, Richard A. Lupoff's on-demand imprint for Ramble House, Christopher Conlon's *The Tell-Tale Soul: Two Novellas* was inspired by the work of Edgar Allan Poe and Eugene O'Neill and came with an Introduction by John Pelan.

Working Stiff by Kevin J. Anderson from WordFire Press collected seven stories about zombie private investigator Dan Shamble. It was reprinted with bonus material by Gauntlet Press in an edition of 500 signed copies and a traycased lettered edition.

Welcome trade paperback reprints from Valancourt Books included the novels *Cold Moon Over Babylon* and *Katie* by Michael McDowell; *The Woodwitch* by Stephen Gregory with an Introduction by Paul Tremblay; *House of Fire* by Arch Oboler with an Introduction by Christopher Conlon, and *Burnt Offerings* by Robert Marasco with an Introduction by Stephen Graham Jones.

Edited with an Introduction by Stephen Jones and featuring new movie-themed Afterwords by Kim Newman, *Fengriffin & Other Gothic Tales* and *The Cell & Other Transmorphic Tales* were original collections from Valancourt of some of the best stories and novellas by David Case.

Other collections from the same PoD imprint included *On an Odd Note*, a reprint of the 1958 volume containing thirteen stories by Gerald Kersh and a new Introduction by Nick Mamatas, and *Antique Dust*, an excellent collection of ghost stories by Robert Westall, with an Introduction by Orrin Grey.

Nightscript: Volume One, edited by C.M. Muller for Chthonic Matter, was billed on the cover as "An Anthology of Strange and Darksome Tales". It lived up to that description with twenty original stories by, amongst others, Daniel Mills, Clint Smith, Eric J. Guignard, Michael Kelly and Jason A. Wycoff.

Edited by Jean-Marc Lofficier and Randy Lofficier for their Black Coat Press imprint, *The Vampire Almanac (Volume 1)* collected twenty-one original pastiche vampire stories. Frank Schildiner's novel *The Quest of Frankenstein* from the same PoD publisher united Mary Shelley's Monster and H.P. Lovecraft's Herbert West in the trenches of the First World War.

Nicole Cushing's first full-length collection, *The Mirrors*, was issued by Cycatrix Press, an imprint of JaSunni Productions. It contained twenty stories (two original) along with a Foreword by S.T. Joshi and a Preface and Story Notes by the author.

Issued by on-demand publisher Hippocampus Press, Josh Kent's *The Witch at Sparrow Screek: A Jim Falk Novel* was about its titular young protagonist using ancient knowledge to rid the land of evil.

A Confederacy of Horrors from Hippocampus was a first collection from James Robert Smith containing twenty-five stories (nine original), along with an Afterword by Smith's former *Deathrealm* alumnus Stephen Mark Rainey.

From the same imprint came the collections *Dreams of Ys and Other Invisible Worlds* by Jonathan Thomas, *The Bloody Tugboat and Other Witcheries* by Robert H. Waugh, and *Dark Equinox and Other Tales of Lovecraftian Horror* by Ann K. Schwader, all featuring a mix of original and reprint material.

Cult of the Dead and Other Weird and Lovecraftian Tales collected twenty reprint stories by Lois H. Gresh with an Introduction by S.T. Joshi, while W.H. Pugmire's *Monstrous Aftermath: Stories in the Lovecraft Tradition* included fifteen reprint stories plus, for no apparent reason, Lovecraft's sonnet-cycle 'Fungi from Yuggoth'.

Translated by Maria Mountokalaki and Elizabeth Georgiades, *Necronomicon: The Manuscript of the Dead* by German-born Greek writer Antonis Antoniades was a historical Lovecraftian novel set in the 10th century and concerned the translation of the blasphemous tome written by the mad Arab, Abdul Alhazred.

Edited by S.T. Joshi, the second issue of the attractively-designed *Spectral Realms* from Hippocampus Press featured more than sixty poems by Donald Sydney-Fryer, Ann K. Schwader, Gemma Files, Darrell Schweitzer, John Shirley, William F. Nolan, Michael Kelly, W.H. Pugmire and many others, along with an article about the poetry of Leah Bodine Drake by Leigh Blackmore and reviews by Sunni K. Brock.

Joshi also supplied the Preface for Ann K. Schwader's poetry collection *Dark Energies* from Australia's P'rea Press. Featuring an interview with the poet by editor Charles Lovecraft, along with an Afterword by Robert M. Price, the book also included a mix of new and reprint poems.

Edited and introduced by Price for Celaeno Press, *Beyond the Mountains of Madness* was a Lovecraftion anthology inspired by the classic novella. It contained fourteen stories (one reprint) by Joseph S. Pulver Sr., C.J. Henderson, Cody Goodfellow, Stephen Mark Rainey, Will Murray, William Meikle and others.

A Lonely & Curious Country: Tales from the Lands of Lovecraft edited with an Introduction by Matthew Carpenter for Ulthar Press featured seventeen original stories about eldritch locations from, amongst others, Pete Rawlik, Christine Morgan, Don Webb, Robert M. Price and Aaron J. French.

Thirteen of the late John S. Glasby's Lovecraftian stories (six original) were collected together in *The Brooding City and Other Tales of the Cthulhu Mythos* from Dancing Tuatara Press, along with an historical Introduction by publisher John Pelan.

Edited with an Introduction by Tony Eccles and published by the Cygnus Alpha creative collective in an oversized softcover format, *Secret Invasion: Tales of Eldritch Horror from the West Country* was another PoD Lovecraftian anthology with fifteen original stories set around Cornwall, Devon and Somerset. It also included an interview with Ramsey Campbell and full colour illustrations by John Swogger, Mark Toner and Steven Tickey. The aim of the book was to raise money for the UK mental health charity MIND.

From Great British Horror Books imprint Black Shuck Books, *Masks* featured thirteen original stories by Adrian Cole, Phil Sloman, James Everington and others. The anthology was dedicated to the memory of American artist James Powell, who did the cover.

From the same imprint, *Wild Things,* edited with an Introduction by publisher Steve J. Shaw, included thirteen stories (three reprints) about the beast within by, amongst others, Anna Taborska and Johnny Mains.

KnightWatch Press was another imprint of Great British Horror and published *Season's Greetings from Theresa Derwin* as an attractive little booklet featuring six comedic Christmas stories by the author, with impressive cover art by Stephen Cooney.

KnightWatch also turned out a slew of PoD anthologies, including *Chip Shop Horrors* edited by Stewart Hotston, *Sunny with a Chance of Zombies* edited by Dion Winton-Polak, *Nice Day for a Picnic* edited by Brian Marshall and Alex Davis, *Once Bitten* by Steve Lewis, *Soul Survivors Volume II* edited by Christine Morgan, *Play Things & Past Times* edited by Steve J. Shaw, and the inevitable volume of Lovecraft pastiches, *New Tales of the Old Ones* edited by Theresa Derwin and Paul Simpson.

Die Dog or Eat the Hatchet from Comet Press featured three novellas by Adam Howe, along with a Foreword by Randy Chandler and Story Notes by the author. Writing as "Garrett Adams", British writer Howe's short story 'Jumper' was selected by Stephen King some years earlier as the winner of his *On Writing* contest.

Edited with an Introduction by Donald J. Bingle and published by 54·40' Orphyte, Inc., *Familiar Spirits* contained eleven original stories "that go bump in the night" by William Peck, Jean Rabe and Sarah Hans, amongst others.

Nightmares Unhinged: Twenty Tales of Terror, the first anthology from editor and game designer Joshua Viola's PoD imprint Hex

Publishers, featured original stories by Steve Rasnic Tem, Stephen Graham Jones, Jeanne C. Stein and others, including four contributions from the editor himself. A portion of the proceeds were donated to the charity Rocky Mountain Cancer Assistance in memory of Melanie Tem, to whom the book was dedicated and who was remembered in a moving Afterword by Edward Bryant.

Edited by Juliana Rew, *Ain't Superstitious* was published by the American/ Scottish print-on-demand micropublisher Third Flatiron Anthologies. A double edition of a series of quarterly themed anthologies, it featured twenty-six stories of the "weird, wild and magical".

From Lethe Press, *The Nameless Dark: A Collection* brought together fourteen stories (five original) by T.E. Grau with an Introduction by Nathan Ballingrud.

The same imprint also published *Daughters of Frankenstein: Lesbian Mad Scientists!* edited by Steve Berman. It contained nineteen stories by Gemma Files, Melissa Scott and others, along with a historical essay by Jess Nevins and an Introduction by Connie Wilkins.

Edited by Rhonda Parrish, *B is for Broken* was the second volume in a series of "Alphabet Anthologies" from PoD imprint Poise and Pen Publishing and featured twenty-six stories based on letters of the alphabet, along with a bonus tale from the previous volume.

The busy Parrish also edited and introduced *Corvidae* and *Scarecrow*, the second and third volumes in "Rhonda Parrish's Magical Menageries" series from Michigan's World Weaver Press. The anthologies contained a mixture of new and reprint stories and poetry by Jane Yolen, Angela Slatter and others.

In *Frozen Fairy Tales* from the same publisher, editor Kate Wolford brought together fifteen original stories based around a chilly theme.

Published by Parallel Universe Publications, *Kitchen Sink Gothic* selected by David A. Riley and Linden Riley contained seventeen "unglamorous" stories (three reprints) by Stephen Bacon, Andrew Darlington, Gary Fry, Kate Farrell, David A. Sutton, Adrian Cole and others.

From Post Mortem Press, *Shrieks and Shivers from the Horror Zine* edited by Jeani Rector contained thirty-one stories by William F. Nolan, Tom Piccirilli, P.D. Cacek, Tim Waggoner and others.

Carus & Mitch was a post-apocalyptic novella by Tim Major, published on-demand by Omnium Gatherum.

Edited and introduced by Ross Warren and Anthony Watson for Dark Minds Press, *Darkest Minds: Stories from the Borderlines* contained twelve stories (one reprint) themed around crossing borders by Gary Fry, Andrew Hook, Stephen Bacon and others.

Peripheral Visions: The Collected Ghost Stories (1986 to 2015) was a huge compilation of Robert Hood's short fiction published by Dark Phases/IFWAG Publishing. The almost 800-page hardcover brought together forty-four stories (three original), along with an Introduction by Danel Olson and a Preface and extensive story notes by the author. Nick Stathopoulos supplied the illustrations.

Edited with an Introduction by Tehani Wessley for Australian PoD imprint FableCroft Publishing, *Insert Title Here* contained twenty-one original tales of speculative fiction by, amongst others, Robert Hood, Alan Baxter, Ian Creasey and Kathleen Jennings.

From the same publisher and co-edited by Wessley and Tansy Rayner Roberts, *Cranky Ladies of History* featured twenty-two original stories and a reprint poem about women who challenged conventional wisdom about appropriate female behaviour by Garth Nix, Jane Yolen, Lisa L. Hannett, Amanda Pillar and others.

Amanda Pillar was also the editor of *Bloodlines: 16 Journeys on the Dark Streets of Urban Fantasy*, published by Ticonderoga Publications. The anthology contained original fiction by Stephanie Gunn, Alan Baxter, Kathleen Jennings and others, along with an Introduction by the editor.

Australia's Brimstone Press published *The Abandonment of Grace and Everything After*, a collection of thirteen "dark fantasy and desolation" stories by Shane Jiraiya Cummings with an Introduction by Stephen M. Irwin.

Illustrated with classic etchings, *Dark Parchments: Midnight Curses & Verses* was an attractive trade paperback from MoonDream Press/Copper Dog Publishing that showcased eighty-five poems (seven reprints) by Michael H. Hanson with a Foreword by Janet Morris.

Finally revived after eighteen years in a slick new PoD format by John Gregory Betancourt's Wildside Press after some social media controversy, the new incarnation of *Weirdbook* was edited by Doug Draa, with founder W. Paul Ganley on board as Consulting Editor. Issue #31 featured fiction and poetry from Adrian Cole, Gary A. Braunbeck, Paul Dale Anderson, Darrell Schweitzer, Jessica Amanda Salmonson, Kurt Newton, Ann K. Schwader, W. H. Pugmire and Dave Reeder, amongst others.

The Winter 2015 paperback edition of *Blight Digest* edited by Bracken MacLeod, Ron Earl Phillips, Frank Larnerd and Jan Kozlowski for One Eye Press featured thirteen stories by Matt Andrew, Tony Wilson and others, along with a Foreword by co-editor MacLeod.

Ably edited by Tom Roberts, *Windy City Pulp Stories #15*—published to tie in with the Windy City Pulp and Paperback Convention in Chicago—was a handsome-looking trade paperback celebrating the 125th Birthday of H.P. Lovecraft and the 75th Anniversary of the Street & Smith Comics. It included fiction by Lovecraft and Robert Weinberg, along with fascinating articles from, amongst others, David H. Keller M.D., F. Paul Wilson, Stephen Jones, Will Murray, S.T. Joshi, August Derleth and Anthony Tollin. Les Edwards did the cover, and Randy Broecker contributed a portfolio of Lovecraftian illustrations.

Lavie Tidhar's episodic *noir* novel *A Man Lies Dreaming*, conceived in the mind of a prisoner in Auschwitz, was issued by PS Publishing in a signed, slipcased edition of 200 copies, along with the author's *Lust of the Swastika*, a spoof pulp novel by "Sebastian Bruce".

A family's holiday in Greece turned decidedly strange in Ramsey Campbell's *Thirteen Days by Sunset Beach*, while *The Unlicensed Magician* was a short novel about magic and a baby rescued from death by Kelly Barnhill.

The Night Listener and Others was a welcome collection from PS of twenty-two tales (two original) by Chet Williamson with an

Introduction by Richard Christian Matheson and story notes by the author.

Other Stories from the same publisher collected fifteen superior tales (two original) plus Story Notes by Paul Park, along with an Introduction by Michael Swanwick.

Thirteen of James Cooper's excellent stories were collected in *Human Pieces*, including tributes to Stephen King and Peter Cushing, while *Frost on Glass* was another fine collection of fiction (two previously unpublished) by Ian R. MacLeod, with new Afterwords to each of the tales.

Second Shift: More Tales from the Word Mines was a thin hardcover containing three stories by the late Graham Joyce. It was a companion to the previous year's retrospective volume, and was available in a 100-copy signed edition.

Visions from Brichester was a collection of fourteen Lovecraftian stories by Ramsey Campbell, who received an honorary fellowship from Liverpool John Moores University in July for his "outstanding contribution to literature". The book also included such bonus material as first drafts, fragments, non-fiction and early poems, along with numerous black and white illustrations by Randy Broecker.

Journalist David Hambling's *The Dulwich Horror & Others* from PS collected seven Lovecraftian pastiches with a distinctly British bent, along with a Foreword by S.T. Joshi and an Introduction by the author.

Probably the last thing anybody needed was yet another anthology of Lovecraftian-inspired fiction, but editor Lois H. Gresh gave us one anyway. *Innsmouth Nightmares* contained a mixed bag of twenty-one stories (one reprint) based around HPL's ichthyic Deep Ones by Lavie Tidhar, Paul Kane, Tim Lebbon, Nancy Kilpatrick, Richard Gavin, Steve Rasnic Tem, John Langan, William F. Nolan, Lisa Morton, James Moore, Nancy Holder, S.T. Joshi and others.

Also from PS, *That is Not Dead: Tales of the Cthulhu Mythos Through the Centuries* was an anthology of historical Lovecraftian fiction edited with an Introduction by Darrell Schweitzer and featuring fourteen original stories by John Langan, Jay Lake, Don Webb (two), Lois H. Gresh, Will Murray, S.T. Joshi, Richard

A. Lupoff, Harry Turtledove and others, including the editor himself.

Edited with an Introduction by S.T. Joshi, *Black Wings IV: New Tales of Lovecraftian Horror* featured seventeen stories and a poem from, amongst others, Fred Chappell, W.H. Pugmire, Richard Gavin, Caitlín R. Kiernan, Darrell Schweitzer, Melanie Tem, Lois H. Gresh, Will Murray and Simon Strantzas.

PS continued its attractive "Lovecraft Illustrated" series of reprints under The Pulps Library imprint with *The Shadow Over Time*, *The Shadow Over Innsmouth* and *At the Mountains of Madness*, all with introductions by S.T. Joshi, full colour illustrations by Pete Von Sholly, and plenty of bonus material from the likes of W.H. Pugmire, Brian Yuzna, Robert M. Price and others.

From the same publisher, *Weird Poems: The Complete Poems from Weird Tales* by H.P. Lovecraft was a reprint of a 2010 collection compiled by Stephen Jones, with new artwork by Sholly.

Edited as usual by Nick Gevers, *Breakout* was volume 34/35 of PS' "Postscripts Anthology" series. It featured twenty-seven diverse stories by Garry Kilworth, Lisa L. Hannett, Simon Strantzas, Kit Reed, Darrell Schweitzer, Anna Tambour and others.

The deluxe 30th Anniversary Edition of Stephen King's second collection, *Skeleton Crew*, was available from PS Publishing in a printing of 974 slipcased copies signed by artist Pete Von Sholley and Stephen Jones, who contributed the Introduction. It came in two alternative dust-jacket designs.

PS also produced a 10th Anniversary Edition of Joe Hill's debut collection *20th Century Ghosts* in various editions, with an Introduction by Ramsey Campbell.

Published as a collaboration between Edgeworks Abbey and PS Publishing, the 52nd Anniversary 9th edition of *Ellison Wonderland* contained almost all the Harlan Ellison^{Æ} stories from the earlier 1974 and 1984 editions, along with the original Introduction and a new (128 page!) one by the author, an Appreciation of Ellison by J. Michael Straczynski, and an Afterword by screenwriter Josh Olson. The 200-copy signed and slipcased edition came with a slim bonus volume, *Pebbles from the Mountain*, which collected eleven obscure and mostly pseudonymous stories by Ellison, originally published in magazines in the 1950s.

A group of acid-folk musicians returned with a documentary filmmaker to the eponymous haunted country house where their lead singer disappeared many years before in Elizabeth Hand's terrific novella *Wylding Hall.*

Equally notable from PS was *In the Lovecraft Museum*, a surreal horror novella by Steve Rasnic Tem in which an American still grieving over his missing son was invited by a mysterious British penpal to visit a bizarre museum devoted to author H.P. Lovecraft and his work.

Marc Laidlaw's *White Spawn* was another Lovecraft-inspired novella, about a young girl's momentous discovery in a backwoods community.

All PS Publishing's novellas were available in 100-copy signed editions, as well as unsigned editions.

Best New Horror #3 edited by Stephen Jones was reprinted in a revised and updated trade paperback edition with French flaps by the PS imprint Drugstore Indian Press.

Originally published in 2001 in serial form as part of the packaging for a series of collectible action figures, Clive Barker's novelette *Tortured Souls: The Legend of Primordium* was issued by Subterranean Press in various hardcover states, including a twenty-six copy lettered traycased edition ($275.00), illustrated by Bob Eggleton.

Subterranean also published *Tonight, Again*, a collection of thirty-one mostly erotic stories and vignettes by Barker, who also illustrated the volume. It was also available in a slipcased edition of 224 copies ($125.00) and twenty-six leather-bound, traycased copies ($350.00).

Beneath an Oil-Dark Sea: The Best of Caitlín R. Kiernan Volume 2 collected twenty-seven stories, a short novel and a poem, with an Introduction by S.T. Joshi. A signed leather-bound edition was limited to 600 copies and came with a hardcover of previously unpublished material.

Perdido: A Fragment from a Work in Progress by Peter Straub was about a legendary mountain resort in Norway. Stephen King and

Gahan Wilson briefly turned up as characters. A signed edition limited to 400 copies was also available.

Bob Eggleton contributed fold-out interior artwork to *Tales of the Primal Land*, an omnibus of Brian Lumley's Lovecraftian novel *Sorcery in Shad* along with the collections *The House of Cthulhu* and *Tarra Khash: Hrossak!* The book was also available from Subterranean in a signed, limited edition of 250 copies.

Joe Hill contributed a new Introduction to a reprint of Alan Moore's 1996 novel *Voice of the Fire*, which was available in a signed slipcased edition and a deluxe twenty-six copy version limited to 750 copies ($350.00).

Subterranean reissued Thomas Harris' 1988 novel *The Silence of the Lambs* in a deluxe slipcased edition, illustrated by Marshall Arisman. Limited to 200 copies signed by the artist ($150.00), there was also a fifty-two copy lettered edition additionally signed by the author for $1,500.

A ship hired by a reality TV crew to search for mermaids discovered something terrible beneath the waves in the novella *Rolling in the Deep* by "Mira Grant" (Seanan McGuire), available from Subterranean in a 1,000-copy signed edition.

Co-published by Borderlands Press and Gauntlet Press, *Family Secrets* was the second book in the young adult "Nocturnia Chronicles" series by Tom Monteleone and F. Paul Wilson. It was also available in a signed edition of 300 copies, and a traycased and lettered edition.

Monteleone's *Submerged* from Cemetery Dance Publications involved a sunken secret Nazi submarine and the secrets it concealed. It was published in a signed edition of 750 copies.

From the same imprint, Bentley Little's satirical novel *The Consultant* was set in a big corporation filled with fear.

Limited to 500 signed copies, the tenth volume in Earthling's annual "Halloween" series was Simon Clark's pseudo-werewolf novel *Rage Master*.

Awaiting Strange Gods: Weird and Lovecraftian Fictions from Fedogan & Bremer collected twenty-two stories by Darrell Schweitzer (including two collaborations with Jason Van Hollander), introduced by the ubiquitous S.T. Joshi.

Limited to 125 signed and numbered hardcovers and an unlimited number of paperbacks, but barely given any distribution when publisher Spectral Press found itself in financial problems, Stephen Volk's novella *Leytonstone* was a homage to Alfred Hitchcock, just as his previous book for the publisher, *Whitstable*, had been a celebration of Peter Cushing. It came with an Afterword by Stephen Gallagher.

Similar distribution problems also afflicted two anthologies from the same publisher: *Darker Terrors* edited by Stephen Jones and David A. Sutton was a "sampler" anthology from the six-volume series that ran from 1995-2002. It contained seventeen stories by Ray Bradbury, Harlan Ellison, Ramsey Campbell, Karl Edward Wagner, Neil Gaiman, Brian Lumley, Poppy Z. Brite, Michael Marshall Smith, Gwyneth Jones and others, along with a new Introduction and Afterword by the Editors. The book was available in a trade paperback edition and a 100-copy hardcover edition signed by both Jones and Sutton.

Spectral's *The 2nd Spectral Book of Horror Stories* edited with an Introduction by Mark Morris also suffered from poor distribution. It featured nineteen original stories by, amongst others, Paul Finch, Tim Lebbon, Lisa L. Hannett, Adrian Cole, Nicholas Royle, Ian Rogers, Simon Kurt Unsworth, Thana Niveau, Ray Cluley, Gary Fry, Stephen Volk and Robert Shearman.

Centipede Press produced a beautifully slipcased set of all Karl Edward Wagner's "Kane, the Mystic Swordsman" books: *Bloodstone, Dark Crusade, Darkness Weaves, Death Angel's Shadow* and *Night Winds* were illustrated, respectively, by Patrick J. Jones, Tom Kidd, Boco, Les Edwards and Grant Griffin. The *Night Winds* volume additionally included artwork by Stephen E. Fabian and Jim Pitts.

Limited to 320 signed copies, *It Only Comes Out at Night & Other Stories* collected more than forty reprint stories by Dennis Etchison, along with an Introduction by S.T. Joshi and story notes by the author. David Ho supplied the illustrations.

James Herbert's trilogy *The Rats, Lair* and *Domain* were reprinted in hardcover by Centipede, with artwork by Ho and Jason C.

Eckhardt, and an Introduction by Stephen Jones. They were limited to 300 signed sets.

Centipede also issued the first North American edition of David J. Schow's 1990 novel *The Shaft* in a 300-copy signed edition, with a Foreword by F. Paul Wilson, an Afterword by the author, and art by David Ho.

Published as part of Centipede's ambitious "Masters of the Weird Tales" series edited by Joshi, *David Case* contained sixteen stories by the titular author, plus a surreal new novella. Ramsey Campbell supplied the Introduction, and there was also an interview with Case by Johnny Mains. The oversized slipcased edition was illustrated by Jason Zerrillo.

The sixth issue of Centipede's excellent *Weird Fiction Review* was a hefty trade paperback featuring, amongst other things, a terrific look at "Spook Show" posters with some great colour illustrations, an interview with veteran horror comics artist L.B. Cole (who died in 1995), S.T. Joshi comparing writers Irvin S. Cobb and Gouverneur Washington, a portfolio of art by Christopher Conn Askew, a look at the photography of William Mortensen, a discussion between Clive Barker and Peter Atkins, and an interview with T.E.D. Klein. There was also fiction and poetry by Richard Gavin, Jonathan Thomas, Michael Aronovitz, Ann K. Schwader, Darrell Schweitzer and many others, along with much more.

Probably Monsters was a collection of twenty stories (three original) by Ray Cluley from ChiZine Publications, with Story Notes by the author.

The same Canadian imprint also reissued Gemma Files' collections *Kissing Carrion* and *The Worm in Every Heart* with new material included, and a former film critic thought he saw a long-missing socialite in a silent movie in Files' novel *Experimental Film*.

Edited by Michael Matheson, *The Humanity of Monsters* from ChiZine featured twenty-six stories by Gemma Files, Neil Gaiman, Joe R. Lansdale and others.

From Egaeus Press, *Soliloquy for Pan* was an illustrated compendium of works "in praise, in fear, in awe of the great goat-god Pan". The anthology featured new stories by, amongst others,

Reggie Oliver, John Howard, R.B. Russell, Lynda E. Rucker, D.P. Watt and Mark Valentine, along with archive material from Dion Fortune, Robert Louis Stevenson, Henry Wood Nevinson, A.C. Benson, Lord Dunsany, Robert Frost, Ivar Campbell and Harry Fitzgerald. Limited to only 300 copies, the book sold out in just two weeks and quickly went into a second edition with a different cover image and endpapers.

Canada's Undertow Publications published *Skein and Bone*, a collection of fourteen stories (three original) by V.H. Leslie, along with one of the finest anthologies of the year, *Aickman's Heirs*, which was nominally a tribute to the subtle "strange stories" written by the late Robert Aickman (1914-81). In fact, editor Simon Strantzas skilfully compiled a volume of fifteen often remarkable stories showcasing some of the very best talent working in the horror field today, including work by Brian Evenson, Richard Gavin, John Howard, Lynda E. Rucker, John Langan, Helen Marshall, Daniel Mills, Nina Allan, Lisa Tuttle and others.

Presumably the culmination of Tartarus Press' ambitious reprint programme of books by Robert Aickman (eight collections of stories and two volumes of autobiography), *The Strangers and Other Writings* was an impressive compendium of the author's previously unpublished and uncollected short fiction, non-fiction and poetry, with a Preface by Aickman's friend and literary executor Heather Smith.

One of the most important books of the year, it was accompanied by *Robert Aickman: Author of Strange Tales*, an excellent DVD documentary about the author by R.B. Russell and Rosalie Parker. It featured, amongst others, Jeremy Dyson and Reggie Oliver, and was a perfect primer for anyone interested in Aickman's complex life and work.

Orpheus on the Underground and Other Stories from the same imprint was a collection of sixteen typically odd tales (one reprint) by Rhys Hughes, illustrated by Chris Harrendence.

Michael Reynier's *Hortholary: Tales from Montagascony* was limited to 300 copies and included four further stories about investigator extraordinary Professor Summanus Hortholary, while

Haunted by Books was a collection of literary-inspired essays by Mark Valentine.

Also from Tartarus and limited to 300 copies, *The Children of the Pool* was a welcome reprint of the 1936 collection by Arthur Machen which featured a new Introduction by Mark Valentine.

As usual edited by Rosalie Parker, the Tartarus anthology *Strange Tales V* collected seventeen new stories by Steve Rasnic Tem, Andrew Hook, John Howard, Mark Valentine, Tom Johnstone and others.

Inspired by the work of Arthur Machen, authors John Howard, Mark Valentine and Ron Weighell contributed three excellent novellas and Afterwords to *Romances of the White Day* from Sarob Press. From the same imprint, *In the City of Ghosts* collected thirteen haunting tales (two original) by Michael Chislett, and *Friends of the Dead* contained ten stories (two previously unpublished) and an Introduction by James Doig.

From Three Hands Press, *Penumbrae: An Occult Fiction Anthology* edited by Richard Gavin, Patricia Cram and Daniel A. Schulke was an attractive hardcover containing thirteen stories (four reprints) in the "emerging literary form" by, amongst others, Hanns Heinz Ewers, Michael Cisco, Brian Evenson, Caitlín R. Kiernan, Don Webb and all three editors.

From Dark Renaissance Books, *The Sea of Blood* collected together twenty-three stories from Reggie Oliver's six collections, along with three original tales. There was also a signed, deluxe edition available ($125.00).

Tanith Lee's *A Different City* was a new collection of stories from Immanion Press, while the same author's *Dancing Through the Fire: A Collection of Stories in Five Moves* appeared from Fantastic Books.

Tachyon Publications celebrated its 20th Anniversary with *The Monstrous* edited by Ellen Datlow. Featuring twenty tales (one original) of "the Other gone wrong", contributors included Peter Straub, Dale Bailey, Caitlín R. Kiernan, Gemma Files, Kim Newman, Brian Hodge, Terry Dowling, Glen Hirshberg, Steve Rasnic Tem and John Langan, amongst others. John Coulthart supplied the interesting interior art.

Death's Sweet Echo was a collection of thirteen ghost stories and strange tales (three reprints) by (Len) Maynard and (Mick) Sims. Published in various formats by the Tickety Boo Press imprint Scarier 51, the signed hardcover was limited to just 150 copies.

The third volume in a series of novellas from Wordcraft, *The Girl on the Swing and At Night in Crumbling Voices* by Peter Grandbois, featured two stories loosely inspired by the 1950s monster movies *The Quatermass Experiment* and *The Mole People.*

Gods, Memes and Monsters: A 21st Century Bestiary, edited with an Introduction by Heather J. Wood for Stone Skin Press, collected short-short essays/stories by more than sixty authors, including Silvia Moreno-Garcia, Sandra Kasturi, Helen Marshall, Nancy Kilpatrick and Nick Mamatas, amongst others, illustrated by Rachel Kahn.

From Resurrection House/Underland Press, Will Elliott's novel *The Pilo Traveling Show* was a belated sequel to *The Pilo Family Circus* (2006), while a student discovered a big hole under the football stadium in Dale Bailey's *The Subterranean Season.* Resurrection's Arche Press imprint produced *The End of the End of Everything*, which collected nine stories by Bailey.

Published by Word Horde, *Cthulhu Fhtagn! Weird Tales Inspired by H.P. Lovecraft* was the third Mythos-related anthology edited by Ross E. Lockhart. It featured nineteen original stories by Ann K. Schwader, W.H. Pugmire, Nathan Carson, Anya Martin, Cody Goodfellow and others.

Edited by Scott Harrison for Snowbooks, *Whispers in the Dark: A Collection of Cthulhu Novellas* collected three original novellas set between the 1940s and the present day by Thana Niveau, Johnny Mains and Alison Littlewood.

Goat Mother and Others from Chaosium collected all nineteen Mythos stories by Pierre V. Comtois, along with an essay and an Introduction by Robert M. Price.

Edited by James Lowder for the same imprint, *Madness on the Orient Express* contained sixteen Lovecraftian stories set on the famous locomotive. Contributors included Christopher Golden and Darrell Schweitzer.

Atomic-Age Cthulhu edited by Owen Glynn Barrass and Brian M.

Sammons contained nineteen original Lovecraftian stories set in the 1950s by Cody Goodfellow, Robert M. Price and others.

Joseph S. Pulver, Sr. edited and introduced *Cassilda's Song: Tales Inspired by Robert W. Chambers' King in Yellow Mythos* for Chaosium. The all-women anthology featured eighteen original stories by Nicole Cushing, Lynda E. Rucker, Helen Marshall, Allyson Bird, Lucy A. Snyder, Anya Martin, Maura McHugh and others.

From Dark Regions Press, *Dreams from the Witch House: Female Voices of Lovecraftian Horror* was edited and introduced by Lynne Jamneck and featured twenty stories (three reprints) by Joyce Carol Oates, Caitlín R. Kiernan, Gemma Files, Lois H. Gresh, Nancy Kilpatrick, Storm Constantine and others.

Produced with money raised from a crowdfunding project, *She Walks in Shadows* from Canada's Innsmouth Free Press contained twenty-five Lovecraftian stories plus impressive artwork by women writers and artists. Co-edited with an Introduction by Silvia Moreno-Garcia and Paula R. Stiles, contributors included Ann K. Schwader, Angela Slatter, Gemma Files, Mary A. Turzillo, Wendy N. Wagner and others.

Boasting an Introduction by Ramsey Campbell and published by Horror Australis, the partially crowdfunded *Cthulhu: Deep Down Under* edited by Steve Proposch, Christopher Sequeira and Bryce Stevens was a handsomely-produced hardcover anthology containing twenty-four Lovecraftian pastiches (six reprints) by such Australian writers as Aaron Sterns, Lucy Sussex, Janeen Webb, Stephen Dedman, Bill Congreve and Robert Hood. Each story in the book was illustrated in full colour by a different artist.

Also produced with the aid of a crowdfunding campaign and published in trade paperback by Canada's Edge Science Fiction and Fantasy Publishing, *nEvermore! Tales of Murder, Mystery & the Macabre*, co-edited with an Introduction by Nancy Kilpatrick and Caro Soles, featured twenty-two neo-Gothic stories inspired by the works of Edgar Allan Poe. Although his influence was not always apparent, the anthology wisely stayed away (for the most part) from fiction that was a slavish imitation or sequel to Poe's own tales. The impressive line-up of contributors included, amongst others,

Margaret Atwood, Chelsea Quinn Yarbro, Lisa Morton, Thomas S. Roche, Nancy Holder, Richard Christian Matheson, Loren Rhodes, Kelley Armstrong, Tanith Lee and David Morrell, while Uwe Sommerlad contributed a "rather scholarly" essay on Poe.

Kilpatrick also edited and introduced *Expiration Date: When Your Time is Up...* for the same publisher. The anthology contained twenty-five original stories about death from Kelley Armstrong, Steve Rasnic Tem and Melanie Tem, Silvia Moreno-Garcia, Paul Kane, Sephera Giron, Kathryn Ptacek, Nancy Holder, Erin Underwood and others.

Nicholas Royle's Nightjar Press published four chapbooks of literary unease: *The Harvestman* by Alison Moore, *The Home* by Tom Fletcher, *The Woman Who Lived in a Restaurant* by Leone Ross and *Last Christmas* by John D. Rutter, each limited to 200 signed copies.

These Last Embers by Simon Strantzas was the first volume in Undertow Publications' attractive chapbook series. It was published in an edition of 200 copies, signed by the author and cover artist Drazen Kozjan.

Lisa L. Hannett's story *Smoke Billows, Soot Falls* was published in a chapbook edition of just 125 signed and numbered copies by Spectral Press.

Charles Coleman Finlay took over the editorship of *The Magazine of Fantasy & Science Fiction* with the March-April issue from Gordon Van Gelder, who remained as publisher. The digest magazine, founded back in 1949, produced its usual six bi-monthly editions featuring fiction by, amongst others, Dale Bailey, Albert E. Cowdrey, David Gerrold, Rachel Pollack, James Patrick Kelly, Ron Goulart, Paolo Bacigalupi, Dennis Etchison, Elizabeth Bear, Tim Sullivan and Jeffrrey Ford, along with all the usual review and opinion columns by such contributors as Charles De Lint, David J. Skal, Elizabeth Hand, David Langford and Douglas A. Anderson.

Andy Cox's bi-monthly *Black Static* continued to put out six solid issues a year with fiction by Steve Rasnic Tem, Cate Gardner, Gary McMahon, James Van Pelt, John Connolly, Jeffrey Thomas, Stephen

Bacon, Andrew Hook, Thana Niveau, Erinn L. Kemper, Simon Bestwick and others. Each edition also featured the regular opinion and review columns by Stephen Volk, Lynda E. Rucker, Tony Lee and Peter Tennant, the latter interviewing Tim Waggoner, Helen Marhsall, Ralph Robert Moore, Ray Cluley, Simon Kurt Unsworth and Nicole Cushing.

Black Static's companion SF/fantasy title, *Interzone*, also produced six issues, which featured yet another interview with Helen Marshall, along with a guest editorial by Christopher Fowler.

The two issues of *Cemetery Dance* included reprint fiction by Stephen King and Norman Partridge; new stories from Gerard Houarner and Keith Minnion; a round-robin interview with Rick Hautala, Ronald Kelly and C. Dean Anderson talking about being published by Zebra Books during the 1980s, and another with Peter Straub, Ramsey Campbell and Robert Weinberg discussing the rise of modern horror fiction in the 1970s. There were also opinion and review columns by Thomas F. Monteleone, Michael Marano, Ellen Datlow, Ed Gorman, Robert Parrish and Mark Sieber, along with numerous Stephen King reviews by Bev Vincent.

The two issues of Hildy Silverman's *Space and Time: The Magazine of Fantasy, Horror, and Science Fiction* contained the usual selection of fiction and poetry, along with interviews with Nancy Kress and Robert J. Sawyer, and some fine artwork from Steven C. Gilberts, Douglas Drapper and Martin Hanford.

Three years after its previous edition appeared, *Allen K's Inhuman Magazine* was back with a sixth issue, published by Centipede Press. The bumper, 200-plus page edition of Allen Koszowski's fiction magazine contained new stories by J.F. Gonzalez, Justin Gustainis, Tim Curran, David A. Sutton, C.J. Henderson, Weston Ochse, Gene O'Neill, Randall D. Larson, Don D'Ammassa and others, reprints from Jason Van Hollander, Chad Hensley and W.H. Pugmire, Gahan Wilson, Darrell Schweitzer and Michael Bishop, plus plenty of examples of the editor's own artwork and a portfolio of illustrations inspired by *The Thing*.

The seventh issue of Adam Golaski's paperback magazine *New Genre* contained five stories plus an essay by the editor.

The glossy Canadian magazine *Rue Morgue* featured interviews with, amongst others, Bert I. Gordon, John Carpenter, Clive Barker, Brian Yuzna, Richard Stanley, Jorg Buttgereit, Joe Dante, Dick Miller, Reggie Oliver, Nancy Kilpatrick, Roger Corman, Guillermo del Toro, Thomas Ligotti, and the late Robert Quarry. The Halloween issue looked at the history of the Ouija board, while the November edition celebrated H.P. Lovecraft's 125th birthday with a discussion about the Old Gentleman of Providence's enduring influence, conducted by Dejan Ognjanović and featuring commentary by Brian Hodge, Stephen Jones, S.T. Joshi, Thomas Ligotti, Simon Strantzas, Charles Stross and Jason A. Weinstock.

The newsstand edition of *Famous Monsters of Filmland* #281 featured a cover painting by Bob Eggleton that pitted Godzilla against Cthulhu. It was to accompany an article by Kelly Dunn that included commentary from Nancy Holder and others.

The June issue of *Classic Images* included a profile of *Famous Monsters* founder Forrest J Ackerman by Deborah Painter, and writer Ed Gorman recalled his cousin, Hollywood child actor Bobby Driscoll.

Having only published two editions in 2014, *Video WatcHDog* was back after a long hiatus with three further issues that looked at, amongst other things, *Dr. Strangelove*, *The Shining* (1980), and various Vincent Price boxed sets.

For those who liked their movies a little more esoteric, there was Timothy Paxton and Steve Fenton's monthly *Monster!* magazine. Amongst the often cluttered contents were fascinating features on Hammer's Frankenstein and Dracula series; films based on Richard Matheson's *I am Legend*; the *Dinosaurs Attack! and Mars Attacks!* bubble gum cards; an in-depth look at the two versions of *Equinox* (1967 and 1970), the latter featuring author Fritz Leiber Jr.; Blaxploitation; the *Puppet Master* franchise, and much more, along with reviews of obscure genre movies from all over the world.

The May 15 edition of *Entertainment Weekly* contained an exclusive excerpt from Stephen King's *Finders Keepers*, nicely illustrated by Jae Lee and June Chung, while the December 31 issue included a brief excerpt from Justin Cronin's vampire novel *The City of Mirrors*.

Stephen King also asked a possibly rhetorical question in the August 27 issue of *The New York Times* with an article entitled 'Can a Novelist Be Too Productive?'.

For Halloween, *The New Yorker* published 'The Scariest Story Ever Told' by writer and voice actor Colin Nissan. Unfortunately, it wasn't.

The monthly issues of *Locus* included interviews with Lauren Beukes, Robert Jackson Bennett, Garth Nix, Joanne Harris and Elizabeth Hand, along with "Spotlight" columns on Black Coat Press publishers Randy and Jean-Marc Lofficier, Edge Science Fiction and Fantasy publisher Brian Hades, and literary agent Fleetwood Robbins.

Edited by Sarah Newton and Ian Hunter, *BFS Horizons* was a new magazine/anthology devoted to fiction, poetry, art and news produced for members of the British Fantasy Society. Newton left after the second issue. Meanwhile, *BFS Journal* edited by Stuart Douglas and chairman Phil Lunt became a fully non-fiction periodical with issue #14. It included articles on Brian Lumley's *Necroscope*, an interview with artist Paul Hanley, and lots of media stuff.

Despite a sometimes-uncertain future, David Longhorn's *Supernatural Tales* celebrated its 30th issue in 2015. The three editions published during the year featured fiction from, amongst others, Rosalie Parker, Katherine Haynes, Helen Grant, Lynda E. Rucker, Mark Valentine, Michael Kelly, Adam Golaski and Steve Duffy, Tom Johnstone, and Mike Chinn, along with book and media reviews by the editor.

The two editions of Rosemary Pardoe's *The Ghosts & Scholars M.R. James Newsletter* featured the usual fascinating mix of articles, fiction and reviews, while Jim Pitts contributed some nice artwork to both issues.

The first issue of *The Hyborian Gazette*, published by Steve Dilks for The International Robert E. Howard Fan Association was an old-school style fanzine that included sword & sorcery stories and poetry by Glen M. Usher, Adrian Cole and Lin Carter, amongst others, along with some interesting non-fiction from Jeffrey Shanks and Tim

Marion and excellent artwork by Jim Pitts, Steve Lines and Yannis Rubus Rubulias.

Co-edited by Justin Everett and Jeffrey H. Shanks, *The Unique Legacy of Weird Tales: The Evolution of Modern Fantasy and Horror* was published by academic press Rowman & Littlefield. It included essays on how "The Unique Magazine" served as a "locus of genre formation and literary discourse community", along with individual chapters on H.P. Lovecraft, Robert E. Howard, Robert Bloch and other authors, and their particular contributions to the pulp.

John L. Steadman's *H.P. Lovecraft and the Black Magic Tradition* from Red Wheel/Weiser Books looked at the author's influence on western occultism.

Published by Hippocampus Press, S.T. Joshi's *The Rise, Fall and Rise of the Cthulhu Mythos*—yet another book about Lovecraftian fiction—was a revised and updated edition of a study first published in 2008.

Rebecca Janicker's *The Literary Haunted House: Lovecraft, Matheson, King and the Horror In Between* from McFarland visited the haunted house genre while, for the same imprint, Tara Prescott edited *Neil Gaiman in the 21st Century: Essays on the Novels, Children's Stories, Online Writing, Comics, and Other Works*. It collected nineteen essays along with an interview with Gaiman.

A revised edition of George Beahm's *The Stephen King Companion: Four Decades of Fear from the Master of Horror* included a sixteen-page gallery of Michael Whelan's artwork.

Issued under PS Publishing's Drugstore Indian Press trade paperback imprint, *Ramsey Campbell, Probably,* edited by S.T. Joshi, was a hefty revised and expanded edition of the 2002 collection of essays, with an Introduction by Douglas E. Winter.

Edited by Christopher Sirmons Haviland for WordFire Press, *The Synopsis Treasury* presented thirty-two novel proposals sent by authors such as H.G. Wells and Robert A. Heinlein to publishers, with selected commentary by those still-living writers.

Compiled by J. Gordon Melton and Alysa Hornick for McFarland, *The Vampire in Folklore, History, Literature, Film and Television: A*

Comprehensive Bibliography chronicled the penetration of the undead into all areas of western society. *Monsters and Monstrosity from the Fin de Siècle to the Millennium* edited by Sharla Hutchison and Rebecca A. Brown looked at how the genre had helped shape popular culture, while Kyle William Bishop's *How Zombies Conquered Popular Culture: The Multifarious Walking Dead in the 21st Century* was also available from the same publisher.

Edited by collector Roland Trenary, *Mahlon Blaine's Blooming Bally Bloody Book* from publisher Grounded Outlet was an auto-biographical memoir illustrated with drawings by the often-controversial artist himself.

Edited by Stephen Jones and featuring a Foreword by Neil Gaiman, *The Art of Horror* was subtitled *An Illustrated History* as genre experts David J. Skal, Jamie Russell, Gregory William Mank, Kim Newman, Richard Dalby, Barry Forshaw, Lisa Morton, S.T. Joshi, Bob Eggleton and Robert Weinberg explored ten iconic themes illustrated with posters, book and magazine covers, and other ephemera, along with original artwork by more than 100 featured artists. These included Clive Barker, Jim Burns, Edd Cartier, Vincent Chong, Peter Cushing, Les Edwards, Virgil Finlay, Gary Gianni, H.R. Giger, Basil Gogos, Graham Humphreys, Alan Lee, Dave McKean, Ian Miller, Bruce Pennington, J.K. Potter, Clark Ashton Smith, Michael Whelan and Bernie Wrightson, amongst many others.

British poster artist Graham Humphreys also had his own retrospective volume out. *Drawing Blood: 30 Years of Horror Art* featured 140 examples of the cult horror film illustrator's work, along with commentary by Sam Raimi and Kim Newman. The book was available in a £150.00 boxed edition of just 500 copies which came with a signed and numbered giclée print. It was supported by an exhibition of the artist's work at London's Proud Camden gallery, which ran from the end of October through to the end of November.

Edited by Mike Hunchback and Caleb Braaten, *Pulp Macabre: The Art of Lee Brown Coye's Final and Darkest Era* from Feral House/Sacred Bones Records was basically a companion volume to the 2005 study *The Life & Art of Lee Brown Coye* by Luis Ortiz, who contributed the Foreword to this book. Concentrating on the pulp and regional artist's later work, it included commentary from Karl Edward Wagner, David Drake, Robert Weinberg, Les Daniels, David Stuart Schiff and others.

Edward Gorey: His Book Cover Art and Design included almost 100 full colour covers by the artist, along with an essay by Steven Heller.

R.L. Stine's picture book, *The Little Shop of Monsters*, was colourfully illustrated by Marc Brown, while Pete Von Sholly contributed the colourful artwork to *Joe R. Lansdale's Christmas Monkeys*.

British artist Jim Kay supplied the art for a new illustrated edition of J.K. Rowling's *Harry Potter and the Philosopher's Stone* (aka *Harry Potter and the Sorcerer's Stone* for those Americans who don't know what "Philosopher" means), the first in a series of editions of the *Potter* books illustrated by Kay. A £135.00 deluxe slipcased edition featured a foldout of Diagon Alley.

Beautifully reproduced from the original 1929 edition by Centipede Press, *God's Man: A Novel in Woodcuts by Lynd Ward* contained a fascinating historical Preface about the artist by Barry Moser and two essays by Ward himself. It was limited to 300 signed copies.

From the same imprint, *Harry O. Morris: A Portfolio* was a career retrospective and autobiography of the American artist who helped popularise photo-collage work.

Having taken over the editorial and publishing reins of the annual *Spectrum: The Best in Contemporary Fantastic Art* with the previous volume, editor John Fleskes' *Spectrum 22* featured more than 450 works by over 240 artists. Gary Gianni contributed a profile of Grand Master Award winner Scott Gustafson.

Perhaps the most bizarre crossover title of the year was Dark Horse Comics' *Archie vs. Predator*, in which the all-American teen and his friends were stalked by the alien hunter.

Mike Mignola and Christopher Golden expanded their 2012 illustrated novel *Joe Golem and the Drowning City* into the five-issue Dark Horse series *Joe Golem: Occult Detective*, and Mignola also teamed up with Ben Stenbeck for same company's *Frankenstein*

Underground, which introduced Mary Shelley's character into the "Hellboy" universe.

Joe Frankenstein from IDW Publishing concerned a teenage Frankenstein and an urbane Monster battling vampires.

The Fly: Outbreak was a five-part sequel to David Cronenberg's 1986 movie (and its sequel), written by Brandon Seiffert and illustrated by the enigmatically named "menton3". IDW offered variant covers on each edition.

The second issue of the same publisher's *Godzilla in Hell* was written and painted by Bob Eggleton and included a special "Inspirations" section by the artist.

For fans of Charles Band's 1980s movies, Action Lab Comics released a new series of *Puppet Master* comics while, over at Dynamite, H.P. Lovecraft's mad doctor battled the servants of Cthulhu in a new series of *Re-Animator* comics.

To celebrate Vampirella's 45th Anniversary, Nancy A. Collins' five-issue mini-series from Dynamite, *Vampirella's Feary Tales*, featured such writers and artists as Joe R. Lansdale, Steve Niles and Stephen Bissette, amongst others, putting the scantily-clad vampire into their own twisted versions of classic fairy tales.

From Space Goat Publishing, *Evil Dead 2: Tales of the Ex-Mortis* featured stories that expanded the movie mythology.

In August, an incredibly rare copy of *Suspense Comics* #3 (Continental Magazines, 1944) realised $173,275 at auction, setting a world record for a non-superhero comic book.

Nancy Holder wrote the official movie novelisation of Guillermo del Toro's *Crimson Peak*. It was also available as a 500-copy signed, numbered and slipcased hardcover from Titan Books.

Before Tomorrowland was a "distant prequel" novel to the Disney movie, set in 1939 and credited to Jeff Jensen and artist Jonathan Case, with story input from film-makers Brad Bird and Damon Lindelof.

Screenwriter Mark Stay's novelisation of the children's SF film *Robot Overlords* also included an original short story and the shooting script.

Alien: River of Pain by Christopher Golden was a tie-in to an enduring movie series, as was Tim Lebbon's *Predator: Incursion*, the first in the "Rage War" series.

Actor Simon Pegg supplied a new Introduction to *Dawn of the Dead*, George A. Romero and Susanna Sparrow's 1978 tie-in to Romero's classic zombie movie.

Jay Bonansinga's *Robert Kirkman's The Walking Dead: Invasion* was the sixth tie-in based on the popular comics and TV series.

Nancy Holder also wrote *Beauty & the Beast: Some Gave All*, and other TV tie-ins included *Once Upon a Time: Red's Untold Tale* by Wendy Tolliver and *The 100: Homecoming* by Kass Morgan.

Doctor Who: City of Death by Douglas Adams and Gareth Roberts was a novelisation of the original TV scripts by Adams, based on an original idea by David Fisher. *Doctor Who: The Drosten's Curse* by A.L. Kennedy, *Doctor Who: Deep Time* by Trevor Baxendale, *Doctor Who: Big Bang Generation* by Gary Russell and *Doctor Who: Royal Blood* by Una McCormack were more tie-ins based on the BBC show.

Joanne Harris was amongst the authors who contributed to *Doctor Who: Time Trips: The Collection*, featuring eight original novellas about the TV Time Lord.

Paige McKenzie's *The Haunting of Sunshine Girl* was a young adult tie-in to the ghostly YouTube web series, credited to the show's leading actress.

Batman: Arkham Knight by Marv Wolfman and *Batman: Arkham Knight: The Riddler's Gambit* by Alex Irvine were based on the comics-inspired video game, while Margaret Stohl's *Black Widow: Forever Red*, Jason Starr's *Ant-Man: Natural Enemy* and *Deadpool: Paws* by Stefan Petrucha were all based on the Marvel Comics characters.

John W. Morehead edited *The Supernatural Cinema of Guillermo del Toro: Critical Essays* for McFarland, with an Introduction by actor Doug Jones. The same imprint published *Classic Horror Films and the Literature That Inspired Them* by Ron Backer, *A Christian Response to Horror Cinema: Ten Films in Theological Perspective* by

Peter Fraser, *Horror Films by Subgenre: A Viewer's Guide* by Chris Vander Kaay and Kathleen Fernandez-Vander Kaay, and *The Creature Chronicles: Exploring the Black Lagoon Legacy* by Tom Weaver, David Schecter and Steve Kronenberg, with an Introduction by Julie Adams.

Brenda S. Gardenour Walter studied the history behind our fears in *Our Old Monsters: Witches, Werewolves and Vampires from Medieval Theology to Horror Cinema*, and editors Markus P.J. Bohlmann and Sean Moreland collected *Monstrous Children and Childish Monsters: Essays on Cinema's Holy Terrors*.

Roberto Curti used information drawn from official documents and original scripts to write *Italian Gothic Horror Films: 1957-1969*. Also from McFarland, Michael R. Pitts' *RKO Radio Pictures Horror, Science Fiction and Fantasy Films, 1929-1956* looked at the Hollywood studio's genre output.

If you don't know who Lionel Belmore, Arthur Edmund Carewe, E.E. Clive, Forrester Harvey, Halliwell Hobbes, Brandon Hurst, Noble Johnson, Edgar Norton, Edward Van Sloan and Ernest Thesiger were, then the answers could be found in Jim Coughlin's *Forgotten Faces of Fantastic Films* from Bear Manor Books, which spotlighted the careers of twenty-two obscure character actors. Gregory William Mank supplied the Foreword.

Thommy Hutson's retrospective in-depth look at the series of Freddy Krueger films, *Never Sleep Again: The Elm Street Legacy*, came with a Foreword by creator Wes Craven.

Brian Taves' *Hollywood Presents Jules Verne: The Father of Science Fiction on Screen* from University Press of Kentucky looked at screen adaptations of the French author's work.

The second volume of *Midi-Minuit Fantastique: Une intègrale augmentèe* edited by the late Michel Caen and Nicolas Stanzick was another hefty, 750-page hardcover from French publisher Rouge Profond. This volume reprinted four more issues of the influential 1960s film magazine and came with with a Prèface by iconic actress Barbara Steele and a bonus DVD.

Perhaps the best indication yet of the paucity of creativity to be found in Hollywood studios these days, 2015 was the year of the remake, the reboot and the re-imagining at the movies.

Gil Kenan's *Poltergeist*, an unnecessary remake of Tobe Hooper's 1982 movie, updated the story about a family moving into a cursed suburban home. Sam Rockwell was the father whose youngest daughter (newcomer Kennedi Clements) was the centre of supernatural attention, and Jared Harris the flamboyant TV ghost hunter called in to help. Sam Raimi was a co-producer, and an extended cut was released on DVD and Blu-ray that included an alternative ending.

In June, Universal's belated sequel/reboot *Jurassic World* took the record for the biggest opening in movie history, with a US debut of $208.6 million and an overseas launch of $315.6 million. This, despite a total lack of chemistry between stars Chris Pratt and Bryce Dallas Howard as they ran around the rebuilt theme park trying to save a pair of young brothers from a genetically-created hybrid dinosaur, "Indominus rex".

Henry Cavill and Armie Hammer were also so devoid of any screen chemistry as super-spies Napoleon Solo and Illya Kuryakin in *The Man from U.N.C.L.E.*, one wonders why director Guy Ritchie even bothered to pretend his film was a reboot when it had nothing in common with the stylish 1960s TV series after which it was named.

The best thing about the time-trippy 3-D *Terminator Genisys* was that Arnold Schwarzenegger was back as not one, but *two* Terminators in an overlong story that attempted to reboot the series in a different timeline.

Thirty years after the last entry in the series, Australian director George Miller brought back his post-apocalyptic anti-hero (now played by Tom Hardy) in *Mad Max: Fury Road*. However, the real star of the reboot was Charlize Theron's mechanical-armed Imperator Furiosa, who lived up to her name amongst the dystopian desert mayhem and destruction.

Set forty years after the first film, Helen McCrory's group of schoolchildren were unwisely evacuated during World War II to the haunted Eel Marsh House in Hammer's disappointing sequel *The Woman in Black: Angel of Death*.

With its alien creatures apparently inserted as an afterthought, Tom Green's disappointing *Monsters: Dark Continent* was set ten years after the events in Gareth Edwards' superior *Monsters* (2010), when "Infected Zones" had spread throughout the world.

Jennifer Lawrence's boring rebel Katniss Everdeen led her band of fighters against the dystopian society of President Snow (Donald Sutherland) in the overlong *The Hunger Games: Mockingjay—Part 2*, which was hopefully the final entry in the derivative YA series based on the books by Suzanne Collins.

Dylan O'Brien's Thomas and his fellow survivors from the first film found themselves in anything but a safe haven in *Maze Runner: The Scorch Trials*, the second film based on James Dashner's series of best-selling young adult novels. Meanwhile, Shailene Woodley and Theo James were on the run from Kate Winslet's evil overlord in *The Divergent Series: Insurgent*, the sequel to *Divergent* (2014) and based on the YA novel series by Veronica Roth.

A misguided attempt to reboot a third incarnation of the Marvel franchise with a new cast of younger and ethnically diverse younger characters resulted in *Fantastic Four* crashing and burning at the summer box-office (it took just $25.7 million on its opening weekend). Director Josh Trank even ended up criticising his own movie on Twitter the day before it was released, which probably didn't help matters.

Unfortunately, Joss Whedon's all-star sequel *Avengers: Age of Ultron* decided to quickly wrap-up its story about the team of bickering superheroes—including Iron Man, Captain America, Thor, The Incredible Hulk, Black Widow and more—trying to bring down HYDRA, and instead pitted them against the titular CGI villain (a sentient robot voiced by James Spader), who looked as if he had wandered in from a *Transformers* movie.

At least J.J. Abrams' eagerly-anticipated *Star Wars Episode VII: The Force Awakens* was the best *Star Wars* movie since the initial trilogy, as original stars Harrison Ford, Carrie Fisher and Mark Hamill (along with Anthony Daniels, Peter Mayhew and a surprise Max Von Sydow) teamed up alongside newcomers Daisy Ridley and John Boyega to prevent the evil First Order from using a planet-destroying device to defeat the Resistance. We may have seen it all before (and we had), but Abrams infused his film with an infectious nostalgia and sense of *joie de vivre* that pasted over the plot-holes.

The Force Awakens grossed almost $248 million during its December opening weekend in the USA, beating *Jurassic World*'s record of six months earlier.

Guillermo del Toro channelled the spirits of Edgar Alan Poe and Roger Corman in his sumptuous-looking Gothic mystery *Crimson Peak*, which trapped Mia Wasikowska's aspiring novelist and Tom Hiddleston and Jessica Chastain's strange siblings in a bizarre *ménage à trois* in the eponymous decaying house.

Despite the title, Paul McGuigan's delayed *Victor Frankenstein* was less about James McAvoy's maniacal doctor seeking the secrets of life, and more about his confidant and assistant Igor (Daniel Radcliffe). Mark Duplass played a researcher who brought his dead girlfriend (Olivia Wilde) back from the dead in *The Lazarus Effect*.

Besides the overblown *Terminator Genisys*, Arnold Schwarzenegger also starred in a much better genre film in 2015. In Henry Hobson's sombre indie debut *Maggie*, he played a grizzled father whose teenage daughter (Abigail Breslin) had been infected by a zombie ("necroambulism") virus.

Enjoyable in an '80s-style *The Goonies* way, Christopher Landon's comedy *Scouts Guide to the Zombie Apocalypse* featured Cloris Leachman as an irascible old zombie.

Jay Gallagher attempted to rescue his kidnapped sister from a mad scientist during the zombie apocalypse in the Australian *Wyrmwood: Road of the Dead*.

In Miguel Angel Vivas' Spanish-made *Extinction* two feuding survivors and a nine-year-old girl waited out the zombie apocalypse in a frozen town. It was based on a best-selling novel by Juan de Dios Garduno.

The disparate inhabitants of a British apartment block discovered they were imprisoned while an epidemic spread outside in the low budget *Containment* (aka *Infected*), while the passengers on a late-night commuter train were attacked by werewolves in the low-budget British horror movie *Howl*, featuring Sean Pertwee.

Filmed in 2014 and based on a novella by Tim Lebbon, *Pay the Ghost* was an effective slice of urban horror starring an unusually subdued Nicolas Cage as a New York father whose young son went missing on Halloween night due to a centuries-old curse.

In the creepy Austrian-made *Goodnight Mommy*, nine-year-old twin boys (Lukas Schwarz and Elias Schwarz) suspected that it wasn't really their mother under the cosmetic surgery bandages, while two siblings (Olivia DeJonge and Ed Oxenbould) went to stay with their strange grandparents (Deanne Dunagan and Peter McRobbie) for five days in M. Night Shyamalan's *The Visit*.

Maika Monroe's gawky teenager discovered that she had contracted a sexually transmitted curse in David Robert Mitchell's critically acclaimed *It Follows*.

Writer/director Carol Morley found herself channelling *Picnic at Hanging Rock*, as girls at a late-1960s English boarding school suddenly began mysteriously fainting in *The Falling*, starring Florence Pugh, Maisie Williams and Greta Scacci.

James Marsden, Thomas Jane and Billy Bob Thornton came up against a Jaws-like killer bear in *Into the Grizzly Maze*, and a group of cub scouts encountered a legendary forest monster in the Belgium-made *Cub*.

Lin Shaye's psychic medium Elise Rainier returned for the third time in the prequel *Insidious 3: Chapter 3*, as she attempted to prevent a demon from possessing the body of yet another unlucky teenager (Stefanie Scott).

A mother and her twin boys moved into an old farmhouse haunted by Nick King's ghoulish bogeyman and his ghostly children in the sequel *Sinister 2*, while Maria Bello's psychologist and Frank Grillo's police detective investigated the murders of a group of teens holding a séance in a haunted Louisiana house in *Demonic*, which was "presented" by James Wan.

Paranormal Activity: The Ghost Dimension supposedly brought an end to the six-film found-footage franchise.

Six high school teens were threatened by the malevolent spirit of a dead friend (Heather Sossaman) who haunted social media in *Unfriended*, which played out through a computer screen in real time.

A group of Nebraska teens putting on a high school play were stalked by the ghost of a former student who died two decades earlier in the found-footage chiller *The Gallows*, while Oren Peli's found-footage *Area 51* finally received a limited release after six years on the shelf.

The Vatican Tapes was basically *The Exorcist* re-imagined as a found-footage demonic possession movie, as a priest (Michael Peña) and two exorcists attempted to save the soul of a young woman (Olivia Dudley).

A London family discovered that their remote Irish mill house was haunted by banshees and demonic fungus in Corin Hardy's *The Hallow*, while Cary Elwes brought some class to *A Haunting in Cawdor*, in which a troubled teen (Shelby Young) discovered an old VHS tape that revealed a murder committed years earlier in a haunted theatre in the Midwest.

Bereaved parents Paul (Andrew Sensenig) and Anne (genre veteran Barbara Crampton) moved into a rural New England house to start a new life and were menaced by a family of vengeful spirits in writer/director Ted Geoghegan's 1970s-set debut *We Are Still Here*, which also featured Lisa Marie, Larry Fessenden, Monte Markham and Susan Gibney.

The busy Crampton also turned up in the multi-director anthology film *Tales of Halloween*, which featured Barry Bostwick, Lin Shaye, Lisa Marie and John Savage; directors Mick Garris, Stuart Gordon, Joe Dante and John Landis; author Cody Goodfellow, artist Drew Struzan, and the voice of Adrienne Barbeau.

William Shatner played a radio host who linked a number of stories—including one involving zombie elves—in the episodic *A Christmas Horror Story*, and the eponymous demon knew if you had been naughty or nice in Michael Dougherty's subversive *Krampus*.

A young woman (Taissa Farmiga) was transported back into the 1980s slasher movie that starred her late mother in *The Final Girls*.

Finally getting a limited release after two years, *The Green Inferno* was Eli Roth's homage to 1980s cannibal movies, as a group of eco-activists found the indigenous population biting back in the Amazon rain forest. Meanwhile, Keanu Reeves' husband and father found his life turned into a living hell by two strange women (Lorenza Izzo and Ana de Armas) who turned up at his door in the same director's *Knock Knock*.

After some film festival screenings, Eli Roth "presented" Guillermo Amoedo's bloody Chilean vampire thriller *The Stranger* in a limited American release.

Hayato Ichihara's yakuza gangster was bitten by his vampire boss in Takashi Miike's bonkers *Yakuza Apocalypse*.

The Human Centipede III (Final Sequence) marked writer/director Tom Six's return to his torture-porn franchise with a surprise appearance by Eric Roberts as the strict governor of a prison where an insane warden (Dieter Laser, returning from the first film) was conducting his revolting experiments on the inmates. Adult movie star Bree Olson was also in the cast.

Matt Damon's cheery astronaut found himself trapped on the red planet and left to fend for himself in Ridley Scott's surprisingly upbeat *The Martian*, based on the self-published novel by Andy Weir. US President Barack Obama declared it his favourite film of the year.

Mila Kunis' Chicago cleaner discovered that she was really an intergalactic princess in The Wachowskis' YA space opera *Jupiter Ascending*, which also featured a slumming Channing Tatum, Sean Bean and Eddie Redmayne.

Margot Robbie, Chiwetel Ejiofor and Chris Pine were part of a post-apocalyptic love triangle in the New Zealand-shot *Z for Zachariah*, which was based on the novel by Robert C. O'Brien and originally filmed by the BBC in 1984.

A pair of engineers (Norman Reedus and Djimon Hounsou) maintained the last breathable air on a dystopian Earth in *Air*, which was co-produced by Robert Kirkman. Also set in a dystopian future, an Asian woman decided to have her consciousness transferred into a younger, more ethnically diverse body, to help her daughter in Jennifer Phang's *Advantageous*.

With a plot lifted from the much better *Seconds* (1966), Ben Kingsley's dying businessman had his consciousness transferred into the healthy body of a young man (Ryan Reynolds) in Tarsem Singh's derivative *Self/Less*. Kingsley also starred, alongside Gillian

Anderson, veteran Roy Hudd and the young cast of Jon Wright's low budget *Robot Overlords*, which was set on an Earth ruled by alien automatons.

Hugh Jackman and Sigourney Weaver turned up in Neil Blomkamp's *Chappie*, in which a futuristic police droid attained consciousness, while a computer programmer (Domhnall Gleeson) found himself interacting with a sexy female artificial intelligence (Alicia Vikander) in Alex Garland's directorial debut, *Ex Machina*.

Thomas Jane's maverick police detective teamed up with a runaway cyborg (Ambyr Childers) to bring down Bruce Willis' titular pleasure resort in the derivative *Vice*, which was a near-future rip-off of both *Westworld* and *Blade Runner*.

Elliot Cowan's near-future police officer uncovered a conspiracy in a city where all recreational drugs were legal in the low budget *Narcopolis*, which also featured Robert Bathurst, Nicky Henson and Jonathan Pryce.

Even John Cusack had the sense to sit-out the sequel *Hot Tub Time Machine 2*, but Chevy Chase needed to fire his agent.

Ethan Hawke's temporal secret agent pursued through time a criminal who had eluded him in The Spierig Brothers' complex *Predestination*, which was based on Robert A. Heinlein's short story 'All You Zombies' and released in both cinemas and on-demand in the UK.

Hawke also starred in Alejandro Amenábar's *Regression* as a detective who believed that Emma Watson's troubled teenager was the victim of Satanic abuse in the 1990s.

Also released simultaneously in cinemas and on-demand, *The Messenger* starred Joely Richardson as a psychiatrist trying to discover if Robert Sheehan's scruffy medium could really communicate with the dead.

Anthony Hopkins' psychic doctor helped Jeffrey Dean Morgan's FBI agent track down Colin Farrell's psychic serial killer in *Solace*, which had sat on the shelf for a year.

Farrell also starred in Greek director Yorgos Lanthimos' surreal *The Lobster* as a man who wanted to turn into the titular crustacean if he couldn't find a partner in forty-five days. Rachel Weisz, Olivia

Coleman, John C. Reilly and Ben Whishaw were amongst the international cast.

Co-director Guy Maddin's fragmented *The Forbidden Room* comprised a number of episodes based on "lost" movies and featured Udo Kier, Geraldine Chaplin and Charlotte Rampling.

Dwayne Johnson and Carla Gugino set out to save their daughter (Alexandra Daddario) as California was wiped off the map by an earthquake in Brad Peyton's enjoyable disaster epic *San Andreas*.

Rupert Friend's genetically engineered assassin was ordered to kill the daughter (Hannah Ware) of a corporate CEO in *Hitman: Agent 47*, the second box-office flop based on the video game.

Taron Egerton's street kid found himself recruited to secret sci-spy organisation of modern-day knights in Matthew Vaughn's *Kingsman: The Secret Service*, which was based on a comic book by Mark Millar and Dave Gibbons. The impressive supporting cast included Colin Firth, Mark Strong, Mark Hamill, Michael Caine, and an over-the-top Samuel L. Jackson as an evil Internet billionaire.

Both *Ant-Man* and *Deadpool* took radically different approaches to the already over-saturated superhero genre, as Paul Rudd and Ryan Reynolds, respectively, actually had fun with their not-so-well-known characters from the Marvel universe.

After a freak meteor storm turned stand-up comedian Brett Goldstein's Peckham postman into a superhero, he set out on his first date for six years in the low-budget Britcom *SuperBob*, which also featured Catherine Tate.

Quentin Tarantino's overlong Western mystery *The Hateful Eight* included elements from the 1968 movie *5 Card Stud* and Agatha Christie's *Ten Little Indians*, as Kurt Russell's bounty hunter was trapped by a blizzard with his prisoner (Jennifer Jason Leigh) and a group of strangers (played by Samuel L. Jackson, Michael Madsen, Tim Roth, Bruce Dern and others), one of whom might be a murderer.

Russell also starred in a much better horror-Western, novelist S. Craig Zahler's *Bone Tomahawk*, which involved a tribe of cave-dwelling cannibals preying on the inhabitants of a frontier town.

Tom Hardy's disgraced military policeman started investigating a series of child murders in Stalin's Russia of the early 1950s in *Child 44*.

Daniel Espinosa's dark thriller was based on the best-seller by Tom Rob Smith and also featured Noomi Rapace, Gary Oldman, Vincent Cassel, Paddy Considine and Charles Dance.

Set in 1947, Ian McKellen played an ageing, retired Sherlock Holmes dealing with early dementia and an unsolved case in Bill Condon's *Mr. Holmes*, based on the 2005 novel *A Slight Trick of the Mind* by Mitch Cullin.

Vin Diesel produced and starred as the immortal sword-wielding warrior Kaulder in Breck Eisner's *The Last Witch Hunter*, which also wasted the talents of Elijah Wood and Michael Caine.

Jeff Bridges and Julianne Moore squared off against each other as rival sorcerers in *Seventh Son*, inspired by Joseph Delaney's series of "Spook" novels, as Tom Ward's farm boy was taught to battle witches and ghouls.

A magic ring allowed Josh Hartnett's marine archaeologist to travel back into the body of a young British captain in 18th century India in Roland Joffé's sumptuous-looking romance *The Lovers* (aka *Time Traveller*).

Justin Kurzel's brutal and atmospheric version of Shakespeare's *Macbeth* starred Michael Fassbender as the cursed Scottish king.

Adam Sandler's bored New York shoe-repairer was able to magic-ally transform into the people whose shoes he repaired in the fantasy *The Cobbler*, which also featured Steve Buscemi, Fritz Weaver, Dustin Hoffman and Ellen Barkin. Meanwhile, Sandler's former arcade player saved the world from retro video-game inspired aliens in Chris Columbus' unfunny *Pixels*.

Jack Black played a fictional version of children's horror author R.L. Stine, whose monsters were accidentally released from his manuscripts in *Goosebumps*, and a trio of children battled an ancient Ice Ghost in the German-made *Ghosthunters on Icy Trails*, based on the book by Cornelia Funke.

Levi Miller's boy-who-never-grew-up battled Hugh Jackman's theatrical Blackbeard while befriending Garrett Hedlund's future Captain Hook in Joe Wright's overblown origin story *Pan*. Estimated to have cost nearly $150 million, it grossed just over £15 million in its opening weekend in the US.

A teenage girl (Britt Robertson) and a disillusioned inventor (George Clooney) visited the titular futuristic utopia in Disney's underrated *Tomorrowland*, while Kenneth Branagh was the surprise choice to direct Disney's live-action remake of the studio's animated *Cinderella*. It starred Lily James in the title role and Cate Blanchett as her wicked stepmother.

Disney/Pixar's animated *Inside Out*, which looked at what really goes on in the mind of a young girl, grossed $90 million at the domestic box-office during its opening weekend, being beaten only by *Jurassic World*. Unfortunately the studio's own prehistoric story, the 3-D *The Good Dinosaur*, fared less well after a troubled production history.

Drac (voiced by the busy Adam Sandler, who also co-wrote this sequel to the 2012 movie) tried to convince his half-vampire grandson he was a true bloodsucker at heart in the animated *Hotel Transylvania 2*, which also featured the voices of Andy Samberg, Selena Gomez, David Spade, Steve Buscemi, Fran Drescher and Mel Brooks.

The banana-loving yellow subordinates travelled to London to work for evil mastermind Scarlet Overkill (voiced by Sandra Bullock) in the eponymous prequel, *Minions*.

An alien fugitive (annoyingly voiced by Jim Parsons) teamed up with a young girl (voiced by Rihanna) in Tim Johnson's animated *Home*, based on Adam Rex's children's book *The True Meaning of Smekday*.

The humour in Seth MacFarlane's *Ted 2* was much more adult, as Mark Wahlberg's character was reunited with his foul-mouthed childhood friend. The impressive supporting cast included Amanda Seyfried, Giovanni Ribisi, Morgan Freeman, Sam J. Jones, Michael Dorn and Liam Neeson.

Nicholas Kleiman and Rob Lindsay's Canadian kickstarter documentary *Why Horror?* was a disappointing look at the psychology of the subject, despite interviews with Alexandre Aja, John Carpenter, Don Coscarelli, Barbara Crampton, Steve Niles, George A. Romero, Eli Roth and Elijah Wood, amongst others.

Belinda Sallin's feature-length documentary *Dark Star: H.R. Giger's World* looked at the life and work of the Swiss surrealist artist and concept designer, filmed a year before his death.

Future Shock! The Story of 2000AD was an overlong documentary that interviewed numerous talking heads about the history of the influential British comic. Much better was Jon Schnepp's kickstarter-funded *The Death of "Superman Lives": What Happened?*, in which excitable host Kevin Smith took a fascinating in-depth look into the 1998 movie that never happened. It featured input from prospective star Nicolas Cage, proposed director Tim Burton, Grant Morrison, Brom, and hilariously egocentric producer Jon Peters.

It was reported in July that the head of German film director F.W. Murnau, who died in a car crash in1931, had been stolen from his family plot in a Stahnsdorf cemetery, near Berlin. It was suspected that the skull of the man who directed *Nosferatu* (1922) and *Faust* (1926) had been taken for some occult purpose, as other tombs were not disturbed.

In October, director George A. Romero revealed to an audience at a convention that he had found a nine-minute section of *Night of the Living Dead*—possibly "the largest zombie scene in the film," according to one source—that was cut from the original movie. The missing footage, which was discovered as part of a 16mm print, could be included in an upcoming re-release of the 1968 cult classic.

The same month, TCM presented the world TV premiere of the "lost" 1916 film version of *Sherlock Holmes*, featuring the only screen appearance by the great American stage actor William Gillette. Discovered in the vaults of the Cinémathèque Française a year earlier, the almost two-hour production underwent extensive digital restoration and colour tinting before being initially screened at film festivals in France and America.

A readers' poll in the UK's *Radio Times* listings magazine to find the "Greatest Movie Monster" came up with the following, not very exciting list: #1 Alien (*Alien*, 1979); #2 Skeleton Army (*Jason and the Argonauts*, 1963); #3 The Thing (*The Thing*, 1982); #4 Freddy Krueger (*A Nightmare on Elm Street*, 1984); #5 Jaws (*Jaws*, 1975); #6 Dracula (*Dracula*, 1931); #7 Godzilla (*Godzilla*, 1954); #8 Pale Man (*Pan's Labyrinth*, 2006); #9 Dementor (*Harry Potter and the Philosopher's Stone*, 2001) and #10 Chucky (*Child's Play*, 1988).

A magical Devil genie idol allowed Anton Yelchin's horrible girlfriend (Ashley Greene) to return from the grave in Joe Dante's lightweight but fun zomromcom *Burying the Ex*. As usual, the director found a cameo role for veteran character actor Dick Miller in this direct-to-DVD release.

Doug Bradley played the owner of a failing amusement park who instigated a series of gruesome murders to generate publicity in Cary Hill's low budget slasher *Scream Park*, and Michael Gross was back as "Burt Gummer", now the star of a low budget reality TV show, in the belated DVD sequel *Tremors 5: Bloodlines*.

Possibly the worst movie of the year (or perhaps even the decade) was Alessandro Capone's *Death Squad* (aka *2047: Sights of Death*), which was set in a repressive future and wasted the questionable talents of Danny Glover, Daryl Hannah, Michael Madsen, Stephen Baldwin and Rutger Hauer.

Made on a budget of just £12,000 and mostly financed by John Herbert, the brother of late horror writer James Herbert, much of Warren Dudley's *The Cutting Room* was filmed in the tunnels beneath Newhaven Fort, East Sussex.

A father and son were forced to squat in a haunted London council estate in Oliver Frampton's feature debut *The Forgotten*, also released on DVD.

The *Jurassic World* Blu-ray set was not only in 3-D, but also came with two dinosaur figures.

The BBC boxed set *Doctor Who: The 10 Christmas Specials* included the mostly disappointing annual festive one-offs featuring both David Tennant and Matt Smith as the Doctor.

Stephen Taylor's video documentary *Jack Pierce: The Maker of Monsters* was a profile of the Universal Studios make-up man who created some of the screen's most iconic creatures.

Danny Trejo was amongst the passengers of a cruise ship menaced by a mutated predator in the Syfy TV movie *3-Headed Shark Attack*, directed by Fred Olen Ray's son Christopher, and the actor also found himself battling lava-filled zombies in *The Burning Dead*.

Steve Guttenberg, of all people, was the hero of *Lavalantula*, in which volcanic eruptions in Los Angeles released an army of gigantic, lava-breathing tarantulas. Ian Zierling had a cameo as his character from the *Sharknado* series.

Speaking of which, author George R.R. Martin was just one of the famous faces who met a bloody end in Syfy's witless sequel *Sharknado 3: Oh Hell No!* Once again directed by Anthony C. Ferrante and starring a game Ziering and a comatose Tara Reid, the pointless parade of "celebrity" cameos included appearances by Frankie Muniz, David Hasselhoff, Bo Derek, Lou Ferrigno, Lorenzo Lamas, Kim Richards, Jackie Collins, Tim Russ, Michael Bolten, Jerry Springer, Teller (but no Penn), Matt Lauer, Al Roker, Kathie Lee Gifford and many other people who apparently have no shame.

Four friends on vacation encountered infected sharks in *Zombie Shark* (aka *Shark Island*), while a giant Russian robot battled it out with a razor-tooth predator in the equally ludicrous *Mega Shark vs. Kolossus*.

Corin Nemec, Yancy Butler and Robert Englund all found themselves drowning in *Lake Placid vs. Anaconda*, and *Martian Land* was a disaster movie set on a colonised Mars in the distant future.

In Syfy's *Avengers Grimm*, fairy tale-characters Cinderella, Sleeping Beauty, Rapunzel and Red travelled through the Magic Mirror to the real world to rescue Snow White and destroy Rumpelstiltskin (Casper Van Dien) and his army of thralls.

Loosely based on a reportedly true story, Sky Living's grim three-part mini-series *The Enfield Haunting* starred Timothy Spall as a real-life psychic investigator looking into apparent poltergeist activity in a drab North London suburban home in 1977. Juliet Stevenson, Matthew Macfadyen and young Eleanor Worthington-Cox provided solid support.

Also inspired by a real-life psychic investigator, along with Neil Spring's novel *The Ghost Hunters*, ITV's *Harry Price: Ghost Hunter* starred Rafe Spall as the titular debunker looking into an MP's apparently haunted house in what could have been an impressive series pilot.

When a teenager (Hazel Doupe) was admitted to Great Ormond Street Hospital in London for life-saving surgery, she found herself transported to the world of J.M. Barrie's *Peter Pan* in the TV movie *Peter & Wendy*. The eclectic cast included Paloma Faith as Tinkerbell and Stanley Tucci as Captain Hook.

The Disney's Channel's *Descendants* was a teen musical about the offspring of such villains as Maleficent, the Evil Queen, Cruella de Vil and Jafar, while a new boy in town (Rahart Adams) pretended to be a vampire to impress the rest of his schoolmates in Nickelodeon's *Liar, Liar, Vampire*.

The 1978 version wasn't all that good, so why did NBC think we needed *The Wiz Live!*, featuring Queen Latifah, Mary J. Blige and David Alan Grier easin' on down the yellow brick road to Oz?

More than any other time that I can remember, television is awash with genre shows on multiple channels and platforms.

The ninth series of the revived *Doctor Who* got off to a shaky start in September when the show lost more than two million viewers on BBC. It might have been down to the later broadcast time or the fact that Steve Moffat's typically complicated plot was aimed at older fans who would have welcomed back the evil Davros (Julian Bleach), the Daleks, UNIT and Missy/The Master (the droll Michelle Gomez).

The mostly two-part stories that followed featured underwater ghosts (scripted by Toby Whithouse), alien mercenaries, Zygon rebels and a "found footage" space mystery (written by Mark Gatiss), before companion Clara (Jenna Coleman) was apparently killed off after three years, only to be snatched out of time in the extended series finale/reboot and flying off in a retro-styled TARDIS with Viking tomboy Ashildr/Me (Maisie Williams), a reluctant immortal created by Peter Capaldi's damaged Doctor.

The enjoyable (for a change) Christmas Day special reunited the Doctor with Alex Kingston's River Song in a fun romcom that also featured comedians Greg Davies and Matt Lucas.

Anna Maxwell Martin starred as glum church exorcist ("deliverance consultant") Reverend Merrily Watkins, who attempted to keep her sulky teenage daughter Jane (Sally Messham) out of the clutches of a cult of upper-class Satanists, in Stephen Volk's three-part adaptation of Phil Rickman's novel *Midwinter of the Spirit* for ITV. David Threlfall turned up as Merrily's even more downbeat mentor.

Martin also turned up as author Mary Shelley, along with Steven Berkoff's William Blake, in ITV's six-part serial *The Frankenstein Chronicles*. It starred Sean Bean as 19th century London policeman John Marlott investigating a series of macabre murders involving the stitched-together corpses of children dragged out of the River Thames and high society experiments to reanimate the dead.

The busy actress also turned up briefly as a housekeeper murdered in her bed in the BBC's three-part adaptation of Agatha Christie's classic mystery *And Then There Were None*. The atmospheric 1939-set thriller also featured Charles Dance, Sam Neill, Miranda Richardson, Toby Stephens and Aidan Turner amongst the potential murder victims invited to an old dark house on an isolated island off the Devon coast. Unfortunately, the production decided to reinstate the author's nihilistic ending.

Bertie Carvel and Eddie Marsan portrayed the titular feuding 19th-century magicians in the BBC's sumptuously produced seven-part adaptation of *Jonathan Strange & Mr Norrell*, based on the best-selling 2004 novel by Susanna Clarke. Set in an alternate history where "practical magic" was restored to England during the Napoleonic wars, Marc Warren played the menacing "Gentleman" from the fairy kingdom.

Loosely based on the Vertigo comics title, The CW's fifteen-episode *iZombie* starred Rose McIver as likeable medical student Liv Moore (get it?), who was turned into a zombie during a wild party on a boat. Her job at the Seattle Coroner's Office not only allowed her to feed her hunger for brains, but also to use her meals' memories to help Detective Clive Babineaux (Malcolm Goodwin) solve crimes.

The terrific supporting cast included Rahul Kohli as Liv's boss, who helped keep her secret, and David Anders as the criminal zombie Blaine who exploited the re-animated dead's need for fresh sustenance. Unfortunately, the show's sophomore season failed to move the plot along.

Drugged-out Johnny Depp-lookalike teen Nick (Frank Dillane) and his dysfunctional Los Angeles family found themselves caught up in the early stages of the zombie apocalypse in the first season of AMC's *Fear the Walking Dead*, which was an equally talky prequel/companion to the same network's lumbering *The Walking Dead*. Following the apparently shocking death of series regular Glenn (Steven Yeun) at the end of that show's fifth season, the sixth series was once again set around the walled-off community of Alexandria, as Rick Grimes (Andrew Lincoln) and the other survivors were menaced by both the humans and zombies outside.

With nowhere near the budget of *The Walking Dead*, the second season of Syfy's *Z Nation* was still a lot more fun as everybody started hunting the duplicitous Murphy (Keith Allan) and the team discovered "Z-weed"—a potent strain of marijuana grown in zombie compost.

However, much more groovy than both was Starz's ten-episode *Ash vs Evil Dead*, which brought back Bruce Campbell's dim-witted hero and teamed him up with a couple of quirky young sidekicks (Ray Santiago and Dana DeLorenzo) to battle the demonic "deadites" in the most gory manner imaginable. Original co-creator Sam Raimi was an executive producer and directed the first episode, and Lucy Lawless turned up as the show's recurring villain.

Featuring a mysterious visitor (Laurent Lucas), the even worse father (Michaël Abiteboul) of cannibal serial killer Serge, and an undead baby trying to fight its way out of the womb, the second eight-part season of the French TV series *The Returned* was set six months after the Season 1 finale, when the town flooded and the dead disappeared into the mountains.

Meanwhile, a ten-episode remake of the first French series aired on A&E Network under the same title, as the inhabitants of a small Pacific Northwest town had to deal with the dead mysteriously returning. It lasted just the one season.

ABC's *Resurrection* wrapped up its increasingly confusing second and final season, as a virus spread amongst the living and the returned dead.

Having exhausted Tom Perrotta's source novel in Season 1, the second series of HBO's *The Leftovers* had a reboot and relocated Justin Theroux's retired cop and Christopher Eccleston's reverend from New York to the small Texas town of Miracle, where other mysteries awaited them.

Instead of the vampire apocalypse of New York City we expected at the end of the previous series, the second season of FX's *The Strain*, based on the trio of novels by Guillermo Del Toro and Chuck Hogan, offered up more of the same as Corey Stoll's increasingly unhinged hero and his bickering allies tried to stop the plans of the Master and his creepy *strigoi*.

Del Toro himself directed the terrific prologue to the season opener that confirmed what we had always suspected about the Master's identity, while Mexican actor Joaquín Cosio joined the cast as former masked wrestling hero "The Silver Angel".

The second season of El Rey's *From Dusk Till Dawn: The Series* was set three months after the lawless Gecko Brothers (D.J Cotrona and Zane Holtz) freed Santánico Pandemonium (Eliza González) from the Titty Twister bar, as they began exacting revenge on everybody.

Having lost its female star (Nina Dobrev), the seventh season of The CW's *The Vampire Diaries* soldiered on with its vampire soap opera plots, while over on the third season of companion show *The Originals*, the New Orleans vampires discovered that poachers were killing werewolves in the bayou.

Set in a boarding school, the Danish vampire series *Heartless* ran for just eight episodes.

While Dean (Jensen Ackles) continued to come to terms with the Mark of Cain, Crowley's (Mark Sheppard) scheming mother Rowena (Ruth Connell, stealing every scene) attempted to usurp her son's position in Hell in The CW's *Supernatural*, which was still going strong after eleven seasons.

After it was revealed that Thomas Jefferson (Steven Weber) still lived on as a hologram and was guarded by zombie monsters, Fox's *Sleepy Hollow* jumped forward six months for Season 3. Abbie (Nicole Beharie) was now an FBI agent, while Ichabod (Tom Mison) teamed up with Jenny (Lyndie Greenwood) and Joe (Zach Appelman) to battle Pandora (Shannyn Sossamon) and her demon lover (Peter Mensah).

The Halloween episode of the same network's appallingly twee *Bones* was a crossover episode with *Sleepy Hollow* that left the two stars of the latter show looking suitably embarrassed.

Based on the Vertigo comics series, the title character in Fox's thirteen-part *Lucifer* (British actor Tom Ellis, being louche and annoying) decided to take a vacation from Hell and teamed up with an LAPD detective (the sulky-looking Lauren German) to solve crimes. Unfortunately, the first season was not nearly as entertaining as it should have been.

NBC's *Grimm* really picked up as it headed towards the end of its fourth season, as Captain Renard (Sasha Roiz) was possessed by the spirit of Jack the Ripper, Juliette (Bitsie Tulloch) turned into an evil hexenbeast, and Adalind (the wonderful Claire Coffee) discovered that she was accidentally pregnant with Nick's baby. It all wrapped up with the shocking deaths of two major characters before the show underwent a reboot. It returned at Halloween with Nick (David Giuntoli) having to deal with becoming a father.

Charlie Higson's ten-part steampunk version of *Jekyll and Hyde* may have been a bit too strong for its intended teatime audience after 800 complaints from viewers that the opening episode was too scary. Tom Bateman played Dr. Jekyll's personality-fluid grandson in 1930s London, who had to contend with, amongst other adversaries, Spring-Heeled Jack, a female vampire, an incubus, Richard E. Grant's head of MIO (Military Intelligence Other) and the dastardly Captain Dance (Enzo Cilenti) from the evil Tenebrae organisation.

After an episode was pulled following the Paris shootings, television watchdog Ofcom agreed that the show broke the rules "requiring children to be protected from unsuitable material by appropriate scheduling", and ITV unfortunately cancelled the series.

A disturbed Los Angeles police detective (Wes Bentley) hunting the "Ten Commandments Killer" found himself sharing the rundown art deco Hotel Cortez with vampires, ghosts, serial killers and deceased silent movie stars, all ruled over by Lady Gaga's blood-drinking Countess, in the better-than-usual fifth season of FX's *American Horror Story*, which was appropriately subtitled *Hotel*.

From the creators of *American Horror Story* and *Glee*, Fox's silly spoof on slasher films, the thirteen-episode *Scream Queens*, was often quite funny, mostly due to Jamie Lee Curtis' over-the-top performance as the promiscuous Dean of a campus where a group of sorority sisters were being gruesomely murdered by a number of serial killers in Red Devil costumes.

In the third and final season of the increasingly bonkers *Da Vinci's Demons* on Starz!, Leo (Tom Riley) and his friends once again encountered Paul Rhys' brutal Vlad the Impaler.

A detective (Moa Gammel) looking for her missing daughter discovered that a creature in the forest was taking children from her hometown in the Swedish-made *Jordskott*, and three people from different centuries were recruited by the eponymous secret agency to travel through time and prevent changes to history in the Spanish series *El Ministerio del Tiempo*.

The second series of BBC2's *Inside No. 9* featured creators Steve Pemberton and Reece Shearsmith in another six offbeat half-hour tales set behind doors with that number, including one about 17th century witches and a finale involving a creepy séance. Guest stars included Michele Dotrice, Jane Horrocks, Sheridan Smith, Alison Steadman and David Warner.

During the improved second season of Sky/Showtime's *Penny Dreadful*, the league of extraordinary monsters found themselves up against Helen McCrory's Madame Kali and her coven of shape-changing witches.

Despite Joe Dante directing an episode of the second season of WGN America's *Salem*, the show remained more of a romantic history lesson. At least someone had some fun naming each episode title after an established genre work.

Catherine Bell recreated her role of Cassie Nightingale from the seven previous TV movies for the eight-part Hallmark series *Good Witch* and the holiday special *Good Witch Halloween*.

When British backpacker Kyle (Joe Layton) and his friend "Budgie" (Theo Barklem-Biggs) travelled to the Cook Islands in the

South Pacific for a vacation, they drank a hallucinogenic ritual drink and became involved in a supernatural murder mystery in the BBC's eight-part *Tatau* (which means "tattoo" in Maori).

The fifth and final season of Syfy's *Lost Girl* kicked off with the surprise death of Bo's sidekick Kenzi (Ksenia Solo), and Famke Janssen returned as the monstrous matriarch in the third and final season of Netflix's *Hemlock Grove*, executive produced by Eli Roth.

The fifth season of MTV's increasingly dark *Teen Wolf* saw its cast of young characters preparing to graduate from high school while also having to deal with a deadly new shape-shifter and the menace of the Frankenstein-like Dread Doctors.

Laura Vandervoort's Elena and her werewolf Pack teamed up with a coven of witches to battle a greater magical menace in the second season of Syfy's *Bitten*, based on Kelly Armstrong's "Women of the Otherworld" series, and Vincent and Cat revealed their relationship to the world and moved in together on the third season of The CW's *Beauty and the Beast*. However, when their wedding was ruined, the couple worked together to prevent Liam (Jason Gedrick) from revealing Vincent's secret.

When Hollywood actor Paul Rudd was killed by a werewolf, the mayor of a strange backwoods-town-with-a-secret hired Jon Glaser's titular character to track it down in The Cartoon Network/Adult Swim's very silly five-part comedy series *Neon Joe: Werewolf Hunter*.

Sarah Alexander's judge found she could communicate with the ghosts of her husband (John Hannah), her lover (Nicholas Burns) and the local vicar (Jo Joyner) in the three-part comedy series *Marley's Ghosts*, broadcast on Gold.

In Fox's ten-part "limited" series *Wayward Pines*, Matt Dillon's secret service agent and his family found themselves in the eponymous Twin Peaks-like town, with no idea how they got there. Unfortunately, it was soon revealed that they were two thousand years into the future and that the rest of the world was populated by cannibalistic mutants. Carla Gugino and Toby Jones also starred, while M. Night Shyamalan was one of the show's executive producers.

A series of brutal murders committed in the strange Arctic Circle community of the title involved polar bears, a graveyard of mammoths, cannibalism, and a science fiction twist in Sky Atlantic's eleven-part *Fortitude*. The ensemble cast included Sofie Gråbøl, Stanley Tucci, Michael Gambon and Christopher Eccleston.

Despite its terrible title, the thirteen-episode *Zoo*, adapted from the 2012 novel by James Patterson and Michael Ledwidge, was undemanding fun as animals all over the world finally turned on mankind, just like they did in the 1977 movie *Day of the Animals*. Unfortunately, CBS decided to end what should have been a limited series on a cliffhanger, leaving it open for a second season.

Christina Ricci was perfectly cast as the acquitted 19th century axe murderer in Lifetime's eight-part *The Lizzie Borden Chronicles*.

After six years, the girls of ABC Family's *Pretty Little Liars* finally came face-to-face with their mysterious transgender tormentor "A" in the mid-season finale, while an entirely new group of teenagers were menaced by a different masked murderer in MTV's ten-episode reboot *Scream: The TV Series*, based on the 1990s movie franchise co-created by executive producer Wes Craven.

Norma (Vera Farmiga) began to realise that her son Norman (Freddie High-more) had an increasingly dark side in the third season of A&E's *Bates Motel*.

After viewing figures dropped 54%, the third and final season of NBC's *Hannibal* saw Mads Mikkelsen's cannibal killer relocate to Italy, alongside his mysterious psychiatrist (Gillian Anderson). However, FBI agents Will Graham (Hugh Dancy) and Jack Crawford (Laurence Fishburn) were finally able to capture him before the plot abruptly jumped forward three years and recounted the events in Thomas Harris' novel *Red Dragon*.

Jennifer Beals' troubled doctor was hired by a dying billionaire (Matthew Modine) to investigate the existence of life after death in TNT's ten-episode *Proof*, and ABC's fan favourite *Forever* ended its twenty-two episode run after just one season, as Ioan Gruffudd's immortal medical examiner met his match in dwindling ratings.

Jason Isaacs' FBI agent discovered a 2,000-year-old conspiracy centred around human cloning in the USA Networks' ten-part *Dig*, which also featured Anne Heche and Richard E. Grant. It was cancelled after just one season, as was ABC's thirteen-episode *The*

Whispers, in which Lily Rabe's FBI child specialist tried to prevent youngsters from luring adults to their death by an imaginary friend named "Drill". It was supposedly based on Ray Bradbury's story 'Zero Hour'.

A young hacker (Emma Ishta) was recruited into a secret government agency that could "stitch" people's minds into the memories of the recently dead to help solve not very interesting crimes in ABC Family's eleven-episode *Stitchers*.

Inspired by much better movies, CBS's twenty-two episode *Limitless* was based on Alan Glynn's 2001 novel *The Dark Fields* and the 2011 film, as Jake McDorman's slacker had his brain expanded by executive producer and original star Bradley Cooper's designer drug NTZ; while in Fox's ten-episode *Minority Report* sequel, inspired by the Philip K. Dick short story and executive producer Steven Spielberg's 2002 movie, Stark Sands' "precog" teamed up with a police detective (Meagan Good) to prevent crimes before they happened.

Based on a novel by Philip K. Dick, Amazon's ten-part series *The Man in the High Castle* was set in an alternate history in which the Nazis and Japanese won World War II and now controlled opposite coasts of America. Ridley Scott was an executive producer.

Unfortunately, just after the show's streaming debut in November, Amazon was forced to remove advertising posters on the New York Subway due to complaints from activists about the depiction of re-designed insignia that resembled the Nazi *Reichsadler*, the heraldic eagle used by the Third Reich, and a wartime Imperial Japanese flag (which was kind of the whole point of the series). Even New York Mayor Bill de Blasio jumped on the bandwagon, calling the ads "irresponsible". Meanwhile, the same posters failed to provoke a similar outcry on the London Underground.

After five relentlessly grim seasons of TNT's *Falling Skies*, the war between the humans and the alien Espheni finally came down to a confrontation between resistance leader Tom Mason (co-executive producer Noah Wyle) and a monster-spider Queen. Not only was the final battle for Earth mostly kept off-screen (presumably for budgetary reasons), but the series ended with a ludicrously jingoistic speech that was completely at odds with the show's previous humanitarian theme.

Clarke (Eliza Taylor) made a final stand against Mount Weather in the two-part finale to the second season of The CW's *The 100*.

CBS wisely decided to reboot its second season of *Extant* with different showrunners, as Halle Berry's astronaut Molly teamed up with Jeffrey Dean Morgan's rugged cop to track down her evolving space baby and stop him procreating. Bizarrely, it all ended happily ever after.

Channel 4/AMC's eight-part *Humans* was set in a "parallel present" where five cyborg servants, including Gemma Chan's creepy-looking nanny-synth, were planning to rebel on their human masters. William Hurt turned up as a kindly scientist. A consolidated audience of six million watched the first episode in the UK.

A family's life changed forever after the eponymous first sentient "artificial person" (Poppy Lee Friar) came to secretly live with them in *Eve*, the BBC's similar-sounding series for children.

After the introduction of a group of male clones (Ari Millen) from Project Castor, BBC America's fan-favourite *Orphan Black* returned for a third season and was available on BBC iPlayer before its terrestrial transmission in the UK.

Six strangers and a cyborg found themselves on a derelict spacecraft with no idea how they got there in Syfy's thirteen-part space opera *Dark Matter*, while the same network's *Killjoys* was about a group of bounty hunters in outer space.

The Votanis Collective waged war on the alien inhabitants of the eponymous outpost in the third season of the increasingly complicated *Defiance*, and Thomas Jane's space station detective uncovered a vast government conspiracy in Syfy's *The Expanse*.

The time-tripping *Continuum* finally came to an end with a truncated six-episode fourth season on Syfy, while Aaron Stanford played the scruffy time-traveller from a post-apocalyptic future who tried to warn about a deadly plague in the same network's *12 Monkeys*, based on Terry Gilliam's 1995 movie.

In fact, 2015 was a funny old year for apocalypses. Matthew Baynton, Rob Lowe, Pauline Quirke, Megan Mullally and Diana Rigg were amongst those who had only thirty-four days until a comet obliterated the Earth in Sky's ten-part comedy-drama *You, Me and the Apocalypse*. June Whitfield turned up as God in the penultimate episode.

After a virus wiped out most of the human race, Will Forte's Phil Miller had plenty of time to amuse himself until fellow survivors started showing up in the first two seasons of the Fox Network's post-apocalyptic comedy-drama *The Last Man on Earth*, while Daniel Lawrence Taylor starred in ITV2's six-part sitcom *Cockroaches*, about a family trying to survive in a post-apocalyptic England.

When a man (Diogo Morgado) fell to Earth, he triggered an energy wave that initially killed five unconnected strangers who then awakened to find they were tasked with averting the Apocalypse in The CW's *The Messengers*, which lasted for just one season.

A diverse group of children were taken to a remote and mysterious Scottish castle as the world prepared to end in the half-hour BBC children's series *World's End*, while the third series of *The Sparticle Mystery* was set on a world where adults had been accidentally banished to a parallel universe by a group of children.

AMC's six-episode *Into the Badlands* was a martial arts Western starring Daniel Wu as a warrior making his way through a post-apocalyptic feudal society.

TNT's *The Last Ship* sailed into a second season, as Commander Chandler (Eric Dane) and his fractured crew joined forces with an underground resistance group, while still trying to develop a cure for the pandemic that wiped out most of the Earth's population.

Following a deadly virus outbreak in Antwerp, a quarantine wall was built around the infected area and 5,000 people left to fend for themselves in the ten-part Belgian-made *Cordon*, and when everybody older than twenty-two in the town of Pretty Lake mysteriously dropped dead, the remaining inhabitants found themselves quarantined by the government in Netflix's *Between*.

Based on the novel by Stephen King, the third season of CBS' *Under the Dome* began with some new residents of Chester's Mill emerging from the tunnels beneath the town. Meanwhile, Julia (Rachelle Lefevre) and Big Jim (Dean Norris) were suspicious of

Christine (Marg Helgenberger), who imposed some draconian new rules on the townsfolk before the dome finally came down.

With new Troubles infecting many of the town's inhabitants, Audrey (Emily Rose) and her friends found themselves in a race against time to defeat Croatoan (William Shatner) in the fifth and final episode of Syfy's ever more convoluted *Haven*, also inspired by a King novel.

Based on a series of superior TV movies starring Noah Wyle, who executive produced and sometimes appeared in the spin-off series, the second season of TNT's *The Librarians* pitted its quirky team of paranormal investigators against the evil Prospero (Richard Cox).

Created by J. Michael Straczynski and Andy and Lana Wachowski, Netflix's twelve-episode *Sense8* concerned eight "Sensates" around the world who were suddenly psychically linked by visions of the suicide of a mysterious woman (Daryl Hannah) before finding themselves hunted by a stranger known as "Mr Whispers" (Terrence Mann).

In the thirteenth and final episode of NBC's *Constantine*, based on the DC Comics character from *Hellblazer*, the psychic investigator once again teamed up with New Orleans detective Jim Corrigan (Emmett J. Scanlan as the future Spectre), to hunt down a Satanist who was kidnapping young girls, and we learned something shocking about the angel Manny (Harold Perrineau).

After deciding to run for Mayor against evil sorcerer Damien Darhk (Neal McDonough), Oliver McQueen (Stephen Amell) was helped by John Constantine (Matt Ryan, crossing networks to reprise his role from the cancelled NBC show) to restore the soul of the revived Sara Lance (Caity Lotz) in The CW's much more mystical fourth season of *Arrow*.

Having travelled back in time in an attempt to change history in the first season finale of the The CW's *The Flash*, the scarlet speedster (Grant Gustin) discovered that he had inadvertently opened a wormhole to Earth 2, which not only allowed all kinds of new supervillains to travel between the worlds, but also another Flash (Teddy Sears) and a new version of the untrustworthy Professor Wells (Tom Cavanagh). The mid-season finale saw the return of Mark

Hamill's villain The Trickster (a role he had originally played in the 1991 TV series).

In 'Legends of Yesterday', an epic crossover between the two shows in December, The Flash, Green Arrow and their various comrades teamed up to save Egyptian immortals Hawkman (Falk Hentschel) and Hawkgirl (Ciara Renée) from the murderous Vandal Savage (Casper Crump) as the individual storylines built towards the 2016 spin-off *DC's Legends of Tomorrow*, which will unite heroes and villains from each series.

From the same stable as *The Flash* and *Arrow*, CBS' more lightweight *Supergirl* starred newcomer Melissa Benoist as Superman's younger cousin Kara, who worked for media magnate Carla Grant (Calista Flockhart, having fun) and the DEO (Department of Extra-Normal Operations) run by David Harewood's J'onn J'onzz, the Martian Manhunter. Although Mehcad Brooks was mis-cast as potential love-interest Jimmy Olsen, Kara's adopted parents were played in a nice piece of stunt casting by previous superhero actors Helen Slater and Dean Cain.

Meanwhile, over at Fox's continually improving *Gotham*, based on DC's Batman, the second season was all about the rise of the villains.

ABC's eighteen-episode *Agent Carter* began life as a "Marvel One-Shot" in 2013. Set in 1946 and following the events in *Captain America: The First Avenger* (2011), Peggy Carter (Hayley Atwell) was reduced to working as a secretary for the SSR (Strategic Scientific Reserve), a secret, male-dominated government agency. When Howard Stark (Dominic Cooper) asked her to discover who was stealing his inventions and selling them to the enemy, she became involved in a deadly cat-and-mouse game with Soviet spies and assassins. The series featured some nice nods to the Marvel universe, including an episode featuring the original "Howling Commandos" and the surprise appearance of an old villain in the first season finale.

Krysten Ritter was a revelation in the title role of Marvel's *Jessica Jones* on the thirteen-episode Netflix series, playing a sarcastic super-powered private eye battling against David Tennant's ruthless mind-controlling villain in a grim New York City. Inhabiting the same Hell's Kitchen *milieu*, Netflix's thirteen-part *Daredevil* was basically an extended origin story, as blind lawyer Matt Murdock (Charlie Cox) was pitted against Vincent D'Onofrio's remarkably complex crime boss Wilson Fisk.

ABC's much better second season of *Marvel's Agents of S.H.I.E.L.D.* not only tied in to the movie *Avengers: Age of Ultron*, but also saw Agent Coulson (Clark Gregg) and his team trying to protect the Inhumans while battling HYDRA. Season 3 featured Powers Boothe as the new head of the evil many-headed organisation.

Based on the graphic novel by Brian Bendis and streamed on the PlayStation Network, *Powers* was about a pair of homicide detectives (Sharlto Copley and Susan Heyward) who investigated crimes involving superheroes.

NBC's thirteen-episode *Heroes Reborn* was an uncalled for reboot/sequel that brought back a number of previous cast members while adding a new batch of "evos" (evolved humans).

The fifth season of HBO's mega-successful *Game of Thrones*—a show almost guaranteed to shock its huge audience with ever-more surprising twists—ended with the apparently fatal stabbing of fan-favourite Jon Snow (Kit Harrington), Cersei (Lena Headey) facing a trial for her sins by the Faith Militant, Daenerys (Emilia Clarke) captured by a tribe of warriors despite her dragons, and Arya (Maisie Williams) having her sight taken away by the mystical Jaqen H'ghar. And if none of that made any sense to you, imagine how George R.R. Martin felt knowing that the next series would extend the TV plot beyond the five novels he had so far written.

Game of Thrones picked-up a record-breaking twelve awards at the 67th Primetime Emmys and Creative Arts Emmys in September, including the top prize for Outstanding Drama Series. The dozen trophies were the most ever awarded to a show in a single year.

The darker second and last season of the BBC's enjoyable *Atlantis* concluded after its delayed final seven episodes, with most of its plot-lines left unresolved. John Hannah joined the cast as Jason's father, but the pilot episode's time-travel story was never explained.

A group of warriors (led by Tom York's "Hero") were banished by the Greek gods to the Underworld in Syfy's thirteen-part series *Olympus*.

The elusive Author (Patrick Fischler) turned out to have been manipulating the fairy-tale characters, and Jennifer Morrison's heroine Emma Swann turned into the evil "Dark Swan" for the fifth season of ABC's *Once Upon a Time*, which revolved around Camelot, Merlin and the legend of King Arthur.

Problems for wife and mother-of-two Debbie Maddox (Martha Howe-Douglas) continued after she was declared the "Chosen One" of the magical world hidden in her larder in the second series of Sky's *Yonderland*. Anthony Head guest starred as Debbie's suspicious father-in-law.

Having become a private investigator during the seventh season of ABC's *Castle*, the eponymous writer (Nathan Fillion) found himself investigating a murder in a Mars simulation and confronting a masked serial killer from his childhood.

Fox's *The Following* returned for a third and final season, as Kevin Bacon's FBI agent was still being plagued by serial killer Joe Carroll (James Purefoy) and his legion of obsessive followers.

An episode of the third season of CBS' *Elementary*, involving a murder victim found instantly frozen to death, revolved around the cult 1966 horror movie *Manos: The Hands of Fate*. Following Holmes' (Johnny Lee Miller) drug relapse, his estranged father Morland (John Noble) arrived in New York at the beginning of Season 4.

Mark Williams' eponymous Cotswolds cleric investigated an ancient Egyptian curse, encountered a man who claimed to have built a time machine, and became involved in a ritual murder in the BBC's enjoyable third series of 1950s-set *Father Brown* mysteries, loosely based on the character created by G.K. Chesterton.

14-year-old Tara Crossley (Naomi Sequeira) found herself grappling with magic while trying to get on with her schoolwork in the Disney Channel's YA series *Evermoor* (aka *The Evermoor Chronicles*).

Based on Raymond Briggs' classic children's book, Sky's three-part adaptation of *Fungus the Bogeyman* starred Timothy Spall as the titular smelly monster, ably supported by Marc Warren, Keeley Hawes and Victoria Wood.

More than forty years after Oliver Postgate and Peter Firmin's original series aired, the BBC revived *Clangers*—about mouse-like aliens living on a distant planet—much to the delight of small children and former university students eveywhere.

The animated *Scream Street* on children's channel CBBC featured a werewolf boy relocated by the government to the titular location, which also housed vampires, zombies, mummies and witches.

Marvel's *Guardians of the Galaxy* was turned into an animated series for Disney XD, as Peter Quill (Will Friedle) and his companions searched for a weapon called the Cosmic Seed.

The second season of Disney's animated *Star Wars Rebels* on the same network kicked off with a feature-length episode, *The Siege of Lothal*. James Earl Jones voiced Darth Vader and Billy Dee Williams reprised his role of Lando Calrissian.

ITV's *Thunderbirds Are Go* was a misguided attempt to reboot the cult 1960s "Supermarionation" series as a half-hour CGI show. Rosamund Pike voiced Lady Penelope, while her chauffeur Parker was voiced by David Graham, who had also played the role in the original show.

The twenty-sixth annual Halloween episode of Fox's *The Simpsons* featured psychopath Sideshow Bob (Kelsey Grammer) killing Bart over and over again in ever more gruesome ways; Homerzilla attacking a city; and Bart, Lisa and Millhouse gaining superpowers. Other episodes included a second Halloween-themed story and the family being transported by an amusement park ride to the planet of tentacled aliens Kang and Kodos.

Meanwhile, Stewie and Brian took Chris back in time and found themselves trapped in the past in the third season of Fox's *Family Guy*, and Stewie built himself a robot friend with homicidal tendencies. In the Series 14 Halloween episode, 'Peternormal Activity', Peter, Cleveland, Quagmire and Joe went to an abandoned asylum to write a horror movie script and ended up accidentally killing a hook-handed war veteran.

The six-episode reboot of Fox's animated *Golan the Insatiable* teamed a young Goth girl (Aubrey Plaza) with the titular Dark Lord (Rob Riggle) from an alternate universe.

Greg James presented the BBC's eight-part reality game show *I Survived a Zombie Apocalypse*, set six months after the 5G phone signal had caused an epidemic of the living dead.

Hosted by yet another comedian, the six-part series *The Fear* featured twenty-eight amateur directors of short horror films competing for a thirty-minute slot on the BBC. A cinema audience gave their verdict each week, and *The Blair Witch Project* co-director Eduardo Sánchez judged the final three highest-scoring films.

In June, Sky Arts presented a fascinating hour-long interview with George R.R. Martin about his writing career and, specifically, *Game of Thrones*, with additional commentary from Lisa Tuttle and Neil Gaiman.

Charlie Lyne's feature-length documentary *Fear Itself* was basically just a montage of short clips. It debuted on the BBC iPlayer.

To commemorate the life of Christopher Lee, BBC2 presented a half-hour documentary, *Christopher Lee: Talking Pictures*, narrated by Sylvia Syms and featuring clips of interviews with the actor from over the years. It was followed by screenings of Hammer's *The Curse of Frankenstein* (1957), *Dracula* (1958) and *The Mummy* (1959).

In *Unmade Movies: Orson Welles' Heart of Darkness*, starring James McAvoy and Jonathan Slinger, Welles' unproduced 1939 screenplay of Joseph Conrad's novel was adapted into a feature-length drama for BBC Radio 4. In the same series, *Hitchcock's The Blind Man* was based on an unfinished script written by Alfred Hitchcock and Ernest Lehman and completed by director Mark Gatiss. Hugh Laurie starred as a blind jazz pianist whose pioneering eye transplant gave him visions of the donor's killer.

Following Naomi Alderman's conversation with the author (along with contributions from Neil Gaiman and David Mitchell) in *Ursula Le Guin at 85*, Judith Adams' adaptation of Le Guin's 1969 novel *The Left Hand of Darkness* was broadcast over two one-hour episodes on Radio 4 in April. The cast included Lesley Sharp and Toby Jones.

The same month saw Adams' version of the first three novels in Le Guin's *Earthsea* saga broadcast in six half-hour episodes on Radio 4 Extra.

In Julian Simpson's *Drama: Fugue State*, sound effects were used to prompt the brain of a hospital patient (Steven Mackintosh) to recall a possible alien invasion that occurred in a remote village.

A TV researcher (Chloe Pirrie) discovered that the eponymous cult horror video she tried to track down had the power to drive people mad in Simon Passmore's drama *Earworm*, while Simon Armitage's half-hour drama *The Raft of the Medusa* was set in a flooded, near-future England.

BBC Radio 4 celebrated Hallowe'en night with two episodes of *Fright Night*: *The Stone Tape* was a re-imagining of Nigel Kneale's classic 1972 TV drama and featured a cameo by that show's star, Jane Asher. Meanwhile, *Ring* was an updated version of Koji Suzuki's 1991 novel that replaced the cursed videotape of the original with social media "shares". The series continued over on Radio 4 Extra, as Robert Glenister starred as Father Karras in an adaptation of William Peter Blatty's 1971 novel *The Exorcist*.

At the beginning of the year, Radio 4's *Book at Bedtime* presented a five-part adaptation of Robert Louis Stevenson's *The Bottle Imp*, read by Ian McDiarmid, and at the end of November the same slot offered a five-part abridgement of Neil Gaiman's award-winning novella *The Truth is a Cave in the Black Mountains*, read by Bill Patterson.

Weird Tales featured a three-part adaptation of 'The House on Pale Avenue' by Richard Vincent, starring Jamie Glover, along with dramatisations of Christopher William Hill's 'Original Features', Richard Vincent's 'The Burial of Tom Nobody', Amanda Whittington's 'Louisa's' and Lizzie Nunnery's 'Night Terrors'.

Haunting Women featured five supernatural tales by Irish novelist and poet Dermot Bolger, while *Wish You Weren't Here* featured readings of three short stories about undesirable residences.

Julia McKenzie played a bad-tempered old woman living and working on a giant recycling machine orbiting Pluto in Iain Ross' SF drama *A Thing Inside a Thing Inside a Thing* on Radio 4.

All the Dark Corners on BBC Radio 4 Extra featured a trio of forty-five minute dramatisations, including Paul Cornell's 'Something in the Water'.

The same station's *Ray Bradbury's Tales of the Bizarre* included half-hour adaptations of the classic stories 'The Man Upstairs', 'The Scythe', 'The Wind', 'And So Died Riabouchinsk' and 'The Day it Rained Forever'.

The five-episode *Elizabeth Jane Howard Short Stories* featured Matilda Ziegler reading 'Child's Play', 'Whip Hand', 'Pont du Gard' and the two-part 'Mr. Wrong'.

During the first week of November, *The Man in Black* featured Mark Gatiss introducing Lucy Moore's tale 'Connect', Nicholas Pierpan's 'The Printed Name', Christopher Golden and Amber Benson's 'Lights Out', Alison Falconer's 'Uncle William's House', and Nick Warburton's 'Perfect Home' starring Toby Jones.

Later in the month there was a welcome re-airing of *M.R. James Stories*, in which Derek Jacobi read James' 'Oh, Whistle, and I'll Come to You, My Lad', 'The Tractate Modoth', 'Lost Hearts', 'The Rose Garden' and 'Number 13'.

David Tennant read such 20th-century vampire stories as Angela Carter's 'The Lady of the House of Love', Fritz Leiber's 'The Girl with the Hungry Eyes', Edith Wharton's 'Bewitched', Richard Matheson's 'Drink My Blood' and Robert Swindell's 'A Lot of Mince Pies' for the Radio 4 Extra series *A Night with a Vampire*.

Ahead of the BBC-TV adaptation, Radio 4 Extra broadcast a ninety-minute version of Agatha Christie's classic whodunnit, *And Then There Were None*, starring Lyndsey Marshal, Sean Baker and Geoffrey Whitehead.

Christie's short story 'The Lamp' was broadcast as part of a re-run of the series *Haunted* on the same station, which also included R. Chetwynd-Hayes' 'The Liberated Tiger' and 'Which One?', J.B. Priestley's 'The Grey Ones', and the anonymous 'The Dead Man of Varley Grange'.

Ian McDiarmid read J. Sheridan Le Fanu's 1839 story 'Schalken the Painter' over two half-hour episodes on BBC Radio 4 Extra, and Ryan McCluskey read H.P. Lovecraft's 'The Tomb'.

Sylvester McCoy recreated his 1980s incarnation of the Time Lord in the three-part *Doctor Who: A Thousand Tiny Wings*, and Peter Davidson's fifth Doctor contributed a DVD commentary to the re-release of a cult 1970s horror movie in *Doctor Who: Special Features*, both on BBC Radio 4 Extra.

The same station also broadcast the hour-long dramas *Doctor Who: The Renaissance Man*, *Doctor Who: The Wrath of the Iceni*,

Doctor Who: Energy of the Daleks and *Doctor Who: Trail of the White Worm*, all featuring Tom Baker and Louise Jameson.

The Scarifyers: The Magic Circle was the latest four-part serial in the supernatural thriller series featuring David Warner, and John Barrowman reprised his rolel as Captain Jack Harkness in *Torchwood: The Lost Files: The Devil and Miss Carew* and *Torchwood: Submission*.

Tom Canton reprised his debut role of Dorian Gray in BBC Radio 3's ninety-minute adaptation of Neil Bartlett's stage play, *The Picture of Dorian Gray*, based on the short novel by Oscar Wilde.

Alan Moore was amongst a number of people who discussed the ancient "Hollow Earth" theory with Robin Ince in Radio 4's *Hollow Earth: A Travel Guide*, and Ben Hammersley explored the global consumption of fictional universes with Marc Zicree, Robin Hobb and Warren Ellis in the documentary *Homer, Hagrid and the Incredible Hulk*.

In *The Essay: The Further Realm*, novelist Andrew Martin looked at the British fascination with ghosts and their stories over five fifteen-minute episodes at Hallowe'en, while actor Jack Shepherd talked with Fiona Shaw, Sir Richard Eyre and others about Britain's spookiest stages in *Ghost Stories from Theatreland*. For those interested, The Theatre Royal in Drury Lane, London's oldest theatre still in use, came out top for ghostly experiences.

BBC Radio 3's *Sound of the Cinema* series included an episode on *Hammer!* in August, in which presenter Matthew Sweet presented scores from the studio's films by James Bernard, Benjamin Frankel, Tristram Cary and others.

The ubiquitous Mark Gatiss was on hand for *Sherlock Holmes—A Musical Mind*, broadcast as part of *BBC Proms 2015* on the same station.

Stephen King was the first of four authors who picked their favourite music recordings for *Paperback Writers* on BBC 6 Music. His choices included AC/DC's 'Stiff Upper Lip', 'Anarchy in the UK' by the Sex Pistols, and 'At the Hop' by Danny and Juniors.

The inaugural release from Syracuse-based Cadabra Records, *Where is Abby? & Other Tales* featured stories (from newspaper columns) and art by famed *Weird Tales* illustrator Lee Brown Coye (1907-81), read by his son, Robert Coye.

Pseudopod marked "Women in Horror Month" in February, and two months later celebrated the work of Thomas Ligotti with stories by or inspired by him. The free weekly podcast of horror fiction also included works by Joe R. Lansdale, Nina Kiriki Hoffman, Lisa Tuttle and Kelly Link throughout the year.

Jim Dale narrated audio versions of all J.K. Rowling's *Harry Potter* books for Audible.

Bruce Willis made his Broadway theatre debut at New York's Broadhurst Theatre in November as injured novelist Paul Sheldon, being held captive by Laurie Metcalf's crazy fan Annie Wilkes in Will Frears' stage version of Stephen King's *Misery*, adapted by William Goldman.

Meanwhile, a refreshed version of the 1988 Broadway disaster *Carrie: The Musical* debuted in London at the Southwark Playhouse, with Evelyn Hoskins as the telekinetic teen and Kim Criswell as her up-tight mother.

Based on Christopher Bram's novel *Father of Frankenstein*, which was filmed in 1998, Ian Gelder portrayed troubled film director James Whale in Russell Labey's stage version of *Gods and Monsters* at London's Southwark Playhouse over February-March.

Nick Mohammed played the deluded star of a fictitious vampire musical in the comedy *Dracula! (Mr. Swallow—The Musical)* at the Soho Theatre during the same period, while the titular fan (Ali Brice) presented the stage version of George R.R. Martin's books he thought should have happened to attract investors in the parody *Graeme of Thrones* at the Leicester Square Theatre.

Tooting Arts Club set its pop-up revival of Stephen Sondheim's musical of *Sweeney Todd: The Demon Barber of Fleet Street* in an actual hot-pie and mash shop, recreated in the heart of London's West End. Jeremy Secomb played the crazed coiffeur, while Siobhán McCarthy was his cookery cohort, Mrs. Lovett.

It was closely followed by the English National Opera's production of the same musical, which opened for a limited run at the London Coliseum. This time the star roles were taken by Bryn Terfel and Emma Thompson.

Sophie Ward starred in a stage production of Aldous Huxley's 1932 novel *Brave New World* with original music by These New Puritans, which opened at the Royal & Derngate theatre complex in Northampton before touring the UK.

Only James Dreyfus' Elwood P. Dowd could see the eponymous invisible white rabbit in a revival of Mary Chase's 1944 fantasy *Harvey*, which also starred Maureen Lipman, at the Theatre Royal Haymarket, London.

On September 17, *Rocky Horror Show Live* was broadcast into cinemas across the UK. Starring creator Richard O'Brien, Stephen Fry, Emma Bunton, Mel Giedroyc, Anthony Head, Adrian Edmondson, and David Bedella as Frank N. Furter, the one-off gala performance was in aid of Amnesty International.

The Generation of Z: Apocalypse from New Zealand was an immersive live zombie experience staged in a warehouse in east London, while *Shrek's Adventure* was launched on London's South Bank in July.

Towards the end of the year, the Old Vic presented Max Webster's two-hour version of Dr. Seuss' *The Lorax*, with the title character represented by a two-and-a-half-feet-high puppet.

Jim Broadbent starred as Ebenezer Scrooge in a seasonal revival of Charles Dickens' *A Christmas Carol* at the Noël Coward Theatre in London.

Following on from the successful 2013 origin reboot, the *Rise of the Tomb Raider* video game featured Lara Croft battling a mysterious organisation that was seeking an artefact known as the "Divine Source", which held the secret of immortality.

Capcom's *Resident Evil: Revelations 2* was initially available through four weekly digital downloads before a full release in March, while *State of Decay: Year-One Survival Edition* was a remake of the zombie survival RPG originally released in 2013, featuring add-ons, new characters and new missions.

Set in a steampunk Victorian London, Ready at Dawn's *The Order: 1886* for PlayStation 4 pitted the Knights of the Round Table ("The Order" of the title) against a rising army of werewolf lycans.

Created by Japan's Hidetaka Miyazaki and developer From Software, *Bloodborne* was set in the Gothic horror town of Yharnam, where monsters lurked around every corner.

Slightly more subtle was Blue Isle Studios' *Slender: The Arrival*, developed in collaboration with Eric "Victor Surge" Knudson, who created the "Slender Man" paranormal phenomenon.

Hayden Panettiere and Peter Stormare starred in *Until Dawn*, an interactive slasher game in which eight teenagers were trapped for the night in a creepy old hotel with a psychotic killer.

Dark Souls II: Scholar of the First Sin was an updated version of the original RPG with added bells and whistles, and *Saints Row: Get Out of Hell* was a stand-alone expansion of the successful game series which sent the Saints to Hell to rescue the US President, who had been kidnapped and forced to marry the daughter of Satan.

Forty-seven years after playing the role on the *Batman* TV series, Yvonne Craig voiced the titular heroine of *Batgirl: A Matter of Family*, a downloadable story expansion for the Rocksteady Studios video game *Batman: Arkham Knight*. Batgirl teamed up with Robin to save her father, Commissioner Gordon, who had been kidnapped by the Joker and his minions.

The new *Godzilla* game was based on the original Japanese movie series, rather than the recent big-screen reboots, and also featured many other classic *kaiju* monsters.

As with the previous two entries in the *Star Wars: Battlefront* series, the third game's photo-realistic action was restricted to events in the original movie trilogy, and players had to assemble the hero's new Magnum Opus car before heading into the post-apocalyptic wastelands in the first *Mad Max* game, which was released in a "Ripper Special Edition".

Released alongside *Paranormal Activity: The Ghost Dimension* in selected AMC movie theatres at the end of October, Beast Media Group's *Paranormal Activity* first-person virtual reality game was rolled out as a free demo for US audiences before its official 2016 release.

To celebrate the movie trilogy's three decades and *Back to the Future II*'s significant time-jump to October 21, 2015, TellTale Games'

Back to the Future 30th Anniversary Edition repackaged the original five-episode sequel games from 2010-11 with added new material for the current generation of consoles.

Peter Capaldi voiced the Twelfth Doctor Who for the TT Games franchise mash-up *Lego Dimensions*, which included everyone from Gandalf and Superman to the *Jurassic World* dinosaurs. Meanwhile, *Lego Jurassic World* featured insufferably cute pastiches of all four movies.

The seven-inch Vincent Price Bobblehead was the first release from the Rue Morgue RIPers series, and limited to 1,500 numbered units.

From home décor company The Bradford Exchange came *The Nightmare Before Christmas* Cuckoo Clock and *The Nightmare Before Christmas* Moonlight Lamp, both of which were issued in limited editions and priced at $199.95 apiece plus shipping. *The Nightmare Before Christmas* Blacklight Village from the same company came with a hand-painted figurine of Jack Skellington and a free blacklight to make everything glow spookily.

The *Game of Thrones* Monopoly came with some nice board pieces, while the red Albert Bartlett Rooster was the official tie-in potato to the UK release of *The Martian* (no, I'm not making this stuff up).

Rhode Island's Narragansett Beer, in collaboration with Revival Brewing, released its Lovecraft Honey Ale on January 19, the birthday of Lovecraft's biggest literary influence, Edgar Allan Poe. The horribly sweet craft beer in a can was described as the first "chapter" in a series of four ales celebrating the 125th anniversary of Providence's most famous native son. The best thing about it was the label artwork produced by graphic designer A.J. Paglia.

It was followed by a much better tasting Innsmouth Old Ale in April, with a label by Jason Eckhardt, and Reanimator Helles Lager in October.

With the release of the new movie imminent, the UK's Royal Mail issued eighteen *Star Wars* first-class stamps the same month.

A 1937 first edition of J.R.R. Tolkien's *The Hobbit* was auctioned by Sotherby's in June, where it sold for a record-breaking £137,000. This was probably in part due to a calligraphic verse inscription by the author, written in Old English.

Meanwhile, a recently discovered map of Middle-earth, annotated in green ink and pencil by Tolkien himself, was put on display at the Oxford store of Blackwell's Rare Books with a price tag of £60,000. The map was found in a copy of illustrator Pauline Baynes' own copy of *The Lord of the Rings*, and she had added her own notes while working on a colour poster map of Middle-earth, published in 1970.

At a vintage movie poster auction in March, a rare *Frankenstein* (1931) three-sheet went for $358,000, while a single lobby card from the same film featuring the Monster's unused make-up design sold for $40,630. A three-sheet for the lost 1927 movie *London After Midnight* made $71,700 at the same sale.

In September, a previously unknown—and possibly unique— insert poster for the 1947 reissue of Universal's *Dracula* (1931) starring Bela Lugosi sold at auction in Chicago for $15,600, which was 50% more than the high estimate. Another rare poster, for Roland West's *The Bat Whispers* (1930), sold at almost twice the lower estimate for $7,800.

Two months later, a collection of movie posters discovered after more than sixty years under a linoleum floor in York County, Pennsylvania, went under the hammer in Dallas, Texas. A one-of-a-kind "Style D" one-sheet for *Tarzan the Ape Man* (1932) sold for $83,650, while a rare one-sheet for *Doctor X* (also 1932) made $23,900.

In the same auction, a window card for the Karloff *Frankenstein* sold for $89,625 and an oversized Swedish poster for *King Kong* (1933) went for $31,070. A *Creature from the Black Lagoon* (1954) one-sheet realised $21,510; a *Things to Come* one-sheet made $20,510; a three-sheet for *Son of Kong* (1933) sold for $17,925, and a Swedish one-sheet for *Bride of Frankenstein* (1935) reached $15,535.

The Troop by Nick Cutter (Craig Davidson) was named as the winner of the inaugural James Herbert Award for Horror Writing at a ceremony held in London on April 1. Aimed to "discover and publicise a new generation of horror authors and celebrate the boldest and most exciting talent in the genre", the winner received a £2,000 prize and a commemorative statuette. The panel of judges included Ramsey Campbell, Sarah Pinborough and Herbert's eldest daughter, Kerry.

The 25th World Horror Convention was held in conjunction with the HWA Bram Stoker Awards Weekend over May 7-10 in Atlanta, Georgia. Author Guests of Honour were Lisa Tuttle, John Farris, Charlaine Harris, Christopher Golden and Kami Garcia. Unfortunately, Tom Piccirilli was unable to attend due to health issues and he tragically died a couple of months later. Bob Eggleton was Artist Guest of Honour, Chris Ryall was Editor Guest of Honour, and Jonathan Maberry was Toastmaster.

The numerous Bram Stoker Awards were presented at a ceremony on the Saturday night, which featured Jeff Strand as "Emcee" (MC) and Dacre C. Stoker as Special Presenter.

Superior Achievement in a Screenplay went to *The Babadook*, the Graphic Novel Award went to *Bad Blood* by Jonathan Maberry and Tyler Crook, and Tom Piccirilli's *Forgiving Judas* won for Poetry Collection.

The Non-Fiction Award was won by Lucy A. Snyder's *Shooting Yourself in the Head for Fun and Profit: A Writer's Survival Guide*, and Snyder also won the Collection Award for *Soft Apocalypses*. Ellen Datlow's *Fearful Symmetries* was awarded Anthology.

Superior Achievement in Short Fiction was a tie between 'The Vaporization Enthalpy of a Peculiar Pakistani Family' by Usman T. Malik and 'Ruminations' by Rena Mason. The Long Fiction Award went to Joe R. Lansdale's 'Fishing for Dinosaurs'.

The YA Novel Award was won by *Phoenix Island* by John Dixon, First Novel went to *Mr. Wicker* by Maria Alexander, and Steve Rasnic Tem's *Blood Kin* collected the Novel Award.

Life Achievement Awards were previously announced for the late Tanith Lee and Jack Ketchum, Canada's ChiZine Publications was the winner of the Speciality Press Award, and Rena Mason received the Silver Hammer Award for outstanding services to the HWA. The Richard Laymon President's Award for Service went to the organisation's publicity team.

Meanwhile, William F. Nolan was named Grand Master at the same World Horror Convention.

Co-editors Eric J. Guignard and Bailey Hunter produced an impressive trade-paperback souvenir book, which was limited to 500 copies and included fiction and articles by all the Guests of Honour, along with Jill Bauman, Joe R. Lansdale, Aaron J. French, Joe McKinney, Nancy Holder, Weston Ochse, Tom Monteleone and Mort Castle, amongst others.

The 2015 Hugo Awards for achievement in science fiction were thrown into chaos when two separate conservative groups, the "Sad Puppies" and the "Rabid Puppies", used campaigns to nominate works they promoted as a response against what they perceived to be a liberal "bias" to the awards in recent years. This resulted in huge amounts of controversy both online and in the mainstream media, leading to some authors withdrawing their work from consideration, while other nominees were disqualified after the initial ballot had been released. In the end, the "No Award" option beat out many of the agitators.

FantasyCon 2015 was held over October 23-25 in Nottingham, England. The Guests of Honour were Jo Fletcher, John Connolly and Brandon Sanderson, while Juliet E. McKenna was Mistress of Ceremonies.

The winners of the British Fantasy Awards were announced after the Banquet on the Sunday. *Guardians of the Galaxy* picked up the award for Best Film/Television Episode. Adele Wearing's Fox Spirit Books was announced as Best Independent Press, *Holdfast Magazine* edited by Laurel Sills and Lucy Smee won the Best Magazine/Periodical Award, *Through the Woods* by Emily Carroll was the Best Comic/Graphic Novel, and Karla Ortiz won for Best Artist.

The Best Non-Fiction Award went to *Letters to Arkham: The Letters of Ramsey Campbell and August Derleth, 1961-1971* edited by S.T. Joshi, *Lightspeed: Women Destroy Science Fiction Special Issue* edited by Christie Yant won the Best Anthology Award, and Best Collection was presented to *Nick Nightmare Investigates* by Adrian Cole.

Stephen Volk's 'Newspaper Heart' won Best Novella, and Emma

Newman's 'A Woman's Place' won Best Short Story. The August Derleth Award for Best Horror Novel went to *No One Gets Out Alive* by Adam Nevill, while Frances Hardinge's *Cuckoo Song* picked up The Robert Holdstock Award for Best Fantasy Novel.

The Sydney J. Bounds Award for Best Newcomer was won by Sarah Lotz for her novel *The Three*, and Juliet E. McKenna was the recipient of The Karl Edward Wagner Special Award.

The 2015 World Fantasy Convention was held in Saratoga Springs, New York, over November 5-8. The many Guests of Honour were Steven Erikson, Chelsea Quinn Yarbro, Glen Cook, Lloyd Currey, David Drake, Kathe Koja and Rick Lieder, with Paul Di Filippo as Toastmaster (replacing the late Graham Joyce). Unfortunately, the organisation left much to be desired, with the result that no souvenir book was ever produced.

The World Fantasy Awards were presented at the Sunday afternoon Banquet. The Special Award—Non-Professional Award went to Ray B. Russell and Rosalie Parker for Tartarus Press while, somewhat confusingly, the Special Award—Professional went to another independent press, Sandra Kasturi and Alexander Savory's ChiZine Publications.

Samuel Araya won for Artist, the Collection Award was a tie between *Gifts for the One Who Comes After* by Helen Marshall and *The Bitterwood Bible and Other Recountings* by Angela Slatter, and Anthology was presented to *Monstrous Affections* edited by Kelly Link and Gavin J. Grant.

Scott Nicolay's 'Do You Like to Look for Monsters' won Short Fiction, *We Are All Completely Fine* by Daryl Gregory was winner in the Novella category, and the Novel Award went to *The Bone Clocks* by David Mitchell.

Ramsey Campbell and Sheri S. Tepper were the previously announced recipients of Life Achievement Awards.

During the awards presentation, it was announced that the World Fantasy Convention Board had bowed to public pressure and was "retiring" Gahan Wilson's iconic awards bust of H.P. Lovecraft (the "Howie") because of the author's alleged racist views. The award had been presented since the first World Fantasy Convention in 1975, but it was only recently that a small number of newer writers complained about it on social media.

The Board opened submissions for a new award to artists "proficient in the three-dimensional form" with the ideal design representing "both fantasy and horror, without bearing any physical resemblance to any person, living or dead".

As some of my readers will know, my mother—Violet—died earlier this year (hence the dedication at the front of this book). Over the years, she met many of the authors I've worked with, and although I don't think she ever quite understood exactly what it is I do instead of having a "proper" job, she always supported me and was always kind and considerate to my friends and colleagues.

Her death got me thinking about family and this great community that we are all a part of . . .

I grew up in London in the 1950s and '60s. Yes, I was one of the post-war "Baby Boomers" so reviled by the post-millennial "Generation Z", but things were tough back then. We were a typical middle-class family, and we certainly had no contact with anyone in either the literary or movie businesses. But my parents encouraged me to read from an early age (which is why we all need to be protecting our local libraries from closure).

I also started reading British comics before moving on to their much more interesting American counterparts from DC and Marvel. From there I discovered the monster movie magazines like Forrest J Ackerman's *Famous Monsters of Filmland* and, especially, the more eclectic *Castle of Frankenstein*. It was in the pages of the latter magazine that I started reading Lin Carter's book reviews, and it wasn't long before I was buying Edgar Rice Burroughs' "Mars" and "Venus" series, Robert E. Howard's "Conan" novels, and Carter's own "Thonger" books.

However, perhaps the book that had the most impact on my teenage self was a British paperback edition of *Dagon and Other Macabre Tales* that I picked up in Woolworth's one afternoon after school (and I still have that exact same copy on my bookshelf today).

Yet as much as I lapped up H.P. Lovecraft's stories of cosmic horror—I had never read anything like them before—what impressed me most was August Derleth's Introduction, where he mentioned *Weird Tales* and the authors who contributed to that iconic pulp magazine: Lovecraft, Howard, Clark Ashton Smith, and so many others.

Not only did this make me seek out the work of those writers, but I was captivated with the idea that authors—and artists, and editors—could all know each other, and socialise together, and collaborate with each other on different projects. That these fabulously creative people shared their lives and careers with one another absolutely thrilled me.

As I've said, my family had zero contacts within the Arts, but that didn't stop me dreaming. I expanded my reading horizons and became a regular moviegoer. I started writing and drawing, although I had no idea what to do with the results outside my school magazine.

And then, in the early 1970s, I lucked out. While working at a part-time job, one lunch break I called in to a small specialist bookstore in south London. It was run by a young guy and his mum and, seeing that I was interested in the various British and American magazines they stocked, they kindly suggested a few titles to me, which I duly bought. By the way, that guy turned out to be Stan Nicholls who, many years later went on to become the best-selling author of the "Orcs: First Blood" series. But back then, he was just a store manager helping out a young fan.

In one of the magazines I bought that day I found an advertisement for The British Fantasy Society. It sounded like a cool thing, and so I joined. And I quickly discovered that there were many other people out there who, just like me, were also interested in this horror, fantasy and science fiction stuff. Pretty soon I was contributing to fanzines and, within a couple of years, I was editing my own.

I had been going to some comic conventions in London, but while attending my very first science fiction convention I met two men who were to have a huge influence on my life—editor David A. Sutton and writer Ramsey Campbell. They recognised my name from some snotty letters I had had published by the BFS, and yet still they invited me to join them at their table in the bar. And for the rest of that convention they took me under their wings and introduced me around.

And that's how it works. It was through the British Fantasy Society that I first met Karl Edward Wagner, and he introduced me to Manly Wade Wellman, and David Drake, and H. Warner Munn, and Dennis Etchison. And Dennis introduced me to William F. Nolan, and George Clayton Johnson, and Roberta Lannes, and Richard Christian Matheson, and Nancy Holder, and Lisa Morton. Ramsey Campbell introduced me to Clive Barker, and Clive in turn introduced me to Peter Atkins. Charles L. Grant introduced me to Alan Ryan and Tom Monteleone and Douglas E. Winter, and they introduced me to so many others. And so it goes on and on . . .

I got to meet—and work with—Robert Bloch, Fritz Leiber, Ray Bradbury, Richard Matheson, Michael Moorcock, Brian Lumley, James Herbert, Brian Aldiss, Stephen King, Peter Straub, Tanith Lee and so many other legends of our field.

And that's because we are a community. A family. And like any family, we need to look after each other. Over the past forty years I have grown up within this genre that I adore. The writers, and artists, and editors are the creative family that I wished I could join while reading August Derleth's Introduction to that Lovecraft book all those years ago. And it actually happened. With the help of so many people, I managed to carve out a career for myself doing the one thing I love most in a genre that I care about more than anything else.

And in turn, I've done my best to bring other, newer writers into the fold: Kim Newman, Neil Gaiman, Joel Lane, Nicholas Royle, Michael Marshall Smith, Joe Hill, Angela Slatter, Robert Shearman . . . the list goes on and on. But I hope that, in some small way, I have been able to influence their careers and helped them become the talents they were always destined to be.

Which is why it truly saddens me when I see what is happening to our community these days. I am bitterly disappointed when any group with their own political axe to grind highjack awards systems for their own selfish ends, or when an iconic award honouring not just one but two giants of our genre has to be replaced by something innocuous just so that it doesn't offend people who are unable to put historical events into context.

I'm saddened when people who have so much to offer to our genre are attacked and ostracised for beliefs they renounced decades ago or things they might, possibly, could have said but never did; or when people we trust behave in ways that betray that trust. Everybody in our community should feel safe at all times, no matter who they are; no matter what their beliefs; and no one should expect to be cheated by someone they considered to be a colleague or even worse, a friend.

As a family, that is not what we should be about. Sure, all families have problems. All families have arguments. But there's no need for us to be dysfunctional. We, as a genre, are better than that.

We—the horror community—should be more understanding, more accepting of our diversity, and embrace it. In America, the two major political parties tore themselves apart this year because of differing ideology. The same happened in the UK over a public referendum.

We—the dreamers, the fiction-makers, the Creatives—should always be above that kind of behaviour.

And personally, I like to believe that we are.

The Editor
October, 2016

ROBERT AICKMAN

THE COFFIN HOUSE

ROBERT FORDYCE AICKMAN (1914-81) was an acclaimed writer of "Strange Tales", which were collected in *We Are for the Dark: Six Ghost Stories* (with Elizabeth Jane Howard), *Dark Entries: Curious and Macabre Ghost Stories*, *Powers of Darkness: Macabre Stories*, *Sub Rosa: Strange Tales*, *Cold Hand in Mine: Eight Strange Stories*, *Tales of Love and Death*, *Intrusions: Strange Tales* and *Night Voices: Strange Stories*. He was also the author of the slightly mystical novel *The Late Breakfasters* and the posthumous novella, *The Model: A Novel of the Fantastic*.

Although much of his time was taken up with the Inland Waterways Association, which he co-founded to preserve and restore England's inland canal system, Aickman also edited the first eight volumes of *The Fontana Book of Great Ghost Stories* (1964-72).

One of the author's best known stories, 'Ringing the Changes', was adapted for television in 1968 for the BBC2 anthology series *Late Night Horror*. Four further tales were filmed in the late 1980s for the HTV *Night Voices* series, and Tony Scott directed 'The Swords' for a 1997 episode of *The Hunger*. In 2002, Jeremy Dyson directed a short film of Aickman's 'The Cicerones' starring Mark Gatiss.

Robert Aickman was the first Guest of Honour at the British Fantasy Society's Fantasycon in 1976. His short story 'Pages from a Young Girl's Notebook' had received the World Fantasy Award the previous year, while 'The Stains' won the British Fantasy Award in 1981.

In recent years, Tartarus Press has done a marvellous job of bringing Aickman's eight collections and two-volume autobiography back into print and, in 2015, they added *The Strangers and Other Writings*, a collection of previously unpublished and uncollected stories, non-fiction and poetry, from which the following "Strange Tale"—originally written circa 1941—is taken.

The author's friend and literary executor Heather Smith notes in her Preface to the book: "Various themes, familiar in the later work, are foreshadowed in these stories; for example, an outing which turns out to be other than expected, leading to a need for shelter and sustenance. (Robert loved expeditions!) Just at the point of despair, the characters come across a refuge—and always a strange one at that.

"In 'The Coffin House', there are two young girls, spending precious free time from their war-work as Land Girls, on a rather miserable walk, when they are caught in a storm. They come across a ramshackle hut where they are offered shelter.

"Both the dwelling and the occupants of the 'Coffin House' are every bit as scary as in the later tales such as 'The Hospice' and 'The Unsettled Dust', their strangeness well described and subtly emphasised by the tea the woman produces for the guests. There is even an 'inner room' where the coffin-maker plies his trade."

It is my great pleasure to open this volume of *Best New Horror* with a "lost" tale by one of our most important and influential authors of subtle chills...

D URING THE THIRTIES Jessica Yarrow had found a publisher for no fewer than four volumes of verses, and the pleasant little parties in her studio had led to her being regarded with affection by many of the more subdued Bohemians; but now, it being 1941, she had been in the Women's Land Army for nearly a year, and seemed to have only a single friend in the world, her resigned fellow-sufferer, Bunty Baines, daughter of a veterinary surgeon in Shropshire, and one to whom animals and the land seemed truly the order of nature. Mr. Honister, the farmer, a widower and a Methodist, worked both of them as strenuously and as systematically as he could. At Christmas, even Bunty had revolted at the sombre, elderly festivities (to which, moreover, they had barely been invited); and the two women found themselves on a long lonely walk together across the bulrush-green fells. Their land girls' costume stood them in good stead against the heavy, ranging gusts which blew from horizon to horizon every other minute, but they had been able neither to bring much food nor to find shelter in which to eat with comfort the little they had. They had eaten as they walked; but they had started early in the hope of avoiding arguments, and once more were hungry when, shortly after half-past three, the heavy wind fulfilled its threat of heavy rain.

Jessica had never seen such rain. "We must get out of this."

"Where?"

"Look!" Jessica pointed to a small wooden cabin which stood alone and exposed on the hillside.

The two women ran towards it, down and up the intervening fold in the hills.

The windows were boarded up, but there were the remains of a primitive verandah. The two women pressed themselves against the black dilapidated woodwork while the rain beat at them. It was darkening all the time with the premature-seeming darkness of Christmas Day.

Suddenly Jessica noticed that the door of the hut was open. Standing in it was a very large elderly woman with grey hair drawn back into a bun, and strong bony features. She was muffled in a vague, navy-blue wrapper, and appeared indifferent, perhaps habituated, to the weather. She was looking at the two land girls from grey commanding eyes.

"I should come in if I were you." She spoke in the accents of the district, but with much self-possession.

They entered. The cabin, small though it was, appeared to be divided into at least three compartments by partitions of dark wood.

The outer door led into a centre section; from which other doors opened on either side. The windows being boarded up, the tiny chamber was lighted, it was to be presumed at all times, by a single oil lamp hanging from the roof. The lamp was cheap, crude and old; its chimney grimed; its illumination wavering.

"I should take off your coats and sit down."

Although the room seemed unheated, they removed their heavy waterproof. The only place to sit was on planks, unusually dark and roughly hewn, which stretched between trestles on the far side of the room. Jessica expected the planks to bow when they sat on them, but in fact they remained as firm as the trunk from which they had been cut. Jessica now perceived that the table which filled the rest of the room was a carpenter's bench. It was deep in dust.

"I should have some tea."

"We couldn't possibly trouble you on Christmas Day," said Jessica.

But Bunty's knee struck her sharply; and in any case the elderly woman had disappeared through the door on the right.

"I'm *dead*," said Bunty. She looked around. "Do you think she lives here permanently?"

Jessica, faithful to the habits of a lifetime, was combing her wet hair. She found it impossible to see in her little mirror. She said nothing but "God knows".

"I wonder if she's good for an egg," continued Bunty. "I could use an egg."

"No hens," said Jessica, trying to smarten her tie.

In a moment the elderly woman was laying tea on the dusty carpenter's bench. The cheap white china was chipped and cracked; the teapot spout jagged as a broken tooth. The genteel penny bazaar knives were serrated and rusty.

"I should start."

Jessica lifted the pot to pour. Immediately she realised that it was empty. Plainly, also, there was no food of any kind. Even the sugar basin contained only a discoloured slime.

The elderly woman was silently watching them from her grey commanding eyes.

Jessica perceived that she could prevent them from working round the heavy carpenter's bench and reaching the door. For a moment she thought; then she put down the teapot.

"I'm so sorry. My friend and I both take milk."

The elderly woman nodded and retired.

"Come away," said Jessica, more softly than a mouse. "Bring your mackintosh."

But Bunty was tightening her belt, and this delayed them, so that before they could reach the door the woman was back. Bunty screamed sharply. The woman had discarded her navy blue wrapper and was dressed in the uniform of an old-fashioned policewoman, with tunic and long skirt. Jessica associated the costume with the previous world war.

"I shouldn't try any funny business."

She had her back to the door. In the heavy clothes she looked more massive than ever. Her voice was sharply menacing.

"When my father passed away, his job became mine. I'm the only village policewoman in England. You didn't know that, did you?"

Jessica could only shake her head; but she was trying to think. She noticed that Bunty was very pale, and seemed as if under a spell.

"Mr. Honeyman!"

At the elderly woman's call, the remaining door in the room opened for the first time and disclosed a small bent figure in working clothes. Occasional long grey locks hung from under his black cloth cap and his trousers were strapped beneath the knees. His face was old and yellow, but he was smiling like Mr. Punch. His hands were shiny with beeswax. He nodded affably to each of the land girls in turn, then beckoned.

"I should have a look," advised the elderly woman.

Neither of the girls moved.

"I don't want to have to use the darbies." Jessica saw that she held two pairs of heavy handcuffs.

The old man beckoned again. "Easy does it," he said in a voice like a small cracked bell. They went in.

The inner room was lighted by four tallow candles, the bases of which had been liquefied and stuck on the floor. Placed so that there was a candle on each side of them, were two open coffins. They seemed made of the same dark wood as the rest of the place, and they were deeply and newly padded with glossy, blood-red satin. Set upright behind them stood their tops, each with a polished and engraved silver plate, which reflected rectangles of light from the candles on to the wooden walls of the room. The elderly woman was again in the doorway behind the two land girls.

"Do you know what this is?" Mr. Honeyman was holding out a very long, very thin knife which conjured the reflections on the walls to harlequin activity. "This is a coffin maker's knife. There's only one place I know where you can get them."

"Shall I prepare them, Mr. Honeyman?" enquired the elderly woman.

"I'm quite agreeable, Hagan," said Mr. Honeyman. "After all, I only work on Christmas Day."

It was beginning to thunder.

"Look at this," cried Mr. Honeyman in his cracked triumphant voice. He had laid down the knife and was bringing up a wheeled object from the dusky corner of the little room. It was heavily though tastelessly carved in the same dark wood.

"You don't see a thing like that every day."

He was standing behind the cabinet, so that only his head and yellow face appeared above it.

"It's full of live silkworms. They're necessary in my business."

As he spoke he was unrolling a bale of soft white silk.

The two land girls were clinging together.

"I should take off your ties," suggested the elderly woman. Jessica saw that she had put down the handcuffs, and held in one hand a tiny piece of thin red string, such as chemists use for small parcels.

Still as if spellbound, Bunty began to comply. She took off her tie, and unbuttoned her shirt to the waist.

Suddenly Jessica's hands, rough from the fields, were round the old man's throat. In a moment the long thin knife was hers.

Instantly the elderly woman was blowing her police whistle. She blew rendingly, mercilessly, until it seemed that the elements outside the tiny dark cabin picked up the alarum. There was a screaming, cleaving crash and a bright white light. The storm had struck the exposed hut. Or perhaps it had not been thunder but guns.

Jessica awoke in what she took to be a hospital. Certainly there was a nurse standing by her bed.

"Where's Bunty?"

"I should rest, if I were you."

Jessica was not in pain, but, on the contrary, felt wholly and completely numb. Outside they were faintly singing 'Auld Lang Syne'. Perhaps it was New Year's Eve.

"Where have I got to?"

"You'll soon learn."

The woman, Jessica reflected drowsily, must be not a nurse but a sister, as she was middle-aged and wore a dark blue dress buttoned to the chin. She held a hypodermic syringe, larger then Jessica had ever seen; but it appeared to be empty.

DANIEL MILLS

THE LAKE

DANIEL MILLS is the author of *Revenants: A Dream of New England* (Chômu Press, 2011), *The Lord Came at Twilight* (Dark Renaissance Books, 2014) and of the forthcoming *Moriah* (ChiZine Publications, 2017). His work has appeared or is forthcoming in various magazines and anthologies including *Black Static, Nightscript* and *The Year's Best Dark Fantasy and Horror*. 'The Lake' marks his third appearance in *Best New Horror*.

"I first encountered the work of Robert Aickman in my high school library (of all places)," recalls Mills. "I was fifteen or sixteen and happened upon a Book Club edition of *Cold Hand in Mine* which some enterprising librarian had thought to purchase back in the 1970s. In hindsight it seems an unlikely acquisition for a high school in Vermont, but the fact remains that it was there and I was drawn to it instantly on account of the Edward Gorey cover.

"The contents, of course, proved every bit as arresting, but I believe I was most struck by 'Niemandswasser' with its haunting depiction of Lake Constance and the Bodensee as a 'thin place' or borderland between the real and the unreal, waking and dream.

"Inevitably I was reminded of the lake just five miles from my house, a freshwater reservoir shared between three adjacent towns with the boundary lines running somewhere in the water. I had fond memories of swimming there as a child, most often at the old dam and, in the years after reading 'Niemandswasser', there came to be a sense of abiding mystery about the lake itself. Of particular relevance, perhaps, is a night when I was eighteen and walked up to the lake from a friend's house. I remember we saw the stars and Milky Way reflected on the water, shining back with such clarity as to conceal the lake-bottom.

"Even then I was conscious of a certain parallel with childhood and with the nature of memory, generally. In remembering we see ourselves plainly, but reversed, and the glass hides at least as much as it reveals—through a glass darkly and all that. Childhood, then, must remain essentially mysterious. There are moments which can never be reclaimed, wrongs which can never be righted. In looking back, we see only the surface of the lake: we cannot guess at what might lie beneath."

A UGUST, 1997.
Samuel is twelve. He despises himself: his thin limbs, his hairless body. His friend Jason is thirteen but looks older. Jason is a Boy Scout and natural athlete, pitcher for the town's Little League team. The boys have known each other for years.

Samuel's house is less than a mile from the lake. Most evenings the boys ride bikes to the dam, but tonight they will walk, because Nick is coming with them.

They met Nick in July at church camp where Samuel's father was pastor. Nick lives with his father in the next town and attends a different middle school. He is pale, heavy, asthmatic. He wheezes when he runs, breasts bouncing in the shirts he wears to swim.

It is early evening, not yet suppertime. Samuel and Jason watch for Nick from the living room window. His father's truck pulls up short of the house. Its red body gleams, the hubcaps like silver sunbursts. The driver is visible through the windshield, the dark glasses that hide his eyes. His skin is shockingly pale, hands white where they grip the wheel.

Nick dismounts from the cabin and totters up the lawn. His father pulls out, the engine roaring as it gathers speed.

The boys pelt outside, anxious to swim. They meet Nick on the porch and set off with him, following the road along the lakeshore, its floating docks and ranks of summer cottages. Samuel and Jason go first, nearly running, while Nick trails behind, panting, pleading with them to slow down, to wait. They do not.

Eventually, they reach the dam. It is long disused: the sluices blocked with rust, the concrete chipped and pitted. The boys remove their shoes and socks. They scale the hemlock which overhangs the dam and lower themselves to the ledge.

Jason goes first, then Samuel, then Nick, who trembles as he releases his grip on the hemlock and stands unsupported on the dam. A motor boat passes, startling the gulls from a nearby thicket. The noise of the engine tails off to a drone then silence though the waves continue to move in its absence, spreading over the lake's surface like the cracks in a mirror.

The ledge is slick, wet with spray from the lake five feet below. Samuel, cautious, steps carefully over the dam, hooking his toes in the crumbling concrete. He goes from pockmark to crater, listening all the while for Nick's breath behind him: the catch in the other boy's throat, the occasional wheeze.

Jason is far ahead of them. Confident of his footing, he walks the ledge with an acrobat's grace, slowing only as he nears the centre of the dam. Samuel has not been out so far, has never dared, but Nick is behind him and he does not want to appear afraid and so says nothing.

They reach the dam's centre. The ledge is highest here. Behind them an old streambed runs downhill past a cottage shuttered for season's end then bends out of sight beyond a stand of hemlocks. The dark trees shimmer. The day's rain webs their foliage, hangs from branch and needle. The lake is calm, all waves dissipated. Samuel looks down at his reflection far below.

Jason strips off his shirt. The muscles show in his arms and shoulders as he raises his hands, joining them together over his head. He turns his wrists one against the other and stretches, bending himself from side to side.

Samuel asks: "What are you doing?"

"Limbering up."

"Why?"

"We're going to dive."

"Here? It's too high."

"Ten feet, maybe. No more than that. Same as the diving board at the Y."

"I don't know."

"Don't dive, then. I'll do it alone."

Jason drops to a squat. His legs tense. He straightens, readying himself for the jump.

Nick says: "Wait."

Samuel wheels around. He watches dumbly as Nick snorts from his inhaler and shuffles forward past him. The fat bunches at his elbows. His nipples show through his T-shirt.

He says: "I'll jump with you."

Jason grins. "Okay, then," he says.

Samuel reddens and retreats down the ledge. He turns his back on the others, faces the boarded-up cottage. The windows are shut, the doors padlocked.

Behind him Jason and Nick line up at the edge of the dam. He hears them, their breathing. Jason counting down from three. "One."

They jump. Samuel glances behind him, sees Jason fall with his back curved in upon itself and hands thrust out even as Nick steps forward timidly and drops from the ledge feet-first.

The air rushes up toward Nick, unbalancing him as he falls and flipping him onto his back. His T-shirt inflates, rides up, revealing his chest: the breasts like lumps of dough, the lines of yellow bruising near the waistband of his trunks. He strikes the water and plunges toward the bottom. Samuel's reflection unravels with the impact, shattered in the whorl of rising bubbles.

Jason breaches the water. He is some distance from the dam and making for the lake's centre. His strokes are perfect: he cleaves the water with the ease of a boat's prow, his wake rippling behind him.

Samuel waits. Nick does not resurface.

The water re-knits itself, becoming smooth as glass. Samuel's face floats within it, a perfect image: the lines round his mouth, the lips wide as he yells for help. His throat yawns before him, black with the shadow from a dying eddy.

His voice is broken, shrill. It is enough. Jason hears him and turns round. He swims back toward the dam, shouting to Samuel as he draws near. He urges Samuel to jump in, to help, but Samuel cannot. His legs refuse to move, his eyes to close.

Jason dives, surfaces. There are weeds in his hair, water streaming down his face.

"Where is he?" he demands. "Can you see him?"

But the lake is a mirror, obscuring all save Samuel's own pinched face, the tongue flapping uselessly against the dark of his throat. Jasons swears and forces himself under again—longer this time though he comes up gasping, alone. He treads water briefly, breathing hard. Two deep breaths and he submerges himself for a third time, disappearing behind Samuel's reflection.

At last he resurfaces, Nick's head lolling on his shoulder. The other boy is limp in his arms, pressed close to his chest as he holds him up, kicking them both toward shore.

Samuel runs to meet them. He sheds his paralysis and sprints along the dam, forgetting his earlier caution. His bare feet sting as they slap the concrete.

Jason reaches the rocks near the end of the dam and pulls himself from the water. He drags himself forward with one hand then turns to hauls up Nick behind him.

There is blood in the boy's scalp and his T-shirt hangs loosely from his neck. His exposed chest appears soft, rubbery, white but for the bruises at his waist. They form a mottled line, purple and yellow, which disappears into his underwear.

Samuel sees them first, then Jason.

They look at each other, look away.

Jason takes Nick's wrist in hand and listens for the pulse. He cradles the boy's neck between his legs and leans forward, covering Nick's lips with his mouth.

He breathes in, out.

Nick startles and coughs. Jason exhales heavily, falling back. The strength drains from Samuel's legs, and he drops to his knees.

The coughing subsides. Nick's eyelids flutter and open.

His eyes are bulging, wild and white.

Samuel tells no one what happened that day. Jason, too, is silent but only because Samuel begs him not to tell. His fear still eats at him, his shame or something more.

Fall comes and with it school, the seventh grade. Nick disappears from their lives, and it is winter, January, when Samuel sees him again.

Early morning: sun coming up, grey smudges on thick cloud cover. Samuel sits in his mother's car at the end of the driveway, waiting for the school bus.

The morning is cold, below zero. The heat vents rattle. Samuel's head rests against the window, his breath misting on the pane.

Through that fog he watches the red pick-up truck come barrelling down the road, driving too quickly for the ice on the roads. Nick's father. Samuel recognises the black glasses, the pale hands on the wheel, and then the truck is past them.

A face at the rear windshield: Nick. He is as pale as his father and his mouth is open, a black circle.

The years pass and Samuel is seventeen, a senior in high school. In the spring he gets his license and takes to driving the lake-roads at night, circling round and round the lake.

Most nights, Jason rides with him, the water-pipe in hand and the windows down, the night-air breaking like waves around them. Jason offers the pipe to Samuel but always he refuses, thinking of his father's disapproval, and weeks pass in this way before he caves.

Tonight they trade hits from Jason's water-pipe and park below the dam. "Leave the music on," Jason says, and Modest Mouse is playing as they climb out, slam the doors.

The car's headlights shine on the wall of the dam before them, the hemlock-branches through which they climb. They reach the dam and lower themselves down. Stand side-by-side on the ledge, their shadows stretching ahead of them into the water.

The night is clear. The stars are out, the bow of the Milky Way visible. It joins with its reflection on the water to form an ellipse, an open mouth.

"Well, shit," says Jason. "That's really something."

Samuel is slow to respond. When he does he says it is like the future that waits for them, ready to swallow them whole. He is thinking of the coming autumn, when Jason will leave for college, but Jason, laughing, tells him he is stoned.

So they talk of other things: Boy Scouts and church camp and summers spent swimming at the dam. One morning in particular when they donned goggles and snorkels and swam out to the centre of the lake which marked the boundary between two towns. They crossed the border, Samuel remembers, then turned round and swam back to shore.

Jason asks: "You think you still have those snorkels?"

"Sure. Back at the house."

"What do you say we try them out?"

"Tonight?"

"Yeah."

"Alright."

It is after midnight. They walk back to the house and let themselves into the mudroom. The snorkels are in the closet along with two sets of goggles, the lenses grey with dust and spider silk. Samuel hands one set to Jason and takes the other for himself.

Silently, then, they slip outside, drawing the door shut behind them. Returning to the dam, they strip to their boxer shorts and climb the hemlock. Jason squats and leans forward to rinse his snorkel in the lake-water. Samuel follows suit then takes the mouthpiece between his lips. He gags at the taste: mud, mildew, puddled snowmelt.

Jason laughs, his face hidden behind his goggles. Samuel turns from him and looks out toward the lake, its centre. His breath moans in the snorkel.

The moon is waning. The stars cut brighter for the ranks of darkened cottages all around, and the Milky Way is on the water, rippling, opening from itself to receive them as they step forward and drop from the edge.

Samuel hits the water. The lake closes over him, colder than he expected. It sloshes over the snorkel-top and fills his mouth so that he comes up coughing, blind where the lake has seeped into his goggles.

He treads water. "Jason?" he manages.

A voice drifts back to him. "Yeah?"

Jason is ten feet away, nearer the shore, where the lake is shallow enough for him to stand. His bare chest is visible where it thrusts from the water, a web of stars.

Samuel says: "Nothing."

Jason leans forward and submerges his head. He wades along the shore, parting the water before him with his hands.

Samuel empties his goggles and snorkel and begins to swim. The lake-bottom rises out of the blackness as he nears the shallows, the shore.

His toes touch mud and he continues at a walk, wading as Jason did with his goggles submerged in the water. Beyond the glass the lake-bottom appears as a moonscape, lit by stars and cratered where his feet break through it, raising plumes of muddy debris.

He rotates his head toward the lake's centre, the line dividing his town from Nick's. The water is deepest there, he knows, and before him the darkness draws itself into thin bands interspersed with beams of light, stars shining through from above.

All is quiet. Samuel is conscious of no sound save the whistle of air in the snorkel, the slow and even lapping of the lake. The weeds ripple beyond his goggles, the mud blossoming before him at each step. He spreads his arms and brings his hands together, dividing stars from darkness from whirling mud.

The silence is broken.

Samuel hears a heavy splash behind him, as though someone else has fallen from the dam. Panting, grunting. The sounds of frantic swimming.

He spins round, startled. He tears the goggles from his head.

Jason is halfway out of the water, running. He reaches the rocks and scrambles up them, and he must have lost his boxers somehow, because Samuel sees that he is naked, his buttocks showing, white and wiry. He vanishes over the lip of the dam.

Samuel goes after him. He thrashes a path through the shallows and bolts up the wet rocks. He falls once, twice, cutting open his foot. He reaches the dam and vaults over the edge, swinging himself down from the hemlock.

Jason is in the car. The passenger-side door is open and he has draped himself in a red gingham picnic blanket. He holds the pipe between his teeth with the lighter in one hand and the other hand cupped round, trying to coax a spark.

"It's nothing," he says, mumbling. "Freaked myself out, that's all."

"All? You scared me."

"Thought I saw something. In the water."

"What did you see?"

Jason shakes his head, will say nothing more.

Samuel retrieves their clothes from the dam. When he returns to the car, he finds Jason seated with eyes closed and pipe lit, smoke curling up from his open mouth.

Samuel starts the car, pulls out. Jason dresses himself in the dark while Samuel averts his gaze, watching the road unfold in the glare of the high-beams.

Jason's breathing is unnaturally loud to him. Samuel turns on the radio.

Jason's house. Jason crosses the lawn with his hands in his pockets and mounts the steps to the screened-in porch. Samuel watches. The headlights strike through the screens, making shadows like nets which close over him, catching Jason as he turns, waves, disappears inside.

The separation happens slowly, by degrees. On Friday, Samuel calls Jason's house and speaks to his mother. She tells him Jason is out. "Lauren came by and picked him up."

Lauren? The name means nothing to him. Samuel spends the

night in bed with his headphones on and his face to the ceiling, the fan-blades going around.

The weekend passes with no word from Jason. Sunday night, Samuel goes out walking. His footfalls carry him uphill to the lake, the dam—and that is where he sees them, seated together on the ledge. Jason with his back bent forward, his head in his hands. The girl beside him with her arm extended, hand spread across his back. She is speaking to him softly, almost whispering. Jason's shoulders shake.

Samuel skulks back to the house, says nothing of what he saw. In school the boys continue to greet each other, passing in the hallway, but Jason takes to spending the weekends with Lauren and week-nights, too, once summer arrives.

In the autumn Jason leaves for college on a baseball scholarship and Samuel goes to work for his uncle, who owns a contracting business. He sees Jason around the holidays, but only then, and soon they lose touch altogether.

Samuel is twenty-one, twenty-two. Sometimes, at night, he remembers the lake as it was on that night in May with the stars in its folds and the Milky Way on its surface, yawning, joining its reflection to receive him as he fell.

In dreams he stands on the dam, cold concrete between his toes. He hears his own breathing, strained and whistling, and Nick's face is in the water below. It shimmers in place, floating on the dark that whirls up from beneath.

The image stays with him on waking, a trapped melody. One night, late, he staggers out of bed and tiptoes downstairs to his father's office. He digs the address book out of the desk and flips through it until he finds Nick's number.

He takes down the phone from the wall and dials the number. He raises the receiver to his ear, waits for a ringing from the other side. He has no idea what he will say, how he will begin.

Four beeps in sequence. A woman's recorded voice.

The number has been disconnected.

2012. Samuel is a manager in his uncle's contracting business, a youth pastor in his father's church. He teaches Sunday School, arranges field trips to the lake in summertime. He lives alone. His apartment is in the next town but he drives up to the lake on Sundays for dinner with his parents. From them he learns that Jason is engaged. His mother says: "He's coming home for the wedding. They're getting married at the lake."

He does not expect an invitation, does not receive one. At dusk on the night of the wedding he cruises round the lake at twenty miles per hour, watching for signs. He spies one, slows. JASON + AMANDA, it says, the words in green letters on a yellow background. An arrow points up a driveway to a big house overlooking the water. Rented for the occasion, he thinks.

A tent has been erected on the lawn, tables laid with champagne flutes and electric candles. The wedding, it seems, is over, but the dancing continues, men and women whirling together beneath strings of Christmas lights. They are beautiful, achingly so, wearing their best clothes and dancing, pairing off to music he can't hear and always the lake behind them, its awful stillness. The water is calm, un-rippled. Purple with the reflection of a sky that isn't there, not really, and he thinks of his childhood, the years since high school. The surface of his life and the memories it hides. The bruises at Nick's waist. His father's black glasses.

Jason's voice. *Thought I saw something. In the water.*

Samuel backs out into the road. He straightens the wheel and depresses the gas pedal, anxious to be away. Thirty-five, forty. He rounds the northwest corner of the lake just as a pick-up truck pulls out from a side-street, cutting him off.

He slams the brakes. Taps the horn as he approaches, but the truck does not increase its speed. Twenty miles per hour. He is ten feet from the other vehicle, less. The tailgate flaps up, down— groaning, broken—and the truck itself is filthy, half-decrepit.

Samuel strains his eyes. He leans into the glow of his headlights but cannot discern the colour of the pick-up for the layers of rust and mud. The license plate is similarly indistinct, a grey rectangle, while the truck's rear windshield is fogged over, opaque but for a swath where someone has wiped it clear from inside.

Samuel glimpses movement in the cabin, the flutter of something white. He flashes his high-beams. Glimpses a face at the window, a boy.

The child's eyes are black, or appear so, as is the mouth that drops open, crying out, screaming for help while the tailgate bangs up and down.

Samuel brakes, hard. His car shudders, screeches. Stops.

The truck drives away.

Samuel's mouth is dry. His hands shake as he fumbles for the stick-switch, his brights. He sees it again: that face at the window, an open mouth. Screaming even as the truck vanishes beyond the cone of his headlights, leaving the empty road, the windblown trees. The leaves and the patterns they make like ripples in water.

He stomps down on the accelerator. The engine responds, pushing up toward forty. The lake drops away to his left, the north shore visible through a lattice of birch-branch and pine, and again the pick-up is before him.

The tailgate falls open, releasing a cloud of dust from the truck-bed. It rears up before him, white and fine where his headlights strike through, illuminating the interior of the cabin. The driver's head is visible, a shimmering in the truck's rear-view, but only for a moment before it is gone, eclipsed by a hand at the back windshield: a child's hand, the fingers spread.

Samuel slows, his bumper five feet from the truck's tailgate.

He turns on his high-beams, flooding the pick-up's interior, revealing the dark stains on the dashboard and headrests, the mould sprouting from the upholstery. The cabin swims with damp, trapped breath whirling like smoke before the light.

The hand vanishes, reappears.

It thumps feebly at the glass.

The truck accelerates. The chassis shakes as the driver up-shifts, shedding flecks of paint or rust which spatter Samuel's windshield and skitter away into the night.

Samuel speeds up to maintain his distance, punching his horn all the while. He flashes his brights, but the truck will not slow, will not pull over, and together they follow the road as it curves to the south, away from the lake, dark trees yielding to farm-fields, fence-posts.

He presses down the gas pedal. The speedometer jumps to fifty-five, sixty, bringing him within two car-lengths of the truck. The road ahead of them is clear. He jerks the wheel sharply to the left and pulls into the other lane. He continues to accelerate, draws level with the cabin.

The driver-side door is rusted out, sealed over. The window is misted with breath, smeared with fingerprints. The windshield, too, is completely obscured, though the truck continues to accelerate, pushing seventy as they approach the straightaway.

Samuel rolls down his window. He shouts across the seat, but the other driver pays no heed. With the window down, Samuel hears a thudding from the truck and sees the boy's face at the window. There are bruises about the mouth and neck but the features are familiar, somehow, the eyes, though in this moment, he cannot be sure if it is Nick's face, or Jason's, or his own—and then the road is sliding out from under him.

He hits the ditch. Flips, keeps rolling. Tumbles end-over-end through the hay-fields. The airbag explodes from the steering column and he hears a sound like waters churning, sees the stars come rushing toward him: the Milky Way, its open jaws.

He survives. A young woman, driving behind him, witnesses the accident and phones for help from her car. Later, in her statement, she says that he was driving erratically: changing lanes, shouting out his window. She makes no mention of a second vehicle.

He is in the hospital. The days pass and he is discharged, sent home to recover. Home: his parents' house, where he is treated as a sickly child. His mother hovers by the bedside, reading passages aloud from the Bible or *Reader's Digest*. His father kneels by the bed with his hand folded round Samuel's, offering up prayers for his recovery.

Some of his Sunday School students come to visit, three boys in T-shirts and swimsuits. They linger in the doorway, their limbs white and hairless. One boy is heavier than the others, the fat forming dimples where it overhangs his knees. They sing songs from church, their faces like masks showing nothing, and afterward, the fat boy says they are going swimming.

"Off to the beach, then?" Samuel's father asks.

"No," the boy says. "We'll probably just go up to the dam."

The final song is sung—*let the lower lights be burning, send a gleam across the wave*—and his father ushers them from the room. Samuel listens for their voices as they retreat downstairs, the door closing behind them.

The boys are gone.

He heaves himself onto his side, turns his face to the wall.

RICHARD GAVIN

THE BARNACLE DAUGHTER

RICHARD GAVIN is a Canadian author of horror and esotericism. His supernatural fiction has been selected for various "Year's Best" anthologies and has been published in five collections, the most recent being *Sylvan Dread: Tales of Pastoral Darkness* (Three Hands Press, 2016). His latest non-fiction work is *The Benighted Path* (Theion Publishing, 2016).

"I've always felt strongly connected to the water," reveals the author. "Swimming in a lake, gazing out at the ocean, listening to the night tide; all of these things rejuvenate me and stir in me a sense of wonderment. Envisioning kingdoms beneath the sea becomes incredibly easy at such times.

"I've also always loved tales of ghost ships and sea lore in general. So when Lois Gresh approached me about writing an Innsmouth-themed story for her anthology *Innsmouth Nightmares*, I seized the opportunity and tried to channel all my nautical fascinations into a single tale."

I. Leaves

GRIEF BLOOMS WITHIN the girl. It sprouts up from the once-fallow acre of confusion that padded her heart. To her, death was but a word, something distant and vague and ill-defined. "*Your father has died, Rose*," her aunt had said. "*He's left this world, gone to live with the angels.*"

Though the reality of death was new to her, Rose could appreciate its mystery notwithstanding. Born and raised in this smallish town that hemmed the sea, it was not difficult to experience the ineffable, for the water was wide and deep and sat darkly, even on the sunniest of days. Rose had been taught inside the tiny chapel (which served as a primary school on secular weekdays) that the water tables had shifted over great spans of time. Parts of the entire continent had been slowly ingested by the sea, taken below into the churning unknown. Since learning this, even after the teacher had assured her that such changes occur in what he called "deep time", Rose felt that the ground beneath her feet was not so stable after all.

To say nothing of the daily rituals that took place far from shore, when Innsmouth's trappers and fishermen would press out in their boats (all of which seemed battered, brittle, and ancient) to plunge nets and wooden traps and threaded hooks into that heaving expanse in order to trawl up strange and wriggling things that dwelt beneath the surface. These living prizes would be carted back each day, delivered to the lines of women and men with their aprons of soiled rubber and their knives that were marred with rust or old blood or both.

Only once had Rose gone to the pier in order to watch her father work. The sight of those creatures scurrying sideways, or groping their surroundings with antennae, or flogging the gutting table with their ropey tentacles, was too much. She not only shunned the docks where the moored fishing boats bobbed like tethered coffins awaiting burial at sea, Rose also refused to ever swim at Innsmouth Beach.

There was a *world* out there below those waves of bottle-green, of midnight-blue. What were its laws, Rose wondered? How did those alien things make sense of their world? Did they have customs, a faith?

Sailing out to snatch away these creatures from their habitat seemed not only wrong but dangerous.

And so it was. For now the sea had taken her father. He had been deemed lost at sea, but Rose's fertile imagination had been assailing her with images of her father being hooked and dragged downward; fished away from the world of men.

II. Auld Wytcherie

Whenever the mist rolled in off the water it would smudge the boundary between sea and land. On such days Rose liked to play a little game where she would close her eyes and creep deeper into the fog, trying to guess at where the waves began. Never once had she guessed accurately. The tide was always playful, ebbing farther than she'd anticipated, or pressing too near too soon.

If the mist could blur these things, why not others?

It was a child's reasoning, to be sure. But it was enough to inspire Rose to escape from the wake in her aunt's cottage and make her way to Elmira, the grey witch of Innsmouth.

Everyone in Innsmouth knew of Elmira, and though many scoffed at the bulk of the lore that circulated around her, caregivers were uncertain enough to warn their charges to steer clear of her shack on the bluffs.

Rose was confident that if even one tenth of the things she'd heard about Elmira's powers were true, her father could well be brought back.

She went to the shack and she knocked. Elmira answered, but refused to hear the girl's story until a tariff was paid. Rose gave what little money she had in her pocket; two silver coins of the lowest denomination. They sufficed.

Elmira listened as the child expressed her desire.

From a battered sea trunk Elmira produced a bundle of netted rope, and from this, a conch shell.

"On the new moon, face the sea and blow into this horn. It will rouse your father from the deeps."

Unaware of what a new moon was, Rose asked for clarification and received a cursory explanation complete with appointed time.

Elmira then looked hard into the child's fresh face. She gave her the requisite warning that came with this form of incantation. Rose nodded, but the old witch was cunning enough to see that the child neither understood nor cared about any negative consequences.

One week later the time came 'round and Rose heeded it, sneaking away from her aunt's cottage (her home just until Father returned) while her aunt snored upon the living room sofa bed.

The beach was springtime vacant. Rose shivered as she crept along the lunar-dappled sandbanks. The chloral stench of high tide was especially strong tonight, or perhaps it was the nature of the girl's task that made the night so unseemly.

Rose had hoped for a fog-laden atmosphere tonight, so that the boundary between sea and land, between dead and quick, would not feel so harsh, so impassable. But the new moon's glow was untrammelled by mist or cloud. Even the stars seemed nearer and clearer, glinting at the child's work as if conscious, maybe even judgmental.

A cluster of night-fishing boats moved in the far distance, their spotlights gleaming like low-lying embryonic moons. Rose knew they were too far from shore to see her as she freed the conch shell from its netting. Beside this she set a photograph of her and her father, along with a bottle of his favourite cologne and one of his caps.

She righted herself, brought the shell to her mouth. The rim of its horn was spiky. It cut her unsteady lip. Rose closed her eyes and exhaled.

What emitted from the twisted shell was a faint and strangled sound. It was neither musical nor shrill; simply a gust of squeaky air that came and went. Rose tried to blow a second call but this time her breath could not muster any noise at all. Disappointment scooped at her insides. She slumped down before her hurried and haphazard shrine.

She thought back to the warning the old witch had given her: "*When one is called back from the deep, they do not always return alone...*"

Rose gathered her items and sneaked back home. Though she was deflated, she still could not bring herself to glance back over her shoulder to see what (if anything) might have begun a shoreward journey.

III. The Incanted

The Deep has its cities, its customs, its denizens. To the eyes of the living the ocean near Innsmouth's shore appeared as anything but uncommon, an expanse of lilting weeds, sea-life great and small, and human wreckage.

Those who perceive with the eyes of the heart, however, witness an altogether more phantastical scene. For there, in the submerged city of Y'ha-nthlei, stood temples whose grandeur was scarcely conceivable, columned galleries where all the knowledge of this Deep race was preserved in a seemingly endless epic narrative that had been carved into the walls of drowned marble. Theirs was a wisdom too nuanced and un-human to ever be grasped by the tender grey matter of humankind, and because of this, a great wedge was placed between their world and yours. To the landlubber, the Deep Ones were rare enough to become mere myth. Their gods, their labyrinthine city, their treasures, all became tall tales with which the sea-hardened regaled the fresh-faced youths. As with all yarns of the water, most were nothing more than products of the imagination of dullards. A keen ear can perceive the all too human yearnings embedded within such stories: the lust for great riches, for the touch of an exotic and impossibly beautiful feminine creature, for battles befitting *The Eddas*.

Occasionally warnings would surface about the dangers of those who heeded the Siren song and mated with one of the denizens of Y'ha-nthlei. It's been said that their progeny are misshapen hybrids, things that suggest two worlds but do not fully belong in either. It is this taint that gives the locals what has been dubbed "that Innsmouth look". This taint also could explain how certain land-lubbers, such as the witch Elmira, developed the powers that were deemed uncanny to those who lacked it.

But the Sirens beckon still. And sailors are often only too willing to answer.

How exquisitely rare it is for the call to come from shore!

To hear that shrill and extended note sail from the land, dive down and down and down to romance the dwellers of the sunken city.

This particular call was born of a heart that had been broken in a specific way. Each pain bends the call in a unique manner. The wail of a desolate lover differs from that of a mourning mother. This particular call was unmistakably child-like. Thus, what responded was a parental soul.

This soul rose up. It clothed itself in the debris of the ocean floor; coral for its bones, its flesh; crustaceans and seaweed. Fine anemones formed a nervous system.

This father rose, swam, climbed, and eventually shambled across the fog-smeared *terra firma*.

IV. Wayfaring

It took the father a day-and-a-half to reach shore. Thule Fog swirled about all of Innsmouth, obscuring the creature as he went wayfaring among the dunes that lay past the sea.

In time he found the oblong cabin. Only nominally more auspi-cious than a shed, this clapboard structure was home to an old woman who introduced herself as Elmira. Her face, which resem-bled withered fruit, seemed forever in danger of sliding free from the skull on which it was mounted. Her fingers were unnaturally long and resembled the boughs of a willow tree; knotty with arthritis. Her voice was akin to the sound of water struggling down a clogged drain. Her breath smelled strongly of anise.

The father had ventured to Elmira's hovel because of its window light. Through those endless banks of pale mist, the guttering light through the grimy pane of the cabin's only window seemed as bright and rare as a fallen star. The cabin door had suddenly flung open and the father had seen the spindle-thin woman, her arm scooping the air again and again in a desperate gesture of beckoning. Elmira was back-lit by several wan candles or lamps; a crude and crooked impression of some haloed saint.

The incline was steep. His waterlogged feet worried across deep divots and stones made greasy by rain and moss. One of these rocks caught him mid-step, forcing him to practically stumble right into the old woman's home. Immediately Elmira pressed the door closed behind him and guided the father to an upturned crate on the floor.

"Rest now," she urged in that brackish voice of hers. Elmira curled her willow fingers around the father's arm. "Rest..."

A proper respite was difficult to achieve hunched upon that bowed and splintery box. He did what he could to tame his shivering and tried to pretend that the few sputtering candles that sat about the room were actually warming. Those tin can lamps were crude to the point of ugliness, but the father was grateful for their light, for it had been so long since he'd seen light. He also enjoyed the curiously cosy fragrance they emitted, so much as his altered nostrils would allow.

"That's it, my child," she said, "breathe it all in, let it nourish you."

The scent was reminiscent of cooking meat. The candles were in fact cans of congealed meat dripping, which the old woman had collected and fastened with slow burning wicks. There were greasy hisses of the warmed animal fat.

Elmira settled into a rocking chair with a cracked runner. She began to rock, slowly, like a creaking pendulum.

"You know why you're here?" she asked the father.

She pointed to the wall. He noticed the water stains and the rivulets of rain that were breaching the cabin with ease. "In that lighthouse out there, right on the point, that's where it's gonna happen, where she'll come to you."

V. Lighthouse

The old woman had taken her leave. The tin can lanterns had been snuffed by the pooled fat, and the rain seemed to have ceased. The father gazed out the window, using what were only nominally eyes to study the brackish glimmer that radiated through the fog. He rose and shuffled to the door.

The mist was still settled over the heath. For all the father knew it covered every inch of the world. Somewhere beyond this pulsating shroud the sun struggled to shine.

He stood and allowed the noises of the terrain to be collected and amplified within his seashell ears. All he could hear was the susurrus of the distant surf calling him back to his deep home.

The father knew nothing of this village, but Elmira had mentioned the lighthouse last night, with its beacon that swept the water with a wand of white light.

The land was even more treacherous in the fog than it would have already been for the father's naïve feet. He went wayfaring for hours, unsure which way to go. He did not spot a single living soul.

Only after he heard the sound of a foghorn, that deep lamenting wail, did he begin to navigate. That low sonorous call gave a primordial voice to the mist.

At length, he found the lighthouse.

With great care he made his way to the end of the stout pier and searched for the door.

It was hanging ajar. The damp gusts rolling in off the water wobbled the iron door back and forth, but were not strong enough to slam it shut. The father slipped through the opening and stood within the cone-shaped hull of the lighthouse, listening. A loaded, anticipatory silence held fast within the oblong chamber.

His tedious ascent up the staircase of spiralling iron ended in a welcome increase of light. For although the fog was just as thick at this perch, the lighthouse chamber was panelled almost entirely in windows, allowing much of the stormy glow to illuminate the wooden console with its primitive gauges and switches, a table hosting a metal coffee urn and hot plate, and a cot. The lighthouse was abandoned. Here the foghorn was uncomfortably loud. Its two-tone signal made his chest ache.

The father moved to the cot and noticed that the pillow was soaked with water. It was also brightened with an artefact, a curled thing like a stillborn seahorse. A shell, its inner folds the colour of warm living flesh.

He raised it to where his mouth should be.

VI. Roused

A cry like the trilling of a thousand mad birds wrenched Rose off the wave of beige sleep she'd been savouring for what seemed to be years. Grief often swaddles its victims in a soothing oblivion, protecting them from assailing dreams. So when Rose roused to a darkened bedroom she was certain that the noise was not a product of her imagination.

She slipped out of her bed and passed by her snoring aunt.

Out the back door and across the dewy lawn, Rose moved like a rat of Hamelin, lured and lulled by a monotonous music only her charmed ears could perceive.

She shuffled toward the waterfront, where none of the drunken revellers or the whores even noticed the barefooted form dressed in a nightgown that was almost phosphorescent within the unsavoury shadows of the wharf.

The lighthouse soon met her gaze. It was enrobed in a strange fog, luminous and animated. As the damp wind teased out thin tendrils of smoke from the vertical fog bank, they curled like fingers in a gesture of beckoning. Rose heeded, hooked upon those curling clouds until she found herself standing at the tower's open door.

By now the high note had ceased and all was silent, save for the tides that plopped and clapped against the floodwall and the pillars of the docks.

She entered and looked up the fog-brightened staircase. A mannish silhouette stared back at her. It raised the shell.

Rose raced up the steps, crying out "Daddy! Daddy!"

Breathless, she reached the summit and ran toward the figure that stood with open arms.

Or things like arms.

The first warning Rose received was olfactory; the chloral stench of decaying marine life, the cloying smell of brine.

What stood before her was a patchwork thing, a doll of flotsam and squirming membranes of sea life. The eyes were pits that pulsed with grey oysters and the flesh was an armour of shellfish and other scuttling things. The mouth was an aspect of jellyfish that flexed like a *yoni*. Rose was horrified to hear that the creature was trying to speak.

The father-thing scooped her up with ease and carried her limp form down the coiling steps. Somewhere deep in her consciousness, like the memory of a distant dream, images of an impossible city began to flower before her mind's eye. It was as if whatever fell intelligence animated this abomination was attempting to reassure her, to tempt her with the glories of what laid in wait for her many leagues below.

Rose wondered if this was in fact her father after all, transformed by the taint of Y'ha-nthlei. She hoped the city was as glorious as it seemed. And then she thought no more.

VII. Requiem

Rory O'Fey had scarcely been conscious for the better part of a week once the crew of the *S.S. Imperium* had fished him out of the waters. They'd spotted him at the last possible second. The surging bow of their great ship would have halved him had some of the men not rushed to the side of the vessel and frantically pushed the prostrate man aside with their oars.

Exactly how long he'd been floating upon the slab of driftwood the men of the *Imperium* never did ascertain. The man had only the shorn clothes on his back and nothing in the way of identification.

The medic estimated by Rory's severe dehydration, his blistered and near-purple flesh, and general delirium that he'd been adrift for approximately a week. It took ten days of near-constant care to bring the rescued man back to a state of lucidity, at which time he told the captain and medic his story:

He'd been night-fishing off the shore of Innsmouth when a freak gale assailed the tiny schooner he and his friend had been in. The boat had not only capsized but had cracked in two. Rory had managed to cling to one of the wooden shards, but his partner, he knew, was gone. He'd floated, he'd prayed that the good Lord send an angel to watch over his daughter Rose, and he'd waited for his inevitable demise.

The *Imperium* was unable to re-route its course back to Innsmouth, so instead they messaged the nearest port and arranged for Rory O'Fey's transport back to his New England fishing village.

The exaltation of his homecoming was short-lived. Rory's sister broke the news to him as soon as he stepped off the bus. Dear Rose had also gone missing.

As to what came next, one can only go by the local gossip and the eventual published obituary.

Rory O'Fey was committed to the State Lunatic Hospital at Danvers just seventy-two hours after returning home to Innsmouth and learning of his daughter's disappearance. That first night, after having imbibed a great quantity of rum, Rory claimed that he had heard his daughter calling to him from the pier. He rushed to the waterfront to meet her.

Rory was discovered at dawn the next day, laughing and gibbering nonsense. He claimed that he had seen his Rose rise up from the churning sea. She had reached for him with arms of limp, dripping kelp. Her hair was a tangled mass of seaweed, her eyes the wide doll-dead orbs of a beached fish. Her face was a pattern of crustaceans, her mouth a pulsing barnacle that sang to him, that beckoned him, that yearned to kiss his cheek and begged him to return with her to her new home.

Rory O'Fey died laughing in a padded cell. Rose was never discovered; her fate yet another of the secrets that swim into the cold deeps of legend.

HELEN MARSHALL

Exposure

H ELEN MARSHALL is a Lecturer of Creative Writing and Publishing at Anglia Ruskin University in Cambridge, England. Her first collection of fiction, *Hair Side, Flesh Side*, won the British Fantasy Society's Sydney J. Bounds Award in 2013, and *Gifts for the One Who Comes After*, her second collection, won both the World Fantasy Award and the Shirley Jackson Award in 2015.

She is currently editing *The Year's Best Weird Fiction* to be released in 2017, and her debut novel will be published by Random House Canada the following year.

"I wrote this story after a trip to see the island of Delos, near the centre of the Cyclades archipelago in Greece," Marshall explains. "A former holy sanctuary and mythological birthplace for Artemis and Apollo Delos, it was absolutely gorgeous: full of collapsed temples, cobbled pathways, and ruined statuary. We were told there was a rule that after the Athenians purified the land, no one was allowed to be born or die on the island.

"I was allowed to wander wherever I wanted, and, of course, having climbed to the highest point of the island, I noticed with some shock that I only had about ten minutes to make it to the harbour before the ferry departed. I was lucky enough not to have been left stranded, but something about the place, the entire situation, captured my imagination."

∞

"**D**ID YOU BRING the sunscreen?" The boat was unsteady, hurled up the height of the enormous waves cast off in the wake of the cruise ships heading to more popular destination, sliding down with a lurch that made Serena feel like fucking hurling. Not her mother, though, no, Serena's mother had a smile like a clenched fist.

"The sunscreen, Serena. Did you bring it? It's important, I told you it's important."

Nothing.

"Serena, I asked you a question: did you bring the sunscreen?"

"Yes, Mom—Jesus!—I brought the sunscreen!"

A long pause. Serena squinted. The glare of the ocean was bleak and blinding. It should have been beautiful, being out on the ocean like this, it should have been glorious—but then, Serena should have been on one of the cruise ships, she should have been wearing a neat little black bikini, should have been sunbathing on the deck, should have been staking out the side of the pool and working on her tan.

Should have been.

"That's it, it must be, in the distance, Serena, don't you think that must be it?"

"I guess."

"You guess? You guess? Ha, she guesses."

Serena rolled her eyes, and her mother ignored it for once, too fucking happy to be here, too fucking happy to be part of the crowd of tourists. Not that there were all that many of them—there wouldn't be, would there? Really, only a handful, German, Italian, English, American—all middle-aged men with bald patches, bulbous sunburnt noses—fucking gross. Some of them clutched at guide-books and cameras. Her mother didn't have a camera. Her mother didn't want anything as crass as a camera. Whatever she wanted, she wanted to see on her own.

Serena didn't understand it. This had never been *her* thing, this had always been her mother's thing. When Serena was twelve her mother had dragged her to Athens. Last year it had been Istanbul. And, okay, maybe those places had a certain charm. Maybe there had been something to the Acropolis, watching the marble changing from gold to rose to white to pale blue as it reflected the last glow of the twilight—maybe that had been just a little bit nice—but then it got back to the way things always were between them, her mother screaming at her for forgetting the sunscreen, her mother freaking out when she talked to anyone for even ten seconds. Like the hotel concierge was some paedophile. And he wasn't, of course he wasn't! It was just cultural, right? It was just how they were in Greece!

Fucking Carcosa.

She could have gone to Venice.

She could have gone to Barcelona. Or Paris.

Carcosa was nothing but rocks, ruins—no one went to Carcosa, not now, not anymore. A few outcroppings, a few standing pillars. Once, Serena had read, the place had been beautiful. Once they had written about the towers. They had written about the Lake of Hali.

Dim Carcosa. Lost Carcosa. Strange the night where the black stars rise.

That's what the guidebook had said.

But what was left of it now? Rubble. An ancient junkyard. No looming towers. No Aldebaran. No Hyades. No Alar. No Hastur. No Hali. A hundred years ago the French team of archaeologists had drained the fucking thing, and why? Malaria! The Lake of Hali had been breeding fucking malaria-infested mosquitoes!

"*The sunscreen*," her mother reminded her, this time her voice was sharp, cutting.

Serena looked over her shoulder at the cruise ships heading for Mykonos—the white sand beaches she'd been staring at for months in the brochures—and tried desperately to discover the secret of self-teleportation, to will herself onboard *that* ship and not this one, not this dinky little boat fighting the waves, the sailors all dark-haired and dark-skinned, speaking whatever fucking language they spoke, and the tourists with their cameras primed and ready—like Carcosa really meant something to them, like this was it, this was *it*, this was fucking Carcosa!

Fucking losers, Serena thought.

Quiet now.

Blessed, fucking peace.

Serena walked along the shoreline. Her mother was somewhere—anywhere—not here, and thank God for that. Their split had been predictable: the spilled sunscreen, her mother scrubbing away at the oil-slick sand to find something usable, rubbing gravel and who knows what else into her arms until they glistened and blistered at the same time. She was mad, absolutely mad! Serena had been ecstatic to see her storm off, arms and legs crusted like a panko chicken breast, with a trio of tourists from Germany.

Five hours, she had been told. That was all.

Five hours to kill.

Serena kicked a rock. It rolled lazily for a moment, crushing the tiny shells that littered the beach. Serena had examined them earlier, strange spiralled things, flat, gleaming shards in the shape of fans, and amongst them the petrified husks of insects. It sent a shiver up her spine, the thought of what might be wriggling in the waters.

Serena did not like the waters. They were not blue waters as they should have been, but purplish like a fed tick. The algae, she had read. Something like that. And the light here was different. Too bright, but somehow thick, like mist, substantial—you could never see too far. The black stars, a trick of that same light, because they weren't black, not really, not stars really—something to do with the atmosphere, some sort of dust in the air, like how the northern lights could make the sky seem alive and crawling, the black stars were like that, except they made the sky seem dead, they made the sky seem like a giant bloated corpse crawling with flies...

How the black stars seemed to move.

Serena didn't like it.

She remembered the bus ride they had taken to the harbour city.

Bouncing along on broken vinyl-covered seats, padding spilling out, her mother ignoring her, staring at the guidebook, not letting her see.

"You don't care, Serena," she had said, "so just fucking sit there, would you?"

So Serena had been staring out the window, watching the lights of the villages they passed. They were high up. The island was mostly mountainous, mostly volcanic rock, she remembered being thrilled by the heights when there had been daylight, looking out at the red rock beneath them, the tiny houses clustered together on sharp, improbable plateaus.

But then the storm blew in—sudden, furious—and it frightened her how high up they were. How the roads had gone slick and Serena could feel the back of the bus beginning to fishtail as they took the curves. She experimented with news headlines in her head: *Two Americans Dead* or *No Survivors* in *Tragic Crash*. Began to see if she could make them feel real to her, if she could envisage that future—but it all sounded too senseless. Prosaic in a way that made it ridiculous. Those kinds of stories didn't involve Americans. It was always people from somewhere else—India, perhaps, or China. It couldn't happen to her. She watched the lights of the villages like constellations below her. If they were there, she knew she would find her way home.

And then abruptly, terrifyingly, the lights were gone.

For a moment Serena fumbled for her mother's hand—a moment, that was all it was, a single moment of desperation, a single moment of wanting her mother to hold her and tell it would be okay.

"Jesus, Serena," her mother had said at last, rolling her eyes, "the drivers do this all the time. They know the way."

Whatever.

She fucking hated it here.

The sun was lower now. The pillars cut jagged lines into it, brightness spilling out all around.

Boarding time, thank God. Serena waited by the boat. It bobbed up and down lazily. The sailors were moving around cargo containers.

Two of them leaned against the rail, smoking a single cigarette between them that stank something fierce.

"Hey," Serena called. That one looked up—the one that, maybe, no promises, she would like to fuck. He had the cigarette between his fingers. "Hey—can I?"

He shrugged. He smiled at her, and held up the cigarette.

"That's right. Yes, a smoke. I can—good, okay."

She walked up the ramp, and he caught her around the waist when she stumbled in the unstable rhythm. His grip was strong. It lingered. She didn't shake herself free but instead casually plucked the cigarette out of his hand. The smell of it made her choke, but she liked the way the smoke curled in the air like a cat's tail. She liked the way the sailor had held her around the waist.

"Well, Nameless," she said, passing the cigarette back with a smile. "You seem alright."

"Alright," he intoned.

"Some English then?"

He shrugged, and smiled around a second cigarette.

"This is such a crock, isn't it? Carcosa. Fuck."

He sucked on the cigarette casually.

"They say the island is haunted."

"Ah," he said, "the island." He shrugged. "Haunted?" Then gave a lazy wink.

"But you don't believe that, do you? Ha, if you do."

"Ha," he said. The cigarette dangled precariously off his lower lip.

Just beyond them now a small crowd was forming on the pier. They all wore a look of irritable disappointment—not at leaving, but having ever arrived in the first place. In Athens, they had that look, in Venice, in Barcelona. In Paris, they had it too but they were all too afraid to show their true feelings: instead, everyone had exclaimed over the buttered croissants, the quality of the wine all the while doing their best to pretend the Seine hadn't stunk with urine. They had snapped pictures. God, they loved taking pictures, even though they hated whatever they were looking at, even though it disappointed them so hugely. What were they snapping pictures of? A bunch of broken rocks? Whatever they thought they had captured, someone else had been there first. If there was anything Serena had learned, it was the endless disappointment of the already discovered. The great glories of the past—gods and poets, conquerors, angels, artists, all the filthy, dangerous *romance* of the world—had drained away like water through a sinkhole.

The crowd grumbled. Weary men, sunburnt and angry, their flab a glistening mound under their cotton shirts. Women fanned themselves with brochures, their faces still twisted into unnatural shapes from smiling into the sun.

Serena sniffed delicately, plugged away at the cigarette, as Nameless the sailor and the others began shuffling these cows onboard. They huddled together in little clots.

Where was her mother?

Nameless clicked a little tally with every tourist who stepped on board. *Click,* went the tally. *Click, click, click.* Each numbered and accounted for.

But where was her mother?

There was the German trio with their fingers thick as Bratwursts and their Kommandant scowls glowing in the guttering light.

"Hey," Serena called to them. "You there."

They bristled as a unit, and Serena flinched away.

"Hey," Serena tried again—this time to Nameless. He was grinning happily at his tally as the others began to close the gate. "My mother's still out there."

"Mother?"

"Yes. She hasn't come back yet onto the boat yet."

"No," he grinned. He pointed at the tally.

"We can't leave yet."

"We leave." He pointed at the tally again.

"Jesus, I'm trying to tell you, she's still out there. She hasn't come on board yet."

Serena hated his uncomprehending stare.

"We leave," he insisted, "*now.*"

"You said—" she gritted her teeth "—no one stays on the island. My mother is on the island."

It was ridiculous. Fully ridiculous. Of course, they couldn't leave.

She looked around for allies, but they had all turned against her. They had reservations for dinner, appointments, there were cocktails waiting for them in quiet cafés, and the afternoon's exertions were over—they should be abandoned as quickly and efficiently as possible.

She felt a coldness slither down her spine, a sense of how alone she was at that moment and how utterly unprepared she was for it. Her mother kept their passports in her purse, had only given her enough cash for tips...

Nameless shrugged his shoulders comically, waggled his eyebrows at her, and for a moment Serena thought it had all been a joke. She smiled. The tight knot at the centre of her belly began to lose, and her relief was such that she felt a sudden urge to throw her arms around the Germans and kiss them on their sweaty, schnitzel faces.

Then Nameless pulled her in close again, so close she could smell the smoke on him and the salt and the sweat and something else, rancid, sweet as rotting meet. In that moment she was afraid, suddenly, that he was going to kiss her. Instead, he whispered into her ear—and the smell of him was so much worse, it was like smelling a dead animal—"I come back," Nameless said, "an hour or two. No more. No one stays on the island, but you stay, for now, and I come back."

And he gave her a small but deliberate push. Serena stumbled forward onto the gangway, her sandal catching awkwardly in the planking and nearly sending her for a nasty spill. She turned and stared at the sailor, all doe eyes and hurt, but he merely took his cigarette from his mouth with a flourish. Casually, he flicked the edge of it into the water.

The tourists smiled. It would be easier this way, for them, and she would be fine. Of course she was fine. After all, whatever the city was, it was in a guidebook now, and they all damn well knew that for a place such as this a guidebook was as good as a eulogy.

They left her on the shore, standing in the wavering sunlight, feeling naked and exposed as they watched her, each of them smiling, each of them with their fucking cameras, each of them grasping after one final, fatal shot of the shoreline.

Serena stumbled through the columns, calling, but she could not think where to look. Her mother had always wanted to go to Carcosa but that was it. There was no special part of Carcosa she had always wanted to see, as far as Serena could remember. It was just Carcosa. The entirety of it. It was a thing that could not be divided up. No piece would be enough.

Serena's mother was not one to miss appointments. She had a pocketbook in which she kept everything in order. That pocketbook ruled her life: every hour perfectly accounted for, traffic snarls anticipated, emergency phone numbers recorded. Whatever was happening was clearly impossible.

That meant only one thing. Serena's mother was dead.

Once the thought slipped around her like a noose she could not escape it. It was logical. It fit the facts. Serena seized up with shivers. She could not breathe.

Her mother was dead.

Her mother was dead.

Serena had never been one for sustained momentum. She was fickle, and she liked being fickle. Now she was tired. The rocks felt hot to the touch. It felt like she was running over fucking coals. Her skin was starting to burn even though evening had swept in already, she could feel it itching, that telltale sign she'd been out too long. She was thirsty. She was hungry. She was crying and that was a fucking waste of water, wasn't it?

Serena sat on the shore and she stared up the sky. Hours had passed, how many she didn't know. Her fear was like amnesia, but even that was starting to wear off. She dug her fingers into the sand. There were shells there. They had been left behind too, like she had been left behind. Something had crawled out of them, naked, and decided that life would be better without any protection. The shells shattered against her fingertips. They would have made bad protection anyway.

The sky was black. The stars were black. It made the water black too, black and slick as blood in an unlit room. She was watching for lights now because she couldn't watch for shapes anymore. She imagined the Germans wherever they were guzzling beer and staring up at the moon. She imagined them drunkenly stumbling back to their rooms to fuck. The wife would be too tired. She'd spent the day exploring Carcosa after all. It was too much to ask of one person: Carcosa *and* fucking.

Serena thought about the husband, sad and still horny. She thought about him standing in front of the toilet, his thick sausage fingers wrapped around his thick sausage penis.

But then Serena stopped thinking those things because the first body had drifted onto the shore.

It wasn't one of the Germans, she would have recognised the Germans anywhere. But she was sure he had been with them, this fucking guy now with his hair tangled up in the seaweed, his face still fresh but his cheeks starting to bloat as if he'd been holding his breath. He bobbed gently in the water. There were air pockets hiking up the armpits of his brightly-coloured shirt. A camera tugged at his neck. It was an anchor now that he had found the sandy ridge of the beach. It held him in place.

There were two more not far behind him. A woman. She had a wedding ring, big and gaudy. She had bridal eyes, but they were frozen up, staring up at the black sky. Then a much fatter walrus of a woman just behind her.

Serena stepped into the water. Her feet slouched into the mud. There were more of them coming, bloated shapes that broke the pale gleam of the waves apart. She couldn't see them properly, not in the darkness, but she knew they were out there, slowly drifting toward her. She rummaged through the pockets of the closest one for money, documentation, anything, then she realised what she was doing, rummaging through the slick and heavy pockets of dead people, and she stumbled away. Fell over backwards. Now she was lying half in the water, half out, damp cut-off jeans and the salt licking the sunscreen from her thighs.

Her toes bounced gently off the toes of the dead man.

Her revulsion was immediate. Serena scrabbled back onto the sand. Every part of her dripped, even the parts that hadn't been in the water. She was sweating heavily. Shaking. She got to her feet and started to run. Her sandals weren't very well-equipped for this sort of business, so eventually she tossed them aside and ran on her bare feet the way she had when she was twelve years old. The rocks cut her feet to ribbons but she kept running.

"Mom," she screamed, "Mom!"

No one answered her.

"Mom!"

Still no one. She squeezed her eyes shut.

"They're all dead! You can come out now!"

But for one brief second she thought she heard something in reply, something like heavy breathing, and she almost wept in relief. That was it then. Her mother had just been waiting for them to die, and now that they were gone she would reveal herself and take Serena home.

"Mom!" she screamed again.

In the silence that came after her screaming she realised it wasn't heavy breathing at all. It was the sound of the waves beating against the shoreline, and it wasn't even that sound. It was the sound of the silence between the beats. The sound of the great lung of the ocean inhaling.

Her own lungs were heavy now. The black air was too thick to breathe properly. She couldn't get enough oxygen and so, slowly, her frantic pace stumbled to a crawl. She wandered directionless, completely adrift.

Then there were lights in the distance—like a constellation, some sort of hope in the darkness. She tried to remember what else she had read in the guidebook about Carcosa. Who else lived on the island? What language did they speak? She couldn't remember. She hadn't cared at the time. She hadn't even wanted to come here, not to fucking Carcosa, dead Carcosa, lost Carcosa...

She knew she was leaving a bloody set of footprints behind her, but she didn't care. There were lights ahead. That was something.

Lights and then sounds. A series of dense bass notes that reverberated through the rock, shook her ankles, shook her knees, sent her pelvis swinging.

She hadn't expected to find a party here. In fact, it was just about the last thing she had expected to find, but even from a distance, she could recognise the pattern of the flashing lights, the way the earth shook and jived.

Something about it all—the loss of her mother, the horror of the dead bodies, those dark, insectoid stars—began to crack her up, and between the cracks the single word "*Party!*" rose out of her subconscious. Instinct kicked in. Even though she was soaked from the waist down and barefoot, there was a subtle but electric trans-formation taking place. She knew it. This was where she was supposed to be. This was always the place she was supposed to be. Maybe it was fucking Carcosa, but it was also *fucking* Carcosa, baby, or it could be—she thought—it could be, just like Mykonos, just like Paris, everywhere had a nightlife, right?

The music was loud, and she couldn't understand the language of the people around her. That didn't matter. What mattered was the way she smiled, that glow she had, how she could make soaked cut-offs seem like that's the way they were supposed to be worn. She glinted and glimmered in the darkness. She was like a gem.

"Hey," she said to the dark-haired man at the bar. He had long hair and teeth white like bleached bone. His arms were ripped and bulging, and for one brief moment the shape of his muscles reminded her of the pockets coming out of the dead man's pants, filled up with air, bulbous. She didn't care though. She let her finger touch his finger. She paid with the dead man's money, which turned out to be hundred dollar bills. That didn't matter because the bartender said she didn't need to pay anyway.

"Fuck it," she said, flashing a smile at him. "It's a tip."

She went out onto the dance floor, trailing blood-stained foot-prints behind her. Her feet slid, and she made that seem cool too. Pretty soon there were men all around her, exactly the way she wanted there to be. One of them was pressing up against her from behind. She could feel his erection pressing against her ass. His hands touched her wrist. His hands touched her neck.

"See, I come back," he said, and Serena recognised the voice, the slight hiss of it. Nameless the Sailor. He had come back for her after all. Fucking perfect. Everything would be all right. This was all as it was supposed to be.

"What happened to everyone?" she asked him.

"Threw them overboard," he said and started laughing. She couldn't tell if he was serious or not. She liked the feel of him against her, and she pressed herself hard against his crotch. He smelled like cigarettes. He looked dirty, but dirty in a kind of hot way.

"Why did you do that?" Serena asked him over her shoulder. She was trying hard to concentrate, but something inside her was heating up like a pot with the lid clamped down, first steam frothing at the edges, then the hissing as it hit the metal plate and vaporised instantly. That's how she felt. She was the pot. She was the boiling water. She was changing inside.

"The cameras," he said, still smiling, "you know, *click click.*" His teeth bit together as he made the noises.

"They were doing it wrong, huh?" she whispered, and she knew she was onto something there. Them with their stupid cameras. Their fat, sausage fingers, their eyes wanting to devour Carcosa, their disappointment...

"Wrong." He brought his mouth close to her ear and the way he said it made it seem sexy. He was sliding his hands down her hips, underneath the belt of her jeans. "Ha."

Serena arched her hips against him. It seemed as if he was everywhere now and the feel of his hands against her made her wet. She wanted to fuck him. She wanted to fuck him oh so badly but whenever she turned he turned too and so they were dancing like that, movement for movement as if they were already fucking and she just hadn't noticed when they started.

"And my mother?" she managed to ask him, the breath coming like liquid out of her mouth.

"Not her," he said. "Not your mother. Come."

Suddenly his arms were like cabling and he was leading her off the dance floor. She stumbled, big smears of blood painted the tiles, but no one else seemed to notice. When she looked behind herself she could see every place she had been. She could see the pattern of her dancing, and where Nameless had stood behind her. The sight was shocking. It pulled her back into herself. She grew afraid of him, his gargantuan presence, larger than life. It was as if he slipped out of his body and into something more suited to himself. Reverse evolution. He looked as if he had only recently crawled his way out of the ocean.

But it was not only him. It was everyone. They were massive, towering creatures with slab-like faces and jutting jaws, composed of a soft jelly that shook and quivered to the music. Their bodies glistened. They left their own trail as they moved, thin threads of silk that criss-crossed the stonework. They were beautiful in the way that strangers are beautiful, soft-shelled creatures.

Here it was, the filthy romance of the world. Here was everything. Everything.

For a brief instant she wanted to touch them: wanted it painfully, wanted it more deeply than she had ever wanted anything before in her life. They had stripped her down to pure craving. The air was hot in her lungs, everything was hot, and she knew how easy it would be to strip off her shorts, her soaked top, to move naked amongst them. To feel their bodies pushed up against her, the raw, manic energy of it.

Their bodies were so soft, softer even than the bodies of the tourists floating in the water. Serena did not know where they had come from, but she knew, instinctively, that they were weak. She knew this because she was good at sensing weakness. She knew it the way her mother knew it. She knew they were reaching for her the way she had reached for her mother's hand, fumbling around in the darkness, wanting someone to hold. And knowing that made her powerful. It made her disdainful. It made her hate them a little bit for being so fucking weak that they would want her. They were as soft damageable as newborn's skull.

Nameless tugged her forward.

To see her mother.

To see her mother now.

This was what her mother had wanted. This. Carcosa. This was what *she* had been looking for all this time.

She loved these fucking *things*.

"Your mother?" said Nameless, but Serena could feel that his grip had grown spongy. She brushed it off without any problem at all. "Please?" he looked hurt. Bewildered. A kicked puppy.

"Just fuck right off, would you?" Serena said. "My mother's fucking dead."

Serena followed the trail of her blood away from the party.

Eventually the noises grew quiet around her. The lights grew dim. As midnight devoured the rocks and pillars, the crumbling foundations, Serena came to the shore. The bodies were still there. A whole crowd of them had gathered. They made her feel worshipped, the way they clustered around her. She decided she liked them better like that. She liked them better than she had liked them while they had been alive. What a fucking drag they had been then.

She gathered up the cameras one by one. Most of the cameras were busted or drenched. A few shed sparks when she clicked the power buttons. Only one worked, it was practically antique, mechanical. There were canisters of film, little plastic waterproof jars, tucked away. Serena had never used a camera like this, but it felt right, somehow, holding this ancient thing, spilling its guts out. She wanted to know what it was *they* had seen. What had drawn them to this place. She peered at the frames one by one. She expected to see the crumbling rocks. Stupid German faces smiling blandly into the camera, dumb piggy eyes, not knowing how close they were to death, how it would be such a small push to send them overboard...

She laughed at what she saw. Just fucking laughed.

Night washed in. The darkness was nearly complete. Serena sat down heavily amidst the stones and the shells, and, making a necklace of the film, one long winding ribbon of pure black, she settled down to wait for the light to find her.

NICHOLAS ROYLE

The Larder

NICHOLAS ROYLE has won three British Fantasy Awards. He is the author of seven novels, including *Counterparts*, *Antwerp*, *Regicide* and *First Novel*, and a short story collection, *Mortality*. He has also edited twenty anthologies and is series editor of *Best British Short Stories* for Salt Publishing.

A senior lecturer in creative writing at the Manchester Writing School at Manchester Metropolitan University, and head judge of the annual Manchester Fiction Prize, he also runs Nightjar Press, publishing signed, limited-edition chapbooks.

Recent stories have appeared in *Dead Letters* (Titan Books), *Being Dad* (Tangent) and *Stories* (PowWow Festival of Writing). His latest publication is *In Camera* (Negative Press London), a collaboration with artist David Gledhill.

"This story was commissioned by Ellen Wiles for *Ark*," explains the author, "an 'experimental project to push the boundaries of live literature into immersive theatre and live art'. I performed it at 'A Literary Bestiary' at Swiss Cottage Library, north-west London, in collaboration with flautist and project leader Ellen Wiles, who played excerpts from Messiaen's 'Le Merle Noir' during natural breaks in the reading. It was later published in *The 2nd Spectral Book of Horror Stories* edited by Mark Morris."

∾

NOT LONG AFTER we got together, she mentioned that when she was a child her older sister had taken her treasured copy of the *Observer's Book of Birds* and destroyed it. She could still picture the two thrushes on the cover.

I tried some second-hand bookshops, but could only find a later edition, so, although I knew it would be easy to locate online, I decided to give her my own, featuring on the dust-jacket what I knew, more precisely, to be a pair of fieldfares. I had bought it second-hand a year earlier, having decided to start collecting the *Observer's* books, but only those of a particular vintage, reissues from the late 1950s and early '60s.

A week after I had given it to her, I found myself briefly on my own in her kitchen and happened to spot the book lying on the worktop. I picked it up and noticed that the front jacket flap had been inserted between two pages—between the garden warbler and the Dartford warbler—like a bookmark.

I heard the creak of a loose floorboard on the landing outside the kitchen and immediately put the book down again and knelt to get the milk out of the fridge. As she entered the kitchen, I saw her eyes flick to the book momentarily.

"Cup of tea?" I offered.

"Thanks."

While the kettle was boiling, I visited the bathroom. I heard her leave the kitchen. When I came out, I saw that the book had gone from the worktop.

As I was pouring the tea, she re-entered the kitchen and stood behind me. I turned around.

She was standing very close. I handed her one of the mugs.

"Thank you," she said as she took a sip.

"You're welcome."

She didn't back away.

"I like your flat," I said.

"Good," she said. "I want you to feel at home."

She took another sip of her tea and I tried my own, but it was too hot.

"Where do those doors lead?" I asked, inclining my head towards two doors off a narrow vestibule leading to the bathroom.

"The green door leads outside," she said. "Back yard. There are steps down. It doesn't get much use over the winter."

"It's spring now," I pointed out.

"Shall we go and sit in the sitting room where we can be more comfortable?" she said.

"Okay," I said and followed her, with a backwards glance at the other door, which had been stripped and coated in wood stain.

The walls of the sitting room were bare apart from a framed pastel of heathland dotted with clumps of gorse.

"I know I've asked you before," I said. "Is that of somewhere in particular?"

"The New Forest," she said.

"Ah yes, that's where you're from, somewhere down there."

Later, she was in the kitchen preparing a snack for us to have before we went out for a drink. She sang to herself as I listened from the bedroom. She had a lovely, rippling singing voice with just an occasional harsh, almost scolding, note to it. I saw the book by her side of the bed and picked it up. The jacket flap remained in the same place. *This uncommon little warbler is the only resident bird of its family*, I read from the description of the Dartford warbler. *It is found only in a few southern counties.* I scanned down the page. *HAUNT. Gorse bushes and copses.* Then, hearing her approaching from the kitchen, I put the book back down, making sure the flap stayed in the same place.

We saw each other only once a week, as we lived in different cities. On a Monday or Tuesday, I would catch a train and we would spend the night together.

The following week, I arrived in the afternoon while she was still at work. I made a pot of tea and while it was brewing I looked idly around the kitchen, pretending to myself I wasn't looking for the *Observer's Book of Birds*. I looked at the door to the back yard; it was actually painted the greenish blue of a small number of British birds' eggs—heron, dunnock, redstart, whinchat. (I had recently acquired a fine copy of *The Observer's Book of Birds' Eggs*.) There was a key in the lock. I looked at the door next to it, which did not have a key in its lock, but then maybe it wasn't locked.

I poured out the tea, then went over and grasped the handle of the wood-stained door. I turned the handle. The door was locked. I moved to my right and unlocked the greenish blue door. Wooden steps led down to another door at the bottom. I went down, unlocked that door and found myself in a yard no more than six feet square. There was a little round table and two chairs. It was a fine day, warm enough to sit outside. I went back upstairs for my tea.

There wasn't much else in the yard. A washing line hung down from a hook. Its other end lay coiled on the concrete flags next to a hefty stone around which I noticed a number of smashed snails' shells. I sat and drank my tea until the sun disappeared behind a cloud and I went back inside.

When she came home we went out to the pub. I watched her as she walked to the bar for our second round. She was wearing a deceptively simple dress that flattered her. She had wide hips and narrow ankles; her bare arms tapered to slender wrists and long, elegant fingers that rested on the edge of the bar the way they might settle on a piano keyboard.

I smiled at her as she returned with our drinks.

Later, in the flat, I leaned back against the kitchen sink and she pressed into me. I threaded my arms around her waist and kissed her.

"I sat in the yard this afternoon," I said.

"Really?" she said, returning my kiss.

"Yeah. It's nice."

She laughed.

"What's that other door?" I asked, indicating with a nod the one I meant.

"That's the larder," she said, pulling away from me and taking both my hands in hers. "Shall we go to bed?"

"I can't think of a good reason not to," I said and let her lead me out of the kitchen. I had only a very limited view from behind, but her expression looked strangely fixed and almost alien as her sharp features cut through the still air. We both in turn stepped on the loose floorboard.

In the middle of the night I woke with a pounding head. She stirred as I got up, but her breathing remained slow and steady.

I found some paracetamol in the bathroom and gulped two down with a glass of water. Sensing that I would struggle to get back to sleep, I went into the sitting room. On the coffee table was the *Observer's Book of Birds*. I picked it up. There was enough light from the streetlights, the blinds having not been lowered. The flap had been moved on by a single page to the thrushes—mistle thrush and song thrush. My eyes moved over the text until they snagged on a short paragraph towards the bottom of the page devoted to the song thrush: *FOOD. Worms, slugs, snails, grubs and insects; also berries. The bird smashes the snail-shells on a stone known as an "anvil".*

The following week the papers were talking about a heatwave. She texted me, saying did I fancy meeting her by the canal and we could walk back up towards her neighbourhood, perhaps getting something to eat.

When I reached the canal she was already there, standing on the road bridge looking down into the water. Unaware of my approach, she appeared to be staring with almost murderous intensity at a moorhen and her chicks.

"What did they ever do to you?" I joked.

She snapped her head round and her smile of recognition took a moment to arrive. She pecked me on the lips and we headed in a north-easterly direction, ending up walking through the market. I had previously seen the lock-up shops down there only after the end of trading, all the units hidden away behind roller shutters covered in vivid graffiti. Every other business, it seemed, was an African butcher's, their trestle tables practically lowing under stacks of cows' hooves.

"Look at these," she said, pointing to yet more hooves hanging from lethal meat-hooks just above eye-level. She took hold of my hand for the first time during the walk, intertwining her long fingers with mine. I looked down involuntarily and was aware of her turning to look at me, so I met her gaze. There was a strange half-smile on her lips that didn't quite meet her eyes. She looked back at the meat-hooks. The butcher approached from the shadows, asking if he could help us, but she turned away without answering him and we walked on.

When we reached the main road, she asked if I was hungry and without waiting for an answer headed for the first of several Turkish restaurants that lined the high street.

She tore at a shish kebab with her teeth as I tried to keep pace, then we bought some beers from the off-licence across the road and took them back to hers, where we drank them slouched on the sofa in front of the television. Without warning, she stood up and put out her hand. I let her pull me to my feet and followed her into the bedroom, where she quickly undressed and got into bed. I looked down at her, becoming aware of the *Observer's Book of Birds* on her bedside table.

"I just need to go to the bathroom," I said.

As I passed through the kitchen I looked at the two doors on the left. My eye was drawn to the stained door, which in the light from the window appeared a dark rusty red. For the first time since I had been coming to the flat, this door had a key in its lock.

I walked on into the bathroom, where I emptied my bladder and quickly cleaned my teeth before going back through the kitchen and on to the landing, where the loose floorboard creaked beneath my feet.

As soon as I got into bed, she sat up and knelt over me, then kissed me. I felt her teeth pressing behind her lips. I kept thinking about the book that was within arm's reach, plus my stomach had started to ache, presumably from the meat-heavy meal. We soon finished and she got up to go to the bathroom while I reached over and picked up the book. The cover flap had been moved forward about ten pages.

I glanced at the nightingale on the left-hand page, then turned to the red-backed shrike on the right. I read: *This summer visitor from Africa is well named "Butcher Bird", as it butchers birds, mice and insects, and impales them on thorns and spikes, known as its "larder".* I heard the creak of the loose floorboard and quickly closed the book and put it back.

She went to sleep within minutes of getting back into bed, whereas I lay awake for what seemed like hours, unable to relax.

The pain in my gut woke me in the night. I thought at first it was serious, but as I came fully awake I realised it had not got any worse. I could hear her breathing, low and regular.

I got out of bed and walked softly out of the room. I stepped around the loose floorboard and entered the kitchen. I went into the bathroom but failed to make anything happen that might have eased my stomach ache. Instead I returned to the kitchen and stared at the door to the larder. I looked at the key in the lock. The next thing I knew I was holding the rough-textured key between my finger and thumb, turning it, then twisting the door-handle.

As I started opening the door I heard a noise—not the squeak of a hinge that needed oiling, but the familiar creak of the loose floorboard on the landing.

LYNDA E. RUCKER

THE SEVENTH WAVE

L YNDA E. RUCKER grew up in a house in the woods full of
books, cats and typewriters, so naturally, she had little choice
but to become a writer.

She has sold more than two dozen short stories to various maga-
zines and anthologies, won the 2015 Shirley Jackson Award for Best
Short Story, and is a regular columnist for *Black Static* magazine.
Her first collection, *The Moon Will Look Strange*, was released by
Karōshi Books in 2013, and Swan River Press published her second,
You'll Know When you Get There, three years later. She has appeared
multiple times in *Best New Horror* and in other "Year's Best" antholo-
gies, and her forthcoming projects include a monograph from
Electric Dreamhouse Press on the film *Let's Scare Jessica to Death*,
and a novella from Horrific Tales.

"I was flattered when Paul Finch asked me to contribute a story
his *Terror Tales* series," Rucker explains, "and eagerly accepted the
opportunity to write about the ocean—and, as it turned out, I wrote
it while I was by the sea as well, on England's south-east coast.

"My feelings about the sea actually mirror the feeling I get from
many of my favourite horror stories—a mix of awe and terror. I
knew from the start, however, that this would not be a cosmic type
of horror tale but a more human one, for as soon as I began thinking

about the story, the narrator strode in with her strong voice and recited the opening lines for me.

"In addition to its more visceral terrors, it's also a story about another profound and pervasive horror: the hypocrisies conventionally expected of women around such sacred institutions as marriage and mother-hood."

I

*D*O YOU KNOW *the story about the girl who walked into the sea*

Did she drown?

No, she didn't drown. They pulled her out.

That's good.

No it's not. It was the worst thing in the world they could have done.

I want to begin this story in this way: I have always loved the sea. But then I stop and I think: which sea? There are so many of them. There is the sea of my childhood: the flat blue glass of Florida's Gulf Coast, the dirty ocean off Galveston Island in Texas. There are the seas of my later years, the freez-ing Atlantic smashing against the shores of western Ireland, the windswept grey waters of the Oregon coast outside my home right now. And there are the seas of my imagination, the seas I read about in books and never saw, or saw and was disappointed by so that the sea remains forever extant only in my memory. There is the sea of the Greek isles, a sea I somehow always thought would indeed be *wine-dark*, and it was not. There is what I think of as the Gothic sea: it is somewhere off an English coast, surrounded by cliffs and moors and castles with family secrets and brooding men lurking about. This sea, too, does not exist except in my mind. Then we have the metaphorical sea: we can be all at sea, which is bad, or in a sea of love, which is good, I guess.

But my story is about the sea, and about love, and it is not a good story at all. Or rather, the story itself is a good one, I suppose, if you are not in the story, because the things that happen in it are very bad indeed.

Because I am old, and because tonight I *feel* old, and because it is forty years to the day from another, terrible night, I am going to set down here the story of myself and the sea, and all that it took from me.

Every thing and every person that I ever loved taken from me.

II

Do you know the story about the girl who walked into the sea?

Women and men have been throwing themselves at death on account of love for as long as there have been humans and some concept of love, or maybe for longer: when I was a child, I had a dog who mourned the passing of its mate by refusing food for so long it nearly died itself. Before our not-yet-human ancestors were capable of the kind of planning that hastening death requires, they probably still starved themselves, or lay out in the elements, or let themselves get eaten by sabre-toothed tigers rather than bother trying to carry on.

Anyone who isn't terrified of love is either a fool or has no idea what it means. For myself, I'd sooner be flayed alive than fall in love again. You might say there is little chance of either of those things happening. At four score and five I am supposed to be preparing to die, but not from love, and certainly not from *la petite mort*—just from ordinary decay. At my age, the capacity for that quickening of the heart and the spirit and the loins is supposed to be long gone. And yet it happens. It happens to those my age and even those older than me, the ninety-year-olds, the hundred-year-olds.

The human heart is never too old for passion. It is the very young who believe otherwise, but then, the very young believe everything is for them and them alone. There is the old, true adage that every generation believes it has discovered sex for the first time: and yet there is no act, no position, no method of penetration or manner of stimulation or path to ecstasy or perversion that men and women have not been doing to one another in various combinations for at least as long as they have been dying for love.

I find this extraordinarily heartening. I wonder how different humans might be if we wrote history as a chronicle of significant orgasms rather than political intrigues, poisonings, betrayals, battles won and lost. I take a wicked pleasure in saying this sometimes to people because it shocks them. "*Abigail!*" they tut, or "*Mrs. Brennan!*" if they are on less familiar terms with me, clearly believing I am one of those elderly people who has taken leave of my senses and is now just saying any old thing that pops into my head.

And none are ever so shocked as the young. For all their posturing, the young really are terribly conservative, because they *are* so young, and so hopeful, and so they've yet to figure out that nothing at all ever really matters much in the end.

But where was I? I am old, you see, and I digress so readily. Ah, yes. The sea. The ghost story. Lost love. And the girl who walked into the sea, the girl they pulled back out again.

You may or may not have surmised by now that the girl was me, and if so, you are correct. Had they not pulled me out again, I might have been the ghost in this story. And a terrifying, vengeful ghost I would have been as well. I'd have smashed ships against rocks, rent sailors limb to limb, drowned swimming lovers. I was so consumed with sorrow and pain on that day that I walked into the sea. Those things would have felt almost like an act of mercy to me, as though I were doing those people a favour, showing them the true face of the world, and that at the end of it all there is only suffering and fear. Sparing them one more single agonising second of living.

Despite all this, it would, as I said, have been better had they left me there to drown.

I am certain as well that you do not need to be told *why* I walked into the sea that day: for love, of course. For the sake of a man. I was twenty-five years old, a late bloomer, as they say, but then I was possessed of a lethal combination of being both intelligent *and* unattractive.

These days a woman can buy permission to be smart or talented or successful with good looks for as long as she remains young, at least; in my day, being pretty meant you couldn't possibly be bright while plainness was just an affront to everyone. By everyone, of course, I mean men.

I must have been almost unfathomably easy prey for Philip, the married man at the office where I worked who set his sights on me. (Philip, how funny to think of him now! He is either very old or, more likely, very dead. I cannot imagine encountering him now, doddering and senile.) In those days, for me, both virginal and naïve, he was the height of dashing sophistication. I had never even kissed a man, had presumed I would be a spinster my entire life, and as for sex, that was something I gave little thought to, and never in connection with myself.

The result of all this was that a man I later came to understand was very ordinary was able to seduce me and convince me that without him, my life was worthless. After two months of surreptitious rendezvous in his car, twice in the office, once in a hotel room (I told myself then he must *really* love me), he informed me that he had no intention of leaving his wife; two weeks later it was clear he'd taken up with the nineteen-year-old secretary hired a week before he dumped me.

I was, as I said, naïve. I had imagined that there was something extraordinary in what passed between us, in the pleasures of sex, that anything that seemed so intimate must surely *be* intimate. I was in love, though not with him—people say *in love with love*, and that's wrong too. I was in love with the man I thought he was, and in those short two months, I believed I was the best version of myself I have ever been although in fact I was alternately neurotic, terrified, giddy, hopeless, and consumed. Love can do that to you. And then it ends.

When it became clear to me that I had been no more than a passing fancy that he quickly tired of, I resolved to kill myself, both to send him a message and because I truly did feel that I would not be able to live with my pain. Better that he had cut me open and literally torn my heart from my body than this agony of drawing breath after breath. I did not yet understand how the most appalling pain can recede over time even if it never goes away. Time doesn't heal, but enough of it and it begins to tell us lies that let us live in the present, if we allow it.

If the past does not come to you. Did you hear about the girl who walked into the sea? Did you hear what became of her children?

The story of my suicide that wasn't is routine and not very interesting. I did very little planning. In those days, I lived in Savannah, Georgia, where my family had moved to in my teens, and so I drove to Tybee Island, and found what I mistakenly believed to be a deserted bit of shoreline. Fully clothed in a skirt and a sweater and heavy shoes, I walked out into the ocean. Had I put more thought into it, I would have chosen a more reliably empty beach; I would have weighted my pockets to ensure I did not bob to the surface. I would have forced myself to drink the salt water into my lungs. That I did none of those things, however, was no indication that my suicide attempt was merely a cry for help. I was serious; but with suicide as with sex, I was a complete novice.

Novice that I was, I was spotted, and saved by a nearby fisherman. I spent two nights in the hospital, and I believed that Philip would come to me there, having seen the error of his ways. When he did not, I understood at last that I had been a very silly girl, and that I was no different from many very silly girls who had come before me. I quit my job and found a new one and resolved to stay far away from men for the rest of my days.

I told myself that I had survived not because of my rescuer, but because as I loved the sea, the sea loved me back.

I have, you understand, been mistaken about love throughout my life.

Do you hear that? Some would say it is only the howling of the wind and the crashing of the waves, but I know the sound of my children's cries. I must move along and finish my story for you before they come for me.

III

I had sworn to stay away from men, but the revolving door of dull office jobs that were available to no-longer-so-young women in the 1950s eventually brought me into the path of an even duller man named Bernard. He was everything Philip had not been; where Philip had been charming and smooth, Bernard was awkward and fastidious. But he had other qualities. He was steady and dependable. And we did have one thing in common: Bernard loved the sea as well. The first time he took me sailing, I thought this was a man who would never betray me as Philip had, because there was no room in his life for another love.

And so it was that almost five years to the day after they pulled me from the sea, I walked down the aisle with Bernard. No one could say that I had not done well for myself. In those days, I was considered an old bride, and fortunate to snag such a reliable man.

Bernard's boring nature extended to the bedroom. I told myself I didn't care; with Philip, I had seen what passion got you. Having said that, it seems surprising to me to this day that we managed to conceive three children. I told myself I was content, and I settled into an unremarkable domestic life that was exactly the same as the content and unremarkable domestic life that most of my peers had as well. I no longer had to work or worry about the future.

But appearances deceive, do they not? Because then I met Clive, and of all the dull, content, settled people around us, I would have said that Clive was the dullest of them all. Not that I am making myself out to have been a remarkable specimen myself: my oldest child, Deborah, was twelve, and I had long since passed from young and unattractive into ageing and matronly, or so I felt.

Clive said that was not the case; he said I kept myself trim enough to pass for at least ten years younger and that any man who could not see the unkindled fires banked in me must be blind. But he would say that, wouldn't he? He said a lot of other things, too, things married men say in affairs, but I believed they were true: that Stella, his wife, was frigid and moreover didn't love him. I couldn't have been more different from her, he said, and what he meant was there was almost nothing I wouldn't do for him, and he was right.

He even begged me to leave Bernard. And I might have; I told myself that Bernard, preoccupied with sailing and his accounting work, would hardly notice my absence. We no longer lived as husband and wife; we hadn't slept together since before our third child, Joann, now six, had been born. We even had separate bedrooms. Because I had long ago proved myself to be a poor first mate, too dreamy by far, he hadn't taken me sailing with him in years.

It was just as well. I was content to sit on the shore or wade into the shallows with the children. The truth is, I liked the sea less with the children along. There seemed so many more hazards with these tiny, vulnerable people at my side: stinging things, and big waves, and tropical storms and hurricanes, and the sea itself, always pulling away from shore, too eager to take everything with it. The idea of its unfathomable depths, which had once exhilarated me, had come to terrify me instead. I suppose you could say that motherhood made me dull but I would argue instead that motherhood made me *aware*. The world was so full of danger. It was a wonder any of us managed to navigate it for any time at all.

And the sea is terrible in other ways, haunted as well—by millennia of drowned sailors. By pirates and their prey. By captains and their passengers and their crew, by mercenaries and soldiers and lost explorers, by unwary fishermen and swimmers and beachcombers and people who did not notice the tide drawing in. The sea is heaving with corpses and dead souls. It is a stew of old bones and rotten flesh.

It is my single consolation: that wherever they are out there, my children are not alone.

But still they need their mother. All children need their mother, do they not?

I know what you are thinking. That they are going to be horrors when they come in from the sea. That the loving embraces I imagine will be grips of death. That they will be foul, decayed, mad creatures, that they will fall on me with salt-puckered eyes and mouths and suck the life out of me.

Or that I am mad myself: old, and mad, delusional, that I ought to have been put into a home long ago, and that I need *help*. *Help you*, hang you, burn you. You are ugly, female, and old: three strikes and you're out, but you are worse, you are alone, you are reclusive, you are not kind and grandmotherly and comforting. Your eyes do not twinkle. We are too enlightened to call you a *witch* but we will steal your life away from you anyway and lock you away and feed you drugs and call it a mercy.

So, you see, this is a risk I am willing to take. And what mother would not willingly give up her own life for her children's?

I would have, you know. What happened to them was not my fault. I couldn't have saved them. No matter what anyone says. I loved them and I lost them but I did not kill my babies.

IV

They say that you never really know a person, and they are correct. Case in point: my Bernard. I thought him incapable of passion, save for his love of the sea. I thought the children and I were little more than props in his dull life. I even thought he might be the kind of man to turn a blind eye to the fact that his wife had a lover. What did he care? He didn't seem to want me.

I was wrong. Bernard found out about us, not in a dramatic fashion. He didn't stumble upon the two of us in bed together or anything so crass. He saw a look here, a touch there, noticed an absence or two that could not be explained. He is an accountant, after all, and he added it all up, and he knew.

He need not have done anything. Ours was a business arrangement, I had explained to Clive, but a business arrangement with children involved, and as such, I couldn't think of leaving him, at least not until little Joann was off to college. It wasn't fair to either Bernard or me or to the children, who adored their father.

Why could that not have been enough for Bernard? Why could he not have allowed us to go on living with a small lie within the much larger lie that we were all living, the one that said we were a happy, contented family?

Even now, I do not believe what Bernard discovered inside himself was a passion for me, or for his family. There is a certain type of man who has a passion for the things he believes to be his. His own feelings for the things are not the issue; his ownership of the things is.

I do not know how long he was aware before he took action, but he did not give me any indication that he had noticed anything. One late-spring day, I went to pick up the children at school, only to find that none of them were there. Their father had come and taken them out of class in the middle of the day.

From the moment they told me, an icy lump of fear settled in my belly. *He knows.* I told myself it was something else, something innocent, but I knew better. And yet even then, the worst-case scenario that I could imagine was that he would divorce me and be able to keep the children, because what judge would leave children with an adulterous mother? And then Clive would abandon me as well, and there I would be, middle-aged, alone, unskilled, unemployed, a pariah among all who knew me and with no resources to seek out a new community. My parents were dead, and I had no family left. Where would I go? How would I live? *Why* would I live? What would be the point of anything at all?

I phoned Bernard's office; his secretary told me he was not in. I couldn't bring myself to speak to Clive. It was as though if I did not say anything to anyone, whatever was happening would not be happening, would not be true.

I sat there in our home and I waited. I didn't know what else to do. I didn't eat or drink anything. I didn't read, or watch television. I couldn't. I smoked, compulsively, one cigarette after another. It grew dark. And then I heard the sound of Bernard's car in the driveway, the doors slamming—and the children's voices. I almost sobbed with relief. I had half-convinced myself I would never see them again.

They came tumbling in ahead of him, and immediately it was clear to me that they knew nothing was amiss; moreover, they'd had a fantastic day. All of them were sunburned and windswept, having spent the day on their father's boat, a rare treat, and they were all talking to me at once, and I started to think that perhaps I had been wrong. Perhaps Bernard had had a single unpredictable moment out of his entire life and decided that he and the children would enjoy spending a day sailing, with no ulterior motives or secret knowledge behind it all.

Then he walked in, and I looked at him, and I knew.

He said quietly, "Joann, Kevin, Deborah—go brush your teeth and go to bed. Your mother and I need to talk."

They all stopped short at the sound of his voice, and I remember thinking how much like wild animals children are. Their emotions are one with their bodies, and they had been so excited as they all jabbered to be heard above the others that they were contorting themselves, jumping up and down, making hilarious faces, all long brown limbs and sun-bleached hair and laughter. But at the moment their father spoke, everything changed. They were suddenly as wary and watchful as a deer who has sensed a hunter in a nearby stand. They froze; their eyes twitched; their mouths closed. They knew that of all the moments there had ever been, this was not one to argue.

They hugged and kissed me in a perfunctory way and left the room. At any other time, I'd have scolded Bernard for speaking to them so sharply and cutting off their joy. But I had no speech left in me. I had nothing in me.

Or so I thought. Until Bernard spoke, and of all the terrible things I had imagined in the hours leading up to this moment, I never imagined anything as terrible as what he said to me:

"I took the children sailing today so that I could murder them."

He let that sentence hang between us for a few moments before he continued. And as he did so, I thought some part of him was loving this. Meek, inadequate Bernard had the floor in a way he'd never had before in his life, in a way he'd never dreamed. I was as captive an audience as anyone could ever hope for.

"I thought it would be the best way to hurt you most. And it's still what I want to do to you—hurt you, as badly as I can, in as many ways as I can. I was going to go through with it, and I actually had Joann in my arms, ready to toss her over the side, and do you know what stopped me? It wasn't love of the children. I don't love them and have never loved them, and I want you to be very, very certain of that, because one of the things I want you to know is that your beloved children are going to grow up with a man who does not love them at all. I know how much that is going to hurt you. I think it might hurt you even more than if they were dead, knowing I am going to bring them up, poison them with lies against you, and loathe them because they are the spawn of such a filthy, deceptive creature as you."

He went on in that vein for a very long time. I do not remember for how long, or what all the things he said were, because it was impossible for me to move past that first point. *He was going to kill the children. He was going to kill the children.* And he had not done it today, but what was there to stop him changing his mind in the morning, or in a week or a month or a year? And what was this reservoir of pain and anger and hate that I had never seen in Bernard, who had never so much as raised his voice to any of us? Who was the man I had married?

Looking back, I suppose he was thinking something similar about me.

He kept on like that, haranguing me, and sometimes he would require me to respond, and I would, as best I could. I remember thinking that I had to keep him there, keep him talking, and morning would come and he would have to go to work—because surely he would not allow his routine to be disrupted for a second day in a row—and then I could do something. I didn't know what, but I had to do something. He didn't shout at me; didn't raise a hand to me; in a way he was still my mild-mannered, soft-spoken Bernard, and that was what made it all the more terrible.

Even the most awful things come to an end, and that night did at last as well. Bernard went to shower and dress for work and I went to wake the children for school. Their tired, drawn faces, so different from the elated ones that had greeted me when they burst into the house the previous night, told me all I needed to know about how much they may have overheard and understood.

V

My plan—I did not have a plan, or not much of one. I told the children we were taking a vacation and that Daddy would be joining us later. I do not think they believed me, but they knew something was wrong and they were too frightened to put up a fuss although Joann did timidly ask me once if I was going to tell her teacher why she had missed school. She was only in first grade, and was still very excited about it all. I snapped at her, which I will always regret, and she retreated miserably into herself.

I left Deborah to oversee their packing while I went to the bank. I was terrified that Bernard would make or had made this stop before me, and so as soon as possible after they opened I was there to draw as much money as I could out of our joint account. I remember how troubled the teller, a lady named Mrs. Cook, looked as she counted bills out to me, like she knew that something was wrong. Of course it was; married ladies did not turn up alone and make enormous withdrawals like that without some cause.

I do not like to include this part, but I am trying to be as honest as possible here—I knew there was a chance that shortly after I visited the bank, Bernard might stop in as well, in the interest of vigilance, and find out what I had done. For all I knew, they might phone him and tell him themselves. And I knew that if such a thing happened, he would immediately go home, and all would be lost. This was my one chance, the only chance I would ever have for a decent escape.

And so when I returned home, the first thing I did was to make sure that Bernard's car was nowhere in sight; the second thing I did was park my own some blocks away, and walk home from there. And the third thing I did was position myself near the window while the children finished gathering their things so that if Bernard did come home, I would have some warning; I would be able to flee, I would be out the back door and away up the street to my own car before he even realised I was there. I would make my getaway, alone. It was not what I wanted, but it was what I would do if it came to that.

I told myself this was the next best thing. I told myself this was better than being trapped here with the children, that the children would be fine without me, so what if they were taught to hate me, that my presence would make him more volatile and they'd be safer with him and they would be okay. They would grow up okay. They would never know how he felt, or didn't feel, about them. These are the lies I told myself to make it okay for me to abandon my children with their insane father if it came down to it, a choice between them or me.

Other women are not like this, are they? It's documented—it's why women stay in terrible marriages, in deadly situations, in order to protect their young or just to avoid being separated from them. I loved my children more than anything in the world; I loved them so much I found that love almost unbearable; and yet surely there is something wrong with me, that I could do this cold mental arithmetic that would permit me to leave them behind if I had to. But I am not a monster. I said it forty years ago and I say it here, again, I did not hurt my children. I would never hurt my children.

It was the sea; the ghosts; the dead things. The seventh wave.

VI

I didn't know what to do, so I just drove. The children were subdued. They knew everything I'd told them was lies. There was no vacation, there was no Daddy joining us later, and something was terribly, terribly wrong.

That first day, I was so afraid that I drove for eighteen hours straight, keeping on back roads. I was sure that he would have reported us missing and that law enforcement everywhere would be combing the highways in search of a car of my description with my license plate number. But I was so exhausted that I began hallucinating—imagining people stepping out in front of us on the road—and I finally pulled off and paid cash for a motel room, pulled the car round the back, and piled us all inside where we slept.

We lived like that for a week or more—me, driving until I couldn't any longer and then a motel. I kept heading west. Isn't that where people go to reinvent themselves? I'd never been west of Texas or north of the Mason-Dixon line. I imagined the entire West Coast as a glittering paradise where we would be safe.

I bought spray paint to inexpertly disguise the colour of our car, and somewhere out in the desert, at one of the many low-end, no-questions-asked types of places where we'd spend a night or two to rest up, I asked a shifty-looking desk clerk if there was some way I could get a different license plate for my car. I could barely get the words out; it was such an alien thing for me to do, but he reacted as though customers asked him for things like that all the time, and they probably did. He told me he'd have something for me when I checked out in the morning. After that I relaxed a lot more. Not only were we thousands of miles away from Bernard, but we could not be casually identified either.

Yet I still didn't feel safe. We got to southern California and I couldn't stop; it was as though movement had become a compulsion. I turned north, and we went up through the state and then crossed into Oregon and the Cascade Range. And then we were out of the mountains and by the coast, and it was a sea like I had never seen before. The sea I was used to was on the edge of hot white sands, and it was warm for swimming. This sea was icy, washing up on pebbled beaches or crashing against rocks and cliffs. It was grey and roiling. In comparison to the sea I was accustomed to, it felt wild and untamed.

And I finally felt safe.

Those days were such a blur that I don't know how long we were on the run for. Ten days, two weeks, three weeks? I have never known. But I thought, we can do this, we have done this, I have done this. We can disappear. We *have* disappeared. And I think for the first time ever in my adult life I felt a sense of exhilaration and possibility, that the life that had been written for me was not the one I had to live.

True; the children were disoriented and traumatised; they missed their father, and cried for him and for their lost home. But children are resilient. I would find us a place to live, get them enrolled in school in the fall, and things would be better. I still wasn't sure how I would find work or support us, but I had enough cash to at least buy myself a few weeks, and surely in one of these resort towns on the coast I could at worst get a job cleaning hotel rooms.

It was in that exhilarated spirit that we'd had an evening picnic on the beach. It had been windy, and a little on the cool side for our Southern bones, but the sun sinking into the ocean had been beautiful, and the children seemed almost happy for the first time since that evening they had come in from sailing with their father. They had begun to run about and play on the rocks jutting up from the water. The tide was actually on its way out, and the waves were choppy but not nearly of a size to alarm.

I didn't actually see the moment it happened. I had turned away and was tidying up the remnants of our picnic, was thinking idly rather than in a panicky way for a change about what I would do the following day, that I would start to look for work, when I heard a piercing shriek—

And all of my children were in the water, and were being carried out to sea.

I ran in after them. I tried to save them.

You must believe me.

They must believe me.

VII

People tell a story in these parts about the seventh wave. It is not something I ever heard of in my childhood growing up along the south-east coast. The dangerous sneaker waves that snatch people to their death here do not exist where I come from.

Here, though, the ocean is crueller. These waves come out of nowhere, out of a placid sea. They say that every seventh wave is the one to watch out for, that it is the unexpectedly large and dangerous one.

I read about the seventh wave, all those years ago. I even called an oceanographer at a university here and talked to him about it. I was so distraught for so many years, and I felt that if I could only understand why it had happened, it would lessen my pain. What I learned was that science and superstition do converge, that patterns do exist in which roughly the seventh wave or thereabouts will be the largest. But sneaker waves lie statistically outside even this estimation. They cannot be explained. No one can say when one will rise like a great hand out of the sea and pluck people from dry land and drown them. No one can say why.

I do not know when, but I understand why. The gods and the demons and the ghosts that live in the sea demand human sacrifices. What could be lonelier than being dead? And down there in the ocean depths where pale eyeless things swim, beasts that are nothing but tubes and mouths lurk, where monsters that have thrived since the planet was young and all of evolution's nightmares converge under cover of darkness and deep, deep water, down, down, down they dragged my three babies, creatures of sun and light.

It is so late here. It is as late as the ocean is deep, as dark as the depths of the ocean and the blackness of space.

But, you say to me, *you say you love the sea. How can you love such a terrible thing?*

Have you not been reading the story I am telling you? Have I not always loved terrible things? My love has been nothing if not misguided and unwise. And how could I not love the sea, when my children are a part of it? No matter where I go in the world, I can touch the sea and touch some part of them, the atoms of their being.

On that day, twenty years after I walked into the sea in my attempt to die there, I ran screaming into the sea demanding that it bring back my babies. Ancient and implacable, it did not reply. And it was so calm. You'd have never guessed that such an act of inexplicable violence had just occurred.

Everything came out after that, of course: my flight with the children, and accusations from Bernard that I was unhinged and had killed them. Because of him, they investigated, but they said they found no reason to think that what had happened was anything but a tragic accident. Bernard said he would never believe that. I think it is because he had a guilty conscience. I would never have hurt them. What kind of a mother, what kind of a person would that make me? I am not that kind of person.

All of the publicity was strangely advantageous for me. A local innkeeper took pity on me and did give me a job cleaning rooms.

From there, I worked my way up to supervising the maids, and then over to the front desk, and at the end of it all, I was running the inn myself. Somehow, from all that horror and despair, I made a good life for myself. I could never have imagined such a life.

And I travelled the world, and I visited the sea everywhere I went, and every year, on the night of my children's death, I walk down to the shore where it happened and I talk to them. I tell them what the last year of my life has been like and I tell them stories about how their lives would be now. The first few years it was easy, but the older they get the harder it is; I cannot imagine my babies, even little Joann, in their forties and fifties now! They would have families of their own, of course. Their lives would be blessed. I would have seen to it. I would have given them good lives. I would have.

This is the first year I am not able to go down to the beach and talk to them. The weather is too bad, and I have done something to my right foot that makes it difficult for me to walk. I am hesitant to see a doctor about it. I have remained what people call "surprisingly spry" throughout my older years, and I know how they are, these medical people, how they take one look at you and diagnose you with "old", and everything that comes after that is secondary to the disease of "old", and the next thing you know they are poking you and prodding you and trying to put you away, and you with nothing to say about any of it.

But I have a little house that is right on the coast, on the edge of a cliff with a path leading down to the shore, and I can hobble out onto my front porch and see the sea smashing against the rocks below. I don't dare go any further than that. This storm is very violent; it feels as though the wind itself could pick me up and toss me into the ocean. They *would* collude in that way, the elements, to get me back to the sea, to do away with me like that.

I have not gone out just yet, though. For some time now the wind has been howling in a way that sounds like the children crying. They are calling for me over and over: *"Mother! Mother! Mother!"* Children get so angry, and they must be disciplined. They must not be allowed to run wild and do whatever they like, don't you think? It spoils them, and above all, children must not be spoiled.

It was better for them this way. We saved them from love, saved them from passion, the sea and I. My only lover, my one true love, vast and unfathomable and savage, subject to the whims of the moon and the vagaries of the wind, oh my darling brutal sea.

Something thumps on the front porch. A single thin line of seawater has trickled from under the front door and across my floor to stop now at my foot. Their voices on the wind are so loud now, shrieking for me, and their little fists are beating at my door. My children have come home. Suddenly, for the first time, I feel afraid. *I never meant any harm to come to them.*

Can you believe that?

Will they believe that?

JOHN LANGAN

THE UNDERGROUND ECONOMY

JOHN LANGAN lives in the New York's Hudson Valley with
his wife and younger son. He is the author of two novels, *House
of Windows* (Night Shade, 2009) and *The Fisherman* (Word Horde,
2016), and two collections of short stories, *Mr. Gaunt and Other
Uneasy Encounters* (Prime, 2008) and *The Wide, Carnivorous Sky
and Other Monstrous Geographies* (Hippocampus, 2013). With Paul
Tremblay, he co-edited *Creatures: Thirty Years of Monsters* (Prime,
2011).

Currently, he reviews horror and dark fantasy for *Locus* maga-
zine, and forthcoming is a new collection, *Sefira and Other Betrayals*
(Hippocampus, 2017), and a re-issue of *House of Windows*
(Diversion).

"One of the strategies Robert Aickman employed in his fiction
was to begin with something that's already an obvious metaphor,
and then to push past that layer of meaning to another level altogether," Langan observes. "The result is fiction that is unlike almost
anything else I've read.

"His story 'The Swords' is a fine example of this technique. In
it, a group of men take turns thrusting swords into a beautiful
naked woman who is somehow unharmed by their violence. It's as
over-the-top, blatantly Freudian a trope for male heterosexuality as
you're likely to encounter. But that's only part of the story, as the

narrator subsequently goes on a date with the woman that veers into surreal nightmare.

"When Simon Strantzas offered me the chance to contribute to his Aickman tribute anthology, *Aickman's Heirs*, I thought of 'The Swords', and had the idea of approaching its material from a different point of view. The resulting story swerved into unexpected territory, which seems entirely appropriate."

T HAT'S NOT WHAT I want to talk about. If you're interested in hearing about the day to day of a stripper, there are plenty of books you can read. Some of them are pretty good. Or you could watch *Showgirls*. Not, it's not accurate, but it's the kind of movie most of the girls I danced with would have made about themselves. So there's that.

It's a person—Nicole AuCoeur, the girl who told me I should try out at The Cusp, they were hiring and I could make some serious cash. I want to talk about her, about this thing that happened to her.

We weren't friends. We'd been in a couple of classes together at SUNY Huguenot. Both of us wanted to be writers. Nikki said she was going to be a travel writer. I was planning on writing screenplays. We took the same fiction-writing workshops, and were in the same peer-critique group. I read two or three of her stories. They were pretty good. The teacher was into fantasy, *The Lord of the Rings*, *Game of Thrones*, so Nikki turned in that kind of story. She was that type of student. Figure out what the professor likes and play to it.

I didn't know she was working at The Cusp. She was always late for class, and she always showed up stoned. She drenched herself in some kind of ginger-citrus perfume, to hide the smell, but it clung to her hair. She had long, brown hair that she wore in long bangs, like drapes. If anything, I thought she was some kind of dealer. I remember this one time, in the middle of class, she opened her purse and started to root through it—I mean, frantically, taking stuff out of it and piling it on her desk. The professor asked her if everything was okay. She said, "No, I can't find my stash." The guy didn't know how to respond to that. The rest of us tittered.

Anyway. I ran into her the summer after that class. I was sitting in Dunkin' Donuts, making lunch out of a small coffee and a Boston cream donut. Nikki sat down across from me. I hadn't realised she was still in town. I assumed she'd gone home for the summer. She said she'd stayed in Huguenot to work. I asked her what she was doing. She said dancing at The Cusp.

I blushed. Everyone knew about the club. It was on 299, on the way into town, a flat-roofed cinderblock building. We used to call it The Cusp juice bar, because they couldn't serve alcohol there, on account of the girls dancing fully nude. I hadn't known anyone who worked there—well, not that I was aware of—but I knew people who'd known people. Although what I'd heard from them had concerned the professors who were regulars at the place. There was a story about this one old guy who'd paid for a girl to come to his place and pee on him, so I guess I had an idea of the place as one step up from a brothel.

Nikki ignored my blush. She said the money was fantastic, and the club was hiring. If I was interested, there were auditions the following Wednesday. We made conversation for a couple of minutes, then she left.

To make a short story shorter, I tried out, was offered the job, and took it. Money—yeah, the money was better than I could make anyplace else in town without a college degree, and in a lot of cases with one. I had been working part-time as a cashier at Shop Rite, but I couldn't get enough hours to cover the rent, my car—which was a piece of shit that spent as much time at the mechanic's as it did on the road—and groceries. Not to mention utilities. And going out. My Dad had wanted me to come home for the summer, and when I didn't, he got pissed and said if I wanted to stay in Huguenot so bad, I could find a way to pay for it.

So I did. I had to shave my crotch, which was no fun, and kept it shaved, to give the customers a clear view of what I was waving in their faces. The dancing wasn't, not really. It was wriggling around on stage, teasing I was going to undo my top, wriggling some more, removing my top with one hand but keeping my boobs covered with the other, wriggling some more, etc., until I was down to my shoes. Oh, and the garter the guys stuffed their dollar bills into. The air stunk of cigarette smoke, mostly from the dancers. All the same, I smiled at everyone. Not because I was enjoying myself, but because it made me more money if the customers thought I was enjoying myself. It intimidated some of them, too, which did please me.

I wasn't especially nervous working at The Cusp. Probably, I should have been. But I was sure I could handle any creeps who tried anything with me. My Dad had been a Marine, and a martial arts nut, and I had grown up knowing how to punch an attacker in the throat, tear off his ears, and gouge out his eyes. Plus, there were always at least two bouncers in close proximity, in case things in the private rooms got seriously out of hand.

That was where the real money was. Private dances. Lap dances, mostly, which were forty dollars for five minutes plus whatever you could convince the guy to tip you. Some girls could keep a customer in there for two or three dances in a row. I didn't, not usually. There was also a room at the back of the club, the Champagne Parlour. Two-fifty for half an hour with the girl of your choice. And a complimentary bottle of non-alcoholic champagne. That was mainly for the guys whose buddies had brought them to The Cusp for their bachelor parties.

Nikki was the queen of the private dances. She had this routine. The DJ would announce her as, "Isis", which was the stage name she used. (Mine was "Eve". I know: subtle, right?) She would walk out onto the stage in a long, transparent gown that trailed along the floor behind her. She danced to Led Zeppelin, 'The Battle of Evermore'. I think she'd studied ballet at some point. There were a lot of ballet moves in her routine. She stood on one leg and held the other leg out in front of her, or behind her, or to the side. She skipped across the stage on the tips of her toes. She half-crouched, leapt, and came down in another half-crouch. She twirled, sometimes on her toes, her arms stretched above, sometimes with one leg bent behind, her head thrown back, her arms curved in front.

The gown floated after, whipped around her. She let it drift away. Underneath, she was wrapped in scarves, each of which she undid and sent fluttering to the floor. Throughout, she went from customer to customer, bending towards them, giving them a closer look at what lay beneath the remaining scarves.

By the end of the song, all she had left on was a pair of fairy wings. I guess that's what you'd call them. They were like something from a Halloween costume, one for adults. Sexy Tinkerbell or whatever. A pair of clear straps looped them around her shoulders. They weren't that big, and they were made of thick plastic. When the lights played over them, they filled with a rainbow of colours that slid about inside them like oil. Something to do with the plastic. They weren't butterfly wings, which is what most fairy costumes come with. They were long, narrow, shaped like blades. Hornet wings, or an insect from that branch of the family. If I thought about them that way, they almost freaked me out.

Nikki danced stoned—she did everything stoned, from what I could tell—and the glaze the pot gave her eyes made them resemble the hard eyes of an insect. Together with the wings, they lent her the appearance of an extra from a grade-Z sci-fi flick, *Attack of the Wasp Women* or something.

None of the customers noticed this. Or, if any of them did, he had a kink I don't want to think about. Nikki never danced more than one song. As Zeppelin faded away, she was off the dance floor, followed by one and sometimes two guys. Most of them went for lap dances, which took place in one of a row of booths set up opposite the club's bar. Yeah, the juice bar. The booths were basically large closets with small couches in them. The customer reclined on the couch, and the dancer did her thing. Each booth had a camera mounted high in one of its corners. For the safety of the dancers, supposedly, and to ensure no one went from lap dance to out-and-out hooking. Part of the bouncers' jobs was to keep an eye on the video feed; although I never saw any of them cast more than a glance in the monitors' direction. I don't think Nikki ever unzipped anyone's jeans, but there's a lot you can do before you reach that point. To be sure, as far as tips went, none of the rest of us could keep up with her.

Not that she was stingy with her money. If it was a night the club closed early, a bunch of us would head into one of the bars in town, and Nikki would cover our drinks. If we were working a late night, once the last customer was out and the front door locked, she'd produce a bottle of Stoli for us to mix with the juice bar's juices. Those times—sitting around the club, shooting the shit—were better than being at an actual bar, more relaxed.

Most of us changed into our regular clothes, jeans, T-shirts, wiped the make-up off our faces. Not Nikki. She stayed naked as long as she could. Except for her wings. She wandered around the club, a drink in her hand, the wings bouncing up and down with each step, clicking together. She would lean against the bar, where I was sitting with a cup of coffee because I had an 8:00 a.m. class I'd decided to stay awake for. We didn't say a lot to one another. Mostly, we traded complaints about the amount of reading we had to do for school. But having her beside me gave me an opportunity to study the tattoo that decorated her back, so I did what I could to keep the conversation going, such as it was.

That tattoo. All of the girls had ink. In most cases, it was in a couple of places, the lower back and the shoulder, say. That's where mine were. I had a pair of coiling snakes on my back, and the Chinese character for "air" on my right arm. There's a story behind each of them, but they're not part of this story. One girl, Sheri, had ink on most of her body, brightly-coloured figures that were enacting an enormous drama on her skin.

Nikki had a single tattoo, a square panel that covered most of her back. It was difficult to see clearly, warped by the plastic wings lying over it. The artist had executed the image in black and dark blue, with here and there highlights of pale yellow and orange. There was a car in the middle of it, an older model with a narrow grille like the cowcatcher on a train. The headlights perched high on either side of the grille. The car stretched along a foreshortened road, its rear wheels and end dropping behind the horizon. I wasn't sure if the distortion was supposed to represent speed, or just an extra-long car. To the right of the car, a cluster of tall figures filled the scene.

There were five or six of them. They were dressed in black suits, and black fedoras. Their faces were the same pale oval, eyes and mouths empty circles. To the left of the car, a steep hill led to a slender house whose wall was set with a half-dozen mismatched windows. Within each frame, there seemed to be a tiny figure, but I couldn't make out what any of them were. A rim of orange moon hung over the scene in a sickly smile. The picture had been done in a style that reminded me of something from *Mad* magazine, exaggerated in a way that was more sinister than comic.

It fascinated me. I asked Nikki what it was supposed to be. She said, "Oh, you know, just a picture." Which could have been true, for all I knew. At the same time, that was a lot of investment in a random image.

The customers didn't mind it. Not that I heard, anyway. Most of them were too timid to say anything. They acted as if they were cool, confident, but it was obvious they weren't. It was as if they were tuning forks, and our bare skin was what they'd struck themselves on. They vibrated, made the air surrounding them quiver. There were exceptions, sure. One guy who was a long-haul trucker. Not too big. Kept his hair short, his beard long. Had on a red flannel shirt every time he entered the club, which was about once a month. He was quiet, polite, said, "Yes ma'am", "No ma'am". But there was a stillness to him. It was what you'd expect from a wolf, or one of the big cats, a tiger. The utter focus of a predator.

That I know, he hadn't tried anything with any of the girls before I started at The Cusp. He behaved himself while I was there, too. If I'd heard he owned a cabin in the woods, though, whose walls were papered in human skin, I would not have doubted it. I gave him a lap dance, once, and spent the five minutes planning the elbow I'd throw at his temple or throat when he grabbed me. He didn't, and he tipped pretty well. That said, I wouldn't have done it a second time.

The other exception was a group of guys who squeezed into the club one Thursday night. There were five of them, plus a man who said he was their driver. The bouncer who was working the front door said he saw them pull up in a white van. The five guys were huge, the biggest men I'd ever seen in person. I'm going to say seven feet tall, each, three feet and change wide. Three fifty, four hundred pounds. All dressed in the same khaki safari shirts, khaki shorts, and sandals. They had the same style, crew cuts that squared the tops of the heads. Their faces were blank, unresponsive. They stared straight ahead, and didn't so much as glance at any of the girls. In the club's mix of white and blue lighting, their skin looked dull, grey. They could have been in their early twenties. They could have been twice that. They stood beyond the front door in a group and did not move. They reminded me of the stone heads on Easter Island. They weren't still—they were inert.

Not their driver, though. He was smaller—average-sized, really. It was standing in front of his passengers that made him appear diminutive. He was wearing a beige, zip-up jacket over a white dress shirt with a huge collar and brown bell-bottom slacks. His hair was black, freshly-cut and gelled, but his skin had the yellow tinge of someone with jaundice. He was younger pretending to be older. I figured he was in charge of the five guys. Actually, what I thought was, the five passengers were residents of one of the local group homes, and the driver had decided to treat them to a night out. I know how it sounds, but things like it happened often enough for it not to seem strange, anymore.

The driver didn't waste any time. He spoke to the front door guy, who pointed him to the bartender. She leaned across the bar to hear what he had to say, then motioned to one of the girls who was killing time with a cranberry spritzer to fetch someone from the dressing room. I read her lips: Isis. Nikki. The driver nodded at the bartender, and passed her a folded bill. I'm pretty sure it was a hundred.

Nikki emerged from the dressing room wearing her assortment of scarves, but without the long gown. She looked across the club to where the driver was standing with his hands in his trouser pockets. Her head jerked, as if she recognised him. When she walked up to him, she kept her expression neutral, which only seemed to confirm that she knew the driver. He tilted forward to speak into her ear. Whatever he had to say didn't take long, but she took a while to respond to it. She stared at the driver, as if trying to bring him into focus, then nodded and said, "Sure".

Apparently, what the driver wanted was a lap dance for each of his five passengers, all of them provided by Nikki. He gestured for the nearest of the huge guys to come forward. Nikki took hold of one enormous hand and led the guy to the middle lap dance booth. He had to stoop to enter it; I wondered if he'd fit inside. He did. His four buddies didn't register his departure in the slightest. The driver stationed himself midway between the rest of his passengers and the booth. He gazed into space, and waited.

I didn't see Nikki emerge from the booth with the first giant in tow, because I'd been called to the dance floor. It took me two songs into my three-song routine to sell a customer a private dance. He was a college student. I almost thought I recognised him from one of the big lecture classes. He was free with his money, and it wasn't difficult to keep him in the booth for two dances. We were to the right of Nikki and whichever of the enormous guy she had with her. The walls of the booths weren't thick. All kinds of sounds leaked through from the adjoining spaces. That centre booth, though, was silent. I noticed this, but I don't know if it seemed strange to me or not. I'm not sure. I was busy with the college student. I want to say that there was something off about that lack of sound. It was as if it was a gap in sound, a blank spot in the middle of a song, rather than the end of it.

Nikki and I finished our dances at the same time. I didn't notice anything wrong with her, then, standing naked outside the booths. She was flushed, but she'd been working hard for almost thirty straight minutes. She was sweaty, too, which was odd. The club was air-conditioned, in order to keep the dancers' sweat to a minimum. I wondered if the driver was going to ask for his turn, next. He didn't. He passed Nikki the biggest roll of bills I had and have ever seen, collected his giant cargo, and exited The Cusp without another word. Nikki gathered her scarves from inside the booth and retreated to the dressing room.

She didn't stay there long. She dropped the scarves on the floor, stuffed the roll of money into her purse, and returned to the club. The first customer she approached was a middle-aged guy wearing

grey slacks and a white button-down shirt. He was sitting back from
the stage, so he could watch the show and not have to pay out too
much cash. Nikki straddled him in his chair and ground her pelvis
against him. Whatever prudence he'd imagined he possessed flew
out the window. He trailed behind her to the lap dance booths.

A minute later, he was screaming. The booth's door flew open, and
Nikki stumbled out of it. There was blood all over her legs, her ass.
She stopped, found her balance, and walked towards the dressing
room. As she did, her customer emerged, still screaming. The front
of his slacks was dark with blood. Of course I assumed he'd done
something to her. His face, though. He was wide-eyed, horrified. One
of the bouncers was already next to him. I went to check on Nikki.

She was bent over one of the make-up tables, attempting to roll
a joint. The backs of her legs, the cheeks of her ass, were scarlet.
Closer to her, I saw that her skin had been scraped raw. It reminded
me of when I'd been a kid and wiped out on my bike, dragging my
palms or shins across the blacktop. The air smelled coppery. Blood
ran down Nikki's legs and pooled on the floor. Blood flecked the
bottoms of the plastic wings, the tattoo. She wasn't having any luck
with the joint. Her hands wouldn't do what she wanted them to. I
pushed in beside her, and rolled the spliff as best I could. I passed
it to her with fingers that weren't trembling too much, then held
her lighter for her.

I didn't know what to say. Everything that came to mind sounded
inane, ridiculous. Are you hurt? Her legs and ass looked like
hamburger. Do you need a doctor? Obviously. What happened to
you? Something bad. Who were those guys? See the answer to the
previous question. I couldn't look away from the ruin of her flesh.
When I'd started working at The Cusp, I'd thought that I was entering
the world as it really was, a place of lust and money. Now I saw
that there was a world underneath that one, a realm of blood and
pain. For all I knew, there was somewhere below that, a space whose
principles I didn't want to imagine. I mumbled something about
taking her to a doctor. Nikki ignored me.

By the time one of the bouncers and the bartender came to check
on her, Nikki had located her long gown and tugged it on. She

checked her pocketbook to be sure the roll of cash was there, took it in the hand that wasn't holding the joint, and crossed to the fire exit at the opposite end of the dressing room. Without breaking stride, she shoved it open, triggering the fire alarm. She turned left towards the parking lot as the door clunked shut behind her.

The bouncer, the bartender, and I traded looks that asked which of us was going to pursue her. I did. I hurried along the outside of the club and across the parking lot to where Nikki parked her Accord. The car was gone. I ran back towards the building, which everyone was pouring out of. I could hear a distant siren. Most of the customers were scrambling for their cars, hoping to escape the parking lot before the fire engines arrived and boxed them in. I considered making a dash inside for my keys, and was brought up short by the realisation that I didn't know where Nikki lived. I had an approximate idea—the apartments down by the Svartkill—but nothing more. I could drive around the parking lots, but what if she'd gone to the emergency room, or one of the walk-in care facilities? I didn't even have her cell number, another fact which suddenly struck me as bizarre.

Why couldn't I get in touch with her? Why didn't I know her address? The strangest sensation swept over me there in the parking lot, as if Nikki, and everything connected to her, had been unreal. That couldn't have been the case, though, could it? Or how would I have found out about the job at The Cusp?

I didn't see Nikki for the rest of the time I worked at the club. I stayed through the end of the fall semester, when I graduated early and moved, first back in with my Dad, then down to Florida. The five enormous guys, their jaundiced driver, didn't return during those months. The customer whose pants had been soaked with Nikki's blood did.

Less than a week later, he appeared at the front door, insisting he had to talk to her. His face was red, sweaty, his eyes glazed. He looked as if he had the flu. The bouncer at the door told him that the girl he was looking for no longer danced here, and no, he didn't know where she'd gone. The guy became agitated, said he had to see her, it was important she know about the cards, the hearts. The bouncer placed his hands gently but firmly on the guy's chest and told him the girl wasn't here and he needed to leave. The guy broke the bouncer's nose, his right cheek, and three of his ribs.

It took the other two bouncers on duty to subdue him, and they barely managed to do that. The cop who answered the bartender's 911 call took one look at the guy and requested back-up. The cop said they would transport the guy across the Hudson, to Penrose Hospital, where there was a secure psych ward. As far as I know, that's what happened. I don't know what became of Nikki's last customer, only that I didn't see him again.

Years went by. I left Florida for Wyoming, big sky and a job managing a bank. I bought a house, a nice car. The district manager was pleased with my performance, and recommended me for a corporate event in Idaho. I took 80 west to Utah, where I picked up 84 and headed north and west into Idaho. Somewhere on the other side of Rock Springs, a white van roared up behind me and barely avoided crashing into the back of my rental. I swore, steered right. The van swung wide to the left, so sharply it rose up on its right wheels. I thought it was going to tip over, roll onto the median. It didn't. It swerved towards me. I should have braked. Instead, I stomped the gas. The rental surged past the van. As it did, I glanced at the vehicle's passengers.

Its rear and middle seats were filled by a group of enormous men whose crew-cut heads did not turn from the road ahead. In the front seat, a driver with black hair and yellowed skin laughed uproariously along with a woman with long brown hair. Nikki. Together, she and the driver laughed and laughed, as if caught by an emotion too powerful to resist. He wiped tears from his eyes. She pounded on the dashboard.

I pulled onto the shoulder and threw the car into *Park*. My pulse was hammering in my throat. I watched the van speed west down the highway until it was out of sight. I waited another half-hour before I shifted into *Drive* and resumed my journey. The remainder of the drive to Idaho, and all of the way home, I didn't see the van. But I was watching for it.

I still am.

For Fiona, and in memory of Joel Lane.

LOREN RHOADS

THE DROWNING CITY

L OREN RHOADS is the author of a space opera trilogy entitled "In the Wake of the Templars" and co-author of a series
called "As Above, So Below", about a succubus and her angel. Her
"Alondra" stories have appeared in the anthologies *Fright Mare:
Women Write Horror, Sins of the Sirens, The Haunted Mansion Project:
Year One* and *nEvermore!: Tales of Murder, Mystery, & the Macabre,*
as well as in the upcoming volume *Strange California.*

"Alondra DeCourval came out of my love for the old psychic
detectives like Dion Fortune's Dr. Taverner, Manly Wade Wellman's
Silver John, Algernon Blackwood's John Silence and William Hope
Hodgson's Carnacki," reveals the author. "Because I love to travel,
I've been setting Alondra stories in cities I have visited and loved.
So far she's had adventures in Tokyo, Prague, New Orleans, Los
Angeles, and San Francisco, with more to come.

"'The Drowning City' was inspired by a trip to Venice, where I
discovered the Jesuit church of Santa Maria Assunta. It really does
have a balcony draped in fabric made of marble. I'm prone to ear
infections and I've had my ear-drums punctured more than once
(but only once in both ears at the same time, thank goodness), so
I wanted to spin something positive out of that experience.

"I was a Kickstarter supporter of Nancy Kilpatrick's *nEvermore!*

project, at a level that allowed me to submit a story for consideration. I pulled Edgar Allan Poe's *Tales of Mystery and Imagination* off the shelf, looking for inspiration, and reread his story 'The Assignation'. There were correspondences between that story and 'The Drowning City', because I've loved Poe's stories since I was a child. I was surprised and thrilled when Nancy accepted my story for her anthology."

T HE WET WINTER air swirled around Alondra DeCourval, slipping icicle fingers under her collar. As she walked back from the boat landing at the Fondamenta Nuove, her nose felt raw, her throat ached, and her head throbbed. It had been a long time since she'd gotten sick while travelling. At least the trip to Murano had been worth it. Her new glass beads were warm under her shearling coat.

Venice was a maze during the best of times, one she enjoyed unravelling on a sunny day. Tonight, with the fog hastening an already early twilight, she wanted only to curl up beneath the comforter at Guilietta's *palazzo* on the Grand Canal, sip *cioccolata calda*, and be swarmed by cats. Instead, she took a wrong turn and found herself in a little dead-end square dominated by a stone cistern and surrounded by 16th-century apartment buildings. Lost.

Alondra pulled off a wine-coloured glove to wipe her nose. She felt nearly miserable enough to knock on a stranger's door to ask for directions. Instead, she replaced the glove, wrapped the scarf tighter around her throat, and retraced her steps.

A brief meander brought her to a paved square ringed by a few sad olive trees in marble planters. The trees had been carted to the sinking city and left to fall to ruin. Alondra brushed droplets of fog from one's sagging leaves.

A Baroque church loomed over the square. Age stained its white marble façade to the colour of spoiled milk. Black lichen gnawed permanent shadows beneath the pediment. Above the gutters stood a row of saints on soapboxes, clutching the instruments of their martyrdoms.

Alondra had never grown entirely comfortable with churches. She no longer felt personally threatened by the survival of the institution that had tortured and killed her ancestors as witches, but she didn't assume modern Christians were better behaved. It was a prejudice she'd inherited at her grandmother's knee and she had not looked for a reason to challenge it. Let the Christians beseech their god to work his magic on their behalf and Alondra would work her own. The less contact between them, the better.

Be that as it may, the unnamed church was open and bright inside. Alondra had no better concept of the time than she did of the direction of the Grand Canal. She was sure, however, that it was Thursday night. Whatever was going on inside the church, she guessed it wouldn't be preaching. Rather than drift around in the cold any longer, she climbed the steps and entered the sanctuary.

To her continual surprise, she did not burst into flames as she crossed the threshold. The earth, even liquefied as it was in Venice, did not tremble. The Christian god never betrayed any displeasure when the witch set foot in his house.

Alondra's gaze went immediately to the chancel at the opposite end of the nave, but everything behind the choir rail was blacker than the night outside.

And what a splendid building it was: the ceiling rose in a series of domes, every surface adorned in contrasting relief with urns or acanthus leaves or dentition. The columns that stood sentry around the chancel were inset with green stone that morphed and grew in kaleidoscopic horticultural patterns. Swaying dizzily, Alondra sank onto a vacant pew at the back of the room.

Perhaps a hundred people sat in clusters, chatting. Alondra studied the congregation, trying to define their commonality. She saw rough-looking fishermen in patched wool coats. Unabashed society women in mink. A knot of too-handsome men with black eyes, laughing together. Teenaged girls watched them enviously, craving their attention.

Alondra heard nothing spoken but Italian. Apparently this was not a show church, drawing tourists to an evening concert. These parishioners felt as comfortable in their neighbourhood basilica as they would at the local *ristorante*. Alondra wondered that they hadn't interrogated the outsider in their midst. Just as well. She had enough trouble gathering her thoughts. Conversing in Italian might be beyond her. She promised herself that she'd sit for another minute, then seek a teenaged girl—surely they'd learned English in school—and ask directions. She loathed being reduced to a tourist bumbling along in a single language.

A balcony attached to the marble wall on her left caught her eye. Alondra realised the damask drapery that flowed from its canopy and hung in graceful folds from the balcony's lip had been carved from white marble inset with green. The jagged edge of the canopy's valance: stone. The large tassels hanging from the valance: stone. The fringe on the curtains: stone.

The exuberant detail slaved over by the stone carvers made her want to laugh. She wondered if their god took the same amusement in it.

She touched chilly fingertips to her forehead, suspecting she was feverish. Everything sounded out of focus, as if cotton wool wrapped her head. She had better get back to Guilietta's. She reached out toward the girl across the aisle.

To the rattle of polite applause, someone cleared his throat. Alondra prepared to flee, rather than sit through a sermon. As she rewound her scarf, however, she realised that she'd blundered into a recital rather than a religious service.

It was difficult to make out the speaker's words as they bounced around the stone space. The congestion in her head didn't help. Still, Alondra understood "voice like an angel". That persuaded her to settle back in the pew.

A woman gestured grandly to the audience nestled inside their winter coats in the unheated church. She wore a spotless white gown that fell in a single shining piece. An ornate gold brooch accented the shoulder. Her bare arms were an olive tone that spoke of sun and summer and the warmth of islands farther south.

The singer turned to her accompanist, who lifted a flute to her lips and quietly began to play. Her smoky voice was deep enough to be masculine, dark and strong as espresso. Alondra struggled to follow the words, garbled by echoes from the uneven stone walls.

The emotions behind the song were clear. The singer held a deep reverence for something Alondra couldn't decipher, as well as pride in her talent.

The first aria finished to an enthusiastic ovation. Alondra joined in. The voice had been lovely, as far as she could tell, but not spectacular. Maybe the singer was one of the congregation's own.

The accompanist exchanged her flute for some kind of lute. The singer's voice entered the music with a sustained high note that soared through the church, silvery and radiant. The tone dove back down into the depths, then rose again like a dolphin playing in the waves.

Around Alondra, people chuckled and swayed, enjoying themselves immensely. She wished she could hear better. Obviously she was missing something remarkable.

Alondra had grown up listening to vocal music, attending operas with her guardian. Victor taught her to appreciate the nuances of tone and colour in various voices, the ways different singers could flavour a familiar song. She pushed down a stab of grief, one in a long series, for the guardian she'd lost. She swore she would not cry in public.

The third piece changed mood again. This was some kind of threnody, for a love that was gone and would not—could not?—return. Alondra watched a tear roll off the nose of a weathered fisherman. Black-clad grandmothers dabbed their eyes with lace-edged handkerchiefs. Younger couples clung to each other and sobbed.

Alondra felt terribly out of place amidst the stricken crowd. What had reduced these people to such a state? As the song built in intensity, so did the crowd's lamentation. One young woman flung herself to the travertine floor, screaming in distress that eerily paralleled the soprano's melody. Those around her nodded, unable to offer comfort through their own suffering.

Perhaps she'd misunderstood and the recital was really a memorial service. Whatever the case, Alondra felt she was intruding.

She gathered her gloves and crept out of the church.

The fever worsened as she staggered through the empty streets. Fog muffled every sound but the quiet lapping of water in the canals.

The sound reverberated around her, confusing her sense of direction even more. The streetlights cast halos in the fog that hurt her eyes. Inside her shearling coat, her flesh felt clammy, but she was too chilled to open her collar or loosen her scarf. She vowed that if she ever saw another soul, she would beg him to escort her to Palazzo Schicchi.

But she'd never seen a Venetian night as uninhabited as this. It seemed every god-fearing citizen was tucked safely into bed, shades drawn, lights out.

Gooseflesh crept up Alondra's arms. *Something* walked the night, something ancient and malevolent. She hunched into her black coat and hid in the shadows. Tears prickled her eyes. She'd never felt so alone or so frightened in her life, so incapable of protecting herself.

She stumbled over a little bridge that arched like a cat's back, above a narrow canal cutting knife-like between the houses. Beneath her, black water flowed, not a sparkle of reflected light to break its inky surface.

Alondra leaned over the spiral pillars of the balustrade, willing her eyes to focus. There had to be *some* reflection. A white streetlight burned at either terminus of the bridge. The fog above her held in enough light that she could see even when streetlights were scarce. She should at least be able to see a shadow of her own reflection.

Her scarf uncoiled from her throat and dangled one fringed end toward the water. As Alondra reached out to wind it tight again, the scarf slipped from her shoulders and fluttered downward. She lunged after it, nearly losing her balance on the slick stones.

A pallid hand stretched out from beneath the bridge, fingers cupped around the black water in its palm. The hand was attached to a wrist in a shabby wool coat. Slowly, the corpse bobbed out of the shadows. Alondra recognised the crying fisherman.

His mouth gawped open. Several of his teeth were blackened and rotting.

Another body nudged his: the young woman who'd flung herself to the church's floor. Behind her drifted one of the handsome men

Alondra had unconsciously labelled Gondoliers. With eyes closed, he seemed to be still listening to the angelic voice.

Alondra reeled to the other side of the bridge to gaze down on bodies glutting the narrow canal. They stretched back as far as she could see.

Slipping, falling, picking herself up, she ran.

The flight through the city evaporated instantly from her memory. Alondra remembered only the stitch in her side and the terror that stole the laboured breath from her lungs. Finally she lurched through the courtyard of the correct *palazzo* and flung herself at the bell cord.

Guilietta Schicchi answered the door herself, a flannel robe thrown over her beribboned nightdress, silver hair loose around her shoulders. Alondra collapsed at her hostess' slippered feet.

Guilietta's knees snapped with a sound like breaking twigs as she knelt at Alondra's side. In English, she asked, "Oh, my dear one, what's happened?"

"They're dead!" Alondra whispered hoarsely. "They're all dead."

Guilietta touched fingers soft as wrinkled silk to Alondra's brow. "You burn," she said sympathetically. She looked up to where her two remaining servants stood on the stair. "Help her to bed, Cesare. Maria, call Dr. Serafin. Then bring us some tea and that *torta* from dinner. I'll sit up with her tonight."

Alondra woke with a sensation of water inside her head, like swimmer's ear. Tossing onto her side, she hoped the water would just drain out. With dazed affection, she noted Guilietta sleeping in the armchair beside the bed.

Instead of draining from her ear, the infection festered. The pain in her head flickered so vividly she could almost see it. Alondra writhed beneath the duvet, disturbing the cats, unable to find comfort.

In the back of her mind, she heard the melody sung at the fantastical church. She picked at the song, trying to learn its tune, anything to distract herself from the swollen burning ache inside her head.

Dawn painted streaks of rose outside the window, as bubbles crackled like fireworks behind Alondra's eardrum. The pain crescendoed, nearly unbearable, before liquid dribbled from her ear. She fainted.

When she woke again, watery blood streaked her pillowcase. The cats guarding her had changed and Guilietta had gone from the chair. Pain ramped up in her left ear, so Alondra flung herself onto that side and implored her eardrum to rupture already.

Alondra bolted awake, disoriented and dizzy. As Guilietta spoke, her words seemed to come from a great distance. "This is Dr. Serafin. He will help."

The doctor had striking black eyes, fringed with velvet lashes. He set an old- fashioned black bag down on the armchair where Guilietta had spent the night. Alondra whispered, "*Buongiòrno*." Her voice sounded loud inside her skull.

"*Buongiòrno*," the doctor replied.

"I can't hear you very well, but I can read lips," Alondra said. "I think my eardrums burst."

He rubbed his hands together, warming his fingers before he touched her forehead.

"The fever has not broken. I will give you something to bring it down."

He squatted down to insert an instrument into her right ear. Alondra appreciated that he didn't make her sit up. Even lying still gave her vertigo.

He touched her face gently so she would look at him. He spoke slowly, so she could understand. "I see small punctures in your eardrums. They allow the fluid to drain. This used to happen all the time before antibiotics." He smiled reassuringly. "Allow Guilietta to fuss over you and take the pills I give you. You will be well soon."

As the doctor repacked his bag, Alondra asked, "The bodies...?"

His head snapped toward her. "What did you say?"

"Last night I saw...perhaps I hallucinated...a canal full of bodies. As if a hundred people drowned."

He took her hand. "This is true. This was why I couldn't come to you sooner. Rio di Santa Caterina was choked with corpses."

Alondra shuddered. "How did they die?"

"Drowning," the doctor said. "We don't know why."

The doctor touched her face again so she would look up. "Do not worry about this. Sleep, get well, and try to erase this horror from your mind."

Guilietta roused her to drink some broth and take her pills. Congestion prevented Alondra from guessing the broth's flavour. Her hearing had become entirely internal. Every swallow was full of gurgling like the tide going out.

Drinking the broth exhausted Alondra. She curled up and surrendered to sleep again.

The Siren's lament wove through her dreams. *The others were gone. The others were at peace now.* Why hadn't she gone with them? Tears welled under her closed lids.

Alondra wrenched herself awake. Ringing filled her head, different pitches in each ear.

She tottered to the window, praying that the view would distract her. On the Grand Canal below stretched a parade of gondolas. Each shiny black boat held a long wooden box.

Seagulls wheeled above the procession. Alondra could not hear their screams.

The gondoliers must be ferrying the Siren's victims to San Michele in Isola, the cemetery island where Venice buried all of its dead.

So many caskets floated by. Alondra didn't count them. She stood witness, a pallid spirit in a white nightdress at the Gothic window of a 15th-century *palazzo*.

She had no tears left for the unknown dead. They were beyond her help now. Even if she had her full strength, she wouldn't dare go to the graveyard and ask the ghosts what she might do for them. The weight of all that pain, grief, and hunger would blow her out like a candle.

After *vaporettos* full of mourners passed, reflections danced on the wavelets, colours muted by the mist curtaining the sun.

Alondra returned to bed.

What could she do? Something evil had happened, something she'd accidentally observed. However the singer caused the audience's despair, whatever magic had been in her song, Alondra had escaped. She wondered if she was the only survivor.

She tried to envision the congregation leaving the church. They must have come out soon after she fled. Had they taken their leave of each other, kissed one another goodbye? Or had they simply filed to the canal and flung themselves into the gelid water?

Where was the Christian God to prevent the suicides? Why had he allowed the Siren to sing in his house? Why hadn't he intervened?

Alondra shivered under the duvet, tossing so fitfully that the cats sought peace elsewhere. The soprano stalked her dreams. Alondra remembered the shining white garment she wore, like a goddess on a Roman urn. Had she seen Alondra leave the church? Would she come after her, after Guilietta? Alondra was so weak now; it would be better to capitulate than to fight.

Guilietta brought a tray of tea and toast. Alondra ate dutifully, but the sound her teeth made as they crunched the toast filled her head with ominous rumbling.

"Do they know why they died?" she asked.

Guilietta examined Alondra's face, gauging what she was strong enough to hear. "No," the old woman said at last. "There were people from every walk of life: shopkeepers, charity wives, fishermen . . . They had nothing in common."

"They were all at a church somewhere in the Cannaregio the night I got sick. It had a balcony with stone drapery. There was a woman who sang to them."

"You were there?"

"This infection"—Alondra waved toward one ear—"I think it saved my life."

"Then let us count your blessings," Guilietta said. "I have heard of these things, these women who sing people to their deaths."

"This has happened before?"

"Oh, yes. Three times that I know. When I was a little girl, at the end of the First World War, the authorities said it was the flu that killed them, but it was not. Years later, they blamed a bomb, then invisible gas…Each time, there were rumours of a woman in a shining white dress with a golden ornament upon her shoulder. *La Sirena."*

"What is she?" Alondra asked.

"That would have been a question for your guardian," Guilietta said, gently patting Alondra's hand. "Victor would have consulted his books and found the answer. We are left with guesswork and rumours. If it's the same woman, she must be immortal. Or else there are several women, one a generation, trained to lead people to take their own lives."

"But why?" Alondra whispered, sinking back to the bed. "There were children in that church, widows…What could anyone have against them?"

"Perhaps simply that they were Venetian. Perhaps the vendetta is against the city itself."

Guilietta smoothed tangled flame-orange hair back from Alondra's eyes. "You must not worry about this. There are some evils in the world that are too ancient to fight. To them we are candle flames— *phfft*—too easy to blow out. You must do what you can do; this is what Victor taught you. Save your strength for the battles you must fight, fight with all your mind and all your heart…but you cannot win every battle. In the end, you must not mourn those you cannot save."

After the old woman had gone, Alondra considered Guilietta's final words. Alondra had been mourning Victor, dead now six weeks. She'd done everything in the world that she could think of to save his life, but in the end—in pain, exhausted—he'd crossed the threshold with a smile on his face, anticipating those he loved awaiting him.

She'd spent all her strength battling Death for him, then she'd spent the last six weeks mourning her failure. Victor was certain he'd gone to a better place. And she, however miserable she made herself, could not throw her life away just to join him. If nothing else, he hadn't invited her to.

Alondra rolled onto her left side and stared at what she could see of the sky. The fog swirled and eddied, a vortex that drew her out of herself, out of her sick weak body and into her stubborn, determined centre where she could puzzle over the Siren without distraction.

Sirens were first mentioned in Homer's *Odyssey*. The sorceress Circe warned Odysseus to stop up the ears of his men with beeswax, lest the Sirens seduce the sailors to their deaths. Odysseus directed his men to bind him to the mast so he could listen to the Sirens' song, knowing that it would suck the joy from his life, that he had "no prospect of coming home and delighting his wife and children".

In some tales, after Odysseus and his men escaped them, the Sirens flung themselves into the sea and drowned in a fit of pique. That implied that the Sirens were mortal and could be outwitted. Stopped. Perhaps, as Guilietta suggested, there was not a single woman, but a chain of them revenging themselves slowly on the city that had wronged them.

Odysseus' advantage was that he knew the Sirens' isle lay ahead. He could protect his men. Maybe, Alondra thought sleepily, that was her role in this tale: to be the Circe who warned the next generation of Venetians before the vendetta came due once more. Perhaps she could end it once and for all.

A generation later, the train no longer ran out to the historic part of Venice. Its causeway lay submerged beneath the surface of the lagoon, a hazard to navigation. The Venetians-in-exile refused to demolish it, to concede that *la Serenissima* would not be stolen back from the sea. Paolo, whose father—God rest him—had been a gondolier in Alondra's youth, pointed the tracks out to her as they followed them in his little motorboat.

The city still rose out of the lagoon like something from a dream. Most of it lay abandoned, inhabited only during the day by tourists. Life in the crumbling buildings had been challenging before, but now, with the lowest floor of every building under a foot or more of saltwater, living quarters were accessible only by partially-submerged staircases. Most residents that stayed slept on yachts moored to their ancient *palazzos*.

Water filled the city streets so that there were few places boatmen could not go. Only the highest bridges rose above the waterline,

islands in themselves, bridging nothing. Paolo handed over his handkerchief with a complicated smile. Alondra wiped tears from her
cheeks.

She had an appointment with Casio, a mad musical genius who
recorded the creaks and gasps of Venice in its death throes. She'd
heard his music via the Internet, told him what she needed, and he
promised to be ready. Based on the timing of the previous attacks,
Alondra figured they had three days.

She recalled her last visit with Guilietta, more than two decades
ago, so soon after Victor's death. Stumbling upon the Siren's concert
had changed Alondra's life. She thought back over the adventures
she'd had, the wonders she'd seen, the creatures she had come to
fight because of the monster in the Cannaregio. The Siren had inadvertently given Alondra's life purpose: to protect as many people as
she could from creatures against whom they could not defend themselves. She had inspired Alondra to become a champion.

While Paolo spread word of the recital to the remaining denizens
of the city, Alondra and Casio rappelled from the inside of St. Mark's,
mounting public address speakers to the bases of the domes. They
built a small stage from scavenged lumber in front of the chancel.
Casio had Alondra stand upon it, singing pop songs and anything
else that came into her head as he learned the acoustics of the cathedral.

Alondra careened between worry that her calculations had been
wrong and the Siren would not come, and dread that she had been
right and was luring all who remained in Venice to their deaths.

As late afternoon fog swallowed Venice, Alondra assumed her
place in the rickety gallery above the flooded sanctuary. Casio played
one of his compositions while Venetians arrived in little motor-
boats, rowboats, kayaks, and a pair of scuffed gondolas. Each boat
brought a pitch-soaked torch to light the cathedral, sparking the
13th-century mosaics to life.

If *La Sirena* harboured any suspicions about having been led to
St. Mark's Basilica, they didn't ruffle her serene exterior as she
ascended the makeshift stage. Alondra marvelled again at the shining

white garment that accented the creature's curves, giving grandeur and mystery to her body. She did indeed look like a goddess of antiquity.

The accompanist was a hunched crone now. Still, she somehow summoned enough wind to play her flute. The recital soared, even lovelier than Alondra remembered. With clearer hearing, she appreciated the crystalline purity of the Siren's high notes, the controlled depth of her lows. The voice spanned four octaves effortlessly, no seams between the registers.

The Venetians appreciated the performance, too. They cheered, encouraging, enthusiastic, but not with the hysteria that Alondra had witnessed so many years ago. Casio's sonic magic was working.

Alondra didn't understand the finer points of the electronics, beyond that Casio's recorder analysed the frequencies of the vocal performance, graphing them as it committed them to memory. Simultaneously, his sound generator flipped the frequencies and broadcast their inverse through the public address system.

The audience could hear the Siren's voice, lovely as it was, but the extra-auditory control frequencies—the tones beyond hearing she used to manipulate her listeners to despair and suicide—were cancelled out. Alondra could not have been more pleased. She'd staked too many lives, her own included, on the recording engineer's skill.

Alondra lifted her opera glasses to study the Siren's gold brooch. As she'd suspected, the tightly coiled spiral unravelled to reveal a mermaid with a sinuous tail. And the Siren was the exact same woman Alondra had seen twenty-five years ago: un-aged, undiminished, her hair as luxuriant and black.

The Siren lifted her gaze. A smile flickered across that cold, self-assured face. Alondra nodded, acknowledging the recognition.

The Siren sang the same programme as before. The audience grew increasingly impressed, although without histrionics. Amused, the Siren added extra flourishes, additional *arpeggios*. In contrast, her accompanist struggled and sweated, pressed to the limits of her skill to keep up.

At last the performance ended. The Venetians' ovation thundered back from the domes. *La Sirena* inclined her head and did not move from the stage. When it became clear she would grant no encore, the Venetians turned their boats and filed out through the basilica's doors, taking their torches with them into the deep black night.

Alondra ignited her flashlight and crept carefully down the stone stair from the women's gallery. Paolo's boat was not waiting at the foot. She sat on the steps, unconcerned. He and Casio probably had equipment to pack up.

The ancient basilica reverberated with the lapping of tiny wavelets against its marble-faced walls. Alondra had the sense that something moved in the night, but it was not the malevolence she remembered. This was melancholy embodied. Snuffing her light, she crab-walked back up the stair, out of reach of the water.

"I'm the last of my kind," the Siren said from somewhere below, her Italian strangely accented. "You have murdered me." She sounded perversely glad.

"I don't require you to follow the ancient ways," Alondra told the darkness. "All I ask is that you cease your vendetta against the people of *la Serenissima*."

Something large splashed in the cavernous basilica. The echoes took forever to subside.

Moonlight filtered through the windows in the domes, reflecting cold radiance from the spectacular golden ceiling. Alondra shivered in the damp old church, which—though it appeared to be vacant—was not quite empty.

The long cold night gave Alondra plenty of time to think. Over the years, she had set foot inside many churches. She'd dealt with a spectrum of Christians, even loved a few. Their faith told them that sometimes a witch could work God's will. She had seen nothing to disprove that, but she wasn't comfortable being used by anyone, even a god.

When dawn finally came, Alondra found four bodies floating in the hip-deep water inside the nave. The Siren and her accompanist she expected. Casio did not surprise her—listening to the recording had been too much of a temptation for the sound engineer. Unfortunately, Alondra had needed him too much to tie him to the mast.

Paolo's death saddened her, though. He still wore the headphones Casio lent him, plugged into the recorder. Like Odysseus, Paolo chose to hear the Siren's voice unmasked. Knowing what she was, what she wanted, hadn't protected him.

Four dead, rather than a hundred, and these would be the last: that counted as a triumph.

Alondra waded through the chilly waters, careful not to slip on the submerged floor. She fumbled the Siren's corpse into Paolo's little motorboat.

As she motored back to the mainland, Alondra paused halfway. She weighted the Siren's corpse with Casio's electronics and dumped the creature into the lagoon. The others would be discovered by police on their daily patrols.

She would never know the source of the vendetta.

RON WEIGHELL

THE CHAPEL OF INFERNAL DEVOTION

R ON WEIGHELL lives in Horndean, Hampshire, with his wife
Fran. Individual stories have appeared in many anthologies,
including those published by Michael O'Mara Books, Ash-Tree Press,
Tartarus Press, Ex Occidente Press and Hieroglyphic Press. Past
stories have been selected for *Best New Horror* and the late Karl
Edward Wagner's *Year's Best Horror Stories*.

His published collections include *The White Road*, *The Irregular
Casebook of Sherlock Holmes*, *Tarshishim* and *Summonings*. Two
novellas, 'The Letter Killeth' and the story reprinted here, have
recently been published in the Sarob Press anthologies *Pagan Triptych*
and *Romances of the White Day*, respectively. He is now working
on a third novella, 'The Asmodeus Fellowship', for the next anthology
in the series.

Other future publications include a story in the forthcoming
anthology *Booklore*, and a short verse tribute to Mervyn Peake for
another anthology, *Midwinter Entertainment*. He is also working,
with crossed fingers, towards the publication of a new edition *of
The White Road*.

"'The Chapel of Infernal Devotion' is a conclusion to the novella
'The White Road,'" explains the author, "which was included in the
collection of the same name, published in 1997. Both were prompted

by the narrator's hint, in Arthur Machen's 'The White People', that the girl in the story had left other diaries, passages from which I have had great pleasure in concocting.

"Other Machen plot themes that I have continued to explore here include the true nature of the ritual called "The Marriage Beneath the Shade", and of the Alchemical First Matter in the *Lumen de Lumine* of Thomas Vaughan, in the light of the myths of metamorphosis surrounding the symbolism of Pan and Proteus in Orphic Polytheism.

"Although the character and music of the fictional Eva Malas has elements of Diamanda Galas, Lisa Gerrard and latter-day Marianne Faithfull, she is inspired in the main by the legendary Nico who, with John Cale, charted strange seas of musical thought in the heady days of the 1960s counterculture.

"The night when things 'went bad' in the story once happened pretty well exactly as described, possibly invoked by the first of their wonderful collaborations, *The Marble Index*.

Then, as now, when the doors of perception are opened, interesting things come in."

"In this book I will write the most secret things, and some of the words that were taught me at Voor."

—*The White Road*

I WAS AT a viewing at Bullinger's auction house entitled "Original Book Illustrations and Classic Illustrated Books", where, among a dazzling selection of drawings, paintings and first editions by the likes of Arthur Rackham, Edmund Dulac, Harry Clarke and John Austen, I spotted a small pen-and-ink drawing so richly detailed it could have been mistaken for an engraving. It was listed in the catalogue as "untitled", and attributed to an artist with the highly unlikely name of Adam Midnight.

It depicted, you might have said, some kind of ritualised activity taking place in an enclosed space, but neither the ritual nor the space resembled anything earthly. The location looked unpleasantly organic, a hollow growth, or the intestines of a monster. The congregation appeared to be growing out of, or melting into, the walls and floor, taking root, merging, dividing from some common matter, putrescent but horridly alive. The "Priest" in this "rite", a quite indescribable creature of insectile, yet somehow semi-liquescent, form, was elevating an object that might have been a drinking vessel of contorted, asymmetrical shape, suggestive at once of a chalice and some soft bodily organ.

That dark corruption of the moral sense long sought by the Decadents had been achieved utterly in this tiny drawing. I felt nauseated and seduced in equal measure, making me look too long at details I should not have found so fascinating. And it wasn't just me. Everyone who looked at it commented how disgusting it was, but it didn't seem to stop them looking.

That first glimpse should have occurred in devout silence, because I knew I was looking at a little masterpiece.

Even among a roll call of the Golden Age of book illustration, it seemed to me a remarkable piece of work. There was, however, nothing silent or devout about Bill Sherborne, a book dealer who had attached himself to me like a limpet, and who was running off at the mouth about how horrible the drawing was. Like the others, he neither stopped looking nor moved away, so my subsequent memory of that moment was doomed to be played out to the soundtrack of his inane commentary.

As he droned on, I allowed myself to wonder whether the lack of a title, the ridiculously pseudonymous creator and the conventionally repulsive subject matter might conspire to guide it under the radar of the assembled big beasts of collecting, and give me a chance at the auction.

In any case I knew that in the collecting of Golden Age book illustration, ravishing beauty was more often than not the touchstone. Those of us who favoured the truly grotesque were in a minority. Whether that would make what competition there was any less intense remained to be seen.

When the crowd drifted on I looked at the back of the frame, and on lifting a dried-out flap of detached lining paper, made out very faint pencil script along one edge of the backboard. Casually producing my pocket magnifier, I scanned the place as surreptitiously as I could, and made out the words *Chapel of Infernal Devotion*.

It was a bad slip on the part of Bullingers to list it as untitled. That might, I thought, be just the bit of luck I needed.

On the day of the auction I turned up full of hope, and managed to avoid a place near Bill, who had set his heart on what I thought was an understandably rejected Rackham drawing for *Peter Pan in Kensington Gardens*. The illustrated book Mafia were out in force. Thomas Sorbie would be after the Henry Weston Keen entitled *Female Nude with Skulls*. Paul Appleby nurtured an excessive devotion to Leonard Sarluis, so would target some suppressed drawings for Baudelaire's *Petit poèms en prose*. Bidding for some first quality Dulacs and Neilsens would be intense. Attention was definitely elsewhere.

I really thought I had the *Chapel* drawing. My bid was almost knocked down when a familiar voice from the back of the room attracted the auctioneer's attention, and I knew my number was up.

It was William Bentliff: with his entry I gave up gracefully and accepted that I had lost the day, and that furthermore I would never see the drawing again. When he bought a work, no one ever did. It would disappear into the oblivion of his private collection of the suppressed, withdrawn, never offered and banned, a Cabinet Secret of Social Taboo. Requests for access from even the most exalted of scholars researching the most noble of projects were always met with contemptuous silence.

I had often pondered how a man could combine such a fine eye for magnificent examples of unappreciated and scorned art with such a mean and selfish personal ethic. He seemed to be on a personal campaign to remove works he considered "corrupt" from the world one by one. Why he was so keen to obtain this disturbing, but hardly erotic, work was a puzzle. He usually sought and gathered in mythological pictures of gods mating with humans, such as illustrated editions of Ovid's *Metamorphosis* and so on. He was divorced, lived

alone, and was usually described as an angry, antisocial man. The
ridiculous prices he was prepared to pay at auctions, and his subsequent secrecy, led to the general conclusion that he had gone bonkers
at some point, and was pursuing a private obsession.

None of us could have guessed how right we were.

The disappearance of *Chapel* meant that I was one of few people
who would ever see it. Those moments I had spent gazing at it were
therefore doubly precious, if marred by that banal monologue in
my ear. What I would have given then for five more minutes in
silent contemplation of its wondrous horror.

I brooded quite a bit about the auction in the days that followed.
Foolishly I had allowed myself to consider a spot on my wall where
the drawing might go, and the empty space shouted at me every
time I entered the room.

Later in the week I dropped into the shop of a bookman *par excel-
lence*, Rupert Gildney. I was wondering about the identity of "Adam
Midnight", and if anyone would know, it would be Rupert.

I could say I was a book runner, but that would flatter me. Book
runners are an impressive breed, something of a race apart, widely
knowledgeable about a wide range of books and accomplished when
it comes to sniffing out the highly collectable. At its height it is an art,
and many book dealers wouldn't function half so well without them.

I was merely an impecunious book collector who regularly came
across interesting items outside my own field of interest, and sold
them on to Rupert, or someone he recommended. He probably had
a few people like me bringing him finds. I could never have made
a living from the proceeds, as so many had.

Rupert Gildney was very much of the old school, a gentleman
book dealer with the bearing and fruity tones of the classic "actor
manager", a resemblance in no way diluted by his habit of addressing
me as "laddie". It was hard not to imagine him massaging one's
shoulder while asking if "one could possibly find one's way to cash
a small personal cheque".

Not that Rupert was really questionable in his finances. He was
highly regarded in the trade for knowing not just the price but the

value of everything, and for pitching his prices at that magic point where his customers never felt alienated, his business flourished, and his stock rotated with the effortless regularity of seasons and planets. The generosity with which he shared his knowledge extended to largesse in the matter of the best cups of tea I have ever tasted, made only with "white tips" purchased at eye-watering expense from Harrods.

I had barely got through the door of the shop before his voice boomed out. "Commiserations, laddie. I hear you've been Bentliffed! *Nil carborundum illegitimi*, as they say. It's happened to us all at some time. If you hang around illustrated book auctions long enough, you lose your virginity eventually. I've been Bentliffed so often I've stopped going to them altogether. I leave a bid and hope for the best. At least I don't have to see his gloating face."

Before long I was absorbing steaming cups of white tips, and inside information about Adam Midnight.

"Your assumption is wrong, as it happens. Midnight is a real enough name. I've known a couple of Midnights in my life, and like the equally real Midday, the name probably originates in the exact time of an ancestor's birth. However, rather annoyingly, you are right in this particular case. It is a pseudonym used by Phillip Youlden. No, I don't suppose you've heard of him. An obscure artist, but born in Gwent, and a devotee of Machen's work, which once proved a useful qualification.

It was the main reason he was chosen to illustrate a projected deluxe edition of Arthur Machen stories planned by John Lane in the 1920s. Machen's work had something of a resurgence at that time, here and in America, and Lane had the idea of following up his Harry Clarke-illustrated *Selected Poems of Swinburne* with the Youlden Machen. Then there was some unpleasantness. Lane thought one of Clarke's drawings, for the poem 'Aholibah', too erotic, and left it out of the published volume without even telling Clarke. In case you don't know, it depicts a demon getting very intimate with a naked woman. Clarke was naturally hurt about not being told, and harsh words were probably spoken. Right after, Lane was shown the Youlden drawings for the Machen, and had kittens. They evidently made the Clarke drawing look quite mild by comparison. He'd had enough trouble, I suspect, and eventually dropped the Machen project. I don't think Youlden's career ever recovered."

I told him about my discovery of the title. He didn't seem surprised.

"Yes, Bullingers can be sloppy with their examinations at times. It isn't their first mistake by any means. They once described an Austin Spare pastel depicting someone who looked like a heavyweight boxer as a "self-portrait"! *Chapel of Infernal Devotion* isn't a known Machen title, though Youlden could have given it that after the project was dropped. It does sort of resonate with some of Machen's subject matter, I suppose.

"Just imagine if Lane had continued with the project, though. Full vellum, hand-made paper; that lovely Machen signature done with a fountain pen that sometimes bled a little into fine soft surfaces! I can just see it, can't you?"

I raised my empty tea-cup.

"To books that never were."

Rupert took the hint and refilled the cup.

"Harry Clarke's *Rhyme of the Ancient Mariner*," I offered, "put paid to by fire in the Easter Uprising in Dublin."

He nodded. "And the books he wanted to do but never did: *Jekyll and Hyde*, the *Arabian Nights*, *À rebours*, *The Turn of the Screw*, and of course *Dracula*! Did you know he longed to illustrate *Dracula*?"

Rupert loved Clarke's work as much as I did. The very idea of this had him channelling Vincent Price.

"God in Heaven! *Dracula*! Think of his illustrations for Faust and Poe, and imagine it. 'Holy was the grave to him, saintly its darkness, pure its corruption'. There would have been nothing to touch it, nothing! The rats and the abominations, the brooding darkness and the hungry corpses; the walking corruption and the beauty of decay. Clarke was born to do it. I would have given my blood to see his *Dracula*!"

"You should have seen that Youlden!"

He looked at me strangely, but said nothing.

"So the Lane Machen didn't even get to the proof stage?" I prompted hopefully.

"I can assure you that it did not."

"If that *Chapel* drawing was anything to go by, it would have been something."

"Yes, but unlike the equally alluring Austin Spare de Sade, it doesn't exist."

He said this with a fruitier than usual rumble in his voice. I was in two minds how to respond to it. Here was a man who had once annoyed and tantalised me in equal measure with the straight-faced claim to have seen, and handled, a lavishly bound Hodder & Stoughton collaboration between the two Arthurs, Machen and Rackham, entitled *The Great God Pan in Kensington Gardens*. Nobody in their right mind would really believe it existed, but he knew damn well that I would want it to, so he had sown the seed.

"A de Sade," I heard myself saying, "illustrated by Austin Spare? That was an invention of Kyril Bonfiglioli wasn't it?"

"You think so? Well I've seen the book in question, a goatskin-bound large paper copy, hand-decorated in pen and watercolour by Spare throughout. The most staggering depictions of demonic sex magic I have ever seen. And don't waste your time fishing for more information, because I am sworn to secrecy, and my very faint, and fading, chance of ever being allowed to see it again depends on me keeping my mouth shut. So you do the same, or you'll never darken my door again."

I knew when to change the subject.

"How did you come to know Midnight's real name, anyway?"

"I knew someone who was close to him. No one you would know. Remember that Machen story, 'Out of the Picture'? About an artist who paints landscapes full of horror and doom inhabited by a twisted figure that seems to be able to emerge into the real World. Well I'm pretty sure Machen based the painter on Youlden."

"Did they know each other, then?"

"I don't know, but I do know Youlden did other drawings for Machen stories, because I've seen some."

There was no hint of a fruity chortle this time. He seemed to be stating a fact.

"You're familiar with the Knopf *Ornaments in Jade*?" he went on.

"Lavish thing isn't it? Three blank sheets before you even get to the contents at the front and three more after the limitation and signature at the back. That is to say six sides, or what the ordinary reader calls 'pages', in each case, making twelve in all.

"Well, I've seen a copy with all twelve 'pages' decorated by Youlden—ten full-page drawings, one for each story, a frontispiece and an elaborate end piece or colophon.

"They were all remarkable, but some, 'The Idealist', 'Witchcraft', 'The Ceremony' and 'Midsummer', were very unpleasant. And the one for 'The Holy Things' didn't deal with even the '90s Machen's idea of 'Holy'.

"It must have been a commission from a private collector. One thing I do know; if the sample John Lane saw had been anything like the *Jade* drawings, he would have had a coronary. They were in many ways similar to your description of the drawing at Bullingers: no clear distinction between animal, vegetable and mineral; loathsome-looking creatures performing ritualistic—I might almost say Eucharistic—actions in spaces that were mid-way between constructions and half-natural, or rather decidedly unnatural, growths.

"There was just one, for 'The Ceremony', that was set in a normal room; a child's bedroom. The child was asleep in a big four-poster bed. Something long and thin with its head and limbs in subtly wrong places had come through a kind of living orifice in the wall, and was standing over the bed. The idea of it reaching out and touching the child was so unpleasant my flesh crawled. It struck me as strange that he hadn't depicted the central event of the story, but some childhood experience not even referred to. It was the only one that had anything more than the title written below it. Youlden had written in pencil, *The Alala*.

"That was odd in itself, because that is a reference to 'The White People', not to anything in *Ornaments in Jade*!"

"Was it a penchant for the occult that made Youlden choose a pseudonym like Midnight?"

"No, I don't think so. Apart from the obvious fact that it made his initials the same as Arthur Machen, I think he may have chosen

Adam Midnight because it also resonated with the name of someone who may have been an intended collaborator, a writer called Owen Maddock."

"Never heard of him."

"I'm not surprised. He was spectacularly unsuccessful; Celtic mysticism, sub-Machen stuff, but not without interest. A few people have heard of a couple of his poems; 'Epsilon'—very pessimistic, with a supposedly hidden meaning I've never deciphered—and 'Sabazius', on the Thracian Mysteries. I actually keep a list of some of his works here on the desk in case something turns up. *The Island in the Sunset, A Coracle of Glass, The Luminous Union, The Tavern of Elysium* and *The Night Before Winter.*

"I've never had so much as a glimpse of any of them. He was born in Caermaen, and moved to London with high hopes of a writing career; had a hard time of it, evidently. Suffered some sort of nervous breakdown and came close to suicide. Something stopped him and he went back to Gwent; stayed with a local family called Howell; a father and daughter. The father supposedly had in his possession a stone head with some sort of oracular power, and a diary of a girl that had inspired Machen's 'The White People.'"

"How do you know this?"

"Because Maddock wrote a pretty fantastical account of it, and subsequent events, in a slim volume of fifty-odd pages called *The White Road.* That title I don't have to have written down, because I have a copy of it; I'll dig it out and let you read it. Some of the descriptions resemble Youlden's drawings. Cross-fertilisation, I suppose. It's hard to say who influenced whom.

"Anyway, Youlden just vanished one day, and very little was made of it. Can you imagine if any of the really well known book illustrators from the time had ever just disappeared off the face of the Earth? They'd still be writing about it today."

When I asked why Youlden was not better known, he was uncharacteristically tight-lipped.

Rupert proved true to his word, and in due course sent me the Owen Maddock volume. It was a modest affair, in paper wrappers, but well enough printed.

The contents were broadly similar to that recounted by Rupert up to the return to Gwent. It was the following part that I found most fascinating. Owen returns to his birthplace in Gwent, and stays with a Professor John Howell and his daughter Morwyn. At first his stay is idyllic, but he begins to suspect that father and daughter are conniving in keeping secret dark dealings with the Twlydd Teg.

Following their method, Owen uses a stone head, "The Brute Stone", to cross over, and has to be rescued by Morwyn. The account of the faery realm was written with such conviction and detail—much of it disturbing—that I found it strangely persuasive.

It made me want to know more, but accessible sources on the life and work of Phillip Youlden proved limited and repetitive. What little they said was either wrong or already known to me, except for the tantalising snippet that he had exhibited once in a joint show with John Austen, Harry Clarke, Alan Odle and Austin Osman Spare at the Osney gallery in the 1920s. I managed to locate a copy of the catalogue by library loan, but was disappointed to find only two works by him were illustrated, and they were fairly tame subjects, based on classic stories for children, quite unlike *Chapel*.

After that the necessities of earning a living intruded, and for a while the matter ceased to be at the forefront of my mind.

It was a sad event that changed this. Rupert Gildney died quite suddenly.

The funeral was a dismal affair. It rained incessantly. One of those occasions where the ritual of casting earth into the grave left more mud on the mourners' hands than on the lid of the coffin. There were drinks and sandwiches afterwards, with everyone unsure of the right mood to strike. Strident laughter was as common as muted conversation.

If we should judge a person by their friends, the gathering made a case for Rupert being a pretty remarkable person. I had the feeling that at any moment I might have been amazed, educated, seduced or murdered, or all of them at once.

I was approached early by a large, florid woman trying to look much younger than she was, and failing valiantly. She seemed to have attained a remarkable degree of inebriation in so short a time. She introduced herself as Nicola Ottoway.

"Dear Rupey was quite insistent that we meet. He said you are interested in Adam Midnight."

I was about to reply when someone called for silence and launched into a rambling impromptu speech about the deceased that bordered on the embarrassing. My attention was further distracted by a decidedly peculiar-looking individual in ragged period costume gorging himself on the buffet. It was difficult not to speculate whether he was one of Rupert's more "iffy" book sources, or even a sexual fling.

I almost asked who he was, but something about him made me think better of it, and a few moments later he was not to be seen.

I made a couple of attempts to talk to Ms. Ottoway after that, but she was always in conversation.

As I left, though, she pressed a piece of paper into my hand.

"Give me a call, and we'll arrange when you can come round for a drink and a chat."

I was, to say the least, wary. Rupert had tried to play matchmaker before; his complete lack of interest in women meant that his choices had been utterly disastrous. I suspected I was being set up.

However, the lure of the artist's name, so redolent of darkness and secrets, was too strong. Armed with a ready excuse to leave at short notice, I duly arrived at her house, and soon found that I had done Rupert a grave injustice. He had not been up to his old tricks. Nicola Ottoway really had known "Adam Midnight".

A drink was the first order of the day. Or rather another drink in her case. She was well gone already.

"I knew his real name was Phillip, of course, but I always thought Adam Midnight suited him better—all that beautiful hair and dark good looks. He was getting on when I met him, much too old for me, but I was smitten. Of course he wasn't interested in me. It crossed my mind at the time that he might be gay. Still, you can't choose who you fall for, can you? I hung around. You could say that I became an interested observer.

"His indifference wasn't because he was gay, as it turned out. It was just that he didn't fancy me. He ended up falling for some weird folk singer, or pop star or something, hideous woman with a foreign name.

"What was I about to say? Yes, people don't talk much about Adam because unpleasant things tended to happen around him, and around his pictures.

"For instance, I bet Rupey didn't tell you how he came to burn a book, did he? I didn't think so. The "Crown Prince of Bibliophiles", Rupert Gildney, of all people, burning a rare, beautiful book, would you believe? Yes, and it was a Youlden."

She paused to refill her glass.

"When Rupert was a young man, just starting out in the trade, he came across a folio-size sketchbook of drawings by Adam, *The Mad God's Call.*

"Mesmerising stuff, he claimed: strange creatures, some of them with goaty bits, cavorting in desert landscapes. Meaningless strings of words written around the border of every page. Just the kind of horrible, weird stuff people like Rupey seem to be attracted to. Don't understand the appeal myself. Well, he sat drinking and looking at the book—Rupey always drank too much—and he tried reading out the words. You know, aloud.

"He said he felt strange, and fell asleep, and had an unpleasant dream, very vivid. He was running through woods at night, under a bright moon. I remember he said that vines were sort of coiling up the trees like snakes as he passed, and there were wild animals running with him. Not ordinary ones, leopards and bears and such. He said he'd never felt so alive.

"He was chasing a woman who was wearing a kind of white robe. Caught her. Saw absolute terror in her eyes."

"Not the sort of dream I would expect Rupert to have," I couldn't help saying.

"I know, but it wasn't an ordinary dream, according to him. He wouldn't say any more about it in detail, but there was a report of an attack on a girl in a public park, and one of the papers was rotten enough to publish a picture of her. He took one look at it and immediately tore the sketchbook up and burned it.

"Of course when he had time to think about it, he regretted it. It had just been a coincidence, he said, but coincidences tended to happen where Adam was concerned; and worse.

"He grew up in South Wales, and as a child he befriended a local boy who was—well, you know—we're not allowed to say 'deformed' these days are we? Badly disabled, shall we say? The kid evidently had a very odd appearance and even odder ways. He whistled to himself and muttered all the time, and laughed about nothing. Evidently he was an altar boy, though, very devout, and absolutely obsessed with the Mass, always mumbling about eating the body and blood of God all the time. What was it Adam said they called him? *Plentyn newid*. The Change Child. That was it. The Change Child.

"No one else would have anything to do with him, but Adam evidently loved him. They were inseparable. Played at the Mass with Adam as the priest and the Child serving. And other games involving local children. One day the Change Child did something to one of them that got him locked up in a secure mental hospital. Adam was given an alibi by a local girl, so he didn't become involved."

She paused for a refill.

"All of Adam's old studios are still haunted, did you know that? Dark, twisted shapes processing round and round in a circle in the middle of one; something that rises up, slowly revolving and howling, out of the floor in another. I can believe it."

"Stories of that kind have a way of taking on a spurious life of their own," I offered.

"Oh yes? Well it's a different matter when you've seen for yourself, when something happens to you."

She lit a cigarette and sucked in the smoke hungrily.

"One day when I was staying near the house he was sharing in Wales—on a visit, just hoping I suppose—I called in on Adam when his ugly, weird girlfriend was away somewhere. I walked into the basement, which Adam was using as his studio at the time, without knocking. The air was thick with the smell of something burning on a brazier. We were always smoking or inhaling something or other, but I didn't recognise it. Very unpleasant.

"And there was a sort of television screen on, too. No, there were no televisions that big in those days, were there? I suppose it was a projector screen, shiny and flickering, showing film of countryside, I think.

"I don't know why it was on, because he wasn't watching it. He was working, drawing a still life. He worked with all kinds of peculiar things, to introduce unusual details into his pictures: objects he'd found, fragments arranged as still life subjects, and so on. This seemed to be a big statue, or sculpture of sorts. A modern type of thing, as if a disciple of Giacometti had ditched metal and worked in white marble. A life-size stick figure in white marble. I thought it must have come from the garden, because it had discoloration in places, and clumps of moss on it. And I remember it had rough, horny protuberances like coral sticking up like a crown on its head, and the most remarkable greenish, facetted crystal the size of a fist embedded in its chest, as if it had been fired into it and stuck there. I thought how typical it was of Adam to find something so unusual, and wondered what part it would play in some projected painting."

She stopped and crossed to the sideboard, poured herself another drink without offering me one. When she gulped it, the glass rattled against her teeth.

"Then it turned its head very slowly and blinked its eyes like a sloth. Made a sort of noise, stepped forward and raised an arm, or whatever it was. Very smoothly—horrible. It was alive. It walked towards me. After all these years I can't stop seeing it and hearing the noise it made.

"Adam was furious. I've never seen him so angry. I just got out. I had to get out. We never spoke of it. I've never been able to forget it, but I've never understood exactly what it was I'd seen."

She became distracted, and I left soon after.

It was fascinating, but I had a living to earn. The necessities of everyday life intruded, and for a while the matter faded from the forefront of my mind.

Then Rupert's estate was sorted out, and I found he had left me a few things.

I was surprised and touched. It could hardly have been the modest business I had brought his way that merited such generosity. I could only conclude that our conversations over tea had been as congenial to him as they had been to me.

There was a copy of that *Selected Poems of Swinburne* illustrated by Harry Clarke, inscribed with typical depth of knowledge:

> *Sorry this isn't one of the two copies that Clarke had the suppressed drawing bound into, laddie!*
> *Rupert.*

He also left me what I thought must be a supply of his Romeo y Julieta Cuban cigars, but the box had been reused to hold a small stone carving of a head, and some photocopied pages of written text.

The carving was rather ugly, not at all to my more classical taste, but it was certainly interesting, and clearly old, despite the rather modern fluid lines.

Turning to the pages, it was immediately apparent that they were not Roger's handwriting. I was a little relieved that he had not seen fit to burden me with a record of scurrilous gossip from the book trade or, even worse, some intimate memoir.

The contents were far more interesting. The writer, clearly a child, was describing how her nurse told her of a lady who cried at happy things, and laughed at a funeral, and that when she did so she was doing a very important ceremony for those who understood that good could be bad, and bad good, and that only special people could understand, and that was the secret of the Comedies. She said the White People sometimes took human babies and left their own babies in exchange, and there were people who could live and walk in both worlds without humans knowing. Their work was very secret, and they were called something that meant "Interpreters".

The pages had clearly been copied from a diary very much like that described in Machen's 'The White People'. Such a work had also been described in Owen Maddock's book, and there had been mention of a stone head.

Rupert had explicitly linked Maddock with Youlden. He must have altered his will after our conversation with the intention of encouraging me to pursue the connection.

The box also contained a yellowed newspaper cutting about Phillip Youlden—apparently missing long enough to be presumed dead—reporting that his "personal effects" and surviving artwork would remain in the keeping of Katarina Garside at his last place of residence, *Plas Gwyllion*, in South Wales.

Rupert had underlined the name "Katarina Garside", and the name of the house.

This seemed to be a useful source of further information, but all my initial attempts to contact the woman failed. She appeared to live completely cut-off from the outside world.

I sent several letters, and eventually received a frosty reply in the form of a standard printed note explaining that the collection was not currently available for viewing. I wrote yet again, telling of my experience at Bullingers, and the effect that the *Chapel* drawing had on me.

In a matter of days I received a reply in a large and expensive-looking envelope, written in spidery copperplate, from Katarina Garside herself.

She had not thought, she wrote, that she would ever see *The Chapel of Infernal Devotion* mentioned again. She knew the picture well, and was very keen to know who had bought it.

It struck me that if she was hoping to prise it from the icy hand of Bentliff, she was deluded.

She added that she would be willing to see me at any time.

It didn't seem to occur to her that I would not be able to drop everything at a moment's notice.

As it happened, I was temporarily unemployed at the time, and had a little saved up. The opportunity to see more of Youlden's work was a prospect I couldn't resist. A short stay at *Plas Gwyllion* was arranged, and reassuringly detailed directions sent.

The day of my journey began misty and cold, and visibility gradually degenerated so badly that I eventually reached the Severn Bridge with my lights on full-beam. By the time I crawled past Tintern Abbey, the ruins were swathed in dense fog.

I was none too keen on negotiating narrow, unfamiliar lanes in such conditions, but as I followed the directions I began to climb into clearer, if still misty, regions. Passing through dense pinewoods, I emerged briefly only to turn between high banks littered with grey limestone rocks. The car juddered over slabs of the same material. The banks were crowned with Thorn trees distorted into grotesque shapes by the prevailing winds.

I came out at length onto the mountainside with a wide prospect before me, hollows still shrouded in fog, the higher ground dark and formless except for the odd clump of pines, or far glimpses of falling water.

A single column of stone towered against the sky. As if recoiling from its threat, the road bucked and twisted away, back into the trees. Creeping around the umpteenth sharp bend, I was suddenly confronted with a massive house set in a natural amphitheatre of sombre forest.

The effect was to make me brake hard and sit for a moment, peering through the labouring windscreen wipers and laughing out loud.

"It's actually happened." I thought to myself, "Finally, it's actually happened."

I had lived out my favourite opening to a story.

There was no getting away from it. Through the whole of what had undeniably been a dull, dark and soundless day in the autumn of the year, I had been travelling alone (by car, not horseback, admittedly), through a singularly dreary tract of country, and had found myself, as the shades of evening drew on, within view of the melancholy House of Usher.

It was, of course, *Plas Gwyllion*, but in all conscience it was close enough.

The first impression was of a mausoleum for giants. Some mad genius had built a compact little château in French Renaissance style, then thought what it really needed was to be smothered in stone carvings of heraldic beasts, gods, gargoyles, warriors, spiral columns, and a variety of disturbingly convincing anguipedes.

It would have been no surprise at that point to glimpse Pan amongst the trees, or a monstrous face, *à la* 'The Inmost Light', at a window.

After minutes of knocking repeatedly at the heavy Venetian door knocker, I got the uneasy feeling that my arrival had been forgotten. Eventually the door was opened by an elderly maid, who explained that Mrs. Garside was unavailable, but that a meal had been set up in my room upstairs. She led me up to a cold, damp bedroom with a massive four-poster bed and a barely edible cold repast.

Although I was tired, I slept fitfully, and awoke repeatedly in the night to the sound of some bird shrieking far off.

I breakfasted alone in a huge dining room on porridge, kippers and lapsang souchong from a massive pivoting silver teapot with a lion spout that must have been worth a fortune. Having still not seen my host, I decided that I might as well explore.

The foul weather had passed, and a pallid sun was glinting inter-mittently between dark clouds as I skirted the house, getting satu-rated by dense shrubbery, and walked through a formal garden long gone to seed. Weeds were rampant. I struggled through briars, edging around a choked-up fountain. In the distance there was a summer-house that must have been quite elegant once, but was now ramshackle, with a partly caved-in roof. Statues were being slowly throttled by creepers.

In the middle of what might once have been lawn, now waist-deep in weeds, stood, of all things, a scarecrow. It was clad in an old dress, its head an explosion of saturated straw, gangling arms hanging limp, its oversized hands clawed threateningly.

I felt a distinctly M.R. Jamesian qualm when it turned and moved towards me. Then the figure called out, and I realised I must be looking at Katarina Garside.

Her uncombed mane really did look like straw. The thinness of her bare arms made her bony hands, which were of a span sugges-tive of a pianist, look even more enormous. She was tall, well over six feet in her rain-sodden sandals, and had wrinkled, big-boned features. Her almost skeletal physique was draped in a washed-out dress of Fortuny fabric that must once have been of spectacular richness and colour, gathered at the breast by a massive cameo broach of classical design. She had an air of unkempt elegance and mournful distraction about her that just stopped her being ridiculous.

Her voice had the deep rasp of a long-time smoker as she invited me in.

The room into which she led me was obviously her quarters. It was all Persian rugs, brocade throws, massive mirrors with carved frames, and a profusion of stone and metal gods and goddesses looming through clouds of incense. It took me back at once to many rooms in which I had sat and smoked dope in the late 1960s.

There must have been a big bird either trapped, or given free rein in that huge room, because something was flapping and scraping up in a dark corner.

Katarina Garside perched somewhat precariously on a club fender in front of a roaring fire. The surround was marble, with bearded caryatids that had once been painted in bright colours, but were now faded and peeling into a state of corpse-like decay. Steam was already rising from her saturated skirts as she gestured me to sit before her. As she did, a quite massive cat appeared out of the darkness and draped itself around her shoulders, like a sentient fur stole.

Fronting the fire was a high-backed settle that proved upright and uncomfortable to the point of torture, suitable only for awaiting a judicial sentence. It was as I sat down that I saw for the first time the huge charcoal drawing that hung above the fireplace.

At first glance, it might have been a depiction of a woman asleep at full-length in a dark room. On closer examination, I could make out a host of pulpy, worm-like creatures looking on. The "cover" under which the sleeper lay was a living mass so wonderfully drawn that it seemed to coil and undulate over the body; its upper part, which reared over the woman's face, was a mad combination of gigantic mantis and decaying crustacean, its claws, or tendrils, locked upon her flesh. She was surrounded by what might have been guttering, half-melted candles, or ejaculating members half-gone in rottenness.

The smothering assailant was horribly boneless, disgusting, but the depiction was clearly not one of unwelcome assault. The features of the woman were subtly distorted, but in a way that suggested ecstasy rather than pain or fear. It was in the same style, and had the same unpleasantly attractive effect, as *The Chapel of Infernal Devotion*.

I recognised the face of the reclining figure as a younger version of the woman perched on the fender. I also realised with a shock who Katarina Garside was, or more accurately, who she had once been.

Grainy photographs in magazines and music papers; gauze-filtered images flushed with psychedelic colours on album sleeves: Katarina Garside had once been that "lethal muse of poets", Eva Malas.

Whether or not people of a certain age recognised the name was to me the acid test of just how truly "underground" their musical tastes had once been. To respond positively was to identify oneself as an initiate, a celebrant of deep mysteries; an explorer in recondite musical realms.

Many were the *thyrsus* bearers, but few were the *bacchoi*.

I still loved her songs, like incalculably ancient funeral chants intoned from the deck of some black barge plying strange waters; cries of despair echoing repetitiously through corridors of freezing stone, usually accom-panied by a range of instruments from sources obscure even by the experimental standards of the day, such as the sordun, darbuka, shawm, conch shell, Dong Chen, sackbut, shakuhachi, swaramandal, shofar and rackett.

I had always thought that if Ligeia or Madeline Usher played and sang, the result would have sounded like Eva Malas. Looking at the woman perched on the fender, it struck me that she had finally come to resemble what she had always sounded like: the emaciated doppelgänger of some once-grand creature, haunting its own house while yet alive.

In those psychedelic images on the gatefold LP sleeves, it had not been easy to form a clear idea of her appearance. She was usually in hieratic postures, swathed in layers of robes and fantastic head-gear like a Shinto priest, sometimes even riding camels, or restive stallions, in desert locations. Even in her prime we had not thought her beautiful; interesting in a dangerous way, perhaps. I had always assumed she was foreign, not just because of her name, and her curious pronunciation, but because of her slanting eyes, high cheekbones and odd complexion. The set of her mouth had always suggested callous indifference, if not cruelty.

Suddenly the incredible exterior of the house made perfect sense. Drawing a line through Jimmy Page with his Gothic Revival pad in London, and his purchase of Crowley's Boleskine House on the banks of Loch Ness, nothing seemed more understandable to me than that Eva Malas should have chosen to "get it together in the country" in such a crumbling palace bedecked with gods and monsters.

I was exploding with questions inspired by a life of singular strangeness. Above all, I wanted to ask her whether any recordings existed of 'Altar-wise by Owl Light', the barely publicised live performance of poems by Dylan Thomas to music by Eva and John Cale— an occasion evidently so redolent of Celtic twilight that a journalist from *Melody Maker* had risen to new heights of combined racial and musical bigotry by dismissing it as the "Eistedfodd of the Spheres".

Strangely, some instinct told me not to mention the fact that I recognised her. Possibly it was that dignified reserve that made me reluctant to appear crass. Instead, I pointed out the picture and said it was a wonderful example of a Youlden.

She replied flatly, "Of course it is. What else could it be?"

I was to grow all too familiar with that brusque, dismissive tone, so devoid of sensitivity to the feelings of others.

When I asked her the title of the picture, she stared deep into the fire, one bony hand caressing the cat, and muttered.

"My husband always called it *The Sperm of the World*, but its proper title is *The Marriage Beneath the Shade*."

So my stay did not begin particularly auspiciously, and it got worse before it got better. It soon emerged that she had only invited me because she hoped to get hold of the *Chapel* drawing, and my admission that it was now inaccessible made her very angry. I pointed out that I had not claimed anything to the contrary, which she was unable to deny.

It was when I mentioned the buyer was Bentliff that she exploded with rage, sending the cat leaping to the floor.

Her anger was a truly frightening experience. She was a towering figure, and her great mop of hair made her look bigger still. She clawed the air and poured a stream of invective mingled with unrecognisable words, or more accurately snarling, hissing sounds that bordered on the animalistic. I had never seen anyone so completely consumed with fury. As I cowered there, fearing that my visit was over before it had begun, I made out the accusation that I had come on Bentliff's behalf. I lost no time in assuring her that there was no love lost between me and the man.

She crouched over me like a great bedraggled bird of prey.

"Are you telling me you didn't know that he used to be my husband?"

I was stunned. For a second all I could think was, *what has Rupert got me into?*

It was probably my obvious dismay that eventually convinced her I was not some spy in the war that was apparently still raging between the estranged couple. My sincere dislike of Bentliff, very enthusi-astically expressed, did no harm either. The fool had evidently been trying to get his hands on the collection for years, and had been held at bay only by the legally watertight nature of Youlden's will.

In the end, my obvious hatred of Bentliff and my unfeigned admi-ration for Youlden calmed things, and I was actually allowed to enter the "Holy of Holies", where the collection was kept.

The massive book-lined room—once Bentliff's library, I would guess, and only later appropriated as a studio by Youlden—had clearly been left exactly as it had been on the day the artist disap-peared. His pipe was still sitting in an ashtray, and his spectacles and an expensive-looking fountain pen lay on a page of half-finished notes. There were substantial spaces around the shelves, probably where Bentliff's books had been removed, but there were still many hundreds of old volumes. A massive tome on Welsh folklore on a lectern, entitled *Untrodden Tracks and Faery Paths*, by Professor

Edward Poole, was interleaved with hundreds of scraps of paper, the pages annotated so densely in fountain pen—"sedgy with citations" in fact—that the text looked besieged. Opposite the title page he had written an encouraging inscription beloved of Talmudic scholars: *Delve into it, and continue to delve into it, for everything is in it.*

Books on similar lines lay all around. *The Testimony of Tradition* by David MacRitchie, *A Relation of Apparitions and of Spirits in the Ancient Realm of Gwent* by Professor John Howell and so on were stacked close by, along with an odder choice, a much-thumbed paperback of the *Lumen de lumine* of Thomas Vaughan.

Some of his notes reflected the old argument whether the local belief in the Twlydd Teg was based on memory of an aboriginal race or a distor-ted belief in fallen angels. Another, not in Youlden's hand, was more cryptic:

Brute Stone and spell—do not go near the tunnels of Saksaksalim— one who quivers in a horrible manner—a shib show?—On every tumulus the totems of Dagdagiel—can the Jeelo use them, as in sacrament of the hollow, to raise the pyramid of Shaliku?—Reversion to Primal Slime—power over bodily form—Proteus as a function of Pan?

In an open copy of Evans-Wentz's *The Fairy-Faith in Celtic Countries* I found underlined some words relating to chants, magic sounds and the magician's will that must have resonated strongly with the art of Eva Malas.

There was even a letter from Doctor Anne Ross comparing the nature of Celtic stone heads in their possession, referring to the *têtes coupées* from Entremont, and discussing long, thin figurines, all of a strikingly similar appearance, from as far afield as Argyllshire, County Cavan, Teigngrace in Devon and Montbuoy in France.

I was both surprised and impressed by the seeming extent and seriousness of Youlden's researches. They were frankly excessive for a mere book illustrator, but they might well constitute a separate, if related, obsession.

The collection proved to be immensely impressive. There were dozens of large-scale paintings, many hundreds of drawings, as well as diaries and personal effects, including many old photographs of Katarina and Youlden. She looked, of course, much younger than him. He must have been well past middle-age by then, but Nicola Ottoway's panting description of him had not been entirely unjustified. He still had the look, and the casual self-assurance, of an ageing film star—reminiscent, perhaps, of the Conrad Veidt of *The Spy in Black*.

Most stunning of all the pictures were a number of rough charcoal sketches, obviously drawn very quickly, of creatures from Celtic faery lore. In a stroke of great originality, Youlden had placed them in recognisable surroundings, such as the house and grounds. One, inscribed *The Dol's House*, was apparently a formal architectural study of *Plas Gwyllion*, but the view through the windows revealed the interior to be full of decayed flora and fauna of fantastic size.

Over the following days I settled into a routine, spending most of my time in the library, and seeing little of Katarina. My nights were uncomfortable, my days hardly better. The only form of heating were wood fires, and then only in any room currently occupied by Katarina. *Plas Gwyllion* did have electricity, but either the wiring was faulty, or the local supply was erratic, because I spent an inordinate amount of time in candlelight, which was atmospheric, but inconvenient. The huge cat, named "Cath Paluc", often visited me, sometimes to try and lay on whatever I was looking at, sometimes to annexe my lap for heat, until my legs went numb.

My attention was, of course, mainly focussed on the works of Youlden, but there were occasional distractions, such as the day I found a truly remarkable bundle of letters, tied up with red string, sent to Katarina from the Surrealist poet and author Ithell Colquhoun. One sought her advice on such matters as the obsessive effect of the word "Ishakshar" in *The House of Souls*, and thanking her for the warning concerning the subject of the Sime drawing on the binding. Others dealt variously with automatism as a means to open the way to unseen worlds, Henry and Thomas Vaughan, the meaning of the "Green Diamond" in the ancient wisdom of the Silures, something called *The Children of the Mantic Stain*, and whether Katarina knew that *Plas Gwyllion* stood upon a *mundane chakra* of great telluric power.

I would have given a great deal to read Katarina's replies.

I also found myself giving more time than I should to several small diaries in handwriting similar to that of the photocopied pages left to me by Rupert, which I now thought of as the work of the unnamed child in 'The White People'. The first volume was solely text, but from the second on drawings began to appear—little water-colours delicate and quite well drawn. Gentle views of Gwent, alto-gether charming, like those in Rex Whistler's *An Anthology of Mine*, if a little less accomplished. It was possible to recognise, in the small vignettes in the corners, or in the middle of the text, definite land-marks such as Netherwood, the Black Mountains, a certain ring of stones on a hill that overlooked the distant Severn. Sundials, grave-stones, wall fountains and a stone head set into a wall. She favoured a dark and muted palette.

The text was even more remarkable:

Yesterday, before the storm broke, it was hot, and the sun was the colour of old brass, with a fume around it as if it was burning the flesh of the sky. Nothing moved; even the trees looked as if they were stamped out of tin, and I said aloud, "This is just like deep Dendo." Mother looked at me strangely, and Nurse told me to be quiet, and told Mother that I was not well. Nurse says that I must be careful, and not say things like that, but it was so like Dendo, where every-thing is still and even the clouds never move, not ever, and though the air is warm the deep pools are always very cold. The light there looks as if it had been turned inside out, and things only pretend to be the shapes they are to trick you.

It continued in this vein, very familiar to any reader of Machen. She wrote of the tall, thin Dols, who spoke the Chian language, which she understood because she had learned it from her nurse, who they referred to as "half-sister". There was mention, too, of a carved head called The Brute Stone that could be made to speak, and open the way to deep Dendo, and even awaken something called the Jeelo.

She wrote of the "Voorish domes", where they sang "the hidden songs" that could be tasted and felt. She hated the "smooth, snaky songs". When the Jeelo was angry, it could sing songs that could be seen. They frightened her most of all.

One of these faery creatures was described as a white lady with big eyes and long, long fingers, and "a big stone like an emerald growing out of her flesh".

I thought at once of the drunken, frightened Nicola Ottoway, and what she claimed to have witnessed in Youlden's basement studio: a vision so alien she could not grasp what she was looking at, save that it was the colour of marble, very thin, and with a greenish stone embedded in its chest.

Gradually the drawings changed. Monstrous figures began to predominate, some with the same shifting, protoplasmic character as the protagonists in Youlden's *Chapel* and *Marriage* pictures.

During these days I would see Katarina only at dinner, swathed in ornate shawls and muffled about the shoulders with the half-sleeping form of Cath Paluc.

Conversation was unpredictable. On one occasion she suddenly blurted out: "Someone asked me once if Phillip was out of his mind! We were hardly ever in our minds! Have you any idea what a meagre, narrow prison of perception the normal concept of 'the mind' is?"

The random, disjointed nature of Katarina's monologues seemed all of a part with her old persona, the incantatory Priestess whose art had served strange gods. I only briefly suspected that her eccentricity might actually be mental illness on being awakened one night and descending the stairs to find her crouched before an ancient radiogram that Youlden had decorated so the speaker that issued its sound was transformed into the open mouth of a grotesque face. She seemed to be trying to tune it, but there was something wrong with the reception, producing nothing but shrieking and rasping, interspersed with shrill explosions of metallic sound. She was rocking on her heels, staring intently at the apparently howling face as though mesmerised by its streams of gibberish, muttering to herself and laughing. I leant in and caught the manic flood of her words.

"Black Hell. Those who dwell under the water. Shadowland. Family of the deep..."

Later I examined the radiogram dial, and found Youlden had person-alised that, too, by replacing the station names with a strip of parch-ment marked at intervals in exquisite script. When the dial was turned to them, the band selector picked up nothing but some decidedly odd interference. *Cyhy raeth* resulted in groaning sounds; *Ufferndu* produced roaring, like thousands of voices in agony, while *Gwragged Annwn* offered unpleasant gurglings. *Plant Rhys Dwfen* seemed to be a badly tuned talk channel, and *Aderyn Y Corff* nearly deafened me with blood-chilling shrieks. When I tuned to a station marked *Coblyanan*, it produced only voices chanting the same vaguely Middle Eastern-sounding words in a never ending round: *"Nashtaraan ashgraak shamash ossaam reechmaak..."*

And suddenly a memory came back to me, like a bubble of foul gas released from something better left submerged to burst on the surface of consciousness. Night in a bed-sitting room on the top floor of a massive old house; a gathering of hippy friends, all stoned and mellow with mesmerising music and dope, utterly entranced. Suddenly a girl screamed, got up and ran crying hysterically from the room.

Taken something stronger, we thought; *having a bad trip*. Her boyfriend, who ran after her, later swore that she hadn't.

Then someone went down to the toilet on the next floor, and said something he couldn't see had reached up out of the stairwell and gripped his leg as he came back up the stairs.

And later, when everyone else had crashed out, and I was slumped against the boarded-up fire place, a weak clawing began, and a dry, evil little voice began to whisper from the enclosed space right behind my resting head. Something about the monotonous, repet-itive nature of that voice reminded me of the chanting from the radio.

Retreating to the farthest end of the room, I had spent the dark hours listening to the sounds as they gradually subsided into faint scraping, and with the first light of dawn, silence.

The mesmeric music that had been playing when the evening turned bad had been an LP by Eva Malas called *The Separable Soul.*

Plas Gwyllion was like Prospero's island, full of noises. At times the corridors seemed filled with shuffling footfalls. Tapestries shifted when there was no breeze to move them. Something other than Cath Paluc seemed to be abroad in the passages and stairways, but I could never get a clear view. One room had at some time been given over to the storage of fruit, which had been left to wither and rot, filling the air with a tainted sweetness. Moth-eaten banners hung everywhere, too faded to decipher.

The same desolate strangeness reigned outside. At night no light was visible outside for as far as the eye could see. We might have been on the edge of the world. Shaggy, ancient-looking ponies wandered, apparently wild, in the grounds, grazing among outcroppings of stone that reared like monoliths from a wilderness of weeds. There was a wooded mound in the woods on which carvings, like larger versions of the stone that Rupert had left me, stood half-buried in the earth. Some were leaning over at odd angles in their holes like decayed teeth. Strangely, someone had marked the loose stones with the initials A.M. which could have stood for "Adam Midnight", but might just as easily been some kind of tribute to Arthur Machen.

Once I came upon a forlorn gathering of very fine classical statues in an outhouse, crammed together behind wire mesh like forlorn prisoners of war.

Aside from the maid, the only other servant seemed to be an elderly Jack-of-all-trades, who looked haggard, distracted and care-worn enough to be an old "roadie" hanging on from better times. These two were not always present, and in any case hardly seemed capable of the work necessary to serve even our modest needs, but although there was no sign of activity, tables were always laid, food cooked and crockery cleared away like clockwork. On this matter Katarina was characteristically gnomic.

"They come and help."

One night I awoke to the sound of an old clavicord echoing through the house. She was playing John Ireland's 'The Scarlet Ceremonies'. Of course, it had been written for piano, but the silvery, metallic sound, glittering like showers of "sparks from the afflicted flint", was somehow right in that house, bringing a resonance of trance-like gamelan to the piece.

When I got closer, I could hear that she had tuned the radiogram to one of those non-existent channels and was accompanying the indescribable noises with rippling accompaniments that sometimes quoted Ireland and sometimes went off on their own, punctured by her harsh, guttural vocalisations, until it became impossible to separate the strands of classical quotation and crazy invention, of droning voice and monstrous radio noise.

Once, for a while, before necessity forced me to part with it to Rupert, I had owned a lovely edition of the *De situ orbis* of Pomponius Mela, and would dream for hours over my favourite passage until it had become fixed forever in my memory:

All day heavy broods the silence. Hidden terrors abound. But with the fall of night, firelight flickers, the incantations of Aegypans resound on all sides. The shrill sound of flutes and the clash of the cymbals of the Bassarids resound all along the desolate shore.

That was what Katarina conjured up that night: wind-ravaged beaches, funeral pyres, the Bakcheia, or Dionysiac frenzy of the women called Khairei, the Deerslayers.

If Eva Malas was mad, it was akin to Plato's telestic madness, or Mirandola's "divine frenzy". It was the *pneuma enthusiastikon* of the Pythia crazed on laurel leaves and the fumes of Hades.

Her songs had always been that for me, spells and incantations. This was how Sirens entranced, and sibyls prophesied. I remembered all the inner journeys her music had launched. How could anyone claim to be oblivious to the dark sorcery of such maledictive psalms?

She greeted my appearance with regal indifference, but when she stopped playing and turned off the radio, a verbal flood burst out of me. I told her of my love for her music, all it had meant to me.

It could have been disastrous, of course: the tedious fan inviting the humiliation of the cold shoulder. But artists who have ploughed a lonely and unappreciated furrow without full recognition often harbour a great longing for informed praise and true understanding. I went in seconds from being a tolerated presence to a dear friend.

At first our conversation was like a collision of two torrents, my memories of concerts and treasured albums half-drowned by her accounts of the sources of certain inspirations, the challenges of recording them. Some old myths were debunked, others even more jaw-dropping took their place. She had, it turned out, been with Brian Jones on the trip to Morocco to experience the 700-year-old invocation of Pan performed by the master musicians of Jajouka. After days of trance invoked by the weird hypnotic wail of their flutes, Bou Jeloud had manifested to them, filling the camp with the overwhelming stench of he-goat.

He was the king of the satyrs, she said, who was revered as Azâzil, ruler of the ancient goat-legged *djinn*, called *se'irim* in Arabic lore.

That night she had seen what Machen called "the Great God Pan", and had devoted her life to his service.

I learned of her early life with Bentliff in the 1960s, and of the appearance of Youlden, not in his youthful persona of the black-clad "Adam Midnight", but that of a man entering old age, though still vital and charismatic. They were thrilled that he had once actually met their hero Machen, and had come so close to illustrating his works.

It was clear to me that a *ménage à trois* had developed early, though I resisted prying too deeply for fear of stilling the flow of reminiscence. She was adamant that they had all been happy together, and that it had been a time of great creativity for them all.

An image of Shelley, Byron and Mary at Villa Diodati sprang to mind, to be followed swiftly by the thought that I was flattering Bentliff.

There could be no doubt, though, that this distinctly Anacreontic arrangement was also bound together by a shared love of the works of Arthur Machen. Their talk, like that of the girl in the diaries, was always of the Aklo letters, the Chian language and the nature of the Jeelo.

Youlden was revered not just for his art, but his status as a living link with the great man, though this had not precluded some heated arguments about Machen's views on the nature of the faery realm. Bentliff favoured the ancient pygmy race theory most often referred to by Machen himself. Youlden was equally committed to a belief in them as supernatural beings, though he believed that a "squat, hissing race of pre-humans" had co-existed with them.

Katarina had sided with Youlden, perhaps an early glimpse of the way things were going. The exact parallels between the faery lore of Britain and the *djinn* lore of Arabia, experienced so pungently at first-hand in Morocco, had, she said, convinced her of their reality.

The rift had widened as time went on.!!!!

Bentliff, for instance, believed that the girl in 'The White People' had poisoned herself to escape a "worse fate" that had befallen her as a result of "The Marriage Beneath the Shade". Youlden and Katarina, on the other hand, favoured the view that she had not regretted her actions, and that her death had been an accident with a "Sabbatic drug", such as belladonna, which was traditionally used to assist passage between worlds.

For many, such matters would have been abstruse literary discussions of little moment. I got the impression that things were going on at *Plas Gwyllion* that made the subject central to their daily experience.

If access to the library had been a huge leap forward in relations with Katarina, it was nothing to what happened a few days after.

She led me to a door which I had always known to be locked, and down a flight of stairs into a huge basement room dominated by a spectacular doll's house, in the form of a perfect scale model of *Plas Gwyllion*, on a table in the middle of the floor. Behind it ran the console of what must have been her recording studio in years gone by. A host of exotic instruments still lay scattered around the floor among low couches and beaded cushions. There was a massive animal horn, resembling a Jewish ritual shofar, but of fantastically contorted shape, and of unnaturally vivid colour. I could not imagine what animal it came from.

Against the wall opposite the console stood a large picture, clearly a Youlden, its sombre colours painted onto a massive piece of slate the size and shape of a door. The rough surface had been used brilliantly to give selected features in the picture a three-dimensional depth. It depicted a night landscape, strangely stylised so the hills seemed drawn up unnaturally into steep pyramidal mounds crowned with misshapen obelisks. The valleys between were choked with weird vegetation, and there appeared to be many small moons in the sky.

Katarina could see my fascination.

"One of his earliest works. This was his studio at one time, and he always had it with him. He called it *The Dweller on the Old Hill.* We always called it *The Silver Screen.*"

That was such an odd choice for so dark an image, for there was nothing silver about it at all. I said as much, and she just smiled thinly.

Perhaps it was because we had been getting on so well that she chose that moment to open up, in a roundabout sort of way, about Youlden's disappearance.

"You've heard the tales about people who ate faery fruit, or picked a faery flower without permission, and suffered a terrible punishment. The Twlwydd Teg are like children in some ways. Dangerous, powerful, but children. Their laws sometimes make no sense to us, but break them and the consequences can be terrible.

"There's a steep little hill in the grounds, with figures that look like stone carvings all over it. Oh, you've seen it! Well it's a place sacred to *them*, and the figures aren't sculptures. They somehow form themselves, grow like mushrooms in the night. Some solidify, others are constantly moving and changing. They are sometimes called 'serpent stones'.

"You must have wondered about Phillip's disappearance. Something terrible happened here, something personal that I can't talk about, but Phillip was badly affected by it. He became depressed and couldn't work. The ability to draw and paint just left him. It was dreadful for someone as creative as him.

"He dug up some of the serpent stones and brought them into the house. A visitor saw them and mistook them for his work. He said nothing to correct them. Then I found his initials cut into some of them. He said they stood for 'Arthur Machen', as a tribute, but it was a lame excuse.

"I don't believe he ever planned it, it just happened. He was trying to pretend he could still create, I suppose. I convinced him to have them put back on the mound, but the damage was already done.

"To move them had been bad enough. To claim them as his own work was a kind of blasphemy. It was inevitable that he would be made to suffer for it."

"You think he killed himself because his mind was disturbed?"

"Don't be ridiculous. Phillip didn't kill himself. They punished him."

"Like the Furies you mean? His own guilt destroying him subconsciously?"

"Is that what you really think? God, you people can be so blind. And what makes you think he's dead?"

"Wait, are you trying to say that Phillip Youlden is still alive?"

"Not exactly. Well, yes, he is, but…"

She paused and strode around the room, then stopped and faced me.

"Yes, perhaps it's time. There's only one way I can make you understand."

She took off a heavy pendant, hung it around my neck and muttered some words.

Crossing the room, she switched on a tape machine, and the swirling incantations of *The Separable Soul* began to pulse and boom.

Lighting a massive brazier, she cast powder on it until the room was full of an unpleasant smelling cloud that made my head swim. Katarina breathed deeply of the vapours for some seconds, and began to chant.

"I am the goddess who kindles the senses with sacred smoke."

As Katarina spoke, the inhaled clouds escaped in lazy billows that poured up her face in a dark flood.

Youlden had once done a painting called *Gwragedd Annwn*, of a vampiric water fairy deeply submerged, with the sucked blood of a drowned victim escaping from her smiling lips and streaming up her face. In that moment the painting lived.

The words changed, though still in rhythm with the music. Familiar words—the painted radiogram's rasping message from another world:

"*Nashtaraan ashgraak shamash ossaam reechmaak aakraamaa saamaaraa...*"

It sounded like many voices.

And Katarina began to change. Before my eyes I swear the years fell from her, until her wrinkled face was smooth. Her body somehow became healthily fleshed, with the curves of a young woman, her tangled mane of hair gathered up into some kind of tall turban.

She was, and yet was not, Eva Malas.

Taking up that massive coiling shofar of mysterious origin, she blew it.

The sound was of a depth and immensity that seemed to shake the whole room.

She blew again.

A silver glow blazed on the face of the doll's house, as if the moon had come from behind a cloud. I turned to the source of the light and saw that the picture on the wall was no longer dark. It had actually become what Katarina had said it was: a silver screen.

She laid her hand on my back, whispered in my ear. I felt a gentle but insistent pressure between my shoulder blades.

That was all; nothing more, and then we were standing among an apparently endless succession of smooth, unnaturally steep hills topped with columns that seemed to have the texture of stone, but writhed as though alive. Our way wound between the hills through tall, feathery foliage that winnowed the breathless air. New stems erupted noiselessly from the ground, and in their rising they released luminous globes that floated like thistledown all around, giving off the rich vibration of distant bells and the light that had turned the whole landscape to quicksilver.

A fine dust, or pollen, fell from them, too, and when I breathed it in, it intoxicated like sweet wine. My heart began to ache with a deep, unfocussed yearning.

Katarina moved close alongside me, and I saw that she had changed again.

She seemed now to be completely composed of opalescent light. Veins of fire ran like rivers through her body, overflowing from her head and body in wings of light. Just to look at her filled me with an exquisite feeling of joy.

When she laid her hand on me I moved at her will, through the elongated, wispy foliage. It showered us with a thick, noxious-smelling syrup. Katarina offered her radiant face up to it, as if welcoming the cool touch of rain.

The memory of what followed is fragmentary and confused. I was looking into a hollow like a great weeping ulcer, filled with a multitude in flux, a sea of living things that merged and separated. All over its surface shapes of flaccid softness would rise up, then fall back to an undifferentiated ocean of rottenness that lapped against a block of stone on which was squatting a figure more spider than human, its whole body a-swarm with glittering parasites. The crowd boiled and rolled in ecstatic adoration as the thing raised its forelegs and gestured with a weirdly sacerdotal grace. There was something Eucharistic in the gesture, and I knew that I was witnessing the enactment of some secret liturgy of sacred putrescence. The sea of bodies rose to devour the offering.

Then I was peering down into immense depths, where gigantic domes blazed with strange light. There were living heads trailing luxuriant hair, floating, and their song was at once exquisite and agonising. And I remember a series of caves ablaze with a chill corpse-light, an icy labyrinth in whose walls creatures of various kinds were trapped, their limbs veined with glittering minerals, their flesh fused with the cold rock.

One trapped body that was all but consumed, its chest facetted with ugly crystalline growths. The face, though mottled, veined and crazed with tiny radial fractures, was still recognisable as that of Phillip Youlden.

The eyes looked deep into mine, and, locked as they were in agonising sockets of stone, they were alive.

I found myself on the floor of the basement. Katarina was sitting on a cushion, strumming a fat-bellied lute.

"You had better wash that off now," she said, "unless you want to gradually become what the human race is pleased to call 'insane.'"

The thick, noxious syrup shaken from the trees by our passage was still spattered all over me.

That harsh initiation into the faery realm had the effect that Katarina had intended all along. I would be haunted ever after by the memory of what I had seen, or more particularly by a deep, unfocussed yearning which would never leave me, ingested with the dust of a hundred singing moons.

I left *Plas Gwyllion* the next day. Katarina made it clear she looked on my departure as some kind of betrayal, but then her reactions could be exaggerated.

I readjusted, as much as I could, to normal life. My half-hearted book dealing proved less enjoyable now Rupert was gone. Rarely was there tea on offer, and the conversation was pretty poor. Many things that had given me pleasure now seemed stale and unprofitable.

Katarina Garside died later that year. Her passing went unnoticed by the press, even by the music papers, who had long ago embraced a very different set of musical criteria. I heard about it from a fellow fan, weeks after her death. Her body, he said, was found in her basement recording studio, sprawled in front of a "big painting".

In the absence of any written details of her preference, and of any surviving relatives, her ex-husband, William Bentliff, had kindly supplied the information that it had been her wish to be cremated, and her ashes scattered on a certain wooded mound in the grounds of *Plas Gwyllion*. This was duly done.

I may have been doing him a disservice, but I suspected this might be a last, spiteful act of revenge. It was certainly not the flamboyant Baroque ritual I would have expected her to choose.

In one respect at least Katarina had thought ahead. A few months after, I received a letter from her solicitors, Embley and Yewbert, informing me that I had been named as permanent curator of the Youlden collection.

Despite some inner turmoil, I knew before I finished reading the letter that I would accept the position. As I saw it, Bentliff's past behaviour meant that if it wasn't me it would very probably be him, and I wanted Youlden and Katarina's works to be seen and remembered.

Besides, don't the fairy tales agree that the place you fear to enter holds the treasure you most ardently seek?

So it was that I found myself returning, on a day no more clement than on my first journey, to *Plas Gwyllion*, where I found I would be residing alone, her faithful "staff" having long-since departed.

On the first night in my customary sleeping place I was awakened by a weight on my feet. As I sat up it shifted, dropped to the floor and ran out. When I got a light on, the room was empty.

I concluded that poor Cath Paluc was still in the house, living on god-knew-what.

Watching for signs in the days that followed, I caught only those sounds and fleeting glimpses of dark movement. I put down bowls of food, but they were never touched.

As I worked ceaselessly on the cataloguing which Katarina had never been disciplined enough to even attempt, my admiration for Youlden grew, convincing me that I should publish a volume of his *oeuvre*.

I was aware, though, that much of the late work was of too unpleasant a nature to be popular, even among connoisseurs of the grotesque, for its subject matter had gradually narrowed to an obsessive focus: endless variations on *The Marriage Beneath the Shade*.

Everywhere the intimate union of the human and the unhuman, and its unthinkable results.

I was in danger of turning into a Bentliff sympathiser.

Those columns on the mound that were the cause of Youlden's terrible demise had somehow rooted themselves again, and had grown in all manner of fantastic ways, and the letters he had carved upon them were gone.

In leisured moments, I developed vague plans for the release of Katarina's—that is Eva Malas'—unpublished music, much of it surviving on antiquated reel-to-reels and cassettes. In these works I could catch, deeply inter-fused with Celtic harmonies, the strains of raga, gamelan, Gnawas and the exorcisms of Aisha Kandisha.

Some pieces—'Songs of the Frantic Lupanar', for instance, and 'Mystic Dances of the Aegypans', both influenced by her Moroccan Jajouka experience—and the equally remarkable 'Dol Chants', were as weirdly haunting as anything from the 1960s. Others, like verses from *The Secret Glory* set to harpsichord accompaniment, and a brief tune entitled 'Change Child', were almost classically restrained. A lighter piece using themes from John Ireland's *Legend*, with lyrics based around a Machen tale, was entitled 'The Happy Child'.

Either she was a remarkably versatile musician, or there had been distinguished visitors of a musical bent over the years.

Out of the blue I received a letter from Katarina's maid and the "old roadie", explaining they had taken Cath Paluc with them when they left. They had grown to love him over the years, and hoped I would not mind.

So whatever had climbed onto my bed in the dark had not been the cat.

I took to sleeping downstairs on a day bed in the library, with the lights on.

Then, in Katarina's bedroom, I came across a large Welsh Bible, on the flyleaf of which a family had recorded births, deaths and marriages through the years.

In the 1920s, Owen Maddock had married Morwyn Howell, and had two children, a boy Arthur, who died early, and Gwen, who grew up to marry one John Garside. Katarina was their daughter, the granddaughter, then, of Owen and Morwyn, the woman credited with strange powers in his most heartfelt book: Cassap, wise in the faery ways, one of a partly-human species called an "Interpreter".

So Katarina Garside, weaver of the musical magic that had entranced me, had the blood of the Twlydd Teg in her veins.

I also found what I thought was a beautiful old book bound in brown leather decorated in gold and bronze. It had a vaguely Byzantine look about it.

Only it wasn't actually a book at all. It was one of those boxes made to look like a book, and it was full of photographs. *Plas Gwyllion*, of course, in all seasons and weathers; Twmbarlwm, Mynydd Maen, and snow-shrouded hanging woods. Katarina with a younger, happy Bentliff, she much as I remembered her from old LP sleeves. Youlden was often to be seen brooding in the background, dark sorcerer from *The Thief of Bagdad*.

One snap at the bottom of the pile had been taken in the basement, in front of that marvellous scale-model of *Plas Gwyllion*. Katarina was sitting upright, on a hard chair, face a frozen mask, with an unspeakably horrible doll sitting on her lap; it might have been autonomatonophobia personified.

But even in an old Polaroid it was clear that it was no dummy, but a living thing, malformed, repellently cadaverous and utterly grotesque.

Sin, according to Machen, is an esoteric, occult thing, an infernal miracle: an attempt to gain knowledge intended only for "the angels", and it makes a man a demon. It is sorcery, the penetrating of other spheres in a "forbidden" manner, "a re-enactment of The Fall". Yet even he was torn. The attempt might be a "powerful and deadly poison", yet it could also be "a precious elixir" for those who had "fashioned the key".

The combined arts of Youlden and Katarina had undeniably fashioned a potent key, and released what Sir Thomas Browne once called "the hidden Pan in the ever-changing Proteus".

Sometimes, it seems, the very thing that gives purpose to your life can also be your curse.

God alone knows what demons Katarina had struggled with through the subsequent years, but her sullen indifference on my arrival now seemed, in retrospect, a sort of quiet patience.

I worked diligently in my new position, preparing a *catalogue raisonné* of the unseen works of Adam Midnight, and arranging theoretical collections of Eva Malas songs in expectation of a hoped-for future release.

The latter was made harder by a growing reluctance on my part to spend time in the basement. I always had the feeling I was being watched, and never felt comfortable when my back was turned to the Silver Screen.

Nicola Ottoway may have been right about Youlden's former studios being haunted; this one certainly was. The most disconcerting manifestations were sounds, disturbing enough when I was close by, but increasingly audible even from other parts of the house, such as instruments being plucked, blown or knocked over, and slamming, like wood on wood. There was, too, the occasional shrieking, like a living thing in pain.

One afternoon I was almost lifted from my seat by the distant blast of that strange shofar, and made up my mind that things had gone far enough. I had grown sick of perpetually living on my nerves.

Even from the top of the stairs, I became aware of a pale radiance illuminating the basement, and knew at once it was the Silver Screen. As I stood there, plucking up my courage, I heard the sound of footfalls swiftly crossing the floor. That familiar glow was shut off abruptly, and by the time I switched on the light and got down the stairs, the basement was empty, offering only scattered instruments and a dark painting on slate.

Out of the Picture.

Yes, quite literally, out of the picture.

There was an odd sound on the air, which I took only a second to identify as every stringed instrument in the basement, gently vibrating.

It was then I noticed that the front of the massive *Plas Gwyllion* doll's house had been left open, and saw inside it for the first time.

The furniture and miniature occupants of the rooms, if there at all, had been buried under mounds of strange detritus: oddly shaped stones, dried leaves, the desiccated remains of small birds. Plaited knots and balls of human hair, withered fruits and berries, some poisonous, and dead spiders pierced with thorns. A small sheet of lead rolled into a tight tube; a few painstakingly poured pyramids of sand and earth, each one topped with an ugly torpedo-shaped pellet of excreted bones and hair. A wasp nest, many odd gloves filled with earth, like a cluster of fat groping hands. Teeth, many and various.

And little manikins and poppets crudely made either of wax, or of plaited straw, branches and fine red cord, some with their necks broken, or pierced through the chest and head with feathers.

In that moment, I would have gladly filled the whole basement with St. John's Wort, planted an impenetrable hedge of Prickly Furze around *Plas Gwyllion*, and never looked back.

It was days before I could bear to go down there again, and much longer before I could look at the contents of the doll's house with equanimity.

But they have a strange fascination. It is tempting to see something poignant about the placing of them, though I know that is probably sentimentality. Does such a creature even know what a doll's house is? It might just as well think it an altar for treasured offerings, or an elaborate pyx in which to keep its sacred relics.

The contents change. Additions are made in my absence. Sometimes what is left is a concoction so strangely beautiful that I am tempted to remove it and keep it with me. I resist that temptation. If the present condition of Phillip Youlden is indeed a punishment for theft, I have no wish to even accidentally risk some similar fate. As there is no way of knowing if these objects are being given, lent, or displayed in some obscure ritual observance, I am scrupulous in leaving everything as I find it, with the exception of the small gift I occasionally add as a gesture of friendship.

Some of the objects I leave are taken away, some show no signs of ever being touched. No pattern is discernible; no application of human logic could anticipate what does or does not please my unseen visitor.

And unseen it has remained. Part of me longs to know what manner of creature it is that passes back and forth through the Silver Screen, but part of me dreads to.

That faded Polaroid alone haunts my nights.

Lately it has occurred to me that this placing and removal of small objects has assumed the nature of a kind of stilted conversation between two solitary creatures who share no other language, bound together by unfathomable devotions.

KATE FARRELL

ALMA MATER

KATE FARRELL lives in Edinburgh. As she is pathologically indisposed to describe a happy ending, the former actress now principally writes *contes cruels* wherein bad things happen to bad people; sometimes the innocent suffer too. Her stories have appeared in the *Black Books of Horror, Terror Tales, The Screaming Book of Horror* and *Best British Horror 2014*.

Kate's debut novella, *My Name is Mary Sutherland*, appeared from PS Publishing in 2014. *And Nobody Lived Happily Ever After*, published by Parallel Universe Publications at the end of 2015, was her first collection of short stories.

"I was a chubby schoolgirl," recalls Farrell, "though not asthmatic; a day girl and not a boarder. Rubbish at sports and needlework (one of the teachers told me that I didn't sew, I harpooned), my friends and I really did hide in a snug, dank hole known as the "Drying Room" at school on cold and wet days and make up horror stories.

"We considered the Stationery Cupboard, but dismissed it as too bright, too cold, and it was often locked, for the nuns trusted no one. I wonder where Louise, Karen and the others are now..."

NOW. THE GOTHIC pile has become a luxury development of lifesty\] apartments with an on-site gym and a concierge; in the 1960s the conver\ of Stella Maris in Romsey was a boarding school for girls aged eleven to eigh\

teen. A large picture of the Virgin Mary spreading her blue cloak like celestial wings dominated the entrance hall and gave the school its motto: *Sub tuum præsidium.* Under Thy Protection.

Converted from a vast Victorian house with a jumble of later additions, it was unwelcoming and unforgiving then, whereas now it is double-glazed and desirable. Halogen lights create intimate corners in the individual apartments; Apple computers glow seductively; granite worktops sleekly gleam, and antiqued leather sofas placed on floors of reclaimed burnished oak create a pleasing ambience for the residents.

Commute over, the building is a haven from the workplace, a veritable sanctuary where the demons of the day are exorcised.

Then. The building was home to an order of teaching nuns, the bequest of a devout spinster who died in the middle of the 19th century. Despite the warm red brick, mullioned windows and gabled roofs, by the early 1960s the convent school was a cold, forbidding place. Spartan and sunless, with badly lit hallways and corridors and an antiquated heating system, it offered little in the way of comfort to the pupils who were separated from their families during term time.

On school days during break periods, the junior girls congregated out of doors. As they were not quite children, yet still not women, the Sisters hoped they would burn off some of that terrifying prepubescent energy. The older students were allowed to remain inside ostensibly to study for their A-levels, though more usually they would droop around and moan about the boy-friends they had left behind. Or compare and contrast the relative merits of their favourite Beatle.

Because of their age, twelve-year-olds Louise, Barbara, Jennifer and Karen were meant to spend their recreation periods outdoors. Only torrential rain would permit them entry to the relative warmth of the gymnasium. On days that were cold but dry, they wore coats and scarves outside and ran around more than usual to keep from freezing. Louise, their leader, thought this was barbaric and would hug a temperamental radiator before being shooed outside with her peers.

Then one day she happened accidentally upon a warm spot indoors that she thought might provide the perfect refuge.

It happened thus: she had been to swimming lessons in the town with her class. Upon return, the usual procedure was to take wet swimwear to a special small area called rather grandly the "Drying Room". The space measured some four feet by twelve feet and was at the end of a long, dark corridor; it was windowless and very warm because of the antiquated heating pipes that ran its length. Racks of pegs had been attached to the walls for damp towels and black regulation bathing suits. There was a light switch on the wall outside which Louise flicked on, while she looked for an available peg. As the door closed behind her, the twenty-watt light bulb flickered and went out. She was not one to panic, and felt her way in.

The door opened again and there was her friend Karen fiddling with the switch. Ever the joker, Louise draped her towel over her head and extended a hand to Karen to drag her into the darkened space, while she gave a shuddering, low moan, in the manner of a ghoul from a horror film. No one heard Karen's scream, Louise's snigger, or her terrified friend's shriek that turned into laughter.

Silly Tom, the school janitor-cum-handyman-cum-dogsbody, pushed a broom in the vicinity, yet paid them no heed. How could he when his head was still full of that place called the Somme? Although nearly fifty years past, its noises and its colours were all he knew: white for the rocket flares and artillery advance; blue for the dead horses in the trenches; red for the place where Victor Cotton's head had been. And so on.

"Listen, Karen," said Louise. "The weather's horrible. We could come in here during breaks and keep out of the cold; we'll stay lovely and warm and they'll never find us. I don't know why I didn't think of it before!"

The pair reported back to their other friends, Barbara and Jennifer, and also to fat little Geraldine who was hanging around, as she so often did. She wasn't really in their gang for although pretty enough, she was too chubby and asthmatic for their tastes. Sometimes she was allowed to tag along when one of them, usually Barbara, showed her a little kindness. And she shared her sweets and her transistor radio, and often helped with their Latin or French homework.

So the girls gathered in the warm and musty hole while their peers shivered outside. To avoid discovery, they had to confine their visits to days when none of the other classes went swimming, yet enjoyed it all the more for that self-imposed restriction. Besides, it gave them something to look forward to.

It became an event. Karen came with crisps, Jennifer brought pop and they let Geraldine bring toffees. They always put the light out lest one of the prefects catch them hiding, and Barbara provided a torch for emergencies, so once their eyes grew accustomed to the dark, it was fun.

Geraldine, although desperate to be included, was a little nervous about the venture. Hadn't they heard the story about Sister Bernadette, she asked, the old blind nun whose ghost walked the corridors? Maybe even this very one.

The tale of the sightless Sister was part of school legend, though some of the seniors put it down to propaganda. The girls were banned from visiting parts of the building that were not included in their daily routines, and individuality of expression was not encouraged. The Drying Room was merely for the storage of swimming kit, it was not a recognised recreation area.

Louise gave the nuns some headaches as she was often caught in places she was not meant to be. The detention she had earned for talking to the gardener's boy was the talk of her year for some time.

"Nah," she said, "it's just the old girls trying to put the frighteners on us, stop us having any fun."

She was not entirely wrong, as fun was a commodity sorely lacking at their seat of learning.

"You think?" asked Karen. "It could well be true. Didn't they say the Sister had a wonderful singing voice and sometimes you could hear her singing the 'Ave Maria'?"

Unseen by Geraldine in the confined space, she nudged Jennifer, who was happy to continue in similar vein.

"Don't know about that, but I heard when it was a private house years and years ago there was some story about a bride who was buried alive in the walls in her wedding dress." Jennifer warmed to her theme. "She was bricked-up by a mad husband. He thought she'd been unfaithful to him before the wedding."

Geraldine did not disappoint them with her gullibility.

"No!" she gasped. As she reached for her inhaler, the other girls roared until Barbara assured her it was only a story. Still, they were all rather glad to be out in the daylight and the fresh air afterwards. Bricked-up brides and blind nuns indeed!

A few days later, the girls were once more taking shelter from the fine November drizzle that turned the hair of their classmates to nut-brown fuzz.

Once they were settled on their nests of dried towels, Jennifer, the literary star of her year, said, "I came across this tale about a blind beggar and how he took his revenge on a boy who had stolen from his begging bowl. It happened in London, years ago when it was still really foggy. He recognised the robber from his smell and knew he could follow his scent. Anyway, one night the robber was walking home with some more money he'd taken from the poor box at St. Vincent de Paul's."

Geraldine said that it was terrible to steal from the blind and the poor too.

Louise shushed her and bade Jennifer continue.

She told them how the robber heard the *tap tap tap* of the blind man's cane in the fog and, every time he stopped and turned to check who was following, he could see nothing. *Tap tap tap*, then stop, turn, still nothing. *Tap tap tap*. All around him the fog swirled and thickened, and the streetlights gave only spectral outlines of distant buildings; a dog howled somewhere—even Louise shuddered at this—yet still, *tap tap tap*.

"Who's there?" said the robber.

Tap tap tap.

"Show yourself!"

Tap tap tap.

"Why are you following me?"

Although he quickened his pace, the tapping still continued. He started to run; he ran down a side street, then another, losing his bearings and slipping over the cobblestones that were damp and greasy. Stopping to listen, all he could hear was the river slapping against the boats, and the sound of a ship's ghostly horn somewhere on the water. And always:

Tap tap tap.

Because he could see only inches in front of him, he didn't realise how near the river was, or how low the embankment wall was, and the *tap tap tapping* grew closer. He stumbled, fell into the water, and because his pockets were so full of stolen coins he sank quickly, dragged down to the muddy bottom by the weight in his pockets.

There was no one else to hear his attempted cries, and once the robber's desperate thrashing was over, the blind man turned and walked away.

Tap tap tap, finished Jennifer.

They all were quiet.

"Wow," said Louise at last.

"Jen, that was horrible," said Karen, full of admiration. Typical of many twelve-year-olds, they welcomed the *frisson* of fear in the dark because soon they knew it would be light again. Barbara's torch shone on all the girls' faces as they breathed once more, though Geraldine sat open-mouthed and fumbling for her inhaler.

"Relax, Geraldine, it's only a story," said Barbara. And they all, even Geraldine, laughed at last.

For their next visit, as they huddled together surrounded by drying towels and swimsuits, Karen took her turn with the storytelling. She thrilled her small audience with a Gothic tale of a strange priest who came to say the Mass, and fed communicants real blood and dried flesh from children he'd murdered. As she described the moment when one young innocent was slain with a hunting knife and pieces of his body were cut up into bite-sized portions, Geraldine actually screamed out loud.

Sister Benedict happened to be thereabouts, looking for Silly Tom to perform some other mundane task. The nun flung open the door to the Drying Room to find five girls sequestered there during the lunchtime break.

They were summoned to appear before Reverend Mother who issued lines, penances, principally in the form of decades of the Rosary, and banned them from entering the space again, other than to hang their damp swimming togs. She saved her flintiest gaze for Geraldine, at whom she was particularly surprised and not a little disappointed. A prolonged spell in such a place was injurious to her fragile health, and she was seriously minded to inform the girl's parents.

"You will confine yourselves to the prescribed places at the appropriate times. We cannot, we shall not, permit you girls to wander around the school at will. It is for your own good. You would do well to recall the school's motto," said the Superior.

A week or two passed. In December the temperature dropped, sleet fell, and the junior girls were permitted to spend their recess hours in the vast assembly space of the gymnasium. They still wore their coats indoors, but finally there was shelter from the fiercer elements of the weather during the short days leading up to Christmas.

Louise felt it would be safe to resume visiting their favourite haunt; they would not be missed in a gymnasium heaving with young girls killing time in the dinner break.

She said that the stories would continue, and they were to take on a new tone as a result of the dressing down from Reverend Mother. Henceforward, all must feature nuns as the victims or villains.

Louise herself decided to kick-off the new regime. To add theatricality to the proceedings, she took a towel from the rack, and placed it over Barbara's torch, which she held under her chin. A ghastly green light suffused her face and she was unrecognisable, with sunken eye-sockets and hollowed cheekbones.

The scene was set for the story of Sister Marinella from the Philippines and her evil voodoo doll. With its shadows thrown on the convent walls, greatly magnified by some trickery, it frightened the Mother Superior into a heart attack, which Louise described in all its awful detail. A similar fate befell her successor and, ultimately, Sister Marinella became head of the convent. However, one night, as she was in the chapel alone, she too was visited by this horrible sight, this giant silhouette. The thing was beyond her control, and she was found the next day, features twisted into a howl of fear and her eyes staring madly at some distant spot. At her side was a small broken puppet doll.

Brilliant, they all declared.

Louise asked Geraldine to prepare a tale for the next session, but she refused, she didn't think she had the imaginative flair. Also, her time was otherwise engaged as she had chosen to transcribe the stories from memory and planned to give each of the others a copy as a surprise Christmas present. It was a lot of work, five copies in all including her own, though she felt it would be worth the effort and the others would be pleased. If she couldn't add to the collection, at least she could give them all a keepsake.

So it was the turn of Barbara. Her story concerned a deranged nun who was the only survivor of a war. All the Sisters in the tales by definition were deranged, damaged or just plain evil. She stayed on in the ruins of her convent, eking out what little food she could find and praying for deliverance. Weeks passed by, and one night the Devil appeared to her in a dream and told her if she wished to continue with the Lord's work there was only one hope of survival for her: she must drink the blood of innocents.

Very soon after, some children who were fleeing the advancing armies took refuge at the convent. She shared her bread with them and made them comfortable as best she could, and when they were asleep she slit their throats. She caught the blood that flowed in a chalice salvaged from the ruined chapel and drank her fill. And as more small groups of children came in search of sanctuary, her health and strength continued to improve. Until one day she drank the blood of a poor little boy who had a terrible sickness, and his blood was infected. She too fell victim to the infection and died alone, covered in horrible sores and crying out for God's mercy.

Shudders of approval all round.

When they were gathered for their next session, they waited for Karen, who had still not joined them. They only had the lunch-break hour, and an afternoon of rehearsing Christmas antiphons and parsing French verbs loomed. They sat in the dark on the beds made from dried towels wondering where she was, for time was precious.

There was a sound of running feet, the door opened and in she burst.

"Look out girls, they're calling the class registers and going to do a fire-drill, in the gym in ten minutes, so get a move on, we'll have to pretend we've been in there all along!"

After some furious scrabbling around, the girls scooped up pop bottles and crisp packets, which they rushed to stow in their lockers. There was no time to tidy up the towels, and they made it into the gym just as Sister John Bosco rang the bells to announce the fire-drill and called everyone to their assembly points.

Though Geraldine was a little red-faced after the slight panic, part of her enjoyed the thrill of nearly being caught out a second time with her friends. She was one of them! She belonged at last!

As Gerladine prepared for bed that night, she checked her inhalers. There were always two, an extra one in case the first should fail, the consequences of which were too awful to contemplate. There was one on top of her bedside table, and the second, which was always in or near her school bag, she couldn't locate.

She went through her pockets, turned her satchel upside down, and rearranged all her exercise books and bits of paper, including the loose leaves of the story collection. Nowhere could it be seen.

While the other girls brushed their teeth and said their night-time prayers, Geraldine mentally retraced her steps that day. The inhaler. Where was it? Was in it the dining hall? The gymnasium? Had she dropped it when they ran to the muster for the fire drill? No, if she'd dropped it or left it some place, someone would have found it and handed it in. The pupils and staff were aware of the importance of her small life-support system.

Where could it be?

Could it perhaps...oh no, not there! Not in the Drying Room! She couldn't go there, not now, it was late!

However there was no choice.

She hissed over to Barbara. Too much chatter in the dormitories was forbidden.

"Bar, could I get a lend of the torch for a bit?"

Barbara handed it over.

"What's it for? If you want to read in the bed you won't get far, I think it needs a new battery, it's getting faint."

"I only want to look over the verbs for tomorrow; I don't think I've got them off right..."

Geraldine was the star French pupil, so this didn't quite have the ring of truth to it, but aged-twelve Barbara was not yet the astute judge of character she was to become in later years.

"Okay. Don't let it die on you though."

"Cross my heart, Bar," said Geraldine. And she did.

She waited until most of the dormitory was settled, and looked over her verbs to pass the time. Then just after eleven o'clock when all was silent and dark, she slid from the hard cotton sheets and scratchy woollen blankets that made up her bed, put on slippers and a dressing gown, and set off for the Drying Room.

A building in the dead of night, however familiar during daylight, can be a foreign country to the most stout-hearted, let alone a small asthmatic girl armed only with a flickering torch. Corridors become unnaturally long; corners conceal unknown perils and must be approached with caution. Sounds are magnified, mouths are dry and pulses race. She pushed all thoughts of Louise's story and the voodoo doll's giant shadow from her mind.

Geraldine sent up a silent word of thanks to St. Christopher when she reached her destination on the ground floor. There were no windows at this end of the corridor, and had there been, it would have made precious little difference as the night was moonless, and as black as the raven's wing. The silence was palpable, not even Silly Tom's broom could be heard, nor the slightest rustle of a nun's robes, nor yet the whispered clack of rosary beads that hung from their belts.

The night was cold, but she wiped moist palms on her dressing gown and fought the urge to gasp in short, fast, shallow breaths.

As Geraldine opened the door to the Drying Room, the torch winked, once, twice, then died. She switched on the light, hurried inside lest someone, a nun or a prefect, be patrolling and switched it off immediately, though she left the door open a tiny crack to relieve the unremitting darkness that would otherwise envelope her.

She gave the torch a shake, and mercifully it shone once more. Directing it across the floor area amongst towels and swimwear, the inhaler was not immediately apparent. She switched off the torch to save what little of the battery remained, then dropped to her knees and felt around.

From somewhere beyond, from the inky stillness of the convent, there came a sound. Geraldine listened. It was of a voice, though not quite a human voice; it seemed too wavery and high-pitched.

At first she wasn't sure even if it was human, so distorted was it by the walls and corridors and the distance it had to travel. She stopped scrabbling on the floor a moment to concentrate on it as it became stronger. Clearer.

And closer.

Then the footsteps. Faltering, irregular steps. As if someone was unsure of their passage perhaps. Or couldn't see where they were. Cheated of the light, not unlike little Geraldine herself.

Finally she could hear the voice properly: it was the purest soprano, perfect in pitch, singing a hymn.

'Ave Maria.'

Geraldine made out the words:

"*Sáncta Maria, Máter Déi
óra pro nóbis peccatóribus. . .
nunc, et in hóra mórtis nóstrae. Ámen.*"

It was the most beautiful thing she had ever heard.

The singing stopped. The footsteps stopped. Just by the slightly opened door to the Drying Room.

No other sound then except breathing; unlike the purity of the singing voice, this was deep, rasping, and jagged. Whoever it was, it was as if they had forgotten how to breathe.

Her own breathing now in shallow pants, her mouth as dry as bone, Geraldine stood and switched on the torch for whatever illumination it might provide.

The door opened wider, ever wider, and she shone the pencil-thin beam on the long dark folds of a sleeve. But the fabric was ragged and had marks on it: crusted, indefinable stains. As the door was opened fully, she trained the light from the arm to the body, and clad in rotting raiments from the charnel house, there stood what once had been a nun, shrouded by a foul and foetid odour, the stench of decomposition.

The tunic, the wimple, the veil, all were tattered, smeared and mildewed with filth from decades in the tomb. The face was not a face, nor was it a skull; it was in some unholy place between the two. Blackened, leathered flesh still adhered to it, and small brown teeth showed in the open maw that was the mouth; the torch's dying light revealed shrunken lids half-closed over milky eyes, like dead opals. The thing, the nun, blocked the doorway, its head turned slowly this way, slowly that, as if searching for something.

The creature stretched a hand in, scraping at the air between herself and the child, reaching towards her. Not so much fingers, withered claws, that may have been fingers once, pecked at the space as the nun leaned in and brushed the cheek of the small girl.

When they found Geraldine several hours later, it was not possible to do anything for her. Her crumpled body was wedged inside the door to the Drying Room, one hand holding a torch and the other outstretched, mere inches from her inhaler.

Police and medical examiners were summoned, questions were asked in the most reverential of tones, and all protocols duly observed.

The nuns washed her, dressed her, and laid her out in the sick bay to await her parents. They placed rosary beads in her hands, but her father removed them and flung them across the room as he beheld his only daughter.

All her belongings were hastily packed up by Sister Ursula, her form mistress: some exercise books, her missal, her clothes, her transistor radio that was permanently tuned to Radio Luxembourg.

She had smuggled it into the school, her one small act of defiance.

Also, there were several hand-written copies of what appeared to be horror stories. As they were not official schoolwork, Sister Ursula presumed they were rubbish and placed them in a wastebasket.

At Geraldine's Requiem Mass, Sister John Bosco sang the 'Ave Maria', her voice piercing the chapel's dusty air.

It was a sweet soprano, though not as sweet as another.

L.P. LEE

HIBAKUSHA

L.P. LEE was born to a British father and South Korean mother, and she grew up travelling between South London and South Korea. A trained sinologist and anthropologist, her short fiction has appeared in such periodicals as *Litro*, *Eastlit*, *Space Squid*, *BFS Horizons*, *The Fabulist* and *Popshot Magazine*.

Lee shares an artistic synergy with acclaimed UK contemporary artist Annie Ridd, who has produced several illustrations based on her short stories, including 'The Man Root', 'The Feast' and 'Call of the Cicadas'. Ridd's artwork often accompanies Lee's stories in print and was exhibited at the Riverside Gallery, Richmond, in 2015.

"I began writing this story because of something I had come across, several years ago, that still haunted me," reveals the author. "I wanted to go deep into a mysterious island, and uncover a secret. A secret that would draw attention to a forgotten people, and a horrific past."

THE CLOSER I get to the island, the more of a dream Tokyo becomes. The obelisks of high glass, the polished people, their nails and shoes so clean. The neon canopies, the subtle dishes, the cab drivers with white gloves on their hands. I leave it behind on the train ride down. Down to the fishing town with its immaculate streets and kindly grandmother, who hosted me in her *ryokan* and made me a breakfast of rice and fish. Now the fish scatter before my boat, clean waves break against the hull, and the green island looms ahead, rising from the horizon like an old god.

Our boat hurtles through the sea. Sounds surround us: the roar of the engine, the whipping spray, the cackle of birds overhead, but my heart beats loudest of all. A drum-beat, rhythmic in my blood; a constant drum, a war drum.

The waves crash and I remember:

His face and body, so white. White paint on his unclothed skin. His bald head, white as a peeled egg. He squats on the floor, except you cannot see the floor. It is a black space, maybe a black sea. The black space surrounds him. He sits hunched over, head bowed, cradling his knees against his chest, rocking.

Slowly he lifts his head in an unnatural movement. The face reveals itself, eyes wide, staring with the blankness and malleability of a baby. The mouth hangs open, spittle on the chalk white lips. He begins to grin. Spit oozes over his chipped white teeth. Close up, into the emptiness of his eyes, or are they holes? Holes torn into white paper, and on the other side is a black space, empty as the space that surrounds him.

The sun and sea dazzle; I raise my hand, shield my eyes from the sight. The island looms closer.

"She's seen us now," the captain shouts.

I lean forwards, plant my hands on the boat's ledge only to sharply withdraw. I turn up my palm to find a splinter has pierced my skin.

The island jumps closer. When I look up again, the trees are now clearly distinguishable. The black volcanic rocks jut from the shore.

It is a small island, a Pluto of the sea, empty of people.

As our boat approaches, the captain tries again to sway me. "What research can you do here? There's nothing to see."

"I just want to understand."

The beach ahead is pristine; it seems like a paradise. Waves lap at the shore, birds swoop overhead.

But the captain's concerns seep into me. Perhaps there's something about the island, like they say, something darker than what meets the eye, lurking just beneath the surface. But I can't let my imagination be provoked, and besides, I won't let myself turn back now. I've been working on this project for months, and there are a few questions that remain, that will wrap up my research on Kaita Morimura.

Gradually I've chipped away at the mystery that surrounds him, unpicking his background and gaining insight into his thinking. Now I want to see where Morimura spent the last years of his life, secluded away from the world; see the writing that he etched onto the walls of his solitary home. I want to understand why the other island inhabitants fled from him. What was it about him, his death, that caused the island to become deserted?

The roar of the engine dulls to a throb. The boat bobs in the water, keeping its distance from the shore. The captain frowns at the green trees and volcanic rocks. His face, tanned a dark nut-brown, betrays a look of apprehension.

Slowly we approach the dock. The wood is not in good condition; parts of it have fallen into the sea.

The captain moors the boat and helps me onto the pier. His hand is weathered, his manner firm and gentle. His physical presence has been sculpted by a life at sea; eyes used to looking across vast distances rather than small, confined spaces, and a way of standing and moving that seems accustomed to the rhythm of the boat.

My own body has atrophied from a life of written words. My muscles are soft and underdeveloped, my stature is slight. I wouldn't be good at lifting heavy objects. My skin is pale from university lecture halls and from working indoors. While the captain has a sense of energy spread evenly across his body, all my energy is concentrated in my head. I get headaches often; my tensions reside there too.

"You'll be all alone," the captain says.

I smile and tap my camera. "I'm not alone."

He smiles too but there is concern in his eyes. I begin to make my way across the pier, onto the island.

I'm wearing sturdy boots and a rucksack. In the rucksack I have a notebook, a tape recorder and a collection of tapes.

On one of the tapes is an interview with a dancer who knew Morimura. I replayed it this morning, over the breakfast of rice and fish. It went like this:

"*Sometimes when I looked into his eyes, I felt that there was nothing on the other side. Just an emptiness, like his face was a paper mask, or his eyes were holes into outer space. Black and cold, empty of other people.*

"*I thought it was because of what had happened. After Hiroshima and Nagasaki, people didn't really understand. They thought that the survivors might be infectious, that they wouldn't be good employees because of their ill health, and that they wouldn't make good marriage partners because of the risk of deformed children. The survivors were called* hibakusha, *'bombed persons'.*"

A bird squawks above me, in the trees. The sun is blinding; I feel its summer heat on my face and neck. But the sky is a beautiful blue.

The boat is now far away. The captain bobs disapprovingly in the distance.

There is a narrow dirt track that disappears into trees. I follow it and am swallowed up by the forest.

"*He came from Hiroshima. Survived the vapours but his family didn't. Sometimes I thought I saw this in his dancing.*

"*While he was with us, he was invited to put on a show to commemorate Hiroshima. But he refused.*

"*There was a businessman called Mr. Tanaki. He came out of Morimura's performance looking very shaken. He thought he could launch Morimura, and reach a lot of people around the world. Never let people forget.*

"*But Morimura didn't even say no. He just ignored the offer. Went silent for a long time. I don't think he spoke to any of us for a few months. Just ate with us, drank with us, and danced. But it wasn't the same after that. Mr. Tanaki's generosity would have been very good for us, as a group, and Morimura's rejection caused bitterness. It started off small but gradually it simmered. Then there was Morimura's big performance, and he left.*"

The forest clears and there is a cluster of houses. They're small, modern, whitewashed houses. There's a road behind them, leading to the other side of the island which is more developed.

A ginger cat slinks through the grass. It has a collar on but it looks skinny and malnourished. It moves nimbly, close to the earth. When it sees me, it freezes. The amber eyes fixate on my face. I crouch down and make coaxing noises, hoping it will come closer. But the amber eyes show no memory of ownership. In a moment it's gone; dashed away, out of sight again.

Hesitantly I approach the houses and peer in through the windows. They're all deserted.

I return to the dirt path and climb further up the hills, into the forest again.

The trees close behind me until I cannot see the white houses anymore. And beyond them, I can no longer see the sea, the bright waters and the little boat waiting. The canopy above my head grows denser and plunges me into shadow.

"Morimura had his own style. We never questioned it. Right from the start, Hijikata made it clear that the dance form was a reaction to structure and 'fixity'. We were fed up with the rules of noh, and with the upright physiques of ballet, the Western ideals that were taking root in Japan.

"Our way of dancing was a return to the essence of the body. Letting out what was in us, raw and unconstrained. In the 1960s this was a big deal. It was a new bodily aesthetic, overturning our post-war values of refinement and understatement. But it was also a return to an older kind of body."

The forest clears again and I can see a house. A plain, modern, whitewashed house like the rest, but much smaller. It's a relief to see the sky blue and expansive again. I squint as the sun beats down.

My eyes have not adjusted to the bright clearing yet, but as the house comes into focus, I realise that the windows are broken.

This is where Morimura lived.

After his performance in Tokyo, his last performance and his greatest, he came here, secluding himself away from the world.

I am at the house. I can't remember crossing the clearing. I circle the house in a daze.

On the walls I find a line of writing. I hope that it is Morimura's hand.

I take a photo. My Japanese is not good enough to translate it here and now—I'll save it for when I'm back on the boat.

I circle back to the front of the house, and try the door.

I look for a rock and clear the jagged glass that remains on one of the windows. I heave myself through the window and into the dark room.

The noon sun is directly above the house; little light filters in and again my eyes must adjust, this time to darkness.

"His last performance involved all of us, as a group. He'd never asked for our help before, and some people were reluctant at first. But we allowed him to choreograph us, and straight away, after the first session, we knew that it was going to be big. It's still the most important piece of work that I've ever done.

"We were very excited, and we put a lot of resources into publicising the show. We didn't have much money, but with some help we rented a space in downtown Tokyo. Whatever we thought of Morimura as a person, we had faith in him as an artist. We knew that he was going to make an impact."

The inside of the room is bizarre. Whoever broke the windows before me didn't do it for theft. Everything is neat and orderly, everything except for the talismans...

Strips of white cloth fill the room, draped over the seats, hanging from the light bulb, and strung up along the walls like bunting. They are embellished with stark calligraphic strokes; energetic black ink on white, calling for an expulsion.

These writings are *ofuda*. What happened here was an exorcism.

I take out my camera. The camera flashes are like lightning strikes, and they make me shudder. I feel as if I am waking up a tomb.

Quickly I look around for any notes that I must make. I want to get out of here as fast as possible.

I feel my heart pounding.

I search through the room, and find nothing.

My gaze drifts to the door.

I edge my way into the corridor, and there are talismans here too. They are like long ribbons of noodles, or a crowd of white birds whose feathers obscure my view, or stretched out ghosts.

I look up the stairs.

My heart pounds harder.

I creep up the stairs.

Why am I creeping? There is no one here.

I tread gently. I don't make any sudden movements. The hairs on the back of my neck are standing on end.

I am holding my breath.

As I ascend the stairs, the question comes into my mind...

Do I really have the right to be here?

I'm on the landing now. There are no talismans here.

The door to the bedroom is open.

I creep in and find that there is another line of writing, this time on the wall above the bed.

I take a photo.

Again the lightning strike, and the sense of awakening.

I delicately look through the items in the room. Under the bed I discover a box. It is wooden and the size of a shoebox. Gingerly I lift the lid open, and find papers and a black and white photograph inside.

Kneeling next to the bed, I lift out the photograph.

It is of a man and a woman, with a small child between them.

They look at the camera with the unsmiling expressions common at the time for photographs. But the woman is wearing a dress that makes me confused.

It is a style of dress that comes from Korea. It's a *hanbok*, a traditional Korean dress with a long-sleeved top and a bouffant skirt.

I put down the photograph and pick up the papers. The writing is in Japanese. It starts out neatly, and then becomes wilder. Morimura's last words?

I feel very urgently now that I must leave.

But I spread the photograph and papers on the floor and lift up my camera. My grip on the camera seems unsteady.

Something compels me against pressing the shutter, but I fight against it. I press down anyway.

I take a photo and the lightning strikes again.

I spread out the documents, and take more photos. In that final flash, I see something. Under the bed...

Out, out! Down the stairs, the talismans are alive, a flock of white birds awakened whose wings flap in my face, obscuring the way ahead. Down, I almost trip on the last step, turn right, into the room where the talismans shake.

Through them, tearing away the white cloths that hinder me, towards the broken window. And out, falling onto the lawn outside, and stumbling across the clearing, blinded by the sun, until I am in the darkness of the forest again.

Down the dirt track I run, so fast and so panicked and on a declining hill that I risk losing my footing and stumbling. Hurtling down through the trees until I reach the next clearing with the small, white, modern houses. Past them, and down again. Finally, the sea! The boat bobbing up ahead, the captain reading a newspaper at the helm.

He looks up and sees me running. Immediately he is on his feet and coming towards me.

My feet clatter across the pier. He extends his hand wordlessly, and supports me back onto the boat.

I turn my face away from him and collapse and sit with my head in my hands.

Behind me, I hear the captain's footsteps, the rumble of the engine starting. The boat begins to move.

I lift my head and see the shore receding, the island sinking slowly back into the sea, falling away on the horizon.

Around my neck, the camera hangs heavily.

Back in Tokyo, I disembark the night train and take a taxi. We drive through glittering streets and modern high-rises. The streets shine with fresh rain; puddles reflect the neon colours, the faces of people. I look out the window at the fluorescent monoliths rising high above.

The taxi driver wears white gloves and sits with a straight back. There's a disciplined polish to his crisp, clean movements.

At the hotel, I sit on the narrow bed looking out at the view of Tokyo. It's midnight. I fish the camera out of the suitcase and try to bring myself to turn it on.

But again that sense of resistance...Something stops me.

I put the camera down quickly as if it's hot.

Instead I take out the tapes from my interviews and put on my headphones.

"*On the day of the performance, the venue was packed. We had people standing all along the walls, crowding at the back, and kneeling on the floor before the stage.*

"*We plunged the room into darkness with only a faint grey light on the stage. There was a lot of chatter in the room when the lights went out, but once Morimura began dancing, everyone fell silent.*

"*He started off standing upright, elegant, and then gradually moved himself closer and closer to the earth, bent-backed and squatting, like so...All of his movements were slow but hyper-controlled.*

"*When he reached the floor, there was a strong flash of light that illuminated everyone's faces.*

"*Then the smoke machines began billowing, and you could barely see Morimura through all of the smoke. But there he was, lifting his arms and legs and looking at himself as though surprised that he was naked.*

"*He picked invisible shards out of the palms of his hands. Then he raised his mouth skywards, opening and closing it as if to catch precious rain.*

"*We crawled in at this point, our whole group of dancers, surrounding Morimura with our ash-white bodies. Raising ourselves up, swaying with our arms held out. We turned up our heads to drink the invisible rain.*"

I saw a photo of the performance. With their arms held out, they looked like zombies in an apocalypse.

I take off my headphones and pick up the camera again.

After that performance, Morimura disappeared. He resurfaced months later on the island.

I switch on the camera.

People tried to interview him. The performance had caused quite a stir. But he refused to talk to anyone. It didn't seem like any kind of snobbery. He just wanted to vanish.

On the camera, the image comes up of the writing that was on the wall of his house. I flick through to the line of writing in his bedroom, and I realise that the two texts are the same.

Character by character I look them up on my phone.

The text reads: What is worse than a *hibakusha*? A *zainichi hibakusha*.

I write down the words and frown at them. My head begins to reel.

I move onto the photos of the documents, and decipher them. It takes hours of looking up words, checking the grammar and piecing the meanings together. But finally, after midnight, I am sitting with a messy translation in my hands, the paper filled with crossed out lines and rewordings.

It reads:

I was lying sprawled out on the floor of my room. I had just finished my night shift and was contemplating whether I had the energy to crawl into bed.

Suddenly, there was a flash of light... A strong, otherworldly light... I had never seen anything like it before. It was beautiful, but also frightening...

When I came to, I realised that I was in the middle of rubble. I had to scramble my way out of the building. I understood that a bomb had fallen, and as I made my way outside, I saw how lucky I was. The windows had blown straight in, and shards of glass punctured the walls opposite them. But I had only a splinter in the palm of my hand, and minor cuts and bruises.

The strange thing was that my clothes had vanished. I was naked! Where had my clothes gone?

By the entrance I found my friend Park Sun-il, who was badly injured and couldn't walk. He was fourteen; two years younger than me, and he called me *hyung*, "older brother". I felt ashamed that I was relatively unscathed.

I helped Sun-il out of the building, and then I felt a wave of nausea. I had to stop. Standing there, I couldn't believe my eyes. The people on the street were burned from top to toe, and everyone was naked. Many people were holding their arms out, and I realised that it was because they didn't want their burned skin to touch anything.

Buildings had collapsed and fires were everywhere. It was hot and difficult to breathe.

I carried Sun-il on my back. He was in a bad way, and he was desperate for water. I also felt an extreme thirst like I had never felt before. I decided that we should go to the river.

As we went through those streets, everyone was silent. No one made a sound.

Many of us were heading in the same direction, to the river.

I saw old women with peeling skin, young boys, mothers with their babies...

Schoolgirls with blisters on their faces... gathering around a police box, weak...

I heard sounds now... Young people, lying on the ground, calling for water...

In the distance I saw a tornado. It whipped through the streets, and everything that it touched was burned. Everyone tried to get away from it.

At the river, there were crowds of people. People were everywhere. Here there was a great commotion, and people crying out. More and more people were coming up behind us, crashing against us. The air was so hot that I felt my skin burning, and the water was a cool relief.

But as I dipped my head into the water, the water sucked me down, and I lost my grip of Sun-il. I tried to get out but the water was suddenly so strong. I thought for a moment that I would not be able to get out alive.

I heard Sun-il shouting my name, and I managed to grab hold of him, and drag us onto the other side of the river. I was so frightened that I hurried in taking us away from that scene before I stopped to think about what direction we should take.

I saw that many people were going in the same direction, and Sun-il said that it must be because they knew where a hospital was. So we joined them.

Soon it began to rain. The rain was black, and the raindrops were big. Everyone opened their mouths. They were all opening their mouths as wide as possible because they were so thirsty.

But the rain was sticking to everything. And it felt heavy, like oil. It hurt when it touched my skin. I begged Sun-il not to drink it, but he was so thirsty. He drank it.

I was beginning to shake from the effort of carrying Sun-il. Eventually we found a hospital, but it was overcrowded with people, and when they heard our accents, they knew that we were not one of them...

I didn't know what to do. I seemed to be walking through Hell. On the streets, there were not just bodies of humans, but also of birds, cats and dogs, even horses...

I took Sun-il out of the city, and tried to help him myself. I tried to stop the bleeding, and to comfort him. I tried to keep him calm. He seemed to recover for a while, but then he grew weak, and spots appeared all over his skin, like mosquito bites...

I felt very alone. I buried Sun-il. He had wanted to grow up to become a botanist. But he'd been forced to come to Japan, to work in the factories.

After a few weeks, I also became ill. My hair fell out, and I became bald...I was very weak. I felt angry that I had no control over my own body.

I recovered, and when the war ended, I returned to my hometown. But back in my homeland, I was an outsider because my Korean was not good enough. Then the Korean War broke out.

Returning to Japan, I did all that I could to hide my identity. If they knew what I was, it would be difficult to work and find a place to belong in society.

Today, I try to find meaning in what happened. But I only find absurdity.

Yes. It is the essence of absurdity.

After I finish translating the document, I stand up and open the window. The room has suddenly become very stuffy. It feels suffocating and hard to breathe.

I gulp down the outside air.

Then I return to my bed, sit down, and pick up my camera again.

I hesitate for a long time before finally pressing the button, moving onto the final image.

Is this what frightened me so much?

There's nothing in the frame except for Morimura's documents, laid out on the floor, and the shadowy recesses under the bed.

I breathe out in relief. I realise that I've tensed up, and now I try to relax my shoulders, to slow my heart rate down, but my eyes are drawn back to the image.

There's a strange and subtle sense of movement... At the back of the picture, in the shadows under the bed.

My chest tightens.

A miniature hand slowly creeps into sight, then another... Two ash-white hands, crawling cautiously forwards...

Hurriedly I switch off the camera. The screen goes black.

I don't dare to breathe. I drop the camera.

But down, at my feet, a finger tickles.

I jump up, back away from the bed.

Slowly, two large hands inch into sight, the fingers waving and feeling ahead like the sensitive legs of a spider.

The hands are shy at first, tentatively becoming familiar with the floor, then they pounce forwards, and behind them the arms appear, stretching out.

The top of a bald head surfaces.

Morimura pulls himself out from under the bed and crouches opposite me. He looks down at the floor, hunching his shoulders, squatting.

Then he rises, straightening his shoulders, straightening his back, and his sad expression changes to one of calm.

I look into Morimura's eyes and see that they are not eyes but holes torn through white flesh, opening out onto endless space; black as rain.

CONRAD WILLIAMS

THE OFFING

CONRAD WILLIAMS lives in Manchester with his wife and three sons. He is the author of nine novels: *Head Injuries*, *London Revenant*, *The Unblemished*, *One*, *Decay Inevitable*, *Loss of Separation*, *Dust and Desire*, *Sonata of the Dead* and *Hell is Empty*, and his short fiction is collected in *Use Once Then Destroy* and *Born with Teeth*. He is currently working on a haunted house novel and an interactive video game.

Williams has won the British Fantasy Award, the International Horror Guild Award and the Littlewood Arc Prize.

"'The Offing' was the result of a number of factors," he recalls. "I'd not long before written a story for the anthology *Weirder Shadows Over Innsmouth* called 'The Hag Stone', which played upon similar ocean-based fears.

"It reminded me of various things: cutting open a squid to find a slowly-digesting fish within; watching swimmers while outflow pipes spewed God-knows-what into the waters on numerous beach visits around the UK as a child; James Cameron's *The Abyss*, and that quote about our knowledge of the ocean compared to the moon; and what we're doing to the sea and the great reckoning that is due us.

"The story crystallised not long after when I asked my youngest son, Zac, to draw me a picture of the ocean. He worked hard on it, and did a great job. I have it hanging on my bedroom wall: a sea filled with sharks and octopi and...other things, swimming in the deep. Things with curved teeth and spines and eyes the size of footballs. There's a guy in a small boat on the surface with a speech bubble, and all it says is: '*Help!*'."

F EARNE GATHERED HER treasures into the blue handkerchief and picked her way up the beach to where her mother was lying in the shingle. It was early evening—summer's terminal breath— but even so Fearne could see the skin of her mother's arms stippled with goosebumps; she had always been sensitive to a chill in the air. She didn't seem to mind. By her side lay the remnants of their picnic tea: a few pastry crusts from the quiche, an empty packet of crisps, Pinot Grigot dregs gleaming in the base of a sand-blasted bottle.

"What did you find?" her mother asked. Her voice carried traces of sleep, although whether it was that already taken or yet to come, Fearne couldn't be sure. The skin above the collar of her blouse was blotchy, a sure sign she had drunk too much. She always did when Dad wasn't around, as if she was making up for lost time.

For a moment Fearne was reluctant to list her acquisitions. She felt the insecurities of childhood rise up even though she had turned thirteen last birthday; a fear that what was uttered would become desired by the other. Mum shouldn't be interested in bits of sea-junk. She loved wine and shoes and hard rock. Fearne sometimes wondered why she had chosen to have children at all. The question alone was a surprise: Mum hardly ever showed any interest in what she was up to. The reluctance remained, however.

"I found some rusting chain. A blue stone. And a fossilised twig."

"Nice," her mother said, but her voice was as flat as the horizon. "That stone isn't stone, it's glass, polished by the sand. And that isn't a fossilised twig, you ninny. It's some kind of coral. White. Which means dead. And you're not bringing that rusty old piece of rubbish home. If it scratches you: lockjaw. I don't think you've had a tetanus shot since you were little."

Fearne had found a shell too, a pretty one that reminded her of the ice cream that Mr. Nardini swirled on to the top of a sugar cone at the parlour near the guesthouse. She hadn't intended to show it to her mum, convinced she would want it for herself, but she felt undermined; she had nothing of worth to show for her search and she didn't want her mum thinking she was useless. She withdrew it from her pocket and held it out for inspection.

"Ooh, that's gorge-o," her mum said, holding the shell up to the hard, midday light. "It wasn't a wasted trip after all. Lovely colour. Very unusual. Carmine, I'd say. Or a cochineal red. Very earthy. Very organic. I could make that up into a pretty necklace if you'd like."

"Okay," Fearne said, knowing full well that she'd not see the thing again. Her mother fancied herself as a craftswoman. Barb the Boho jeweller, she said. She had a little corner of the kitchen set up with various pieces of hardware: pots of glue, a little rotary power tool, a soldering kit, endless tubs of beads. Whenever she got to work on something, it would invariably be accompanied by a large goblet of wine. There'd be more wine than work, especially if one of her wine-by-day friends called for a chat. Jules, say, or Kat, or Loz. The shell was destined to end up as just so much calcium dust when Mum inevitably introduced the Dremel too enthusiastically.

"Although it's a little weird, isn't it, when you think about it? This shell... every shell was once home to something all wet and squidgy. Bit morb-o when you look at it like that."

Fearne gazed out at the compressed edge of sea, like a beaded line of hot solder. It must have been five miles away. The sand was the colour of cooked cream. To the south, the power station sat fat and toad-like, steam rising from its cooling towers like the lazy pre-launch vapour of a sleeping rocket.

She too was tired. Originally she'd planned to march all the way out there to the water's edge. The distance formed a layer on her own fatigue. She imagined striking out to try to meet it before nightfall, the effort it would take, and her posture slumped. She'd never been to the beach by herself or encountered the sea alone before. It was high time, she kept saying to her mum and dad, when they were driving out here. They teased her about that for hours afterwards.

Dad, unpacking his things in a room filled with sailor's paraphernalia: coils of rope, a propeller on the wall, a dressmaker's dummy in a Breton shirt. "It's high time I put my jacket in this wardrobe."

Her mother, fingering the corkscrew already, though breakfast had been only a couple of hours before. "It's high time we thought about lunch."

Very funny. Very *fucking* funny.

She coloured now, as she thought of that prohibited word. She had never sworn in front of her parents; would not dream of it. But she had been angry, and what made it worse was that they registered that and did nothing to placate her.

"Shall we go back to the room?" her mother asked. "It's getting a bit nipply."

"Will Dad be there?"

"I don't know, avocado pip. It's likely. He's been out longer than we have. It'll be time for dinner soon. If he's anything like me he'll be starv-o."

The thought of food made her feel even more tired. She wished they had come here during a proper holiday. Dad's work—he was a wildlife photographer for a number of international travel and nature magazines—meant that they were forever slinking off during school term time. It would be nice to play with some other kids in the pool rather than sit with grown-ups all the time.

The wind began to swell as they trudged back along the seafront. Tiny twisters of sand stung their legs. By the time they got back to the pale blue guest house, Fearne's long hair was matted with silica; it would take an age to wash it out.

Their room was empty. No note from Dad. No camera gear. "He must still be working," her mum said. "I guess the light is better for him at this time of day. Less harsh."

"What does he do at midday, then?" Fearne asked.

"Drink beer. Lech the local talent. I don't know."

"What about dinner?"

"If he misses it, he misses it. But I'm having a shower and a cocktail and then I'm eating seafood until it leaks out of every orifice."

"Ew, *Mum*," Fearne said, but she couldn't keep the smile from her mouth.

They showered together, her mother helping to get the worst of the sand out of her hair. She seemed to grow a little wistful at the sight of her daughter's coltish body, and she complimented her on her long, slender legs.

"Better legs than me," her mother said. "But I've got the best bust, my little cherry stone."

Fearne felt herself reddening again. Her mother seemed to want to steer whatever discussion they had towards talk of her burgeoning sexuality. *Got any boyfriends? Kissed anyone yet?* and once, mortifyingly, *Ever masturbated?*

She exited the shower and dried herself quickly, then dressed before her mother reappeared to pry more about the curves and bumps that were making themselves known in her body. She felt pulled in too many directions at once. Sometimes, she would come to, as if from a trance, to find herself playing with dolls, or reading a comic aimed at children much younger than she. She'd push these things away from her, guilty, embarrassed, but sad too, as if acknowledging that in her resting state she wanted to remain a girl; hormones seemed to be taking the decision out of her hands.

At the window she peered into the distance and wished the sea closer. Her mother said, when she was a child, the tide hardly ever went out beyond the old, weather-bleached groynes. But in the last decade or so, the waters around the coast had steadily retreated, and the shape of the island had changed to the point where all the maps had to be radically redrawn. Doom-mongers talked of fatally damaged eco-systems, unlikely to repair themselves again. The concept of four seasons already seemed like some nostalgic joke.

Where are you, Dad? she asked herself, craning her neck to look up and down the front. She wondered if he was off beachcombing. That irritated her, because he knew how much she loved to do that, and they'd spent many happy hours in each other's company trying to outdo each other. She wondered, not for the first time, if there was some trouble—some serious trouble—going on between her mum and dad. Over the years there'd been some nasty back and forth, but it had mostly been hot air. They loved each other, she was watertight sure of that—although she couldn't for the life of her understand what it was about her mother that secured such devotion. No, his departing like this must be connected to his work. He'd said as much, hadn't he, before they set off? Busy, busy, busy. Lot on my plate. No rest for the wicked. Any heartache lost to the easy roll call of clichés.

They ate outside at one of the restaurants that boasted an extension on the esplanade. It was too cold, but her mother insisted. Under a canopy that flapped alarmingly they ordered clams and swordfish and hot, garlicky lobster tails.

"How are the fishermen finding this if the sea is receding? Where are the boats?"

"Maybe it's from the freezers," her mum explained, hoovering up a fantail of opaque white flesh.

The salt on the back of Fearne's hand was like the smear of dust transferred to a fingertip upon handling a moth. She dipped her tongue into it.

"Don't do that," her mother said. "That salt...you don't know what's in it."

The waiter was a young man with high cheekbones, a half-mask of light stubble and a tattoo in burgundy and ochre that peeked out from the rolled-up sleeve of his shirt. He kept yawning and rubbing his eyes. Her mother allowed Fearne a diluted glass of the white Burgundy she was washing her bivalves down with. Each time she heard a boot gritting on the pavement she lifted her head in case it was Dad, but he didn't appear. Her mother flirted with the waiter, her chin slicked with butter. Fearne wanted to be in her room listening to music through her headphones, reading her book, anything else.

"Do you live around here?" her mother asked the waiter. Fearne turned her face away.

"Yeah, just up the road in Mapleton. But I'm aching to get out. I'm busting a nut. I don't trust the power station. I don't trust the sea. This place is a ghost town and nobody here realises that yet."

"What's wrong with the sea?" Fearne asked. Her mother arched her eyebrow, evidently amused that she'd engaged with another human being, and a boy at that.

"It's like a tsunami, only in super slow-motion. Tide goes out. Comes back with interest. I don't want to be around come that reckoning."

"Oh don't be so apocalyptic," Mum said. "Guy your age. You shouldn't be worrying about stuff."

"Yeah well," he said, "I've been here all my life. I'm not just a tourist." He seemed about to say more but he pressed his lips together and collected plates instead. "How was the meal?"

"Lovely," Fearne said. "What's wrong with the power station?"

"Nothing," said the waiter. "Guy my age? I shouldn't be worrying about stuff."

"People around here," her mum continued (Fearne recognised the drawl that alcohol lent her voice), "and I've heard them, still talk about the sea as if it should be placated. As if we should be sacrificing our first-born sons or daughters. Flinging them piecemeal into the waves, like rubby-dubby. Like chum. What do you think of that?"

"You don't have to worry," he said, smiling at Fearne. She felt her cheeks burn. "Your daughter is no child."

"She's my little girl," her mum said, archly. "She always will be. My baby."

For a moment Fearne thought her mother might cry, but she cut it off with another gulp from her wine glass. Thirteen years old. On the cusp. Like this place. Her hips were becoming wider, like the bay. Her breasts were swelling, like the ocean. She felt something like the tide pulling at her insides. Childhood was something she had wanted to escape for so long, but now that time was here, she feared it. She wanted infancy back. The comfort and simplicity. The lack of confusion and doubt.

It grew so dark that it was impossible to see the sea any more. Her mother finally paid the bill and they retreated to their room, but not before Fearne had to experience the ignominy of her mother's offer to the waiter of a nightcap when he finished his shift.

She said goodnight and closed the door on her mother before she became morose and began to tearfully list her regrets, a recurring process that took hours and usually the best part of another wine bottle.

Fearne quickly pulled on her pyjamas and scrambled under the duvet. It was cold in the room; frost was spreading across the windowpanes. It was more like the Sahara here these days; hot afternoons and bitter nights. She switched on the little portable TV and turned down the sound. News items showed boats stranded in motionless seas where slob ice had turned the water to sludge. She wished she had the shell so she could trace its patterns with her fingertips. Though sleep was some time off, she felt on the edge of a terrible dream. Every surface was hard and flat yet refused the weight of her gaze. Her view slid away and would only hold when it met that uncertain, treacly shift of thickening water.

Things moved within it, agonisingly slowly, black mouths agape in a bid to swallow oxygen that was no longer there. Now sleep was settling, but she had not recognised the shift from wakefulness. She dreamed of creatures beyond the limits of vision regurgitating the brittle bones of animals they had eaten, the slurry of waste filling the seas, condensing them like cornflour added to gravy. Everything was cold and brittle. She thought of the waiter, but even his wolfish beauty was mottled with bruises of frostbite.

She touched herself in the night and she was like a cast of sand, fragile, friable. She was scared to explore more forcibly in case parts of her caved in. At one point, when sleep was secure inside her, she tried to cry out but her throat seemed filled with ice.

Unable to find sleep, she crept into her parents' room. Her father had still not returned. Her mother was snoring, and in last night's clothes, make-up smudged on her face and turning a patch of the pillow the colour of tea. She saw that the wardrobe was opened and feared that her father had returned while they were asleep to pack his things and abandon them. Even as she moved towards the crack she knew that would not be the case; he would never do that, no matter how bad things became.

There: his suitcase. She felt guilty to have doubted him. She went to it and pulled it open, not worried about the racket she was making; after wine, her mother could sleep through noise that would have alarmed patients in a hospital for the deaf. Her relief was short-lived, here it was: evidence that her dad had been treasure-hunting without her. The base of the suitcase was gritty with sand. Within it sat objects he had acquired. Intricately patterned shells and polished stones and odd pieces of bleached wood.

She took a handful of them back to her bedroom and studied them in the moonlight. They were strange, jointed things; strange globular things. They hinted and haunted, and she fell asleep with their smooth hollows beneath her fingers, and dreamed of buried skeletons scrabbling through the soil for a gulp of air.

She was wakened by the sound of seagulls shrieking outside the window. She watched a pair wheel around a woman trying to fend them off from the baguette she was carrying under her arm. Last night's trinkets seemed ordinary now. Whatever mystery and magic the night had suffused them with was gone. She still could not iden-tify them, though, in this hard, unflattering light.

She went to wake her mother, but thought it would be much nicer to do it with croissants. Checking her money, she dressed and slipped on her shoes. The bakery was part of a row of shops set back from the road behind a narrow buffer of parking spaces slowly being adopted by weeds. There were no cars. She saw someone move behind the large window of the bakery, a ponderous figure now collecting up the display of cakes, pastries and tarts arranged lovingly on silver trays and bone china platters. Salt caulked the corners of the windows. Drifts of it created brackets at the foot of the door. The name on the awning had been bleached to invisibility.

She reached the bakery just as he was flipping the OPEN sign around to CLOSED. He saw her and stood aside to let her in. The bell tinkled and she was put in mind of icicles dropping to the path at the angry slam of a door.

"Oh," she said, "am I too late?"

"No, no," he said. His lips were chapped and there were shrouds of dry, white skin on his fingertips. Sleep was collected in the corners of his eyes like sticky wads of pollen. "I have a couple of customers in the morning, but that's pretty much it. I was going to shut up shop and get on with my jigsaw puzzle."

"I just wanted two croissants," she said.

"Two croissants it is, young lady."

She breathed an internal sigh of relief when he pulled on a pair of latex gloves to handle the bread.

"Holiday?" he asked.

"Kind of. My dad's taking photographs for a magazine. It's his job."

"Nice. Although nothing much to photograph here, wouldn't you agree?"

She nodded her head. "It's for a geographical magazine, I think. Rugged coast."

"Everyone's leaving," he said, appearing not to hear her. He placed the croissants in a paper bag and tenderly twisted it shut. It was warm in her hands. "It used to be a busy little place, this. But now all the windows are getting boarded up. People are trying to sell their properties. The sand and the salt are coming. It'll bury us, you watch. We're all going to sleep."

"You're still here."

"Not for long. Business is terrible. I'm going to be out by the end of the year. I can retire, at least. I'm going to go north and help my brother. He keeps bees. Makes his own honey."

She felt bad now that she had not ordered more food, but she only had so many pennies. He took them from her now and let them cascade from his dry fingers into the open mouth of the cash register. For some reason she thought of sacrifices.

"Seaside towns die when the sea disappears," the man said, his voice edged with sorrow. For a moment she thought he might start weeping. "It's kind of the point, isn't it? 'I do like to be beside the seaside' and all that. What have you got without the water? It's just a walled-in desert, it's little more than a sandpit."

He walked her to the door.

"Mind how you go," he said.

"What is it?" she asked, impulsively.

"Sorry?"

"Your jigsaw puzzle. Is it a big one?"

"My yes," he said. "Ten thousand pieces. I've been working on it since New Year. A picture of the harbour at Antibes." He stared out of the window at the denuded skyline. "A lively harbour. A place with real get-up-and-go. I miss the sea," he said.

"I'm sure it will return," Fearne said, but she could offer no logical reason why.

It seemed like a good moment to leave; she didn't like the mild horror that had arisen in his face at her words. She glanced back once she'd crossed the road and descended, by way of the stone steps next to her guesthouse, to the sand. He was stock-still by the window, as if stricken by the salt he had warned her about.

Her mother was not on the terrace; a glance up at their room confirmed that her curtains remained shut. She was about to head inside, eager to surprise her with the warm croissants, when her attention was drawn to a set of footsteps in the sand stretching off into the distance where the sea gleamed like a line of silver thread. She recognised immediately the tread of her father's boots, that and the size of them. *Claude Hopper*, Mum called him. And she would tease him by saying: *If only it were true what they say about men with big feet.*

The footprints moved away from the low sea wall in a large arc, as if he had been on his way back to the guesthouse only to be diverted by something at the critical moment. Perhaps he had seen something worthy of his lens; a sea bird of some sort, or an unusual play of light on the scenery. She decided to follow the prints, determined to find him and give him some grief for leaving her with her mother for so long. If she left it any later, the prints would be erased by the incessant dance of sand heated loose by the strengthening sunshine. She experienced an unpleasant image of her father becoming lost should she fail to track his prints properly, mummified by the salt winds driving in from the north.

Bit morb-o, she thought, in her mother's voice, and shuddered. *Bit morb-o, my little pineapple ring.*

At least it was not so cold now. Daylight lifted the temperature to a point where her light cardigan was adequate protection. She was worried about her dad though. He had been wearing his short-sleeved shirt yesterday. If he hadn't sought shelter by evening, he would have frozen to death.

Stop it, she thought. *He's not a child. He would have found somewhere warm.*

Of course he would. And of course he would have called to let them know. The fact that he had not done the latter kept her nagging at the likelihood of the former.

She glanced behind her at the properties along the sea front and tried to spot her mother in the window of the guesthouse. No such luck. Still asleep. She'd be amazed if Mum raised her head before lunch.

From here the guesthouse looked pretty as a button. It was only when you got up close to it that you saw the cracks and the dust and the stains. A bit like Mum, she thought, and laughed. If it had been her guesthouse, she decided, she would have given it a name. *Clouds* or *Dunes* or *Breakers*. Something to suggest the coast and holidays. Something a bit dramatic. Mrs. McKenzie, who owned it, was as dull and tired as the beige towels that hung from the rails in the bathroom. Maybe she had been enthusiastic, once upon a time. But now she could barely muster a smile when she took their breakfast orders.

Something glinted in the sand. She bent down and swept with her fingers until she had unearthed her father's watch. Now she found it hard to swallow. It was as if the ice from her dream had returned to lodge in her throat. She felt the prick of tears as fear jangled its nails up and down her back. The watch face was scoured opaque, as if the sand had been working it for years. She held it to her ear; it was still ticking. What to do? She ought to go back. She couldn't understand why, but her father couldn't have just simply dropped his watch. He must have been attacked. But his were the only set of footsteps around and there was no sign of a struggle.

"Dad!" she called out. Her voice was ripped from her lips by the eager wind, as if it had been waiting for her to say something. She felt a bizarre urge to dig in the sand, convinced that he had been sucked down. She didn't remember there being any concern about this beach in terms of quicksand, but that didn't mean there weren't any hazards.

She was weighing up the pros and cons of going on or heading back when she heard her mother calling her name.

"Mum!" She raced towards the figure, waving the watch as she weaved through the sand.

Her mother was carrying a bag laden with food. "We'll have another picnic," she said, unaware of Fearne's panic. "It might not be the warmest day of the year, but even scant sunshine means outdoor eating in my book. Right, peach fuzz?"

"Dad's gone," Fearne said. "Look!" She pressed the watch into her mother's hands. The older woman stared at it as if she had never seen it before, but it was she who had bought it for her husband, for his fiftieth birthday. Fearne reminded her of that but the perplexed look remained.

"I'm tired, grapeskin," her mother said. "Can't we just pretend to be having a nice time? Can't we just eat this bread and cheese and sit in the sand and rub sun cream on each other's shoulders?"

"But what about Dad?"

"Daddy's a rock, applesauce. This isn't the first time he's gone walkabout. I remember some time in the late '80s he went missing for a whole week."

"But his watch..."

"Maybe he dropped it. It was always a bit too big for his wrist anyway. Sweaty weather. Not concentrating. It happens. Give it to me. I'll look after it for him. Now, I thought we could nip up to those rocks over there and—"

"No!" Fearne shouted. "I'm going to find Dad. You do what you want."

"But pumpkin..."

Fearne ignored her and marched after the footprints, clutching the watch more tightly. Behind her she heard the metallic screw top lid easing off a bottle, and her mother sighing as she reclined in the sand.

Rocks crumbled from the headland towards that gleaming seam of silver, like cake fragments on to a tea-time salver. She searched frantically for some vertical stripe of colour and movement within the still, horizontal mass but could see none. The leaves on the trees were grey with salt. Then, on to the stripe of gunmetal road curling around the bluff, she saw someone running in a pair of black shorts and a lime-green vest. Even at this distance she could tell it was the waiter from the previous evening. He skipped down a set of steps, the lower risers of which were disappearing into the sand, and began jogging across the beach, presumably back towards the restaurant.

He slowed when he spotted her, and removed a pair of white buds from his ears. When he smiled at her she was emboldened to ask him what music he was listening to.

"Not music," he said. "It's a recording. Of a lecture I went to in London last month."

"What lecture?"

"Oh, just some stuff about environmental effects on communities. Behaviour. Health. That sort of thing. Linked to global warming. Or the possible dangers of nuclear power plants."

"I don't see any gills on you," she said, meaning it as a joke. He laughed, a bitter little snort, but his fingers absently went to the side of his neck and plucked at the flesh.

Fearne checked behind her; her mother was lying back in the sand, having kicked off her shoes. To her mortification, she had also removed her blouse to reveal a black satin push-up bra that shimmered in the hazy light.

"Is anything wrong?" the waiter asked. Fearne remembered the previous night he had been wearing a shirt with his name on a badge, but the badge was grimy, or the light wouldn't allow her to read what was upon it. She wanted to ask his name now, but also she wanted to know what things he had found in the sand, or whether he was tired all the time, and whether he believed that the nuclear power station was dangerous, or that there really was a tsunami poised to engulf the town.

Instead, she said: "I'm trying to find my dad. Did you see anyone, up on the road?"

"I saw nobody," the waiter said. And then: "I only run for twenty minutes in the mornings, but by the time I get to work, my hair is stiff with salt, and it's in the creases of my skin. It's like being attacked."

"You're scaring me."

"You should be scared. You know we understand more about the Moon than we do about our oceans?"

"What could we do if we knew everything?"

He stared at her. Sweat had dried to thin cakes on his skin. A muscle jumped in the shadowed flesh beneath his left eye.

"You're probably right," he said. "The sea comes back. The sea doesn't come back. Either way makes me scared to the point of shitting myself."

"I just want my dad," she said. "Will you help me?"

"I can't. I'm already late. Where's your mum?"

"You'll run straight past her if you go the way I came. So I'd run fast if I were you."

He made a strange, stilted noise, a laugh, perhaps, though hobbled by mild guilt at finding her mother a figure of amusement.

"Okay," he said. "Mind how you go. The rocks can be treacherous."

Fearne watched him settle back into the rhythm of his run, and felt her skin tighten and flush as she caught herself admiring the jut of his buttocks against his close-fitting shorts, his slender, toffee-brown calves. She turned her back on him and marched towards the collapsed headland, angry with herself for becoming sidetracked. The watch in her fist was hot. Her father needed her and she had chosen instead to flirt with a guy who had not one iota of interest in her.

She reached the rocks ten minutes later. At some point there would have been pools here, little bowls of trapped seawater where kiddies would poke around with their nets, hoping to capture a stranded tiddler, or a crab. Now they were only tinder-dry crucibles littered with the translucent bones of sea creatures she could not identify. They reminded her of glass noodles; of thin, fractured patterns in puddles of ice. Some of the creatures seemed deformed, and she thought of what the waiter (Eric, was it? Eddie?) had said about the nuclear power plant. They used seawater as a cheap, readily available coolant, apparently. What came in was eventually discharged. She imagined water warmed by the reactor core going back into the ocean. She wondered if salt water meant that corrosion was a problem. She thought of all that water flushed with scintillas of uranium; irradiated fish spawning for generations. Imperfections upon imperfections. There might come a future where the fish returned to the land to avenge their crippled ancestors.

Maybe they were already in the process. She imagined a great piscine army jealously drawing back the waves. A power station without coolant could not survive for long, and she guessed uranium did not simply have an OFF switch.

Too many prawns before bed, she thought. *How shellfish of me.*

She picked a way through the potholes, looking out for any striking counterpoint to the dun landscape. She found a shoe as she was making her way down the side of a rock scarred with what looked like a million tiny ash-white limpets. Was it her dad's shoe? She couldn't be sure. It was big enough, but it was badly damaged: leather hung like a flap of torn skin from the vamp. Dried blood ringed the collar. She called out for him again but her voice was as dry and cracked as the scenery.

On the other side of the fallen shoulder of land, a bay stretched away to what looked like marshlands, and a narrow, stunted fringe of trees with weather-beaten canopies like back-combed hair. Salt made Christmas of everything. No figures here, though Fearne could see the marks Eric (Ernie? Is the name Ernest still going?) had made in the sand with his prissy gait before angling up on to the bluff.

There were no buildings here either, save a small wooden hut that might have served as a coastguard's retreat but was now dilapidated, its door wailing grittily in the breeze. She approached it anyway. Inside she found a chair with its vinyl seat torn, sunburned foam frothing from it like fat from an opened gut. A newspaper had been whitened to illegibility. Ink from a pen had oozed across a page creating a thought bubble of furious black. The sound of something tapping or flapping against the wood at the back of the hut made her think of restless sails knocking against masts in deserted harbours. The beat matched that of her heart, and, she imagined, of the tide creaming against a shore many miles away. She remembered wiggling her toes in the crashing waves at anonymous beaches all over the world. Her father with a Nikon in his hand. She remembered a holiday—an assignment—when she was constantly worrying about her parents. It was around the time she began to understand what mortality was. After the reassurances, after the cuddles, her father—never one for sentimentality—had taken her for a walk along the beach.

"The waves are like us, Fearne," he told her. "They move through their short lives placidly, unnoticed, but at the end, near death, they gather pace; they struggle and roar. Never think that death is easy, sugar lump. The body might be tired and old, but it fights like fury. It does not go gentle."

The hasp of the padlock that had kept this hut closed was shattered; anything of value was long gone. She closed her eyes. The smell of the vinyl from hot days gone by had remained in the air. There was a smell too of burnt dust, and of skin that has been touched by the sunshine.

When the tapping became more of an irritation than she could cope with, she stepped outside and walked around to the rear. The rocks had reached this far in their collapse from the promontory. They formed a loose circle. She found her father within it, like a fragment trapped in a ring of teeth. Something had been at him in the night; most of his face was missing. She stared at the pale skin where his watch had been. The wind blew the fastener on his camera bag against the shed's rim joist. She watched that for a few minutes, until the numbness inside her felt too much like the frost creeping across her bedroom windowpanes. Sand was shifting over her feet, and she struggled to free them. She moved away and the horizon was suddenly closer, as if viewed through binoculars. The sea was returning.

Fearne hurried back the way she had come, and only when she hit the shield of the headland did she realise that she was crying. She pressed the heels of her hands against her eyes and wiped her nose. The surf was alive. It did not move in the way those waves from her childhood had moved. There was no rhythm or poetry to it. It was a shambling collapse, filled with angles and shadows: were they fins? Tentacles? Teeth? She thought she saw a serrated hook on the end of what looked like pistoning white muscle unsheathed from a tube of blood-red chitin. She thought she saw something globular turn in on itself, revealing a skirt of nacreous tissue, like oyster flesh hanging off a bed of shells. The water billowed and foamed with the *exuviae* of a billion things either dead, or grown too big for what had housed them. The sound of the sea was nothing that she recalled. No ozone crash and hiss; no skitter and chuckle of surf on pebbles. This was a sickly slithering, a jumble of keratin and collagen, a slick of ink and membrane and cartilage. She thought she saw remnants of ancient meals on the barbs and claws of what thrashed beneath the surface. But she could not concentrate on them. They looked too much like fingers. Too much like the things that she'd found in the base of her father's suitcase. Her eyes would not fasten on the eyes that fastened all too readily upon her: they were too soulless, too intent. There were too many of them.

Her mother was half-asleep, singing snatches of a song half-remembered from the radio. Sand had claimed her to the groin. It played in the pleats and crevices and wrinkles of her flesh. Her lips made a ring of dry white elastic; her tongue was a forgotten bivalve on a half-shell, desiccating in the sun.

The perils of the cockle harvest. The collapse of a tunnel bored through a dune with cheap red plastic and tiny hands. Quicksand. *A man was dragged from the pier.* Tsunami. Riptide. *The shark attack occurred in just three feet of water.* Bodies still missing. You'd be forgiven to believe that such things as accidents did not occur.

She moved toward the water and her pace increased. She felt herself turning brittle under the cold stare of what shivered just beyond that frothing black tide.

The beach was no place for a child.

KURT FAWVER

MARROWVALE

KURT FAWVER is a writer of horror, weird fiction and dark fantasy. His short fiction has appeared in publications such as *The Magazine of Fantasy & Science Fiction*, *Strange Aeons*, the *Lovecraft eZine*, *Weird Tales* and *Nightscript*. He has also released one collection of short stories, Forever, in Pieces (Villipede Publications, 2013), and his non-fiction has been published in periodicals such as *Thinking Horror* and the *Journal of the Fantastic in the Arts*.

Fawver holds a Ph.D. in literature and teaches at a large state university where, every semester, he tries to impart to his students the necessity of horror.

"The primary inspiration for my story was my hometown," he explains, "which, like the eponymous 'Marrowvale', is an unassuming, slowly eroding backwater village nestled in central Pennsylvania. The people there are largely xenophobic and highly protective of their customs and culture—a culture that, above all else, revels in tromping about the wilderness (whether to hunt game, go camping, ride all-terrain vehicles, or hold alcohol-fuelled bonfire parties).

"Growing up, I always suspected that the people of my hometown were belligerent to outsiders because they were hiding some sort of deep, dark secret—maybe about themselves, maybe about their town. This secret would most naturally manifest itself in the wilderness and be latently (if not openly) hostile toward anything from the 'outside' world.

"'Marrowvale' provided an opportunity to glimpse such secrets, and to explore the uneasy insularity that binds together small, rural towns like the one I grew up in."

From the unpublished manuscript of *The Candle-Lit World: A Travelogue of Unusual Halloween Traditions* by Charlotte Halloran

Entry: Marrowvale, Pennsylvania, U.S.A.

DEEP IN THE forgotten foothills of central Pennsylvania lies the impoverished, weather-beaten town of Marrowvale. It's a speck on the map—little more than one nameless bar and a dozen enfeebled, paint-stripped houses wheezing toward demolition. Barely what you could even call a "town". Surrounded by dark, rolling forests and tattooed with fallow cornfields, Marrowvale impresses passers-through—if it impresses them at all—only as a fleeting image of exploded dreams and withered hopes. It's the sort of place where America has worn itself to a nub, the sort of place where "living" and "dying" are the same word, the sort of place that the future has stopped visiting.

Within this decrepit hamlet reside thirty-three men, women, and children—each and every one a crumbling watchtower standing sentinel over the remains of a savaged kingdom, each and every one refusing to accept that the battle for their tiny hometown was lost decades before they were even born. These are people the outside world might call "rustics", "yokels", or "sons and daughters of the soil". They wear wrinkled, sweat-stained flannel shirts with crusted jeans and speak in a slow, distant manner. Many struggle with the bottle. Even more struggle with obesity. They are people who hunt deer and squirrels and even groundhogs for food and work themselves into early graves. Their industries are the industries of sawdust and grease and heavy lifting. They express little concern for the world beyond their valley because the world certainly expresses no concern for them.

On its surface, Marrowvale doesn't seem the sort of place that I would have visited for this book. As small and relatively remote as it is, it doesn't seem like the sort of place anyone would visit for *any* reason. But Marrowvale conceals an inexplicable and, if I'm being honest, terrifying Halloween tradition that few outsiders ever witness.

In my last book, *Burying Ourselves: Funeral Practices Across the World*, I'd mentioned in my epilogue that I was thinking about writing a future volume on the topic of Halloween. As it so happened, a fifteen year-old girl who lived in Marrowvale—one Kristina Taylor Pittlebach—had read that book and decided to e-mail me about her hometown, a tiny nowhereville with what she claimed was *a super weird and freaky thing that we all do at Halloween*. She said that I absolutely had to come and see it; she said no one but the people of Marrowvale knew it happened.

Of course my curiosity was piqued. I responded to Kristina and asked if she could provide any more details, stressing that if the tradition really was out of the ordinary, I'd be happy to swing by her town and check it out. To my query, she sent a grainy black and white photo of two dozen people posed in graduated rows, as though they were taking a class picture. Everyone in the photo wore strange cylindrical helmets that entirely engulfed their heads. A chaos of jagged lines lay engraved about the circumference of each helmet. Where one would have expected eyeholes, a pair of spiked, elongated pyramids protruded from every face. I wasn't sure how anyone could see out of the things. Considering that there were no visible nose or mouth apertures, I wasn't sure how anyone could breathe in them, either.

To accompany her photo, Kristina wrote only one cryptic line: *We all have to wear them to the meeting place every year.*

As I stared at the picture and imagined an entire town wearing headgear that resembled 1950s sci-fi robots by way of a medieval torture device, a deep sense of unease washed over me. I couldn't quite pinpoint what it was about the helmets or masks or whatever they were that set my nerves on edge; I could only say that they didn't *feel right*. They didn't give the impression of objects any sane human would ever design, let alone want to wear. It was exactly the kind of weirdness I was in search of, and it convinced me to include Marrowvale in my Halloween itinerary.

To reach Marrowvale, I had to fly into Harrisburg and then drive a rental car north-west from the city for almost two hours. Along my route, I encountered a profusion of nameless villages without so much as a single working stoplight or chain convenience store. I passed farmhouses and barns that, while still clearly operational, were flaking and splintering into nothingness. I drove over surprisingly steep hills cowering in the shadow of even more surprisingly steep mountains. And everywhere, everywhere I was met with autumnal foliage not bright and inflamed like the leaves in more northerly climes, but the same withered brown as rotting fruit and ancient parchment.

When I finally rolled into Marrowvale the day before Halloween, I was greeted by two sights: one, the town bar—a sagging two-storey Gable Front house which was only distinguishable as a bar because of the neon Coors and Budweiser signs that hung in its dusty windows—and two, a shirtless old man riding a lawn mower on the berm of the road.

As I neared him, the old man pulled his mower into the gravel parking lot that fronted the bar to let me pass. But I had no interest in passing. I, too, needed to visit the bar. I swerved in behind him and collected my thoughts. Curious as to the people of the town, I sat in the car and stared at the man. He turned in his seat and stared back. His right eye was entirely missing and he made no attempt to cover over the injury with a patch or a glittering prosthetic. His gaze split my attention in equal halves. On one side, a hollow gaped wide and deep and beckoned its viewer to crawl inside and explore a vacancy that might easily extend far beyond the reaches of the old man's skull. On the other, an electric blue eye shot forth concentrated, penetrating scrutiny that felt as though it could carve through any length of time and space. I wasn't sure which side I should meet.

As I stared in fascination, the old man's cracked, blistered lips tightened and quivered. It seemed he was about to break into either tears or a murderous rage. He shook his head once, slowly, then swivelled forward, threw open the mower's throttle, and motored away.

Clearly, Marrowvale wasn't in the business of tourism. I jumped from the car and hurried into the bar.

In Kristina's first email, she mentioned that the bar's owner—a Mr. Dale Schwartz—kept a collection of what she termed "Halloween Meeting Treats" in one of the bar's upstairs rooms. I wanted to check out this collection before I visited the Pittlebachs, so that I wouldn't arrive on their doorstep entirely ignorant of their traditions. So the bar was my first stop.

Most likely due to the fact that it was only three o'clock in the afternoon, the rustic watering hole sat empty. The hardwood floor of the place was scuffed and cracked and its boards groaned under my every step. I counted eight tables set up around the main bar area, but I doubted they were ever all filled at the same time. Behind the bar slouched a doughy man with a shaggy walrus moustache and heavy circles draped beneath his eyes. He glanced up from the magazine in his hands—a yellowed *Reader's Digest*—and asked, slowly, as if uncertain how to approach someone who wasn't a regular, "What can I getcha?"

I asked the man if he was the owner of the bar and, when he hesitantly nodded, I launched into my journalism routine. I explained that I was a writer from Chicago and that I was writing a piece on Marrowvale and its unique Halloween rituals for an upcoming book. I said I needed to talk to people around town, to glean a sense of who they were, what they believed, why they did what they did. When you tell people you're writing about them or their homes, most crack wide open like clams in a steamer, ready to regale you with embellished anecdotes and personal details that you wouldn't otherwise be able to touch. But Mr. Schwartz didn't spill his mind.

He simply closed the *Reader's Digest* and stared at me in much the same way the old man on the lawn mower had.

"So you want to see the museum, then?" he asked. I nodded and, trying another tactic, slid a twenty onto the bar.

He stared at the bill, eyes narrowed, then pushed it back toward me.

"Money doesn't have much value here," he said. "But let me show you what does."

He hobbled out from his post and beckoned me to follow. I patted the switchblade in my pocket—a gift from my father on my four-teenth birthday and a precautionary tool I always carry when I'm in unfamiliar territory—and fell in behind Mr. Schwartz. I didn't sense any menace from the barkeep, but I've read too many police blotters to simply accept invitations from strange men without reservation.

Mr. Schwartz led me up a flight of rickety stairs to a darkened hallway and, from there, shuffled into a small adjoining room lit by a single dingy lamp. Dust motes swirled in his wake like minuscule galaxies. I burst through them, into the room, and was instantly mesmerised by the assortment of objects laid out before me. On three long tables covered in white crushed velvet and set up in a "U" formation rested things for which I had no name. Here, a thing that looked like a leaf, but with a holographic sheen and a thick-ness closer to cardboard. There, a thing that resembled a butcher-knife but pulsed like a still-living heart. Here, a dull blue sphere cut in half, with hundreds of glittering, black needle-like shards protruding from its core. There, a metal square scoured with jagged lines similar to those etched upon the helmets in Kristina's picture. Here, an inverted pyramid with drooping points that, defying gravity and physics, somehow stood upon its bottom vertex. There, a thing that mixed equal parts dollbaby and viral microbe, limbs contorting into spirals and wavy ropes.

The room was filled with craftsmanship and artistry, certainly, but it was craftsmanship and artistry of a completely unknown form. Each and every object in the room looked out of place, felt out of place, and caused my stomach to clench with an anxiety I'd never experienced in my entire life. It was like suddenly waking up in a room you've never been inside in a building you've never visited in a city inhabited only by the machinery of a long-forgotten people.

I stood gaping for several minutes, then finally asked, "What *are* these?"

Mr. Schwartz's eyes narrowed. "You don't know? They're treats from the meetings."

"Treats, yes," I said. "But what are each of them supposed to represent? What are they used for?"

Mr. Schwartz shrugged. "I try not to find out. It's for the best."

"And why is that?" I asked.

"Because," Mr. Schwartz said, fingers gently tracing the outline of one of the objects, "people who find out tend to end up in a bad way."

"A bad way?" I pressed, though my imagination supplied plenty of horrifying imagery. I pictured my head locked inside one of the bizarre helmets from Kristina's photo.

Mr. Schwartz nodded and tapped his forehead. "Up here."

I murmured an assent and let the subject drop. I didn't want to talk about the objects anymore, and I certainly didn't want to be in the same room as them any longer. I was a journalist, a professional writer. I should have been overcome with curiosity. Yet, ridiculous though it may sound, I was beginning to feel disconnected from my own time and place, from my own thoughts and feelings. Terror rose up in my chest and I pinched the back of my hand to make sure I was still corporeal. I had a fleeting suspicion that somehow I might not be, even though I could feel the softness of my flesh twist in my fingers.

I hurriedly thanked Mr. Schwartz for the opportunity to view the collection and ran to my car. I sped away from Marrowvale and refused to glance in the rear-view mirror. Thirty miles and a separate world later, I parked at the shabby motel where I'd made a reservation. I checked in as quickly as possible and, forsaking my luggage, dashed inside my room. I bolted the door and collapsed on the bed—a bed that, while foreign and hard and tinged with the unmistakable scent of mildew, still reflected something crucially human, something that had been utterly absent in Mr. Schwartz's "museum".

Before long, sprawled on the bed, I fell into a deep slumber and dreamed.

In my dreams, I found myself in a stately edifice crammed full of glass display cases that housed two distinct types of artefacts: broken, twisted mirrors of ornate design and tiny human beings pinned to foam boards like so many insects. I wandered among those cases for the rest of the night, half-frightened to examine their contents but compelled to see the entire exhibit.

I also felt another presence in the edifice—a distant, ever-vigilant thing, like a night watchman at a bank of security cameras. I worried that I might be as broken and twisted as the mirrors, as pinned and skewered as the tiny people; I worried that the vigilant thing might see fit to include me in the displays. And so I tried to run from the edifice. I fled through thousands of rows of display cases, but encountered no end, no exit. I couldn't escape the exhibit. I could examine the mirrors and take notes on the characteristics of the little people forever, but I could never leave. It appeared that I was inextricably trapped in my own curiosity. I threw myself to the floor, pounded the hard surface beneath me, and screamed myself into the morning.

The next afternoon found me in a better state of mind. Although it had taken a morning's worth of writing, two hot showers, and a perfectly grilled hamburger at a quaint roadside diner called The Country Kettle to expunge my previous night's dreams, I was prepared to return to Marrowvale to witness its Halloween festivities. I'd arranged to meet Kristina Pittlebach and her family before the celebration began and to accompany them to the mysterious "meeting" that Kristina refused to discuss in any detail. In the course of our exchanges, Kristina had also promised to let me examine "the heads"—her term for the bizarre helmets in the old photograph—and to interview any member of her family if I so desired.

As I drove toward Marrowvale, enthusiasm leaped beneath my skin. Something about the chill in the air shouted promise. I felt close to a discovery of monumental proportion, even though I wasn't quite sure what that discovery might be. By the time I reached the Pittlebach homestead, a ranch-style house missing half its siding, my heart was racing.

I parked in the Pittlebachs' driveway, which was gravel stained black by used motor oils, and made my way to their door. Innumerable rusted yard tools and shards of broken lawn statuary littered the path between driveway and door. I had to step carefully so as to not trip and impale myself on an ancient blade or the point of an eroded jockey. When I finally arrived on the Pittlebachs' doorstep, a short, preternaturally pale girl with fiery red hair was hanging out over the threshold. I thought perhaps I'd stumbled across a wayward fey princess.

"Ms. Halloran," the girl said, voice surprisingly grave. "I'm Kristina. I've been waiting." She ushered me inside and slammed the door behind me.

We exchanged pleasantries—the usual "Oh, it's so good to finally meet yous"—and she introduced me to the rest of her family, none of whom seemed pleased at my visit. Her father, a wisp of a man with a long, straggly beard, stared at me without speaking. Her mother, a buxom lady with a pronounced harelip, smiled and nodded. Puffy red rings beneath her eyes told of either seasonal allergies or a story of recent sadness. Kristina's grandmother, a squat woman with uncontrollable tremors, was the only one to actually greet me with words.

"Hello," the old woman said, "I hear you're a writer. You know, writers have to be careful. Some things don't want to be written. And some things simply *can't* be written. You don't want to end up lost forever, dear."

Kristina pulled me away, clearly embarrassed, and whispered, "Everyone around here is like Grandma. Especially this time of year." She hurried me into the basement—a space that looked as though a flea market had exploded within it—and drew my attention to a gun safe that stood against one wall. Kristina fiddled with its dial and, after a few spins, its door squeaked open. She stepped back to let me peer inside. There, setting on makeshift shelves, were four of the helmets I'd seen in Kristina's photo. For no reason I could have possibly explained, my stomach twisted in knots.

Struggling to maintain my composure, I leaned in and examined the headpieces. None of them had any forging marks or soldered seams or any other signs of metallurgy. Instead, they seemed almost organic, like an insect's carapace, only composed of a material more rigid than chitin. In colour, they were a shade I'd never seen, a hue that shifted from bronze to grey and grey to bronze depending on the angle at which it reflected light. I didn't want to touch one, but I knew I had no choice. I ran a finger along the inscrutable etchings—which, up close, reminded me of seismograph readings or the ECGs of heart attack victims—and felt a bolt of panic crash through my chest.

I flinched away and, desperate to remain objective, asked Kristina what the helmets were supposed to represent.

She laughed. "They're not supposed to represent anything."

"Then why wear them?" I asked, breathing hard, pulse pounding.

She shrugged. "Because we have to."

"Did you make them?"

Again she laughed, as if what I'd asked was the most infantile question ever uttered.

"Of course not."

The room began to spin and sway. I stepped away from the helmets and asked if I could sit down.

Kristina nodded and led me back upstairs. Somehow, I managed to navigate my way to a chair, where I vomited and collapsed. Every nerve in my body twitched and screamed. Some atavistic code in my chromosomes told me to run, to hide. But from what? Some bizarre Halloween masks? I was too professional to allow primordial fears to erase a potential chapter in my book.

Kristina brought me a glass of water and patted my shoulder. "I guess trying one on is probably a bad idea, then," she said. "Grandma said it would be."

I shuddered at the thought of the helmet being placed upon my head, my every perception being encased in a device of such indescribable foreignness. *What would the world look like from inside?*

I wondered. *Would it even still be this world, or would it be some other place? Would the sun or the moon or the stars be recognisable inside those helmets or would they be radically contorted variations of themselves?* I sat and stared at the Pittlebachs' chipped wooden floors, contemplating both these questions and nothing at all.

After minutes, hours, or, perhaps at the very end of time itself, I shook myself from the fugue and asked Kristina, who was still sitting nearby, "When do we go to the meeting place?"

Kristina looked at me askance. "At dusk," she said. "So pretty soon."

I glanced at a window and was shocked to find the sky beginning to bruise. Had I really been inside my own head for that long?

"It's about a mile up one of the hunting paths in the hills," Kristina continued. "But are you sure you want to? I think you might be sick."

I assured Kristina that I'd be fine. I told her I occasionally experienced panic attacks—not a lie, actually—and that it just took me a while to regain my composure after I'd suffered one. I knew very well that what had happened to me in the basement couldn't be chalked up to misfiring neurons or chemical imbalances, though. Like the objects in Dale Schwartz's "museum", the helmets radiated an uncanny otherness so powerful that it warped the fabric of thought. These were not simple Halloween masks. They were something else entirely.

Before long, Kristina's father descended into the basement with a large, empty velvet sack and returned with it bulging full. As he passed, I could sense the "heads" in the bag, gazing at me with their pointed eyes.

"Time to go," Kristina's grandmother called out, spurring us into action. Mr. Pittlebach led the way and was already out the door, traipsing up a gentle, forested hill behind the Pittlebachs' house. Kristina and I followed, with her mother and grandmother lagging behind.

While we walked, Kristina asked me about my last book, about the death rituals I'd witnessed. She wanted to know if there really were places where corpses served as bird food, where people danced with the deceased, where the bereaved amputated their own fingers to more physically approximate the loss of a loved one. I said yes, and that I'd even watched a young boy raised from his grave.

Kristina nodded. "I saw something like that once, when I was really little. A kid forgot his mask."

"And what happened to him?" I asked.

Kristina shrugged. I wasn't sure whether she didn't remember, didn't know, or didn't want to tell me. We walked on, in silence.

With Kristina ensconced in quiet contemplation, I sensed an opening.

"So what *are* the heads?" I asked. "The masks?"

Kristina stopped and turned to look for her mother and grand-mother. Softly, in the near darkness, she said, "Depends on what you're willing to believe, I guess."

"What do you believe?"

Softer yet, "That in the right time and place anything is possible, though most things are inconceivable due to the complexity and magnitude of their horror."

I smiled, but I doubted that Kristina could have seen me. She'd quoted from my book. I'd been referring to the varied and innu-merable ways we could die. I didn't think she'd meant it in quite the same way.

"Why did you ask me to come here?" I pressed. "I don't get the sense that your fellow townsfolk are too eager to share their traditions."

Kristina shrugged again. Such a teenager.

"I think someone like you should see it. I think someone like you might understand. People think nothing happens here. People think this is one of America's many buttholes. But it's so much stranger than that. I think everyone should know."

Hometown pride. Who would've guessed?

I reached out and squeezed Kristina's arm. She jumped away, as though shocked.

Huffing, her mother and grandmother caught up to us and we continued stumbling onward.

After close to half an hour of hiking under night's silken fabric, I saw a bright light flickering within the dense forest.

"We're meeting the rest of the citizens of Marrowvale out here?" I asked. "Sort of a town festival with a bonfire and hotdogs? Something like that?"

Kristina's voice dropped into a deeper register. "Yeah," she breathed. "Something like that."

We broke through a copse of trees and entered a field strewn with boulders the size and shape of which I'd never experienced. Each boulder stood twenty or thirty feet high and had been chiselled into complex star-shapes that resembled Goliath anemones and sea urchins. Near the centre of the cluster of boulders raged a fire and around the fire gathered the people of Marrowvale, all of whom had already donned their "heads". Everyone stood silent and motionless and I shuddered at the spectacle.

Kristina motioned to an alcove in one of the megaliths. "You should probably wait here," she whispered. "Try to stay out of sight. Some of our neighbours don't know that I invited you to the meeting place and they might not like it."

My throat tightened. "I'm a shadow," I said, probably even less convincing to Kristina than to myself. I crawled into the alcove and gave Kristina a thumbs-up. Satisfied, she strode to the circled townsfolk and received a helmet from a person I assumed was her father. When her mother and grandmother passed by, the older lady paused for a moment. She glanced at my hiding spot and said, very casually, "If I were you, I'd sneak off now. They'll know you're here, and they won't allow it. They don't have a head for you and yours isn't going to be good enough." Then away she puttered.

I crouched between the star-megalith's legs and waited, fearful in the way of a child hopelessly lost in a department store. More people arrived. The air gained a serrated chill. I counted the number congregated before me. Thirty-three. The exact population of Marrowvale.

And so it began.

When the last straggler arrived and slid a "head" over his own, the townspeople aligned themselves into a large triangle, with each side comprised of eleven individuals. Then they did nothing. They stood in the field, their fire roaring without purpose, and did nothing.

But something was happening all the same.

The air in the field suddenly grew indescribably cold and sharp. It tore at my lungs and shredded my nostrils as I breathed in. Even having lived through a handful of tornado touchdowns, I'd never felt air so hostile, so bent on eradicating me from the inside out. I brought a hand to my face and found blood leaking from my nose. At the same time the air was gaining malicious sentience, a wide dark line appeared, floating, behind the triangulated people of Marrowvale, as though a strip of reality itself had been cleanly sheared away with a razor.

I stared at the dark line, blood now flowing freely from my nose, and began to seriously consider Kristina's grandmother's advice. This wasn't a place I should be. This wasn't a place anyone but the people of Marrowvale should be—and perhaps not even them.

The dark line didn't undulate or widen or even suck us all into oblivion. It simply waited, like me, like the townspeople. Frozen. Neither alive nor dead.

I began to climb out of my alcove, blood dripping onto my jacket, my shirt. A wave of nausea pounded my abdomen and white dots spotted my vision. The air grew even colder. The thought "absolute zero" flitted around my mind.

The old lady had been right. Kristina was young, hopeful. She thought she might be able to let the outside world break into her town. Her grandmother knew better. I had to flee.

I took one last look at the dark line hovering over the good citizens of Marrowvale and what I saw set me running from the field. Somehow, from *within* the line were emerging long, whip-like arms the same odd colour and hue as the helmets. These arms ended in perfectly human hands that held out to the masked people of Marrowvale an assortment of unnameable and unclassifiable objects. Treats.

As soon as I gazed upon those spindly arms stretching out from the line, the hands so bizarrely human yet clearly not, I turned to the forest and sprinted. I wasn't a journalist or a travel writer then. I was a human fighting to remain human.

Though my thoughts came fuzzy and my vision still popped with bright dots, I managed to follow the path we'd taken to reach the field. I fell over stumps and roots, skinning my hands, bruising my knees, but the farther I crept from the dark line in the forest, the warmer the air became and the more alive I felt.

I arrived in the Pittlebachs' backyard exhausted and near the verge of collapse. My nose had stopped bleeding, so I felt sure that I could drive, that I could make my getaway. I dragged myself to the rental car and blasted away from Marrowvale. I drove for hours; I drove until my eyes drooped and I nearly ran off the road.

When I finally stopped at a large, well-lit chain motel, I asked the desk attendant where I was.

"Almost in Pittsburgh," she said. "Just ten miles out. Where are you coming from?"

I considered telling her. I considered asking her if she knew about Marrowvale. I considered not speaking at all.

"Nowhere you've ever heard of," I said, and paid for a room.

GEMMA FILES

HAIRWORK

G EMMA FILES was born in England and raised in Toronto, Canada. She won a 1999 International Horror Guild Award for Best Short Fiction for her story 'The Emperor's Old Bones', and five of her stories were adapted into episodes of *The Hunger*, an erotic horror anthology TV show produced by Tony and Ridley Scott.

Her first novel, *A Book of Tongues* from ChiZine Publications, won the 2010 Dark Scribe Magazine Black Quill Award for Best Small Press Chill; it was followed by two sequels, completing the "Hexslinger Series". She has also published two short fiction collections, two chapbooks of poetry, and a story cycle (*We Will All Go Down Together*, 2014). Her latest book, *Experimental Film*, won the Shirley Jackson Award for Best Novel of 2015.

"The minute I heard about the anthology *She Walks in Darkness*, a project specifically aimed by its editors (Paula R. Stiles and Silvia Moreno-Garcia) at re-interpreting H.P. Lovecraft's monstrously feminine characters through a slightly less male-slanted lens, I started thinking about what story I'd like to re-tell, and from whose POV.

"Naturally, my mind went to 'Medusa's Coil', because Jesus, is that a doozy: a one-two punch of racism and gynophobia combined, with what has to be the single most skeevy last line in weird fiction history, even though Lovecraft co-wrote it with Zealia Bishop (under whose name it first appeared in *Weird Tales*, two years after his death).

"One way or the other, I thought that if any one character in Lovecraft's stable deserved the opportunity to speak for herself, it was that story's Marceline Bedard de Russy. I really liked the idea of doing something similar to what Joe Lansdale did with his graphic novel adaptation of Robert E. Howard's equally dicey 'Pigeons From Hell', in which he deliberately made the characters contemporary descendants of the central family, mixed-race, almost like a living rebuke to or reflection of the tangled historical issues at the tale's heart.

"I wanted Marceline to be the revenge of generations of slaves upon their slave-owners, a karmic bitch-slap the de Russys had literally bred for themselves and still not seen coming. Because this is why we don't just let Lovecraft lapse into obscurity, from my angle: we keep him around specifically to be subverted, to look unflinchingly at the things he could only approach metaphorically. Hopefully I succeeded; if I didn't I guess we all know why, but I'm glad I had the chance to try.

"No plant can thrive without putting down roots, as nothing comes from nothing; what you feed your garden with matters, always—be it the mulched remains of other plants, or bone, or blood. The seed falls wherever it's dropped and grows, impossible to track, let alone control. There's no help for it.

"These are all simple truths, one would think, and yet, they appear to bear infinite repetition. But then, history is re-written in the recording of it, always."

"*ICI, C'EST ELLE,*" you tell Tully Ferris, the guide you've engaged, putting down a pale sepia photograph printed on pasteboard, its corners foxed with age. "Marceline Bedard, 1909—from before she and Denis de Russy met, when she was still dancing as Tanit-Isis. It's a photographic reference, similar to what Alphonse Mucha developed his commercial art pieces from; I found it in a studio where Frank Marsh used to paint, hidden in the floor. Marsh was Cubist, so his paintings tend to look very deconstructed, barely human, but this is what he began with."

Ferris looks at the *carte*, gives a low whistle. "Redbone," he says. "She a fine gal, that's for sure. Thick, sweet. And look at that hair."

"'Redbone?' I don't know this term."

"Pale, ma'am, like cream, lightish-complected—you know, high yaller? Same as me."

"Oh yes, *une métisse, bien sur.* She was cagey about her background, *la belle Marceline*, liked to preserve mystery. But the rumour was her mother came from New Orleans to Marseilles, then Paris, settling in the same area where Sarah Bernhardt's parents once lived, a Jewish ghetto; when she switched to conducting séances, she took out advertisements claiming her powers came from Zimbabwe and Babylon, darkest Africa and the tribes of Israel, equally. Thus the name: Tanit, after the Berber moon-goddess, and Isis, from ancient Egypt, the mother of all magic."

"She got something, all right. A mystery to me how she even hold her head up, that much weight of braids on top of it."

"Mmm, there was an interesting story told about Marceline's hair— that it wasn't hers at all but a wig. A wig made *from* hair, maybe even some scalp, going back a *long* time, centuries...I mean, *c'est folle* to think so, but that was what they said. Perhaps even as far *as* Egypt. Her mother's mother brought it with her, supposedly."

"Mummies got hair like that, though, don't they? Never rots. Good enough you can take DNA off it."

You nod. "And then there's the tradition of Orthodox Jewish women, Observants, Lubavitchers in particular—they cover their hair with a wig, too, a *sheitel*, so no one but their husband gets to see it. Now, Marceline was in no way Observant, but I can see perhaps an added benefit to her *courtesanerie* from allowing no one who was not *un amant*, her intimate, to see her uncovered. The wig's hair might look much the same as her own, only longer; it would save her having to...relax it? *Ça ira?*"

"Yeah, back then, they'd've used lye, I guess. Nasty. Burn you, you leave it on too long."

"*Exactement.*"

Tully rocks back a bit on his heels, gives a sigh. "Better start off soon, you lookin' to make Riverside 'fore nightfall—we twenty miles up the road here from where the turn-off'd be, there was one, so we gotta drive cross Barker's Crick, park by the pass, then hike the rest. Not much left still standin', but I guess you probably know that, right?"

"Mmm. I read testimony from 1930, a man trying for Cape Girardeau who claimed he stayed overnight, spoke to Antoine de Russy. Not possible, of course, given the time—yet he knew many details of the events of 1922, without ever reading or hearing about them, previously. Or so he said."

"The murders, the fire?"

You nod.

"Yeah, well—takes all sorts, don't it? Ready to go, ma'am?"

"If you are, yes."

"Best get to it, then—be dark sooner'n you think and we sure don't wanna be walkin' 'round in *that.*"

A mourning sampler embroidered in fifteen different de Russy family members' hair once hung upstairs, just outside my husband's childhood bedroom door: such a pretty garden scene, at first glance, soft and gracious, depicting the linden-tree border separating river and dock from well-manicured green lawn and edging flowerbeds—that useless clutter of exotic blooms, completely unsuited to local climate or soil, which routinely drank up half the fresh water diverted from the slave quarter's meagre vegetable patch. The lindens also performed a second function, of course, making sure de Russy eyes were never knowingly forced to contemplate what their *negres* called the bone-field, a wet clay sump where slaves' corpses were buried at night and without ceremony, once their squeamish masters were safely asleep. Landscaping as *maquillage*, a false face over rot, the skull skin-hid. But then, we all look the same underneath, no matter our outward shade, *ne c'est pas?*

In 1912, I took Denis' hand at a Paris *soirée* and knew him immediately for my own blood, from the way the very touch of him made
my skin crawl—that oh-so-desirable *peau si-blanche*, olive-inflected
like old ivory, light enough to shine under candle-flame. I had my
Tanit-wig on that night, coils of it hung down in tiers far as my
hips, my thighs, far enough to brush the very backs of my bare
knees; I'd been rehearsing most of the day, preparing to chant the
old rites in Shona while doing what my posters called a "Roodmas
dance" for fools with deep pockets. Frank Marsh was there, too, of
course, his fishy eyes hung out on strings—he introduced Denis to
me, then pulled me aside and begged me once again to allow him
to paint me "as the gods intended", with only my ancestors' hair for
modesty. But I laughed in his face and turned back to Denis instead,
for here was the touch of true fate at last, culmination of my mother's
many prayers and sacrifices. Mine to bend myself to him and bind
him fast, make him bring me back to Riverside to do what must
be done, just as it'd been Frank's unwitting destiny to make that
introduction all along and suffer the consequences.

Antoine de Russy liked to boast he kept Denis unworldly and I
must suppose it to be so, for he never saw me with my wig off, my
Tanit-locks set by and the not-so-soft fuzz of black which anchored
it on display. As he was raised to think himself a gentleman, it would
never have occurred to Denis to demand such intimacies. By the
time his father pressed him to do so, I had him well-trained:
Something odd about that woman, boy, I heard him whisper more
than once, before they fell out. *Makes my blood run cold to see it.
For all she's foreign-born, I'd almost swear I know her face...*

Ha! As though the man had no memory, or no mirrors. Yet, I
was far too fair for the one, I suspect, and far too... different, though
in "deceitfully slight proportion"—to quote that Northerner who
wrote your vaunted *testimony*—for the other. It being difficult to
acknowledge your own features in so alien a mirror, not even when
they come echoing back to you over generations of mixed blood,
let alone on your only son's arm.

You got in touch with Tully last Tuesday, little seeker, securing his services via Bell's machine—its latest version, any rate—and by yesterday, meanwhile, you'd flown here from Paris already, through the air. Things move so *fast* these days and I don't understand the half of it; it's magic to me, more so than magic itself, that dark, mechanical force I hold so close to my dead heart. But then, this is a problem with where I am now, *how* I am; things come to me unasked-for, under the earth, out of the river. Knowledge just reveals itself to me, simple and secret, the same way soil is disturbed by footfalls or silt rises to meet the ripple: no questions and no answers, likewise. Nothing explained outright, ever.

That's why I don't know your name, or anything else about you, aside from the fact you think in a language I've long discarded and hold an image of me in your mind, forever searching after its twin: that portrait poor Frank did eventually conjure out of me during our last long, hot, wet summer at Riverside, when I led my husband's father to believe I was unfaithful expressly in order to tempt Denis back early from his New York trip...so he might discover me in Frank's rooms, naked but for my wig, and kill us both.

Workings have a price, you see, and the single best currency for such transactions is blood, always—my blood, the de Russys' blood, and poor Frank's added in on top as mere afterthought. All of our blood together and a hundred years' more besides, let from ten thousand poor *negres'* veins one at a time by whip or knife, closed fist or open-handed blow, crying out forever from this slavery-tainted ground.

After Denis' grandfather bred my mother's mother 'til she died— before his eyes fell on her in turn—*Maman* ran all the way from Riverside to New Orleans and further, as you've told Tully: crossed the ocean to France's main port, then its capital, an uphill road travelled one set of sheets to the next, equal-paved with vaudeville stages, dance-floors, séance-rooms, and men's beds. Which is why those were the trades she taught me, along with my other, deeper callings. Too white to be black, a lost half-girl, she birthed me into the *demi-monde* several shades lighter still, which allowed me to climb my way back out; perception has its uses, after all, especially to *une sorciére*. From earliest years, however, I knew that nothing I did was for myself—that the only reason I existed at all was to bring about her curse, and her mother's, and her mother's mother's mother's.

There's a woman at Riverside, Marceline, ma mie, my mother told me before I left her that last time, stepping aboard the steam-ship bound for America. *An old one, from Home—who can say how old? She knew my mother and hers; she'll know you on sight, know your works, and help you in them.* And so there was: Kaayakire, whom those fools who bought her named Sophonisba—Aunt Sophy— before setting her to live alone in her bone-yard shack, tending the linden path. It was she who taught me the next part of my duty, how to use my ancestors' power to knit our dead fellow captives' pain together like a braid, a long black snake of justice, fit to choke all de Russys to death at once. To stop this flow of evil blood at last, at its very source.

That I was part de Russy myself, of course, meant I could not be allowed to escape, either, in the end. Yet only blood pays for blood, so the bargain seemed well worth it, at the time.

But I have been down here so long, now—years and years, decades: almost fifty, by your reckoning, with the de Russy line *proper* long-extirpated, myself very much included. Which is more than long enough to begin to change my mind on that particular subject.

So, here you come at last, down the track where the road once wound at sunset, led by a man bearing just the barest taint of de Russy blood in his face, his skin, his veins: come down from some child sold away to cover its masters' debts, perhaps, or traded between land-holders like a piece of livestock. One way or the other, it's as easy for me to recognise in Tully Ferris by smell as it'd no doubt be by sight, were I not so long deep-buried and eyeless with mud stopping my mouth and gloving my hands, roots knot-coiled "round my ankles" bones like chains. I'd know it at first breath, well as I would my own long-gone flesh's reek, my own long-rotten tongue's taste.

Just fate at work again, I suppose, slow as old growth—fate, the spider's phantom skein, thrown out wide, then tightened. But the curse I laid remains almost as strong, shored up with Kaayakire's help: Through its prism, I watch you approach, earth-toned and many-pointed, filtered through a hundred thousand leaves at once like the scales on some dragonfly's eye. I send out my feelers, hear your shared tread echo through the ground below, rebounding off bones and bone-fragments, and an image blooms out of resonance that is brief yet crisp, made and remade with every fresh step: you and Tully stomping through the long grass and the clinging weeds, your rubber boots dirt-spattered, wet coats muddy at the hem and snagged all over with stickers.

Tully raises one arm, makes a sweep, as though inviting the house's stove-in ruin to dance. "Riverside, ma'am—what's left of it, anyhow. See what I meant?"

"Yes, I see. Oh, *pute la merde!*"

Tree-girt and decrepit, Riverside's pile once boasted two storeys, a great Ionic portico, the full length and breadth necessary for any plantation centrepiece; they ran upwards of two hundred slaves here before the War cut the de Russys' strength in half. My husband's father loved to hold forth on its architectural value to anyone who'd listen, along with most who didn't. Little of the original is left upright now, however—a mere half-erased sketch of its former glory, all burnt and rotted and sagging amongst the scrub and cockle burrs. Like the deaths of its former occupants, its ruin is an achievement in which I take great pride.

"Said this portrait you come after was upstairs, right?" Tully rummages in his pack for a waterproof torch. "Well, you in luck, gal, sorta...upstairs fell in last year, resettled the whole mess of it down into what used to be old Antoine's ballroom. Can't get at it from the front, 'cause those steps is so mouldy they break if you look at 'em the wrong way, but there's a tear in the side take us right through. Hope you took my advice 'bout that hard-hat, though."

You nod, popping your own pack, and slip the article in question on: It even has a head-lamp, bright-white. "*Voilà.*"

At this point, with a thunderclap, rain begins to fall like curtains, drenching you both—inconvenient, I'm sure, as you slip and slide 'cross the muddy rubble. But I can take no credit for that, believe it or not; just nature taking its toll, moisture invading everything as slow-mounting damp or coming down in sheets, bursting its banks in cycles along with the tea-brown Mississippi itself.

Ownership works both ways, you see. Which is why, even in its heyday, Riverside was never anything more than just another ship, carrying our ancestors to an unwanted afterlife chained cheek-by-jowl with their oppressors, with no way to escape, even in death. No way for *any* of us to escape our own actions, or from each other.

But when I returned, Kaayakire showed me just how deep those dead slaves had sunk their roots in Riverside's heart: deep enough to strangle, to infiltrate, to poison, all this while lying dormant under a fallow crust. To sow death-seeds in every part of what the de Russys called home, however surface-comfortable, waiting patient for a second chance to flower.

Inside, under a sagging double weight of floor-turned-roof, fifty years' worth of mould spikes up the nose straight into the brain while shadows scatter from your twinned lights, same as silt in dark water. You hear the rain like someone else's pulse, drumming hard, sodden. Tully glances 'round, frowning. "Don't like it," he says. "Been more damage since my last time here: there, and there. Structural collapse."

"The columns will keep it up, though, no? They seem—"

"Saggy like an elephant's butt, that's what they *seem*... but hell, your money. Got some idea where best to look?" You shake your head, drawing a sigh. "Well, perfect. Guess we better start with what's eye-level; go from there."

As the two of you search, he asks about *that old business*, the gory details. For certainly, people gossip, here as everywhere else, yet the matter of the de Russys is something most locals flinch from, as though they know it to be somehow—not sacred, perhaps, but *significant*, in its own grotesque way. Tainted and tainting, by turns.

"Denis de Russy brought Marceline home and six months later, Frank Marsh came to visit," you explain. "He had known them both as friends, introduced them, watched them form *un ménage*. Denis considered him an artistic genius, but eccentric. To his father, he wrote that Marsh had 'a knowledge of anatomy which borders on the uncanny.' Antoine de Russy heard odd stories about Marsh, his family in Massachusetts, *la ville d'Innsmouth*...but he trusted his son, trusted that Denis trusted. So, he opened his doors."

"But Denis goes travelling and Marsh starts in to painting Missus de Russy with no clothes on, maybe more. That part right, or not?"

"That was the rumour, yes. It's not unlikely Marceline and Marsh were intimates, from before; he'd painted her twice already, taken those photos. A simple transaction. But this was...different, or so Antoine de Russy claimed."

"How so?"

You shrug. "Marsh said there was something inside her he wanted to make other people see."

"Like what, her soul?"

"*Peut-être*. Or something real, maybe—hidden. *Comme un*, eh, hmmm..." You pause, thinking. "When you swallow eggs or something swims up inside, in Africa, South America: it eats your food, makes you thin, lives inside you. And when doctors suspect, they have to tempt it out—say 'aah,' you know, tease it to show itself, like a...snake from a hole..."

Tully stops, mouth twitching. "A *tapeworm?* Boy must've been trippin', ma'am. Too much absinthe, for sure."

Another shrug. "Antoine de Russy wrote to Denis, told him to come home before things progressed further, but heard nothing. Days later, he found Marsh and Marceline in Marsh's rooms, hacked with knives, Marceline without her wig, or her, eh—hair—"

"Been scalped? Whoo." Tully shakes his head. "Then Denis kills himself and the old man goes crazy; that's how they tell it 'round here. When they talk about it at all, which ain't much."

"In the testimony I read, de Russy said he hid Marsh and Marceline, buried them in lime. He told Denis to run, but Denis hanged himself instead, in one of the old huts—or something strangled him, a big black snake. And then the house burnt down."

"Aunt Sophy's snake, they call it."

"A snake or a braid, *oui, c'est ca. Le cheveaux de Marceline.*" But here you stop, examining something at your feet. "But wait, what is—? Over here, please. I need your light."

Tully steps over, slips, curses; down on one knee in the mud, cap cracking worryingly, his torch rapping on the item in question. "Shit! Look like a...box, or something. Here." As he hands it up to you, however, it's now his own turn to squint, scrubbing mud from his eyes—something's caught his notice, there, half-wedged behind a caryatid, extruding from what used to be the wall. He gives it a tug and watches it come slithering out.

"*Qu'est-ce que c'est, la?*"

"Um...think this might be what you lookin' for, ma'am. Some of, anyhow."

The wet rag in his hand has seen better days, definitely. Yet, for one who's studied poor Frank Marsh's work—how ridiculous such a thing sounds, even to me!—it must be unmistakable, neverthe-less: a warped canvas, neglect-scabrous, all morbid content and perverted geometry done in impossible, liminal colours. The body I barely recognise, splayed out on its altar-throne, one bloated hand offering a cup of strange liquor; looks more the way it might now were there anything still unscattered, not sifted through dirt and water or filtered by a thousand roots, drawn off to feed Riverside's trees and weeds with hateful power. The face is long-gone, bullet-perforated, just as that skittish Northerner claimed. But the rest, that coiling darkness, it lies (*I lie*) on—

You make a strange noise at the sight, gut-struck: "Oh, *quel dommage!* What a waste, a sinful waste... "

"Damn, yeah. Not much to go on, huh?"

"Enough to begin with, *certainement*. I know experts, people who'd pay for the opportunity to restore something so unique, so precious. But why, why—ah, I will never understand. Stupid superstition!"

Which is when the box in your hands jumps, ever so slightly, as though something inside it's woken up. Makes a little hollow rap, like knocking.

As I've said, little seeker, I don't know you—barely know Tully, for all I might recognise his precedents. Though I suppose what I *do* know might be just enough to feel bad for what must happen to you and him, both, were I any way inclined to.

Frank's painting is ruined, like everything else, but what's inside the box is pristine, inviolable. When my father-in-law disinterred us days after the murders, too drunk to remember whether or not Denis had actually done what he feared, he found it wound 'round Frank's corpse, crushing him in its embrace, and threw burning lamp-oil on it, setting his own house afire. Then fled straight to Kaayakire's shack, calling her slave-name like the madman he'd doubtless become: *Damn you, Sophy, an' that Marse Clooloo o' yours...damn you, you hellish ol' nigger-woman! Damn you for knowin' what she was, that Frog whore, an' not warnin' me...'m I your Massa, or ain't I? Ain't I always treated you well...?*

Only to find the same thing waiting for him, longer still and far more many-armed, still smouldering and black as ever—less a snake now than an octopus, a hundred-handed net. The weight of every dead African whose blood went to grow the de Russys' fortunes, falling on him at once.

My cousin's father, my half-uncle, my mother's brother: all of these and none of them, as she and I were nothing to them—to him. Him I killed by letting his son kill me and set me free.

I have let myself be dead far too long since then, however, it occurs to me. Indulged myself, who should've thought only to indulge them, the ancestors whose scalps anchor my skull, grow my crowning glory. Their blood, my blood—Tully Ferris' blood, blood of the de Russys, of owners and owned alike—cries out from the ground. Your blood, too, now.

Inside the box, which you cannot keep yourself from opening, is my Tanit-Isis wig, that awful relic: heavy and sweet-smelling, soft with oils, though kinked at root and tip. You lift it to your head, eyes dazed, and breathe its odour in, deeply; hear Tully cry out, but only faintly, as the hair of every other dead slave buried at Riverside begins to poke its way through floors-made-walls, displace rubble and clutter, twine 'round cracked and half-mashed columnary like ivy, crawl up from the muck like sodden spiders. My wig feels their energies gather and plumps itself accordingly, bristling in every direction at once, even as these subsidiary creatures snare Tully like a rabbit and force their knotted follicles inside his veins, sucking de

Russy blood the way the *lamia* once did, the *astriyah*, demons called up not by Solomon, but Sheba. While it runs its own roots down into your scalp and cracks your skull along its fused fontanelles to reach the grey-pink brain within, injecting everything which ever made me *me* like some strange drug, and wiping *you* away like dust.

I *would* feel bad for your sad demise, little seeker, I'm almost sure; Tully's, even, his ancestry aside. But only if I were anyone but who I am.

Outside, the rain recedes, letting in daylight: bright morning, blazing gold-green through drooping leaves to call steam up from the sodden ground, raise cicatrice-blisters of moisture from Riverside's walls. The fields glitter like spider-webs. Emerging into it, I smile for the first time in so very long: lips, teeth, muscles flexing. *Myself* again, for all I wear another's flesh.

Undefeated, *Maman*. Victory. I am your revenge and theirs. No one owns me, not anymore, never again. I am...my own.

And so, my contract fulfilled, I walk away: into this fast, new, magical world, the future, trailing a thousand dark locks of history behind.

NEIL GAIMAN

BLACK DOG

NEIL GAIMAN is the author of more than thirty books and graphic novels for adults and children, including *American Gods, Stardust, Coraline, The Graveyard Book* and *Trigger Warning: Short Fictions and Disturbances*.

His most recent novel, *The Ocean at the End of the Lane*, won several awards, including being voted Book of the Year in the National Book Awards 2013.

Gaiman's work has been adapted for film, TV and radio. He has written scripts for *Doctor Who*, collaborated with authors and illustrators including Terry Pratchett, Dave McKean and Chris Riddell, and *The Sandman* is established as one of the classic graphic novels.

"We first met Baldur 'Shadow' Moon in *American Gods*," the author explains, "in which he gets caught up in a war between gods in America. In 'The Monarch of the Glen', a story in the *Fragile Things* collection, Shadow found himself a bouncer at a party in northern Scotland. He is on his way back to America, but in this story has only made it as far as Derbyshire's Peak District.

"I want to thank my friends Colin Greenland and Susanna Clarke for taking me to the Three Stags Head pub in Wardlow, which, cat, lurchers and all, inspired the opening, and to Colin for telling me that Black Shuck walked The Lane, when I asked him about black dogs.

"There is one last story to be told, about what happens to Shadow when he reaches London. And then, if he survives that, it will be time to send him back to America. So much has changed, after all, since he went away."

There were ten tongues within one head
And one went out to fetch some bread,
To feed the living and the dead.
—Old Riddle

I. The Bar Guest

OUTSIDE THE PUB it was raining cats and dogs. Shadow was still not entirely convinced that he was in a pub. True, there was a tiny bar at the back of the room, with bottles behind it and a couple of the huge taps you pulled, and there were several high tables and people were drinking at the tables, but it all felt like a room in somebody's house. The dogs helped reinforce that impression. It seemed to Shadow that everybody in the pub had a dog except for him.

"What kind of dogs are they?" Shadow asked, curious. The dogs reminded him of greyhounds, but they were smaller and seemed saner, more placid and less high-strung than the greyhounds he had encountered over the years.

"Lurchers," said the pub's landlord, coming out from behind the bar. He was carrying a pint of beer that he had poured for himself. "Best dogs. Poacher's dogs. Fast, smart, lethal." He bent down, scratched a chestnut-and-white brindled dog behind the ears. The dog stretched and luxuriated in the ear-scratching. It did not look particularly lethal, and Shadow said so.

The landlord, his hair a mop of grey and orange, scratched at his beard reflectively. "That's where you'd be wrong," he said. "I walked with his brother last week, down Cumpsy Lane. There's a fox, a big red Reynard, pokes his head out of a hedge, no more than twenty metres down the road, then, plain as day, saunters out onto the track. Well, Needles sees it, and he's off after it like the clappers. Next thing you know, Needles has his teeth in Reynard's neck, and one bite, one hard shake, and it's all over."

Shadow inspected Needles, a grey dog sleeping by the little fireplace. He looked harmless too. "So what sort of a breed is a lurcher? It's an English breed, yes?"

"It's not actually a breed," said a white-haired woman without a dog who had been leaning on a nearby table. "They're crossbred for speed, stamina. Sighthound, greyhound, collie."

The man next to her held up a finger. "You must understand," he said, cheerfully, "that there used to be laws about who could own pure-bred dogs. The local folk couldn't, but they could own mongrels. And lurchers are better and faster than pedigree dogs." He pushed his spectacles up his nose with the tip of his forefinger. He had a mutton-chop beard, brown-flecked with white.

"Ask me, all mongrels are better than pedigree-anything," said the woman. "It's why America is such an interesting country. Filled with mongrels." Shadow was not certain how old she was. Her hair was white, but she seemed younger than her hair.

"Actually, darling," said the man with the mutton chops, in his gentle voice, "I think you'll find that the Americans are keener on pedigree dogs than the British. I met a woman from the American Kennel Club, and honestly, she scared me. I was scared."

"I wasn't talking about dogs, Ollie," said the woman. "I was talking about... Oh, never mind."

"What are you drinking?" asked the landlord.

There was a hand-written piece of paper taped to the wall by the bar telling customers not to order a lager "as a punch in the face often offends".

"What's good and local?" asked Shadow, who had learned that this was mostly the wisest thing to say.

The landlord and the woman had various suggestions as to which of the various locals beers and ciders were good. The little mutton-chopped man interrupted them to point out that in his opinion *good* was not the avoidance of evil, but something more positive than that: it was making the world a better place. Then he chuckled, to show that he was only joking and that he knew that the conversation was really only about what to drink.

The beer the landlord poured for Shadow was dark and very bitter. He was not certain that he liked it. "What is it?"

"It's called Black Dog," said the woman. "I've heard people say it was named after the way you feel after you've had one too many."

"Like Churchill's moods," said the little man.

"Actually, the beer is named after a local dog," said a younger woman. She was wearing an olive-green sweater, and standing against the wall. "But not a real one. Semi-imaginary."

Shadow looked down at Needles, then hesitated, "Is it safe to scratch his head?" he asked, remembering the fate of the fox.

"'Course it is," said the white-haired woman. "He loves it. Don't you?"

"Well. He practically had that tosser from Glossop's finger off," said the landlord. There was admiration mixed with warning in his voice.

"I think he was something in local government," said the woman. "And I've always thought that there's nothing wrong with dogs biting *them*. Or VAT inspectors."

The woman in the green sweater moved over to Shadow. She was not holding a drink. She had dark, short hair, and a crop of freckles that spattered her nose and cheeks. She looked at Shadow. "You aren't in local government, are you?"

Shadow shook his head. He said, "I'm kind of a tourist." It was not actually untrue. He was travelling, anyway.

"You're Canadian?" said the mutton-chop man.

"American," said Shadow. "But I've been on the road for a while now."

"Then," said the white-haired woman, "you aren't actually a tourist. Tourists turn up, see the sights and leave."

Shadow shrugged, smiled, and leaned down. He scratched the landlord's lurcher on the back of its head.

"You're not a dog person, are you?" asked the dark-haired woman.

"I'm not a dog person," said Shadow.

Had he been someone else, someone who talked about what was happening inside his head, Shadow might have told her that his wife had owned dogs when she was younger, and sometimes called Shadow *puppy* because she wanted a dog she could not have. But Shadow kept things on the inside. It was one of the things he liked about the British: even when they wanted to know what was happening on the inside, they did not ask. The world on the inside remained the world on the inside. His wife had been dead for three years, now.

"If you ask me," said the man with the mutton chops, "people are either dog people or cat people. So would you then consider yourself a cat person?"

Shadow reflected. "I don't know. We never had pets when I was a kid, we were always on the move. But—"

"I mention this," the man continued, "because our host also has a cat, which you might wish to see."

"Used to be out here, but we moved it to the back room," said the landlord, from behind the bar.

Shadow wondered how the man could follow the conversation so easily while also taking people's meal orders and serving their drinks. "Did the cat upset the dogs?" he asked.

Outside, the rain redoubled. The wind moaned, and whistled, and then howled. The log fire burning in the little fireplace coughed and spat.

"Not in the way you're thinking," said the landlord. "We found it when we knocked through into the room next door, when we needed to extend the bar." The man grinned. "Come and look."

Shadow followed the man into the room next door. The mutton-chop man and the white-haired woman came with them, walking a little behind Shadow.

Shadow glanced back into the bar. The dark-haired woman was watching him, and she smiled warmly when he caught her eye.

The room next door was better lit, larger, and it felt a little less like somebody's front room. People were sitting at tables, eating. The food looked good and smelled better. The landlord led Shadow to the back of the room, to a dusty glass case.

"There she is," said the landlord, proudly.

The cat was brown, and it looked, at first glance, as if it had been constructed out of tendons and agony. The holes that were its eyes were filled with anger and with pain; the mouth was wide open, as if the creature had been yowling when she was turned to leather.

"The practice of placing animals in the walls of buildings is similar to the practice of walling up children alive in the foundations of a house you want to stay up," explained the mutton-chop man, from behind him. "Although mummified cats always make me think of the mummified cats they found around the temple of Bast in Bubastis in Egypt. So many tons of mummified cats, that they sent them to England to be ground up as cheap fertiliser and dumped on the fields. The Victorians also made paint out of mummies. A sort of brown, I believe."

"It looks miserable," said Shadow. "How old is it?"

The landlord scratched his cheek. "We reckon that the wall she was in went up somewhere between 1300 and 1600. That's from Parish records. There's nothing here in 1300, and there's a house in 1600. The stuff in the middle was lost."

The dead cat in the glass case, furless and leathery, seemed to be watching them, from its empty black-hole eyes.

I got eyes wherever my folk walk, breathed a voice in the back of Shadow's mind. He thought, momentarily, about the fields fertilised with the ground mummies of cats, and what strange crops they must have grown.

"*They put him into an old house side*," said the man called Ollie. "*And there he lived and there he died. And nobody either laughed or cried.* All sorts of things were walled up, to make sure that things were guarded and safe. Children, sometimes. Animals. They did it in churches as a matter of course."

The rain beat an arrhythmic rattle on the windowpane. Shadow thanked the landlord for showing him the cat. They went back into the taproom. The dark-haired woman had gone, which gave Shadow a moment of regret. She had looked so friendly. Shadow bought a round of drinks for the mutton-chop man, the white-haired woman, and one for the landlord.

The landlord ducked behind the bar. "They call me Shadow," Shadow told them. "Shadow Moon."

The mutton-chop man pressed his hands together in delight. "Oh! How wonderful. I had an Alsatian named Shadow, when I was a boy. Is it your real name?"

"It's what they call me," said Shadow.

"I'm Moira Callanish," said the white-haired woman. "This is my partner, Oliver Bierce. He knows a lot, and he will, during the course of our acquaintance, undoubtedly tell you everything he knows."

They shook hands. When the landlord returned with their drinks, Shadow asked if the pub had a room to rent. He had intended to walk further that night, but the rain sounded like it had no intention of giving up. He had stout walking shoes, and weather-resistant outer clothes, but he did not want to walk in the rain.

"I used to, but then my son moved back in. I'll encourage people to sleep it off in the barn, on occasion, but that's as far as I'll go these days."

"Anywhere in the village I could get a room?"

The landlord shook his head. "It's a foul night. But Porsett is only a few miles down the road, and they've got a proper hotel there. I can call Sandra, tell her that you are coming. What's your name?"

"Shadow," said Shadow again. "Shadow Moon."

Moira looked at Oliver, and said something that sounded like "waifs and strays?" and Oliver chewed his lip for a moment, and then he nodded enthusiastically. "Would you fancy spending the night with us? The spare room's a bit of a box-room, but it does have a bed in it. And it's warm there. And dry."

"I'd like that very much," said Shadow. "I can pay."

"Don't be silly," said Moira. "It will be nice to have a guest."

II. The Gibbet

Oliver and Moira both had umbrellas. Oliver insisted that Shadow carry his umbrella, pointing out that Shadow towered over him, and thus was ideally suited to keep the rain off both of them.

The couple also carried little flashlights, which they called torches. The word put Shadow in mind of villagers in a horror movie storming the castle on the hill, and the lightning and thunder added to the vision. *Tonight, my creature,* he thought, *I will give you life!* It should have been hokey but instead it was disturbing. The dead cat had put him into a strange set of mind.

The narrow roads between fields were running with rainwater.

"On a nice night," said Moira, raising her voice to be heard over the rain, "we would just walk over the fields. But they'll be all soggy and boggy, so we're going down by Shuck's Lane. Now, that tree was a gibbet tree, once upon a time." She pointed to a massive-trunked sycamore at the crossroads. It had only a few branches left, sticking up into the night like afterthoughts.

"Moira's lived here since she was in her twenties," said Oliver. "I came up from London, about eight years ago. From Turnham Green. I'd come up here on holiday originally when I was fourteen and I never forgot it. You don't."

"The land gets into your blood," said Moira. "Sort of."

"And the blood gets into the land," said Oliver. "One way or another. You take that gibbet tree, for example. They would leave people in the gibbet until there was nothing left. Hair gone to make bird's nests, flesh all eaten by ravens, bones picked clean. Or until they had another corpse to display anyway."

Shadow was fairly sure he knew what a gibbet was, but he asked anyway. There was never any harm in asking, and Oliver was definitely the kind of person who took pleasure in knowing peculiar things and in passing his knowledge on.

"Like a huge iron birdcage. They used them to display the bodies of executed criminals, after justice had been served. The gibbets were locked, so the family and friends couldn't steal the body back and give it a good Christian burial. Keeping passers-by on the straight and the narrow, although I doubt it actually deterred anyone from anything."

"Who were they executing?"

"Anyone who got unlucky. Three hundred years ago, there were over two hundred crimes punishable by death. Including travelling with Gypsies for more than a month, stealing sheep—and, for that matter, anything over twelve pence in value—and writing a threatening letter."

He might have been about to begin a lengthy list, but Moira broke in. "Oliver's right about the death sentence, but they only gibbeted murderers, up these parts. And they'd leave corpses in the gibbet for twenty years, sometimes. We didn't get a lot of murders." And then, as if trying to change the subject to something lighter, she said, "We are now walking down Shuck's Lane. The locals say that on a clear night, which tonight certainly is not, you can find yourself being followed by Black Shuck. He's a sort of a fairy dog."

"We've never seen him, not even on clear nights," said Oliver.

"Which is a very good thing," said Moira. "Because if you see him—you die."

"Except Sandra Wilberforce said she saw him, and she's healthy as a horse."

Shadow smiled. "What does Black Shuck do?"

"He doesn't do anything," said Oliver.

"He does. He follows you home," corrected Moira. "And then, a bit later, you die."

"Doesn't sound very scary," said Shadow. "Except for the dying bit."

They reached the bottom of the road. Rainwater was running like a stream over Shadow's thick hiking boots.

Shadow said, "So how did you two meet?" It was normally a safe question, when you were with couples.

Oliver said, "In the pub. I was up here on holiday, really."

Moira said, "I was with someone when I met Oliver. We had a very brief, torrid affair, then we ran off together. Most unlike both of us."

They did not seem like the kind of people who ran off together, thought Shadow. But then, all people were strange. He knew he should say something.

"I was married. My wife was killed in a car crash."

"I'm so sorry," said Moira.

"It happened," said Shadow.

"When we get home," said Moira, "I'm making us all Whisky Macs. That's whisky and ginger wine and hot water. And I'm having a hot bath. Otherwise I'll catch my death."

Shadow imagined reaching out his hand and catching death in it, like a baseball, and he shivered.

The rain redoubled, and a sudden flash of lightning burned the world into existence all around them: every grey rock in the dry stone wall, every blade of grass, every puddle and every tree was perfectly illuminated, and then swallowed by a deeper darkness, leaving afterimages on Shadow's night-blinded eyes.

"Did you see that?" asked Oliver. "Damnedest thing." The thunder rolled and rumbled, and Shadow waited until it was done before he tried to speak.

"I didn't see anything," said Shadow. Another flash, less bright, and Shadow thought he saw something moving away from them in a distant field. "That?" he asked.

"It's a donkey," said Moira. "Only a donkey."

Oliver stopped. He said, "This was the wrong way to come home. We should have got a taxi. This was a mistake."

"Ollie," said Moira. "It's not far now. And it's just a spot of rain. You aren't made of sugar, darling."

Another flash of lightning, so bright as to be almost blinding. There was nothing to be seen in the fields.

Darkness. Shadow turned back to Oliver, but the little man was no longer standing beside him. Oliver's flashlight was on the ground. Shadow blinked his eyes, hoping to force his night vision to return. The man had collapsed, crumpled onto the wet grass on the side of the lane.

"Ollie?" Moira crouched beside him, her umbrella by her side. She shone her flashlight onto his face. Then she looked at Shadow. "He can't just sit here," she said, sounding confused and concerned. "It's pouring."

Shadow pocketed Oliver's flashlight, handed his umbrella to Moira, then picked Oliver up. The man did not seem to weigh much, and Shadow was a big man.

"Is it far?"

"Not far," she said. "Not really. We're almost *home*."

They walked in silence, across a churchyard on the edge of a village green, and into a village. Shadow could see lights on in the grey stone houses that edged the one street. Moira turned off, into a house set back from the road, and Shadow followed her. She held the back door open for him.

The kitchen was large and warm, and there was a sofa, half-covered with magazines, against one wall. There were low beams in the kitchen, and Shadow needed to duck his head. Shadow removed Oliver's raincoat and dropped it. It puddled on the wooden floor. Then he put the man down on the sofa.

Moira filled the kettle.

"Do we call an ambulance?"

She shook her head.

"This is just something that happens? He falls down and passes out?"

Moira busied herself getting mugs from a shelf. "It's happened before. Just not for a long time. He's narcoleptic, and if something surprises or scares him he can just go down like that. He'll come round soon. He'll want tea. No Whisky Mac tonight, not for him. Sometimes he's a bit dazed and doesn't know where he is, sometimes he's been following everything that happened while he was out. And he hates it if you make a fuss. Put your backpack down by the Aga."

The kettle boiled. Moira poured the steaming water into a teapot. "He'll have a cup of real tea. I'll have chamomile, I think, or I won't sleep tonight. Calm my nerves. You?"

"I'll drink tea, sure," said Shadow. He had walked more than twenty miles that day, and sleep would be easy in the finding. He wondered at Moira. She appeared perfectly self-possessed in the face of her partner's incapacity, and he wondered how much of it was not wanting to show weakness in front of a stranger. He admired her, although he found it peculiar. The English were strange. But he understood hating "making a fuss". Yes.

Oliver stirred on the couch. Moira was at his side with a cup of tea, helped him into a sitting position. He sipped the tea, in a slightly dazed fashion.

"It followed me home," he said, conversationally.

"What followed you, Ollie, darling?" Her voice was steady, but there was concern in it.

"The dog," said the man on the sofa, and he took another sip of his tea. "The black dog."

III. The Cuts

These were the things Shadow learned that night, sitting around the kitchen table with Moira and Oliver:

He learned that Oliver had not been happy or fulfilled in his London advertising agency job. He had moved up to the village and taken an extremely early medical retirement. Now, initially for recreation and increasingly for money, he repaired and rebuilt dry stone walls. There was, he explained, an art and a skill to wall building, it was excellent exercise, and, when done correctly, a meditative practice.

"There used to be hundreds of dry stone-wall people around here. Now, there's barely a dozen who know what they're doing. You see walls repaired with concrete, or with breeze blocks. It's a dying art. I'd love to show you how I do it. Useful skill to have. Picking the rock, sometimes, you have to let the rock tell you where it goes. And then it's immovable. You couldn't knock it down with a tank. Remarkable."

He learned that Oliver had been very depressed several years earlier, shortly after Moira and he got together, but that for the last few years he had been doing very well. Or, he amended, relatively well.

He learned that Moira was independently wealthy, that her family trust fund had meant that she and her sisters had not needed to work, but that, in her late twenties, she had gone for teacher training. That she no longer taught, but that she was extremely active in local affairs, and had campaigned successfully to keep the local bus routes in service.

Shadow learned, from what Oliver didn't say, that Oliver was scared of something, very scared, and that when Oliver was asked what had frightened him so badly, and what he had meant by saying that the black dog had followed him home, his response was to stammer and to sway. He learned not to ask Oliver any more questions.

This is what Oliver and Moira had learned about Shadow sitting around that kitchen table:

Nothing much.

Shadow liked them. He was not a stupid man; he had trusted people in the past who had betrayed him. But he liked this couple, and he liked the way their home smelled—like bread-making and jam and walnut wood-polish—and he went to sleep that night in his box-room bedroom worrying about the little man with the mutton-chop beard. What if the thing Shadow had glimpsed in the field had *not* been a donkey? What if it *had* been an enormous dog? What then?

The rain had stopped when Shadow woke. He made himself toast in the empty kitchen. Moira came in from the garden, letting a gust of chilly air in through the kitchen door. "Sleep well?" she asked.

"Yes. Very well." He had dreamed of being at the zoo. He had been surrounded by animals he could not see, which snuffled and snorted in their pens. He was a child, walking with his mother, and he was safe and he was loved. He had stopped in front of a lion's cage, but what had been in the cage was a sphinx, half-lion and half-woman, her tail swishing. She had smiled at him, and her smile had been his mother's smile. He heard her voice, accented and warm and feline.

It said, *Know thyself.*

I know who I am, said Shadow in his dream, holding the bars of the cage. Behind the bars was the desert. He could see pyramids. He could see shadows on the sand.

Then who are you, Shadow? What are you running from? Where are you running to?

Who are you?

And he had woken, wondering why he was asking himself that

question, and missing his mother, who had died twenty years before, when he was a teenager. He still felt oddly comforted, remembering the feel of his hand in his mother's hand.

"I'm afraid Ollie's a bit under the weather this morning."

"Sorry to hear that."

"Yes. Well, can't be helped."

"I'm really grateful for the room. I guess I'll be on my way."

Moira said, "Will you look at something for me?"

Shadow nodded, then followed her outside, and round the side of the house. She pointed to the rose bed. "What does that look like to you?"

Shadow bent down. "*The footprint of an enormous hound*," he said. "To quote Dr. Watson."

"Yes," she said. "It really does."

"If there's a spectral ghost-hound out there," said Shadow, "it shouldn't leave footprints. Should it?"

"I'm not actually an authority on these matters," said Moira. "I had a friend once who could have told us all about it. But she..." She trailed off. Then, more brightly, "You know, Mrs. Camberley two doors down has a Doberman pinscher. Ridiculous thing." Shadow was not certain whether the ridiculous thing was Mrs. Camberley or her dog.

He found the events of the previous night less troubling and odd, more explicable. What did it matter if a strange dog had followed them home? Oliver had been frightened or startled, and had collapsed, from narcolepsy, from shock.

"Well, I'll pack you some lunch before you go," said Moira. "Boiled eggs. That sort of thing. You'll be glad of them on the way."

They went into the house. Moira went to put something away, and returned looking shaken.

"Oliver's locked himself in the bathroom," she said.

Shadow was not certain what to say.

"You know what I wish?" she continued.

"I don't."

"I wish you would talk to him. I wish he would open the door. I wish he'd talk to me. I can hear him in there. I can hear him."

And then, "I hope he isn't cutting himself again."

Shadow walked back into the hall, stood by the bathroom door, called Oliver's name. "Can you hear me? Are you okay?"

Nothing. No sound from inside.

Shadow looked at the door. It was solid wood. The house was old, and they built them strong and well back then. When Shadow had used the bathroom that morning he'd learned the lock was a hook and eye. He leaned on the handle of the door, pushing it down, then rammed his shoulder against the door. It opened with a noise of splintering wood.

He had watched a man die in prison, stabbed in a pointless argument. He remembered the way the blood had puddled about the man's body, lying in the back corner of the exercise yard. The sight had troubled Shadow, but he had forced himself to look, and to keep looking. To look away would somehow have felt disrespectful.

Oliver was naked on the floor of the bathroom. His body was pale, and his chest and groin were covered with thick, dark hair. He held the blade from an ancient safety razor in his hands. He had sliced his arms with it, his chest above the nipples, his inner thighs and his penis. Blood was smeared on his body, on the black and white linoleum floor, on the white enamel of the bathtub. Oliver's eyes were round and wide, like the eyes of a bird. He was looking directly at Shadow, but Shadow was not certain that he was being seen.

"Ollie?" said Moira's voice, from the hall. Shadow realised that he was blocking the doorway and he hesitated, unsure whether to let her see what was on the floor or not.

Shadow took a pink towel from the towel-rail and wrapped it around Oliver. That got the little man's attention. He blinked, as if seeing Shadow for the first time, and said, "The dog. It's for the dog. It must be fed, you see. We're making friends."

Moira said, "Oh my dear sweet God."

"I'll call the emergency services."

"Please don't," she said. "He'll be fine at home with me. I don't know what I'll... please?"

Shadow picked up Oliver, swaddled in the towel, carried him into the bedroom as if he were a child, and then placed him on the bed. Moira followed. She picked up an iPad by the bed, touched the screen, and music began to play. "Breathe Ollie," she said. "Remember. Breathe. It's going to be fine. You're going to be fine."

"I can't really breathe," said Oliver, in a small voice. "Not really. I can feel my heart, though. I can feel my heart beating."

Moira squeezed his hand and sat down on the bed, and Shadow left them alone.

When Moira entered the kitchen, her sleeves rolled up, and her hands smelling of antiseptic cream, Shadow was sitting on the sofa, reading a guide to local walks.

"How's he doing?"

She shrugged.

"You have to get him help."

"Yes." She stood in the middle of the kitchen and looked about her, as if unable to decide which way to turn. "Do you...I mean, do you have to leave today? Are you on a schedule?"

"Nobody's waiting for me. Anywhere."

She looked at him with a face that had grown haggard in an hour. "When this happened before, it took a few days, but then he was right as rain. The depression doesn't stay long. So, just wondering, would you just, well, stick around? I phoned my sister but she's in the middle of moving. And I can't cope on my own. I really can't. Not again. But I can't ask you to stay, not if anyone is waiting for you."

"Nobody's waiting," repeated Shadow. "And I'll stick around. But I think Oliver needs specialist help."

"Yes," agreed Moira. "He does."

Dr. Scathelocke came over late that afternoon. He was a friend of Oliver and Moira's. Shadow was not entirely certain whether rural British doctors still made house calls, or whether this was a socially-justified visit. The doctor went into the bedroom, and came out twenty minutes later.

He sat at the kitchen table with Moira, and he said, "It's all very shallow. Cry-for-help stuff. Honestly, there's not a lot we can do for him in hospital that you can't do for him here, what with the cuts.

We used to have a dozen nurses in that wing. Now they are trying to close it down completely. Get it all back to the community."

Dr. Scathelocke had sandy hair, was as tall as Shadow but lankier. He reminded Shadow of the landlord in the pub, and he wondered idly if the two men were related. The doctor scribbled several prescriptions, and Moira handed them to Shadow, along with the keys to an old white Range Rover.

Shadow drove to the next village, found the little chemist's and waited for the prescriptions to be filled. He stood awkwardly in the over-lit aisle, staring at a display of suntan lotions and creams, sadly redundant in this cold wet summer.

"You're Mr. American," said a woman's voice from behind him. He turned. She had short dark hair and was wearing the same olive-green sweater she had been wearing in the pub.

"I guess I am," he said.

"Local gossip says that you are helping out while Ollie's under the weather."

"That was fast."

"Local gossip travels faster than light. I'm Cassie Burglass."

"Shadow Moon."

"Good name," she said. "Gives me chills." She smiled. "If you're still rambling while you're here, I suggest you check out the hill just past the village. Follow the track up until it forks, and then go left. It takes you up Wod's Hill. Spectacular views. Public right of way. Just keep going left and up, you can't miss it."

She smiled at him. Perhaps she was just being friendly to a stranger.

"I'm not surprised you're still here though," Cassie continued. "It's hard to leave this place once it gets its claws into you." She smiled again, a warm smile, and she looked directly into his eyes, as if trying to make up her mind. "I think Mrs. Patel has your prescriptions ready. Nice talking to you, Mr. American."

IV. The Kiss

Shadow helped Moira. He walked down to the village shop and

bought the items on her shopping list while she stayed in the house, writing at the kitchen table or hovering in the hallway outside the bedroom door. Moira barely talked. He ran errands in the white Range Rover, and saw Oliver mostly in the hall, shuffling to the bathroom and back. The man did not speak to him.

Everything was quiet in the house: Shadow imagined the black dog squatting on the roof, cutting out all sunlight, all emotion, all feeling and truth. Something had turned down the volume in that house, pushed all the colours into black and white. He wished he was somewhere else, but could not run out on them. He sat on his bed, and stared out of the window at the rain puddling its way down the windowpane, and felt the seconds of his life counting off, never to come back.

It had been wet and cold, but on the third day the sun came out. The world did not warm up, but Shadow tried to pull himself out of the grey haze, and decided to see some of the local sights. He walked to the next village, through fields, up paths and along the side of a long dry stone wall. There was a bridge over a narrow stream that was little more than a plank, and Shadow jumped the water in one easy bound. Up the hill: there were trees, oak and hawthorn, sycamore and beech at the bottom of the hill, and then the trees became sparser. He followed the winding trail, sometimes obvious, sometimes not, until he reached a natural resting place, like a tiny meadow, high on the hill, and there he turned away from the hill and saw the valleys and the peaks arranged all about him in greens and greys like illustrations from a children's book.

He was not alone up there. A woman with short dark hair was sitting and sketching on the hill's side, perched comfortably on a grey boulder. There was a tree behind her, which acted as a wind-break. She wore a green sweater and blue jeans, and he recognised Cassie Burglass before he saw her face.

As he got close, she turned. "What do you think?" she asked, holding her sketchbook up for his inspection. It was an assured pencil drawing of the hillside.

"You're very good. Are you a professional artist?"

"I dabble," she said.

Shadow had spent enough time talking to the English to know that this either meant that she dabbled, or that her work was regularly hung in the National Gallery or the Tate Modern.

"You must be cold." he said. "You're only wearing a sweater."

"I'm cold," she said. "But, up here, I'm used to it. It doesn't really bother me. How's Ollie doing?"

"He's still under the weather," Shadow told her.

"Poor old sod," she said, looking from her paper to the hillside and back. "It's hard for me to feel properly sorry for him, though."

"Why's that? Did he bore you to death with interesting facts?"

She laughed, a small huff of air at the back of her throat. "You really ought to listen to more village gossip. When Ollie and Moira met, they were both with other people."

"I know that. They told me that." Shadow thought a moment. "So he was with you first?"

"No. *She* was. We'd been together since college." There was a pause. She shaded something, her pencil scraping the paper. "Are you going to try and kiss me?" she asked.

"I, uh. I, um," he said. Then, honestly, "It hadn't occurred to me."

"Well," she said, turning to smile at him, "it bloody well should. I mean, I asked you up here, and you came, up to Wod's Hill, just to see me." She went back to the paper and the drawing of the hill. "They say there's dark doings been done on this hill. Dirty dark doings. And I was thinking of doing something dirty myself. To Moira's lodger."

"Is this some kind of revenge plot?"

"It's not an anything plot. I just like you. And there's no one around here who wants me any longer. Not as a woman."

The last woman that Shadow had kissed had been in Scotland. He thought of her, and what she had become, in the end. "You *are* real, aren't you?" he asked. "I mean... you're a real person. I mean..."

She put the pad of paper down on the boulder and she stood up. "Kiss me and find out," she said.

He hesitated. She sighed, and she kissed him.

It was cold on that hillside, and Cassie's lips were cold. Her mouth was very soft. As her tongue touched his, Shadow pulled back.

"I don't actually know you," Shadow said.

She leaned away from him, looked up into his face. "You know," she said, "all I dream of these days is somebody who will look my way and see the real me. I had given up until you came along, Mr. American, with your funny name. But you looked at me, and I knew you saw me. And that's all that matters."

Shadow's hands held her, feeling the softness of her sweater.

"How much longer are you going to be here? In the district?" she asked.

"A few more days. Until Oliver's feeling better."

"Pity. Can't you stay for ever?"

"I'm sorry?"

"You have nothing to be sorry for, sweet man. You see that opening over there?"

He glanced over to the hillside, but could not see what she was pointing at. The hillside was a tangle of weeds and low trees and half-tumbled dry stone walls. She pointed to her drawing, where she had drawn a dark shape, like an archway, in the middle of a clump of gorse bushes on the side of the hill. "There. Look." He stared, and this time he saw it immediately.

"What is it?" Shadow asked.

"The gateway to Hell," she told him, impressively.

"Uh-huh."

She grinned. "That's what they call it round here. It was originally a Roman Temple, I think, or something even older. But that's all that remains. You should check it out, if you like that sort of thing. Although it's a bit disappointing: just a little passageway going back into the hill. I keep expecting some archaeologists will come out this way, dig it up, catalogue what they find, but they never do."

Shadow examined her drawing. "So what do you know about big black dogs?" he asked.

"The one in Shuck's Lane?" she said. He nodded. "They say the Barghest used to wander all around here. But now it's just in Shuck's Lane. Dr. Scathelocke once told me it was folk memory. The Wish Hounds are all that are left of the wild hunt, which was based around the idea of Odin's hunting wolves, Freki and Geri. I think it's even older than that. Cave memory. Druids. The thing that prowls in the darkness beyond the fire circle, waiting to tear you apart if you edge too far out alone."

"Have you ever seen it, then?"

She shook her head. "No. I researched it, but never saw it. My semi-imaginary local beast. Have you?"

"I don't think so. Maybe."

"Perhaps you woke it up when you came here. You woke me up, after all."

She reached up, pulled his head down towards her and kissed him again. She took his left hand, so much bigger than hers, and placed it beneath her sweater.

"Cassie, my hands are cold," he warned her.

"Well, my everything is cold. There's nothing *but* cold up here. Just smile and look like you know what you're doing," she told him. She pushed Shadow's left hand higher, until it was cupping the lace of her bra, and he could feel, beneath the lace, the hardness of her nipple and the soft swell of her breast.

He began to surrender to the moment, his hesitation a mixture of awkwardness and uncertainty. He was not sure how he felt about this woman: she had history with his benefactors, after all. Shadow never liked feeling that he was being used; it had happened too many times before. But his left hand was touching her breast and his right hand was cradling the nape of her neck, and he was leaning down and now her mouth was on his, and she was clinging to him as tightly as if, he thought, she wanted to occupy the very same space that he was in. Her mouth tasted like mint and stone and grass and the chilly afternoon breeze. He closed his eyes, and let himself enjoy the kiss and the way their bodies moved together.

Cassie froze. Somewhere close to them, a cat mewed. Shadow opened his eyes.

"Jesus," he said.

They were surrounded by cats. White cats and tabbies, brown and ginger and black cats, long-haired and short. Well-fed cats with collars and disreputable ragged-eared cats that looked as if they had been living in barns and on the edges of the wild. They stared at

Shadow and Cassie with green eyes and blue eyes and golden eyes, and they did not move. Only the occasional swish of a tail or the blinking of a pair of feline eyes told Shadow that they were alive.

"This is weird," said Shadow.

Cassie took a step back. He was no longer touching her now. "Are they with you?" she asked.

"I don't think they're with anyone. They're cats."

"I think they're jealous," said Cassie. "Look at them. They don't like me."

"That's..." Shadow was going to say "nonsense", but no, it was sense, of a kind. There had been a woman who was a goddess, a continent away and years in his past, who had cared about him, in her own way. He remembered the needle-sharpness of her nails and the cat-like roughness of her tongue.

Cassie looked at Shadow dispassionately. "I don't know who you are, Mr. American," she told him. "Not really. I don't know why you can look at me and see the real me, or why I can talk to you when I find it so hard to talk to other people. But I can. And you know, you seem all normal and quiet on the surface, but you are so much weirder than I am. And I'm extremely fucking weird."

Shadow said, "Don't go."

"Tell Ollie and Moira you saw me," she said. "Tell them I'll be waiting where we last spoke, if they have anything they want to say to me." She picked up her sketchpad and pencils, and she walked off briskly, stepping carefully through the cats, who did not even glance at her, just kept their gazes fixed on Shadow, as she moved away through the swaying grasses and the blowing twigs.

Shadow wanted to call after her, but he instead he crouched down and looked back at the cats. "What's going on?" he asked. "Bast? Are you doing this? You're a long way from home. And why would you still care who I kiss?"

The spell was broken when he spoke. The cats began to move, to look away, to stand, to wash themselves intently.

A tortoiseshell cat pushed her head against his hand, insistently, needing attention. Shadow stroked her absently, rubbing his knuckles against her forehead.

She swiped blinding-fast with claws like tiny scimitars, and drew blood from his forearm. Then she purred, and turned, and within moments the whole kit and caboodle of them had vanished into the hillside, slipping behind rocks and into the undergrowth, and were gone.

V. The Living and the Dead

Oliver was out of his room when Shadow got back to the house, sitting in the warm kitchen, a mug of tea by his side, reading a book on Roman architecture. He was dressed, and he had shaved his chin and trimmed his beard. He was wearing pyjamas, with a plaid bathrobe over them.

"I'm feeling a bit better," he said, when he saw Shadow. Then, "Have you ever had this? Been depressed?"

"Looking back on it, I guess I did. When my wife died," said Shadow. "Everything went flat. Nothing meant anything for a long time."

Oliver nodded. "It's hard. Sometimes I think the black dog is a real thing. I lie in bed thinking about the painting of Fuseli's nightmare on a sleeper's chest. Like Anubis. Or do I mean Set? Big black thing. What was Set anyway? Some kind of donkey?"

"I never ran into Set," said Shadow. "He was before my time."

Oliver laughed. "Very dry. And they say you Americans don't do irony." He paused. "Anyway. All done now. Back on my feet. Ready to face the world." He sipped his tea. "Feeling a bit embarrassed. All that Hound of the Baskervilles nonsense behind me now."

"You really have nothing to be embarrassed about," said Shadow, reflecting that the English found embarrassment wherever they looked for it.

"Well. All a bit silly, one way or another. And I really am feeling much perkier."

Shadow nodded. "If you're feeling better, I guess I should start heading south."

"No hurry," said Oliver. "It's always nice to have company. Moira and I don't really get out as much as we'd like. It's mostly just a walk up to the pub. Not much excitement here, I'm afraid."

Moira came in from the garden. "Anyone seen the secateurs? I know I had them. Forget my own head next."

Shadow shook his head, uncertain what secateurs were. He thought of telling the couple about the cats on the hill, and how they had behaved, but could not think of a way to describe it that would explain how odd it was. So, instead, without thinking, he said, "I ran into Cassie Burglass on Wod's Hill. She pointed out the Gateway to Hell."

They were staring at him. The kitchen had become awkwardly quiet. He said, "She was drawing it."

Oliver looked at him and said, "I don't understand."

"I've run into her a couple of times since I got here," said Shadow.

"What?" Moira's face was flushed. "What are you saying?" And then, "Who the, who the *fuck* are you to come in here and say things like that?"

"I'm, I'm nobody," said Shadow. "She just started talking to me. She said that you and she used to be together."

Moira looked as if she were going to hit him. Then she just said, "She moved away after we broke up. It wasn't a good break-up. She was very hurt. She behaved appallingly. Then she just up and left the village in the night. Never came back."

"I don't want to talk about that woman," said Oliver, quietly. "Not now. Not ever."

"Look. She was in the pub with us," pointed out Shadow. "That first night. You guys didn't seem to have a problem with her then."

Moira just stared at him and did not respond, as if he had said something in a tongue she did not speak. Oliver rubbed his forehead with his hand. "I didn't see her," was all he said.

"Well, she said to say hi when I saw her today," said Shadow. "She said she'd be waiting, if either of you had anything you wanted to say to her."

"We have nothing to say to her. Nothing at all." Moira's eyes were wet, but she was not crying. "I can't believe that, that *fucking* woman has come back into our lives, after all she put us through." Moira swore like someone who was not very good at it.

Oliver put down his book. "I'm sorry," he said. "I don't feel very well." He walked out, back to the bedroom, and closed the door behind him.

Moira picked up Oliver's mug, almost automatically, and took it over to the sink, emptied it out and began to wash it.

"I hope you're pleased with yourself," she said, rubbing the mug with a white plastic scrubbing brush as if she were trying to scrub the picture of Beatrix Potter's cottage from the china. "He was coming back to himself again."

"I didn't know it would upset him like that," said Shadow. He felt guilty as he said it. He had known there was history between Cassie and his hosts. He could have said nothing, after all. Silence was always safer.

Moira dried the mug with a green and white tea towel. The white patches of the towel were comical sheep, the green were grass. She bit her lower lip, and the tears that had been brimming in her eyes now ran down her cheeks. Then, "Did she say anything about me?"

"Just that you two used to be an item."

Moira nodded, and wiped the tears from her young-old face with the comical tea-towel. "She couldn't bear it when Ollie and I got together. After I moved out, she just hung up her paintbrushes and locked the flat and went to London." She blew her nose vigorously. "Still. Mustn't grumble. We make our own beds. And Ollie's a *good* man. There's just a black dog in his mind. My mother had depression. It's hard."

Shadow said, "I've made everything worse. I should go."

"Don't leave until tomorrow. I'm not throwing you out, dear. It's not your fault you ran into that woman, is it?" Her shoulders were slumped. "There they are. On top of the fridge." She picked up something that looked like a very small pair of garden shears. "Secateurs," she explained. "For the rose bushes, mostly."

"Are you going to talk to him?"

"No," she said. "Conversations with Ollie about Cassie never end well. And in this state, it could plunge him even further back into a bad place. I'll just let him get over it."

Shadow ate alone in the pub that night, while the cat in the glass case glowered at him. He saw no one he knew. He had a brief conversation with the landlord about how he was enjoying his time in the village. He walked back to Moira's house after the pub, past the old sycamore, the gibbet tree, down Shuck's lane. He saw nothing moving in the fields in the moonlight: no dog, no donkey.

All the lights in the house were out. He went to his bedroom as quietly as he could, packed the last of his possessions into his backpack before he went to sleep. He would leave early, he knew.

He lay in bed, watching the moonlight in the box room. He remembered standing in the pub and Cassie Burglass standing beside him. He thought about his conversation with the landlord, and the conversation that first night, and the cat in the glass box, and, as he pondered, any desire to sleep evaporated. He was perfectly wide-awake in the small bed.

Shadow could move quietly when he needed to. He slipped out of bed, pulled on his clothes and then, carrying his boots, he opened the window, reached over the sill and let himself tumble silently into the soil of the flowerbed beneath. He got to his feet and put on the boots, lacing them up in the half-dark. The moon was several days from full, bright enough to cast shadows.

Shadow stepped into a patch of darkness beside a wall, and he waited there.

He wondered how sane his actions were. It seemed very probable that he was wrong, that his memory had played tricks on him, or other people's had. It was all so very unlikely, but then, he had experienced the unlikely before, and if he was wrong he would be out, what? A few hours' sleep?

He watched a fox hurry across the lawn, watched a proud white cat stalk and kill a small rodent, and watched several other cats pad their way along the top of the garden wall. He saw a weasel slink from shadow to shadow in the flower bed. The constellations moved in slow procession across the sky.

The front door opened, and a figure came out. Shadow had half-expected to see Moira, but it was Oliver, wearing his pyjamas and, over them, a thick tartan dressing gown. He had Wellington boots on his feet, and he looked faintly ridiculous, like an invalid from a black and white movie, or someone in a play. There was no colour in the moonlit world.

Oliver pulled the front door closed until it clicked, then he walked towards the street, but walking on the grass, instead of crunching down the gravel path. He did not glance back, or even look around. He set off up the lane, and Shadow waited until Oliver was almost out of sight before he began to follow. He knew where Oliver was going, had to be going.

Shadow did not question himself, not any longer. He knew where they were both going, with the certainty of a person in a dream. He was not even surprised when, halfway up Wod's Hill, he found Oliver sitting on a tree stump, waiting for him. The sky was lightening, just a little, in the east.

"The Gateway to Hell," said the little man. "As far as I can tell, they've always called it that. Goes back years and years."

The two men walked up the winding path together. There was something gloriously comical about Oliver in his robe, in his striped pyjamas and his oversized black rubber boots. Shadow's heart pumped in his chest.

"How did you bring her up here?" asked Shadow.

"Cassie? I didn't. It was her idea to meet up here on the hill. She loved coming up here to paint. You can see so far. And it's holy, this hill, and she always loved that. Not holy to Christians, of course. Quite the obverse. The old religion."

"Druids?" asked Shadow. He was uncertain what other old religions there were, in England.

"Could be. Definitely could be. But I think it predates the druids. Doesn't have much of a name. It's just what people in these parts practice, beneath whatever else they believe. Druids, Norse, Catholics, Protestants, doesn't matter. That's what people pay lip service to. The old religion is what gets the crops up and keeps your cock hard and makes sure that nobody builds a bloody great motorway through an area of outstanding natural beauty. The Gateway stands, and the hill stands, and the place stands. It's well, well over two thousand years old. You don't go mucking about with anything that powerful."

Shadow said, "Moira doesn't know, does she? She thinks Cassie moved away." The sky was continuing to lighten in the east, but it was still night, spangled with a glitter of stars, in the purple-black sky to the west.

"That was what she *needed* to think. I mean, what else was she going to think? It might have been different if the police had been interested... but it wasn't like... Well. It protects itself. The hill. The gate."

They were coming up to the little meadow on the side of the hill. They passed the boulder where Shadow had seen Cassie drawing. They walked towards the hill.

"The black dog in Shuck's Lane," said Oliver. "I don't actually think it is a dog. But it's been there so long." He pulled out the small LED flashlight from the pocket of his bathrobe. "You really talked to Cassie?"

"We talked, I even kissed her."

"Strange."

"I first saw her in the pub, the night I met you and Moira. That was what made me start to figure it out. Earlier tonight, Moira was talking as if she hadn't seen Cassie in years. She was baffled when I asked. But Cassie was standing just behind me that first night, and she spoke to us. Tonight, I asked at the pub if Cassie had been in, and nobody knew who I was talking about. You people all know each other. It was the only thing that made sense of it all. It made sense of what she said. Everything."

Oliver was almost at the place Cassie had called Gateway to Hell. "I thought that it would be so simple. I would give her to the hill, and she would leave us both alone. Leave Moira alone. How could she have kissed you?"

Shadow said nothing.

"This is it," said Oliver. It was a hollow in the side of the hill, like a short hallway that went back. Perhaps, once, long ago, there had been a structure, but the hill had weathered, and the stones had returned to the hill from which they had been taken.

"There are those who think it's devil-worship," said Oliver. "And I think they are wrong. But then, one man's god is another's devil. Eh?"

He walked into the passageway, and Shadow followed him.

"Such bullshit," said a woman's voice. "But you always were a bull-shitter, Ollie, you pusillanimous little cock-stain."

Oliver did not move or react. He said, "She's here. In the wall. That's where I left her." He shone the flashlight at the wall, in the short passageway into the side of the hill. He inspected the dry stone wall carefully, as if he were looking for a place he recognised, then he made a little grunting noise of recognition. Oliver took out a compact metal tool from his pocket, reached as high as he could and levered out one little rock with it. Then he began to pull rocks out from the wall, in a set sequence, each rock opening a space to allow another to be removed, alternating large rocks and small.

"Give me a hand. Come on."

Shadow knew what he was going to see behind the wall, but he pulled out the rocks, placed them down on the ground, one by one.

There was a smell, which intensified as the hole grew bigger, a stink of old rot and mould. It smelled like old meat sandwiches gone bad. Shadow saw her face first, and he barely knew it as a face: the cheeks were sunken, the eyes gone, the skin now dark and leathery and if there were freckles they were impossible to make out; but the hair was Cassie Burglass's hair, short and black, and in the LED light, he could see that the dead thing wore an olive-green sweater, and the blue jeans were her blue jeans.

"It's funny. I knew she was still here," said Oliver. "But I still had to see her. With all your talk. I had to see it. To prove she was still here."

"Kill him," said the woman's voice. "Hit him with a rock, Shadow. He killed me. Now he's going to kill you."

"Are you going to kill me?" Shadow asked.

"Well, yes, obviously," said the little man, in his sensible voice. "I mean, you know about Cassie. And once you're gone, I can just finally forget about the whole thing, once and for all."

"Forget?"

"Forgive *and* forget. But it's hard. It's not easy to forgive myself, but I'm sure I can forget. There. I think there's enough room for you to get in there now, if you squeeze."

Shadow looked down at the little man. "Out of interest," he said, curious, "how are you going to make me get in there? You don't have a gun on you. And Ollie, I'm twice your size. You know, I could just break your neck."

"I'm not a stupid man," said Oliver. "I'm not a bad man, either. I'm not a terribly well man, but that's neither here nor there, really. I mean, I did what I did because I was jealous, not because I was ill. But I wouldn't have come up here alone. You see, this is the Temple of the Black Dog. These places were the first temples. Before the Stonehenges and the standing stones, they were waiting and they were worshipped, and sacrificed to, and feared, and placated. The Black Shucks and the Barghests, the Padfoots and the Wish Hounds. They were here and they remain on guard."

"Hit him with a rock," said Cassie's voice. "Hit him now, Shadow, *please.*"

The passage they stood in went a little way into the hillside, a man-made cave with dry stone walls. It did not look like an ancient temple. It did not look like a gateway to Hell. The pre-dawn sky framed Oliver. In his gentle, unfailingly polite voice, he said, "He is in me. And I am in him."

The black dog filled the doorway, blocking the way to the world outside, and, Shadow knew, whatever it was, it was no true dog. Its eyes actually glowed, with a luminescence that reminded Shadow of rotting sea-creatures. It was to a wolf, in scale and in menace, what a tiger is to a lynx: pure carnivore, a creature made of danger and threat. It stood taller than Oliver and it stared at Shadow, and it growled, a rumbling deep in its chest. Then it sprang.

Shadow raised his arm to protect his throat, and the creature sank its teeth into his flesh, just below the elbow. The pain was excruciating. He knew he should fight back, but he was falling to his knees, and he was screaming, unable to think clearly, unable to focus on anything except his fear that the creature was going to use him for food, fear it was crushing the bone of his forearm.

On some deep level he suspected that the fear was being created by the dog: that he, Shadow, was not cripplingly afraid like that. Not really. But it did not matter. When the creature released Shadow's arm, he was weeping and his whole body was shaking.

Oliver said, "Get in there, Shadow. Through the gap in the wall. Quickly, now. Or I'll have him chew off your face."

Shadow's arm was bleeding, but he got up and squeezed through the gap into the darkness without arguing. If he stayed out there, with the beast, he would die soon, and die in pain. He knew that with as much certainty as he knew that the sun would rise tomorrow.

"Well, yes," said Cassie's voice in his head. "It's going to rise. But unless you get your shit together you are never going to see it."

There was barely space for him and Cassie's body in the cavity behind the wall. He had seen the expression of pain and fury on her face, like the face of the cat in the glass box, and then he knew she, too, had been entombed here while alive.

Oliver picked up a rock from the ground, and placed it onto the wall, in the gap. "My own theory," he said, hefting a second rock and putting it into position, "is that it is the prehistoric dire wolf. But it is bigger than ever the dire wolf was. Perhaps it is the monster of our dreams, when we huddled in caves. Perhaps it was simply a wolf, but we were smaller, little hominids, who could never run fast enough to get away."

Shadow leaned against the rock face behind him. He squeezed his left arm with his right hand to try to stop the bleeding. "This is Wod's Hill," said Shadow. "And that's Wod's dog. I wouldn't put it past him."

"It doesn't matter." More stones were placed on stones.

"Ollie," said Shadow. "The beast is going to kill you. It's already inside you. It's not a good thing."

"Old Shuck's not going to hurt me. Old Shuck loves me. Cassie's in the wall," said Oliver, and he dropped a rock on top of the others with a crash. "Now you are in the wall with her. Nobody's waiting for you. Nobody's going to come looking for you. Nobody is going to cry for you. Nobody's going to miss you."

There were, Shadow knew, although he could never have told a soul how he knew, three of them, not two, in that tiny space. There was Cassie Burglass, there in body (rotted and dried and still stinking of decay) and there in soul, and there was also something else, something that twined about his legs, and then butted gently at his injured hand. A voice spoke to him, from somewhere close. He knew that voice, although the accent was unfamiliar.

It was the voice that a cat would speak in, if a cat were a woman: expressive, dark, musical. The voice said, *You should not be here, Shadow. You have to stop, and you must take action. You are letting the rest of the world make your decisions for you.*

Shadow said aloud, "That's not entirely fair, Bast."

"You have to be quiet," said Oliver, gently. "I mean it." The stones of the wall were being replaced rapidly and efficiently. Already they were up to Shadow's chest.

Mrr. No? Sweet thing, you really have no idea. No idea who you are or what you are or what that means. If he walls you up in here to die in this hill, this temple will stand forever—and whatever hodge-podge of belief these locals have will work for them and will make magic. But the sun will still go down on them, and all the skies will be grey. All things will mourn, and they will not know what they are mourning for. The world will be worse—for people, for cats, for the remembered, for the forgotten. You have died and you have returned. You matter, Shadow, and you must not meet your death here, a sad sacrifice hidden in a hillside.

"So what are you suggesting I do?" he whispered.

Fight. The beast is a thing of mind. It's taking its power from you, Shadow. You are near, and so it's become more real. Real enough to own Oliver. Real enough to hurt you.

"Me?"

"You think ghosts can talk to everyone?" asked Cassie Burglass's voice in the darkness, urgently. "We are moths. And you are the flame."

"What should I do?" asked Shadow. "It's hurt my arm. It damn near ripped out my throat."

Oh, sweet man. It's just a shadow-thing. It's a night-dog. It's just an overgrown jackal.

"It's real," Shadow said. The last of the stones was being banged into place.

"Are you truly scared of your father's dog?" said a woman's voice. Goddess or ghost, Shadow did not know.

But he knew the answer. Yes. Yes, he was scared.

His left arm was only pain, and unusable, and his right hand was slick and sticky with his blood. He was entombed in a cavity between a wall and rock. But he was, for now, alive.

"Get your shit together," said Cassie. "I've done everything I can. Do it."

He braced himself against the rocks behind the wall, and he raised his feet. Then he kicked both his booted feet out together, as hard as he could. He had walked so many miles in the last few months. He was a big man, and he was stronger than most. He put everything he had behind that kick.

The wall exploded.

The beast was on him, the black dog of despair, but this time Shadow was prepared for it. This time he was the aggressor. He grabbed at it.

I will not be my father's dog.

With his right hand he held the beast's jaw closed. He stared into its green eyes. He did not believe the beast was a dog at all, not really.

It's daylight, said Shadow to the dog, with his mind, not with his voice. *Run away. Whatever you are, run away. Run back to your gibbet, run back to your grave, little Wish Hound. All you can do is depress us, fill the world with shadows and illusions. The age when you ran with the Wild Hunt, or hunted terrified humans, it's over. I don't know if you're my father's dog or not. But you know what? I don't care.*

With that, Shadow took a deep breath and let go of the dog's muzzle.

It did not attack. It made a noise, a baffled whine deep in its throat that was almost a whimper.

"Go home," said Shadow, aloud.

The dog hesitated. Shadow thought for a moment then that he had won, that he was safe, that the dog would simply go away. But then the creature lowered its head, raised the ruff around its neck, and bared its teeth. It would not leave, Shadow knew, until he was dead.

The corridor in the hillside was filling with light: the rising sun shone directly into it. Shadow wondered if the people who had built it, so long ago, had aligned their temple to the sunrise. He took a step to the side, stumbled on something, and fell awkwardly to the ground.

Beside Shadow on the grass was Oliver, sprawled and unconscious. Shadow had tripped over his leg. The man's eyes were closed; he made a growling sound in the back of his throat, and Shadow heard the same sound, magnified and triumphant, from the dark beast that filled the mouth of the temple.

Shadow was down, and hurt, and was, he knew, a dead man.

Something soft touched his face, gently.

Something else brushed his hand. Shadow glanced to his side, and he understood. He understood why Bast had been with him in this place, and he understood who had brought her.

They had been ground up and sprinkled on these fields more than a hundred years before, stolen from the earth around the temple of Bastet and Beni Hasan. Tons upon tons of them, mummified cats in their thousands, each cat a tiny representation of the deity, each cat an act of worship preserved for an eternity.

They were there, in that space, beside him: brown and sand-coloured and shadowy-grey, cats with leopard spots and cats with tiger stripes, wild, lithe and ancient. These were not the local cats Bast had sent to watch him the previous day. These were the ancestors of those cats, of all our modern cats, from Egypt, from the Nile Delta, from thousands of years ago, brought here to make things grow.

They trilled and chirruped, they did not meow.

The black dog growled louder but now it made no move to attack. Shadow forced himself into a sitting position. "I thought I told you to go home, Shuck," he said.

The dog did not move. Shadow opened his right hand, and gestured. It was a gesture of dismissal, of impatience. *Finish this.*

The cats sprang, with ease, as if choreographed. They landed on the beast, each of them a coiled spring of fangs and claws both as sharp as they had ever been in life. Pin-sharp claws sank in to the black flanks of the huge beast, tore at its eyes. It snapped at them, angrily, and pushed itself against the wall, toppling more rocks, in an attempt to shake them off, but without success. Angry teeth sank into its ears, its muzzle, its tail, its paws.

The beast yelped and growled, and then it made a noise which, Shadow thought, would, had it come from any human throat, have been a scream.

Shadow was never certain what happened then. He watched the black dog put its muzzle down to Oliver's mouth, and push, hard. He could have sworn that the creature stepped *into* Oliver, like a bear stepping into a river.

Oliver shook, violently, on the sand.

The scream faded, and the beast was gone, and sunlight filled the space on the hill.

Shadow felt himself shivering. He felt like he had just woken up from a waking sleep; emotions flooded through him, like sunlight: fear and revulsion and grief and hurt, deep hurt.

There was anger in there, too. Oliver had tried to kill him, he knew, and he was thinking clearly for the first time in days.

A man's voice shouted, "Hold up! Everyone all right over there?"

A high bark, and a lurcher ran in, sniffed at Shadow, his back against the wall, sniffed at Oliver Bierce, unconscious on the ground, and at the remains of Cassie Burglass.

A man's silhouette filled the opening to the outside world, a grey paper cut-out against the rising sun.

"Needles! Leave it!" he said. The dog returned to the man's side. The man said, "I heard someone screaming. Leastways, I wouldn't swear to it being a someone. But I heard it. Was that you?"

And then he saw the body, and he stopped. "Holy fucking mother of all fucking bastards," he said.

"Her name was Cassie Burglass," said Shadow.

"Moira's old girlfriend?" said the man. Shadow knew him as the landlord of the pub, could not remember whether he had ever known the man's name. "Bloody Nora. I thought she went to London."

Shadow felt sick.

The landlord was kneeling beside Oliver. "His heart's still beating," he said. "What happened to him?"

"I'm not sure," said Shadow. "He screamed when he saw the body—

you must have heard him. Then he just went down. And your dog came in."

The man looked at Shadow, worried. "And you? Look at you! What happened to you, man?"

"Oliver asked me to come up here with him. Said he had something awful he had to get off his chest." Shadow looked at the wall on each side of the corridor. There were other bricked-in nooks there. Shadow had a good idea of what would be found behind them if any of them were opened. "He asked me to help him open the wall. I did. He knocked me over as he went down. Took me by surprise."

"Did he tell you why he had done it?"

"Jealousy," said Shadow. "Just jealous of Moira and Cassie, even after Moira had left Cassie for him."

The man exhaled, shook his head. "Bloody hell," he said. "Last bugger I'd expect to do anything like this. Needles! Leave it!" He pulled a mobile phone from his pocket, and called the police. Then he excused himself. "I've got a bag of game to put aside until the police have cleared out," he explained.

Shadow got to his feet, and inspected his arms. His sweater and coat were both ripped in the left arm, as if by huge teeth, but his skin was unbroken beneath it. There was no blood on his clothes, no blood on his hands.

He wondered what his corpse would have looked like, if the black dog had killed him.

Cassie's ghost stood beside him, and looked down at her body, half-fallen from the hole in the wall. The corpse's fingertips and the fingernails were wrecked, Shadow observed, as if she had tried, in the hours or the days before she died, to dislodge the rocks of the wall.

"Look at that," she said, staring at herself. "Poor thing. Like a cat in a glass box." Then she turned to Shadow. "I didn't actually fancy you," she said. "Not even a little bit. I'm not sorry. I just needed to get your attention."

"I know," said Shadow. "I just wish I'd met you when you were alive. We could have been friends."

"I bet we would have been. It was hard in there. It's good to be done with all of this. And I'm sorry, Mr. American. Try not to hate me."

Shadow's eyes were watering. He wiped his eyes on his shirt. When he looked again, he was alone in the passageway.

"I don't hate you," he told her.

He felt a hand squeeze his hand. He walked outside, into the morning sunlight, and he breathed and shivered, and listened to the distant sirens.

Two men arrived and carried Oliver away on a stretcher, down the hill to the road where an ambulance took him away, siren screaming to alert any sheep on the lanes that they should shuffle back to the grass verge.

A female police officer turned up as the ambulance disappeared, accompanied by a younger male officer. They knew the landlord, whom Shadow was not surprised to learn was also a Scathelocke, and were both impressed by Cassie's remains, to the point that the young male officer left the passageway and vomited into the ferns.

If it occurred to either of them to inspect the other bricked-in cavities in the corridor, for evidence of centuries-old crimes, they managed to suppress the idea, and Shadow was not going to suggest it.

He gave them a brief statement, then rode with them to the local police station, where he gave a fuller statement to a large police officer with a serious beard. The officer appeared mostly concerned that Shadow was provided with a mug of instant coffee, and that Shadow, as an American tourist, would form a mistaken impression of rural England. "It's not like this up here normally. It's really quiet. Lovely place. I wouldn't want you to think we were all like this."

Shadow assured him that he didn't think that at all.

VI. The Riddle

Moira was waiting for him when he came out of the police station.

She was standing with a woman in her early sixties, who looked comfortable and reassuring, the sort of person you would want at your side in a crisis.

"Shadow, this is Doreen. My sister."

Doreen shook hands, explaining she was sorry she hadn't been able to be there during the last week, but she had been moving house.

"Doreen's a County Court judge," explained Moira.

Shadow could not easily imagine this woman as a judge.

"They are waiting for Ollie to come around," said Moira. "Then they are going to charge him with murder." She said it thoughtfully, but in the same way she would have asked Shadow where he thought she ought to plant some Snapdragons.

"And what are you going to do?"

She scratched her nose. "I'm in shock. I have no idea what I'm doing any more. I keep thinking about the last few years. Poor, poor Cassie. She never thought there was any malice in him."

"I never liked him," said Doreen, and she sniffed. "Too full of facts for my liking, and he never knew when to stop talking. Just kept wittering on. Like he was trying to cover something up."

"Your backpack and your laundry, are in Doreen's car," said Moira. "I thought we could give you a lift somewhere, if you needed one. Or if you want to get back to rambling, you can walk."

"Thank you," said Shadow. He knew he would never be welcome in Moira's little house, not any more.

Moira said, urgently, angrily, as if it was all she wanted to know, "You said you saw Cassie. You *told* us, yesterday. That was what sent Ollie off the deep end. It hurt me so much. Why did you say you'd seen her, if she was dead? You *couldn't* have seen her."

Shadow had been wondering about that, while he had been giving his police statement. "Beats me," he said. "I don't believe in ghosts. Probably a local, playing some kind of game with the Yankee tourist."

Moira looked at him with fierce hazel eyes, as if she was trying to believe him but was unable to make the final leap of faith. Her sister reached down and held her hand. "More things in Heaven and Earth, Horatio. I think we should just leave it at that."

Moira looked at Shadow, unbelieving, angered, for a long time, before she took a deep breath and said, "Yes. Yes, I suppose we should."

There was silence in the car. Shadow wanted to apologise to Moira, to say something that would make things better.

They drove past the gibbet tree.

"*There were ten tongues within one head,*" recited Doreen, in a voice slightly higher and more formal than the one in which she had previously spoken. "*And one went out to fetch some bread, to feed the living and the dead.* That was a riddle written about this corner, and that tree."

"What does it mean?"

"A wren made a nest inside the skull of a gibbeted corpse, flying in and out of the jaw to feed its young. In the midst of death, as it were, life just keeps on happening."

Shadow thought about the matter for a little while, and told her that he guessed that it probably did.

STORM CONSTANTINE

IN THE EARTH

S TORM CONSTANTINE is the creator of the "Wraeththu
Mythos", the first trilogy of which was published in the 1980s.
She has written more than thirty books, including full-length novels
(*Hermetech, Burying the Shadow* etc.), novellas, short story collec-
tions and non-fiction titles, such as *Sekhem Heka*. She is currently
working on a new novel and several short stories.

Constantine is the founder of the independent publishing house
Immanion Press. She lives in the Midlands of the UK with her
husband and four cats.

"'In the Earth' was primarily inspired by my recollections of a
childhood friend," she recalls, "who was an unusual person to say
the least, but exciting company. Several of the escapades described
in the tale are drawn from my own experiences, although embellished for this piece.

"I was always a little frightened but so intrigued and awed I
never wanted to say no to any of my friend's ideas and lose her
respect. This friend didn't disappear from my life because of doing
something terrible, she merely moved away with her family. But
only a few years ago, I met someone who still knew her, and when
I suggested getting in touch with her, the response I got had to be
included in the end of this story."

∾

THE CENTIPEDE WAS cut in two. "Why did you kill it?" Mawde asked.

Jeryl pursed her lips. She was squatting in the dirt of the lower cellar, the frilly skirt of her white Sunday dress pulled up over her knees. "Don't you know what they *do*?" she said.

Mawde shook her head. "Run about?"

"They *burrow*—into *any* hole of your body, and then they start eating."

Mawde grimaced. She couldn't believe that. Why would a humble creature like a centipede do that?

"They *do*," said Jeryl. "I've seen pictures. They ate a woman's eyes from the inside."

Mawde was sentimental about all creatures, whereas her cousin Jeryl seemed fixed with the idea that if anything was small enough to slaughter with a quick stamp of the foot or a blow from a trowel, then it was her treat—or perhaps her duty—to kill it. Mawde's mother said that all animals, however scary and unpleasant they might look, were all part of Nature's creations and must be respected. Loved.

Jeryl's mother didn't believe in anything. Now Jeryl poked the centipede parts with a stick she'd found.

Outside, the summer was gloomy and thundery, pressing down on the tall wooden house, making its labyrinth of cellars a cauldron of shadows and lifeless air. A smell of old earth surrounded the girls; pungent and musty. Jeryl was staying with Mawde's family for a whole month during the school holidays. She liked to play in the cellars. She said there were tunnels down there, hidden behind the sagging wooden racks and shelves, which snaked right into Pike Mountain, dating back to the start of time. Even when dressed in feminine flounces, within this confection lurked the heart and mind of a grubby little boy. No amount of dressing up would change that.

Jeryl had been looking for tunnels (hence the digging that had unearthed the doomed centipede), but to Mawde's relief so far none had been found. She liked her cousin's company but wished sometimes her favoured pastimes didn't have to involve danger or fear.

It wasn't enough simply to sit in the sunshine on the porch roof, but Jeryl insisted they had to jump down from this height onto the lawn, which hurt Mawde's ankles and feet. They couldn't just play make-believe in the cellars but had to look for tunnels—undoubtedly haunted, or so Jeryl said. Neither was it enough to climb the tall old yew trees that clustered like hags at the garden's edge; they had to hang upside-down by their knees from the highest branch they could reach... then right themselves and drop to the ground. Jeryl was always on the lookout for higher places from which they could jump and was unconcerned that yew wood was relatively soft and therefore not the best support for weight, even of a child.

She was obsessed with heights, but also like to push herself physically. "This *could* be too high," she might say solemnly, before holding out her arms and throwing herself into the air. Mawde was afraid of these antics—demands, even—but couldn't bring herself to refuse them. Jeryl's scorn was worse than her challenges. But that aside, she was the most fascinating playmate, unlike any other girl Mawde knew.

Neither set of parents were aware what the girls got up to during their holidays. In all the households Mawde knew, it was common for the children to be shooed out of adult company after breakfast, tolerated briefly at lunch, then sent out again until tea. Unless it was bad weather when they were allowed to play indoors, but out of adult hearing, such as in the attics or cellars. Bizarrely, neither Jeryl nor Mawde had ever hurt themselves, which perhaps—Mawde thought—meant that her mother's stories about guardian angels must be true.

That night another storm came up from the south, crotchety and fevered. When lightning pierced the hot sky it had the look of bruised flesh being punctured by needles. The heat, the anxiety of the sky, infected the old house. It groaned in what sounded to Mawde like dread.

Her cousin Jeryl slept in a bed on the other side of the room, but had fallen asleep soon after the curtains had been drawn, and did not wake, even when flickering storm light illumined the room. The unseen inhabitants of the house—vermin and insects—were skittish, pattering behind the walls and in the cavities above the ceilings, below the floors. Mawde lay awake, thinking of the centipede her cousin had killed, how the halves had curled in on themselves. The creature had felt pain, and it had been so big. What if...?

No, Mawde told herself, *no. It was an insect. Didn't have feelings.*

The rain, when it came, was of the kind that Mawde's grandmother often referred to as "the tears of the world"—that is, a deluge beyond measure. Even through the curtains, the stormlight now seemed watery, running down the walls of the room, threading between the somehow sickeningly large roses of the wallpaper. Despite the rain, the air was hot and Mawde's body felt sticky and uncomfortable beneath her light summer blanket.

She drifted in and out of sleep, images flickering across her mind's eye, her head aching. She dreamed of earthy tunnels and myriad feet in the dark. On her hands and knees she crawled through the dirt, then it was as if she slithered along it on her belly, and the scent of loam and rot was like the sweet hearth of home. She was comfortable in this dream, neither scared nor excited, simply... doing her business.

Then, as dreams do, the world shifted, and she was standing barefoot in the middle of her bedroom with the watery light over the walls and the blanket-cocooned hump of her cousin's shape in the bed before her.

Was this a dream?

"Jeryl?" Mawde breathed.

The hump in the bed twitched and a strange little sleeping-noise came out of the blankets, such as a slumbering dog might utter, as it ran across its dream-fields.

Mawde went to the bed and placed a hand on her cousin's shoulder, shook it. "Jeryl?"

Another noise came out, like dead branches rubbing together, or a bowl of dried peas being thrown down the stairs. Dream-Mawde pulled back the blankets, saw what lay there. A centipede, cut in half, the size of an eleven-year-old girl, the parts curled in on themselves. But the face between the feelers at the head was Jeryl's, and now she looked up at her cousin with all the pain of the world, its deluge of tears in her eyes.

Mawde woke with a cry. She felt sick, wanted to vomit, but then the feeling passed. She sat up, glanced fearfully at the bed to her right. "Jeryl?" she murmured. And then louder: "Jeryl!"

"Wassamatter?" came a grumpy reply.

"I had a dream," Mawde said.

Jeryl sat up in her bed too, scraped hair from her eyes. "You're awake now. Open the curtains."

Mawde shuddered. "No!"

Jeryl expressed a disappointed sigh and clambered from her bed, went to the window.

"Why?" Mawde asked.

"There might be angels in the windows," Jeryl said. "I see them a lot at home, especially when I wake up from a dream."

Mawde had not heard Jeryl mention this before. "You *see* them?" she asked timorously.

"Yes, they fill the window, very tall. They tell me things, but I never want them to step out and get into the shadows. It's important to keep them where they are, because then you can see them. They can't hide and whisper things."

An angel is a kind, beautiful creature, Mawde thought, but in that moment the idea of seeing one seemed the most terrifying thing possible.

But all that was in the window was the fluid mosaic of running water and Jeryl's face, half-asleep, dripping with the light.

The storm passed away moodily to the north, and summer returned in its wake. The morning was magnificent, inviting, and any echoes of the disturbing dream and its unsettling aftermath faded from Mawde's mind.

Now the weather was better, the cousins could ride their bicycles out into the country lanes around Mawde's home, which were empty of traffic during the week, except for the occasional farm vehicle or someone riding a horse.

No longer required to wear what Jeryl referred to as "stupid doll dresses", they were attired in shorts, T-shirts and pumps, riding their bikes from village to village. In nearby Elmslane was a tiny shop that sold ice cream, which they always aimed for before returning home for the day. In every village, Jeryl was drawn to the moss-robed old churches, looking for ghosts or evidence of people being buried alive. She would examine headstones for mysteries. "Look, this woman died two days before her baby, and she wasn't much older than *us*. The father killed the baby because it had killed her. That's obvious."

Ever since Jeryl had started visiting her cousin in the holidays, one of her favourite pastimes was to hide and frighten people, especially those who came to tend graves. As graveyards were often thick with yew trees—Jeryl's favourite kind—she would order Mawde to climb into the branches and stay very still. A woman might come, or an elderly man, and then Jeryl would coo something sinister, such as, "Nooo, nooo, tooo soon". Or simply hoot like an owl or utter a sound like an exclamation from a startled dog or cat.

They were rarely caught, and if the victim did spy them, the girls would throw themselves from the tree and run off like deer. Mostly, the people would pay no attention, but it was satisfying when a frightened face looked up, glanced around themselves, hurried away. Then the cousins would giggle uncontrollably. "Let's go to the next place," Jeryl would say.

But that day, the graveyards were empty of sport and Jeryl became restless. She suggested a visit to another of their haunts.

At the western end of Dappleheath, Mawde's home village, was a row of old houses with long gardens. At the bottom of these summer-time jungles was a "no-man's-land" that didn't appear to belong to anybody. This was a narrow ribbon of woodland—holly, birch, thick stands of elderberry, some domesticated fruit trees that had perhaps escaped the gardens—through which a stream ran. On the other side of the trees was a school playing-field that seemed inordinately huge and was rarely used. Not that Mawde ever saw it that often in term-time; her school was somewhere else.

After heavy rain, one section of the stream would swell to fill a shallow sandy pool. Naturally, as the pool's width varied, and offered on some occasions a greater challenge, Jeryl liked to take a run and jump it. Mawde was afraid of getting wet, even though the water was hardly treacherous and less than three inches at its deepest point. There was simply something disturbing about the way it was so important to Jeryl that they succeeded in their jumps; as if, should they fail, some calamity would happen.

Today, of course, after the storm, the waters would be engorged and swift—as much as they ever could be—and Jeryl was eager to see how wide the pool would be.

Mawde liked the wood, even if she didn't enjoy the jumping that much. There was such a variety of life within it, as if it were a minia- ture, and therefore magical, ancient woodland. Rabbits braved the boundary between this small wilderness and the shorn playing-field. A woodpecker lived there; always heard, sometimes seen. The petals of flowers—periwinkle, forget-me-not, campion—seemed more vivid there amid the emerald forest grass that was springy underfoot. Mawde liked to think it was a sanctuary for benign magical creatures, but to Jeryl it was the fortress of capricious fairies, who would steal babies, swap them for a blackened tree stump. They could suck out a beautiful girl's youth, or curse a man to fall in love, then go blind, mad. Jeryl searched for the spoor of these beings relentlessly.

On that day, as Jeryl rooted in the soft, dark earth, like a terrier rummaging for a buried bone, Mawde wondered why—for her— angels were golden and good, and fairies were simply aloof and mysterious, yet for Jeryl these creatures were always cruel and vengeful, full of hate for humanity.

"Look at this," Jeryl said, wonder in her voice. She had uncov- ered something beneath a stone, perhaps evidence of a fairy atrocity.

But before Mawde could come to look, a harsh male voice rang out. "Hoi! Get out of there! This is private property! Gerrout!"

The cousins stared at each other in alarm, before jumping to their

feet. Mawde had a glimpse of an unfriendly male face—elderly—
staring over the fence at the bottom of the nearest garden.

"Don't you come back here, you little pests!" he roared as Jeryl
and Mawde scampered away. "Private property, you hear?"

Usually, when caught out, and a swift retreat was called for, Jeryl
laughed and poked fun at whoever had yelled at them, but this time,
when they emerged through a hole in the fence by the lane, where
their bicycles lay hidden in the long grass and cow parsley, Jeryl's
face was pinched.

"Stupid old git," Mawde offered, hoping Jeryl would then smile
and say something even more insulting.

"I'll get 'im," Jeryl said simply, not even with darkness in her tone,
just stating a simple fact. She lifted her bicycle from the grass. "No
one uses that land. It's wild. No one should stop us."

"*How* will you get him?" Mawde asked.

Jeryl said nothing. She mounted her bike and jerked her head to
indicate Mawde should follow.

They went to another woodland place they liked—a copse of oaks
and beeches in a hollow in the middle of a hay field. But sometimes
other children were there, which neither Mawde nor Jeryl liked
particularly. Today, mercifully, they had it to themselves.

Jeryl was still not speaking, despite Mawde's efforts to lighten the
atmosphere. Jeryl simply rooted, clawing at sodden dead wood and
beneath the bracken. She turned over a large log that had to be
pulled forcibly from the earth, making a sucking sound. Beneath,
the ground teemed with insect life—woodlice, beetles, centipedes.
"Oh, look," Mawde murmured. "So many of them."

Jeryl stood up; then, methodically, she began stamping on the
tiny creatures, grinding her foot against the soil, all the time making
a soft, grunting sound.

"Stop it," Mawde said. "Stop, Jeryl."

Jeryl wouldn't stop, and for the first time, Mawde ran away from
her cousin, out of the shade of the wise oaks, across the sun-soaked
hay field, and went home alone.

Jeryl did not reappear until teatime. To protect her cousin from any parental chastisement, or indeed herself for leaving Jeryl alone in the copse, Mawde hid in the garden until she heard the whirr of Jeryl's bicycle wheels on the gravel of the drive. Then, Mawde ran from her hiding place, across the lawn.

At that moment, Mawde's mother came out the house, no doubt to advise them their tea was ready. She caught sight of Jeryl, muddied and unkempt, then glanced briefly at her tidier daughter. "What have you been doing?" she snapped. "Where have you been?"

Jeryl stared defiantly, shrugged.

Horrified at what this insolent response might evoke in her normally fair-minded mother, Mawde said, "We went fishing and Jeryl fell over in a muddy place."

"Mud?" said Mawde's mother in a voice that might easily have been saying "entrails?" so disgusted was her tone. Mawde realised then— one of the chiming epiphanies of childhood—that although her mother considered nature beautiful and to be respected from a distance, in her view no girl had any place getting *into* it and letting it dirty her.

"Get changed," she said severely to Jeryl. "And wash yourself as best you can. Bath later." She turned to Mawde, "As for you, young lady…"

"I'll wash and change too," Mawde said, even though she wasn't very dirty. She ran after Jeryl, who was stomping into the house.

In the bathroom, Jeryl was still quiet, although she hummed to herself softly. "Are you all right?" Mawde asked.

"Of course," Jeryl answered.

"Jeryl…" Mawde began. She knew she had to speak, say *something*, but the words were reluctant. "You shouldn't kill things like that."

Jeryl flicked a sharp glance at her. "They don't mind dying for me. They expect it."

"*Dying* for you…?"

"How else can I tell them what I want? Beetles don't have brains, but they have eyes. You have to show them." Jeryl threw water over her face, rubbed mud from her arms.

Mawde remembered her dream then, the insect Jeryl in the bed, cut in half. "You're wrong," she said.

Jeryl expressed a contemptuous snort. "*You* don't know anything. Keep your trap shut."

The look in Jeryl's eyes was frightening, so cold and dark, like winter earth; small scuttling things moving behind it. A distinct thought formed in Mawde's mind: *don't make her angry with you.*

"Sorry," she said, and went to the bath where she washed her hands. She didn't want to share the sink Jeryl was using.

That night, Mawde slept deeply and did not wake. To her, it was an ordinary night and the morning that followed it equally ordinary. Jeryl seemed brighter now, for which Mawde was grateful. The sullen, quiet Jeryl frightened her; she'd never been like this on previous visits.

While they were washing-up for Mawde's mother after breakfast, a knock came at the back door. Friends and family never used the forbidding front door, which was rarely opened. This visitor came right inside without waiting to be invited—a friend of Mawde's mother called Mrs. Cherry. She had a sickly son, who went to the same school as Mawde and was excused sports and swimming.

After the ritual offering of tea, and with Mrs. Cherry established at the kitchen table, the woman lit a cigarette, inhaled purposefully and on her exhale, announced with relish, "The Hensons had dreadful trouble last night."

"Who?" asked Mawde's mother.

"Live in End Lane, the one with the green door."

"Oh...yes...I don't know them personally. What trouble?"

Mrs. Cherry chewed her words with satisfaction before sharing them. "Vandals got in their garden. Made a terrible mess. Ruined it, you know. Ruined it! Even the greenhouse gone. It's just a mud patch now, I heard. And you know what?"

"What?"

"They didn't hear a *thing*. Got police round now, of course."

"How dreadful..."

Mawde's head had begun to buzz. She felt strangely dizzy and disorientated. End Lane . . . the wood at the back of the houses where she and Jeryl had been yesterday. She knew her face had gone bright red, and that it was important her mother didn't notice this.

Jeryl was still washing dishes in a serene manner, as if her mind was far away, as if she hadn't heard.

"Susan Ross just told me that May Henson's kitchen was absolutely crawling with beetles this morning. Unearthed, I expect. They were in *everything*."

Mawde put away carefully the last dish she was drying. "Can we go now, Mum?"

Mawde's mother nodded distractedly. "Yes, sweetheart. Don't be late for lunch."

Outside, as the cousins walked to the shed where the bicycles were stored, Jeryl was again quiet, although she was smiling—a private expression she clearly had no intention of sharing.

Mawde wanted to say something, *ask* something, desperately, but was afraid to do so. She sensed endings and change, the summer fading, without understanding why.

At the shed, as she wrestled with the padlock—unlocked but as recalcitrant as if it were stuck fast—she said, "Wonder if it was the man who shouted at us . . . whose garden was wrecked?" She glanced up at her cousin.

Jeryl stared back for a moment, the put out her tongue. Mawde jumped backwards. There was a centipede on Jeryl's tongue, still and wet, just lying there. Jeryl uttered a squawk of laughter, then spat. Mawde winced away.

"Told you," Jeryl said.

After that summer, the cousins grew apart. Further details of the holiday became blurred in Mawde's mind, but then perhaps Jeryl had returned home only a couple of days after the garden-wrecking incident—a crime for which no one was caught.

Later that year, Mawde overheard a couple of whispered, coded conversations that her mother held on the phone with friends. Listening carefully from concealment, Mawde deciphered Jeryl had been in severe trouble at school. Phrases such as, "difficult child" and "a bit touched" were breathed down the line. Mawde gleaned that for Jeryl a new and different kind of school had been in order; her mother and father had moved a couple of hundred miles away to be near her.

There had been no further holiday visits, and the relationship between Mawde's mother and her sister inexplicably cooled. Mawde couldn't divine the reason, and her mother kept her secrets until she died, quite young.

Mawde had no idea where her aunt lived, and any questions made to her father resulted only in "Let it lie, Mawde. They don't want us contacting them."

Jeryl became a childhood memory; a strange yet intriguing girl. Mawde never spoke about her, and eventually forgot her, except for moments during summer storms, when she lay awake in the dark at night and heard insects in the walls.

Then, by chance, many years later when Mawde was in her late thirties, her work brought her into contact with Meredith Jones, a woman who'd known Jeryl as a child. Mawde had even met her a couple of times at gatherings of Jeryl's family, not that she recognised Meredith's grown-up face, and—unlike Mawde—she had married, so her name was different.

After an office meeting, as both women were putting away their laptops, Meredith said, "You're not the Mawde Emsley who's a cousin of Jeryl Ashman, are you?"

"Yes, I am," Mawde said, surprised. In an instant, the past came hurtling back and she felt faintly disorientated. She smelled earth.

"You probably don't remember me," Meredith said. "I was a friend of Jeryl's." She laughed. "Well, went to the same school, and was invited to birthdays and so on, but Jeryl didn't really have friends, did she?"

"I . . . well . . . it was a long time ago," Mawde said, in a colder tone than she intended.

Meredith blinked in a nonplussed manner, clearly unsure what to say.

Mawde made a vague gesture with one hand, looked away, fiddled with her computer bag. "Family thing. There was a rift..."

"Ah." Meredith sighed, then ploughed on bluntly. "Can't say I'm surprised. They had a terrible time with her, terrible. So sad for the parents, having to move away and virtually take on new identities." She offered a pitying expression. "But of course, you must know that."

Mawde grimaced, which she trusted would indicate she didn't wish to speak further on the matter, although part of her was itching to interrogate this stranger. The problem was, she didn't know *anything*. This childhood acquaintance of Jeryl's knew more.

"Are you still in touch with the family?" Mawde asked, as lightly as she could muster.

"My mother is," was the reply.

"I wonder..." Mawde now spoke impulsively. "Jeryl and I had no say in...becoming estranged when we were children. I wonder whether I should contact her?"

The woman gave Mawde a glance that was full of meaning, bursting with it: a keen arrow of a glance. "That's up to you," she said carefully, "but...she's a very *troubled* person, Mawde."

Polite euphemism, Mawde thought. She nodded. "Yes," she said, "I expect she is. Cut in two." She hadn't meant to say those last few words, but Meredith Jones nodded.

"Yes, you could put it like that," she said. "Tragic."

Mawde muttered a hasty goodbye and fled the room. Outside, it was thundery, the lawn beyond the office building oozing and mulchy. Mawde saw a brief image before her mind's eye of Jeryl crouching in the dirt, glancing up, her smile as secretive and cruel as that of the fairies in which she believed. There were insects on her skin, like a living tattoo. Then she sank into the wet earth until only her eyes remained, peering out.

STEVE RASNIC TEM

IN THE LOVECRAFT MUSEUM

STEVE RASNIC TEM's last novel, *Blood Kin* (Solaris, 2014), won the HWA Bram Stoker Award. His next, *UBO* (Solaris, January 2017), is a dark science fictional tale about violence and its origins, featuring such historical viewpoint characters as Jack the Ripper, Stalin, and Heinrich Himmler. He is also a past winner of the World Fantasy and British Fantasy Awards.

A handbook on writing, Y*ours To Tell: Dialogues on the Art & Practice of Writing*, written with his late wife Melanie, is due from Apex Books. Further into the future, Colorado-based HEX Publications will bring out his young adult Halloween novel, *The Mask Shop of Doctor Blaack*.

"The initial seeds for 'In the Lovecraft Museum' were planted in 1988 on my first trip to the UK. Our son had died earlier that year and frankly I was no longer quite sure who I was anymore—life had become something strange and absurd. I was fascinated by the British, particularly by how they seemed to have come up with different solutions for such basics as electricity, plumbing, foods, and yet they spoke English!

"Even at the time I realised this was a pretty naïve and unso-phisticated way to look at cultural differences—chalk it up to trauma, but Britain felt like an alternative universe. At our first B&B I started looking behind things, taking things apart, lifting up rugs, examining fixtures, bolts, fasteners, and taking off the lid of the toilet tank to see what lay within—I wouldn't have been surprised to find a creature wedged in there, tubes leading in and out. When I started to remove one of the electrical plates to peer behind it Melanie stopped me, quite rightly pointing out that it would ruin our vacation if I electrocuted myself.

"Someday I knew I would write about this—I wrote down the title 'Flying to England' in one of my notebooks. Subsequent trips (including one early morning arrival at a Gatwick under new construction, walking down an endless series of halls with no one else in sight) solidified the idea.

"Years later, after writing a number of Lovecraft-themed stories, it occurred to me how strange he must have felt at times, how vulnerable, how alienated. I felt I understood that feeling, and recognised how oddly it was manifested in others—their paranoia about the government, their belief in secret causes and dynamics, the cosmologies they manufactured to explain it all. 'Flying to England'

"The most merciful thing in the world...is the inability of the human mind to correlate all its contents."
                                        —H.P. Lovecraft

"Paranoia is just having the right information."
                                        —William S. Burroughs

I. The Park

THE YOUNG MAN at the front door looked wall-eyed and fish-faced through the peephole. Even knowing that if he opened the door that distortion would disappear, Jamie sensed that what he saw through the peephole was in some way the truth, and that everything else was a lie and a disguise.

But he was being uncharitable. Jamie was never as kind as he wanted to be, and if people liked him it was because they didn't understand him. He didn't want to let the fellow in—he suspected that people who travelled door to door had nothing good in mind— but he didn't want to be one of those old men who spoke to people only from the other side of a wall. He turned the knob and dragged the slab of heavy door inside. The sudden glare of sky against his face was painful.

"Hello!" the skinny young man said, too eagerly. "Sorry to bother you." And of course that was a fib. "But are you registered to vote?"

Jamie didn't answer because he wasn't sure. But he doubted it. He never signed things because when you signed things you were put on a list. It wasn't that he thought all politicians were monsters; he just didn't trust any of them. He looked at the young man's scrawny chest, bejewelled with buttons. The names were unfamiliar, perhaps, maybe not. Without thinking of the consequences, he blurted out, "Who's running this time?"

The young man stared at him, looking shocked or embarrassed— Jamie could no longer tell the difference between the two. Then the fellow recovered, said, "I'm supporting..." and rattled off a list of names and elective offices.

Jamie thought he might have heard of one or two of the gentlemen, one of the women. Or perhaps it was simply the last names. Politics ran in families, it seemed. He looked past the young man at the street, looking for partners, fellow travellers, mob. He leaned slightly forward to try to get a glimpse of the park where his son Henry used to play, to see if shadowed figures were waiting there, or just people staring at his home, but saw no one. The nearby buildings and the pavement looked even shabbier than he remembered, purposeful or accidental gaps in the concrete and asphalt permitting earth and vegetation to show through, the occasional ragged pedestrian stumbling down the walk like a refugee from a disaster, vehicles belching smoke and rattling as they negotiated the poorly maintained lanes. He thought about how inappropriate the human presence was on this planet.

"Unopposed, are they?" Jamie asked. This time he recognised the embarrassment (or was it frustration?) in the campaign worker's face. He obviously didn't want to say the names of the ones on the other side of his arguments. No doubt they were evil, sinister characters who plotted the destruction of everything good and holy about America.

As the young man visibly perspired, Jamie noticed the skin tag at the side of the thin neck, obvious now as it grew and elongated and began feeling its way toward the Adam's apple, which seemed oddly shaped for an Adam's apple, actually, being too rectangular, too sharp-edged, too blue beneath the thin skin of the throat. The tentacle of flesh probed and stroked, then straightened and swung away from the neck and toward Jamie like some sort of alerted pseudopod. Jamie stepped back and pushed the door closed, retreating into the dim interior of his house. Sometimes all it took was to be in the wrong place at the wrong time to see something you never wanted to see, to watch your life change around you.

He'd wanted to be both a good husband and a good father, but he'd learned long ago that the universe did not care what he wanted.

Much of the time the world was speechless. And when it did speak it whispered, and you never knew where its voice was coming from, and it always had the most terrible things to say.

Jamie stumbled as he tried to rush through the rooms. It wasn't safe, but he wanted more house between him and the front door. Everything had filled with even more clutter since he'd retired. Everything had filled and overfilled, and he'd been swallowed up by too much of everything. His health could withstand the tide no longer.

Henry had been small like him, but raven-haired, pale, and quite unable to resist whatever illnesses passed through their crowded urban neighbourhood. He did not appear to mind, however, and would cough and read for hours, sniffle over his drawings, and drip clouded fluids onto the page. He rarely slept late, seemingly eager to get up and explore even from the small chair by the bay window, crowded together with his collection of broken vehicles, stuffed creatures with odd modifications, and stack upon stack of old books and papers altered with paint, glue, and miscellaneous scraps, and all of it layered over with his incessant, unreadable scrawl.

Jamie had always thought their house singularly unsuited for a child, even though it was the kind of house he'd always hoped to live in. Too many bookcases, too many books, tomes crashing down at random because he'd constructed the bookcases so poorly. There had always been a spill of papers across some passageway or another, patterned with shoe prints and travelling along beneath their feet because nobody ever bothered to gather them up.

Chloe had been a meticulous housekeeper before they were married. But each day of their marriage she'd become more like him.

He had to move several pieces of home-made taxidermy—a squirrel, a rabbit, a bat, the back half of a deer (or some other, less familiar creature; it was hard to tell now)—and several boxes of disintegrating pulp magazines to get to the desk he'd made for himself out of a small, re-purposed bathroom door. It was piled high with correspondence from Clarence, his British pen pal and founder of the British Lovecraft Appreciation Society. (Jamie had no idea how many members there were, but sometimes suspected the entire roll consisted of Clarence.) An old computer precariously balanced along one edge, for research and the rare e-mail. Like Jamie, Clarence was old-fashioned enough to prefer hand-written correspondence mailed in fine, personalised envelopes.

He sat down on the wobbly kitchen chair and tried to catch his breath. His collection of outdated medical devices loomed over him from an alarmingly leaning nearby bookcase. Henry had last played with them how long ago? Henry's own childhood collection of natural specimens—shells and dried plants and bottles of bugs—was scattered among the mix. Jamie hadn't the heart to dispose of them, or even to touch them. The overall effect was like the shabby remains of some abandoned museum.

When he was little, Henry had sympathised with Jamie's interests. It had been that way almost from the beginning. "I think I know this one," he'd say, again, moving some odd-looking fossil back and forth between his small hands. "It's some sort of erect—walking, I believe—amphibian."

"An erect amphibian?" Jamie would shudder. His son would nod enthusiastically.

Henry had played very little with the neighbourhood children. Jamie knew this was partly his fault—he'd never really encouraged those interactions, and he himself had been a poor example, with few friends, and none were ever invited to the house. But Henry was also a solitary child by nature, his rich imagination no doubt far more stimulating than a room full of similarly aged children.

By this time, Chloe had begun to complain. "I'm afraid for him. Did you know he talks to himself?"

"I talked to myself when I was his age."

She stared at him oddly for a moment. "I've been paying attention, Jamie." *Did she mean he wasn't?* "Some days he murmurs to himself almost constantly. And in the back garden he talks to the plants, or to the ground, or to the air. And he digs."

"Digs? What do you mean? Boys dig—they enjoy getting dirty."

"It's not like he's digging holes or anything. It's like he's sculpting, making art. But not really. More like—I don't know—tracing? He's very deliberate about it. But I can't make sense of the designs, whatever. It's not like he's playing—he's just *so* serious. I think some of the designs are still out there in the garden. Come on, see for yourself."

He felt silly, but he could hardly say no. He followed her into the small plot back of the house, dense with vegetation dripping from the recent rain. He winced involuntarily as she crouched into wet leaves and spread them with her hands. The damp had coagulated into something like a cloudy bodily fluid that dripped and stained and ran across everything. Random bits of dead vegetation stuck to the backs of her hands like broken, angular insects.

"Here, what do you make of this?" She twisted her head around awkwardly and stared up at him.

The furrows in the dirt with the slightly rounded areas between them looked like tubes, or veins. They appeared to go everywhere, crossing back over themselves now and then like fossil images of garden hose. "I can't really make out anything," he lied.

She stood up, slightly bent, somewhat frantically wiping her wet, dirty hands and forearms on her blue-jeaned thighs. "Well, *I'm* really worried."

"Well, then." He actually felt no alarm, but he wasn't about to tell her that. "What do you suggest?"

"He needs more exercise. He needs to be away from this house more."

This was probably true, but the idea made him uncomfortable. "I don't believe this neighbourhood is entirely safe."

"Just an occasional afternoon in the local park. I'll go with him," Chloe said.

And so it began, the daily visits to the park, many of them hours long, just Chloe and Henry. They always came back looking happy but subdued.

Jamie'd never visited that park while Chloe was still alive. He'd considered it, thinking it his responsibility to check out his son's favourite playground. It wasn't right that Chloe had to do everything, including taking care of her own husband. "You wouldn't dress, bathe, or eat properly if I weren't around to tell you when and what," she'd always said. And she'd been right.

He really should have escorted Henry sometimes. It wasn't as if the park were inconvenient. One corner with its tall, leaning trees was actually visible from the house. Double doors opened from their upstairs bedroom onto a balcony attached to the ornate front façade. Some Saturday mornings he would sit on that balcony sipping his tea and reading some odd bit of fiction populated by eccentric and lonely characters, watching below as Chloe walked Henry to the diminutive park for an hour or two of play. If they were later coming back than he had anticipated he might stand up on the balcony and lean in that direction, trying to make his eyes see what they could not. He would see the edges of those trees, and perhaps a bit of the wall that enclosed a portion of the grounds, but little else. He was never able to leave the balcony until his wife and son returned.

Over time, the existence of this park only a short distance away became an unreasonable challenge to his coping skills. What was he afraid of? Other people walked about in city parks all the time with no untoward results. Why should this park be any different? But disaster was without logic or morality. The terrible mechanics of the universe were beyond *both* our control and our understanding. We were not a consideration.

Leaving their son's outdoor play completely in Chloe's hands had been irresponsible. And certainly once she'd shown the initial symptoms of her illness, he should have insisted on taking their son to the park himself. After his wife died he told Henry he was sorry but he could never go there again.

"That is all very interesting," the man in the rumpled suit and sloppy tie said. "But what does any of this have to do with the events which occurred in the Lovecraft Museum?"

He felt embarrassed, as if he'd made a terrible mistake. But of course, he had made many terrible mistakes. "I'm just trying to be as co-operative as possible. You asked me to relate anything I thought might be relevant to your inquiries. Well, this is where it all started for me—those visits my wife and son made to the park, and my wife's illness, her death. Everything started then. I don't understand, but I thought you would. That's your specialty, isn't it? Figuring things out? Making them fit?"

The man in the suit conferred with the soft-spoken man in uniform. The man in the suit took out a pack of cigarettes, removed one, brought it partway to his mouth, then put it back. Apparently he was trying to quit and hadn't found anything to replace it. We all need something that relieves the tension, Jamie thought, but he himself had never had anything. He had always been out there exposed with nothing to comfort him.

The man in the suit looked unhappy. "Please continue. Anything you can think of. Anything you think might help us understand. I apologise for my previous question. Please don't hold anything back."

Jamie looked up from his chair, felt his face. He'd been weeping without even realising it. He gazed around the room—so much evidence of Henry, of Jamie's own obsessions, but nothing of Chloe's.

All these years he'd been so consumed by Henry's disappearance that his memories of Chloe had been overwritten.

Jamie's first conscious exposure to his wife's illness had occurred on a Friday, when she remained in bed, sending Henry with the news that "Mother doesn't believe she can join us today."

His wife's message alarmed him. Her habits had always been exact and predictable—if she had been sick at any other time in their marriage, she'd certainly not told him about it. Jamie sent Henry to his room while he went to his wife's door.

"Come in." Her voice was like dry wings against her pillow.

At first he wasn't completely convinced that was his wife in the bed. Her head seemed too small, her hair like old straw scattered across the sheet. "Chloe?"

Two dark marbles in the shrunken face rolled his way. "Sit by me," the face said.

He dragged a straight-backed chair through a scattering of exhausted tissues on the floor and up to the edge of the bed. He sat and leaned over. "Chloe, you need to go to the doctor." His fear made him a bit more forceful than usual. "I've never seen you like this."

A small hand appeared, pushing a faded green notebook out of the covers toward him. "I've seen a great many doctors, these past few months."

"How—"

"I took the time off work. They had no choice, really—I'm told I kept fainting. They're lawyers—they don't take chances."

"And you didn't tell me?" He asked this, even though he wasn't surprised.

"What would be the point? How would it—" She started coughing then, the entire bed heaving convulsively. "I've written it all down: what they said, Henry's schedule, reminders, everything I could think of. Jamie, you need to study this, or you won't know what to do."

"This is *crazy*. Shouldn't I take you to the hospital?"

"Jamie, I need you to *focus*. You're so…*fuzzy* sometimes. But you have to take care of Henry. Don't be an *idiot*. *Please*."

He grew dizzy, clutched the edge of the bed. She *couldn't* have been ill without his knowing it—he didn't care how oblivious he might be. She was simply being cruel. But he couldn't be trusted to do things correctly on instinct. She understood him perfectly.

Two days later, she went into the hospital. And a week after that she was dead.

Chloe's notes had outlined Henry's needs precisely. It was embarrassing how little Jamie knew about his own child.

"That's not the way you make toast, Dad." Henry threw away the burnt pieces, tried again with fresh pieces, which he buttered after they came out a golden brown. He could probably see the frustration in Jamie's face because then he said, "You'll get it. It took a while for Mom to teach me."

Jamie gradually learned how to handle the household routine. He also learned that he and Henry liked the same kinds of movies, shared a few favourite foods, and had books they enjoyed reading out loud.

And these few things got them through five or six years together, until Henry was in his teens, and all the things he had seemed to forgive his father for became cold resentments, and disrespect, and the occasional rage Jamie thought tinctured with an unreasoning hatred he could never quite adjust to.

Their first trip to England was supposed to mend some of that growing rift between them. But instead Jamie had had to return home without his son.

Twenty years after forbidding Henry from going to his favourite playground anymore, and almost ten years after his disappearance, Jamie visited that nearby park for the first time. He didn't completely understand the need. Once he'd become alone in the house without the informing influence of family, he could not be sure of any of his motivations.

The drab park was much smaller than he had always imagined it. A cracked, dark sidewalk wound through a scattering of weathered benches, circling an ill-kept playground with a solitary swing, rust-coloured slide, old-fashioned see-saw, and rickety roundabout.

Numerous old bushes and shaggy trees, poorly kept. A rough hedge blocked a clear view of the street on one side. The other three sides were bound by rough stone walls with deteriorated edges framing the gates east and west. The gates themselves had been swung back and bolted to the walls for permanent passage. They bore elongated seahorses, which might have once kissed when the gates were closed, and on the other side narrow stalks of iron seaweed attached to broken hinges, the centre sections decorated with starfish and segmented limbs attached to a corroded mess which might have been the creature's body. The motif was more fitting for a public aquarium than a family park. He couldn't imagine what about it had interested his son, other than its proximity.

Each visit, Jamie sat quietly on a particular bench for several hours. Perhaps because it was slightly wider and deeper than the others, or because it was slightly less weathered, or received a bit more sun. What was clear was that it was the one bench where you weren't forced to look at either of those ugly gates, or those less-than-attractive walls. Instead there were bushes and shrub to gaze at, and glimpses of street traffic beyond.

Sometimes he came to the park and someone else was already sitting there. On those days, Jamie would walk around awhile, feigning interest in the vegetation or some section of the stone enclosure, or sit on another bench biding his time. If the interloper seemed prepared for a lengthy stay, Jamie would eventually leave.

During one of these enforced periods of wall-gazing, he became aware of the interesting details on many of the stones. Although these walls appeared soiled and dingy from a distance, closer examination revealed large areas of scarring. He supposed this might have been caused by the process of cutting the individual pieces from their source, but that would have suggested consideration and method, whereas these marks were more consistent with frenzy and the unfocussed strokes of desperation. And very few of them were sharp-edged—it appeared that for the most part something duller and softer had been applied, as if the stone had been punished over a long period by countless fleshy yet determined fingers. Then at some point the bruised source rock had been cut up into individual blocks for construction. Now and then a series of more deliberate marks appeared in their midst, regularly spaced and more uniform, like language.

On Jamie's final visit to the park, he was sitting on his favoured bench, watching as a few young children cautiously tried out the playground equipment. Two small boys climbed aboard the see-saw, travelling on it once up and down before scrambling off again. It had made a sound—high and screechy, as if it were pulling apart. A little girl touched the seat of the swing, then wiped her finger on her pants and wandered away. Two others—sexless in their bundles of clothing—stared at the rusty slide, one of them furiously shaking his/her head.

A white-haired gentleman, possibly early seventies, slid onto the bench beside Jamie. Jamie felt himself stiffen, wanted to get up immediately, but didn't want to be so obvious about it. "It's a shame they won't use the playground," the man said. "I don't know a kid who will."

Jamie thought to mention how much Henry had loved this park, but did not. "Why don't they... Well, can't the city replace it?"

"I think nobody wants to mess with it. The park is one of those ideas which seemed good at the time, a make-lemonade-out-of-lemons type situation. But it's just a tad too morbid, don't you think?"

"I'm not sure I know what you're talking about."

The old man glanced at him with the beginnings of a smile, but cheeks reddening with embarrassment. "Sorry—I thought every-body around here knew the story. You must be from outside the neighbourhood."

Jamie blinked at that, said, "Yes. Yes I am."

"Well," the gentleman leaned back, looking pleased to be able to tell the tale. "If you look at these walls, see how thick they are, and old? They weren't built to enclose the park; they were here long before. We're sitting in the middle of what used to be the McNally Mansion—once upon a time, the biggest private residence, I'm guessing, in this whole half of the state. Those walls used to be part of the foundation. The park here was the basement, after they filled it in some. Those gates were part of the iron fence that fronted the street. Prime real estate here. I know there was a fellow wanted to put in a big hotel. But nobody was having it, not after what happened."

The man clearly wanted Jamie to ask what happened, but he just couldn't see himself doing that. He replied, simply, "I see."

The man blinked. "Thirteen children killed. At least. I'm thinking more. I wouldn't be at all surprised if some day they dig up a lot more bodies. One of those wacko religious groups. They claimed there was a race of creatures living in the countryside here long before human beings came to be. Their idea was to use the children to lure these creatures back into the world, whatever that's supposed to mean. Most of the bodies had little holes drilled into the backs of their little skulls, poor kids."

Jamie shifted uncomfortably on the bench. "What happened to the people in that group?"

"A few were executed, some got life sentences. A bunch went crazy, I hear—or crazier, killed themselves or got locked up in one of the asylums—there are a right many asylums around here, just in case you ever need one." He laughed, a little too hard and a little too long. "A few got away, maybe. A lot of debate about that, as I'm sure you'd imagine. In any case, people around here at the time just couldn't abide the idea of another house going up on this lot—or worse, some kind of business. The idea of a study centre was discussed, a kind of museum dedicated to human cruelty. But that would have cost too many tax dollars. Besides, who'd want to go to a museum like that? They eventually demanded a park, and I guess the city council thought it prudent to agree. There used to be a plaque on one of these old foundation walls, but it's long gone. I don't know why they never replaced it."

"It's not maintained very well," Jamie said.

"Hard to, I hear. I think they just gave up on it. The equipment kept breaking, supposedly. And I guess there was a serious graffiti problem. Nonsense words that they were always painting out, plastering over, but then the words would come back again."

That evening, Jamie was unable to sleep. It seemed he was clear on very little, understood very little. Perhaps all he was convinced of was how easily a culture might become infected, how anything, given the right fortunate or unfortunate circumstances, might become a virus and spread through architecture or religion, design or politics; how little the dreams we created each night were in fact our own.

Over the next few years he kept close to home, stayed inside for the most part. It was a brave new world—almost anything could be purchased on computer for delivery.

He read even more vociferously than before, spending a good portion of his retirement income on rare and esoteric volumes. But the book which finally determined the overall direction of his readings was a collection by M.R. James, *Ghost Stories of an Antiquary*. He was taken by both the author and the approach of the stories— quiet tales about studious and lonely men, characters very much like himself. They came to sorry ends for the most part, which seemed perfectly realistic as far as he was concerned, but he kept reading in part to study the manner in which they dealt with their tormentors and the varied ways in which they met those terrible ends.

He read all the M.R. James he could get his hands on, then the works by the writers James had influenced, gradually moving on generally to tales of the weird or outré. In his youth he'd found such stories a bit silly, or uncomfortably self-involved, in any case incompatible with the mindset he believed he needed to have in order to become a successful person. But that ship had sailed, had it not? Being a successful person, in any sense of that term, no longer seemed a possibility.

Now he regretted his time away from these stories, savouring their descriptions of mysterious hidden realities, grotesque denouements, and both gruesome and transcendent fates. He almost never ventured outside, so he ceased to worry about his appearance. If there was a body attached to his thoughts, he wasn't always aware of it.

Eventually he became particularly intrigued by H.P. Lovecraft, whose 1939 Arkham House edition of *The Outsider and Others* was one of the most valuable books in his collection. The montage-cover by Virgil Finlay thrilled him with its monstrous faces, naked woman, and descending stars, suggestive of matters both celestial and hideous.

Despite the valuable and delicate nature of this volume, Jamie determined that this was one he must read and reread in its original state, even though printings of the individual stories were readily available in various cheap paperbacks. He was perfectly aware that every time he picked up this collectible book and began to read, he was decreasing its value, but he had decided not to care. This was the way he wanted to experience these stories, and he revisited such tales as 'Dagon', 'The Strange High House in the Mist', 'The Statement of Randolph Carter', 'The Lurking Fear', and 'The Shadow Out of Time' many, many times. Some profound emotional and psychic weight behind the author's expressions inevitably strained and warped the language, which thrilled Jamie.

Uncharacteristically he initiated correspondences, initially with dealers specialising in the genre and later with fellow fans, scholars, other enthusiasts. A little over a year later his letter-writing activity consumed most of his time, other than those sacrosanct periods set aside for rereading these canonical texts. He would wake up every morning realising he had just a little more to say about a particular obscure aspect of a favourite text, and this usually involved sending a dozen or so letters and e-mails to a varied network of recipients. The afternoon was often spent replying to letters and e-mails received that morning. The majority of his evenings were devoted to reading, often under the dimmest light possible. When he went to bed, whatever was left in his brain fuelled a tangle of complicated and feverish dreams.

All of it, of course, was an avoidance. Not that he had no genuine interest in these materials—their themes struck strong emotional and spiritual chords. But they kept him from thinking about Henry, missing all these years, now dead or a young man.

And then Clarence came along five years ago and quickly became a favourite correspondent, and the letters and messages between them soon filled random boxes. Eventually an invitation was offered. Clarence insisted that Jamie come to England. Clarence claimed there were a great many things related to their shared interests that he wanted to show him there. Finally, after years, Jamie agreed.

Once in England again, would he renew his search for his son? It seemed futile, but how could he not? And yet he didn't believe he could revisit that wound again. The details and meaning of Henry's disappearance kept him sleepless once again.

Jamie had not travelled in years, and had little idea how to begin or plan or carry out his preparations. He did realise he needed a new passport, and did nothing else until it arrived, struggling and failing to control his conviction that his government would find him undesirable for some reason and determine he should be kept in country, where they might maintain surveillance.

Finally the passport did arrive and Jamie purchased a number of books on the subject of vacationing in the British Isles: things to see, things to watch out for, basic preparations to make. Often these guides contradicted one another so badly he suspected their real purpose was to increase the anxiety of people travelling abroad as a method of behavioural control.

The several weeks leading up to Jamie's trip were infected with a kind of dissolution, the minute details of preparations, errands, finances, architecture, streets, security, gradually separating, ungelling, so that finally he felt on the verge of cancelling and retreating into his house again. At least inside his house he had been surrounded by the familiar, however strange that familiarity made him feel.

But didn't he owe it to Henry to go, even if he didn't continue to search for him there? He would go, but not as Jamie. Suddenly the name grated—a child's name, the name of someone trapped inside his own house. Once he boarded that plane he would think of himself as James.

II. Flying to England

James sailed above the world in a kind of twilight. The clouds lacked the complex variegation of real clouds. These were the clouds of two-dimensional animation, overlapping icons of cloud multiplied into a beautiful complexity, each filled with a different shade of grey.

And below these the ocean, vast and immeasurable as it obliterated the horizon, depthless and arrogant in its denial of time.

On that ill-fated trip of ten years ago, before he even knew Clarence, he hadn't been so calm. His nervousness then had largely involved the length of the trip and the fact that for most of its distance it was over water. Henry had never flown before, and had insisted on looking down from their window, trying to find the ocean, thrilled when he did. But James had either locked his eyes forward or closed them, trying to pretend he was on a large bus. The plane rode more smoothly than a bus, certainly, but with most of the window shades closed, he could not tell much of a difference.

But he'd wanted to be brave for Henry, and not spoil the experience for him, considering how poorly they'd gotten along during the previous year. Henry had grown into an edgy teenager, and had dyed a section of his hair in front a bright crimson colour, so that it looked like he had a serious, bleeding head wound. It made him look almost... demonic. Hardly human at all. James had guessed it was supposed to signify rebellion, something you did to let people know you weren't the same as everyone else. Henry was every bit as odd, as eccentric as he. Why did you need to rebel when you were already some kind of outcast?

On this solo trip he need not worry if Henry was happy or not, if he was having a good time, if he had what he needed. This trip he didn't need to know if Henry was prepared, or if he was still angry with him. There was some relief in that, but it brought James only anguish.

Sometimes on this trip when he peered down it was as if a peephole has been cut into his bubble of protective reality. Below, he could see the shadow of the airplane cast against those cartoon clouds, a great fish that had grown wings on its way to heaven. Nervous spectres of the temporary fluttered by, giving chase to that huge flying fish before falling away, the shadows suddenly robbed of reference.

Inside the plane's cabin, life was a live-action movie, the colours the brilliant and dirty hues of enhanced photography, the passengers with their ruddy and asymmetrical faces obsessed with their narrowly confined comforts with pillows and blankets and small packets of food.

Almost as long as James could remember, he had had these flights of surrealistic fantasy, if fantasy they were. He'd come to the arbitrary point of view that they were fantasy only if he shared them with other people, which he never had. But if not fantasy, what were they? Was it possible they were like special instruments for looking at the world? To view an object in infra-red was not to view it realistically, at least in the normal sense of that term using the everyday human sensory apparatus, but it was hardly a fantasy, either.

These visions might be a kind of spiritual fine-tuning, but of course there was no way to test for such a thing. Instead, he contented himself with simply experiencing them, whether they occurred at night in his dreams or grabbed his attention during some idle moment during the day.

His list of things which felt completely understandable had shrunken drastically over the years, until now it was not much longer than a grocery list for a quick stop at a convenience store.

James figured this to be a normal evolution, however—the longer you lived, the more you knew how little you knew.

If he still had a child he might have told him this. His added perspective might have made some small difference.

"So you assumed at this point that your son had passed away?" The man questioning him looked beyond weary, almost to the point of tears.

"On this second flight over, yes, I was thinking that. I concluded he had been kidnapped on that first trip, years ago, and killed."

"And why do you suppose someone would do that? And who? Perhaps you're thinking it was someone having to do with the Lovecraft Museum?"

"Well, no. The museum didn't even exist back then. Unless it was in the planning stages, do you know?"

The man rubbed his face. "I have no such information. But tell me, this madness you admit to having experienced—is it possible this came into play at the Lovecraft Museum, and might have been responsible for what occurred there? Is it possible your madness was related to your son's disappearance?"

James was alarmed. "No, no! I wasn't describing a psychological illness of any kind! Just a different way of seeing! Mystics, saints, philosophers—you wouldn't accuse them of being mad, would you?"

"James, James," his questioner gazed at him sadly. "Surely you are not suggesting you are some sort of saint?"

James hadn't been able to sleep on the flight to London, and got up to wander back and forth to the toilet several times. He had read that deadly blood clots were possible on transatlantic flights. But there were always so many things to worry about that he was unable to favour any one potential calamity. He wondered if they had ever thought of taking larger planes, with room for a compact gym, or at least a space where you could run in place, or do jumping jacks. But that would reduce the number of seats, and therefore the airline's income. Not likely, he supposed. He wondered if they ever under-fuelled these planes. Certainly they oversold the seats. He wondered if any of these planes had ever run out of fuel mid-flight and dropped into the ocean like a bird with a heart attack. Avian heart attacks seemed a distinct possibility, given the smallness of their hearts, and how hard it must be to *flap flap flap* all day long.

His flight had been delayed for hours, providing him with ample opportunity while lying about in the airport, thousands of passengers arrayed as if in some vast heavenly waiting room, to compare his two trips to England. That first trip had been enveloped in turmoil, beginning long before his arrival at the airport, and had ended in despair. Now he wondered if the strangeness he felt were a clear indication that this was a journey he should not be making.

"The world always feels strange to people who are unhappy," said his wife's voice into his ear. He would have shushed her if she had only been there to hear. He'd been hearing her voice ever since he began his preparations for this trip, and it was disturbing. She'd always been relatively quiet, even when she had been alive. Why speak up now? But theirs was a one-way communication—he could not actually speak to her and hope she would listen.

There was undeniable truth in her statement, as there was truth in most everything his wife said, but there was also dismissal, and he had long ago lost all tolerance for dismissal. If he could have replied to her, if it wouldn't have made him look crazy to any passenger awake enough to hear, he would have said, "Human beings are poor mind readers. And because of that, we can never know another person's real story."

Perhaps he *had* spoken aloud, for he saw several passengers staring at him. He made a silly little smile and an awkward wobbling movement, and either because he had convinced them he was in fact the sandman or because they were embarrassed for him, they all closed their eyes again.

He remembered little about the interior of the plane from his last flight years ago. On this flight he wondered about the small details: if the instruments in the cockpit were similar to or vastly different from the instruments on that previous plane, if the pilot and copilot had less or more facial hair than the pilots of that former era, or if the basic ergonomics of the passenger compartment had changed due to subtle evolutions in human physiology, or perhaps just advances in understanding. He and his fellow passengers were so completely enclosed they could actually have been anywhere; they might have been in some warehouse with blackened windows and hydraulics rocking the craft in order to simulate flight. He had to remind himself that he was actually flying, although he felt reluctant to do so. He might have preferred that warehouse to this endless, featureless night.

Although this was his first trip back to England since that other lifetime, James had returned many times in his dreams, in his daylight fantasies, and in a series of notes he had written to himself over the years during idle moments at work or solitary dinners at home.

My hope in undertaking this trip is for a profound and positive change.

The journey will be implausibly long. The flight may require months, even years, and may likely be followed by additional legs involving a variety of transportation: boat, train, automobile.

Endless journeys through the Underground may be involved. But I'm not bothered by the time investment required, as it may be necessary for a positive outcome.

I might actually arrive in England an old man. Or due to a variety of meta-physical and scientific reasons, I might land at the airport younger than when I began. Or perhaps I may step off the plane an entirely different person.

"And were any of the crewmembers aware of your hallucinations? The flight attendants took no notice of your surprising behaviour? Or perhaps at the gate—were you having these hallucinations at the airport prior to departure?"

"Well, no, no. I'd hardly call this kind of thing hallucinating. Really, I'm not crazy."

"What would you call them then?"

"I don't know... Idle thoughts, maybe? There's nothing wrong with that—people have the craziest thoughts when they're sitting, waiting for a length of time. I think we all do that."

There was a pause as the interrogator conferred with his uniformed colleague. When he came back he said, "Most people do not confess their idle thoughts, particularly to those in authority. Perhaps that is our issue. Do you understand why that might surprise us?"

"You said to tell you anything, anything that might help. And I do want to help you find my friend. And if you could help me find my son, that would be just wonderful. So I'm telling you everything I know. And these idle thoughts? I'm not sure I would have come to England if I hadn't been thinking these things.

"It's really the dirty little secret of all individuals, isn't it? This ocean of illogic swishing about in our skulls. These mad ruminations, these flights into the unimaginable. We dare not speak of them, really, because the authorities, well, they might lock you up for them, eh?

"I read the particular books I do because of those kinds of thoughts. I suspect Lovecraft must have had similar thoughts, crazy thoughts, but of course much more elaborate than anything I've ever thought of. Much, much crazier.

"But I think he understood that those insane idle thoughts pointed

to a reality beyond this one, that perhaps those thoughts were simply a vibration created by movements in that other world. And if you follow them, well, perhaps we can find out where my friend has gone. And if my son, well, what if my son is in that same awful place?"

"So you are convinced they must be in an 'awful' place? 'Awful' is the word you would use?"

"Oh yes, putting it in its mildest terms. I think they must be in a terrible, terrible place."

The curtains were closed at the end of each aisle to block the lights in use by the flight attendants. Such curtains had been used when he was a child to separate the rooms in their tiny house. He and his parents, a grandmother, aunt and uncle, three brothers and two sisters had lived together in one small crate of a home—you always knew what the others were doing, however trivial or banal. You were a direct witness to their daily desires and despairs. But at least you knew. You thought you understood.

He found himself pacing the narrow aisles. The flight attendants eyed him suspiciously. He tried to reassure them with sly smiles, but he was sure he'd only made matters worse. He tried not to look into the faces of the sleeping passengers. He was uncomfortable with the facial expressions of sleeping people, wondering what they might be dreaming. But still, on that long night over the dark ocean he was able to walk around in his stockinged feet, sleeplessly padding back and forth between his seat and the toilet. It was like being at home, but better.

He warned himself to be cautious and alert. What if during one of his mindless strolls he accidentally walked directly into the land-scape of some other passenger's dream? With that in mind, he was careful where he stepped, and there were certain passengers whose proximity he deliberately avoided.

Here he was in a capsule hurtling through space, surrounded by comatose bodies, and the most disturbing thing was that this was not a circumstance which felt foreign to him.

He tried not to look into their sleeping faces, but sometimes he simply could not help himself. A child suddenly opened her eyes and stared at him. He realised there were several children on the plane, ranging in age from toddlers to teens. It angered him how parents could just yank their children out of comfortable surroundings to travel on some dangerous foreign journey. Children rarely had a choice in such matters, and every day they were exposed to the unpredictable jeopardy of travel. The girl fluttered her eyes closed, no doubt thinking he was a dream. Beside her, her mother opened her eyes partway in order to peer at him, her face tense, alert.

He knew how he must look to such a mother. Despite his age, he knew that his face was childish, puffy, his eyes always wet, red, irritated. And he had a boy's body: short, awkward, his chest under-developed. People took one look at him and they knew something was wrong, they just didn't know what. They didn't want their children around him. He nodded, attempted a reassuring smile, but left before it was complete.

A number of the passengers wore clothing covering almost every inch of skin, even when they were sleeping. He had noticed several of them during boarding, bandages peeking out of their long sleeves and high collars, visible on cheeks and foreheads under their floppy, low-slung hats. He didn't think they were American, but it would be difficult to say why. Something about their size and the way they held themselves, he supposed. He imagined they might have travelled from their homeland for treatment in the US and were now returning. The edges of exposed skin near the tightly wrapped bandages appeared raw, red, and not-to-be-touched. He imagined some accident affecting an entire village, or some long-standing abnormality genetically linking these unfortunates. Were such perceptions prejudiced? He hoped not.

He returned to his seat, his thoughts multi-tracking as his brain attempted to sort through a confusing array of contradictory memories, dreams, and impulses. This didn't feel odd to him, but simply part of the physics involved when flying across a vast expanse of ocean.

He had been lucky enough to find an empty seat beside him, where he spread out his books and made a transatlantic nest for himself. He had brought along three by Lovecraft—*The Shadow Over Innsmouth, At the Mountains of Madness, The Colour Out of Space*—out of which he read paragraphs at random during the flight. This exercise had a meditative effect, enabling him to somewhat control the anxiety. He believed this method also had the potential to reveal aspects of the great author's work which he had been hitherto unaware of.

Also spread open on the seat was a collection of e-mail printouts he'd carefully hand bound inside an attractive blue cloth cover. This was the majority of his correspondence with Clarence, who'd first told him about the construction of the Lovecraft Museum somewhere north of London, including random reports concerning the progress of the project and a chronicle of what Clarence had witnessed and experienced there on opening day. This, too, he dipped into at random:

I cannot imagine who must be funding such a project. Obviously some wealthy enthusiast of the author must be involved. Doubtless some British peer with considerable clout, intent to honour, on British soil, a rather eccentric American author of narrow appeal, of all things. Already it is obvious that millions of pounds have been spent. The land may be some distance outside London, but surely it cannot have come cheap.

Not that I am complaining, actually. As a lover of all things Lovecraftian, it will be quite thrilling to have such an institution so close at hand.

They refuse anyone entry to the building site, but some photographs have been leaked (see the link). There appears to be a great, glass-domed foyer whose individual pieces are joined by means of an intricate webbing of brass...

One of the more startling details to emerge is the excavation and filling of a large artificial lake behind the museum, which places the museum on its shore. Rumours abound that *several* rich patrons are involved, all with an obsession with weird fiction, Lovecraft in particular. I also remember reading a random late-night internet posting claiming that the lake had been populated by a number of unusual aquatic species, but since that time I have been unable to track down this particular comment, despite my usual good luck with search engines...

Attendance was quite small on opening day. But that gave those who were there more opportunity to study the exhibits. Some are specific to Lovecraft personally—an array of pens, manuscripts, his favourite hat—there are also a number of artworks inspired by his stories. Other authors—their artefacts, their inspirations—are represented to a lesser degree. A large collection of mechanical devices seems unrelated to anything else housed here, except for the compelling sense of strangeness one feels when trying to rationalise their functioning. On that first day we all spent a great deal of time in the gift shop...

I am having the most difficult time explaining the ambience of the museum. It *is* true to Lovecraft, but not in the most obvious of ways. This is not the old musty facility a reader of his fiction might expect. It is a thoroughly modern, even hyper-modern construction, as if Lovecraft's ideas and views had been allowed to develop into something a bit more mainstream, a projection into an alternate future in which his aesthetics have informed the predominant modes of popular entertainment...

The e-mails had been long, enthusiastic, and detailed. But James was able to discern very little in the distant, out-of-focus pictures Clarence had provided. When he grew tired of reading, he slid open the window shade and looked out: endless black cloud outlined by the occasional flashes of lightning coming, apparently, from underneath. In the distance they appeared to be shredding into nothing, but he could not determine the origin of this effect. His fraying nerves buzzed in his ears.

He had begun to wonder if his fantasies of a near-endless plane flight could possibly be based in reality, when he pushed himself awake through a cloud of static-charged imagery to the pilot's announcement that they were less than a half-hour from landing at Gatwick.

III. Anarchy in the UK

The walk to passport control with his carry-on luggage seemed unnecessarily long and complicated. The occasional signs from the international arrival gates led them up some stairs and down a series of long, declining corridors which were otherwise empty, their windows providing desolate early morning views of vast fields of tarmac. But for lengthy stretches there were no signs at all, and James could only assume the arriving passengers were supposed to stay within the confines of corridors and not take any of the several closed doors that led away from the main route from the planes. He thought about trying a door every now and then to make sure it was locked and not an available option, but he was afraid to. Surely cameras were everywhere, and it seemed quite possible this was somehow part of the airport's security system. Foreign passengers who tried the doors might be considered troublemakers and hauled off for questioning based on their persistent curiosity. And anyone contemplating committing any sort of havoc in Britain would have a great deal of time to ponder the possible consequences, building anxiety to a level of maximum discomfort.

How could a passenger who was physically handicapped deal with these distances? Possibly there were separate accommodations for those with special needs. Or perhaps it was intended that their travel be curtailed. So far he had seen no motorised carts or wheelchairs.

The arriving passengers proceeded at their own individual paces, and very soon James lost sight of the young man far ahead of him and could detect no signs of the couple following behind. He was alone in the echoing halls, with no evidence of fellow humanity, and as he entered a series of passages which showed extensive signs of construction, flowing sheets of clouded plastic making more walls and openings to go through, he was increasingly agitated, almost to the point of panic.

Was this what they wanted? Was this how they weeded out those who came into the country with a guilty attitude, with secret yearnings for destruction, or those who in general did not belong?

"You seem to have been very concerned about our methods of security as you entered the country," his interrogator said.

"No, not so much." James shifted nervously under the man's gaze. "I just didn't really understand why the distance, and, well, the apparent lack of supervision. I'd actually have felt more at ease if there had been armed guards stationed at regular intervals. But perhaps that is part of the design, to maximise anxiety while perhaps saving on personnel costs?"

His interrogator was silent for a few moments. Finally he spoke. "That isn't my department. My only concern is why your particular level of anxiety."

"All those empty corridors. I kept looking for signs, for cameras. It made me paranoid."

"Why would you be paranoid if your intentions were innocent?" The man glanced back at his uniformed partner.

"Why not? People don't have to be guilty of anything to feel paranoia. Really, why the lack of signage? What if I were from a foreign country and knew no English, here in Britain for the first time?"

"If you did not speak English then the signs would hardly have helped."

"But you could have used symbols, signs with graphics. There are international symbols for things."

"Symbols mean different things to different peoples. What you might find innocent and comforting might fill another with terror. There are pitfalls everywhere."

James' anxiety reached its peak as he passed through passport control. He felt like a smuggler. All he had to smuggle in were his thoughts. What if they asked about Henry? What if they wondered why he had left Henry behind? He did not mention the museum, not wanting to seem an eccentric, stating simply that he would be sightseeing and his ticket home was for two weeks from his arrival. At that moment, he was not absolutely sure he would be using this return ticket, but he withheld that information because he had no idea why he might even think such a thing. He had no intention of skirting any laws, he simply could not imagine himself returning to America.

Walking the corridor that would lead him officially into England, he was struck by the posters of British children of all ages arranged on the walls, each holding a different small animal. All were smiling, but many of the smiles failed to convince. He recognised most of the animals: various cats, various dogs, a lamb, a large bird, a fawn, but some sparked no recognition at all. Perhaps these were rare animals native to the British Isles, or to some old colony, but wouldn't he have encountered pictures of these creatures during his extensive reading? Several appeared to be of some unusual species of mole, the neck on one deformed or broken. One might have been a small otter with its teeth bared, its mouth alarmingly close to the slight, nervously grimacing red-headed little girl holding it.

"I take it you do not care for animals?"

"Oh, I like animals well enough. Cats, dogs, that sort of thing. I don't care to have pets in my own house, but I know they give many people a great deal of pleasure."

"Perhaps you have an issue with children?"

"Of course not! Why would you think such a thing? I may not spend a great deal of time with children—I have no children in my life right now—but I loved my own son and it would be wonderful to have him in my life again."

"And yet the posters at the airport disturbed you?"

"Well, I think some of those children were disturbed, frightened, to be holding such creatures. You could see it in their faces."

"Those posters are up all over England. It is part of the current RSPCA campaign. I have seen them many times, and those children have always looked very happy to me, blissful even, holding their lovely pets."

"But some of those pets—well, they are a bit unusual, don't you think?"

"No, no, not at all. They are quite standard British pets in these times. I take it you do not have such pets in America? I've never been to your country, but I would have imagined that you had pets like those as well."

"No." James sat, thinking back, wondering if he might have missed some trend because he didn't watch television, or because he read the wrong newspapers, or simply because he had been so preoccupied. But he really didn't think so. "No, we do not."

Ahead of him, one of the overdressed passengers with a floppy hat and hanging edge of bandage walked vigorously, carrying a battered leather suitcase heavy enough to distort his or her stride. Around the turn, James was confronted by a mass of back-lit, shadow-swollen British heads atop ill-defined bodies, and he realised he and Clarence had never communicated how they would recognise one another.

He was on the edge of that seething conglomerate when a tall sliver peeled off and whispered, "James?"

He couldn't see the person's face for the glare, so he awkwardly tried to sidle around to an angle where the shadows fell helpfully. But he was blocked by someone else's luggage. "Clarence, is that you?"

The tall figure bent down out of the light. He had a broad pale face with close-cropped blond hair. "At your pleasure." A large hand trapped his own, trembling as it pumped his arm lightly. Then the glare was gone completely and he was staring up at Clarence in his old-fashioned brown suit and matching vest. James couldn't help thinking of his own clothes: blue jeans and blue checked shirt, a Western-style belt, beat-up tennis shoes. It felt as if his father had come to pick him up at the airport for summer vacation. They looked at each other until a point of discomfort had been breached, then Clarence picked up James' bag. "The station is this way," he said, and strode away. James felt he should object to Clarence's help with his luggage, but he couldn't find the right words.

He ran to catch up, self-conscious about his lack of grace. He almost never ran, and imagined everyone must notice. His progress felt impeded by all the faces watching. He felt an irrational need to register every face he saw, especially the children's, the young men's. Perhaps Henry had secretly come to the airport to see him. But that made no sense—Henry couldn't know he was coming. But still, there were many young men with jet-black hair. Henry *could* have been among them. James tried not to search the crowd for his son, but he could not help himself. It was all starting up again—the anxiety, the constant search. No wonder people viewed him with suspicion. He tried to avert his eyes but could not. His eyes continued to search the crowds. Would he even recognise him, ten years later and all grown up? Would it be like this the entire trip?

From the length and ramped-up enthusiasm of so many of Clarence's e-mails, James had expected virtually non-stop conversation on a variety of interesting and/or esoteric topics. But his new acquaintance seemed reluctant and quiet in person.

They boarded the Overground, the car moving along with a roller-coaster shimmy. Several of those odd, overdressed, bandaged people were on the train. *Just how many are there?* James thought, not really desiring to speculate, but wondering if they might have arrived in other planes besides his.

"You've never asked me about all those bandaged people I saw on the plane, and after."

His interrogator conferred with the man in uniform. "What about them?"

"Well, usually you question me when I've told you about unusual things I've witnessed on my trip."

"We did not consider this unusual. Patients fly into London all the time for advanced medical treatment. It's a normal occurrence—much like a child holding a favoured pet, I might add."

"But so many in body bandages?"

The interrogator shrugged. "Terrible things happen to people, in many countries, especially in this day and age. Your friend, Clarence, did he comment on these bandaged people?"

"Well, no, no. Maybe he just didn't notice them."

"*A psychologist might suggest that since you feel yourself a wounded individual, you see wounds everywhere. But then, I am not a psychologist, simply a low-paid police officer of little consequence. You, sir, are the one at the centre of attention.*"

Clarence made no overtures of friendship and did not even attempt small talk. He seemed obsessed with parsing the details of James' trip as quickly as possible, and as far as James could tell had not looked at him once since their initial meeting.

"I have booked you into a B&B near the British Museum," Clarence stated, staring directly ahead. "Inexpensive, but clean. I would offer you lodging at my flat, but it is much too small, not big enough for me alone, really."

"Oh, no problem. Thank you."

"Unfortunately I have things on my schedule this afternoon, a deadline on an indexing assignment. I don't believe we have ever discussed our respective livelihoods, even after five years of correspondence, but I am a professional indexer. That does not mean I simply assemble a list of words and attach page numbers to it. There is a great deal of analysis involved. I not only read the text, I interpret it. I attempt to determine what the author is really saying, what images and themes obsess him, and I design an index to reflect that. If the author uses language and vocabulary in a manner outside the norm, I use alternate look-up strategies to enable the average reader to better navigate the text. I attempt to separate opinion from fact, explication from obvious obscuration. If you were to examine one of my indices closely, you would find the qualities of a critical essay, albeit in a highly structured, at times cryptographic form. I'm not sure the author would always appreciate what I have to say, but most are a bit too linear to really grasp what I am suggesting about their work. All of which is to say you must find your own entertainment this afternoon. But there are many things to see. I assume you have studied the many brochures I have sent you."

It wasn't a question, so James did not attempt to answer. Many of the fellow's letters and e-mails had been like this—endless lectures on sometimes quite esoteric subjects. Despite his statement to the

contrary, he had actually expounded many times in his correspondence concerning his indexing-profession-cum-philosophy. For the
most part, James had learned to ignore vast amounts of what Clarence
had to say until some nugget floated to the top. Clearly, Clarence
was another socially awkward human being. Was there something
about weird fiction that brought this quality out in its aficionados?

"Were you disappointed by his lack of social graces?"

*"Well, no—they were about as I had expected. We've been corre-
sponding for five years now, and his e-mails have been quite informative, but—well—rather awkward. He seems to have led a rather
solitary existence, much like myself, but he does seem like a nice person
under all that."*

*"Still, to come all this way, to come alone into a foreign country,
some friendly companionship would have been nice, particularly on
your first day."*

"Yes, well, of course. But you do the best with what you have."

"And you were able to maintain this attitude with no resentment?"

*James tried to consider the question seriously. He always tried to be
so flexible, so amenable to other people's eccentricities. Did this blind
him to what he actually felt? More importantly, did they think he'd
wished Clarence harm?*

Their trip had entered its Underground portion, the train dropping
into a tunnel as they approached London's urban sprawl. Soon they
were stopping at tube stations and a mesmerising flow and exchange
of commuters began. James was pleased to see that this part of
London city-life, at least, had not changed since his previous trip a
decade ago. Even the overdressed bandaged people with their
inflamed skin—still in evidence as they boarded and disembarked
the train at various stops—seemed more like eccentric immigrants
now, here in London to do the jobs the native Brits didn't want to
do.

Familiar yet exotic names like Hammersmith and Gloucester and
Knightsbridge appeared suddenly on fields of black-and-white tile.

These names did not sound like foreign places, but still they weren't the kinds of places you expected to find in America. It was an observation he'd also made on his previous trip. These English-speaking countries with their different governments and measuring systems, their different solutions for electrical connections or how an automobile might be driven, seemed at times like alternate world versions of America. Or like strangely distorted dreams of America. It was a terribly American-centric perception, of course (and relegated non-Americans to illusory status), and that thoroughly embarrassed him, but at least it was an honest admission.

"I hadn't realised you were married," Clarence suddenly said beside him.

James looked up, slightly red-faced. Did Clarence know he'd been ignoring him? "Pardon me?"

"You have a ring."

James looked down at the wire-thick band. His finger had fattened around it. Soon he wouldn't be able to take it off at all. He considered briefly that the finger itself might actually have to be removed someday, which felt oddly appropriate. "She died, some years ago."

"Oh, I apologise."

"No need. It was relatively sudden. An undiagnosed leukaemia." He glanced up at Clarence's puzzled face and frowned. "I'm sorry— that sounded abrupt. I suppose you didn't really want to know any specifics. Chloe once said, 'If anybody lives long enough, they die of something.' I think it was her way of saying the body has a time limit, and it's not designed to exist beyond a certain point. It seemed to help her deal with the anticipation of it—I think even though it was undiagnosed, she somehow knew. But it didn't help me. Not at all."

"*Very* interesting." Clarence was suddenly animated. "The human body reaches its design limits, which will vary from model to model, if you will excuse the terminology. After that, some mutation at a cellular level is bound to occur, the tissues reorganising themselves into something else entirely."

James felt an alarming impulse to slap him. He supposed he might have encouraged the man's insensitivity—perhaps he'd been too glib in sharing that bit of personal information. Since they had first begun their e-mail exchanges, Clarence had periodically veered off into fantastic biological speculations—it was apparently one of his obsessions. But this seemed so oblivious. James wondered if his new friend was even less equipped for decent, normal conversation than he was—a situation James had hitherto considered impossible.

Clarence insisted on carrying James' bag up the two flights to his room at the B&B, and James, who was thoroughly winded even without the bag, let him. For an indexer, Clarence was impressively fit, his feet pounding up the stairs, arms aggressively clutching James' large bag to his chest as if it were a rescued child. The urgency in his action puzzled James.

After a series of rambling apologies Clarence walked out the door. James could hear his feet once again thundering on the stairs. He collapsed onto the edge of one of the beds—three were crammed into this long, narrow room—and looked around.

The room smelled like his grandmother's house, and the furnishings were apparently of that same vintage. Besides the beds, two mismatched dressers were pushed together along one side, and the room seemed to be oversupplied with towel warmers mounted on the walls—he counted four. A coin-operated television was attached to one wall near the ceiling. He dropped the requested coins into the slot and watched a few minutes of news concerning personalities and issues he'd never heard of, before flipping among a variety of gardening and housekeeping shows and several American reruns.

Over on BBC 0—Had there been such a channel during his previous trip? He didn't think so—a smiling, red-faced man held up a giant vegetable unlike anything James had ever seen before, but the programme appeared to be about financial issues. Next, two men in period costume gesticulated angrily, set fire to papers in their hands, then danced merrily until their sleeves also caught fire before the men stumbled out of camera range. Next, an old man held up one of the toothy otter creatures, which screamed continually as the man stroked its belly. No eyes were visible in the creature's head. In a following segment, several figures in heavy clothes and floppy hats laboured in a field. There was a close-up of bandaged, reddened hands holding the tools.

All this had a narrative voice-over in English, but the vocabulary for the most part was unfamiliar to him.

James did not go far for dinner, afraid he might not find his way back along the unfamiliar dark streets. He ordered fish and chips at a small local café. He didn't recognise the names of any of the fish varieties on the menu, so ordered something in the middle of the price range. The fish had a faint smell of cloves and cinnamon. When he got outside he spat and spat in an attempt to get rid of the taste. The crowd walking through the intersection eyed him with displeasure. He stared back at them, searching for the face of a familiar young man. It was ridiculous—he wouldn't simply find Henry by random accident. Eventually he found he could straighten up and walk more or less upright, although with each step nausea came to lap at the back of his eyes.

London was every bit as crowded as he remembered, people walking elbow to elbow, some dazed like himself, many proceeding rapidly on one mission or other. When he reached a row of shops, every other window invariably displayed one of those humane society posters with the strange animals. No one stopped, or appeared to notice in any way, so he assumed these creatures were indeed common household pets.

With one exception. He passed a smaller bandaged person close to a window with a poster featuring the mole-like creatures, one arm raised to the glass and a tiny appendage which might have been a finger except it looked so thin, so red, touching the area in front of the mole's head.

There appeared to be more beggars and homeless people in evidence than the last time he'd been in this city. Every block or so there would be a gathering huddled around the corner of some old building. Passing a group, he heard musical mumblings in a foreign tongue he did not recognise.

At the edge of a park a rag-swaddled figure had climbed up on a bench and was humming a loud atonal composition into the smoky evening air. Very few passers-by paid attention.

Just as he remembered, the night fell quickly during this part of the year. Shadows grew increasingly complicated until James felt an urgent need to get in off the streets. Low movements whipped across the broken stone pavements. There were garbled complaints followed by running into buildings he could not quite see. People began to leave the streets quickly and he did his best to follow suit.

Back in the B&B, James searched out the water closet on his floor. He shut the door and stayed there for a long time. Now and then he could hear footsteps outside in the hall, sometimes pacing right in front of the door, going away, coming back. He stayed as quiet as possible.

He stared at the electrical outlet on the wall. It was slightly different from ones he had seen before—he wasn't sure how but wondered if they were now pandering to a new group of foreign tourists. A ticking inside the wall sounded both vaguely electrical and mechanical, but he could not quite pinpoint the source.

Before he left the WC he stood on top of the toilet to get a closer look at the light fixture. He'd never seen a bulb like this before. Something swam around inside it, turning over and over, occasionally resting against the bottom of the bulb. He traced a long narrow tube that led to a star-shaped electrical junction box in one corner by the door. He climbed down from the toilet and gazed at the large ceramic tank mounted on the back of the toilet bowl. Nervously sliding off the heavy lid, he tried not to make any noise as he leaned it against the wall. Something big and furry was fixed to the centre of the tank, with sharp steel hooks piercing various portions of fur and hide. Numerous tubes encircled and entered the mass, which quivered rhythmically. Now and then there appeared to be a quick, violent shudder, and then the rhythm resumed.

Sleep the first night came with the speed of a drawn curtain. He woke into brilliant light, instantly aware that he'd forgotten to take off his shoes.

"You were exhausted after the long trip. Most visitors take a nap right away. I am sure that must explain your, let us say, unusual obsession with plumbing."

"Then that thing in the toilet tank. That wasn't real?"

After consulting with the man in uniform, his questioner replied, "We are hardly plumbing experts. You would have to ask someone in the trades. London is an international city. Many household devices from other countries, a variety of engineered solutions, new styles and approaches, all of it ends up here in our buildings and their furnishings. There is much—cross-pollination? Nothing should surprise you here. Nothing."

IV. The Lovecraft Museum

The next morning, walking with Clarence down the cold grey lane toward the tube station, James smelled roasting chestnuts. A vendor was set up in front of the British Museum, an unusually tall man in a top hat and oversized Elton John glasses. His hands looked swollen in pale gloves, so enormous James wondered how he could handle anything at all. Looking a bit gloomy, he dispensed bags that quivered as if they held something alive. The customers, however, devoured the contents with obvious pleasure and alacrity, surprising when James remembered how hot and chewy roasted chestnuts were.

The bricks and stones of sidewalks and buildings appeared wet and oily, but as far as he could tell it hadn't rained. The sky was low over the building tops, pregnant with threatening grey masses of shadow. The sun was nowhere to be seen, the ambient light a submerged glow. The air had the clarity of a dirty aquarium. This was basically the kind of weather he had expected in London, yet he found it discomfiting.

The city seemed unusually busy for a Saturday. The streets and sidewalks were jammed with people in all manner of clothing, a good deal of which he supposed displayed a recent European influence, with an increased use of plastics and metals. Some of the outfits looked more like furniture designs than something human beings would wear.

The lady ahead of him wore an outfit which consisted, appar-

ently, of numerous cloth bags sewn together into pants and a voluminous poncho. Objects in some of these bags shifted as she walked,
unbalancing her, the edges of metal or cloth or some bit of vegetable
matter peeking out of the pocket openings now and then.

Several gentlemen in the crowd wore business suits made out of
a stiff-looking, rubber-like material, with moulded lapels, ties, fake
buttonholes. They walked with sometimes aggressive, exaggerated
movements, sweating profusely. Skin rashes rose up their necks.

The crowd surged into the tube station and through the turn-
stiles. James struggled for balance. Clarence appeared to be having
no trouble at all and led the way confidently, his head visible above
the crowd, making James grateful for his friend's unusual height.
The crowd spilled onto the down escalators, where there were more
posters of distressed-looking British children embracing not-quite-
recognisable pets.

As the escalator descended, James was struck by the varying styles
of the collars, and the different relationships between neck and collar.
The proportions unsettled him. He might almost think none of
these people had worn clothing before, like dogs forced into human
outfits.

He found himself drawn to the back of a particular young man's
head several yards below him. The youth had dark, dark hair. James
suspected it must have been dyed in order to get it that black. He
wasn't quite sure what about the youth had attracted his increased
attention—but people do change, especially after so many years.
Other than his small size, was there anything about James that
someone who had known him years ago would recognise as undeniably him? He doubted it. Some very serious things had happened
to him during his life—he was hardly even the same person.

But he had focussed on this young man for some reason, and
that in itself compelled him to take a good long look. There seemed
to be a certain glow about him. A bit of scalp peeked through in
back. His immediate thought was that he'd been sick, cancer perhaps,
and the very idea filled him with dread.

He attempted to will the young man to turn around. Even after
so many years, it might be the face he remembered, and he knew

if he were to see that face right now he might very well collapse onto this escalator, causing injury to others, not to mention the potential damage to his own body, but he did not care—it would be both the most wonderful and the most awful thing.

As he stared at this head, praying both that the young man would and would not turn around, he observed that here and there a squiggle of pink appeared in his hair, and he gasped, convinced that these were worms rising out of his scalp, then realised those thick pink marks must be evidence of some sort of scalp disease. And as the raven-black strands moved and separated, wounds seemed to be exposed, and those wounds formed still-bleeding letters, written on the scalp beneath the roots even as James watched. The message might have been meant for him, or might have been the young man's private thoughts instantly transcribed as a missive for the universe at large. There was no way to know unless this strange young man were to take out a razor right then and there and shave his head, and it seemed indicative of this trip to England that this did not feel outside the realm of possibility.

When the youth reached the bottom of the escalator, James was determined to follow, but he walked among some of those over-dressed people with the peekaboo bandages and the floppy hats—and James instantly lost track of him. Was he with them? Was he with them willingly?

"So, why didn't you shout after this young man? Why didn't you raise an alarm?"

"What? What do you mean?"

"Obviously you thought this young man might be your lost son, correct?"

James stalled, trying to gather his thoughts. Well, of course he had, but that would have been unreasonable. "I wasn't sure. There was no way to know—he was much older. But his appearance triggered something, I admit."

"Then why not shout his name?"

"I—I would have been embarrassed. I obviously couldn't know for sure. I needed to make sure."

"If it had been my son, if I had had a missing child, I would have been unstoppable! Perhaps I would have been mistaken, perhaps not. But a mistake is forgivable, is it not, when the stakes are so high? Your only child, missing all these years—couldn't you have taken the chance?"

"You don't understand. There was a time after he first went missing, I was seeing him everywhere! I was stopping every child on the street who even vaguely resembled him. The children cried out, the parents were quite upset. Police officers were called. I spent a few hours in jail—I had to go to court numerous times. Both here, and especially in the US after I got back. Never mind the unlikelihood that he might have made it back to the States on his own—I still thought I saw him everywhere. It was a nightmare!"

"I just think," the interrogator said quietly. "We just think, you might have behaved differently, if you indeed wished to find him again."

A hand tugged gently at his arm. At first he thought it was meant to reassure, but then he recognised the impatience in it. "James, we need to go this way." Clarence led him beneath a staircase and into a large circular opening. They appeared to be the only ones taking this particular exit.

The tunnel seemed no different than any other in the London Underground, tiled in black and white, lined with posters advertising cryptic local events, books, and musical acts he'd never heard of, featuring unlikely combinations of personnel and instrumentation. Scattered among these advertisements were more of the posters with the children and their disturbing pets—sometimes showing just the pets with their disproportionate eyes, large teeth, and asymmetrical heads, and sometimes just the children with their stricken faces. James felt he would weep, although he was not exactly sure where his sadness was coming from. It felt like some sort of virus that had suddenly evolved under the right conditions and now made him unusually sensitive to these images. He struggled to control himself in front of Clarence, whom he knew only through all that correspondence, sharing their enthusiasm for weird fiction, and who seemed completely oblivious to these odd disturbances in their environment.

Which raised the question of whether they were, in any way, odd, or merely the shadow effects of a foreign community as perceived by someone of heightened sensitivity and exaggerated empathies, especially one whose grief had never been satisfactorily discharged.

He had no idea, and no hope of eventually feeling comfortable with any of it. But why should this place be any different? James did not feel comfortable anywhere.

Music had begun to thread its way from around the curve ahead of them, and James was so pleased at the prospect of encountering something as normal as a typical tube musician, he reached into his pocket to make sure he had change to give. But as they made the bend there was no musician in sight, just another one of those men (or women?) in dark, rough clothing that almost completely swallowed them, floppy hat hiding the face as he or she sat slumped over on the floor, back against the wall.

But James could still hear the music, louder than ever, reverberating off the floor and curved walls, entering his abdomen and vibrating inside his body cavity so that he began to feel ill.

As they approached the figure, James could see the surface of the voluminous cloak rising and falling, the chest inflating, deflating, causing the dropped-forward head to nod in time with the music—windy, reedy sounds like sighs and weeping, mournful moans and distant cries, a chorus of loss and disappointment. The music sounded something like a pipe organ out of tune, something like bagpipes with ruptured bladders.

Clarence stopped in front of the hunched figure and studied the exaggerated breathings, and once James saw that the lower part of the figure's face and mouth were buried inside the folds of material around his neck, he was sure this creature must have been blowing into some hidden mouthpiece, and this was in fact the musician after all.

There was no hat or cigar box or guitar case for offerings, and James was surprised to see Clarence reach out his hand to drop a folded note that would join a number of other notes at the man's feet, then walk quickly away down the tunnel.

James rushed hard to catch up with the long-legged Clarence. "What was that? Was that a cheque?"

"No, simply a hand-written note, like the others."

"But what did it say?"

Clarence shrugged. "I'm not sure—I always prepare dozens in advance for just such occasions. Prayers, promises, exaggerations. But primarily good wishes, sympathetic hopes for good luck on life's voyage, for the most part. That sort of thing. That's what they expect, or so I've been told."

"You carry them around with you?"

Clarence opened his coat. Hundreds of folded bits of paper were pinned to the lining.

Suddenly they were at the platform, and despite the fact that they had encountered no one along the way but that lone busker, it was crowded. Several people stared at them with what James felt was suspicion, but since the majority of these people appeared to be foreigners, he couldn't be sure of their body language. He hoped this was not a racist perception—certainly he did not want to be racist, but at times like this he was painfully aware of how little he knew about the rest of the world and its customs.

The signage here was older than what he had seen in other parts of the Underground, with missing letters and words and everything overlaid with an obscuring scrawl of graffiti. The platform itself appeared to have been recently repaired—cracks filled, exposed pipes mended, one large section of concrete resurfaced. Almost all the signs were illegible, except for a small poster pasted on the wall near the middle of the platform. It mostly consisted of a pen-and-ink sketch depicting a peaceful lake scene with a futuristic tower erected nearby. And at the bottom:

VISIT THE LOVECRAFT MUSEUM

The train arrived screaming into the station. James had to struggle to maintain his balance against the crush of the crowd, aware of Clarence's head floating above it all, seemingly unperturbed. No one spoke. For its size and aggressiveness, the crowd settled surprisingly quickly. People went right into their seats. And still no one was talking. James squirmed a bit to get more comfortable, then stopped, aware that he was the only one moving.

The car rocked through a series of flashing lights, alternating periods of heat and cold, but at no point could James say he felt comfortable. For a while there was dust in the air. He was aware of faces staring at him through the haze, but as the fuzziness dissipated no one met his eye.

He was shocked at how quickly they reached the outside edge of metropolitan London, the train emerging from a hillside tunnel into light and grass and sky. He wondered at the flatness, and the sparseness of structures—only a house or barn here and there. It looked more like the American Midwest than venerable English countryside.

The train picked up speed, whipping around an extended curve, which allowed him to see the landscape ahead, or the lack thereof—bright mist with cooler, bluish fog hanging just over the grass. Like a blind spot in the eye. The passengers were more active now, turning their heads, stretching, murmuring to one another as if they had just risen from the same bed. James was surprised by the number of young men in this car, most of them heavily made up, punk-looking, exhausted, disappointed. He didn't recall seeing such a collection of men on the platform, and he wondered if they'd already been on the train—and why hadn't he noticed them before?

One of the men was paying particular attention to him, it seemed, and it was difficult to look at anyone else while this man was staring at him. He found himself looking for something familiar in his eyes, in the chin and set of mouth. But so many young men that age seemed to resemble each other, he couldn't be sure if he'd seen this one before or not. Did *he* recognise something in *him*?

James wasn't quite sure what to make of the fact that, after that initial trip from the airport, Clarence had had very little to say to him, had become more than taciturn—he had practically turned to stone.

As if to deny the observation, Clarence spoke to him now. "You can see it," he said, and pointed.

James actually thought his companion was deliberately lying, for some reason, as he could detect no change in that distant bright vista. But then a shiny crack in the brightness materialised, like a sudden flaw in his eye, which quickly resolved itself into a distant tower, and that stretch of blue-grey around it could only be the lake he'd heard so much about.

Most of the passengers transferred to buses at the next station, labelled LOVECRAFT in tall red letters. But a few remained on the train. "What's the next stop for them?" James asked.

Clarence shrugged. "I had no idea there was one."

It was another half-hour before their bus arrived at the actual facility. They travelled through several groves of increasingly abundant trees, their views of both the sky and what was ahead of them almost completely annihilated, until the trees suddenly ended and an apron of knee-high grasses swept the eye, leading downwards toward the huge concrete *mandala* with the spire rising so sharply at its centre it seemed a violent assault on the sky. It certainly did gleam. A particular combination of metal and glass caught the sun and sent it away, painful to look at for more than a few seconds, making it difficult to fully grasp details.

Most of the tower consisted of twisted stretches of some sort of cast material, iron-like but definitely not iron. James suspected this might be some sort of recently developed synthetic, and certainly nothing he'd ever seen as a building material before.

The patterns appeared vaguely organic, like segmented stems or perhaps spinal columns, with occasional branching, or reproduction. Here and there he spied a gill-like structure, a segmented leg, an ocular organ. The effect of the structure as a whole was of a slight asymmetry, as if the tower were a stalagmite built up from the floor of the world.

The tower compelled him to trace its upward progress into the sky far above it, where he would have sworn he saw flying creatures the size of double-decker buses, flapping their sail-sized wings with stop-motion rhythms, their gigantic cartoony googly-eyes keeping track of everything going on below. Quickly he became convinced it was some sort of live special effect. Still, he looked away, sensing that to make eye contact might have terrible consequences.

A narrow lane bordered by sculptured shrubs led up to the ornate gate. It was covered by a variety of asymmetrical characters cast in brass, resins, aluminium, and iron. "Sculptured" was a theoretical term used in regards to the shrubbery—the trimming *looked* purposeful, but James had no idea what these figures were meant to represent. Everyone seemed a shape in transition, halted or frozen by exhaustion or death or a petrifying fear.

Along the edges of the road pedestrians walked slowly toward the museum, many of them in coarse robes, their heads and necks wrapped or otherwise covered. "Some of the groups who come here do not trust motorised transportation," Clarence said beside him. "So they visit on foot."

"Their clothing—where are they from? Or is it some religious thing?"

"I suspect they are foreign born. Something about the eyes, don't you think? The way they appraise you, as if they have never encountered your kind before. And I agree, there is this worshipful air about them—sometimes I see them in the museum with their eyes closed for long periods of time, as if they're praying. But they never say anything—at least nothing a person with average hearing might hear. I believe myself to be a tolerant man, with very few prejudices. But I do not like them, I am afraid—they make me uneasy. People like that, you never know what they have come from, what they are thinking, what they might do."

James was shocked. He could hardly say he himself was comfortable with these people. But he hadn't really been comfortable since his arrival in England.

The gate opened for the buses that had come from the train. They descended into a huge circular lot, parking along its circumference. The buses emptied quickly and the passengers climbed the concrete stairs to the grand entrance, double doors two-storeys tall, each carved with several very tall figures. From a distance the figures appeared to be women, but as James got closer he thought perhaps they were some sort of animal with a tall neck, walking upright.

Their mouth-parts were disturbingly complicated. He could not look into their faces long.

The bus drivers had become ushers, standing at the top of the stairs and between the crowd and the closed doors. They admonished the visitors to be patient and assured them that the doors would open soon. The vast collection of visitors milled about in their restricted space, murmuring to one another, looking anxious. Suddenly there was an explosive, metallic sound, like that great foghorn trumpet the alien tripods made in Spielberg's film version of *War of the Worlds*. A few people cried out in alarm. There were scattered chuckles during a brief pause. Then the rest began moving forward. The great doors were easing open.

James was frustrated at being able to see so little from his position in the mass of moving bodies, but as soon as the crowd flowed inside, it thinned and separated rapidly. He found the ticket booths just inside the doors, each containing an ornately lettered sign: FREE TODAY.

"I hear those signs have become permanent fixtures," Clarence said above him.

"How do they make any money?"

"The gift shop appears somewhat popular, but I doubt that income makes much of a dent in the operating costs. I don't know—perhaps they don't need the income. Since no one understands where the money to fund the construction came from in the first place, I suppose any scenario is as likely as the next."

From the size of those exterior doors and just the general aspect of this grand building, James had expected the entryway to be equally grand, and in its way it was—every inch of the rock-like walls and ceiling appeared to be inscribed with delicate, fussy script, a kind of intricate lettering, but if these were letters they were from a language unlike any he had ever encountered before, and the length of some of the words surely made them impossible to articulate within the space of a single breath. The lighting in the room was remarkably deceitful, changing drastically depending on where he stood, transforming inch by inch so that as the initial room revealed itself, he realised that some of the walls he'd thought perfectly straight were in fact curved, and that the ceiling was inconsistent and in places much lower than he had first thought, dipping down so far in spots Clarence actually had to walk hunched over with legs bowed.

By the time they got to the centre of this first room, James had begun to realise that there was something nautilus-like about the architecture. Chambers appeared to spiral into chambers off this main entryway, and the various openings to each one were of non-uniform size.

No one else seemed amazed by this arrangement. Even Clarence, for all his hunching and bowing, proceeded across the room as if this were an everyday stroll. James looked in vain for some sort of directory.

"How do we find our way around?" Some parts of his speech were amplified and some parts distorted by the strange acoustics.

"I believe it is intended that you discover your own path." Clarence looked around intently with barely a glance spared for James. "The intention, I gather, is that every visitor's experience be different, and that with successive trips a sense of the whole is, I suppose, accumulated."

"Are there guides?"

"I believe so, although I've never encountered any. I gather they find you, if they will, rather than the reverse."

"It all seems..." James stopped himself. He didn't want to be critical. He wanted to reserve any sort of judgement.

"In keeping with the design, I suggest that we separate, and find our individual ways through the exhibits," Clarence said. "We should attempt to honour the intention of the Lovecraft Museum. I think that would be particularly beneficial for you, James."

"Oh, why so?"

"I simply mean that as an American you're accustomed to an alternative way of doing things. But if you are forced to simply follow the architecture of the museum, if you are pressured into its patterns, it will be, oh, much more rewarding, I think."

James felt vaguely annoyed, condescended to. Obviously Clarence simply wanted to go about by himself. Fine, then. "Of course, naturally," he replied, and headed off in the direction of the nearest opening, the one that appeared to have the fewest number of visitors crowding through.

But before going he turned around briefly, looking for Clarence in the scattering crowd. He saw him on the other side of the room, or at least he saw much of his head rising above the shorter examples of humanity surrounding him. He appeared to be uncharacteristically smiling, reaching out to their shadowed, dark heads.

Immediately inside this next hall, the texture of the walls changed into something less refined, less finished. If this hadn't been a brand-new building, in fact, James would have thought he'd entered a much older, less well-maintained part of the structure. The corridor narrowed to three feet or less, and now the flooring was wooden planks so scuffed they looked as if livestock had been driven over them. The wall grew spotted with mould, and wept an amber colour. Fine plaster powder gritted under his shoes. He was sure he'd taken a wrong turn somewhere, or perhaps an employee had left a door open, allowing access to an area the public wasn't meant to see. The air became a little breezy, bringing with it the sour rot of fish and vegetation standing in stagnant ocean-side pools, and hints of a worst stench waiting just underneath. He thought to turn and retrace his steps, but then he came upon the window.

It was smallish and filthy with a yellow oil scum, and much of its area layered over with old boards and rusted scrap nailed in place, but it did give a distorted sense of the outside, which was nothing like the outside James had just come from. He glimpsed a line of weathered buildings and docks. How had they managed it?

A few more steps brought him to a sagging staircase dropping down a flight, ending in a shabby, peeling door. He took those crumbling steps two at a time and used his momentum to push the warped door open, the top of it bowing out as the bottom scraped across a trash-littered threshold. He didn't imagine he'd ever be able to get it closed again.

He wasn't sure if what surrounded him was intended to be Innsmouth—the curators hadn't bothered to erect a sign, but it was certainly as James had always imagined that rundown seacoast town. Although there had been no attempt at creating a convincing sky, the high ceiling was vaulted and draped with cloth stained a variegation of whites, greys, and blues, and some source of moving air was evident in the ways the cloth periodically bent and warped to provide some illusionary cloud movement. The unpainted and weatherworn structures below spread in all directions, so that James really couldn't quite see the end of them. Perhaps some matte painting was involved, or strategically positioned mirrors? Otherwise the setting would seem to go on for miles, and that was impossible, wasn't it?

The space was densely constructed, with building after building crowding into each other until the edges spilled into the sea, their lower levels drowned. Some areas had been patched and repaired, supported and reinforced by ingenious home-made means so that the boundaries between buildings were blurred.

The detailing was remarkable—no single surface appeared wholly intact. Broken windows were stuffed with oily rags of an almost beautiful foulness. Here and there, shells with slimy tissue hanging from their openings had been strategically placed, and dead fish were scattered in the oddest locations atop roofs and snagged in closed doors. Weeds and the dead remains of aquatic plants had taken root in thresholds and along gutters, wedged between clapboards and growing out of window-frames.

Very few people were about, unless they were hiding deep inside the structures. Among the figures visible, it was difficult to distinguish between museum personnel made up to look like Innsmouth citizens and tourists unusually dressed for a holiday visit. A number of the bandaged people moved about in ways that suggested physical damage. And the way they moved in and out of doorways—suddenly appearing in some high window or other, or sitting down by the edge of the pier, dangling their clothed limbs nonchalantly in that foul amber water—was disturbing to watch.

Three tall steeples towered above all the gables and gambrel roofs, one's clock dials replaced with howling holes, the other two collapsing, their timbers imploding. They made a convincing simulacrum of decay, as did the patch-worked collection of ruins below them, but here and there James spied the faint traces of minute activity among these poor materials, the kind that an infestation of vermin might account for, so that he had to wonder if some of the progressive devastation might be actual. Of course there were finer houses—Georgians and stately Queen Anne's—but they were set so far back from the waterfront they were likely part of the painted scenery designed to give depth to this elaborate illusion.

He moved down the wooden walkways cautiously, afraid that at any moment the supports would break and dump him into that terrible foul-smelling liquid. He tried to pay attention to everything, but there really was too much to see. Finally he followed a family clump of four or five of the bandaged, crooked folk as they made their way through a tall pair of church doors carved with figures of an unrecognisable and unlikely morphology. And found himself in another juncture of the museum, the rock walls cold and dripping a briny, gelatinous secretion.

From this mercifully brief and unpleasant tunnel, James travelled through a series of much smaller rooms apparently meant to in some way represent some of Lovecraft's short stories. In the 'The Dreams in the Witch House' room, a young scholar was having his heart eaten out of his chest by a giant rat. The rat might have been an automaton of some sort, or something rigged up out of wax, rags, and pumps. Or it might have been an actor in a hideous costume, just like the actor portraying the poor student himself.

Almost as bad was the 'Shadow Over Innsmouth' room, in which the young man turned into something vaguely subhuman, fish-like, reptilian, all the while delivering this terribly sad and delirious monologue running the gamut from repulsion to outright celebration.

A long portrait gallery featured not only a variety of photographs taken of Lovecraft over the years, but also interpretations of the man and his family in paint, sculpture, and other media. The tall, gaunt figure looked pretty much the same in every image, although some interpretations exaggerated his chin or his facial blemishes or both. In several paintings, he was portrayed as walking about the streets of Providence, Rhode Island, under the cover of darkness, peering from around hedges or the corners of old buildings.

On an elaborate Grecian stand at the end of this exhibit hall was Lovecraft's fedora beneath a bell jar, labelled with a flowing inscription engraved on a brass plate. The hat was layered in a thick grey fur of dust, preserving both hat and dust together. James thought he had seen a picture or two of Lovecraft wearing this hat, and didn't think it particularly suited the man.

In the warren of rooms and alcoves and intersecting corridors that followed, various items from Lovecraft's house, along with antiques belonging to relatives and friends, even odd associational objects from the Providence of Lovecraft's time were displayed. But although a few of Lovecraft's own things were properly labelled—toiletries and clothing and books and the like—most appeared to have simply been dumped, overflowing the rooms and stacked dangerously high with only narrow passages contrived between them to accommodate visitors.

James was astounded that they actually allowed the public into this area. These particular acquisitions seemed obsessional, more the results of the hoarding of anything even vaguely Lovecraftian than the careful selections of a serious collector and sane museum curator. What kind of person would put so much time and money into transplanting this eccentric slice of Rhode Island kitsch to England, of all places? And then to care so little about how these dubious collectibles were presented?

Visitors to this area acted as if they were at a suburban garage sale. James could hardly blame them. He was sure some of the smaller artefacts were being pocketed. It was shameful.

There was a fine line between what people valued and made some attempt to preserve, and what was simply thrown away as having exhausted its significance. How did you decide? If he died today what would be kept, and more importantly, who would bother to keep it? The objects of a life must necessarily accumulate haphazardly, like the trash that's overflowed the bin, if we've made no rules, devised no strategy for moving on. Not only couldn't you take it with you, but best be careful about what you left behind. It was as if a poet left a final poem for all the world to see, but didn't even bother to edit it.

He thought about life with Chloe and Henry—what they'd had and what they'd done, and how none of that would be truly past, but co-existed, dream-like, with the present. At least as long as James was alive to experience it. His own house was certainly no better organised than this hodgepodge of items—he just lacked a sign that said MUSEUM. But he could take care of that particular oversight. Perhaps it was an odd thing to do, but who would ever see it other than him?

For all its flaws, the museum was wonderful, and James was excited to be there. But an unease had followed him through the various exhibits, indeed had come along with him in his trip out here from London. Some-thing poorly ignored, incompletely avoided. He was in England, where his only child had disappeared. And though the trail was years cold, he had no business enjoying himself, and the self-loathing he'd been so adamantly pushing down came suddenly racing, and he staggered over to the wall, ill. He gasped, holding his chest, choking and crying with his face turned from the crowd, who doubtless would not have paid much attention to him in any case.

If he were any kind of father he'd be back in the city, re-tracing the stops of his first trip, focusing on the things which had fascinated Henry at the time, because perhaps they might fascinate him still. James' chances of finding Henry were negligible, of course, but at least he could tell himself he'd done everything. Perhaps there was a bus that might take him back early. Surely not everyone could be expected to last an entire day. There were old people here, parents with their young children. Not everyone was an obsessive.

James couldn't decide what might be the quickest way out, but could not bring himself to shove his way back through the crowds and clutter. The museum appeared to have a predetermined traffic pattern, a natural flow through the exhibits, and it seemed foolish to struggle against it. So he permitted this tide to push him along into the final room in this particular sequence, before the next voluminous hall.

The room was announced by tall gold lettering on the black mahogany door: MISKATONIC UNIVERSITY: SPECIAL COLLEC-

TIONS. He aggressively pushed his way inside, bumping the people crowded in ahead of him. He wasn't sure that they spoke English—their outfits appeared stylish, but slightly odd. Some avant-garde designer's work, some European maverick, although he really didn't know that much about the subject.

He supposed it wasn't a surprise that this room was so popular. One of the most intriguing aspects of Lovecraft's work was the many strange and mysterious books he and his disciples referenced, and this homage to that mythic Miskatonic apparently housed most of them: the arcane *De Vermis Mysteriis*, the *Book of Eibon*, the *Celaeno Fragments*, *Cultes des Goules*, the *Dhol Chants*, a worn and heavily annotated working play script for *The King in Yellow*, *The Seven Cryptical Books of Hsan*, and various translations of the *Necronomicon* of the Arab Abdul Alhazred.

These were displayed in glass cases scattered throughout the room, which had an extremely tall ceiling with narrow, apparently faux windows at the top of each wall showing a shiny silver sky with reddish highlights. Below these the bookcases towered, the upper shelves accessed by long thin ladders which swayed under the weight of dark-cloaked, diminutive librarians. The shelves were dusty and jammed, and some housed reams of yellowed pages dissolving around the edges, bundled into groups and tied together with old string. Rolls of parchment were jammed side by side with fan-shaped books attached to broken black lacquer handles, books carved into rough planks of wood and woven books created out of discoloured rags.

Something he'd never seen before, or even imagined, were several books floating in glass jars full of a yellowish liquid. Thin wires dipped down through the wide mouths, to stir the pages and cause new words to emerge, as if a variety of invisible inks were gradually being activated, but if one kept agitating that liquid, other words slowly disappeared. A certain care had to be taken. Twist the sheet too much and individual letters would literally pop off the page, float out into the liquid and dissolve.

James saw them at the far edge of the room—his British acquaintance Clarence and the short young man with the shockingly black hair, still sporting that crimson red patch in front. Could that be his Henry? They were talking to each other using abrupt, animated gestures. James couldn't tell if they were arguing or simply displaying their enthusiasm for the subject matter. But at the end of the conversation Clarence put his arm around the young man's back, either in affection or as part of an attempt to force him out of the room. Within seconds they had exited through the far twin doors.

James pushed forward as vigorously as he could, trying to be forceful but hoping not to alarm anyone and cause a panic in this so-crowded room. This proved to be difficult due to both the size of the crowd and the eagerness with which they swarmed the exhibits, chattering away in a number of languages. Ahead of him a group of short figures in green uniforms completely jammed the aisle in front of a case displaying the two oldest editions of the *Necronomicon*. At first James thought it was some sort of scout outing, but then noticed the baldness, the array of wrinkles and weathered faces. And they would not be budged. Finally he pushed himself around the back of the crowd against a squall of protests, then through the other door, hoping to catch up with Clarence and that heart-stoppingly familiar young man.

James found himself in the largest chamber yet, as an enormous array of artistic interpretations of Cthulhu, in all sizes and styles, filled the great space beyond. On the domed ceiling the phrase *Ph'nglui mglw'nafh Cthulhu R'lyeh wgah'nagl fhtagn* writhed in huge dirty yellow letters, moving and distorting under a slowly swirling mist of dark-grey smoke.

He gazed tensely past the bewildering assortment of styles and techniques, seeking the moving forms of Clarence and that important young man. The predominance of sculptures, legs and arms and appendages unidentifiable, confused him, requiring time he didn't think he had to sort through and eliminate stone and metal in search of flesh. He was relieved to be among the paintings, drawings, etchings, block prints, and assemblages, but there were more visitors in this section, pointing, gesturing, gabbing. Where the devil were they? Why had such famous artists as Van Gogh, Picasso, Dali, and Whistler attempted their own interpretations of Lovecraft's themes? That was impossible, wasn't it? Certainly Van Gogh hadn't been alive when Lovecraft had created them.

No doubt there were signs that explained all these puzzles, but James didn't have time to read them. His son—was it possible?— *might* be in this room, and that was the only question that mattered.

Yet, how amazing was it that there were representations of Cthulhu from every artistic movement, from Romanticism to Cubism to Neo-expressionism? And in one well-lit case crude markings on a piece of stone, said to be taken out of a cave in France, showed a fantastic blend of octopus, dragon, and human caricature. Paleolithic Cthulhu.

He pushed through clots and masses of humanity in a blur of facial inventory, looking for his son among aquatic-body Cthulhus, head Cthulhus mounted on humanoid bodies, rudimentary winged figures, scales shaped or scattered with artistic illogic.

He attempted to block it all out so that he might focus on his pursuit, but it proved impossible to keep these bizarre, so compelling impressions away. Despite himself, he was being seduced by this wonderful display of Lovecraftian horror.

Cthulhu's name pronounced in different accents sang from countless tiny speakers. But James was listening for his son's voice, aged, transformed and doubtless impossible to recognise.

The largest, mountain-sized Cthulhus were arranged along the back of the hall. The scaled and rounded walls almost undulated as James searched curve to curve. He was positive he had seen Clarence standing here among the joints and plated hide, doing some terrible thing to a figure much smaller and less determined. Then above one of the taller cases that great eye rose, and James understood that the wall itself was another imagining of Cthulhu, made all the more realistic by whatever mechanicals and special effects engines were being used to supply the puppetry. He pushed ahead, sorting through more faces and moving profiles, and the pair once again came into view ahead of him, always one step beyond, fleeing through the grey irising doors at the other end of the chamber.

The corridor outside was packed with eager tourists. The attraction was a small stand with two clerks behind, the sign overhead:

CTHULHU JELLY SWEETS. People were walking off with bags full. James quickly became disoriented. He watched in some alarm as an elderly man latched his teeth into a couple of multicoloured Cthulhu feelers, pulling until they had stretched almost a foot, his false teeth beginning to edge out past his trembling lips.

But again he saw Clarence and Henry several yards ahead, almost racing. Clarence looked around briefly, still pushing aggressively on the young man's back. James felt a burn of anger and sorrow in his throat. Had Clarence seen him? He paused—their backs were turned again, headed for another large door off the corridor. James charged ahead, afraid he might lose them. The crowds seemed much larger now, so he assumed more buses full of tourists had arrived, from London or perhaps other cities in the British Isles. Such popularity for the man from Providence seemed so unlikely, so impossible. This would never happen in America. He knew that he didn't understand commerce and had no feel for degrees of popularity, but still, this hardly seemed possible anywhere in the world. And yet here it was in all its grand, unsettling magnificence. He reached the door but seconds after they'd gone through.

On a series of well-illuminated, glass-enclosed platforms in the dark room, different figures stood, dramatically posed. Like the kind of action figures little boys and girls liked to play with, only much larger, life-size and bigger-than-life-size. The crowd was sparser here, and he could hear no sounds of running. If anything, the hall was preternaturally quiet. He slowed down, trying to look inconspicuous. Now that they knew he was on to them they must have been hiding among the exhibits. He proceeded cautiously, gliding his head side to side, looking.

Arranged in half a dozen rows, the platforms were filled with figures of Cthugha, Dagon, Glaaki, Hastur, Ithaqua, Nyogtha, Shudde M'ell, Tsathoggua, Yig, Azathoth, Nyarlathotep, Shub-Niggurath, and Yog-Sothoth. Some of these figures had not been created by Lovecraft himself, James knew, but originated with Campbell, Lumley, Derleth, Smith, and others under Lovecraft's influence. They were minutely detailed, and obviously had required enormous time and money to produce.

Dagon was an immense eel whose face had that long-fanged, deep-sea fish aspect. Suckered tentacles and sharp talons covered his body. Hastur changed appearance depending on the angle. From some viewpoints he appeared almost man-like, but his face was wrapped in a tangle of opaque shadow which defied interpretation. From other points he was clearly octopoid, with nothing remotely human about him.

Nyarlathotep was quite pharaoh-like from the front, but when James went around to the back of the figure he saw that both bat wings and tentacles were erupting from the spine, preparing to take over and transform the rest of the body. Shudde M'ell appeared as a burrower, a consumer of earth and rock, whose frightening maw dripped acid. The base the figure was standing on was partially eaten away by the character's drool.

He could hear them, talking in the shadows, Clarence's voice louder than anyone else's, proclaiming—what? James couldn't quite make out the words. He never saw Clarence in this exhibit, or his son, but he certainly heard them. Suddenly off in a dark corner they were moving. They must have seen him approaching. Their clashing voices rising and falling indicated some sort of argument. Again he wasn't sure of the words, something like "you must" and "now" and "no future opportunity". But try as he might he could not connect these vocal bits. When he heard the door open at the back he ran in that direction, tightly focussed on the swiftly narrowing vertical rectangle of door.

Once through, he saw them on the other side of a queue of tourists, running inside a larger crowd, bumping into people, knocking one of the small bandaged types to the floor without stopping to help (and no one else did, either—they all stood around watching, as if afraid to touch). He was sure they had seen him now—why else would they be running? And he felt surer still as they dashed into some sort of sprawling gift shop—ELDER THINGS scrawled in thin, barely legible script over the double glass doors. No doubt they wanted to lose themselves within the mass of shoppers. James was not very far behind, but the entrance was so crowded he had to squeeze through. The number of people jamming the interior, already crowded with tables and other merchandise displays, seemed more than uncomfortable—it felt dangerous.

There were more children here than he'd seen elsewhere in the museum. Many were crowded around the tables, trying out remote-control models of various Yig, Ithaqua, unidentified fish-like people, and of course both simple and complex versions of Cthulhu, the more elaborate having individually moving tentacles. Other children dragged one or more parents from display to display wheedling and threatening.

There were teenagers and adults too, examining the role-playing games based on Lovecraft, the clothing based on Lovecraft, the Lovecraft-influenced music, the calendars, the T-shirts, the action-figures modelled on their larger selves in the great hall, the luggage, the dishware, the toiletries.

There were plastic models of Innsmouth and R'lyeh and Kingsport (with the Strange High House in the Mist hanging above) those so inclined might put together, or you could purchase them pre-assembled if you didn't mind paying the hefty premium. There were expensive chest sets based on the Byakhee, the Great Old Ones, and the Yithian. And a solid gold set based on a range of characters, with Cthulhu as king, glorious in its own expansive case by the nine cash registers, with a price tag stating ENQUIRIES TAKEN.

And of course there were the books, for those who still cared to read Lovecraft in his original words: the standard paperbacks, the still inexpensive cheaply bound hardcovers, and limited editions in leather and materials James did not recognise, with signed, limited-edition prints tipped in, hand-painted interiors, special endpapers, wooden-boxed or slipcased, some in their own special lacquered puzzle boxes guaranteeing you'd spend weeks just trying to figure out how to open them and get to the treasured volumes inside. The prices for these items went up astronomically, accommodating anyone with any amount to pay.

James saw them, standing quietly together among all those colourful stacks of books, Henry looking dwarfed and small again beside the leaning towers of board and paper as he gazed at James with something like sadness, something like defiance, because his son *was* plainly staring at him now, with all pretence that he might just be some random look-alike stranger completely gone. Clarence moved closer to Henry, but James didn't think he realised they'd been found yet. Now he looked strangely—shy, perhaps? Cowed? How were these two people related?

Then the pair walked away from the books and out of the shop, but James couldn't budge—there were far too many customers, far too many spoiled, crying children in his way. He could only follow them with his eyes, watching through the shop's windows as they passed down another corridor into the crowd spilling from another great hall.

In the hours that followed, James wandered in frantic, painful exhaustion from exhibit to exhibit, peeking into rooms in which both real and imagined arcane technologies were displayed, into long aisles arranged like closets with all manner of clothing both showcased and stored, into areas where artists worked live creating fanciful yet tortured imagery, into great open spaces with incompressible sculpture and fountains and benches where he would not sit because of the strange people already sitting there, down elevators and up ramps, through tunnels so narrow the visitors had to trickle through in singles and pairs, into sections half-constructed and vast wings being torn down.

It was not immediately apparent what most of these sights had to do with Lovecraft, although he thought the signage and audio commentary attempted to convince visitors of the connections. But he did not have the will or the heart to hear or read any of that. Apparently he had been led here across the ocean under false pretences, and he had lost his son, his only child, once again. He had only the most general sense of the details, and he had no idea as to the hows and whys. Hows and whys apparently belonged to another reality, to privileged folk who saw the likes of him as props and tools for designs he could not possibly understand.

James spent the balance of the afternoon in a large room labelled THE DEEP ONES. An enormous aquarium filled most of the space at its centre. Observers entered from any of the four doors and were compelled to walk its perimeter while gazing at the tank, most unhurriedly, quiet and fully absorbed by the contents of this tank until they exited the door where they had come in. So he wasn't the only one who spent a great deal of time in this room. Apparently it was expected that everyone would. Long benches had been installed for sitting. There were even doorways to toilets for those whose physical requirements made the occasional break necessary, so they could return to their observations of the tank almost immediately.

Inside the murky green waves, the vague shapes of undersea dwellers drifted in and out of visibility, the smaller ones looking human at times, and at times more fish-like. The bigger ones, at certain angles, were like hallucinations of giant humanoid frogs, the kind of creature in anguish whether in water or air, and so at home nowhere. Some which seemed more human at first appeared to mutate as they moved through the shadowed depths.

Further back in the deep green darkness, larger shapes moved—the ones that these smaller ones no doubt were meant to serve. James could arrive at no clear sense of form—movement in the water might have been caused by some sort of appendage. Occasional stirrings might be due to respiration or a filtration for food. There were broader movements perhaps of a large bulk shifting, and when the smaller companions neared, a vague indication of stillness and focus. And despite seeing very little within that murk, James came away with a conviction of sight, or at least of vision. However busy that presence might be with its own cosmic concerns, it had noticed him. It had seen James and was now watching. He had no doubts of it.

This was the fantastic interpretation of what he was seeing, of course. But when he tried to think about it realistically—because certainly a much more mundane explanation must apply—he could not make good sense of it. He tried to view this tank as just another elaborate illusion within this overly imagined circus that used Lovecraft's name, but it was difficult to figure out what they were doing here. It made the most sense that automated figures would be in the tank, but some of the figures had such individuated and non-repeating movements they certainly had to be actors in costume. But how did they stay underwater for so long?

Inevitably the day wandered on toward dinnertime, and James became quite hungry. In any case he longed for a place where he could simply sit down and collect his thoughts. He took an elevator down to the lower level, where an immense restaurant named Shoggoths took up the entire visible floor space. It had a rustic, Polynesian sort of ambience with rough wooden tables sheltered by thatched roofs, and tiki-style masks, idols, and totems, except the carvings were of Lovecraftian characters and designs. The servers, both male and female, had Joan of Arc-style haircuts and all wore solid black kaftans. They looked somewhat religious, even down to the stylised ways in which they moved about the tables, took orders, and delivered food. He thought of androgynous nuns in cutting-edge designer outfits. What they served at every table was basically the same, the Shoggoth sandwich—a long, sloppy, submarine sandwich sort of food with the diner's choice of meats, mixed with an overabundance of vegetables and unidentifiable sprouts spilling out in all directions. This was topped by the special grey Shoggoth sauce, a pickled saline, brine-smelling goop that inevitably got all over the diners as they attempted to eat it. Even as starved as he was, James wasn't sure he could consume such an unattractive disaster.

His eyes were drawn to the back of the restaurant, where a tall male figure moved swiftly toward a door. A much shorter figure moved with the man, being dragged, or perhaps pushing—at least some sort of struggle was taking place. James moved around trying to see more clearly, and couldn't quite manage it. But he was convinced it was Henry and Clarence.

James made his way through the maze of staggered tables, apologising as he ran into legs, moved chairs, jostled the elbows of people trying to eat. There was an outcry, and several servers were approaching, but he had no time to explain—if that was Clarence and Henry, he probably wouldn't get another chance. He finally reached the door a long time after they'd passed through. He ran in, onto a stairwell platform, steps leading down. Although the steps were well lit, the walls were not, and he could not touch them by stretching out his arms. Given the nature of the echoing footfalls—

he could hear them far below—the walls were some distance away. He felt a moment of panic, then forced himself to descend as quickly as physically possible, focussing only on the steps and the pounding sounds below.

After a few minutes without slowing, he became aware of a rising stench. He thought perhaps they were approaching an area where the museum disposed of its wastes, but there was a sharpness to the stench that did not signify garbage to him. A few more flights down and the smell began to burn his eyes. He realised it had a vague resemblance to the smell of that pickled, briny sauce, although magnified a few thousand times.

At the bottom, the stair became the hub to a wheel of corridor openings. He moved from opening to opening, listening. From several, he heard a lapping as of ocean waves, but no steps. From another there came a regular, distant shush-shushing sound, and a terrible stink, but not the same as what he had smelled before. Several others appeared dead—dark and unlit and with air that tasted deeply of dirt. He was ready to give up when he heard the faint *click click click* inside one of the corridors, like hard soles hitting metal. The briny stench here was terrible, and a breeze from the opening seemed to indicate some passage to outside air. And a low-level, phosphorescent sort of light outlining floor, ceiling, walls. He had no choice, so he raced into it headlong, glancing down just enough to avoid tripping over obstacles: piles of vegetation, loose unravelling of clothing, and other materials—stubby, moving things.

Just ahead of him was a crumbling of the corridor wall, a break that allowed some light in, a mix of impossible ocean beach sounds and two stumbling figures. Suddenly the crumbling hole widened as bits of metal and clay and stone tumbled across the floor. Daylight illuminated the forms: Clarence with his hands on Henry, pushing. James shouted.

Clarence stopped, turned and saw James, reached out one hand, bleeding, grasping at air. At that moment the young man who was clearly Henry shoved him, and Clarence tumbled backwards through the hole and into the outside.

"Henry! Henry, it's Daddy!" James cried.

His son turned and looked at him then, his eyes dark as his hair, his mouth grim, the red streak in his hair damp and shiny as if it might actually be real blood. He just stared. Then smiled a too-wide, most-inhuman, humourless grin. Then he leapt through the hole as well.

James gazed, despairing, and would have fallen to his knees if Clarence hadn't reappeared around the hole's edge, waving his arms. "James!" he sobbed, before being sucked outside again.

James was reluctant to go any further, but would have, would have gone to investigate, would even have followed the pair of them through the hole and outside, if the figures dressed in black hadn't surrounded him and dragged him away.

"Museum security says they found you in an unauthorised area, and when you would not co-operate they were compelled to remove you by force. They also report that there was no evidence that you ever had companions on your visit to the museum."

"Why would there be evidence either way? I certainly didn't expect Henry to be there. And Clarence and I came together, but he thought it would be best if we went off exploring on our own."

"Why would he do that? He is British, you are American, and based on your correspondence it is easy to see he encouraged you to come for a visit. It hardly seems proper he would simply leave you to your own devices."

"Clarence wasn't terribly friendly. He seemed to have his own things going on. Certainly he didn't try to entertain me at all."

His interrogator glanced over at the companion in uniform. "And I imagine you must have resented this? Or did your anger explode when you say you saw him with your son, his hands upon Henry?"

"Wait, no—you actually think I had something to do with his disappearance?"

"No insult intended, but unlike yourself, he was not a loner. He had friends, and a large family he was quite close to. A rather important family, I might add."

"All I wanted was to make one last trip over here." Pleading embar-

rassed him, but he could not help himself. "I wanted to be where I last saw my son. And I genuinely wanted to see the museum. I have this interest in Lovecraft, you see. He certainly speaks to me. And that interest, it has saved me. It has kept me from thinking about other things."

"I understand. I have never been to the museum myself, but I hear it is quickly becoming quite an attraction—a national institution, some might say. But then, I've never been much of a reader. I'm far too busy. And so, was it everything you expected?" The man busily referred to his notes.

"No. Not at all. Nothing here was as I expected it. Not your entire country."

"Well, that is the joy and the interesting thing about international travel, is it not? Or it should be. Visiting other cultures, being taken out of one's comfort zone? What did you expect? England is a wonderful country—many people want to visit us."

"Of course, of course it is. I wanted to visit England—this just isn't the England I expected to visit."

"We do not fit your preconceived notions? Is that it?"

"Where do I begin? Lovecraft of all writers has become a major tourist attraction? Those so-called pets on the posters, held by obviously frightened children? And the foreigners here—the people in bandages, for example, what mythical land do they come from? And have you looked inside the backs of your toilets? What passes here for plumbing? What kind of thing is that? Have you bothered investigating your own plumbing?"

"We are police officers, sir. You would have to go to the municipal engineers with that sort of question. Have you really flown across the Atlantic simply to study the minutest details of our infrastructure? I must say, your two visits to our country have resulted in two unsolved missing persons cases. I should warn you, sir, that providing frivolous and eccentric answers to our inquiries is not likely to improve your situation here. I would simply suggest that, well, there is an old saying. Confession is good for the soul."

"I flew across the Atlantic to be where I last saw my son. Perhaps it was foolish to think I might run into him, but a broken father can *be a very foolish man. I came across the Atlantic to meet someone of like interests, perhaps someone who might in time become a dear friend. Foolish, I know. Perhaps even pathetic. This is the sort of thing that happens to some of us when we are alone."*

"I sympathise, of course. But we are all alone—that is my belief. The other people in our lives, they distract us from that fact, but they do not change it."

"I know, I know—we all have this problem. Believe me, I know I'm not special in this regard. We all feel a certain insignificance. We all feel that things move so fast, events accumulate, that we can truly understand very little of it. We all feel there are processes at work, decisions being made at a higher level which deeply effect our lives, which we cannot even begin to understand. Our ultimate fate is out of our hands, and we cannot run away from it. I would just like to make sense of my small part of it. I would just like to find some small thread of sanity and hold onto it. Other people seem to live out their lives happily—why can't I?"

James hadn't even been aware that he'd put his hands over his face. Embarrassed, he jerked them away. His interrogator wasn't there. He looked around, frightened, and saw the man in deep conversation with his uniformed companion, with occasional furtive glances his way. Finally his questioner returned.

"My apologies, sir, for the interruption. But we were wondering if you would like to go now? It seems your friend has turned up, and apologises for any inconvenience. But he strongly requests that you do not attempt to contact him. He is quite adamant on that point. We encourage you to enjoy yourself in London for another day, but we would like you to leave the country on Friday. All the arrangements have been made, everything has been taken care of. Your belongings have been moved to the International Hotel. You will find your travel documents waiting for you there."

The interrogator and the one in uniform escorted James down to the street. The one in uniform stayed back in the shadows. The one who'd asked all the questions squinted painfully into the dim afternoon light, as if even that little bit of sunshine was too much.

James felt relieved to have some distance from the man. All those questions, delivered with the man's stinking breath. The man's breath reeked of fish and brine and vegetation rotting in salt water. What were they eating over here to cause such a stink?

James did not like to dwell on a person's appearance, and yet the width of the man's head had been so distracting, and those terribly wide eyes, narrowed to razor slits by the heavy lids. The one in uniform had been worse, with the ridges on his neck, and the blinkless way he had looked at James, as if he might leap and devour him at any moment.

V. Flying Home

For his final day in London James walked around Soho and over to Covent Garden and the theatre district. This was where Henry had disappeared on that trip so many years ago. The fact that he might have lost him at any point along the route, that he could not pinpoint a block or a street or even a more specific neighbourhood, was shameful to him now. At the opening to each lane, alley, or walk he imagined that smallish form, shoulders hunched in that hostile way, walking away from him, receding so rapidly he had no time even to call out, even to catch a breath, cry, or gasp. Impossibly fast, the speed at which constellations were formed. A careless blink and his son was taken from him, gone.

That had been a strange day, an unusually incompetent day for himself as a parent, out of—frankly—dozens of other only slightly less incompetent days. He hadn't known what to do. He doubted every decision, to the point where making decisions appeared impossible. He certainly did not hate his son, but that particular day he would have had to admit he didn't like the boy very much.

Henry had been that Sullen Monster almost from the hour they'd stepped off the plane. That's what James used to call him—never to his face—back when the boy was impossible to reach, unpleasant to talk to. The child had developed a sudden talent for distaste, a formidable skill for putdowns, an unending appetite for boredom.

Part of the problem, James knew now, was that he'd needed too much from his son. Needed his conversation, needed Henry to make him a little more human. With a son, family was possible, and James could imagine himself as some part of the community. Henry no doubt had felt the power he'd possessed, and so seized it, wielding it ruthlessly.

"Maybe we could try one of those electronic shops in the Garden?" he'd offered. Henry still loved gadgets—he was always combining them in creative, if not practical, ways. "I'm buying. Anything you want—I've already paid for the ticket home." He laughed then, because he'd meant it to be funny. Henry gave his poor effort what it deserved, which was nothing.

He'd been following Henry much of the day, at his insistence. "Let's go to lunch," Henry would say, and head out at breakneck speed, the angry thrust of his shoulders pushing him forward. It hadn't been a real invitation—it had been a challenge. And James had been too late picking up on that. James had strained to keep up, but he had been afraid of what might happen if he lost sight of his son. Henry had become so impulsive the last couple of years. James fielded calls from the schools (four in two years) every week regarding the things Henry had done, the things Henry had started. Once the boy took some random, ill-considered path, he did so with full commitment. It was almost admirable, in a frightening, edge-of-the-cliff sort of way.

"Henry, wait up!" It was a plea he'd repeated a hundred times a day this trip.

This day, James' last day in London, there appeared to be a large number of young men in their twenties out and about. Henry's age, Henry's size. And neighbouring on Henry's attitude, although of course Henry was the master, the exemplar beside which all other sullenness paled. (Was that a terrible thing to think? Was that the sort of thing a *good* father felt about his child?) A few had dyed streaks in their hair. Many didn't. Many of the young men provided him with his first real-life exposure to those odd pets from the poster campaign, being led about on those child leashes or holding hands with their owners. Although it seemed odd to think you could actually own anything who had a hand you could hold.

Some of these unpleasant creatures rode piggyback on their owners' backs, clutching them tightly, whispering into or occasionally actually licking their owners' ears. Creatures in brown fur, blue fur, yellow fur, golden, like stuffed animals charming on the shelf but more than disturbing when actualised. Long nails, long claws, long teeth. Many of the young men bore extended scratches. James had the distinct impression they bore them proudly.

"You're crowding me, Dad!" Henry had cried out, turning, snarling at him, suddenly not so dissimilar from those disturbing pets.

"I'm several feet away! You've got plenty of space!" It had been foolish trying to reason with his son, but James couldn't help himself. He depended on logic, even when logic was undependable. His son used to be so much like him—surely his sense of logic was still in there somewhere.

"Just *stay back*! Okay?" Henry twisted around, his black-and-red hair flipping violently. He wore a too-small black jacket with aluminium studs inexpertly applied. Before their trip Henry had imagined that was the way the British teens would be dressed, but apparently that style was out that year in London—they saw no one else dressed in anything remotely like it. Henry had been embarrassed, practically humiliated, but he'd stubbornly kept the outfit on, and if James wasn't mistaken, flaunting it.

So James had followed Henry around the squares and through the secretive, named walks and down the quaint alleys more like a puppy dog than like a father, and he'd felt ashamed and incompetent but with no idea what to say to his son to make him stop it. At that moment their relationship seemed far from fixable.

There was a great commotion ahead. Apparently one of those strange pets had gotten away from its young owner and been struck by a car. James lingered around the edges of the crowd, watching. The ape-like creature lay on its back, moving its arms and legs as if it were dancing, as if it were some wind-up toy knocked on its side but still attempting to do what it was designed to do. Its long, worm-like tail wriggled aggressively, trapped beneath its body, looking vaguely tentacle-like, looking as if it had its own intelligence.

The car that had struck the animal looked like four or five enormous pipes bolted together with metal boxes of various sizes attached at random. The driver's head was visible inside a clear plastic bubble mounted on the top. James had never seen anything like it.

James had lost Henry somewhere in those streets during the confusion. He'd turned his head for just a second, and at that moment the boy had raced headlong into the crowd, which opened, then closed again behind him, as if sealing him away from life with his father. James had walked around, circling the blocks and pacing every lane calling Henry's name, stopping complete strangers and questioning them, going into every likely shop with his son's picture clutched in his hand. Henry never answered, and James never saw him again.

Boarding took an inordinately long time. James was among the passengers they called first. A British policeman, his neck wrapped in heavy layers of gauze, was stationed by the entrance to the boarding ramp. James did not know if this was now common practice, or if the officer was there to make sure he got on the plane. In any case, he did not speak to him, but James was pretty sure he'd been the object of a pointed glance or two.

After an uncomfortable length of time, they boarded the bandaged people. Their clothes were extraordinarily ragged—much poorer looking than any he had seen on any of these creatures before. In fact their clothing was so worn that in many cases tiny bits of cloth and bandage littered the aisles in minute fragments. Slices of pale skin were exposed. Now and then a damaged bit of flesh would hang out of a worn opening. The plane began to smell of the ocean. It was all very strange, but then a life alone was always very strange.

The bandaged people filled the front two-thirds of the plane. James wondered if they were being deported as well. Of course he hadn't been deported—he'd simply been asked to leave the country.

The captain announced they would be flying over Iceland. The brilliant light bouncing off water and sky and ice flooded the plane. The bandaged people began to sing, an exalted chorus of damage. James didn't understand any of the words, but convinced himself they were singing of home.

STEPHEN JONES & KIM NEWMAN

NECROLOGY: 2015

MORE THAN EVER, we are marking the passing of writers, artists, performers and technicians who, during their lifetimes, made significant contributions to the horror, science fiction and fantasy genres (or left their mark on popular culture and music in other, often fascinating, ways)...including, this year, too many major authors, two original *Star Trek* actors, and at least a couple of horror movie icons.

AUTHORS/ARTISTS/COMPOSERS

American illustrator and cartoonist **Roy McKie**, best known for callaborating with Dr. Seuss ("Ted" Geisel) on a number of children's books, died on January 8, aged 93. Amongst the titles he illustrated during the 1960s are *Ten Apples Up on Top!* and *My Book About Me by Me Myself!*

French SF writer **Michel Jeury** (aka "Albert Higon") died on January 9, aged 80. He began publishing in 1960, and his books, under both his own name and the Higon pseudonym, include *Aux Étoile du Destin*, *La Machine du Pouvoir*, *La temps incertain* (aka *Chronolysis*), *Les Singes du Temps* and *May le Monde*.

British scriptwriter, producer and author **Brian** (Horace) **Clemens**, best remembered for writing some of the more outlandish episodes of the cult ITV series *The Avengers* (1961-69) and *The New Avengers* (1976-77), died on January 10, aged 83. His film credits include *The Tell-Tale Heart* (1960), *And Soon the Darkness* (1970), *Blind Terror* (aka *See No Evil*), Hammer's *Dr. Jekyll & Sister Hyde* and *Captain Kronos Vampire Hunter* (which he also directed), *The Golden Voyage of Sinbad*, Disney's *The Watcher in the Woods*, *Timestalkers*, *Highlander II: The Quickening* and the 2015 horror short *Surgery*. Clemens also created the TV series *Thriller* (1973-76) and wrote episodes of *Adam Adamant Lives!*, *The Champions*, *The Wide World of Mystery*, *Darkroom*, *Hammer House of Mystery and Suspense* ('Mark of the Devil'), *Worlds Beyond*, *Alfred Hitchcock Presents* (1989) and *Highlander*. As "Tony O'Grady" he came up with the original stories for two episodes of *H.G. Wells' The Invisible Man* (1959) and also co-scripted the film *Curse of the Voodoo* (aka *Voodoo Blood Death*). *The Avengers* was turned in to a short-run stage play in 1971, written by Clemens and Terence Feely. In 2013, PS Publishing issued his short story collection, *Rabbit Pie & Other Tales of Intrigue*.

Romanian publisher and writer **Valentin Nicolau**, who founded the successful Nemira imprint in the early 1990s, died of a heart attack on January 13, aged 54.

American animation artist (Alwyn) **Walter** "Walt" **Peregoy** died on January 16, aged 89. He worked as a background and colour stylist for Walt Disney on the movies *Sleeping Beauty* (1959), *101 Dalmations* (1961) and *The Sword in the Stone*, before moving on to such Hanna-Barbera TV series as *The Lone Ranger* (1966), *Wacky Races*, *The New Adventures of Huckleberry Finn*, *Scooby Doo Where Are You!*, *The Amazing Chan and the Chan Clan* and *The ABC Saturday Superstar Movie* ('The Mini-Munsters'), amongst many other titles. Peregoy was involved in the design of Epcot Center in Florida, and he was named a Disney Legend in 2008.

Alice K. (Kennedy) **Turner**, who was fiction editor at *Playboy* magazine from 1976 to 2000, died of antibiotic-resistant pneumonia on January 17, aged 75. Born in China, where her father was an American diplomat, she also edited the anthology *The Playboy Book* *of Science Fiction* and, with Andrew Greeley, she wrote the 1993 non-fiction study *The History of Hell*. Turner also co-edited a chapbook about the work of John Crowley, and her critical essays appeared in *Asimov's*, *The New York Review of Science Fiction* and *Locus*.

Japanese *manga* writer **Kazumasa Hirai** died on January 17, aged 76. He created the *anime* superhero 8 Man and the *Wolf Guy manga* novel series.

British children's author **Pauline** (Millicent) **Fisk** died of cancer on January 25, aged 66. From her first novel, the Nestlé Smarties Book Prize-winning *Midnight Blue* (1990), much of her work combined social realism with the supernatural. Her other ten books include the "Children of Plynlimon" parallel world trilogy (*Sabrina Fludde*, *The Red Judge* and *Mad Dog Moonlight*) and *In the Trees*, and she scripted six episodes of the Gerry Anderson animated TV series *Lavender Castle*.

American feminist SF writer, poet and linguist **Suzette Haden Elgin** (Patricia Anne Wilkins) died on January 27, aged 78. She suffered from dementia and had been in declining health for some time. Her first story appeared in *The Magazine of Fantasy and Science Fiction* in 1969, and her novels include the "Native Tongue" trilogy (*Native Tongue*, *The Judas Rose* and *Earthsong*); the "Coyote Jones" series (comprising *The Communipaths*, *Furthest*, *At the Seventh Level*, *Star-Anchored Star-Angered* and *Yonder Comes the Other End of Time*), and the "Planet Ozark" trilogy (*Twelve Fair Kingdoms*, *The Grand Jubilee* and *And Then There'll Be Fireworks*). Amongst Elgin's other books are the stand-alone novel *Peacetalk 101* and *The Science Fiction Poetry Handbook*. She founded the ScienceFiction Poetry Association in 1978.

Australian author **Colleen McCullough**, best known for writing *The Thorn Birds*, died on January 29, aged 77. Her SF novel *A Creed for the Third Millennium* was published in 1985.

American screenwriter and producer **Robert** (Sherwood) **Blees** died on January 31, aged 96. His writing credits include *The Black Scorpion*, *Screaming Mimi*, *From the Earth to the Moon*, *Frogs*, *Whoever Slew Auntie Roo?*, *Dr. Phibes Rises Again* (starring Vincent Price) and the TV movies *Curse of the Black Widow* and *Savage*

Harvest, along with episodes of *Alfred Hitchcock Presents* and *Project U.F.O.* (which he also produced).

Emmy Award-winning American screenwriter **Stewart Stern**, best known for writing *Rebel Without a Cause* (1955), James Dean's last movie, died of cancer on February 2, aged 92. The nephew of studio executive Adolph Zuckor and a cousin of the Loews, he began his career in the 1940s as a dialogue director on such films as *The Cobra Strikes* and *The Amazing Mr. X* (aka *The Spiritualist*). Stern also had a cameo in the 1985 version of *Fright Night*. He retired from scriptwriting in the mid-1980s due to anxiety.

American horror writer **Melanie Tem** (Melanie Kubachko) died on February 9, two years after being diagnosed with returning breast cancer, which metastasised to her stomach and bone marrow. She was 65. Presented with the British Fantasy Society's Icarus award for Most Promising Newcomer in 1992, her short fiction is collected in *The Ice Downstream* and *Singularities*, while *In Concert* and the Bram Stoker Award-winning *Imagination Box* both featured collaborations with her husband, Steve Rasnic Tem. They also collaborated on the multiple award-winning novella 'The Man on the Ceiling', which they later expanded into a full-length work, and another novel entitled *Daughters*. Melanie Tem's solo novels include the Stoker Award-winning *Prodigal*, *Blood Moon*, *The Wilding*, *Revenant*, *Desmodus*, *Tides*, *Black River*, *Slain the Spirit*, *The Deceiver*, *The Yellow Wood* and two collaborations with Nancy Holder, *Making Love* and *Witch-Light*.

American artist **Gail J. Butler**, whose work appeared in *Marion Zimmer Bradley's Fantasy Magazine* and *Analog*, died after a short illness on February 13, aged 67. She was Artist Guest of Honour twice at Orycon.

British comic-strip illustrator **Brett Ewins** died on February 16, aged 56. He worked on such strips as 'Judge Dredd' and 'Bad Company' for *2000 AD*, along with *Hellblazer* and *Swamp Thing*. In 1988 he created the independent comics magazine *Deadline* with Steve Dillon.

British comics artist **John Cooper** died after a short illness on February 22, aged 72. He had suffered from chronic obstructive pulmonary disease for some years. The many strips Cooper worked on include 'Lady Penelope', 'Thunderbirds', 'Captain Scarlet' and 'Joe 90' for *TV Century 21*, 'Man from Atlantis' in *Look-In*, 'Judge Dredd' and 'Targ's Terror Tales' in *2000 AD*, and 'Doctor Who' and 'Blakes 7' for Marvel UK.

American author **Ryder Syvertsen**, who wrote the SF survivalist "Doomsday Warriors" series as "Ryder Stacy" (some in collaboration with Jan Stacy), died on February 24, aged 73.

American author **Albert J. Manachino** died on February 28, aged 90. He began his writing career in 1975 and his work appeared extensively in the small press magazines. Manachino's short fiction was collected in *The Box Hunters & Others*, *The Odd Lot* and *Noctet: Tales of Madonna-Moloch*, while his only novel was *The Box Hunters*, published in 2002.

Carnegie Medal-winning British author **Mal Peet** died of cancer on March 2, aged 67. His 2014 adult novel, *The Murdstone Trilogy*, was a satire of the publishing industry, about a children's author forced to reinvent himself as a fantasy writer.

47-year-old American inker **Norman Lee**, who worked for both DC and Marvel Comics, apparently drowned while snorkelling off the Cayman Islands on March 5. His body was not recovered. Lee worked on such strips as 'Supergirl', 'Starman', 'Spider-Man', 'The Avengers' and 'X-Men'.

American artist and sculptor **Tom Loback** died the same day, aged 66. An Elvish linguist, he was best known for his J.R.R. Tolkien-related and gaming work, and he created a line of fantasy figures for Dragontooth Miniatures.

Japanese *manga* artist **Yoshihiro Tatsumi** died on March 7, aged 79. He pioneered the alternative adult *gekiga* style of illustration in such works as *Black Blizzard* and *A Drifting Life*, the latter winning him multiple Eisner Awards.

American writer **Lou Silverstone** (Louis Donald Silverstone), who co-scripted the 1972 *ABC Saturday Superstar Movie* 'The Mad, Mad, Monsters', died on March 9, aged 90.

American newspaper comic strip artists **Fred Fredericks**, who illustrated and wrote *Mandrake the Magician* from 1965 until his retirement in 2013, died on March 10, aged 85.

Best-selling British fantasy author Sir **Terry Pratchett** (Terence David John Pratchett) died of a chest infection on March 12, aged 66. He had famously been suffering from PCA (posterior cortical atrophy), a progressive early-onset form of Alzheimer's disease, for the past eight years. Pratchett wrote more than seventy books, selling over eighty-five million copies in thirty-seven languages worldwide. Best known for his forty-volume "Discworld" series, beginning in 1983 with *The Colour of Magic*, he began his career when a story published in his secondary school magazine in 1961 was reprinted in *Science-Fantasy* magazine two years later. After working as a newspaper journalist and as a press officer in the nuclear power industry, he became a full-time writer in 1987. His books range from YA novels and humorous fantasies, to collaborations with friends Neil Gaiman (the novel *Good Omens*) and Stephen Baxter (the "Long Earth" trilogy). Pratchett received the World Fantasy Life Achievement Award in 2010 and the British Fantasy Society's Karl Edward Wagner Award for Special Achievement the following year.

American comics artist **Irwin Hansen**, best known for creating the 1955-86 newspaper strip *Dondi* (with Gus Edson), died on March 13, aged 96. During the 1940s he worked on such Golden Age strips as 'The Green Hornet', 'Secret Agent Z-2', 'The Flash', 'Green Lantern' and 'The Justice Society of America'. Hansen created the character of Wildcat for National Comics/DC.

Danish author and feminist **Inge Eriksen** died the same day, aged 79. During the 1980s and early '90s she published several SF novels, including *Amanda Screamer's Desire*, *Benedetto and Lllalinini*, *Alice Alice*, and the "Space Without Time" quartet, along with the Gothic love story *The Japanese Millionaire*, and wrote the dystopian stage play *The Wind is Not for Sale*.

Danish-born screenwriter, director and author **Ib** (Jørgen) **Melchior** died in West Hollywood on March 14, aged 97. His scripts include *The Angry Red Planet* (which he also directed), *Reptilicus*, *Journey to the Seventh Planet*, *Robinson Crusoe on Mars*, *The Time Travelers* (another directing credit, featuring Forrest J Ackerman) and the English-language versions of *Godzilla Raids Again* and *Planet* *of the Vampires*. Both the *Death Race 2000* (1975) and *Death Race* (2008) were based on his 1958 short story 'The Racer'. Melchoir was also a technical director on the TV series *Tom Corbett Space Cadet* and scripted episodes of *13 Demon Street* (hosted by Lon Chaney, Jr.), *Men Into Space* and *The Outer Limits*. His books include the novels *The Marcus Device*, *The Halgerloch Project* and *The Tombstone Cipher*, while *Melchior a la Carte: A Collection of Short Stories by the Award-Winning Novelist Ib Melchior* was published in 2009. The writer's unfilmed 1964 script entitled *Space Family Robinson*, along with the Gold Key comic of the same title that preceded it, are controversially claimed to have been the inspiration for Irwin Allen's 1960s TV series *Lost in Space*.

Ted (Edward William) **Ball**, co-founder (with Dave Gibson) and co-proprietor of London's Fantasy Centre bookshop since 1969, died of lung cancer on March 18, aged 72. He was an avid collector of H.P. Lovecraft and Jack the Ripper material. The store closed in 2009.

American children's and YA author **Ellen Conford** (Ellen Schaffer) died of heart failure on her birthday, March 20, aged 73. Her more than forty books include the fantasies *Genie with the Light Blue Hair* and *The Frog Princess of Pelham*.

American fan **Peggy Rae Sapienza** (Peggy Rae McKnight), who co-chaired the 2014 World Fantasy Convention in Virginia, died from complications from recent heart surgery on March 22. She was 70. Sapienza also chaired Bucconeer, the 1998 Worldcon in Baltimore, and the 2011 Nebula Awards Weekend, and she was a committee member on many other conventions. She was Fan Guest of Honour at Chicon 7, the 2012 Worldcon in Chicago.

Karl Alexander, who wrote the time-travel thriller *Time After Time* (1979), died on March 30, aged 70. The novel was turned into a cult movie the same year, a stage musical in 2010 and a TV series in 2016, while a sequel entitled *Jaclyn the Ripper* was published in 2011.

American composer **Milton Delugg**, who accompanied Al Jolson on the accordion and co-wrote the Nat King Cole hit 'Orange-Colored Sky', died of heart failure on April 6, aged 96. The musical director of the Macy's Thanksgiving Day Parade for three decades, he also composed the musical scores for the English-language versions of *Puss in Boots*, *Sleeping Beauty* and *Snow White and the Seven Dwarfs* (all 1955), and *Gulliver's Travels Beyond the Moon*, along with the infamous *Santa Claus Conquers the Martians*.

American author, editor, publisher and Edgar Rice Burroughs fan **Patrick H. Adkins** died on April 7, aged 67. He wrote the "Titan" fantasy trilogy (*Lord of the Crooked Paths*, *Master of the Fearful Depths* and *Sons of the Titans*) and the horror novel *The Third Beast*, and published *The Last Magician*, a booklet of David H. Keller stories.

Polish-born German author and poet **Günter** (Wilhelm) **Grass** died in a hospital in Germany on April 13, aged 87. The Nobel Prize-winning writer often included fantastic elements in his work, including the novels *The Tin Drum* (filmed in 1979), *The Flounder* and *The Rat*.

Herb (Herbert William) **Trimpe**, the first comics artist to draw Wolverine, died the same day, aged 75. Having helped out artist Tom Gill on such Dell comics titles as the movie adaptations of *Journey to the Center of the Earth* and *Mysterious Island*, and inked the second issue of *Boris Karloff Thriller*, Trimpe joined Marvel in 1967. There he worked on *The Incredible Hulk*, *The Fantastic Four*, *Captain America*, *Iron Man*, *Ghost Rider*, *Chamber of Darkness*, *Creatures on the Loose* and numerous other titles. He also illustrated such tie-in titles for the company as *Planet of the Apes*, *Robocop*, *Star Wars*, *Godzilla*, *The Further Adventures of Indiana Jones* and *The Transformers*.

American SF fan **Art Widner** (Arthur L. Widner, Jr.) died of prostate cancer on April 17, aged 97. He was an original member of First Fandom and a founder of the National Fan Federation, and attended the first World-con in New York City in 1939. As one of the founding members of The Stranger Club, the pioneers of Boston fandom, he chaired Boskone I (1941) and Boskone II (1942). Widner published more than 160 fanzines; his one story, 'The Perfect Incinerator', appeared in the Winter 1942 issue of *Science Fiction Quarterly* (as by "Arthur Lambert"), and he also contributed to the letter columns of *Weird Tales, Amazing* and *Unknown* (often as "R. Twidner").

Edgar Award-winning British crime and mystery writer **Ruth Rendell** (Ruth Barbara Grasemann, aka "Barbara Vine") died on May 2, aged 85. She had suffered a serious stroke in January. Two of her stories were adapted for the 1980s TV series *Tales of the Unexpected*. She was made a life peer in 1997 as Baroness Rendell of Babergh.

American screenwriter, director and playwright **Norman Thaddeus Vane** (Norman Theodore Vein) died of heart failure the same day, aged 86. His credits include *Shadow of the Hawk, Horror Star* (aka *Frightmare*), *The Black Room* (1983), *Midnight* (1989) and *You're So Dead*, along with an episode of TV's *The Evil Touch*. During the 1970s Vane was a contributing writer to *Penthouse* magazine while living in London, and he was the second-unit director on the 1978 adult movie *Dracula Sucks*.

Edgar Award-winning American scriptwriter and producer **William Bast** died of complications from Alzheimer's disease on May 4, aged 84. A close friend of James Dean (he wrote two controversial biographies of the actor), his credits include the spy spoof *Hammerhead, The Valley of Gwangi, The Legend of Lizzie Borden, The Big One: The Great Los Angeles Earthquake, Deadly Invasion: The Killer Bee Nightmare* and *The Fury Within*. On TV Bast created the series *Tucker's Witch* (1982-83) and wrote episodes of *The Outer Limits, The Alfred Hitchcock Hour* and *Circle of Fear*.

British SF reviewer, copy-editor and short story writer **Chris** (Christopher) **Gilmore** died on May 6, aged 66. He worked for such magazines as *Interzone* and *Spectrum SF*.

British screenwriter **Christopher** (Hovelle) **Wood** died on May 9, aged 79. Although he wrote the *Confessions of...*series of softcore sex books under the pen-name "Timothy Lea", he is best known for his screenplays and novelisations of the James Bond films *The Spy Who Loved Me* and *Moonraker* (for which he created the character of "Jaws"), along with *Remo Williams: The Adventure Begins*.

Danish SF fan, author, editor, critic and translator **Jannick Storm** died after a long illness the same day, aged 75. Apparently, Storm's translation of Brian Aldiss' *The Atrocity Exhibition* preceded the UK edition by quite some time. His own book on science fiction, *Vor tids eventyr: Katastrofe-området* (*The Fairy Tales of Our Time: Disaster Area*), appeared in 1978.

American surrealist/horror artist **James** (Richard) **Powell** ("JP") was killed by a suspected drunk driver in George County, Mississippi, on May 13, aged 42. His 69-year-old mother, Donna Faye Powell, and 36-year-old girlfriend, April Eugina Livingstone, also died in the head-on automobile accident. Powell designed the badge for the 2015 World Horror Convention in Atlanta, and his artwork graced numerous small-press book covers, including Dean M. Drinkel's anthologies *The Grimorium Verum*, *Demonologia Biblica* and *Masks*, plus many titles by Joe R. Lansdale.

62-year-old **Eric** (Jonathon) **Caidin**, proprietor of the Hollywood Book & Poster Co. memorabilia store on Hollywood Boulevard from 1977, died of an aneurysm on May 18, shortly after attending a *noir* film festival in Palm Springs. Caidin had small roles in the movies *The Aftermath*, *Star Slammers* (aka *Prison Ship*), *Cannibal Hookers*, *Hellroller* and the forthcoming *Resurrecting Doug Dunning*, and he was featured in the documentaries *Flying Saucers Over Hollywood: The 'Plan 9' Companion* and *Confessions of Lemora*. Caidin reportedly inherited the rights to several classic titles in the R.K.O. film library from his father, who was an attorney specialising in intellectual property. Profits from the movies contributed to the running of the store, which closed its doors in early 2015.

American SF fan and reviewer **Yvonne** "Vonnie" **Carts-Powell**, who wrote *The Science of Heroes* (2008), a study of the superhero TV series, died of cancer on May 22, aged 49.

South African-born UK author **Moyra Caldecott** (Olivia Brown Caldecott) died on May 23, aged 87. She wrote many children's and YA fantasies, notably "The Tall Stones" sequence.

Acclaimed British fantasy, horror, SF and children's author **Tanith Lee** (aka "Esther Garber") died after a long battle with cancer on May 24. She was 67. A discovery of Donald A. Wollheim, since 1971 Lee published more than 100 novels and collections, including *The Birthgrave*, *Death's Master*, *The Silver Metal Lover*, *Red as Blood* and the Arkham House volume *Dreams of Dark and Light*. She also scripted two episodes of the BBC series *Blake's 7*, and her story 'Nunc Dimittis' was adapted as an episode of the TV series *The Hunger*. She was a winner of the World Fantasy Award and the British Fantasy Award, and she received Life Achievement Awards from the World Horror Convention, the World Fantasy Convention and the Horror Writers Association.

American publisher, editor, writer and independent bookseller **"Chuck" Miller** (Charles Franklin Miller II) died the same day, aged 62. With Tim Underwood, he co-founded the highly respected small press imprint Underwood-Miller in 1976, which published more than 150 books by such authors as Jack Vance, Philip K. Dick, Robert E. Howard, Harlan Ellison, Clive Barker, Peter Straub, Robert Silverberg and Roger Zelazny, amongst many others. Miller and Underwood chaired the 1980 World Fantasy Convention in Baltimore, and they also co-edited and published a number of volumes about Stephen King, including the Hugo Award-nominated *Fear Itself: The Horror Fiction of Stephen King* (1983), before the partnership was dissolved in 1994.

American author **Robert E.** (Ervian) **Margroff** died after a long illness on May 25, aged 85. His first story, 'Monster Tracks', appeared in *If* in 1964, and he sold a number of other stories (some written in collaboration with Piers Anthony and Andrew J. Offutt) to that magazine, as well as to the anthologies *Orbit* and *Protostars*. Margroff also collaborated with Anthony on the novels *The Ring*, *The E.S.P. Worm* and the five-volume series "Adventures of Kelvin of Rud" (1987-92).

Doris Elaine Sauter, a friend of Philip K. Dick, died the same day, aged 63. In 2000 she co-edited (with Gwen Lee) *What If Our World is Their Heaven? The Final Conversations of Philip K. Dick*.

French-Canadian author and editor **Joël Champetier** died of leukemia on May 30, aged 57. His first adult SF novel, *La taupe et le dragon* (aka *The Dragon's Eye*) was published in 1991, and he also worked as an editor with the French-language *Solaris* magazine. Champetier was a Guest of Honour at the 2007 World Fantasy Convention in Saratoga Springs, New York.

Italian screenwriter **Callisto Cosulich**, who co-scripted the original Italian version of Mario Bava's *Planet of the Vampires* (1965), died on June 6, aged 92.

Former Los Angeles County deputy district attorney **Vincent T. Bugliosi, Jr.** died of cancer on June 8, aged 80. He gained fame for his prosecution of Charles Manson and his followers for the brutal murder of Roman Polanski's actress wife Sharon Tate and six others in 1969. Bugliosi later became a best-selling true crime writer, and he co-authored (with Curt Gentry) the book *Helter Skelter* (filmed twice for TV), about the Manson murders.

American book cover artist **Paul Bacon** died the same day, aged 91. Amongst the more than 6,500 covers he created were those for *Catch-22*, *Slaughterhouse-Five*, *The Andromeda Strain* and Ellen Datlow's anthology *Alien Sex*.

Czech-born German SF editor, publisher and author **Wolfgang Jeschke** (aka "Hansjörg Präger") died on June 10, aged 78. For many years he worked for the German publishing imprint Heyne Verlag, and his first novel, *Der letzte Tag der Schöpfung* (aka *The Last Day of Creation*), was published in 1981. Jeschke edited more than 100 anthologies, and he was one of the Guests of Honour at ConFiction, the 1990 World Science Fiction Convention in the Hague.

92-year-old American artist **Earl H. Norem** died on June 19, shortly after ungoing surgery. During the 1950s and '60s he worked for the men's adventure magazines, illustrating covers and interior spreads. At Marvel, the comics he worked on include *Planet of the Apes*, *Savage Sword of Conan*, *Tales of the Zombie* and *Monsters Unleashed*. Norem also contributed to Charlton Comics' *The Six Million Dollar Man*, the *Worlds of Power Wizards & Warriors* book series, and *Mars Attacks* trading cards sets.

Oscar-winning Hollywood composer **James** (Roy) **Horner** was killed in a light plane crash in California on June 22. Horner was 61, and he composed the music scores for *Up from the Depths*, *Humanoids from the Deep*, *Battle Beyond the Stars*, *The Hand* (1981), *Wolfen*, *Deadly Blessing*, *Star Trek II: The Wrath of Khan*, *Something Wicked This Way Comes*, *Krull*, *Brainstorm* (1983), *Star Trek III: The Search for Spock*, *Cocoon*, *Aliens*, *Captain EO*, *The Name of the Rose*,

*An American Tail, Project X, *batteries not included, Willow, Vibes, The Land Before Time, Cocoon: The Return, Field of Dreams, Honey I Shrunk the Kids, The Rocketeer, An American Tail: Fieval Goes West, We're Back! A Dinosaur Story, The Pagemaster, Casper, Jumanji, Deep Impact, Mighty Joe Young* (1998), *Bicentennial Man, How the Grinch Stole Christmas, The Forgotten, The Spiderwick Chronicles, Avatar* and *The Amazing Spider-Man* (2012), amongst many other movies. His music for *Battle Beyond the Stars* was recycled by producer Roger Corman for such movies as *Space Raiders, Barbarian Queen, Wizards of the Lost Kingdom* and *Deathstalker III: Warriors from Hell.* Horner also contributed music to episodes of TV's *Faerie Tale Theatre, Amazing Stories* and *Tales from the Crypt,* and he created the theme for the 1990-97 Universal Pictures logo.

American comic-strip artist **Leonard Starr**, who illustrated *Annie* from 1979 to 2000, died on June 30, aged 89. He also developed and scripted the Rankin/Bass animated TV series *ThunderCats* (1985-87), but was forced to sue for a share of the merchandising profits.

Reclusive American author and former journalist **Jeff Rice** (Jeffrey Grant Rice), who created the character of rumpled newspaper man Carl Kolchak, died in Las Vegas on July 1, aged 71. He had suffered from depression throughout most of his adult life. In 1972, Rice's then-unpublished novel *The Night Stalker* was adapted by Richard Matheson into the highest-rated TV movie ever aired, with an audience share of 54%. They followed it the following year with a sequel, *The Night Strangler*, which led to two short-lived TV series, *Kolchak: The Night Stalker* (1974-75) and *The Night Stalker* (2005-06), along with a comic book series from Moonstone Books.

Italian screenwriter and director **Sergio Sollima** (aka "Simon Sterling" /"Roger Higgins, III") died the same day, aged 94. He scripted such films as *Ursus, Goliath Against the Giants, The Fury of Hercules, Maciste contro lo sceicco, Ursus il gladiatore ribelle* and other early *peplums*, as well as also writing and directing *Agent 3S3: Passport to Hell, Agent 3S3: Massacre in the Sun* and *Devil in the Brain.*

Walt Disney animator (Ira) **Blaine Gibson** died of heart failure on July 5, aged 97. He worked on such movies as *Pinocchio, Bambi,*

Song of the South, Cinderella, Alice in Wonderland, Peter Pan, Lady and the Tramp, Sleeping Beauty and *101 Dalmations*. He then moved full-time over to Walt Disney Imagineering, where he sculpted many of the iconic attractions and audio-animatronic figures (including *Pirates of the Caribbean, The Haunted Mansion, The Enchanted Tiki Room* and *It's a Small World*) at the Disney theme parks. Gibson was inducted as a Disney Legend in 1993.

American horror and crime author **Tom Piccirilli** (Thomas Edward Piccirilli) died after a long battle with cancer on July 11, aged 50. His novels *The Night Class* and *The Cold Spot* both won the HWA Bram Stoker Award, and his other books include *Dark Father, Shards, A Choir of Ill Children, Coffin Blues, Headstone City, The Midnight Road* and *Shadow Season*. Piccirilli's short fiction was collected in *The Hanging Man and Other Strange Suspensions, The Dog Syndrome and Other Sick Puppies* and the World Fantasy Award-nominated *Deep Into That Darkness Peering*, amongst other titles. Two volumes of his poetry also won Stoker Awards, along with the poetry anthology he edited, *The Devil's Wine*. Piccirilli co-scripted the 1995 vampire movie *Addicted to Murder*.

American comics artist **Alan Kupperberg**, who worked on such titles as *X-Men, Thor, Spider-Man* and *Defenders* for Marvel, and *Justice League of America* for DC, died on July 17, aged 62.

American composer **Van Alexander** (Alexander Van Vliet Feldman) died of heart failure July 19, aged 100. He composed the scores for such William Castle movies as *13 Frightened Girls!, Strait-Jacket* and *I Saw What You Did*, along with *The Atomic Kid* and *Tarzan and the Valley of Gold*, and episodes of TV's *Bewitched* and *I Dream of Jeannie*.

American screenwriter **Douglas S. Cook** died the same day, aged 56. Best known as co-writer of *The Rock* (1996) and *Double Jeopardy* (1999) with David Weisberg, the pair also scripted the 2016 mind-swap thriller *Criminal* starring Kevin Costner and Ryan Reynolds.

American fantasy writer and costume fan **Adrienne Martine-Barnes** died on July 20, aged 73. Her first story appeared in Marion Zimmer Bradley's "Darkover" anthology *Swords of Chaos* (1982), and she went on to write the novels *The Dragon Rises*, *The Fire Sword*, *The Crystal Sword*, *The Rainbow Sword* and *The Sea Sword*. With Bradley, she co-wrote the "Darkover" books *Exile's Song*, *The Shadow Matrix* and *Traitor's Sun*, and she collaborated with Diana L. Paxson of the "Chronicles of Fionn mac Cumhal" trilogy: *Master of Earth and Water*, *The Shield Between the Worlds* and *Sword of Fire and Shadow*.

American author, editor and professor **E.L.** (Edgar Lawrence) **Doctorow** died on July 21, aged 84. Best known for his 1975 novel *Ragtime*, his novels *Big as Life* and *The Waterworks* contain fantastic elements.

American Tolkien fan and filk singer **Renee Alper** died from an infection on July 27, aged 58. She suffered from arthritis and had to use a wheelchair for much of her life, and a car accident in 1989 left her with a broken neck. Alper founded the American Hobbit Association in 1977 and was also a member of the Mythopoeic Society.

81-year-old Disney historian **John Culhane** died of complications from cardiac failure on July 30. His books about the studio include *Walt Disney's Fantasia*, *Aladdin: The Making of an Animated Film* and *Fantasia/2000: Visions of Hope*, and he also wrote the 1986 study *Special Effects in the Movies: How They Do It: Dazzling Movie Magic and the Artists Who Create It*. Culhane also did some uncredited work on the script for Ray Bradbury's *Something Wicked This Way Comes*, and he assisted Richard Williams on the animated feature *The Thief and the Cobbler* (featuring the voice of Vincent Price).

British-American historian, poet and author **Robert Conquest** OBE (George Robert Acworth Conquest) died of pneumonia on August 3, aged 98. Best known for his influential works on Soviet history, he also wrote the 1955 SF novel *A World of Difference* (set in a futuristic 2010), edited *The Robert Sheckley Omnibus*, and co-edited the five *Spectrum* anthologies (1961-66) with his long-time friend Kingsley Amis. He is famous for his epigraph: "SF's no good," they bellow 'til we're deaf. / "But this is good!" / "Well, then, it's not SF."

American artist **Jef Murray**, who illustrated books by J.R.R. Tolkien and C.S. Lewis, died the same day, aged 55.

Rick Obadiah, who co-founded the American independent comics imprint First Comics in 1983 with Mike Gold, died of a heart attack at the gym on August 16, aged 66. First Comics published Howard Chaykin's *American Flagg*, adaptations of Michael Moorcock's "Eternal Champion" series, and translations of the Japanese *manga Lone Wolf and Cub*. Obadiah had also been a producer for Stuart Gordon's Organic Theatre Company.

American SF writer and fan **Jor** (Marjorie) **Jennings** died of a heart attack on August 27. Her short stories appeared in *Galaxy*, *Rod Serling's The Twilight Zone Magazine*, *The Year's Best Fantasy Stories* and *L. Ron Hubbard Presents Writers of the Future*, and she was a quarterly winner of the first Writers of the Future contest in 1984.

American SF fan and collector **Ned Brooks** (Cuyler Warnell Brooks, Jr.) died on August 31 after a fall from his roof while carrying out repairs. He was 77. His fanzines include *It Comes in the Mail* (1972-78) and *It Goes on the Shelf*, which he started in 1985. With Dan Martin he compiled the *Hannes Bok Illustration Index* (1970) and the *Revised Hannes Box Checklist* (1974), and he published two indices of artwork from Vaughn Bode and Tim Kirk by George Beahm. A NASA engineer, Brooks was Fan Guest of Honour at Rivercon IV in 1978 and DeepsouthCon 39 in 2001.

David Marshall, who published a number of independent book titles under the Pumpkin Books imprint in Britain between 1997-99, before fleeing the country for Singapore owing creditors money, most probably died around the end of August or early September. Marshall, who published books by Peter Atkins, Ramsey Campbell, David Case, Hugh B. Cave, Dennis Etchison, Jo Fletcher, Stephen Jones, Nancy Kilpatrick, Jay Russell and Bram Stoker, had been suffering from cancer and reportedly decided to end his life by refusing to drink liquids.

Edgar Award-winning American author **Warren** (Burton) **Murphy**, co-creator with Richard Sapir of the popular "The Destroyer" series (which totals more than 100 titles since 1971), died on September 4, aged 81. The books were adapted into the movies *Remo Williams: The Adventure Begins* (1985) and *Remo Williams: The Prophecy* (1988).

British-born former actress turned best-selling author **Jackie Collins** OBE (Jacqueline Jill Collins), the younger sister of actress Joan, died of breast cancer in Los Angeles on September 19. She was 77. Her books sold more than 400 million copies in forty countries, and she appeared as herself in *Sharknado 3: Oh Hell No!* (2015).

American book publisher and television producer **Jeremy** (Phillip) **Tarcher**, who packaged celebrity volumes and New Age titles, died of Parkinson's disease on September 20, aged 83. In 1969 he and his ventriloquist wife Shari Lewis (who died in 1998) co-scripted the *Star Trek* episode 'The Lights of Zetar'.

British SF fan, critic and artist **D.** (Don) **West** died of cancer on September 25, aged 70. He also published his own fanzine, *Daisnaid* (Do As I Say Not As I Do), from 1976-97.

Austrian-born British TV script-editor and producer **Ruth Boswell** (Ruth Neubauer) died on October 1, aged 86. She co-created the ATV series *Timeslip* (1970-71) with her then-husband James Boswell, and went on to produce such shows as *The Tomorrow People*, *Shadows*, *The Feathered Serpent* and *The Uninvited*. As an author, she published her own books (including the alternate world novel *Out of Time*) under the Muswell Press imprint.

Texas fan **Fred Duarte, Jr.** died after a long illness on October 3, aged 58. He chaired three Armadillocons and was the convention's fan Guest of Honour in 2011. Duarte also chaired the 2000 and 2006 World Fantasy Conventions in Corpus Christi and Austin, respectively.

Árpád Göncz, the former President of Hungary (1990-2000), died on October 6, aged 93. He translated many English books into Hungarian, including *Frankenstein*, *The Lord of the Rings* and many titles by William Golding.

India-born British newsreader and novelist (Ronald) **Gordon Honeycombe** died of leukaemia in Perth, Western Australia, on October 9, aged 79. He resigned as an ITN newscaster in 1977 over his support of the fireman's strike. Honeycombe's superior 1969 supernatural novel *Neither the Sea Nor the Sand* was filmed in 1972 (aka *The Exorcism of Hugh*) from his own script, and his other books include *Dragon Under the Hill*, and the non-fiction studies *The Murders of the Black Museum (1870-1970)* and *The Murders of the Black Museum (1835-1985)*. He also scripted episodes of TV's *Late Night Theatre* ('Time and Time Again') and *Time for Murder* ('The Thirteenth Day of Christmas'). A former member of the Royal Shakespeare Company, Honeycombe had an uncredited role as a stretcher-bearer in the 1958 movie *Blood of the Vampire*, and he appeared as a newsreader in *The Medusa Touch* and other films and TV shows.

American military SF writer **Bill Baldwin** died on October 14, aged 80. Best known for his "Helmsman" series of novels, which began in 1985 with *The Helmsman* and encompassed seven sequels, he also wrote the stand-alone *Canby's Legion*.

Romanian SF writer **Liviu Radu** died on October 16, aged 66. He also translated novels by Isaac Asimov, Neil Gaiman, George R.R. Martin, Dean Koontz and A. Merritt.

Seven months after the death of Ted Ball, his co-founder of London specialist bookstore Fantasy Centre in 1969, Scottish-born bookseller **Dave Gibson** died of cancer on October 21, aged 76. Gibson eventually sold his share in the shop to Erik Arthur and moved back to Scotland in 1991, where he became a successful book-finder.

American comic book artist **Murphy Anderson** , who co-created the character "Zatanna" in 1964 with Gardner F. Fox, died of heart failure on October 22, aged 89. One of the greatest artists of the "Silver Age" of comics, he began his career in 1944, illustrating for such pulp magazines as *Planet Stories* and working on strips at Fiction House. From 1947-49 he illustrated the *Buck Rogers* newspaper strip, but he was best known for his work at DC during the 1950s and '60s. Often an inker for such artists as Carmine Infantino, Curt Swan and Gil Kane, Anderson co-created (with John Broome) 'The Atomic Knights' for *Strange Adventures*, and he worked on *Mystery in Space* ('Adam Strange'), *Showcase*, *The Atom*, *Hawkman*, *Justice League of America*, *The Flash*, *The Spectre* and many other titles. He was presented with the Will Eisner Award in 1999.

British film critic **Penelope Houston**, who edited *Sight & Sound* magazine from 1956-99, died on October 26, aged 88. She also wrote for *The Monthly Film Bulletin*, *The Observer* and *The Guardian*, and was the author of several books on films.

French science fiction and thriller writer **Yal Ayerdhal** (Marc Soulier) died of lung cancer the same day, aged 56. His multi-volume SF novel *La Bohême et l'Ivraie* (*Boohemia and Chaff*) appeared in 1990, and he edited the 1996 anthology *Genèses* before becoming a best-selling thriller writer.

Japanese artist **Noriyoshi Ohrai**, best known for his posters in Japan for the first three *Star Wars* movies and nine *Godzilla* productions, died of pneumonia on October 27, aged 79. Ohrai also created the art for the Japanese *Mad Max* poster, along with many books and gaming projects.

American horror writer and fitness instructor **Nick Kisella** died of a torn aorta on October 28, aged 49. His first novel, *The Emerald and the Blade*, was published in 1989, and he followed it with *The Chalice of Souls*, *Death and the Doomweaver*, *The Beasts and the Walking Dead*, *Under Construction*, *Crossing Lines*, *Morningstars*, *Darque & Obscure*, *The Eyes of the Jackal*, and *Lilith's Apple* (a collaboration with "Scream Queen" Deana Demko), along with such low budget movie tie-ins as *I Spill Your Guts*, *Sheriff Tom vs. the Zombies* and *Mary Horror*. Kisella also made cameo appearances in the movie *Witches Blood* and an episode of the independent TV series *Zombies Incorporated*.

American book and pulp collector **Victor Berch** died on October 30, aged 91. He specialised in paperback books, especially dime novels and Lancer titles.

American horror author **T.M.** (Terrance Michael) **Wright** (aka "F.W. Armstrong") died of Parkinson's disease on Halloween, aged 68. His novels include *A Manhattan Ghost Story*, *The Waiting Room*, *The Last Vampire*, *Goodlow's Ghost*, *The Ascending* and *Cold House*, while some of his short fiction is collected in *Bone Soup*.

American screenwriter **Melissa** (Marie) **Mathison**, who was nominated for an Oscar for her original screenplay for Steven Spielberg's *E.T. the Extra-Terrestrial*, died of neuroendocrine cancer on November 4, aged 65. She also scripted George Clayton Johnson's

'Kick the Can' episode of *Twilight Zone: The Movie* as "Josh Rogan", *The Indian in the Cupboard* and Spielberg's 2016 version of Roald Dahl's *The BFG*. During arbitration in the late 1980s, the Writers Guild of America successfully argued that Mathison should receive a share of revenue from all merchandise featuring E.T., and she was awarded 4%-5% on all products bearing the likeness of the character she created. She was married to actor Harrison Ford, who she first met while working as an assistant on *Apocalypse Now*, from 1983-2004. After their divorce, Mathison received an estimated $100-$115 million in what was then the third highest alimony settlement in history.

Rena Wolner (Rena Meryl Tannenbaum), the only woman in America to become publisher of three major mass-market publishing companies—Berkley Publishing, Pocket Books and Avon Books—died of lung cancer on November 7. She was 70.

68-year-old British artist **Malcolm** (Roy) **Poynter** died from a series of cardiac events on November 14. Related to the painter Sir Edward Poynter and an art school contemporary of Gilbert & George, his underground comics artwork appeared in *Oz*, *International Times*, *Ally Sloper* and other 1970s publications. Poynter's art was also published in *Science Fiction Monthly*, *Radio Times* and *Time Out*, and he worked for Pan Books and other publishers. More recently, he contributed a Foreword to the fifth collected volume of *Adventures Into the Unknown* from PS Art Books.

Swedish SF fan, translator, author and musician **Johan Frick** died of a brain tumour the same day, four days before his 50th birthday. In the early 1980s he published a number of fanzines before becoming a translator for the works of such authors as Philip K. Dick, Katharine Kerr, Patricia A. McKillip and Gene Wolfe, amongst others. In 2001, Frick and Glenn Petersen started the Gothenburg branch of the Stockholm-based Science Fiction Bookstore. He also wrote a series of futuristic *noir* stories, the first three of which were published as e-books.

P.F. Sloan (Philip Gary Schlein), the enigmatic songwriter of Barry McGuire's #1 apocalyptic anthem 'Eve of Destruction' (1965), written when he was just 19 years old, died of pancreatic cancer on November

15, aged 70. Sloan also co-wrote (with Steve Barri) the theme song for the 1960s TV series *Secret Agent Man* (originally titled *Danger Man*), which became a hit for Johnny Rivers.

American artist, designer and film producer **Michael C.** (Curtiss) **Gross**, who co-produced *Ghostbusters* and *Ghostbusters II*, died of cancer on November 16, aged 70. His other credits include the animated *Heavy Metal* and TV series *The Real Ghostbusters* (1986-91). When he was 16, *Famous Monsters of Filmland* published his paintings based on *7th Voyage of Sinbad*. Gross was art director at *National Lampoon* from 1970-74, and he designed the iconic "no ghosts" *Ghostbusters* logo, based on a concept in the original script. He also created a Christmas card and book designs for John Lennon and Yoko Ono.

American author **Ann Downer** died of ALS on November 19, aged 54. Her "Spellkey" trilogy consisted of *The Spellkey*, *The Glass Salamander* and *The Books of the Keepers*, while her other novels were *Hatching Magic* and its sequel, *The Dragon of Never-Was*.

Historian and novelist **Anthony Read**, who was a story editor on such British TV series as *The Indian Tales of Rudyard Kipling* (1964), *Sherlock Holmes* (1965), *Doctor Who* (1977-79) and *Hammer House of Horror* (1980), died on November 21, aged 80. Read also wrote scripts for *The Indian Tales of Rudyard Kipling*, the West German series *Sherlock Holmes* (1967), *The Omega Factor*, *Doctor Who*, *Hammer House of Horror* ('Witching Time'), *Into the Labyrinth*, *Sapphire & Steel*, *The Baker Street Boys*, John Wyndham's *Chocky* plus the original sequels *Chocky's Children* and *Chocky's Challenge*, and *A Twist in the Tale*.

American SF writer **Perry A. Chapdelaine** (Perry Anthony Fabio) died on November 24, aged 90. His first story appeared in *If* magazine in 1967, and his novels include *Swampworld West* and *The Laughing Terran*. With George Hay and Tony Chapdelaine he helped compile two volumes of John W. Campbell's letters.

Award-winning Japanese writer and artist **Shigeru Mizuki**, who is credited with popularising *manga* with his seminal comic *GeGeGe no Kitarō* (which was turned into TV series and video games), died on November 29, aged 93.

Self-taught Northern Ireland-born artist **Gerard A.** (Alphonsus) **Quinn** died on November 30, aged 88. During the 1950s and early '60s he produced numerous covers and interior illustrations for John Carnell's SF magazines *New Worlds* and *Science Fantasy*. Quinn also worked on a number of paperback covers, including those for Robert A. Heinlein's *The Man Who Sold the Moon* (1950) and Arthur C. Clarke's *Prelude in Space* (1951) and *Islands in the Sky* (1952). He later contributed cover and interior art to the Australian/UK magazine *Visions of Tomorrow*.

American artist **Jon** (Douglas) **Arfstrom**, the last surviving *Weird Tales* cover artist, died of lung cancer on December 2, aged 87. In the early 1950s he worked for the iconic pulp magazine for the last four years of its existence, along with such digest magazines as *Other Worlds Science Stories* and *Mystic Magazine*, and the science fiction fanzines *The Fanscient*, *Fantasy Advertiser* and *Space Trails*. During this period he also illustrated the dustjackets for *The Dark Other* by Stanley G. Weinbaum and *Omnibus of Time* by Ralph Milne Farley (both Fantasy Publishing Company, 1950). He left the genre in 1956 to work full-time as a commercial artist, and in the 1970s he became a surrealist painter and portrait artist. Arfstrom returned to the genre the following decade, and his art was used on covers by such specialist publishers as Fedogan & Bremer, Haffner Press and PS Publishing.

Takamasa Sakurai, a leading promoter of Japanese *anime*, fashion and music abroad, was killed by a train on December 4 after falling from a platform at Nishi-Nippori Station in Tokyo. The 49-year-old was reportedly intoxicated when he fell onto the tracks at around 12:30 a.m. Sakurai wrote a number of books about Japan's pop culture, including *Sekai Kawaii Kakumei* (World Cuteness Revolution).

Timothy Seldes, who was Isaac Asimov's editor at Doubleday in the 1960s, died of pneumonia on December 6, aged 88. Finding himself unemployed by the early '70s, he became a successful literary agent until his retirement in 2012.

Spanish comics artist **Luis Bermejo** (Rojo) died on December 12, aged 84. His work appeared in such UK comics as *Tarzan Weekly*, *The Eagle* ('Heros the Spartan') and *Fantastic* ('Johnny Future'), and he was also employed by Warren Publishing, with the entire issue of *Creepy* #71 devoted to his work. In 1980 Bermejo illustrated a Spanish comics adaptation of *The Lord of the Rings*, and he also produced a graphic version of Isaac Asimov's *I, Robot* three years later.

David Grotta-Kurska, whose 1976 volume *J.R.R. Tolkien: Architect of Middle Earth* was the first biography of the author, died on December 13, aged 71. He also had short stories published in *Asimov's* and other magazines.

Australian-born fantasy author **Tom Arden** (David Rain, aka "David Rains") died of brain cancer on December 15. He was 54. Arden moved to the UK in 1990, and his books include such novels as *The Harlequin's Dance, King and Queen of Swords, Shadow Black* and *The Translation of Bastian Test*, along with the *Doctor Who* novella, *Nightdreamers*.

Rhodesian-born British author and poet **Peter** (Malcolm de Brissac) **Dickinson** OBE died on December 16, aged 88. The winner of two Carnegie Medals for his books for children and young adults, his many titles include *The Gift, The Blue Hawk, The Flight of Dragons, Tulka, A Bone from a Dry Sea, The Tears of the Salamander* and *In the Palace of the Khans*. His "Changes" SF trilogy was made into a TV series by the BBC in 1975. Dickinson wrote one adult SF novel, *The Green Gene*, and he was also known for his crime and thriller books. Some of his short fiction is collected in *City of Gold and Other Stories from the New Testament, Merlin Dreams* and *The Lion Tamer's Daughter and Other Stories*. With his wife, Robin McKinley, he wrote two YA collections, *Water: Tales of Elemental Spirits* and *Fire: Tales of Elemental Spirits*.

American comics creator and musician **Carson Van Osten** died on December 22, aged 70. During the 1960s and '70s he created *Mickey Mouse* and *Goofy* comics for Disney Studios, before becoming a vice-president with the company and working on tie-in adaptations such as *Atlantis: The Lost Empire*. He received a Disney Legends award in 2015, along with George Lucas.

American SF fan **Jack Robbins** (Jack Rubinson), one of the last two surviving members of the Futurians group (which he helped create), died on December 23, aged 96. A high school classmate of Issac Asimov, he published ten issues of the fanzine *Looking Ahead* in the 1940s.

American author and scriptwriter **George Clayton Johnson**, who had been suffering from chronic obstructive pulmonary disease, died of bladder and prostate cancer on Christmas Day, aged 86. His death had been prematurely announced online three days earlier. Best known for co-writing the novel *Logan's Run* (1967) with William F. Nolan, and for his scripts for TV's *The Twilight Zone*, *Honey West*, *Kung Fu* and *Star Trek* (the debut episode, 'The Man Trap'), Johnson's short fiction and scripts are collected in *All of Us Are Dying and Other Stories*, *Scripts and Stories Written for The Twilight Zone* and *Writing for The Twilight Zone*. He also co-wrote (with Jack Golden Russell) the original story that formed the basis for the *Ocean's 11* movies and, as an actor, appeared in Roger Corman's *The Intruder*, *The Boneyard Collection*, *Her Morbid Desires*, *Crustacean* and *Saint Bernard*.

PERFORMERS/PERSONALITIES

American actress **Donna Douglas** (Doris Smith), best known for her role as blonde tomboy "Elly May Clampett" in CBS-TV's *The Beverly Hillbillies* (1962-71) and the 1981 spin-off movie, died of pancreatic cancer on January 1, aged 82. The former Louisiana beauty queen's other credits include classic episodes of *The Twilight Zone* ('The Eye of the Beholder') and *Thriller* ('The Hungry Glass'), along with *Mister Ed*, *Rod Serling's Night Gallery* and *Project U.F.O.* In her later years she sang gospel music and gave inspirational speeches to church congregations and Christian organisations.

American actor and stuntman **Bill Hart** (Billy Gene Welch) died of cancer on January 2, aged 80. His credits include *The Wild Wild West Revisited*, *Scrooged*, *Solar Crisis*, *Escape from New York*, *The Sword and the Sorcerer*, *The Beastmaster*, *Hell Comes to Frogtown*, *Army of Darkness* and *Dr. Giggles*, along with episodes of TV's *The Outer Limits* and *The Wild Wild West*.

Korean-born British actor **Khan Bonfils** died of cardiac arrest in London on January 5, aged 43. He had supporting roles in *Star Wars Episode 1: The Phantom Menace, Lara Croft Tomb Raider: The Cradle of Life, Sky Captain and the World of Tomorrow, Batman Begins*, the Bond film *Skyfall*, and *Razors*.

British comedy actor **Lance Percival** (John Lancelot Blades Percival) died following a long illness on January 6, aged 81. Following an uncredited appearance in the 1961 Edgar Wallace *krimis The Devil's Daffodil* (featuring Klaus Kinski and Christopher Lee), his other supporting credits include *What a Whopper, The Weekend Murders* and the 1990 TV version of *Jekyll & Hyde*. He was the voice of "Old Fred" in *Yellow Submarine*, and voiced both "Paul McCartney" and "Ringo Starr" for the 1965-67 animated TV series *The Beatles*. His love of calypso music saw him release a cover version of 'Shame and Scandal (in the Family)', which reached #37 in the UK charts in 1965.

Australian-born leading man **Rod Taylor** (Rodney Stuart Taylor) died in Beverly Hills of a heart attack on January 7, aged 84. He had suffered a fall a couple of weeks earlier. Best remembered as "H. George Wells" in George Pal's classic *The Time Machine* (1960), a role he recreated in the 1993 PBS documentary *Time Machine: The Journey Back*, the actor's other credits include *World Without End, Colossus and the Amazon Queen*, Alfred Hitchcock's *The Birds*, Joe Dante's pilot *The Warlord: Battle for the Galaxy* (aka *The Osiris Chronicles*) and *Kaw*. On TV, Taylor starred in *Outlaws* (1986-87) and appeared in episodes of *The Twilight Zone, Tales of the Unexpected* and *Murder She Wrote* ('Nan's Ghost'). In the early 1950s he played "Tarzan" in an Australian children's radio serial, and he voiced "Pongo" in Walt Disney's *101 Dalmatians* (1961). Taylor was originally considered for the lead in *Planet of the Apes* (1968), a role that eventually went to Charlton Heston.

American comedy actor **Taylor Negron** (Brad Stephen Negron) died of liver cancer on January 10, aged 57. He studied comedy at a private seminar taught by Lucille Ball and appeared in Disney's *Angels in the Outfield* and *Freaky Friday* (1995), *Mr. Stitch, A Kid in Aladdin's Palace, Stuart Little, The Flintstones in Viva Rock Vegas*,

Call Me Claus, Super Capers: The Origins of Ed and the Missing Bullion, Vamps and *Alienated*, along with episodes of TV's *Faerie Tale Theatre, Touched by an Angel, You Wish, G vs E, Special Unit 2* and *Wizards of Waverly Place*.

Swedish-born actress **Anita Ekberg** (Kerstin Anita Marianne Ekberg), best known for her role in Federico Fellini's *La dolce vita* (1960), died in Italy after a series of illnesses on January 11, aged 83. A former Miss Sweden, she also appeared in *Abbott and Costello Go to Mars, The Golden Blade, Screaming Mimi, Sheba and the Gladiator,* Fellini's *Boccaccio '70, Way...Way Out, Fangs of the Living Dead* (aka *Malenka*), *The French Sex Murders, Gold of the Amazon Women, The Killer Nun* and *S+H+E: Security Hazards Expert*. She retired from acting in 2002, but nine years later was destitute after her villa was burgled and badly damaged by fire while she was in hospital. Following a long-running affair with Tyrone Power, Ekberg's marriages to actors Anthony Steel (1956-59) and Rik Van Nutter (1963-75) both ended in divorce.

British-born actor, stuntman and bodyguard **Darren** (Majian) **Shahlavi** died of a heart attack in Los Angeles on January 14, aged 42. His credits include *Legion of the Dead, Beyond the Limits, In the Name of the King: A Dungeon Siege Tale, Alien Agent, Watchmen, Red Riding Hood* (2011), *Aladdin and the Death Lamp, Survival Code, High Moon* and Disney's *Tomorrowland: A World Beyond*, along with episodes of TV's *Reaper, Bionic Woman* (2007), *Smallville, Sanctuary, Mortal Kombat* (2011), *Arrow, Continuum, Once Upon a Time in Wonderland* and *Metal Hurlant Chronicles*.

British character actress **Pauline** (Lettice) **Yates** died on January 21, aged 85. Her credits include episodes of TV's *Out of This World* (hosted by Boris Karloff), *Strange Report* and *So Haunt Me*, although she is probably best known as the long-suffering wife of Leonard Rossiter's Reginald Perrin in *The Fall and Rise of Reginald Perrin* (1976-79) and *The Legacy of Reginald Perrin* (1996). She was married to writer/actor Donald Churchill from 1960 until his death in 1991.

British actor **Barrie** (Stanton) **Ingham** died in Florida on January 23, aged 82. A former leading man with the Royal Shakespeare Company, his film credits include *Dr. Who and the Daleks* (as the leader of the Thals, opposite Peter Cushing's eccentric time-traveller), *Invasion* (1966), Hammer's *A Challenge for Robin Hood* (in the title role), the six *Josh Kirby...Time Warrior* titles and *Jekyll & Hyde: The Musical*. In 1986 he voiced the title character in Disney's animated *The Great Mouse Detective* (which also featured Vincent Price). On TV, Ingham appeared in episodes of *The Indian Tales of Rudyard Kipling* ('A Germ Destroyer'), *Doctor Who*, *The Avengers*, *Randall and Hopkirk (Deceased)*, *The Rivals of Sherlock Holmes*, *Voyagers!*, *Shadow Chasers*, *Faerie Tale Theatre*, *Star Trek: The Next Generation* and *The Triangle*. He was also cast as John Barrymore in a 1985 made-for-TV biopic of Errol Flynn.

American poet-songwriter **Rod McKuen** (Rodney Marvin McKuen) died of pneumonia on January 29, aged 81. He wrote and performed the theme for the animated 1969 movie *A Boy Named Charlie Brown*, based on Charles M. Schulz's popular newspaper strip. As an actor, McKuen appeared in an episode of the TV series *Shirley Temple's Storybook* and turned up in the 2008 horror anthology *The Boneyard Collection*, along with Forrest J Ackerman, Peter Atkins, Brad Dourif, Donald F. Glut, Barbara Steele and others.

82-year-old British actress **Geraldine McEwan** died on January 30, following a stroke. Best known for playing Agatha Christie's sleuth "Miss Marple" in the 2004-07 TV series, she also appeared in episodes of *Out of This World* and *Red Dwarf*, and was the voice of "Miss Thripp" in the stop-motion *Wallace & Gromit: The Curse of the Were-Rabbit* and the short *A Matter of Loaf and Death*.

American actor **Than Wyenn** died on January 30, aged 95. His many credits (often playing scientists) include Bert I. Gordon's *Beginning of the End*, *The Boy and the Pirates*, *The Invisible Boy*, *The Billion Dollar Threat* and Disney's *Splash*. On TV he appeared in episodes of *Terry and the Pirates*, *Ramar of the Jungle*, *Science Fiction Theatre*, *The Twilight Zone*, *Thriller*, *Voyage to the Bottom of the Sea*, *The Alfred Hitchcock Hour*, *The Munsters*, *The Man from U.N.C.L.E.*, *The Girl from U.N.C.L.E.*, *Mr. Terrific*, *The Invaders*, *Get Smart*, *Night Gallery*, *The Sixth Sense*, *Search*, *The Six Million Dollar Man* and *Knight Rider*.

Sultry-voiced Hollywood leading lady **Lizabeth Scott** (Emma Matzo) died of congestive heart failure on January 31, aged 92. Following a national tour of the *Hellzapoppin* stage review, the former model appeared in such movies as *The Strange Love of Martha Ivers*, Hammer's *Stolen Face*, and *Scared Stiff* (with Dean Martin and Jerry Lewis). She all-but-retired from films in 1957, after appearing with Elvis Presley in *Loving You*.

American actress and singer **Mary Healy**, who co-starred in *The 5,000 Fingers of Dr. T* (1953), died on February 3, aged 96. She also appeared in the 1959 TV version of *Miracle on 34th Street* before retiring from the screen in the early 1960s.

American character actor **John Miranda** died the same day, aged 88. Best known for starring as "Sweeney Todd" in Andy Milligan's memorable *Bloodthirsty Butchers* (1970), he also had small roles in *Pinocchio* (1968), *Star Trek IV: The Voyage Home*, *Innerspace*, *The Invisible Kid*, and episodes of TV's *Dark Shadows*, *Mork & Mindy*, *The Greatest American Hero*, *ALF* and *Free Spirit*.

British stage and screen actor **Jeffrey Segal** died on February 5, aged 94. He was in the 1987 Spanish film *Rest in Pieces* and had a recurring role in TV's *Rentaghost*.

American actress **Laura** (Lynn) **Nicholson**, the daughter of American International Pictures co-founder James H. Nicholson, died of complications from pancreatic cancer on February 6, aged 69. During the 1960s she had small roles in her father's movies *Beach Party*, *Pajama Party*, *Beach Blanket Bingo* and *Dr. Goldfoot and the Bikini Machine*.

American voice actor **Gary Owens** (Gary Bernard Altman), best remembered as the on-screen announcer for TV's *Rowan & Martin's Laugh-In* (1968-73), died on February 12, aged 80. The voice of "Space Ghost" and "Blue Falcon" on TV, his credits also include Larry Buchanan's *The Naked Witch*, Disney's *The Love Bug* and *Return from Witch Mountain*, *Dr. Phibes Rises Again*, *It's a Bird...It's a Plane...It's Superman!*, *Hysterical* and *Muppets from Space*, episodes of *The Munsters*, *Mr. Terrific*, *The Green Hornet*, *Batman*, *I Dream of Jeannie*, *Man from Atlantis*, *Galactica 1980*, *Sabrina the Teenage Witch* and *Wizards of Waverly Place*, and such cartoon shows as

Space Ghost, Yogi's Space Race, Dynomutt Dog Wonder, The New Batman Adventures, Buzz Light-year of Star Command, Johnny Bravo and *Batman: The Brave and the Bold.*

KTLA-TV (Los Angeles) announcer **Stan Chambers** (Stanley Holroyd Chambers), who was the TV announcer in Bert I. Gordon's *War of the Colossal Beast* (1958), died on February 13, aged 91. He also appeared in the 1996 giant monster spoof *Zarkorr! The Invader.*

French-born Hollywood leading man **Louis Jourdan** (Louis Robert Gendre) died in Beverly Hills on February 14. He was 93. Jourdan portrayed the suave titular bloodsucker in the BBC's 1977 *Count Dracula*, and his other credits include *Julie* (as Doris Day's psychopathic husband), *Fear No Evil* and *Ritual of Evil* (as psychic investigator "Dr. David Sorell"), *Swamp Thing* and *The Return of Swamp Thing* (as mad scientist "Arcane"), and *Octopussy* (as Bond villain "Kamal"), along with an episode of *ITV Play of the Week* ('Gaslight'). Having once described himself as Hollywood's "French cliché", in 2010 he was given that country's top award, the Légion d'honneur.

British character actress **Pamela** (Isabel) **Cundell** died the same day, aged 95. She had small roles in *Memoirs of a Survivor*, *A Fantastic Fear of Everything*, and episodes of TV's *Pardon My Genie*, *The Borrowers* (1992), *The Return of the Borrowers* and *Goodnight Sweetheart*. Said to have been a descendant of one of the original playing company of William Shakespeare, her third husband (1981-87) was comedy actor Bill Fraser.

British actor **Alan** (Mackenzie) **Howard** CBE, who was the "Voice of the Ring" in Peter Jackson's *Lord of the Rings: The Fellowship of the Ring* and *Lord of the Rings: The Return of the King*, died of pneumonia on February 14, aged 77. The cousin of actor Ronald Howard, he also appeared in episodes of TV's *Tales of Mystery*, *The Return of Sherlock Holmes* and the BBC's two-part *Witchcraft*.

British character actress **Eileen Essell**, who played "Grandma Josephine" in Tim Burton's *Charlie and the Chocolate Factory* (2005), died on February 15, aged 92. Her other credits include *Finding Neverland* and episodes of TV's *Strange*, *Torchwood*, *Clone* and *Demons.*

34-year-old American character actor **Ben Woolf** (Benjamin Eric Woolf) died of a head injury on February 23, after being struck by the wing-mirror of a passing car while jaywalking in Los Angeles the previous week. Best known for his roles in the FX Network's *American Horror Story* and *American Horror Story: Freak Show*, the four-foot, three-and-a-half inch actor was also in *Insidious*, *Unlucky Charms*, *Dead Kansas*, *Haunting Charles Manson* and *Tales of Halloween*.

American actor, poet and photographer **Leonard** (Simon) **Nimoy**, best known for his iconic portrayal of half-human Vulcan science officer "Mr. Spock" in NBC-TV's original *Star Trek* series (1966-69) and various spin-offs, died of end-stage chronic obstructive pulmonary disease on February 27. He was 83 and had been suffering from the disease for some time. Nimoy went on to play the conflicted Spock in the spin-off movies *Star Trek: The Motion Picture*, *Star Trek II: The Wrath of Khan*, *Star Trek III: The Search for Spock*, *Star Trek IV: The Voyage Home*, *Star Trek V: The Final Frontier*, *Star Trek VI: The Undiscovered Country* and J.J. Abrams' 2009 re-boot *Star Trek* and its sequel, *Star Trek: Into Darkness*, along with *Star Trek: The Animated Series* and a two-part episode of *Star Trek: The Next Generation*. He voiced "Galvatron" in the 1986 animated feature *The Transformers: The Movie*, and "Sentinel Prime" in *Transformers: Dark of the Moon*. The actor was also the voice of "Mr. Moundshroud" in the 1993 adaptation of Ray Bradbury's *The Halloween Tree*, and he voiced Dr. Jekyll and Mr. Hyde in *The Pagemaster*. Nimoy's other voice work includes *Sinbad: Beyond the Veil of Mists*, Disney's *Atlantis: The Lost Empire*, *Land of the Lost* (2009) and the TV series *Invasion America*, *Futurama* and *The Big Bang Theory* (as "Spock" again). His other movie appearances include *Francis Goes to West Point*, the serial *Zombies of the Stratosphere*, *Them!*, *The Brain Eaters* (credited as "Leonard Nemoy"), *Baffled!* and *Invasion of the Body Snatchers* (1978). On TV he was a semi-regular in *Mission: Impossible* (1969-1971) and *Fringe* (2009-12), guest-starred on such shows as *The Twilight Zone*, *The Outer Limits* (appearing as different characters in both the 1964 and 1995 versions of Eando Binder's 'I, Robot'), *The Man from U.N.C.L.E.*, *Get Smart*, *Night Gallery* and *Faerie Tale*

Theatre, and hosted the paranormal documentary series *In Search of...*(1977-82). Nimoy also came up with the original stories for *Star Trek IV* and *VI*, and he directed *III* and *IV*. He also directed episodes of TV's *Night Gallery* (Everil Worrell's 'Death on a Barge'), *The Powers of Matthew Star* and the short-lived series *Deadly Games* (1995-96), on which he was also an executive producer. His 1977 autobiography was entitled *I Am Not Spock*, which he followed in 1995 with *I Am Spock*, while his first record album was titled *Leonard Nimoy Presents Mr. Spock's Music from Outer Space*. "Given the choice," he once wrote, "if I had to be someone else, I would be Spock."

American character actor **Daniel von Bargen**, who portrayed the resurrected magician "Nix" in Clive Barker's *Lord of Illusions* (1995), died of complications from diabetes on March 1, aged 64. He was also in *The Silence of the Lambs*, *Shadows and Fog*, *Basic Instinct*, *RoboCop 3*, *Broken Arrow*, *Thinner*, *The Postman*, *Inferno* (1998), *The Faculty*, *Universal Soldier: The Return* and *S1m0ne*. On TV Bargen appeared in episodes of *The Pretender*, *The X Files*, *Fantasy Island* (1999) and *The Fearing Mind*.

American actress **Lynn Borden** (Lynn Freyse) died after a long illness on March 3, aged 77. A former Miss Arizona, she appeared in *The Wrecking Crew* (uncredited), *Frogs*, *Hellhole*, and episodes of TV's *Get Smart*, *The Fantastic Journey* and *Fantasy Island*.

Hollywood leading lady **Sally Forrest** (Katherine Sally Feeney) died of cancer on March 15, aged 86. Plucked from obscurity by actress/director Ida Lupino, she starred alongside Charles Laughton, Boris Karloff and Michael Pate in *The Strange Door* (1951), and her other screen credits include *Son of Sinbad* (with Vincent Price). She retired from acting in 1967.

Mexican character actor **Rico Alaniz** (Americo Zorilla Alaniz) died on March 9, aged 97. He appeared in *Phantom of the Rue Morgue* and *War of the Colossal Beast*, along with two episodes of TV's *The Wild Wild West*.

British TV presenter **Shaw Taylor** (Eric Stanley Taylor) MBE died on March 17, aged 90. Best known for presenting such programmes as ITV's *Police Five* (1962-2014), he began his career with an uncredited bit part in Hammer's *X the Unknown* (1956), and also appeared in *The Medusa Touch* before turning up as himself in a 2008 episode of *Ashes to Ashes*.

Despite a solid career in numerous movies and TV shows (especially Westerns and crime dramas) throughout his forty-year career, American actor **Gregory Walcott** (Bernard Wasdon Mattox), who died on March 20, aged 87, is best remembered for his starring role as hero "Jeff Trent" in Edward D. Wood, Jr.'s infamous *Plan 9 from Outer Space* (1959). "I didn't want to be remembered for that," the actor told *The Los Angeles Times* in 2000, "but it's better to be remembered for something than for nothing, don't you think?" He also turned up in episodes of *The Invisible Man* (1975), *Gemini Man*, *Land of the Lost* and *The Six Million Dollar Man*, the sequel *House II: The Second Story*, and as a potential backer in Tim Burton's *Ed Wood* (1994).

60-year-old Canadian actress (Faith Susan) **Alberta Watson**, who was a regular on the TV series *La Femme Nikita* (1997-2001) and *Nikita* (2011-12), died of cancer on March 21. Her other credits include *Virus*, *The Keep* (based on the novel by F. Paul Wilson), *Murder in Space*, *White of the Eye* and *The Risen*, along with episodes of *The Hitchhiker* and *The Outer Limits* (1995).

Italian actor **Ivo Garrani** died in his sleep on March 25, aged 91. Best remembered for his role as the father of Barbara Steele's character in Mario Bava's *Black Sunday* (aka *The Mask of Satan*), his other film credits include *Hercules* (1958), *The Day the Sky Exploded*, *The Giant of Marathon*, *The Night They Killed Rasputin*, *Atom Age Vampire*, *Hercules and the Captive Women*, *Holocaust 2000* and *Zora the Vampire*. Garrani was also the Italian dubbing voice for Cedric Hardwicke in *The Ghost of Frankenstein*, Brian Donlevy in Hammer's *The Quatermass Xperiment*, and Edmond O'Brien in both *The Hunchback of Notre Dame* (1939) and *1984* (1956).

American actor **Robert Z'Dar** (Robert James Zdarsky), best known for his role as the scarred, homicidal police officer "Matt Cordell" in *Maniac Cop* (1988) and its two sequels, *Maniac Cop 2* and *Maniac Cop 3: Badge of Silence*, died of cardiac arrest on March 30 while attending a convention. He was 64. The distinctive-looking Z'Dar also appeared in *Hellhole*, *The Night Stalker* (1986), *Cherry*

2000, Grotesque, Fresh Kill, Evil Altar, A Gnome Named Gnorm (aka *Upworld*), *Soultaker, The Final Sanction, Dragonfight, Beastmaster 2: Through the Portal of Time* and *Frogtown II.* The hard-working actor eventually found himself (often alongside Joe Estevez, William Smith or Conrad Brooks) stuck in cheap, direct-to-video titles like *Marching Out of Time, The Mosaic Project,* Somtow Sucharitkul's *Ill Met by Moonlight, Run Like Hell, Future War, Guns of El Chupacabra* and *Guns of El Chupacabra II: The Unseen, Total Force, Trance, Body Shop* (aka *Deadly Memories*), *Scary Tales: The Return of Mr. Longfellow, Zombiegeddon, Vampire Blvd., The Rockville Slayer, Super Hell, Drawing Blood, Spaced Out, Voices from the Graves, Deeflowered, Untitled Horror Comedy, La Femme Vampir* and *La Femme Vampir Volume 2, Post-Mortem, The Voices from Beyond, Little Creeps, Monsters on Main Street, Super Hell 3: Dreams of Horror, Easter Sunday* and *A Blood Story.* Z'Dar's infrequent TV appearances include episodes of *The Flash* (1991) and *Beyond Belief: Fact or Fiction.*

American character actor **Tom** (Thomas) **Towles**, who appeared in every movie directed by Rob Zombie, died of complications following a stroke on April 2, aged 65. His credits include *Henry: Portrait of a Serial Killer, Night of the Living Dead* (1990), *The Pit and the Pendulum* (1991), *The Borrower, Fortress, Warriors of Virtue, The Prophecy II,* William Shatner's *Groom Lake, House of 1000 Corpses, The Devil's Rejects, Grindhouse* (trailer for *Werewolf Women of the SS*), *Halloween* (2007) and *Blood of the Highway.* On TV Towles appeared in episodes of *Star Trek: Deep Space Nine, VR.5, 3rd Rock from the Sun, Star Trek: Voyager, The Pretender* and *Firefly.*

British character actor **Robert Rietty** (Lucio Herbert Rietti), the son of veteran Italian actor Victor Rietti, died on April 3, aged 92. His film career began in the early 1930s and he had small roles (often uncredited) in *A Matter of Life and Death* (aka *Stairway to Heaven*), *The Black Rider* (1954), Hammer's *The Snorkel, Bluebeard's Ten Honeymoons, The Omen* (1976), *Never Say Never Again, Sherlock Holmes and the Leading Lady* and *Hannibal,* along with episodes of TV's *H.G. Wells' Invisible Man, One Step Beyond, The Avengers, The New Avengers* and *Hammer House of Mystery and Suspense.* Known as "The Man of a Thousand Voices", Rietty was also a prolific voice and dubbing artist, contributing work to his friend Orson Welles' *Othello*, *Moby Dick* (1956), *The Hunchback of Notre Dame* (1957 and 1982 versions), *Dr. No*, *Castle of the Living Dead*, *Thunderball*, *The Night Caller* (aka *Blood Beast from Outer Space*), *The Night of the Generals*, *Casino Royale* (1967), *You Only Live Twice*, *The Blood of Fu Manchu*, *Barbarella*, *The Valley of Gwangi*, *On Her Majesty's Secret Service*, *Tales from the Crypt*, *The Ruling Class*, Alfred Hitchcock's *Frenzy*, *Gawain and the Green Knight*, *The Golden Voyage of Sinbad*, *From Beyond the Grave*, *Ten Little Indians* (1974), *The Devil's Men* (aka *Land of the Minotaur*), *Gulliver's Travels* (1977), *The Thief of Baghdad* (1978), *Hawk the Slayer* and *For Your Eyes Only*, as well as episodes of *The Prisoner*, *UFO*, *Space: 1999* and the animated webcast series *Doctor Who: Death Comes to Time*.

Dependable American character actor **Richard** (Allen) **Dysart**, best known for his role in John Carpenter's *The Thing*, died of cancer on April 5, aged 86. He was also in *The Terminal Man*, *It Happened One Christmas*, *Prophecy*, *Meteor*, *Pale Rider*, *Warning Sign* and *Back to the Future Part III*, along with the pilot for TV's *Gemini Man*. Dysart was the voice of "Cogliostro" in the animated *Spawn* series.

American character actor **Rockne** (Booth) **Tarkington** died the same day, aged 83. He appeared in *Beware! The Blob*, *The Intruder Within* and *The Ice Pirates*, along with episodes of TV's *The Alfred Hitchcock Hour*, *Bewitched*, *The Man from U.N.C.L.E.* and *Tarzan* (1966-67).

American character actor **James Best** (Jewel Franklin Guy), who played bumbling sheriff "Rosco P. Coltrane" in CBS' *The Dukes of Hazzard* (1979-85) and various spin-offs, died of complications from pneumonia on April 6, aged 88. He starred in the 1959 movie *The Killer Shrews*, and his other films include *Francis Goes to West Point*, *Abbott and Costello Meet the Invisible Man*, *The Beast from 20,000 Fathoms*, *Riders to the Stars*, *Forbidden Planet*, *Shock Corridor*, *The Savage Bees* and *The Brain Machine* (1977). Best also scripted and starred in *Death Mask* and the belated 2012 sequel *Return of Killer Shrews*. On TV, the actor was in episodes of *Men Into Space*, *Alfred Hitchcock Presents*, *The Twilight Zone*, *The Alfred Hitchcock*

Hour (Ray Bradbury's 'The Jar'), *The Green Hornet* and numerous Westerns.

American humorist, voice actor, composer, advertising executive and author **Stan Freberg** (Stanley Victor Friberg) died of pneumonia on April 7, aged 88. A long-time friend of Ray Bradbury and an influence on Stephen King, he began his career voicing Warner Bros. cartoon characters in the 1940s and '50s (including Peter Lorre's mad scientist in the 1947 "Daffy Duck" short *Birth of a Notion* and Chester the dog in the 1954 *Dr. Jerkyl's Hide*). Freberg also contributed voice work to Walt Disney's *The Lady and the Tramp*, George Pal's *tom thumb* and Bob Clampett's *Time for Beany* TV series (as "Cecil", the 300-year-old sea serpent), before turning up in episodes of *The Monkees* ('Monkees vs. Machine') and *The Girl from U.N.C.L.E.* He also lent his voice talents to *Stuart Little*, *Loony Tunes: Back in Action* and the 'Family Dog' episode of *Amazing Stories*, along with *Freakazoid!*, *Duck Dodgers* and many other animated shows. Freberg recorded a number of hit parody records, including 'St. George and the Dragonet' and 'Green Christmas'. His advertising contracts included the clause: "The decision as to what's funny and what is not funny shall rest solely with Mr. Freberg".

Memorable American character actor **Geoffrey** (Bond) **Lewis**, the father of actress Juliette Lewis, died of a heart attack the same day, aged 79. He appeared in *The Todd Killings*, *Moon of the Wolf*, *High Plains Drifter*, *Human Experiments*, *Salem's Lot*, *The Return of the Man from U.N.C.L.E.: The Fifteen Years Later Affair*, *Night of the Comet*, *Annihilator*, *Out of the Dark*, *Disturbed*, *The Lawnmower Man*, *Wishman*, *Trilogy of Terror II*, *Vampire Resurrection* (aka *Song of the Vampire*), *The Fallen Ones*, *The Devil's Rejects*, *Voodoo Moon*, *Fingerprints*, *Wicked Little Things* and *Mommy's Little Monster*, while his TV credits include episodes of *The Name of the Game* ('LA 2017'), *Ark II*, *The Six Million Dollar Man*, *Quark*, *Mork & Mindy*, *The Amazing Spider-Man*, *Blue Thunder*, *Highway to Heaven*, *Shadow Chasers*, *Amazing Stories*, *The X Files* and *Odyssey 5*.

British actor **Dickie Owen**, who played reanimated mummies "Ra-Antef" and "Prem" in Hammer's *The Curse of the Mummy's*

Tomb (1964) and *The Mummy's Shroud* (1967), respectively, also died on April 7. He was 88.

German-born character actress **Judith Makina**, who portrayed "Granny" in *The Addams Family* (1991), died of lung disease in New Jersey on April 10, aged 88. She was the widow of avant-garde actor and director Julian Beck.

Venezuelan-born American actress **Diane** (Shirley) **Chambers** died in California the same day, aged 64. She was in *Sharknado*, *Zombie Night* and *The Coed and the Zombie Stoner*.

British actress **Claire Gordon**, who co-starred opposite Michael Gough in the 1961 giant ape film *Konga*, died of an aggressive brain tumour on April 13, aged 74. She was also in the Bond spoof *Licensed to Kill* (aka *The 2nd Best Secret Agent in the Whole Wide World*, 1965) and claimed to be the first British actress to appear fully naked on stage.

British actor **Joseph Bennett**, who portrayed T.E. Lawrence /Lawrence of Arabia in an episode of *The Young Indiana Jones Chronicles* and the TV movie *The Adventures of Young Indiana Jones: My First Adventure*, committed suicide by hanging the same day. He was married to actress Julie Graham.

British character actor **Rex Robinson** (Reginald Robinson) also died on April 13. He was 89. During the 1970s, Robinson appeared in three series of the BBC's *Doctor Who* ('The Three Doctors', 'The Monster of Peladon' and 'The Hand of Fear'), and he was also in *Superman IV: The Quest for Peace*.

48-year-old Canadian actor **Jonathan** (David) **Crombie**, who co-starred in the 1985 TV series *Anne of Green Gables*, died of complications from a brain haemorrhage in New York City on April 15. Crombie also appeared in episodes of the revived *Alfred Hitchcock Presents*, *Knightwatch*, *The Hitchhiker* and *Earth: Final Conflict*.

British actor **Peter Howell** (Peter Norman Bulmer Howell), who starred in TV's hospital soap opera *Emergency-Ward 10* (1957-67), died on April 20, aged 95. He also appeared, often playing authority figures, in *Tarzan the Magnificent*, *The Hellfire Club* (with Peter Cushing), Hammer's *The Devil-Ship Pirates* (with Christopher Lee) and *Shadowlands*. On TV Howell was in episodes of *The Avengers*,

The Prisoner, Journey to the Unknown, The Champions, The Guardians, Doctor Who, Thriller (1974), *Tales of the Unexpected* and the mini-series *Witchcraft.*

Born in China to missionary parents, American actress and author **Jayne Meadows** (Jayne Cotter), the widow of comedian Steve Allen and elder sister of actress Audrey Meadows, died on April 26. She was 95. Meadows appeared in *The Luck of the Irish* and the TV movie *Alice in Wonderland* (1985, as "The Queen of Hearts"), along with episodes of *Project U.F.O.* and *Fantasy Island.*

Former American child actress **Suzanne Crough** (Condray), who played "Tracy", the youngest daughter on TV's *The Partridge Family* (1970-74), died of arrhythmogenic right ventricular dysplasia on April 27. She was 52. During her short acting career, Crough recreated the role in the animated series *Goober and the Ghost Chasers* and *Partridge Family 2200 AD*, and she also appeared in an episode of *Wonder Woman.*

British variety star and ventriloquist **Keith** (Shenton) **Harris**, best known for his act with his annoying bird puppet "Orville", died of liver cancer on April 28, aged 67. He appeared as himself in a 2009 episode of TV's *Ashes to Ashes.* Harris' grating Orville song, 'I Wish I Could Fly', sold more than 400,000 copies.

Classical British stage and screen actor (Peter) **Nigel Terry**, who portrayed "King Arthur" in John Boorman's *Excalibur* (1981), died of emphysema on April 30, aged 69. His other credits include *Déjà Vu* (1985), *The Hunchback* and *Feardotcom*, plus episodes of TV's *Sherlock Holmes* (with Peter Cushing), *Randall and Hopkirk (Deceased), Highlander, Sea of Souls* and *Doctor Who.*

American actress, singer and dancer **Grace Lee Whitney** (Mary Ann Chase) died on May 1, aged 85. She is best known for her role as "Yeoman Janice Rand" in eight episodes of the first season (1966) of TV's *Star Trek*, the spin-off movies *Star Trek: The Motion Picture, Star Trek III: The Search for Spock, Star Trek IV: The Voyage Home* and *Star Trek VI: The Undiscovered Country*, and an episode of *Star Trek: Voyager.* Whitney, who struggled with alcohol and drug problems during her career and once ended up on Los Angeles' Skid Row, also appeared in a two-part episode of *Batman*, along with

Cimarron Strip (Harlan Ellison's Jack the Ripper episode, 'Knife in the Darkness'), *The Next Step Beyond* and *Diagnosis Murder* ('Alienated'). Her 1998 biography was entitled *The Longest Trek: My Tour of the Galaxy*.

American character actress **Ellen Albertini Dow** (Ellen Rose Albertini) died on May 4, aged 101. She was an acting coach before making her screen debut when in her seventies, and her credits include *Munchies*, *Christine Cromwell: Things That Go Bump in the Night*, *Memoirs of an Invisible Man*, *Space Case*, *Radioland Murders*, *Carnival of Souls* (1998) and *The Invited*, along with episodes of TV's revived *The Twilight Zone*, *Highway to Heaven*, *Beauty and the Beast*, *Freddy's Nightmares*, *Quantum Leap*, *Star Trek: The Next Generation*, *Beyond Belief: Fact or Fiction*, *Sabrina the Teenage Witch* and *Good vs Evil*.

American actress **Elizabeth** (Welter) **Wilson**, who portrayed Dustin Hoffman's shallow mother in *The Graduate* (1967), died on May 9, aged 94. She made her uncredited screen debut in Alfred Hitchcock's *Notorious* (1946), and her movies include the same director's *The Birds*, *Catch-22*, *The Day of the Dolphin*, *Man on a Swing*, *The Incredible Shrinking Woman*, *The Believers*, *The Addams Family* and *Special Report: Journey to Mars*. Wilson also appeared in episodes of TV's *Dark Shadows* and *Tucker's Witch*.

American voice actor **John** (Winfield) **Stephenson**, who voiced the character of "Count Rockula" in TV's *The Flintstones Meet Rockula and Frankenstone* (1979) and "Frank Frankenstone" in *The Flintstones' New Neighbors* (1980) and others specials, died of complications from Alzheimer's disease on May 15, aged 91. The voice of "Mr. Slate" on *The Flintstones* (1960-66) and spin-offs, he also contributed to numerous other cartoon TV shows, including *Jonny Quest* (as "Dr. Benton C. Quest"), *Frankenstein Jr. and the Impossibles* (as "Professor Conroy"), *Birdman*, *Scooby Doo Where Are You!*, *Sealab 2020*, *Goober and the Ghost Chasers*, *The New Scooby-Doo Movies*, *Inch High Private Eye*, *Super Friends*, *Jeannie*, *Partridge Family 2200 AD*, *Yogi's Space Race*, *The Fantastic Four* (1978), *Captain Caveman and the Teen Angels*, *The New Scooby and Scrappy-Doo Show*, *Spider-Man and His Amazing Friends*, *Galaxy High School*, *InHumanoids*,

The Transformers, *Bionic Six* and *What's New Scooby-Doo?*. Stevenson also appeared in Disney's *Herbie Rides Again*, plus episodes of *Science Fiction Theatre*, *The Man from U.N.C.L.E.*, *Get Smart*, *The Invaders* and *The Six Million Dollar Man*.

American actress **Mary Ellen Trainor**, the former wife of producer/director Robert Zemeckis, died of complications from pancreatic cancer on May 20, aged 62. Her credits include *The Goonies*, *The Monster Squad*, *Scrooged*, *Ghostbusters II*, *Back to the Future Part II*, *Death Becomes Her*, *Congo* and *Freaky Friday* (2003), along with episodes of TV's *Amazing Stories*, *Tales from the Crypt* ('And All Through the House') and *Roswell*.

American comedienne and character actress **Anne Meara**, the wife of actor Jerry Stiller and mother of Ben Stiller, died on May 23, aged 85. She appeared in *'Twas the Night Before Christmas*, *The Boys from Brazil*, *Highway to Hell* and *Night at the Museum*. A regular on TV's *ALF* (1987-89), she also appeared in episodes of *Time Express* (with Vincent Price) and *Monsters*.

Australian stage and screen actor **Bob Hornery** (Robert James Hornery), a regular in the soap opera *Neighbours* for more than a decade, died of cancer on May 26, aged 83. Based in the UK for many years, he appeared in *Britannia Hospital*, *Every Home Should Have One*, *Mad Max Beyond Thunderdome* and *Virtual Nightmare*. On TV Hornery's credits also include episodes of *Mystery and Imagination* (Edgar Allan Poe's 'The Telltale Heart'), *Doctor Who*, *Sapphire and Steel*, *The Genie from Down Under*, *Thunderstone* and *Legacy of the Silver Shadow*. In 1965 Hornery appeared on stage in a musical version of *Dracula* at the Dublin theatre festival.

American character actor **William** (MacLeod) **Newman** died of multi-infarct dementia on May 27, aged 80. His credits include *Squirm*, *Silver Bullet* (based on the novella by Stephen King), Wes Craven's *The Serpent and the Rainbow*, George A. Romero's *Monkey Shines*, *Leprechaun*, *The Stand* (another King adaptation), *The Craft* and *Shadow: Dead Riot*. Newman was also in episodes of TV's *Star Trek: The Next Generation*, *Eerie Indiana*, *VR.5*, *Angel* and *The Tick* (as "The Cape").

Japanese actor and screenwriter **Masayuki Imai**, who wrote and starred in the 1995 timeslip movie *Winds of God*, based on his own stage play), died of bowel cancer on May 28, aged 54. He also appeared in and directed the 2006 remake, *The Winds of God: Kamikaze*.

American actress **Betsy Palmer** (Patricia Betsy Hrunek), who played Jason Voorhees' crazed mother in *Friday the 13th* and *Friday the 13th Part 2*, died on May 29, aged 88. A former NBC news reporter in the late 1950s, she also appeared in *Goddess of Love*, *Still Not Quite Human*, *The Fear: Resurrection*, *Bell Witch: The Movie* and episodes of TV's *Inner Sanctum*, *Out of This World* (1987-91) and *FreakyLinks*. Palmer lived with James Dean for eight months.

Japanese actor **Hiroshi Koizumi** died of pneumonia on May 31, aged 88. A former television announcer, he was in *Godzilla Raids Again*, *Mothra* (1961), *Matango* (aka *Attack of the Mushroom People*), *Atragon*, *Godzilla vs. The Thing*, *Dagora the Space Monster*, *Ghidrah the Three-Headed Monster*, *Godzilla vs. Mechagodzilla*, *The Last Days of Planet Earth*, *Godzilla 1985* and *Godzilla: Tokyo S.O.S.* Koizumi was also an executive producer on *Tetsuo II: Body Hammer*.

American actor and former professional wrestler **Mike** (Michael) **Lane**, who portrayed the Frankenstein Monster in *Frankenstein 1970* (opposite Boris Karloff), the 1976 TV series *Monster Squad*, and an episode of *The Monkees* ('Monstrous Monkee Mash'), died of cancer on June 1, aged 82. He also appeared in *Valley of the Dragons*, *Ulysses Against Hercules*, *A Name for Evil*, *Stryker*, *Grotesque* (which he also co-produced) and *Demon Keeper*, along with episodes of *The Outer Limits*, *Batman*, *Get Smart*, *The Sixth Sense*, *Gemini Man* and *Knight Rider*.

British leading man **Richard** (Keith) **Johnson** died on June 5, aged 87. An MGM contract star and an associate artist at the Royal Shakespeare Company from its inception in 1960, his film credits include *The Haunting* (1963), *The Witch*, *The Devil Within Her* (aka *Beyond the Door*), *The Night Child* (aka *The Cursed Medallion*), *The Comeback*, *Island of Mutations* (aka *Screamers*), Lucio Fulci's seminal *Zombie Flesh Eaters* (aka *Zombie*), *The Great Alligator*, *The Monster Club* (based on stories by R. Chetwynd-Hayes), *The Aerodrome*,

Secrets of the Phantom Caverns (aka *What Waits Below*), *The Crucifer of Blood* (as "Doctor Watson") and *Lara Croft: Tomb Raider*. Having appeared (uncredited) in the 1951 film *Calling Bulldog Drummond*, he later portrayed the title character in the sci-spy spoofs *Deadlier Than the Male* and *Some Girls Do*, having reputedly turned down the role of James Bond in *Dr. No*. On TV Johnson appeared in episodes of *Thriller* (1973), *Orson Welles' Great Mysteries*, *Space: 1999*, *Tales of the Unexpected* and *Tales from the Crypt*. On stage, his roles included "Charles Condomine" in Harold Pinter's revival of Noël Coward's *Blithe Spirit* at the National Theatre in 1976. In the mid-1960s Johnson was married to actress Kim Novak for a year.

British actress and scriptwriter **Jill Hyem** died of cancer the same day, aged 78. Best known for co-writing the World War II drama series *Tenko* (1981-84), she also appeared in the forgotten ATV serial *The Voodoo Factor* in 1961.

French actor **Pierre Brice** (Pierre Louis Baron de Bris), who portrayed native American warrior chief "Winnetou" in a series of 1960s West German Westerns (usually opposite either Lex Barker's "Old Shatterhand" or Stewart Granger's "Old Surehand"), died of pneumonia on June 6, aged 86. He was also in *Mill of the Stone Women*, *Samson and the Slave Queen* (as "Zorro"!) and *Night of the Damned*. On TV he starred as "Adam" in the UK/West German SF series *Star Maidens* (1976).

The last of the great horror film stars, Sir **Christopher** (Frank Carandini) **Lee**, died of heart failure on June 7, aged 93. The public announcement of his death was delayed for four days. He made his film debut in the supernatural mystery *Corridor of Mirrors* (1948), but achieved stardom in the classic Hammer horrors *The Curse of Frankenstein*, *Dracula* (and six sequels), *The Hound of the Baskervilles*, *The Mummy*, *The Gorgon* and *She*, all opposite Peter Cushing. The pair also appeared together in *Hamlet* (1948), *Dr. Terror's House of Horrors*, *The Skull*, *Night of the Big Heat* (aka *Island of the Burning Damned*), *The House That Dripped Blood*, *I Monster*, *Horror Express*, *Nothing But the Night*, *The Creeping Flesh* and *Arabian Adventure*. Lee co-starred with Boris Karloff in *Corridors of Blood*, *Curse of the*

Crimson Altar (aka *The Crimson Cult*) and an episode of TV's *Colonel March of Scotland Yard*, and alongside Vincent Price (with whom he shared a birthday) in *The Oblong Box, Scream and Scream Again* and *House of the Long Shadows*. The actor portrayed Sherlock Holmes in *Sherlock Holmes and the Deadly Necklace, Sherlock Holmes and the Leading Lady* and *Incident at Victoria Falls*; Fu Manchu in *The Face of Fu Manchu, The Brides of Fu Manchu, The Vengeance of Fu Manchu, The Blood of Fu Manchu* and *The Castle of Fu Manchu*, and he was James Bond villain "Scaramanga" in *The Man with the Golden Gun* (1974). Later in his career he appeared in the block-buster *Star Wars* series (as the duplicitous "Count Dooku"), the *Lord of the Rings* and *The Hobbit* series (as the evil wizard "Saruman"), and he worked with director Tim Burton on *Sleepy Hollow, Charlie and the Chocolate Factory, Corpse Bride, Alice in Wonderland* and *Dark Shadows*. Lee's numerous other genre credits include *The Man Who Could Cheat Death, Uncle Was a Vampire, The Two Faces of Dr. Jekyll* (aka *House of Fright*), *The City of the Dead* (aka *Horror Hotel*), *The Hands of Orlac, The Terror of the Tongs, Scream of Fear*, Mario Bava's *Hercules in the Haunted World* and *The Whip and the Body* (aka *Night is the Phantom*), *Horror Castle, Crypt of Horror, Castle of the Living Dead, Rasputin the Mad Monk, Circus of Fear* (aka *Psycho-Circus*), *Theatre of Death* (aka *Blood Fiend*), *The Blood Demon, The Devil Rides Out, Night of the Blood Monster, Bram Stoker's Count Dracula, The Private Life of Sherlock Holmes* (as "Mycroft Holmes"), *Death Line* (aka *Raw Meat*), *Dark Places, Poor Devil, The Wicker Man, To the Devil a Daughter, Dracula and Son, The Keeper, Hollywood Meatcleaver Massacre, End of the World, Starship Invasions*, Disney's *Return from Witch Mountain, Circle of Iron, Captain America II: Death Too Soon, Once Upon a Spy, Evil Stalks This House* (aka *Tales of the Haunted*), *Goliath Awaits, Massarati and the Brain, The Return of Captain Invincible, Howling II: Stirba – Werewolf Bitch, Mio in the Land of Faraway, Mask of Murder, Around the World in 80 Days* (1989), *Gremlins 2: The New Batch, The Rainbow Thief, Curse III: Blood Sacrifice, Jackpot* (aka *Cyber Eden*), *Funny Man, The Odyssey* (1997), *Talos the Mummy, Crimson Rivers 2: Angels of the Apocalypse, The Golden Compass,*

Burke and Hare (2010), *Season of the Witch, The Resident, The Wicker Tree, Hugo, Angels in Notting Hill* and the animated Edgar Allan Poe anthology *Extraordinary Tales*. On TV he was in episodes of TV's *One Step Beyond, The Alfred Hitchcock Hour* (Robert Bloch's 'The Sign of Satan'), *The Avengers* ('Never Never Say Die'), *Orson Welles' Great Mysteries* (Arthur Conan Doyle's 'The Leather Funnel'), *Space: 1999, Faerie Tale Theater, The Young Indiana Jones Chronicles, The Tomorrow People* (1995), *Edgar Allan Poe's Tales of Mystery & Imagination* (1995), *The New Adventures of Robin Hood, Gormenghast, Ghost Stories for Christmas* (as M.R. James) and *Les redoutables*, and he was the voice of "Death" in the Terry Pratchett "Discworld" adaptations *Soul Music, Wyrd Sisters and The Colour of Magic*. A classically trained singer, Lee also recorded a number of opera/heavy metal albums.

British actor **Ron Moody** (Ronald Moodnick) died on June 11, aged 91. Best known for his role as "Fagin" in the 1968 musical *Oliver!*, he also appeared in *The Mouse on the Moon, Legend of the Werewolf* (with Peter Cushing), *The Strange Case of the End of Civilization as We Know It, Dominique* (aka *Dominique is Dead*), *Revelation*, and Disney's *The Spaceman and King Arthur* (aka *Unidentified Flying Oddball*) and *A Kid in King Arthur's Court* (both as "Merlin"). On TV Moody was in episodes of *The Avengers, Tales of the Unexpected, Into the Labyrinth* and *Highway to Heaven*, but he turned down the chance to be the third Doctor Who and the role went to Jon Pertwee.

Canadian comedian **Rick Ducommun** (Richard Dennis Ducommun) died of complications from advanced diabetes on June 12, aged 62. He started out as an overweight comedian, but slimmed down to appear in supporting roles in *Spaceballs, The 'Burbs, Little Monsters, The Hunt for Red October, Gremlins 2: The New Batch, Encino Man, Groundhog Day, Last Action Hero, Ghost in the Machine*, Disney's *The Shaggy Dog* (1994), *Dogmatic* and *Scary Movie*. On TV, Ducommun co-starred as "Officer 'Raid' Raider" in the short-lived 1986 series *The Last Precinct* ('I Want My Mummy', 'Never Cross a Vampire' etc.), plus he appeared in episodes of *Amazing Stories, Max Headroom* and *Brimstone*.

Former child actor **George** "Foghorn" **Winslow** (George Carl Wentzlaff)—best remembered for his role in *Gentlemen Prefer Blondes* (1953)—died of a heart attack on June 13, aged 69. At the time of his death he was looking after twenty-five cats in his home. Winslow poratrayed precious children in *Monkey Business* and *The Rocket Man*. He retired from the screen in 1958.

American actress **Carol Shelyne** (Carole Stuppler, aka "Carolyne Barry") died of cancer on June 16, aged 71. She began her career as a bespectacled dancer (1964-65) on the ABC-TV music show *Shindig!* (recording the novelty song 'The Girl with the Horn-Rimmed Glasses' in 1965). Shelyne went on to appear in Universal's sci-spy spoof *Out of Sight* and episodes of TV's *Star Trek* ('Arena'), *The Man from U.N.C.L.E.* and *Star Trek: The Next Generation*. In 1976 she co-wrote and appeared in the horror film *Dark August* starring Kim Hunter and J.J. Barry.

American comedian, scriptwriter and voice actor **Phil Austin** (Philip Baine Austin), best known for his work with the Firesign Theater comedy troupe, died of an aneurysm on June 18, aged 74. Austin's credits include the surreal short films *Martian Space Party* and *Eat or Be Eaten*, *Nick Danger in the Case of the Missing Yolk*, *Victims* and episodes of the animated TV series *The Tick*.

Italian actress **Laura Antonelli** (Laura Antonaz), who starred opposite Vincent Price in Mario Bava's *Dr. Goldfoot and the Girl Bombs* (1966), died of a heart attack on June 22, aged 73. Charged with possessing and dealing cocaine and sentenced to house arrest in the early 1990s (the conviction was later overturned), since 2009 she had been a ward of the city of Ladispoli, unable to take care of herself. During the 1960s Antonelli was a longtime companion of actor Jean-Paul Belmondo.

American comedic actor **Dick Van Patten** (Richard Vincent Van Patten) died of complications from diabetes on June 23, aged 96. His many movie credits include *Charly*, *Zachariah*, *Beware! The Blob*, *Soylent Green*, *Westworld*, *High Anxiety*, *The Midnight Hour*, *Spaceballs*, William Shatner's *Groom Lake*, *The Santa Trap* and the Disney films *The Strongest Man in the World*, *The Shaggy D.A.* and *Freaky Friday* (1976). On TV, Patten starred in the popular sitcom

Eight is Enough (1977-81) and spin-off movies, and he also turned up in episodes of *I Dream of Jeannie*, *The Girl with Something Extra*, *Kolchak: The Night Stalker*, *The Six Million Dollar Man*, *Wonder Woman*, *Lois & Clark: The New Adventures of Superman* and *Touched by an Angel*.

British-born actor (Daniel) **Patrick Macnee**, who starred as dapper secret agent "John Steed" in both TV's *The Avengers* (1961-69) and *The New Avengers* (1976-77), died in California on June 25, aged 93. His film credits include *Hamlet* (1948), *Dick Barton at Bay*, *The Strange Case of Dr. Jekyll and Mr. Hyde* (1950), *A Christmas Carol* (1951), *Three Cases of Murder*, *Incense for the Damned* (aka *Blood Suckers*, with Peter Cushing), *Dead of Night* (Richard Matheson's 'No Such Thing as a Vampire' segment), *The Billion Dollar Threat*, *King Solomon's Treasure*, *The Howling*, *Comedy of Horrors*, *Sweet 16*, *The Return of the Man from U.N.C.L.E.: The Fifteen Years Later Affair*, *The Creature Wasn't Nice*, *Automan*, the Bond movie *A View to a Kill*, *Waxwork*, *Transformations*, *Lobster Man from Mars*, *Around the World in 80 Days* (1989), *Masque of the Red Death* (1989), *Waxwork II: Lost in Time* and *The Low Budget Time Machine*. Macnee portrayed Dr. Watson in the TV movies *Sherlock Holmes in New York*, *Sherlock Holmes and the Leading Lady* and *Incident at Victoria Falls*, the later two opposite old schoolfriend Christopher Lee's Holmes. He played the Great Detective himself in the obscure *The Hound of London*, and a character who thought he was Holmes in an episode of *Magnum P.I.* The actor also starred in the futuristic TV series *Super Force* (1990-92) and the short-lived *NightMan* (1997-98), and he appeared in episodes of *The Veil* (hosted by Boris Karloff), *Suspicion* (William Hope Hodgson's 'Voice in the Night'), *One Step Beyond*, *Alfred Hitchcock Presents* (1959 and 1988), *The Twilight Zone*, *The Unforeseen* ('The Tin-Type'), *Encounter* ('The Invaders'), *Night Gallery* (August Derleth's 'Lagoda's Heads'), *Orson Welles' Great Mysteries*, *War of the Worlds* and *The Ray Bradbury Theatre* ('Usher II'). Macnee was also the voice of the "Imperious Leader" and narrated over the opening credits of *Battlestar Galactica* (1978-79), and he voiced an invisible man in the 1998 movie of *The Avengers*. He recorded the song 'Kinky Boots' with his *Avengers* co-star Honor Blackman in 1964, and he also appeared in two music videos, The Pretenders' 'Don't Get Me Wrong' (as John Steed) and Oasis' 'Don't Look Back in Anger'. Despite his on-screen persona as the quintessential British gentleman, Macnee actually became a United States citizen in 1959.

American character actor and comedian **Jack Carter** (Jack Chakrin), who hosted the first televised Tony Awards ceremony, died of respiratory failure on July 28, aged 93. He made his debut in the obscure voodoo movie *The Devil's Daughter* (1939), and his other credits include *The Extraordinary Seaman, The Resurrection of Zachary Wheeler, Poor Devil* (with Christopher Lee), *Human Feelings, Alligator, Heartbeeps, Arena*, Bert I. Gordon's *Satan's Princess, Cyber-C.H.I.C.* and *Mercy* (based on Stephen King's story 'Gramma'). On TV, Carter appeared in episodes of *Tales of Tomorrow, Alfred Hitchcock Presents, Batman* (1966), *I Dream of Jeannie, The Wild Wild West, Beyond Westworld, Fantasy Island, Darkroom, Amazing Stories, Tales from the Darkside, They Came from Outer Space, Lois & Clark: The New Adventures of Superman, Time Trax, Beyond Belief: Fact or Fiction* and *3rd Rock from the Sun*, as well as lending his voice to many cartoon shows.

British character actor **Edward** "Teddy" (Charles) **Burnham** died on June 30, aged 98. His acting career began in 1938, and he appeared in the films *10 Rillington Place* and *The Abominable Dr. Phibes* (with Vincent Price), along with episodes of TV's *Quatermass and the Pit* (1959), *The Avengers, Doctor Who, Thriller* (1975) and *Tales of the Unexpected*. While a drama teacher at RADA, his students included Peter O'Toole, Siân Phillips, Albert Finney and Alan Bates.

Bermuda-born American actress and former model **Diana Douglas** (Diana Love Dill), the first wife (1943-51) of actor Kirk Douglas and mother of Michael and Joel Douglas, died of cancer on July 3, aged 92. She appeared in *Night Cries, A Fire in the Sky* and *Jaws of Satan*, along with episodes of TV's *Science Fiction Theatre* and *Beauty and the Beast*.

American child actress (Phyllis) **Amanda Peterson**, who starred in Joe Dante's *Explorers* (1985), died of an accidental morphine overdose the same day, aged 43. She retired from the entertainment industry in 1994.

Lithuanian-born actor **Jacques Sernas** (Jurgis Sernas, aka "Jack Sernas") died in Rome, Italy, on July 3, aged 89. His many credits include *Goliath and the Vampires*, amongst a number of *peplums*.

British character actor **Anthony Milner**, who danced to the 'Time Warp' in *The Rocky Horror Picture Show* (1971), died on July 6, aged 68. He also appeared in *Hawk the Slayer* and *Superman II*.

Big American character actor **Irwin Keyes** died of acromegaly on July 8, aged 63. He appeared in *Nocturna* (with John Carradine), *Friday the 13th*, *Bloodrage*, *Zapped!*, *Nice Girls Don't Explode*, *Frankenstein's General Hospital* (as "The Monster"), *Disturbed*, *Adventures in Dinosaur City* (co-scripted by Lisa Morton), *The Silence of the Hams*, *Oblivion*, *The Flintstones*, *Timemaster*, *The Power Within*, *Here Come the Munsters*, *Oblivion 2: Backlash*, *Asylum*, *Timegate: Tales of the Saddle Tramps*, *The Flintstones in Viva Rock Vegas*, *The Vampire Hunters Club*, *Dead Last*, *Legend of the Phantom Rider*, *House of 1000 Corpses*, *The Fallen Ones*, *Neighborhood Watch*, *ShadowBox*, *Horror High* (2005), *Wristcutters: A Love Story*, *Wrestlemaniac* (aka *El Mascarado Massacre*), *Dark Place*, *Dream Slashers* (which he also co-produced), *Mansfield Path*, *Dahmer vs Gacy*, *Evil Bong 3: The Wrath of the Bong*, *Dead Kansas*, *Professor Creepy's Scream Party* and *Portend*, along with episodes of TV's *Outlaws*, *Tales from the Crypt*, *Get Smart* and *Black Scorpion*.

Egyptian movie star **Omar Sharif** (Michael Demetri Shalhoub), who was nominated for a Supporting Actor Oscar for his role in *Lawrence of Arabia* (1962), died of a heart attack in Cairo on July 10, aged 83. He had been suffering from Alzheimer's disease. Sharif's films include *The Night of the Generals*, *The Mysterious Island* (1973, as "Captain Nemo"), *Oh! Heavenly Dog*, *The Rainbow Thief*, *Gulliver's Travels* (1996) and *The 13th Warrior*, and he narrated the 2008 prehistoric adventure, *10,000 BC*. The actor was also a world-class Bridge player, and co-wrote several books about the game.

Tony Award-winning Welsh actor **Roger Rees**, who portrayed recurring villain "James MacPherson" in the Syfy TV series

Warehouse 13 (2009-13), died of cancer the same day in New York City. He was 71. Rees also appeared in *A Christmas Carol* (1984), *The Possession of Michael D.* (aka *Legacy of Evil*), *A Midsummer Night's Dream* (1999), *The Scorpion King*, *Garfield 2*, *The Prestige* and *The Invasion* (2007). He was a regular on the 1994-97 series *M.A.N.T.I.S.* and his other TV credits include episodes of *Tales of the Unexpected*, *The Legend of Prince Valiant*, *Elementary* and *Forever*. Rees became an American citizen in 1989.

British-born actor and painter **Olaf Pooley** (Ole Krohn Pooley) died of congestive heart failure in California on July 14, aged 101. In a career dating back to the late 1940s, he appeared in *The Gamma People*, *Naked Evil* (aka *Exorcism at Midnight*), *Crucible of Horror* (aka *The Corpse*, with Michael Gough) and *Beastmaster III: The Eye of Braxus*. He also wrote, directed and acted in the 1971 children's film *The Johnstown Monster*. On TV, Pooley starred in the children's series *The Master* (1966), along with episodes of *Colonel March of Scotland Yard* ('The Abominable Snowman'), *Invisible Man* (1959), *Sherlock Holmes* (1965), *Doctor Who* ('Inferno'), *Doomwatch*, *Shadows*, *Nightmare Classics* ('The Turn of the Screw') and *Star Trek: Voyager*, making him one of only twenty-five actors who had speaking roles in both the *Doctor Who* and *Star Trek* franchises. His second wife was film and TV director Gabrielle Beaumont.

Wonderful British-born creepy character actor **Aubrey Morris** (Aubrey Steinberg) died in Los Angeles on July 15, aged 89. His film credits include *The Night Caller* (aka *Blood Beast from Outer Space*), Hammer's *Blood from the Mummy's Tomb*, *A Clockwork Orange*, *The Wicker Man*, *Lisztomania*, *The Adventures of Sherlock Holmes' Smarter Brother*, *Lifeforce*, *Project Shadowchaser III*, *Bordello of Blood*, *Legend of the Mummy*, *She Creature* (2001), *Visioneers* and *Necessary Evil*. On TV, Morris was in episodes of *The Moonstone* (1959), *Out of This World* (hosted by Boris Karloff), *City Beneath the Sea* (1962), *The Avengers*, *Mystery and Imagination* ('Carmilla' and 'The Flying Dragon'), *The Prisoner*, *The Champions*, *Journey to the Unknown*, *Catweazle*, *Jamie*, *Space: 1999*, *Ripping Yarns* ('The Curse of the Claw'), *The Hitch Hiker's Guide to the Galaxy*, *Metal Mickey*, *Outlaws*, *Beauty and the Beast* (1987), *Alien*

Nation, *Tales from the Crypt*, *Tarzán* (1992), *Babylon 5* and *The Others*. His older brother, character actor Wolfe Morris, died in 1996.

American character actor **Alex Rocco** (Alessandro Federico Petricone, Jr.) died of cancer on July 18, aged 79. Often cast as gangsters or cops, he made his screen debut in Russ Meyer's *Motorpsycho!* (1965) and went on to appear in *The Boston Strangler*, *Blood Mania*, *Stanley*, Disney's *Herbie Goes Bananas*, *The Entity*, *Return to Horror High*, *Lady in White*, *Dream a Little Dream* (directed by his son Marc, who died in 2009), *Dead of Night* (1996), *The House Across the Street* and *The Other* (2016). Rocco's TV credits include episodes of *Batman* (1967), *Get Smart*, *Circle of Fear*, *Early Edition*, *Sabrina the Teenage Witch* and *Touched by an Angel*. Caesars Palace in Las Vegas payed tribute to the actor by turning off the fountains in front of the hotel for one minute.

86-year-old American actor **George Coe** (George Julian Cohen), who co-starred with Alex Rocco in *The Entity* (1982), died the same day after a long illness. He was in *The Stepford Wives* (1975), *The First Deadly Sin*, *Remo Williams: The Adventure Begins* (aka *Remo: Unarmed and Dangerous*), *Why on Earth?* and *The Omega Code*, along with episodes of TV's *Max Headroom*, *Star Trek: The Next Generation*, *The Pretender*, *The Lone Gunman*, *Smallville* and *Supernatural* (2008). As a voice actor, Coe contributed to *Transformers: Dark of the Moon*, *13 Sins*, episodes of *Star Wars: The Clone Wars*, and the *Star Wars: The Old Republic* video games.

Austrian-born actor and folk musician **Theodore Bikel** (Theodor Meir Bikel) died in Los Angeles on July 21, aged 91. His film credits include *I Bury the Living*, *Dark Tower* and *Babylon 5: In the Beginning*, while on TV he appeared in episodes of *Alfred Hitchcock Presents*, *Play of the Week* ('The Dybbuk'), *The Twilight Zone*, *The Amazing Spider-Man*, *Fantasy Island*, *Knight Rider*, *Beauty and the Beast* (1988), *Star Trek: The Next Generation*, *Babylon 5*, *The Burning Zone* and *The Pretender*.

British actress **Natasha Parry** (Natalie Wills) died in France following a stroke on July 22, aged 84. She was in *Crow Hollow*, *Midnight Lace* (1960), *Haunted: The Ferryman* and an episodes of

TV's *Shadows of Fear* and *Sexton Blake and the Demon God*. Parry was married to writer/director Peter Brook.

73-year-old British actor and stage director **Robin Phillips** died in Ontario, Canada, on July 25. He had earlier undergone quadruple bypass heart surgery and was suffering from diabetes. Best remembered for starring alongside Peter Cushing in the 'Poetic Justice' episode from *Tales from the Crypt* (1972), which was his last screen credit, Phillips also appeared in episodes of TV's *Doctor Who, The Indian Tales of Rudyard Kipling* ('The Tomb of His Ancestors'), *The Avengers* and *Out of the Unknown*. He moved to Canada in 1974, where he became the Artistic Director of the acclaimed Stratford Festival (1975-80) and Director General of Edmonton's Citadel Theatre (1990-95). For four years from 1997 his musical production of *Jekyll and Hyde* by Frank Wildhorn and Leslie Bricusse ran on Broadway.

61-year-old World Wrestling Federation legend "Rowdy" **Roddy Piper** (Roderick George Toombs) died of a heart attack in his sleep at his Hollywood home on July 30. Best remembered as the star of John Carpenter's 1988 satirical SF thriller *They Live* ("I have come here to chew bubblegum and kick ass...and I'm all out of bubblegum."), the Canadian-born professional wrestler-turned-actor's other (often direct-to-video) screen credits include *The Highwayman, Hell Comes to Frogtown, Immortal Combat, Sci-fighters, Shepherd, Ghosts of Goldfield, Street Team Massacre, The Mystical Adventures of Billy Owens, A Gothic Tale, The Portal, Billy Owens and the Secret of the Runes, Lights Out* (2010), *Alien Opponent, Pro Wrestlers vs Zombies* and *Don't Look Back*, along with episodes of TV's *Superboy, Highlander, RoboCop* and *The Outer Limits* (1999).

British character actor **Clifford Earl** died the same day, aged 81. He appeared (often as a policeman) in Hammer's *The Two Faces of Dr. Jekyll, The Body Stealers* (aka *Thin Air*), *The Haunted House of Horror* (aka *Horror House*), *Scream and Scream Again, Diamonds Are Forever* and *Tales from the Crypt*. On TV, Earl was in episodes of *The Monsters* (1962), *The Avengers, Doctor Who* and *Randall and Hopkirk (Deceased)*.

American character actor **Gerald S. O'Loughlin** (Gerald Stuart O'Loughlin, Jr.), who co-starred as "Captain E.G. Boyd" in the short-lived ABC-TV series *Automan*, died on July 31, aged 93. He was also in *Twilight's Last Gleaming* and *The Secret Kingdom*, along with episodes of *The Green Hornet*, *The Powers of Matthew Star* and *Highway to Heaven*.

British singer and entertainer **Cilla Black** (Priscilla Maria Veronica White) died in Spain of a stroke following a fall on August 1. She was 72. In 1972 Black co-starred with David Warner in Peter Hall's surreal fantasy *Work is a 4-Letter Word*, for which she also sang the title song.

American leading lady **Coleen Gray** (Doris Bernice Jensen) died on August 3, aged 92. Although best known for such classic 1940s *film noirs* as *Kiss of Death* and *Nightmare Alley*, her other credits include *The Vampire* (1957), *The Leech Woman* and *The Phantom Planet*. On TV she appeared in episodes of *Alfred Hitchcock Presents*, *Mister Ed*, *The Sixth Sense*, *Whiz Kids* and *Tales from the Darkside* (Pamela Sargent's 'The Shrine').

Beloved British character actor **George** (Edward) **Cole** OBE died after a short illness on August 5, aged 90. Best remembered for his role as "'Flash' Harry" in the *St. Trinian's* films and as "Arthur Daley" in the popular TV series *Minder* (1979-94), his other credits include *A Christmas Carol* (1951) and *The Anatomist*, both opposite his close friend and mentor Alastair Sim, Walt Disney's *Dr. Syn Alias the Scarecrow*, Hammer's *The Vampire Lovers* (with Ingrid Pitt and Peter Cushing), *Fright*, *The Blue Bird* (1976), *Mary Reilly* and *The Ghost of Greville Lodge*, along with episodes of TV's *Out of the Unknown*, *UFO* and *Shadows of Fear*.

American actor **Mark Sheeler** died on August 6, of complications following a stroke. He was 92, and he appeared in the movies *From Hell It Came* and (uncredited) *The Raven* (1963), along with episodes of TV's *Captain Z-Ro*, *Alfred Hitchcock Presents* and *Adventures of Superman*. Sheeler retired from the screen for almost thirty-five years to become a professional wedding photographer and a supervisor for the Los Angeles Department of Water and Power.

American character actor **Terrence** (Horace) **Evans**, who played "Monty" in the 2003 remake of *The Texas Chainsaw Massacre* and its prequel, *The Texas Chainsaw Massacre: The Beginning* (2006), died on August 7, aged 81. He was also in *Pale Rider, Curse II: The Bite, Phantom of the Mall: Eric's Revenge, Terminator II: Judgment Day, Alien Nation: Dark Horizon,* Tobe Hooper's *Crocodile, Last Rites, The Pumpkin Karver, Chain Letter* and *Bigfoot the Movie,* along with episodes of TV's *The Incredible Hulk, The Greatest American Hero, Voyagers!, Monsters* (Manly Wade Wellman's 'Rouse Him Not'), *Hard Times on Planet Earth, Quantum Leap, Star Trek: Deep Space Nine, Dark Skies* and *Star Trek: Voyager.*

British voice actor **Susan** (Haydn) **Sheridan**, who was the voice of "Ellonwy" in the 1985 Disney version of Lloyd Alexander's *The Black Cauldron,* died on August 8, aged 68. She also played "Trillian" in the original Radio 4 series of Douglas Adams' *The Hitch-hiker's Guide to the Galaxy,* and returned for adaptions of the sequel volumes.

Trinidad-born musician **Russ Henderson** MBE (Russell Audley Ferdinand Henderson), who appeared as the steel band leader in the 'Voodoo' episode of *Dr. Terror's House of Horrors* (1965), died the same day, aged 91. He also wrote two songs heard in that film and appeared as another band leader in an episode of TV's *The Avengers.*

American dancer and actress **Tyra Vaughn**, who was in the "Charlie Chan" movie *Shadows Over Chinatown* (1946), died on August 9, aged 92. She also appeared (uncredited) in *Down to Earth* before leaving acting in the late 1950s.

American actress **Yvonne** (Joyce) **Craig**, best known for her iconic portrayal of Barbara Gordon/Batgirl on the cult 1960s *Batman* TV series, died of breast cancer that metastasised to her liver on August 17, aged 78. A former ballet dancer, she began acting in the late 1950s and appeared in her then-boyfriend Elvis Presley's movies *It Happened at the World's Fair* and *Kissin' Cousins.* Her other credits include *Ski Party, One Spy Too Many* (in especially-shot footage as "Maude Waverly"), *One of Our Spies is Missing, In Like Flint* and *Mars Needs Women,* along with episodes of TV's *Voyage to the Bottom of the Sea, The Man from U.N.C.L.E., My Favorite Martian, The Wild*

Wild West, The Ghost & Mrs. Muir, Star Trek ('Who the Gods Destroy'), *Land of the Giants, Holmes and Yo-Yo, The Six Million Dollar Man* and *Fantasy Island*. More recently, she voiced "Batgirl" for the 2015 video game *Batman: Arkham Knight*. Craig's 2000 autobiography was entitled *From Ballet to the Batcave and Beyond*.

American actress **Melody Patterson**, who co-starred in the ABC-TV sitcom *F Troop* (including the 1967 episode 'V is for Vampire' featuring Vincent Price), died of multiple organ failure on August 20, aged 66. She was also in *Blood and Lace, The Immortalizer* and an episode of *The Monkees*. Her second husband (1970-77) was actor James MacArthur.

British "spiritualist medium" Reverand **Colin Fry** died of lung cancer on August 25, aged 53. He received his first psychic message in 1972 and seven years later became a professional medium, touring the world. Fry appeared on such TV shows as *6ixth Sense with Colin Fry, Most Haunted* and *Psychic Private Eyes*. His manager said: "Because of what he does, he had no fear of death."

American light comedy actor **Dean** (Carroll) **Jones** died of Parkinson's disease on September 1, aged 84. Best known for his work on such Disney films as *Blackbeard's Ghost, The Love Bug* (1968 and 1997 versions), *Mr. Superinvisible, The Million Dollar Duck, The Shaggy D.A., Herbie Goes to Monte Carlo, The Computer Wore Tennis Shoes* (1995) and the 1982 TV series *Herbie the Love Bug*, he was also in the Elvis Presley musical *Jailhouse Rock, Two on a Guillotine, Once Upon a Brothers Grimm, Special Report: Journey to Mars, A spasso nel tempo, Scrooge and Marley* and an episode of TV's *Nowhere Man*.

Another 1960s icon, British actress **Judy Carne** (Joyce Audrey Botterill), died of pneumonia on September 3, aged 76. Although best known for her regular appearances on the 1968-70 seasons of TV's *Rowan & Martin's Laugh-In* ("Sock it to me!"), she was also in episodes of *The Man from U.N.C.L.E., I Dream of Jeannie* and *Thriller* (1973). Married to actor Burt Reynolds from 1963-67, Carne's 1985 autobiography *Laughing on the Outside, Crying on the Inside*, destailed her tragic descent into heroin addiction and degredation during the 1970s.

Former American child actress **Jean Darling** (Dorothy Jean LeVake) died on September 4 in Rödermark, Germany, aged 93. A regular performer in numerous "Hal Roach's Rascals" (later "Our Gang" or "Little Rascals") silent shorts, she also appeared (uncredited) in Laurel and Hardy's *Babes in Toyland* (aka *March of the Wooden Soldiers*, as "Curly Locks") and *Jane Eyre* (1934). In the mid-1940s she originated the role of mill-worker "Carrie Pipperidge", singing '(When I Marry) Mister Snow' in more than 850 consecutive performances of the original Broadway production of Rodgers and Hammerstein's *Carousel*. Darling later toured the world with her husband (1954-73), Kajar the Magician (Reuben Bowen), in his show "Magicadabr". After the couple's separation, she settled in Dublin, Ireland, to become a short story writer, selling work to such magazines as *Ellery Queen, Alfred Hitchcock* and *Mike Shayne Mystery Magazines, Fantasy Book, Night Cry*, and Stuart David Schiff's *Whispers* and the anthology *Whispers III*.

Italian muscle-man actor **Alan Steel** (Sergio Ciani) died on September 5, two days after his 79th birthday. His film credits include *Hercules Unchained, The Giant of Marathon, Samson, The Fury of Hercules, Samson and the Slave Queen, Hercules and the Masked Rider, Hercules and the Black Pirates, Hercules Against Rome, Hercules Against the Moon Men, Hercules and the Treasure of the Incas, Samson and the Mighty Challenge* and *3 Avengers*, amongst other *peplums*.

Clean-cut American actor **Martin** (Sam) **Milner**, who starred as "Todd Stiles" opposite George Maharis (and later Glenn Corbett) in the CBS-TV series *Route 66* (1960-64), died after a long illness on September 6, aged 83. The show's 1962 Halloween episode, 'Lizard's Leg and Owlet's Wing', guest-starred Peter Lorre, Lon Chaney, Jr., Martita Hunt and Boris Karloff. Milner's other credits include *Francis in the Navy, On the Threshold of Space*, William Castle's *13 Ghosts, SST: Death Flight* and episodes of TV's *Science Fiction Theatre, The Twilight Zone, Fantasy Island* and *RoboCop*. The actor also appeared in, and associate produced, *Sex Kittens Go to College* (aka *The Beauty and the Robot*, 1960), which also featured Mamie Van Doren, John Carradine and Vampira.

Former American child actor **Dickie Moore** (John Richard

Moore, Jr.) died on September 7, five days before his 90th birthday. He began his screen career at the age of eighteen months in 1927, and he appeared in *Peter Ibbetson* (1935), *The Blue Bird* (1940), *Heaven Can Wait* (1943) and the TV series *Captain Video and His Video Rangers* before going into public relations in the late 1950s. Moore was the first person to give Shirley Temple a widly publicised on-screen kiss (in *Miss Annie Rooney*, 1942), and his third wife was actress and singer Jane Powell. He wrote the 1984 book *Twinkle, Twinkle, Little Star (But Don't Have Sex or Take the Car)*, which looked at the life of child actors in Hollywood.

American adult film-maker and actress **Candida Royalle** (Candice Marion Vadala, aka "Mary Pearson", "Candice Ball", "Bettina Mia", "Candice Chambers", "Sharon Lucas", "Cyntnia Pleschette", "Kathy Silverman", "Jeanne Toller", "Candida Royal", "Candita Royale" and "Candace DeCarlo"), founder of Femme Productions, died of complications from ovarian cancer the same day. She was 64. Her porno films include *Femmes de Sade* and *Ultra Flesh*, and she also turned up in the direct-to-video *Tattoo Vampire* (1988).

American actor **John P. Connell** died on September 10, aged 91. He appeared in the 1964 movie *Fail Safe* and episodes of TV's *Captain Video and His Video Rangers*, *Dark Shadows* (1967) and the unsold pilot *The Solarnauts*, before becoming a prolific commercials voice-over.

American adult film actress, producer and director **Ann Perry** (Virginia Ann Lindsay) died of Alzheimer's disease on September 11, aged 79. She appeared in *House on Bare Mountain* (as "Ann Meyers"), *Dr. Dildo's Secret* and *The Toy Box* (as "Meyers" again), amongst other movies. Perry created her own production company, Evolution Enterprises, in the 1970s, and she was the first woman to become president of the Adult Film Association of America (AFAA).

Florida firefighter and singer **Paul Galloway**, who appeared in the 1970s low budget horror films *Zaat* (aka *Blood Waters of Dr. Z*) and *J.D.'s Revenge*, died the same day, aged 92. Galloway was also the unit manager on *Zaat*.

Veteran American stuntwoman **May** (Raymond) **Boss** died on

September 16, aged 90. The former rodeo rider made her movie debut in 1952, and her many credits include *Mary Poppins, Soylent Green, Cleopatra Jones, Earthquake, Logan's Run, The Shaggy D.A., Exorcist II: The Heretic, Return from Witch Mountain, Blow Out, Deadly Blessing, Blue Thunder, The Lost Boys, Dead Heat, Total Recall* (1990), *The Puppet Masters, The Relic, Soldier, Wild Wild West, Inspector Gadget, Mystery Men, The Flintstones in Viva Las Vegas, Hulk* and episodes of TV's *The Bionic Woman.*

American actor and playwright **Jack** (Edward) **Larson**, who is best known for his portrayal of *Daily Planet* cub reporter "Jimmy Olson" in the TV series *Adventures of Superman* (1952-58), died at his Frank Lloyd Wright-designed home in Los Angeles on September 20. He was 87. After retiring from the screen in the mid-1960s to become a respected playwright and opera librettist, he returned more than a quarter of a century later to make guest-appearances in *Superman Returns* and episodes of TV's *Superboy* and *Lois & Clark: The New Adventures of Superman*. A former boyfriend of actor Mongomery Clift, Larson's life partner, Oscar-nominated screenwriter/director James Bridges, predeceased him in 1993.

British character actor, stunt performer and fight arranger **Derek** (Arthur) **Ware,** who choreographed the chase involving a fleet of Mini Coopers in *The Italian Job* (1969), died of cancer on September 22, aged 77. Founder of the stunt company Havoc, his many credits include *The War Game, Witchfinder General* (aka *The Conqueror Worm*), *Krull, Willow, Revenge of Billy the Kid* and episodes of *Doctor Who, The Avengers* ('The Cybernauts'), *Adam Adamant Lives!, Mystery and Imagination, The Changes* and *The Return of Sherlock Holmes*. An injury ended his stunt career in 1990, after which he became a fencing coach.

American TV paranormal investigators **Mark** and **Debby Constantino**, aged 53 and 52 respectively, died in an apparent murder-suicide the same day. Police had earlier discovered one of their daughter's roommates murdered in another location. The married couple specialised in EVP (Electronic Voice Phenomena) and were featured on the Travel Channel's *Ghost Adventures*, along with an episode of *Paranormal Challenge*.

Japanese voice actor **Eiji Maruyama** died on September 24, aged 84. He worked on such animated TV series as *Super Sentai Zyuranger*, *Sailor Moon R*, *Pokémon*, *InuYasha*, *Yozakura Quartet* and *Shiki*.

American actress **Catherine E.** (Elizabeth) **Coulson** died of cancer on September 28, aged 71. She was an assistant director on David Lynch's feature debut *Eraserhead* as well as a camera assistant on that film, and also appeared in *The Toolbox Murders* (1978) and *Star Trek II: The Wrath of Khan*. However, she is best-known for her portrayal of "The Log Lady" in Lynch's cult TV show *Twin Peaks* (1990-91) and spin-off movie *Twin Peaks: Fire Walk with Me*. Coulson spoofed the role in a 2010 episode of *Psych* ('Dual Spires'), and she also had a small role in the 1982 horror film *Trick or Treats*. She was married to *Eraserhead* actor Jack Nance from 1968-76.

American character actor **Zale Kessler** died the same day, aged 76. He appeared in several Mel Brooks comedies, including *Dracula: Dead and Loving It*, along with *The Clonus Horror*, *The Attic*, *The Poughkeepsie Tapes* and *Scouts Guide to the Zombie Apocalypse*. On TV, Kessler was in episodes of *Darkroom* and *Lois & Clark: The New Adventures of Superman*, and he voiced "Daddy Dracula" in the 1988 animated TV movie *Scooby-Doo and the Ghoul School*.

American actress **Pat Woodell** (Patricia Joy Woodell), who co-starred in the 1972 Filipino movie *The Twilight People*, died on September 29, aged 71. A regular on TV's *Petticoat Junction* (1963-65) as "Bobbie Jo Bradley", she also appeared in *The Woman Hunt* and an episode of *The Munsters*.

57-year-old British character actor **Alex Giannini** (Alexander Von Giannini), who portrayed the Penguin in a touring production of *Batman Live* in 2011, died on October 2. As "Sandy Fontaine" he was the lead singer in the 1980s rockabilly group Coast to Coast, while as "Alex Richardson" he starred in the short horror film *Left Hand Drive*, based on the story by Christopher Fowler. Giannini was married to Harry Secombe's daughter, Jennifer, since 1998.

Former Walt Disney child actor turned assistant director and producer **Kevin** (Anthony) "Moochie" **Corcoran** died of colorectal cancer on October 6, aged 66. As an actor he appeared in *Old Yeller*, *The Shaggy Dog* (1959), *Swiss Family Robinson* and *Babes in Toyland*

(1961), before moving behind the camera. Corcoran was an associate producer on *Return from Witch Mountain, Herbie Goes Bananas* and the *Herbie, the Love Bug* TV series, and was a first assistant director on *Mrs Santa Claus* and episodes of TV's *Quantum Leap*. He was named a Disney Legend in 2006, and returned to acting three years later in the spoof *It Starts with Murder!*.

Welsh character actor **Richard Davies** (Dennis Wilfred Davies), best remembered for his role as sarcastic science teacher "Mr. Price" in the LWT comedy series *Please Sir!* (1968-72), died of Alzheimer's disease on October 8, aged 89. He was also in *The Night My Number Came Up, Twisted Nerve, The Mutations* (aka *The Freakmaker*) and *Blue Blood*, along with episodes of TV's *The Snow Queen* (1955), *Out of the Unknown* (Frederik Pohl's 'The Midas Plague'), *Robert's Robots, Whoops Apocalypse* and *Doctor Who*.

Former Hollywood child star **Joan Leslie** (Joan Agnes Theresa Sadie Brodel) died on October 12, aged 90. She played opposite such actors as Humphrey Bogart, James Cagney, Gary Cooper, Henry Fonda, Randolph Scott and Fred Astaire, and in 1979 she appeared in an episode of TV's *The Incredible Hulk*. After retiring from the big screen in the mid-1950s, she designed a line of her own branded clothes.

American character actor and teacher **Richard** (Bruce) **Hyde**, who appeared as "Kevin Riley" in the original *Star Trek* episodes 'The Naked Time' and 'The Conscience of the King', died of throat cancer on October 13, aged 74.

American character actor and talent agent **Marty Ingels** (Martin Ingerman), the second husband of actress Shirley Jones, died of a massive stroke on October 21, aged 79. His credits include William Castle's *The Busy Body, The Picasso Summer* (scripted by a pseudonymous Ray Bradbury), *Parasomnia* and episodes of TV's *The Addams Family, Bewitched, The Ghost Busters, The Munsters Today* and *What a Dummy*.

Irish-born Hollywood star **Maureen O'Hara** (Maureen FitzSimons) died in her sleep in Boise, Idaho, on October 24. She was 95. Her many credits include the 1939 version of *The Hunchback of Notre Dame* (opposite her mentor Charles Laughton's Quasimodo),

Sinbad the Sailor, *Miracle on 34th Street* (1947), *Bagdad* (with Vincent Price) and *Flame of Araby* (with Lon Chaney, Jr.), She was finally awarded an Honorary Oscar for Lifetime Achievement in 2014.

40-year-old British-born actor and model **Sam Sarpong** committed suicide by jumping off the Colorado Street Bridge in Pasadena, California, on October 26. He appeared in *Nailed* (2006), *Marked*, *Farm House*, *Single Black Female*, *The House That Jack Built* and the 2014 short film *Ross and Gil Are Zombies*.

American fashion model and actor **Scott Wells**, who portrayed a teenage Lex Luthor in the 1988-89 TV series *Superboy*, died of complications from a stroke on October 28. He was 54. Wells also appeared in episodes of *The Bionic Woman* and *Beauty and the Beast*, and he left Los Angeles in 1998 to join a drug and alcohol abuse recovery programme.

American character actor **Al Molinaro** (Umberto Francesca Molinaro), who played diner owner "Al Delvecchio" in the ABC-TV sitcom *Happy Days* (1974-84) and various spin-offs, died in hospital of a gall bladder infection on October 30, aged 96. His other credits include the TV special *It's a Bird...It's a Plane...It's Superman!* (1975) and Disney's *Freaky Friday* (1976), as well as episodes of *Get Smart*, *Bewitched* and *Fantasy Island*.

Former American child actor **Charles Herbert** (Saperstein) died of a heart attack on October 31, aged 66. He appeared in *The Monster That Challenged the World*, *The Colossus of New York*, *The Fly* (1958, with Vincent Price), Bert I. Gordon's *The Boy and the Pirates* and William Castle's *13 Ghosts* (1960), along with episodes of TV's *Science Fiction Theatre*, *Alfred Hitchcock Presents*, *One Step Beyond*, *Men Into Space*, *Shirley Temple's Storybook*, *The Twilight Zone* (Ray Bradbury's 'I Sing the Body Electric') and *The Outer Limits*. Herbert's career ended in the late 1960s, and his life descended into poverty, drugs and alcohol for nearly forty years.

American character actor **Gregg Palmer** (Palmer Lee) died of a heart attack the same day, aged 88. A former radio announcer, during the 1950s he was a contract player at Universal where he appeared in such movies as *Francis Goes to West Point*, *Son of Ali Baba* and *The Creature Walks Among Us*. His other credits include *Zombies* *of Mora Tau, From Hell It Came,* Walt Disney's *The Shaggy Dog* and *The Absent-Minded Professor, Scream* (1981), *Early Warning* (1981) and numerous Westerns, while his voice can be heard in *Abbott and Costello Go to Mars.* On TV he was in episodes of *World of Giants, Get Smart, Tarzan* (1967-68), *The Wild Wild West, Star Trek* and *Kolchak: The Night Stalker.*

73-year-old **Fred Thompson** (Freddie Dalton Thompson), a former United States Senator who appeared in movies and on TV, died after a recurrence of lymphoma on November 1. A regular on NBC's *Law & Order* (2002-07) and spin-off shows, his other credits include *The Hunt for Red October, Cape Fear* (1991), *Thunderheart, Sinister* and an episode of the American *Life on Mars.*

Character actor (Philip) **Stephen Hancock**, who portrayed "Ernie Bishop" in the British soap opera *Coronation Street* for almost a decade, died the same day, aged 89. He was also in episodes of *The Avengers, The Lion the Witch and the Wardrobe* (1963) and *Tales of the Unexpected.*

Mexican singer-songwriter and character actor **José Ángel Espinosa** "Ferrusquilla" died of a stroke on November 6, aged 96. His movies include *Gigantes planetarios, El planeta de las mujeres invasoras, Los jinetes de la bruja, House of Evil* (with Boris Karloff) and *Mary Mary Bloody Mary* (with John Carradine).

Icelandic-born **Gunnar Hansen**, the man behind the skin-masked "Leatherface" in Tobe Hooper's *The Texas Chain Saw Massacre* (1974), died of pancreatic cancer in Maine on November 7, aged 68. The six-foot, four-inch actor also appeared in such direct-to-video movies as *The Demon Lover, Hollywood Chainsaw Hookers, Campfire Tales, Mosquito, Freakshow, Repligator, Hellblock 13, Hatred of a Minute, Witchunter, Rachel's Attic, Next Victim, Chainsaw Sally, Murder-Set-Pieces, Wolfsbayne* (aka *Aconite*), *Apocalypse and the Beauty Queen, The Deepening, Debbie Rochon Confidential: My Years in Tromaville Exposed!, Swarm of the Snakehead, Brutal Massacre: A Comedy, Shudder, Gimme Skelter, Reykjavik Whale Watching Massacre, Won Ton Baby!* and *It Came from Trafalgar,* along with the sequel/reboot *Texas Chainsaw 3D.* Hansen also wrote the original script for the 2016 movie *Death House.*

40-year-old American actor **Nathaniel Marston** died on November 11 after sustaining injuries in a car accident on October 30 in Reno, Nevada. A regular on ABC-TV's soap opera *One Life to Live* (2001-07), he suffered a broken back and broken neck amongst other injuries in the collision, and was fighting pneumonia, a heart infection and an irregular pulse. Marston appeared in the 1996 witchcraft movie *The Craft*.

British character actor **Warren Mitchell** (Warren Misell), best known for his role as Cockney bigot "Alf Garnett" in the TV series *Till Death Us Do Part* (1966-75), *In Sickness and in Health* (1985-92) and various spin-offs, died after a long illness on November 14, aged 89. He was in the films *The Trollenberg Terror* (aka *The Crawling Eye*), *Unearthly Stranger*, *Help!*, *The Night Caller* (aka *Blood Beast from Outer Space*), *Jabberwocky*, *A Christmas Carol* (2000) and Hammer's *The Stranglers of Bombay*, *The Curse of the Werewolf* and *Moon Zero Two*. Mitchell appeared as comedy villain "Ambassador Vladimir Jiroslav Brodny" in two episodes of *The Avengers*, and his other TV credits include episodes of *Gaslight Theatre*, *Out of the Unknown* (Ray Bradbury's 'The Fox and the Forest') and *Gormenghast* (with Christopher Lee).

Indian-born **Saeed Jaffrey** died of a brain haemorrhage in London the same day. He was 86. The Bollywood actor appeared in *The Man Who Would Be King*, *Sphinx* and an episode of ITV's *Tales of the Unexpected*.

American actor and presenter **Don Lamond** (Donald Robert Heilman) died of congestive heart failure on November 15, aged 88. He was the son-in-law of "Stooge" Larry Fine, and is credited with resurrecting the comedy trio's career durng the 1950s and '60s by hosting a Three Stooges show on Los Angeles' KTTV Channel 11. Lamond had small rolls in *Space Master X-7*, *Have Rocket – Will Travel*, *The Angry Red Planet*, *The Three Stooges in Orbit*, *The Three Stooges Go Around the World in a Daze* and an episode of TV's *The Invaders*, and he narrated *The Three Stooges Meet Hercules*.

Italian actress **Nicoletta** (Rangoni) **Machiavelli** died in Seattle, Washington, the same day, aged 71. She appeared in the 1960s Bond spoofs *Kiss the Girls and Make Them Die* and *Matchless*, along with the 1970 experimental film *Necropolis* and *The Man with the Transplanted Brain*.

German-born Hollywood leading man **Rex Reason** (Rex George Reason, Jr., aka "Bart Roberts") died of bladder cancer in California on November 19, aged 86. The baritone-voiced actor's movie credits include Universal's *This Island Earth* and *The Creature Walks Among Us*. Reason retired from the screen in the early 1960s to become a real estate broker.

Rugged Australian-born leading man **Keith** (Joseph) **Michell**, who starred in *The Hellfire Club* (1961) with Peter Cushing, died in London on November 20, aged 88. He was also in a TV version of *Wuthering Heights* (1962) and episodes of *Dow Hour of Great Mysteries* and *BBC Play of the Month* ('The Tempest').

Spanish-born leading man **Germán** (Horacio) **Robles**, the closest Mexico got to a genuine horror star, died of complications from peritonitis and chronic obstructive pulmonary disease in Mexico City on November 21, aged 86. Best known for his role as that country's most famous vampire, "Count Karol de Lavud" in *The Vampire* (1957) and *The Vampire's Coffin* (1958), his other movie credits playing a vampire include *El castillo de los monstruos*, *The Curse of Nostradamus*, *The Blood of Nostradamus*, *The Monsters Demolisher* and *Genii of Darkness*. Robles also appeared in *The Brainiac*, *The Living Head*, *Los murciélagos*, *Neutron Battles the Karate Assassins*, *Rocambole contra la secta del escorpión*, *Los vampiros de Coyoacán*, *Secta satanica: El enviado del Sr.* and *El secreto*. He was also a popular Spanish language dubbing actor, providing the Spanish voice for Bill Nighy's "Davy Jones" in *Pirates of the Caribbean: At World's End* and KITT the car in TV's *Knight Rider*.

Indian-born British actor **Robin Stewart**, who appeared in the popular TV sitcom *Bless This House* (1971-76), died on November 22, aged 69. Stewart began his career as a child actor, appearing in the eight-part children's serial *Masters of Venus* (1962). His other film credits include *The Haunted House of Horror* (aka *Horror House*) and Hammer's *The Legend of the 7 Golden Vampires* (as "Leyland Van Helsing", the son of Peter Cushing's character). Stewart also worked as a voice actor on such cartoons as *A Christmas Carol*

(1982) and *Sherlock Holmes and the Valley of Fear, Sherlock Holmes and the Sign of Four* and *Sherlock Holmes and the Baskerville Curse* (all featuring Peter O'Toole as Holmes).

American actor **Al Markim** (Alfred D. Moskowitz), who starred as Venusian sidekick "Astro" in the early live TV series *Tom Corbett, Space Cadet* (1951-55), died on November 24, aged 88. During its history, the popular children's SF show ran on all four networks of the day: CBS, NBC, ABC, Dumont and then NBC again.

Former Hollywood child actor **Larry Olsen**, who starred as "Curley" in the old dark house mystery *Who Killed Doc Robbin* (aka *Sinister House*, 1948) featuring George Zucco, died the same day, aged 77. He also made an uncredited appearance in *Brigadoon* before leaving showbusiness in the 1950s.

British actress **Beth Rogan** (Jennifer Puckle) died on November 25, aged 84. A former Rank starlet, her few film credits include the Ray Harryhausen version of *Mysterious Island* (1961). She retired from the screen in the 1960s and married into high society.

Australian actor **Kerry** (James) **Casey**, who portrayed "Goldar" in *Mighty Morphin Power Rangers: The Movie* (1995), died the same day, aged 61.

American actor **Robert** "Bob" **Christopher** (Robert Hall), who co-starred in and produced Jerry Warren's *Frankenstein's Island* (1981), died after a brief illness on November 27, aged 93. He was also in *Spook Chasers, The Disembodied, Terror of the Bloodhunters,* Warren's *Creature of the Walking Dead, Agent for H.A.R.M.* and *I Dismember Mama*, along with an episode of TV's *Men Into Space*.

American actress **Marjorie Lord** (Marjorie F. Wollenberg), best known for her starring role in the long-running TV sitcom *Make Room for Daddy* (1953-65), died on November 28, aged 97. She made her movie debut as a teenager in 1937, and her credits include Universal's *Sherlock Holmes in Washington* (opposite Basil Rathbone and George Zucco) and *Flesh and Fantasy*, along with the "Bomba, the Jungle Boy" adventure *The Lost Volcano*. On TV she was also in episodes of *Ramar of the Jungle* and *Fantasy Island*, before she retired from the screen in the late 1980s to become a philanthropist and fundraiser. Lord's first husband was actor John Archer, and their daughter is actress Anne Archer.

British actor **Anthony Valentine** died of Parkinson's disease on December 2, aged 76. A former BBC child actor from the late 1940s onwards, he appeared in *The Flesh and the Fiends* (with Peter Cushing and Donald Pleasence), Hammer's *These Are the Damned* and *To the Devil a Daughter* (with Christopher Lee), *Tower of Evil* (aka *Horror on Snape Island*) and *The Monster Club* (with Vincent Price and John Carradine). On TV Valentine was in *A for Andromeda* and episodes of *The Avengers, Thriller* (1975), *Space: 1999, Hammer House of Horror* ('Carpathian Eagle'), *Tales of the Unexpected, Robin Hood* (1984-85) and *The Casebook of Sherlock Holmes*.

Italian actor **Gabriele Ferzetti** (Pasquale Ferzetti) died the same day, aged 90. His many credits include the James Bond film *On Her Majesty's Secret Service*, Lucio Fulci's *The Psychic, Encounters in the Deep, Julia and Julia, Computron 22, Die ringe des Saturn* and the TV mini-series *Around the World in 80 Days* (1989).

American actor **Will MacMillan** (William George McMillan), who co-starred in George A. Romero's *The Crazies* (1973) as "W.G. McMillan", also died on December 2, aged 71. He was in *Christmas Evil, Cards of Death* (which he also wrote and directed), *Dark Romances Vol.1* and *Monarch of the Moon*, along with episodes of TV's *The Greatest American Hero, Knight Rider, Werewolf* and *The Flash* (1991).

Italian-American actor **Robert Loggia** (Salvatore Loggia), best remembered for dancing on a giant piano with Tom Hanks in the 1988 fantasy *Big*, died on December 4, aged 85. His many movie credits include *The Lost Missile, The Ninth Configuration, Psycho II, The Believers, Amazon Women on the Moon, Innocent Blood, Lifepod, Independence Day, Lost Highway, The Boneyard Collection, Her Morbid Desires, The Life Zone, Bleeding Hearts* and *Sicilian Vampire*, and he appeared in episodes of TV's *One Step Beyond, Alfred Hitchcock Presents* (1960, 1962 and 1986), *The Alfred Hitchcock Hour, Voyage to the Bottom of the Sea, The Wild Wild West, Tarzan* (1968), *Wonder Woman, The Bionic Woman, The Six Million Dollar Man, Fantasy Island, Tales of the Unexpected, Wild*

Palms, The Fearing Mind, The Outer Limits (2000) and *Touched by an Angel.*

Jug-eared British character actor **Nicholas** (John) **Smith**, who played "Mr. Rumbold" in the BBC sitcom *Are You Being Served?* (1972-85) plus various spin-offs, died on December 6, following a fall seven weeks earlier at his home. He was 81. Smith made his first (uncredited) appearance on TV in the serial *Pathfinders to Mars* (1960) and went on to appear in episodes of *Doctor Who, The Avengers, The Champions, The Rivals of Sherlock Holmes, Ace of Wands, Worzel Gummidge* and *M.I. High* (as "Professor Quakermass"). He was also in the 1973 musical version of *Dr. Jekyll and Mr. Hyde*, Hammer's *Frankenstein and the Monster from Hell* and *The Adventure of Sherlock Holmes' Smarter Brother*, and he voiced the eccentric "Reverend Hedges" in *Wallace & Gromit: The Curse of the Were-Rabbit.*

Puerto Rican-born transgender actress **Holly Woodlawn** (Haraldo Santiago Feanceschi Rodriguez Danhaki) died of brain and liver cancer in Los Angeles the same day, aged 69. The subject of Lou Reed's song 'Walk on the Wild Side', Woodlawn appeared in films by Andy Warhol and Paul Morrissey, and was also in the 1993 vampire movie *Night Owl* starring John Leguizamo.

American character actor **Martin E. Brooks** (Martin Baum), who played "Dr. Rudy Wells" in *The Six Million Dollar Man* (1975-78), *The Bionic Woman* (1976-78) and related spin-off movies, died on December 7, aged 90. He also appeared in *Colossus: The Forbin Project* and *The Man*, along with episodes of *'Way Out* ('False Face'), *The Wild Wild West, Rod Serling's Night Gallery* and *Planet of the Apes.*

American actress **Elaine** (Louise) **Riley** died the same day, aged 98. A former beauty queen, she had small roles in *The Falcon and the Co-eds, The Brighton Strangler* and an episode of TV's *Adventures of Superman*. Riley retired from the screen in 1960.

American actor and producer **Tony** (Anthony) **Cardoza** (Jr.) died of complications from a stroke also on December 7, aged 85. He appeared in such films as Edward D. Wood's *Night of the Ghouls, The Beast of Yucca Flats, Lemon Grove Kids Meet the Monsters* and

Bigfoot (1970). He also associate-produced Wood's 1957 short *The Final Curtain*, along with *Night of the Ghouls*, *The Beast of Yucca Flats* (which he also edited) and *Bigfoot*.

American actress **Rose Siggins** (Rosemarie Homan), who played "Legless Suzi" in the TV series *American Horror Story: Freak Show* (2014-15), died of complications from surgery on December 12, aged 43.

Canadian character actor **Ken** (Kenneth) **Pogue** died of cancer on December 15, aged 81. His many credits include *The Neptune Factor*, *An American Christmas Carol*, *Virus*, David Cronenberg's *The Dead Zone*, *Dead of Winter*, *Still Not Quite Human*, *Sherlock Holmes Returns* (as "James Moriarty Booth"), *Bad Moon*, *The 6th Day*, *The Christmas Secret* and *Phenomenon II*. On TV, Pogue appeared in episodes of *Amerika*, *The Twilight Zone* (1989), *War of the Worlds*, *Highlander*, *Sliders*, *Strange Luck*, *The Sentinel*, *The Outer Limits* (1996-98), *Millennium* (as "Tom Miller"), *Viper* (1997-99), *So Weird*, *Mysterious Ways*, *Night Visions*, *Taken*, *The Dead Zone*, *The Collector*, *Fringe* and *Alcatraz*.

Exotic-looking Spanish-born singer, dancer and actress **Lita Baron** (Isabel Beth Castro, aka "Isabelita") died of complications from a broken hip in Palm Springs, California, on December 16. She was 92. Baron appeared in *Jungle Jim*, the Lewtonesque *Bomba on Panther Island* and *Savage Drums*. A featured singer with Xavier Cugat and His Orchestra in the early 1940s, she was married to actor Rory Calhoun from 1948-70.

Italian actor **Carlo de Mejo**, the son of actress Alida Valli, died on December 18, aged 70. His credits include *Equinox* (1971), *The Dead Are Alive*, *Alien Contamination*, *City of the Living Dead*, *The Other Hell*, *The House by the Cemetery*, *Manhattan Baby* and *The Night-Gaunts*.

American actor and scriptwriter **Douglas M. Dick** died on December 19, aged 95. He appeared in episodes of such TV series as *World of Giants*, *One Step Beyond*, *Men Into Space* and *The Man from U.N.C.L.E.* Dick also came up with the story for an episode of *I Dream of Jeannie* and co-scripted four episodes of *Bewitched* with his second wife, Peggy Chantler Dick. In the early 1970s he left acting and became a psychologist.

52-year-old American actor **Brooke McCarter**, best known for his role as the undead "Paul" in *The Lost Boys* (1987), died of alpha-1 antitrypsin deficiency (AAT), a rare genetic liver disease, on December 22. His other credits include Herschell Gordon Lewis' *The Uh-oh Show*, *Emerging Past* and a 1987 episode of TV's *The Twilight Zone*. During the 1990s he was fellow *Lost Boys* actor Corey Haim's manager.

American character actor **Jason Wingreen**, best known as the original voice of bounty hunter "Boba Fett" in the *Star Wars* sequel *The Empire Strikes Back* (1980), died on Christmas Day, aged 95. Wingreen appeared (often playing doctors) in episodes of TV's *The Twilight Zone*, *The Outer Limits*, *Voyage to the Bottom of the Sea*, *The Wild Wild West*, *Get Smart*, *Captain Nice*, *The Green Hornet*, *The Man from U.N.C.L.E.*, *The Girl from U.N.C.L.E.*, *The Invaders*, *Star Trek*, *The Name of the Game* ('LA 2017'), *Night Gallery*, *The Sixth Sense*, *The Six Million Dollar Man*, *Fantasy Island*, *Starman*, *Highway to Heaven* and *Freddy's Nightmares*. He was also in the movies *The Dunwich Horror*, *The Last Child*, *Paper Man*, *Miracle on 34th Street* (1973), *The Terminal Man*, *The Man with the Power*, *Captain America* (1979), *The Golden Gate Murders* and *Oh, God! You Devil*. Wingreen additionally scripted episodes of *Thriller* ('Portrait Without a Face') and *The Wild Wild West* ('The Night of the Torture Chamber').

Lemmy (Ian Fraser Kilmister), the British lead singer and bassist for heavy metal band Motörhead, died in Los Angeles four days after his 70th birthday on December 28. He had been diagnosed with an extremely aggressive brain cancer just two days earlier. The band's music can be heard on the sountracks for such movies as *Zombie Nightmare* ('Ace of Spades'), *Hardware*, *Hellraiser III: Hell on Earth* ('Hellraiser'), *Wishmaster* and *Halloween II* (2009), and Lemmy appeared in *Hardware*, *Terror Firmer*, *Citizen Toxie: The Toxic Avenger IV*, *The Curse of El Charro*, *Return to Nuke 'Em High Volume 1* and the forthcoming *Midnight Show* and *Gutterdammerung*.

Puerto Rican-born actress **Lucinda Dooling** (Lucinda Schiff), who co-starred in the 1983 horror movie *The Alchemist*, died after a long battle with brain cancer on December 30, aged 61. She was also in Steven Spielberg's *1941* and the musical comedy *Surf II* before retiring from the screen in the late 1980s.

American leading man **Wayne Rogers** (William Wayne McMillan Rogers III), who starred as "Trapper John" in the first three seasons (1972-75) of the CBS series *M*A*S*H*, died of pneumonia on December 31, aged 82. His other TV credits include episodes of *Alfred Hitchcock Presents*, *The Smothers Brothers Show* and *The Invaders*, and he was in the movies *Chamber of Horrors*, *Doomsday Machine*, *It Happened One Christmas* and *I Dream of Jeannie... Fifteen Years Later*. Rogers also co-produced and co-scripted *Dr. Sex* (as "Juan Rogero") and *The Astro-Zombies* with director Ted V. Mikels, and in later years he became a very successful money manager and business investor.

FILM/TV TECHNICIANS

Scottish-born TV director **Fiona Cumming** died on January 1, aged 77. A former actress, she directed four 1980s series of *Doctor Who*, along with an epsiode of *The Omega Factor* and two episodes of *Blake's 7* (including Tanith Lee's 'Sarcophagus').

American independent movie producer **Samuel Goldwyn, Jr.**, the son of the infamous Hollywood studio mogul, died of congestive heart failure on January 9, aged 88. Goldwyn, Jr.'s films include *The Visitor*, *Once Bitten*, *The Preacher's Wife* and the 2013 remake of *The Secret Life of Walter Mitty* (his father produced the 1947 original).

American film editor **Frank** (Francisco) **Mazzola**, whose credits include *Demon Seed* and *Annihilator*, died of complications from Alzheimer's disease on January 13, aged 79. The son of a Hollywood stuntman, Mazzola appeared as a child extra in the 1939 version of *The Hunchback of Notre Dame*.

American studio executive **Alan** (James) **Hirschfield** who, while CEO of Columbia Pictures from 1973-78 oversaw the making of Steven Spielberg's *Close Encounters of the Third Kind*, died on January 15, aged 79. He was fired from Columbia after he refused to reinstate embezzler David Begelman on moral grounds. Hirschfield later served as chairman for 20th Century-Fox from 1982-86.

British TV and film editor **Charlie Phillips** died on February 6. His credits include Kim Newman's series *Dr. Terrible's House of Horrible*, *High Spirits with Shirley Ghostman*, *Psychoville*, *Sherlock* and the 2015 movie *Victor Frankenstein*. Phillips also worked on the visual effects for the 2007 TV series *Jekyll*.

55-year-old Danish producer and director **Finn Nørgaard** was shot to death by a fanatical gunman in Copenhagen on February 14. He had been attending a debate on Art, Blasphemy and Freedom of Speech when 22-year-old Omar El-Hussein fired dozens of shots before eventually being killed by police. Nørgaard began his career as a cinematographer on Nicolas Barbano's occult detective short *Adam Hart i Sahara* (1990), and he also appeared in the 1998 SF film *Webmaster*.

American TV executive **Dick Crew** (Richard Edgar Crew), who created and executive produced the Sci-Fi Channel series *Sci-Fi Buzz* (1993-98), *Sci-Fi Entertainment* (1998) and the award-winning *Masters of Fantasy* (1994-98), died of lymphoma the same day, aged 72.

American costume designer **Patricia Norris** died on February 20, aged 83. Her many credits include *Don't Be Afraid of the Dark* (1973), *The Stranger Within*, *Capricorn One*, *High Anxiety*, *The Elephant Man*, *SpaceCamp* and *Bad Dreams*. She was also a production designer for David Lynch, working on the director's *Blue Velvet*, *Twin Peaks: Fire Walk with Me*, *Lost Highway* and the *Twin Peaks* pilot.

British-born **Alexander** "Sandy" **Whitelaw** died of lung cancer in Paris, France, the same day, aged 84. In 1975 he scripted, produced and directed the SF film *Lifespan* starring Klaus Kinski. As an actor, Whitelaw appeared in seventeen movies, and he also worked as a writer of English subtitles on more than 1,000 French and other European films.

84-year-old American film and TV producer and scriptwriter **Harve Bennett** (Fischman), one of radio's original "Quiz Kids", died of complications from a fall on February 25. He co-produced the movies *Star Trek II: The Wrath of Khan*, *Star Trek III: The Search for Spock*, *Star Trek IV: The Voyage Home* and *Star Trek V: The Final Frontier*, and helped create such TV shows as *The Invisible Man* (1975-76), *Gemini Man*, *Time Trax* and the animated *Invasion America*. Bennett was also an executive producer on such series as *The Six Million Dollar Man*, *The Bionic Woman* and *Salvage 1*.

Multiple Emmy Award-winning American TV producer and writer **Sam Simon** (Samuel Michael Simon) died of colorectal cancer on March 8, aged 59. As co-developer, he worked on *The Simpsons* from 1989-93, but was still credited as an executive producer on the animated show. Simon was married to actress Meg Tilly from 1984-91 before being married to *Playboy* model Jami Ferrell for three years.

Italian-born producer, scriptwriter and director **Luciano Ercoli** died in Spain on March 15, aged 85. His films include the 1970s mystery thrillers *Death Walks on High Heels* and *Death Walks at Midnight*, and he produced the 1964 film of *Fantomas*.

American journeyman director and producer **Walter** (Eliott) **Grauman**, who directed more than fifty episodes of CBS-TV's *Murder, She Wrote* (1984-96), died on March 20, aged 93. His credits include *The Disembodied*, *Lady in a Cage*, *Daughter of the Mind*, *Crowhaven Farm*, *Paper Man*, *Are You in the House Alone?*, *The Golden Gate Murders*, *Covenant* and *Nightmare on the 13th Floor*, along with episodes of *NBC Matinee Theatre* ('Frankenstein', 'The Cask of Amontillado', 'The Suicide Club' etc.), *The Twilight Zone*, *Tales of the Unexpected* and *V*. Grauman's first wife (1976-80) was actress Joan Taylor.

Hungarian-born American director and screenwriter **Ivan Nagy** died on March 23, aged 77. His credits include *Mind Over Murder*, *Captain America II: Death Too Soon* and *Once Upon a Spy* (both featuring Christopher Lee), the remake of *Midnight Lace* (1981) and *Skinner*, plus episodes of TV's *The Powers of Matthew Star*, *The Hitchhiker* and *The Highwayman*. Nagy, who was a boyfriend of high-class Hollywood Madam Heidi Fleiss, ended his career in the late 1990s and early 2000s making adult videos.

American screenwriter, producer and director **Richard L.** (Leland) **Bare** died on March 28, aged 101. While studying at the University of Southern California in 1932 he made *The Oval Portrait*, an adaptation of the Edgar Allan Poe story that is considered the university's first student film. Shot for $400.00, it won the Paul Muni Award, a college film competition sponsored by Warner Bros. He went on to make the long-running series of "Joe McDoakes" short films for the same studio during the 1940s and '50s. Bare also wrote, produced and directed the 1973 horror movie *Wicked, Wicked* in "Duo-Vision" and directed several episodes of TV's *The Twilight Zone* (including Richard Matheson's 'Third from the Sun' and Damon Knight's classic 'To Serve Man'). Three of his five wives were actresses Phyllis Coates (1948-49), Julie Van Zandt (1951-57) and Jeanne Evans (1958-65).

Czech director of photography **Miroslav Ondříček** , who often worked with Miloš Forman, died the same day, aged 80. His credits include Lindsay Anderson's *If....* and *O Lucky Man!, Slaughterhouse-Five* (based on the novel by Kurt Vonnegut, Jr.), *F/X* and *The Preacher's Wife*.

Michael Birkett, who was an assistant director on *The Innocents* (1961), died on April 3, aged 85. He went on to be a producer on *Modesty Blaise* (1966), *Marat/Sade* and *A Midsummer Night's Dream* (1968). Birkett, who was Vice-President of the British Board of Film Classification from 1985, was the stepfather of actor Alexander Siddig and brother-in-law to actor Malcolm McDowell.

American TV executive **Walt Baker** (Walter Peter Baker), who helped turn actress Cassandra Peterson into sexy horror hostess "Elvira" for KHJ-TV's late-night horror series *Movie Macabre* in the early 1980s, died on April 7, aged 84.

American producer and director **Dean Whitney** died of a heart attack on April 19, aged 68. His credits include the short films *The Body Bag, Seizures* and *Aberrant*, along with the low budget independent horror movies *Terror House, The Games That Children Play, Ghostline, Arisen, Terror at Crimson Creek* and *Kill Me Once*.

Val E. (Edwin) **Lewton**, the son of R.K.O. movie producer Val Lewton, died of metastatic melanoma on April 24, aged 77. He appeared in the documentaries *Shadows in the Dark: The Val Lewton Legacy* and *Val Lewton: The Man in the Shadows*.

Oscar-winning Australian cinematographer **Andrew Lesnie** died of a heart attack on April 27, aged 59. As a director of photography, his credits include *Dark Age, Babe* and *Babe: Pig in the City, The Lord of the Rings: The Fellowship of the Ring, The Lord of the Rings: The Two Towers, The Lord of the Rings: The Return of the King, King Kong* (2005), *I Am Legend* (2007), *The Lovely Bones, The Last Airbender, Rise of the Planet of the Apes, The Hobbit: An Unexpected Journey, The Hobbit: The Desolation of Smaug* and *The Hobbit: The Battle of the Five Armies*. Lesnie also worked in various capacities in the camera department on *Patrick* (1978), *Mad Max 2: The Road Warrior, Dead End Drive-In, Incident at Raven's Gate, The 13th Floor* and *Dark City*.

Award-winning Canadian music video director **Steven** (Harvey) **Goldmann**, who directed the comic-book adaptation *Trailer Park of Terror* (2008), died of cancer in California on April 30. He was 53.

American TV writer and producer **Robert Foshko** died on May 3, aged 85. His script 'The Monsters' for a 1951 episode of *Tales of Tomorrow* was adapted eight years later for an episode of *The Unseen*. He was also an associate producer on the 1965 season of *The Man from U.N.C.L.E.*

Donald (Malcolm) **Wrye**, who wrote, produced and directed the 1987 ABC-TV mini-series *Amerika*, in which the United States was taken over by the Soviet Union, died on May 15, aged 80. He also directed the TV movies *It Happened One Christmas* and *A Vision of Murder: The Story of Donielle*.

American movie director **Michael Campus**, who directed the 1972 SF move *Z.P.G.* starring Oliver Reed, died of melanoma the same day, also aged 80.

American social and entertainment photographer **Mary Ellen Mark** died of myelodysplastic syndrome on May 25, aged 75. Amongst the films she worked on as a unit photographer are *The Believers* and Tim Burton's *Big Fish* and *Charlie and the Chocolate Factory*. Her pictures appeared in such magazines as *Vanity Fair, The New Yorker, Rolling Stone* and *Entertainment Weekly*.

Spanish writer and director **Vicente Aranda** died on May 26, aged 88. His films include *Left-Handed Fate*, *The Exquisite Cadaver* and *The Blood Spattered Bride*.

Oscar-winning British costume designer (Diana) **Julie Harris** died of a chest infection on May 30, aged 94. The films she worked on include *Mister Drake's Duck*, *Help!*, *Eye of the Devil* (aka *13*), *Casino Royale* (1967), *The Private Life of Sherlock Holmes*, Alfred Hitchcock's *Frenzy*, *Live and Let Die*, *Rollerball* (1975), *The Land That Time Forgot* (1975), *The Slipper and the Rose: The Story of Cinderella*, *Dracula* (1979), *The Great Muppet Caper*, *The Hound of the Baskervilles* (1983) and *The Sign of Four* (1983). After retiring in 1991 she became a successful oil painter.

29-year-old American special effects technician and editor **Kate** (Katherine) **Chappell** died on June 1 after being mauled by a lion through the open window of her vehicle in a Johannesburg, South Africa, safari park. She worked in various capacities on *Gravity*, *Hellbenders*, *The Secret Life of Walter Mitty* (2013), *Gods Behaving Badly*, *Noah*, *Captain America: The Winter Soldier*, *Divergent*, *Godzilla* (2014), *Pan* (2015) and TV's *Game of Thrones*.

Spanish cinematographer **Manel Esteban** (Manuel Esteban Marquilles) died on June 3, aged 74. His credits include the experimental 1971 film *Cuadecuc Vampir* and the 2012 documentary short *Dracula vs. Vampir* (both featuring Christopher Lee and Herbert Lom).

Oscar-winning American movie producer **Robert** (Irwin) **Chartoff** died of pancreatic cancer on June 10, aged 81. Best known for co-producing the *Rocky* films with Irwin Winkler, his other credits include *The Tempest* (2010), *Ender's Game* (based on the novel by Orson Scott Card) and *A Midsummer Night's Dream* (2014). His second wife (1970-83), British actress Vanessa Howard, died in 2010.

American producer-manager **Jack Rollins** (Jacob Rabinowitz) died on June 18 aged 100. He co-produced (often with the late Charles H. Joffe) many of Woody Allen's films, including *Everything You Wanted to Know About Sex* *But Were Afraid to Ask*, *Sleeper*, *A Midsummer Night's Sex Comedy*, *Zelig*, *The Purple Rose of Cairo*, *Alice*, *Shadows and Fog*, *Manhattan Murder Mystery*, *The*

Curse of the Jade Scorpion, Scoop, Midnight in Paris and *Magic in the Moonlight*.

American TV comedy scriptwriter and producer **Chris** (Christopher) **Thompson** died after a long illness on June 26, aged 63. He directed the 1998 SF movie *Meteorites!* starring Tom Wopat and scripted the 1987 beach party sequel *Back to the Beach*.

British film producer **John Dark** died in Spain on June 29, aged 88. He began his career as a production manager on *The Strange World of Planet X* (aka *Cosmic Monsters*), and was an associate producer on the James Bond spoof *Casino Royale* (1967) before joining Amicus Productions in the 1970s as a managing partner on such movies as *From Beyond the Grave, The Beast Must Die, Madhouse, The Land That Time Forgot* (1974), *At the Earth's Core* and *The People That Time Forgot*. He also produced *Warlords of the Deep* and *Arabian Adventure*.

American producer **Jerry Weintraub** (Jerome Charles Weintraub), best known for *The Karate Kid* series and the new *Ocean's...*films, died of cardiac arrest on July 6, aged 77. His other movies include *Oh God!, My Stepmother is an Alien, The Avengers* (1998), *Soldier* and *Tarzan* (2016), along with the new *Westworld* TV series (2016-). As a music manager, his clients included Frank Sinatra, Neil Diamond, Bob Dylan, Karen Carpenter, John Denver and The Moody Blues.

Japanese CEO **Satoru Iwata**, who became the fourth president of games giant Nintendo in 2002, died of complications from a bile duct tumor on July 11. He was 55. Having studied computer science at the Tokyo Institute of Technology, Iwata oversaw the development of such successful video game franchises as *Pokémon, Super Mario, Metroid, The Legend of Zelda, Donkey Kong* and many others.

British production designer **Clifford** (Ronald) **Hatts** OBE died on July 27, aged 93. Best known for his set designs for BBC television, including the original 1958-59 serial of *Quatermass and the Pit* (which he also appeared in), his other credits include *A Midsummer Night's Dream* (1958), *Wuthering Heights* (1962), *Gaslight Theatre* ('Maria Marten or, the Murder in the Old Red Barn') and *Late Night Horror* (John Burke's 'The Corpse Can't Play').

Austrian-born director **Herbert Wise** (Herbert Weisz), who directed the 1989 ITV version of *The Woman in Black* scripted by Nigel Kneale, died in London on August 5, aged 90. His other credits include episodes of TV's of *Mystery Hour* ('The Woman in White'), *The Indian Tales of Rudyard Kipling* ('The Tomb of His Ancestors'), *Out of the Unknown, Tales of the Unexpected* ('Royal Jelly' etc.) and *The 10th Kingdom*. He was married to actresses Moira Redmond from 1963-72 and Fiona Walker from 1988 until his death.

British film and TV producer and director **Jack Gold**, best known for his acclaimed TV film *The Naked Civil Servant*, died on August 9, aged 85. His genre credits include *Who?* (aka *Robo Man*, based on the novel by Algis Budrys) and *The Medusa Touch* (based on the novel by Peter Van Greenaway). A charming man and entertaining raconteur, we had the pleasure of interviewing him for the 2006 DVD of *The Medusa Touch*.

Philippines-born animation layout and character designer **Richard Manginsay** died on August 13, aged 43. He worked on the movies *Anatasia* and *Bartok the Magnificent*, and such TV series as *Futurama* and *The Simpsons*.

Japanese puppeteer, scriptwriter, producer and director **Kihachiro Kawamoto** died on August 23, aged 85. His films include the stop-motion shorts *The Demon* (1973), *Dôjôji Temple* (1976) and *House of Flame* (1979).

Respected American horror screenwriter, producer and director **Wes Craven** (Wesley Earl Craven) died of brain cancer on August 30, aged 75. Best known for creating iconic dream-killer "Freddy Krueger" (memorably portrayed by Robert Englund) in *A Nightmare on Elm Street* (1984), and the "Ghostface Killer" for *Scream* (1996) and its three sequels, his other movies include *The Last House on the Left* (1972), *The Hills Have Eyes* (1977), *Stranger in Our House* (aka *Summer of Fear*), *Deadly Blessing, Swamp Thing, Invitation to Hell, The Hills Have Eyes Part II* (1984), *Chiller, Deadly Friend, The Serpent and the Rainbow, Shocker, Night Visions, The People Under the Stairs, New Nightmare, Vampire in Brooklyn, Cursed* and *My Soul to Take*. He also directed episodes of TV's *The Twilight Zone* (1985-86) and *Nightmare Café*. Craven co-scripted *A Nightmare on Elm*

Street 3: Dream Warriors and *The Hills Have Eyes II* (2007), and he has producing credits on *Mind Ripper*, *Wishmaster*, *Carnival of Souls* (1998), *Don't Look Down*, *Dracula 2000*, *Feast*, *The Hills Have Eyes* (2006), *The Breed*, *The Last House on the Left* (2009), *The Girl in the Photographs* and *Scream: The TV Series*. As an actor, he turned up in *Shocker*, *Body Bags*, *New Nightmare*, *The Fear*, *Shadow Zone: The Undead Express*, the first three *Scream* movies (his scenes were deleted from the fourth), *Jay and Silent Bob Strike Back*, *Paris je t'aime* and episodes of *The Twilight Zone* and *Castle* ('Scared to Death'), while his voice can be heard in George A. Romero's *Diary of the Dead*. Craven was married to actress Mimi Craven from 1982-87, and he published his first novel, *The Fountain Society*, in 1999.

American film editor **Millie Moore**, who began her career working on Dalton Trumbo's 1971 movie *Johnny Got His Gun*, died of lung cancer and complications from dementia on September 10. She was 86. Moore's other credits include *Starship Invasions* (starring Christopher Lee) and the underrated *Halloween III: Season of the Witch*.

Former American theatre critic and financier **William Becker** (Arthur William John Becker, III), who acquired art-house movie distributor Janus Films with Saul J. Turell in 1965 and went on to become president of affiliated company the Criterion Collection in 1985, died of kidney failure on September 12, aged 88. Janus (with its distinctive two-faced logo) later secured the rights to such Hollywood classics as *Citizen Kane* and the original *King Kong*.

42-year-old Polish film-maker **Marcin Wrona** committed suicide by hanging in a hotel room in Poland on September 18. His retelling of the Jewish legend of the dybbuk, *Demon* (2015), which he wrote, produced and directed, had its world premiere at the Toronto Film Festival the week before his death.

Italian screenwriter/director **Mario Caiano**, best known (as "Allen Grünewald") for the Barbara Steele movie *Amanti d'oltretomba* (aka *Nightmare Castle/Faceless Monster*) died on September 20, aged 82. His other credits include *Ulysses Against Hercules*, *Goliath the Rebel Slave*, *The Terror of Rome Against the Son of Hercules* and *Eye in the Labyrinth*. Caiano was forced to leave the set of *Vampire in Venice*

(1988) when star Klaus Kinski refused to work with him, and various other people completed the film (including Kinski himself).

British-born movie writer, producer and director **John Guillerman**, best known for *The Towering Inferno* and the 1976 remake of *King Kong*, died of a heart attack in Topanga Canyon, California, on September 27, aged 89. His other credits include *Strange Stories*, *Tarzan's Greatest Adventure*, *Tarzan Goes to India*, *Sheena* and the belated 1986 sequel *King Kong Lives*.

Veteran American special visual effects technician **Howard A. (Andrew) Anderson, Jr.** died the same day, aged 95. He created the effects for *Prehistoric Women* (1950), *Phantom from Space*, *Curucu Beast of the Amazon*, *Invasion of the Saucer Men*, *The Time Machine* (1960), *Jack the Giant Killer*, *Earth II* and the original *Star Trek* TV series (1966-69).

American cinematographer **Charles** (Delacey) **Rosher, Jr.** died on October 14, aged 80. Amongst the movies he worked on were Roger Corman's *Attack of the Giant Leeches*, *Incubus* (1966), *Hex*, *The Cat Creature* (scripted by Robert Bloch), *Nightwing* and *Heartbeeps*.

Former B-47 bomber pilot **John D. Backe**, who became chief executive of CBS, returning the television network to its #1 status amongst prime-time viewers before he was ousted in a power struggle, died on October 22. He was 83. Backe also engineered CBS' acquisition of Fawcett Publications in the mid-1970s and went on to become president of Tomorrow Entertainment, a succesful TV production company. He is credited as an executive producer on the 1989 movie *Brenda Starr*.

Veteran Polish-born casting director **Rose Tobias Shaw** died on October 27, aged 96. She cast such films as *Ten Little Indians* (1959), *Mumsy Nanny Sonny & Girly* (aka *Girly*), *Tower of Evil* (aka *Horror on Snape Island*), *Lost Horizon* (1973), *Madhouse* (starring Vincent Price), *The Spiral Staircase* (1975), *The Seven-Per-Cent Solution*, *The Cat and the Canary* (1978), *Oh Heavenly Dog*, *Inseminoid* (aka *Horror Planet*), *Merlin and the Sword* (aka *Arthur the King*), Disney's *Baby: Secret of the Lost Legend* and *Around the World in 80 Days* (1989), along with the TV series *The Prisoner*, *Strange Report* and *UFO*.

American "kustom" car designer **George Barris** (George Salaptas) died of cancer on November 5, aged 89. He famously created the iconic Batmobile for the 1960s *Batman* TV series, The Munster Koach and Grandpa's Drag-u-la for *The Munsters*, the Black Beauty for *The Green Hornet* and the talking car KITT for *Knight Rider*. Barris also worked on the movies *The Silencers*, *Batman* (1966), *The Car*, *Jurassic Park* and *Turbo: A Power Rangers Movie*. The original Batmobile sold at auction in 2013 for $4.2 million, and *King of the Kustomizers: The Art of George Barris* was a recent book about his work.

Paul Aratow, best known for writing and directing the unreleased 1975 movie *Lucifer's Women*, which Al Adamson turned into *Doctor Dracula* (1978) starring John Carradine, died on November 15, aged 78. Aratow also produced the comic strip-inspired films *Sheena* (1984) and *The Spirit* (1987).

Oscar-winning American film editor **Elmo Williams** died of heart problems on November 25, aged 102. His credits include *Dick Tracy Meets Gruesome* (featuring Boris Karloff) and Walt Disney's *20,000 Leagues Under the Sea*. From 1970-73, Williams was Vice President in Charge of Worldwide Productions for 20th Century-Fox.

Canadian film producer and director **Denis Héroux**, who directed the 1977 anthology movie *The Uncanny*, scripted by Michel Parry and starring Peter Cushing and Ray Milland, died after a long illness on December 10. He was 75. Héroux also produced *The Little Girl Who Lives Down the Lane* and *Quest for Fire*.

British TV director and producer **Don Leaver** (Donald Alfred Leaver) died on December 13, aged 86. His many credits include episodes of *Out of This World* (hosted by Boris Karloff), the four-part *Dimensions of Fear*, *Armchair Mystery Theatre* ('The Lodger', 1965), *Haunted*, *The Rivals of Sherlock Holmes*, *Zodiac*, *Thriller* (1975), Nigel Kneale's *Beasts* ('The Dummy'), *Hammer House of Horror* ('Witching Time' and 'The Mark of Satan') and twenty episodes of *The Avengers* ('The House That Jack Built' etc.).

Richard Perrin, who directed and produced the 2007 horror film *The Dead Don't Scream*, died on December 19, aged 57.

Academy Award-winning American cinematographer and documentary filmmaker **Haskell Wexler** died on December 27, aged 93. His credits include *The Secret of Roan Inish* and he also contributed additional photography to *Blade Runner*. Wexler is credited with creating the handheld camera shot.

USEFUL ADDRESSES

THE FOLLOWING LISTING of organisations, publications, dealers and individuals is designed to present readers and authors with further avenues to explore. Although I can personally recommend many of those listed on the following pages, neither the publisher nor myself can take any responsibility for the services they offer. Please also note that the information below is only a guide and is subject to change without notice.

—The Editor

ORGANISATIONS

The Australian Horror Writers Association
(www.australianhorror.com) is a non-profit organisation that was formed in 2005 as a way of providing a unified voice and a sense of community for Australian writers of dark fiction, while helping the development and evolution of this genre within Australia. They also publish an excellent magazine, *Midnight Echo*, and offer a mentor programme, critique group and short story competitions. Email: ahwa@australianhorror.com

The British Fantasy Society (www.britishfantasysociety.org/ www.fantasycon.co.uk) was founded in 1971 and publishes the *BFS Journal*, featuring articles and reviews, and *BFS Horizons*, which is devoted to fiction and poetry, along with occasional special books only available to members of the Society. Run by volunteers, the BFS also enjoys a lively online community—there is an email newsfeed, a Facebook community, a forum with numerous links, and a CyberStore selling various publications. FantasyCon is one of the UK's friendliest conventions and there are social gatherings and meet-the-author events organised around Britain. For yearly membership details, Email: secretary@britishfantasysociety.org

The Friends of Arthur Machen (www.arthurmachen.org.uk) is a literary society whose objectives include encouraging a wider recognition of Machen's work and providing a focus for critical debate. Members get a hardcover journal, *Faunus*, twice a year, and also the informative newsletter *Machenalia*. For membership details, contact Jon Preece, 9 Ridgeway Drive, Newport, South Wales NP20 5AR, UK (machenfoam@yahoo.co.uk).

The Friends of the Merril Collection (www.friendsofmerril.org/) is a volunteer organisation that provides support and assistance to the largest public collection of science fiction, fantasy and horror books in North America. Details about annual membership and donations are available from the website or by contacting The Friends of the Merril Collection, c/o Lillian H. Smith Branch, Toronto Public Library, 239 College Street, 3rd Floor, Toronto, Ontario M5T 1R5, Canada. Email: ltoolis@tpl.toronto.on.ca

The Horror Writers Association (www.horror.org) is a world-wide organisation of writers and publishing professionals dedicated to promoting the interests of writers of horror and dark fantasy. It was formed in the early 1980s. Interested individuals may apply for Active, Affiliate or Associate membership. Active membership is limited to professional writers, although a recent change in the bylaws allows self-published work to qualify authors for membership under certain conditions. HWA publishes a monthly online Newsletter, and sponsors the annual Bram Stoker Awards and StokerCon.

World Fantasy Convention (www.worldfantasy.org) is an annual convention held in a different (usually American) city each year, oriented particularly towards serious readers and genre professionals.

World Horror Convention (www.worldhorrorsociety.org) is a smaller, more relaxed, event. It is aimed specifically at horror fans and professionals, and held in a different city (usually American) each year.

SELECTED SMALL PRESS PUBLISHERS

The Alchemy Press (www.alchemypress.co.uk)

American Fantasy Press (www.americanfantasypress.com), 919 Tappan Street, Woodstock, Illinois 60098, USA.

Bad Moon Books/Eclipse (www.badmoonbooks.com), 1854 W. Chateau Avenue, Anaheim, CA 92804-4527, USA.

BearManor Media (www.bearmanormedia.com), PO Box 1129, Duncan, OK 73534-1129, USA.

Black Dog Books (www.blackdogbooks.net), 1115 Pine Meadows Ct., Normal, IL 61761-5432, USA. Email: info@blackdogbooks.net

Bloodshot Books (bloodshotbooks.wordpress.com/), 14 Chase Drive, Sharon, MA 02067, USA.

Borderlands Press (www,borderlandspress.com), POB 61, Benson, MD 21018, USA.

Brimstone Press (www.brimstonepress.com.au).

Celaeno Press (www.calaenopress.com), #403 Tenjin 3-9-10, Chuo-ku, Fukuoka 810-0001, Japan.

Cemetery Dance Publications (www.cemeterydance.com), 132-B Industry Lane, Unit #7, Forest Hill, MD 21050, USA. Email: info@cemeterydance.com

Chaosium, Inc (www.chaosium.com).

ChiZine Publications (www.chizinepub.com). Email: info@chizinepub.com

Chthonic Matter (www.chthonicmatter.wordpress.com).

Comet Press (www.cometpress.us).

Dark Minds Press (www. darkmindspress.com), 31 Gristmill Close, Cheltenham, Glos. GL51 0PZ, UK. Email: mail@darkmindspress.com

Dark Regions Press LCC (www.darkregions.com), 6635 N. Baltimore Ave. Ste. 241, Portland, OR 97203, USA.

Donald M. Grant, Publisher, Inc. (www.grantbooks.com), 19 Surrey Lane, PO Box 187, Hampton Falls, NH 03844, USA.

DreamHaven Books (www.dreamhavenbooks.com), 2301 East 38th Street, Minneapolis, MN 55406, USA.

Earthling Publications (www.earthlingpub.com), PO Box 413, Northborough, MA 01532, USA. Email: earthlingpub@yahoo.com

Edge Science Fiction and Fantasy Publishing/Hades Publications, Inc. (www.edgewebsite.com), PO Box 1714, Calgary, Alberta T2P 2L7, Canada. Email: publisher@hadespublications.com

Egaeus Press (www.egaeuspress.com). Email: egaeuspress@gmail.com

FableCroft Publishing (fablecroft.com.au).

Fedogan & Bremer Publishing LLC (fedoganandbremer.com), 3918 Chicago Street, Nampa, Idaho 83686, USA.

Flame Tree Publishing (www.flametreepublishing.com), 6 Melbray Mews, Fulham, London SW6 3NS, UK.
Email: info@flametreepublishing.com

Great British Horror Books/Black Shuck Books/KnightWatch Press (www.GreatBritishHorror.com), "Hillbrow", Northbourne Road, Deal, Kent CT14 0LA, UK.

Hex Publishers (www.HexPublishers.com), 2628 Redcliff Drive, Broomfield, CO 80023, USA. Email: contact@hexpublishers.com

Hippocampus Press (www.hippocampuspress.com), PO Box 641, New York, NY 10156, USA. Email: info@hippocampuspress.com

Horror Australis Pty Ltd. (horroraustralis.com).

IFWG Publishing, Inc. (www.ifwgaustralia.com).

Innsmouth Free Press (www.innsmouthfreepress.com).

Ja Sunni Productions, LLC/Cycatrix Press (www.JaSunni.com), 16420 SE McGillivray Blvd., Ste 103-1010, Vancouver, WA 98683, USA. Email: JaSunni@jasunni.com

Lethe Press, Inc. (www.lethepressbooks.com), 118 Heritage Avenue, Maple Shade, NJ 08052-3018, USA. Email: lethepress@aol.com

McFarland & Company, Inc., Publishers (www.mcfarlandpub.com), Box 611, Jefferson, NC 28640, USA.

MoonDream Press/Copper Dog Publishing LLC (www.copperdogpublishing.com), 537 Leader Circle, Louisville, CO 80027, USA.

Nightjar Press (nightjarpress.weebly.com), 63 Ballbrook Court, Wilmslow Road, Manchester M20 3GT, UK.

Night Shade Books (www.nightshadebooks.com), 307 West 36th Street, 11th Floor, New York, NY 10018, USA.

Omnium Gatherum (omniumgatherumedia.com).

One Eye Press LLC (www.oneeyepress.com).

Parallel Universe Publications, 130 Union Road, Oswaldtwistle, Lancashire BB5 3DR, UK.

Poise and Pen Publishing (www.poiseandpen.com).

P'rea Press (www.preapress.com) c/-34 Osborne Road, Lane Cove, NSW, Australia 2066. Email: DannyL58@hotmail.com

Prime Books (www.prime-books.com), PO Box 83464, Gaithersburg, MD 20883, USA. Email: prime@prime-books.com

PS Publishing Ltd/Drugstore Indian Press/PS ArtBooks Ltd/Stanza Press (www.pspublishing.co.uk), Grosvenor House, 1 New Road, Hornsea HU18 1PG, UK.
Email: editor@pspublishing.co.uk

Resurrection House/Arche Press/Underland Press (www.resurrectionhouse.com), 310 N. Meridian STE 204, Puyallup, WA 98371, USA. Email: mark@resurrectionhouse.com

Sarob Press (sarobpress.blogspot.com), La Blinière, 53250, Neuilly-le-Vendin, France.

Shadow Publishing (www.shadowpublishing.webeasysite.co.uk/), Apt. #19 Awdry Court, 15 St. Nicolas Gardens, Birmingham, West Midlands B38 8BH, UK. Email: david.sutton986@btinternet.com

Short, Scary Tales Publications (www.sstpublications.co.uk), 15 North Roundhay, Stechford, Birmingham B33 9PE, UK. Email: paulfry@sstpublications.co.uk

Small Beer Press (www.weightlessbooks.com), 150 Pleasant Street #306, Easthampton, MA 01027, USA. Email: info@smallbeerpress **Snowbooks, Ltd.** (www.snowbooks.com). Email: info@snowbooks.com

Spectral Press/Tickety Boo Press (www.ticketyboopress.co.uk), 23 Worsdell Street, North Blyth, Northumberland NE24 ISD, UK. Email: gary.compton@ticketyboopress.co.uk

Stone Skin Press/Pelgrane Press Ltd. (www.stoneskinpress.com), Spectrum House, 9 Bromell's Road, Clapham Common, London SW4 0BN, UK. Email: stoneskinpress@gmail.com

Subterranean Press (www.subterraneanpress.com), PO Box 190106, Burton, MI 48519, USA. Email: subpress@gmail.com

Surinam Turtle Press/Ramble House (www.ramblehouse.com), 3208 Claremont Avenue, Berkeley, CA 94705-2722, USA.

Tachyon Publications (www.tachyonpublications.com), 1459 18th Street #139, San Francisco, CA 94107, USA. Email: tachyon@tachyonpublications.com

Tartarus Press (www.tartaruspress.com), Coverley House, Carlton-in-Coverdale, Leyburn, North Yorkshire DL8 4AY, UK. Email: tartarus@pavilion.co.uk

Third Flatiron Anthologies (www.thirdflatiron.com). Email: flatsubmit@thirdflatiron.com

Tickety Boo Press Ltd./Scarier 51 (www.ticketyboopress.co.uk).

Ticonderoga Publications (www.ticonderogapublications.com), PO Box 29, Greenwood, Western Australia 6924.

Undertow Publications (www.undertowbooks@gmail.com) Michael Kelly Editor, 1905 Faylee Crescent, Pickering, ON L1V 2T3, Canada. Email: undertowbooks@gmail.com
Valencourt Books (www.valancourtbooks.com).

Wildside Press LLC (www.wildsidepress.com), 9710 Traville Gateway Drive #234, Rockville, MD 20850, USA.

Word Horde (www.WordHorde.com).

World Weaver Press (www.WorldWeaverPress.com)

SELECTED MAGAZINES

Allen K's Inhuman Magazine. Paperback magazine, now published infrequently by Centipede Press. No unsolicited submissions. Email: outreart@aol.com

Ansible is a highly entertaining monthly SF and fantasy newsletter/gossip column edited by David Langford. It is available free electronically by sending an Email to: ansible-request @dcs.gla.ac.uk with a subject line reading "subscribe", or you can receive the print version by sending a stamped and addressed envelope to Ansible, 94 London Road, Reading, Berks RG1 5AU, UK. Back issues, links and book lists are also available online.

Black Static (www.ttapress.com) is the UK's premier horror fiction magazine, produced bi-monthly by the publishers of Interzone. Six-

and twelve-issue subscriptions are available, along with a lifetime subscription, from TTA Press, 5 Martins Lane, Witcham, Ely, Cambs CB6 2LB, UK, or from the secure TTA website. Email: andy@ttapress.com

Cemetery Dance (www.cemeterydance.com) is edited by Richard Chizmar and Brian James Freeman and appears intermittently. PO Box 623, Forest Hill, MD 21050, USA. Email: info@cemeterydance.com

Fear is back to being a print magazine. Email: fearmagazine@outlook.com

The Ghosts & Scholars M.R. James Newsletter (www.pardoes.info/roanddarroll/GS.html) is a scholarly journal published roughly twice a year. It is dedicated to the classic ghost story and, as the title implies, to M.R. James in particular. Two-issue subscriptions are available from Haunted Library Publications, c/o Flat One, 36 Hamilton Street, Hoole, Chester CH2 3JQ, UK. Email: pardos@globalnet.co.uk

The Horror Zine (www.thehorrorzine.com) is a monthly online magazine edited by Jeani Rector that features fiction, poetry, interviews and reviews. It is also available in a PoD edition.

Illustrators (www.bookpalace.com) is a beautifully designed and published full-colour periodical devoted to art and artists. The Book Palace, Jubilee House, Bedwardine Road, Crystal Palace, London SE19 3AP, UK. Email: IQ@bookpalace.com

Locus (www.locusmag.com) is the monthly newspaper of the SF/fantasy/horror field. Contact: Locus Publications, PO Box 13305, Oakland, CA 94661, USA. Subscription information with other rates and order forms are also available on the website. Email: locus@locusmag.com. You can also now subscribe to a digital edition at: weightlessbooks.com/genre/nonfiction/locus-12-month-subscription

The Magazine of Fantasy & Science Fiction (www.fandsf.com) has been publishing some of the best imaginative fiction for sixty-seven years. After eighteen years, Gordon Van Gelder has now relinquished the editorship to C.C. Finlay. Published bi-monthly, single copies or an annual subscription are available by US cheques or credit card from: Fantasy & Science Fiction, PO Box 3447, Hoboken, NJ 07030, USA, or you can subscribe via the website.

New Genre (adamgolaski.blogspot.com) is a literary paperback magazine publishing original short fiction.

Nightmare Magazine (www.nightmare-magazine.com/) edited by John Joseph Adams is an excellent monthly online site for fiction (both new and reprint), interviews and podcasts.

Rabbit Hole is a semi-regular newsletter about Harlan Ellison® that also offers exclusive signed books by the author. A subscription is available from The Harlan Ellison® Recording Collection, PO Box 55548, Sherman Oaks, CA 91413-0548, USA.

Rue Morgue (www.rue-morgue.com), is a glossy monthly magazine edited by Dave Alexander and subtitled "Horror in Culture & Entertainment". Each issue is packed with full colour features and reviews of new films, books, comics, music and game releases. Subscriptions are available from: Marrs Media Inc., 2926 Dundas Street West, Toronto, ON M6P 1Y8, Canada, or by credit card on the website. Email: info@rue-morgue.com. Every Friday you can log on to a new show at Rue Morgue Radio at www.ruemorgueradio.com and your horror shopping online source, The Rue Morgue Marketplace, is at www.ruemorguemarketplace.com

Space and Time: The Magazine of Fantasy, Horror, and Science Fiction (www.spaceandtimemagazine.com) is published twice a year. Single issues and subscriptions are available from the website or from: Space and Time Magazine, 458 Elizabeth Avenue #5348, Somerset, NJ 08873, USA.

Supernatural Tales (suptales.blogspot.com) is a fiction magazine edited by David Longhorn, with subscriptions available via PayPal, cheques or non-UK cash. Supernatural Tales, 291 Eastbourne Avenue, Gateshead NE8 4NN, UK.
Email: davidlonghorn@hotmail.com

Tor.com (www.tor.com), publishes new fiction, articles, novel excerpts, artist galleries, reviews and a lot more.

Video WatcHDog (www.videowatchdog.com) describes itself as "The Perfectionist's Guide to Fantastic Video" and is published bi-monthly from PO Box 5283, Cincinnati, OH 45205-0283, USA. One year (six issues) subscriptions are available from: orders@videowatchdog.com

Weirdbook (wildsidepress.com) is a revival of the iconic fantasy and horror magazine published by Wildside Press LCC, 9710 Traville Gateway Drive, #234, Rockville, MD 20850, USA.

DEALERS

Cold Tonnage Books (www.coldtonnage.com) offers excellent mail order new and used SF/fantasy/horror, art, reference, limited editions etc. Write to: Andy & Angela Richards, Cold Tonnage Books, 22 Kings Lane, Windlesham, Surrey GU20 6JQ, UK. Credit cards accepted. Tel: +44 (0)1276-475388. Email: andy@coldtonnage.com

Richard Dalby issues an annual Christmas catalogue of used Ghost Stories and other supernatural volumes at very reasonable prices. Write to: Richard Dalby, 4 Westbourne Park, Scarborough, North Yorkshire YO12 4AT. Tel: +44 (0)1723 377049.

Dark Delicacies (www.darkdel.com) is a Burbank, California, store specialising in horror books, toys, vampire merchandise and signings. They also do mail order and run money-saving book club and membership discount deals. 3512 W. Magnolia Blvd, Burbank, CA 91505, USA. Tel: (818) 556-6660. Credit cards accepted. Email: darkdel@darkdel.com

DreamHaven Books & Comics (www.dreamhavenbooks.com) once again has a storefront (open Tuesday through Saturday) as well as a mail-order outlet, offering new and used SF/fantasy/horror/art and illustrated etc. with regular catalogues (both print and Email). 2031 E. 38th Street, Minneapolis, MN 55406-3015, USA. Credit cards accepted. Tel: (612) 823-6070. Email: dream@dreamhavenbooks.com

Fantastic Literature (www.fantasticliterature.com) mail order offers the UK's biggest online out-of-print SF/fantasy/horror genre bookshop. Fanzines, pulps and vintage paperbacks as well. Write to: Simon and Laraine Gosden, Fantastic Literature, 35 The Ramparts, Rayleigh, Essex SS6 8PY, UK. Credit cards and Pay Pal accepted. Tel/Fax: +44 (0)1268-747564. Email: simon@fantasticliterature.com **Ferret Fantasy**, 27 Beechcroft Road, Upper Tooting, London SW17 7BX, UK. Email: george_locke@hotmail.com. Tel: +44 (0)208-767-0029.

Horrorbles (www.horrorbles.com), 6729 Stanley Avenue, Berwyn, IL 60402, USA. Friendly Chicago store selling horror and sci-fi toys, memorabilia and magazines that has monthly specials and in-store signings. Specialises in exclusive "Basil Gogos" and "Svengoolie" items. Open Tuesday through Sunday. Tel: (708) 484-7370. Email: store@horrorbles.com

Hyraxia Books (books.hyraxia.com), 34 Harwill Avenue, Churwell, Leeds LS27 7QQ, UK. Dealing in rare and collectible modern first editions, including many genre titles. Tel: +44 (0)7557-652-609. Email: shop@hyraxia.com

The Iliad Bookshop (www.iliadbooks.com), 5400 Cahuenga Blvd., North Hollywood, CA 91601, USA. General bookstore that has a very fine selection of new, used and rare books, with an emphasis on literature and the arts. Tel: (818) 509-2665.

Locus Online (www.locusmag.com/news) is an excellent online source for the latest news and reviews.

Porcupine Books offers regular catalogues and extensive mail order lists of used fantasy/horror/SF titles via Email brian@ porcupine.demon.co.uk or write to: 37 Coventry Road, Ilford, Essex IG1 4QR, UK. Tel: +44 (0)20 8554-3799.

Reel Art Collectibles (www.reelart.biz), 6727 W. Stanley, Berwyn, Illinois 60402, USA. Nicely designed Chicago store selling movie material, classic comics, vintage toys and rare books. They also host celebrity signings and have regular warehouse sales. Tel: 1-708-288-7378. Facebook: Reel Art, Inc.

The Talking Dead is run by Bob and Julie Wardzinski and offers reasonably priced paperbacks, rare pulps and hardcovers, with catalogues issued very occasionally. They accept wants lists and are also the exclusive supplier of back issues of *Interzone*. Credit cards accepted. Contact them at: 12 Rosamund Avenue, Merley, Wimborne, Dorset BH21 1TE, UK. Tel: +44 (0)1202-849212 (9:00am-9:00pm). Email: books@thetalkingdead.fsnet.co.uk

Terence McVicker Rare Books (www.batsoverbooks.com) is a mail-order business offering premium rare and collectible items—many H.P. Lovecraft and Arkham House-related. A weekly email reader features additions, updates and news.
Email: info@batsoverbooks.com

Ygor's Books specialises in out of print science fiction, fantasy and horror titles, including British, signed, speciality press and limited editions. They also buy books, letters and original art in these fields.
Email: ygorsbooks@gmail.com

ONLINE RESOURCES

Cast Macabre (www.castmacabre.org) is the premium horror fiction podcast that is "bringing Fear to your ears", offering a free horror short story every week.

Fantastic Fiction (www.fantasticfiction.co.uk) features more than 2,000 best-selling author biographies with all their latest books, covers and descriptions.

FEARnet (www.fearnet.com) is a digital cable channel dedicated to all things horror, including news, free movie downloads (sadly not available to those outside North America) and Mick Garris' online talk show Post Mortem.

Hellnotes (www.hellnotes.com) offers news and reviews of novels, collections, magazines, anthologies, non-fiction works, and chapbooks. Materials for review should be sent to editor and publisher David B. Silva, Hellnotes, 5135 Chapel View Court, North Las Vegas, NV 89031, USA. Email: news@hellnotes.com or dbsilva13@gmail.com

The Irish Journal of Gothic and Horror Studies (irishgothichorrorjournal.homestead.com) features a diverse range of articles and reviews, along with a regular "Lost Souls" feature focussing on overlooked individuals in the genre.

The Monster Channel (www.monsterchannel.tv) bills itself as "the first and only independent interactive horror channel!" The 24/7 streaming channel includes first run indie horror movies, retro VHS gore and hosts horror classics.

Pseudopod (www.pseudopod.org), the premiere horror fiction podcast, continued to offer a free-to-download, weekly reading of new or classic horror fiction by a variety of voices. The site remains dedicated to paying their authors while providing readings for free and offering the widest variety of audio horror fiction currently available on the net.

SF Site (www.sfsite.com) has been posted twice each month since 1997. Presently, it publishes around thirty to fifty reviews of SF, fantasy and horror from mass-market publishers and some small press. They also maintain link pages for Author and Fan Tribute Sites and other facets including pages for Interviews, Fiction, Science Fact, Bookstores, Small Press, Publishers, E-zines and Magazines, Artists, Audio, Art Galleries, Newsgroups and Writers' Resources. Periodically, they add features such as author and publisher reading lists.

Vault of Evil (www.vaultofevil.wordpress.com) is a site dedicated to celebrating the best in British horror with special emphasis on UK anthologies. There is also a lively forum devoted to many different themes at www.vaultofevil.proboards.com.